MW01139730

THE LEGEND OF THE GODS

The Complete Trilogy

AARON HODGES

Edited by Genevieve Lerner
Proofread by Sara Houston
Illustration by Christian Bentulan
Map by Michael Hodges

Copyright © January 2019 Aaron Hodges.
First Edition. All Rights Reserved.
ISBN: 978-09951114-55

ABOUT THE AUTHOR

Aaron Hodges was born in 1989 in the small town of Whakatane, New Zealand. He studied for five years at the University of Auckland, completing a Bachelors of Science in Biology and Geography, and a Masters of Environmental Engineering. After working as an environmental consultant for two years, he grew tired of office work and decided to quit his job in 2014 and see the world. One year later, he published his first novel - Stormwielder.

FOLLOW AARON HODGES...

And receive TWO FREE novels and a short story!

www.aaronhodges.co.nz/newsletter-signup/

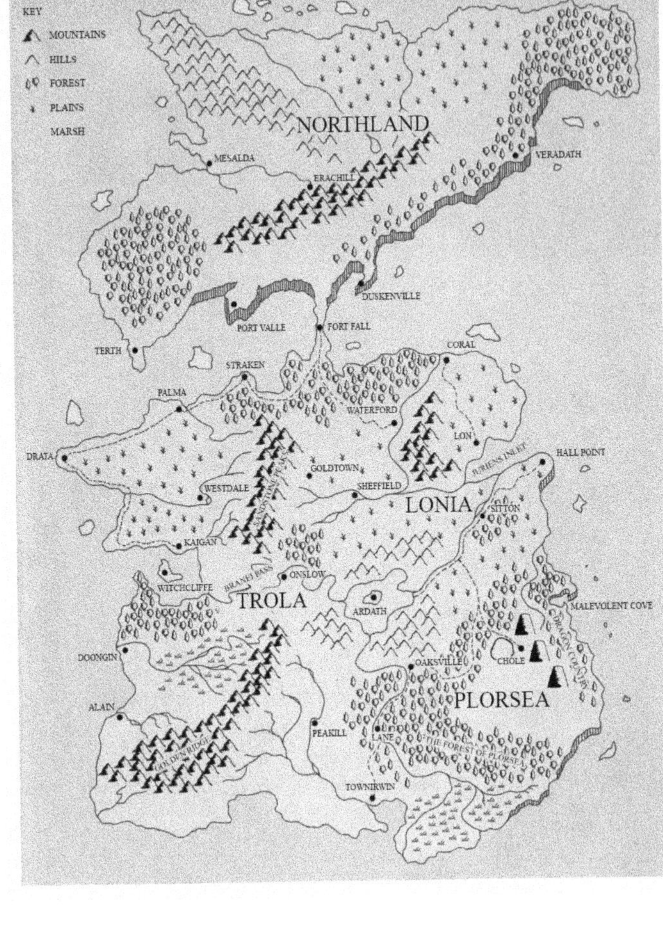

KEY
MOUNTAINS
HILLS
FOREST
PLAINS
MARSH
NORTHLAND
MESALDA
ERACHILL
VERADATH
DUSKENVILLE
PORT VALLE
FORT FALL
TERTH
CORAL
STRAKEN
PALMA
WATERFORD
LON
DRATA
GOLDTOWN
HALL POINT
WESTDALE
SHEFFIELD
LONIA
SITTON
KAIGAN
ONSLOW
WITCHCLIFFE
TROLA
ARDATH
MALEVOLENT COVE
DOONGIN
OAKSVILLE
CHOLE
PLORSEA
ALAIN
PEAKILL
LANE
THE FOREST OF PLORSEA
TOWNIRWIN

NEW YORK TIMES BESTSELLING AUTHOR

AARON HODGES

OATH BREAKER

LEGEND OF THE GODS BOOK ONE

PROLOGUE

The tent was still dark when Devon woke. He lay there for a few minutes, listening to the distant call of the trumpets, knowing he had to rise, but dreading the coming dawn. Finally, unable to delay any longer, he threw off his blanket and rolled from the camp stretcher. Reluctantly he began to dress, pulling on a fresh pair of leather leggings, followed by a woollen gambeson and his chainmail vest. He shivered as the heavy armour settled on his broad shoulders, its icy touch already seeping through to his skin.

Rubbing his hands to fend off the winter cold, Devon laced up his boots and shuffled across to the portable camp brazier. If he was quick, he might have time to reheat last night's gruel before the morning's…festivities began. Bending down, he added kindling to the iron stove, then struck the flint until a spark caught. Allowing himself a smile, he blew gently to stoke the flames before adding a log from his dwindling stack of firewood.

Satisfied the fire had caught, he closed the steel grate and stirred the pot sitting on the brazier. The scent of spiced beef filled the tent, mixing with the stench of smoke and sweat. It had been days since he'd last bathed—but at least that was more than most of his fellow soldiers could say. At twenty years old, his promotion to lieutenant had been hard earned, but at least it had come with a few privileges.

Still, he was quickly growing weary of the fame his promotion had brought him. Devon had once worn his reputation as a badge of pride; but now that a real badge had been pinned to his chest, he found himself weighed down by guilt, shamed by the praise men heaped on him for his exploits on the battlefield.

He shivered, thinking of the festivities planned for the day. Straken, the last Trolan stronghold, had fallen yesterday—its walls sundered, its Magickers crushed, its army shattered. The war was over. Plorsea's supremacy had been restored over the Three Nations. The Tsar finally had his victory.

Devon had played his part, leading the vanguard as they charged through the broken gates. With his warhammer in hand, he had carved his way deep into the ranks of Trolan soldiers. Men had run screaming before the ferocity of his charge, allowing Devon's comrades to scramble through the breach after him.

The shriek of the men dying beneath his hammer echoed through Devon's mind, and closing his eyes, he forced the memories away.

His nose twitched as he caught the stench of burning. Cursing, he lifted the pot from the camp stove. The bottom had caught, but most of the stew remained untouched. Reaching for a spoon, he scooped a piece of meat into his mouth.

The sharp screech of the Tsar's trumpet sounded as

Devon began to chew. He glanced at the pot, his stomach still rumbling with hunger, then returned it to the stove. The rest of his breakfast would have to wait. Leaving the fire to burn down, he took up his half-helm and placed it on his head.

Then he picked up the warhammer from beside his bed. It weighed almost ten pounds, but he hefted it as though it was no heavier than a short sword. The smooth haft of elm felt at home in his meaty hand, more like an extension of himself than a weapon. A dozen runes, worn with age, were etched across its head, written in some long-forgotten language.

He knew what they said, though. Their meaning had been passed down through generations, from father to son, from a time when the heroes had strode the land.

Kanker.

The hammer of heroes. That was what Devon's father had called it, late at night as he told the story of Alan, their ancestor who had stood with the Gods atop the walls of Fort Fall and defied the dark powers of Archon.

Thinking of the legend, Devon's shame returned, and he quickly sheathed the ancient hammer on his back. Times had been simpler back then, when men had followed the paths of the Gods, knowing they fought for the side of good.

Yet the Gods were a hundred years gone. The age of man had come, and with it, the lines between good and evil had blurred. Two years ago, he had joined the Plorsean army as it marched from Ardath, eager to defend his nation, to banish the Trolan invaders. They had done that and more, driving the foreign army back through mountain passes, all the way to the Trolan capital of Kalgan.

Only then, driven to desperation, had the Trolans sued for peace. But by then it had been too late, and the Plorsean armies had razed the city to the ground. It was during that great battle that Devon had earned his promotion to lieutenant.

Just thinking of it now made Devon's stomach tie itself in knots.

After the city's fall, the Tsar had ordered his armies on, marching them north along the Trolan coast. Now, six months and four fallen cities later, the war had finally come to an end. After today, Trola would never rise again.

Shaking his head, Devon cast off his melancholy and stepped through his tent flap. Outside, he squinted into the dawn's light, his eyes struggling to adjust to the sudden brightness. His stomach twisted when he saw the scarlet glow of sunrise.

The beginning of the end.

Silently he started down the hill. Movement came from the other tents as more men stepped out into the open. They walked quickly to join the progression making its way down the hill. Soon the trickle became a flood, as ten thousand soldiers formed up for the day's ceremony.

Straken, like every other city since the fall of Kalgan, had chosen defiance over surrender.

Now its citizens would face the consequences of their choice.

As the light grew, Devon's eyes were drawn out across the silent plains, to where the walled city waited near the sea. So far north, the city's walls were thick and tall, a remnant from the day's when Archon and his hordes had walked the Northern wastelands. Though now a hundred years past, the stone walls remained, unbroken.

Until now.

It hadn't taken long for the Tsar's catapults and siege towers to tear the stone and mortar asunder. As the watch towers collapsed and the gates broke open, Devon had made his charge, leading his fellow soldiers into the storm of battle. Even with their defences shattered, the Trolans had fought like demons, men and women alike standing together against the coming flood.

In the end, it had availed them nothing.

With *kanker* in hand and the bloodlust on him, Devon had sliced through the defenders like a God amongst men. His slaughter had been indiscriminate, his victims reduced to shattered skulls and broken bodies. Only when the end came had he looked back over the carnage and felt the familiar shame.

Now, as he stared out over the broken towers and shattered spires of the temple, the shame swelled. The people of Straken had not been soldiers. The Trolan army had died with the fall of Kalgan. Those who remained here had been civilians, called up to defend their city, their nation, from the foreign army of the Tsar. They had only been trying to protect their livelihood, their families, their homeland.

Yet who was Devon to question the Tsar? After all, the man had been the first to bring peace to the Three Nations, uniting the warring states of Trola, Plorsea and Lonia into a single empire. It had been Trola who'd broken that peace, Trola who'd first marched through the Branei Pass to attack western Plorsea.

They had earned this fate.

So why did he feel so ashamed?

Devon came to a stop as another horn sounded. Standing to attention, he stared straight ahead. The head of his hammer dug uncomfortably into the small of his back, but he did not move to shift it. Around him, ten thousand men stood with him, their eyes fixed to the wooden stage at the foot of the hill.

Movement came from the city gates. Prisoners taken after the fall of the city had been kept there overnight, overseen by a host of soldiers and the Tsar's Magickers. Now the gates were swinging open, and the Plorsean soldiers who'd kept watch were beginning their slow ascent up the hill.

Between them, blindfolded with their hands bound in chains, came the Trolan Magickers who had survived the final battle. They would be marched back to Plorsea, where the Tsar would ensure their magic never posed a danger to anyone ever again.

As the last of the soldiers left the city, the great wood and iron gates swung shut behind them. They had been hurriedly repaired during the night—along with the worst of the breaches in the wall. With the gates barred, Straken's remaining citizens were trapped inside the city.

"People of Straken!" a herald boomed, his voice carrying out over the crowd of waiting soldiers.

Movement came from the men and women surrounding the platform. The royal guards came marching through the crowd, weapons held at the ready. They wore the familiar crimson cloaks of the Plorsean army, but their golden half-helms left no doubt of their identity. Sunlight glinted from their steel-plated armour as they formed two lines leading up to the stage.

"People of Straken!" the herald on the stage repeated as he stepped aside. Lifting a hand, he pointed to a figure now moving through the ranks of royal guards. "Behold, your final judgement!"

Devon shivered as his eyes settled on the Tsar. The man stood no taller than Devon's own six-foot-five, but he carried himself with an aura of invincibility, as if the Gods themselves might bow to his powers. Jet-black hair curled down around his shoulders, while on his head sat a golden crown inset with a dozen diamonds. Thick eyebrows framed his crystal blue eyes. His pale cheeks showed no sign of his fifty years, except where a pale white lock of hair hung across his forehead.

A frown creased the Tsar's brow as he looked down at the enemy Magickers gathered before the stage. Even from where Devon stood, he could see the anger in the man's eyes. He swallowed, his mouth dry as he wondered what it would be like if those eyes were to turn on him.

The crystal eyes swept past the Magickers, to where the city of Straken waited with its paltry gathering of survivors. Not a murmur came from the towering walls. Somewhere within, Devon knew the people waited, praying to long-dead Gods for deliverance. It would not come, he knew. Just as it had not come for Kalgan, or Cascade, or Drata, or Palma before them.

When the Tsar spoke, his words boomed across the fields like thunder, his voice magically projected so all could hear.

"Three long weeks ago, you were offered a choice." The Tsar's tone was soft, sorrowful, as though the city's decision had brought him great pain. "You were told to bow to your one true ruler, or perish. Alas, you chose *death.*"

With his final word, an awful roar came from the hills behind the army. Another followed, then another and another, the sounds merging to create a terrible thunder, a chorus of demonic voices that promised only one thing.

Death.

Devon looked up in time to see the first beast sweep past. The air crackled as great wings rose, sending wind rushing through the men gathered below. The stench of ash and rotting meat filled the air. Clenching his jaw, he watched on as the great beasts flew towards the city.

Moments later, the first flames blossomed.

Even standing far up on the hill, Devon felt the heat of the inferno on his cheeks. He held his breath as the beasts roared again, the sunlight glinting off their blood-red scales.

In Straken, the silence broke as the first screams carried up to the watching soldiers. From the hilltop, little could be seen of the townsfolk huddled inside the city, but there was no mistaking the terror carried by their cries. As the dragons circled back, the flames rushing from their awful jaws, the screams rose, the first traces of agony joining the chorus.

Inside the walls, there was no escape from the dragons' wrath. For weeks the enemy Magickers had held the beasts at bay, driving them back with wind and lightning and light. But with their Magickers defeated, the survivors were defenceless. Trapped within the ancient battlements that had protected them for so many centuries, the city would now become their tomb.

The Plorsean army watched in silence as the flames engulfed the city. Not a man moved as the five Red Dragons circled. They were the Tsar's creatures, taken from Dragon Country, bound and chained by his magic. Once, the Gold Dragons had fought alongside man, willing allies against the powers of darkness. They were extinct now, but with the vicious Reds as slaves, the Three Nations now had little need for their more docile golden cousins.

Overhead, the Red Dragons turned and dove back towards the city. The great jaws opened as one, and the crimson flames rushed down, engulfing the last bastion of refuge within the city. Heat washed over the watching men and women. Sweat dripped from Devon's brow as he listened to the screams slowly die away.

When it was finally over, and silence had returned to the city, the Tsar spoke again.

"It is done." As before, the sorrow was heavy in his voice. "The war is won. Tomorrow, we return to Plorsea."

A cheer went up from the army. Despite himself, Devon joined in, raising a fist skyward in celebration. He had waited so long to hear those words, to know the slaughter was finally over, that he could return to the city of his childhood and hang up his hammer.

Yet now he felt no joy, no happiness—only relief.

He was going home.

But the boy who had left had died long ago.

I

FIVE YEARS LATER

F*ire.*

The thought came to Alana as she drifted through the darkness. Rising from the depths, it sent waves rippling through her consciousness. Comprehension came moments later, as the first tendrils of awareness returned. Heat washed over her, urgent and demanding, drawing her back.

Then the first sounds reached her ears - screams and shouting, the pounding of feet...the crackling of flames!

Touched by panic, Alana fought the pull of sleep and forced her eyes to open. The sight that greeted her was one of pure chaos.

She lay on a smooth stone ledge, looking down over a pit some hundred feet deep. Steps lined the walls of the pit, leading down to the dark waters far below.

A stepwell.

The name rose from the depths of her subconscious, but her mind was already moving on. All around the stepwell, people were fleeing, clambering up the steep stairs, desperate to escape. Sitting up, her gaze travelled down into the depths of the pit, where flames raged on a platform beside the water. There, a small figure was dancing amidst the flames.

She stared as the figure staggered to the edge of the platform and hurled himself into the pool. He vanished beneath the surface, but the fire was undeterred. Its orange tongues danced across the dark waters. Somewhere in its depths, the figure continued to thrash, lit by the flame's glow.

Finally, the figure forced himself to the surface, his desperate screams echoing up from below. High above, Alana shuddered. The cry had not been one of pain or agony, but of fear.

Magic.

As the word formed in her mind, a fresh terror lit in Alana's chest. It was followed by another name, one that sent tendrils of ice coiling around her spine.

Stalkers.

They would be on their way by now, drawn by the pulse of the wild magic below. They could not be allowed to find her, could not be allowed to take her brother.

With the thought, she twisted around, searching for him. Her panic eased as she found her brother lying nearby. He was still unconscious, but gathering herself, she crawled across and shook him.

"Braidon, wake up!" she hissed in his ear.

At fifteen, he was eight years her junior, but he was already closing on her own five foot and seven inches. His eyelids flickered at her touch, and she let out a breath as his blue eyes found hers. His eyebrows knotted into a frown as he looked up at her.

"Alana?" he asked, his voice groggy. "What's going on?"

Brushing the curly black hair from his face, she helped him sit up. "Wild magic."

"Not…mine?"

She shook her head and gestured into the stepwell, where the flames were finally starting to die away. The young Magicker had pulled himself from the water and now lay on the platform once more, his chest heaving. Alana swallowed as her eyes now found the bodies lying on the steps nearby.

"We'd better go," she said quietly.

He nodded, and with her help, regained his feet. Together they turned and made their way up the rows of staircases, legs aching with the exertion. Struggling with her brother's weight, Alana scanned the top of the stepwell, watching as the last survivors of the conflagration disappeared over the lip. There was still no sign of the dark-cloaked Stalkers, but they couldn't be far off. Gritting her teeth, she picked up the pace.

They had just reached the top of the stairs when a shout carried across to them. Twisting, Alana glanced back, and watched as a group of five dark-cloaked figures started down into the pit. She held her breath, waiting for them to look up and spot the two fugitives. But their eyes were fixed on the depths of the stepwell, where the boy had just turned to watch their approach.

Fire lit the boy's hands as he stood. The Stalkers scattered as flames rushed up to greet them. Only one stood his ground. Alana felt a tingle of recognition as the man raised his hand. Around the stepwell, wind swirled, hastening inwards, crackling as it gathered around the Stalker. The inferno roared, then went out as the gale pushed them back down into the waters of the stepwell.

Below, the boy groaned. He swayed on his feet, then his

knees went out from beneath him, and he collapsed face first onto the stone platform. The Stalkers quickly regathered and, drawing their blades, descended towards the motionless figure.

"Alana!" Braidon's voice came from behind her. He tugged urgently at the sleeve of her coat. "We have to go!"

Alana nodded, her eyes still fixed on the Stalker who had turned back to the flames. He led the way down into the stepwell, the winds still swirling around him. His black hair was streaked with blonde, and there was a coldness in his brown eyes as he approached the fallen boy. A golden star pinned to his chest marked him as lieutenant of the Stalkers—the man in charge of capturing rogue Magickers and bringing them before the Tsar's justice. Since the civil war five years before, all magic had been forbidden except by the Tsar's allowance.

Magic like her brother's.

She turned away then, following her brother over the edge of the stepwell. At the last moment, a voice called her back, shrill and filled with pain.

"Please, no, don't hurt him!"

Looking back, Alana glimpsed a woman on the opposite side of the stepwell. Soot stained her face and there were burn marks on her plain dress. She had clearly been caught up in the conflagration below, but now she started down into the pit, face set, eyes fixed on the Stalkers.

"Please," she called again, "he's just a child!"

Across the pit, the lieutenant looked up. His eyes took in the woman with a single glance. He said nothing, but with a gesture, one of his men advanced in her direction. Her face paled as she watched the man stride towards her, but she did not flee. She cried out as the Stalker grabbed her arm and tried to pull away. Before she could resist further, his sword hilt slammed into her head. She collapsed without a sound.

Turning away, Alana grabbed her brother's hand. Together they rushed into the shadows of a nearby building and disappeared into the alleyways of Ardath. The capital of Plorsea was massive, and for what felt like weeks, they had sought anonymity amongst its crowds. Yet now Alana felt exposed, as though with her glimpse of the Stalkers today, she had revealed herself to them. She could feel the noose closing, the hunt drawing near.

Only when they were several blocks away did Alana finally allow them to slow. Heart hammering in her chest, she slipped from the shadows back out into the bustling street, drawing her brother onwards. They had come out in the spice market, and hand in hand, they made their way through the press of bodies.

Alana was still struggling to comprehend what had happened. The events leading up to the explosion were a blur, the memories already fading, as though she were viewing them through a narrow tube. There had been an explosion, a rush of white, then…darkness.

All she knew was they had almost been caught—that pure chance had nearly brought the full wrath of the Tsar down on them. In her mind, she imagined the Stalkers closing in, their swords seeking her flesh, while the lieutenant with his cold brown eyes dragged her brother away.

Shuddering, Alana forced the thoughts away. But she knew they could not ignore the warning. Today the illusion of safety she'd felt in Ardath had been stripped away. There was no doubt in her mind any longer—they had to get out.

If only it were so easy. Ardath stood alone on the cliffs of an island, located in the centre of the largest lake in the Three Nations. The gates were guarded day and night, as were the great granite stairwells leading down to the docks. While she had scavenged enough coin for the ferry crossing, there would be little left to spare. They would travel the Gods Road as paupers, unable to afford passage further down the river to Lon.

At any moment during the long journey, they might be discovered. Then everything would be for naught. She and her brother would be dragged back to Ardath in chains, to face the Tsar's justice. Her life would be forfeit, and her brother…

She shuddered. No, she would not think of that. Tonight, she would visit the inns and pubs frequented by merchants; perhaps there would be one leaving in the next few days with need of extra workers. Alone, she and her brother were sure to draw the attention of the guards. With other travellers, they would blend in with the crowd. Or so she prayed.

Either way, Alana's heart told her they could not wait. They would leave sometime within the week, whether she found a merchant caravan or not. The journey would be long and treacherous, but she had her sabre, even now slapping at her thigh. Together they would make it to Northland, and the safety promised there for rogue Magickers.

2

Devon watched in silence as the couple walked slowly up to the gallows. They moved with heads bowed, shoulders slumped by the weight of defeat. A crowd was already gathering as the excitement in the plaza built. Public executions were becoming a rarity nowadays. The last of the Trolan rebels had been quashed years ago, and few now dared defy the Tsar's rule.

Not these two. He himself had warned them of their folly just days ago, when they had come to him for help. He'd known they were desperate—most were by the time they came seeking his services. But while coin was short, Devon was no fool. It didn't matter how much they offered, no amount of money was worth incurring the Tsar's wrath. Not here in Ardath, at least, in the centre of the empire.

How right he had been. His mood was dark as he watched the scarlet-cloaked guards drape the ropes around the prisoners' necks. Around him, angry murmurs spread through the crowd as the couple looked out over the square. Several bystanders had been killed by the wild magic their son had unleashed, and the mood in the city had quickly turned on them.

Shaking his head, Devon lowered his gaze from the platform, his eyes sweeping the crowd. He picked out several guards moving amongst the clustered bodies, faces alert for danger, hands never far from their sword hilts. With the Tsar's new laws forbidding magic, it had been almost a year since the last outbreak. The sudden return of danger had left people afraid and angry. It wouldn't take much for the mob to turn violent.

Devon's jaw tightened as a black-garbed man joined the couple on the raised gallows. The golden star marked him as a lieutenant, but Devon didn't need such reminders to recognise Quinn. They had fought together five years ago during the civil war, but since then their paths had diverged. Quinn had continued his service with the Tsar, advancing from Battle Magicker to Stalker, and eventually being promoted to lieutenant.

And Devon…

Well, he had chosen his path that cold morning when the dragons had burned Straken.

Up on the platform, Quinn attempted a smile, but even from a distance the gesture looked forced. The man had proved himself a ferocious warrior during the war, aided in no small part by his magic, but charisma had never been a part of his skillset.

"Good citizens of Ardath." He spoke softly, but nonetheless his voice carried to every watcher in the square. Devon guessed Quinn had one of the Tsar's heralds sequestered somewhere in the crowd, magically enhancing his voice. "Thank you for joining me today to witness the Tsar's justice. By his command, these two traitors are to be executed for the destruction of the stepwell. The deaths caused by their betrayal will long be remembered in our hearts, not least because they could so easily have been avoided—if only the condemned had not selfishly kept their son's power a secret."

Around Devon, men and women shouted their approval, their fists raised to the sky. Applause swept through the crowd as Quinn turned to the couple standing at the gallows. The man's eyes were fixed to the wooden trapdoor beneath his feet, but the woman stared back at the dark-cloaked Stalker, her silver eyes untouched by tears.

"Do you have any last words for yourselves?" Quinn asked, his eyes meeting those of the woman.

The woman straightened, her silver eyes flashing out over the crowd. "We were only protecting our son." Her voice carried across the square without any help from the hidden Magicker. "Which of you would not have done the same?"

Despite himself, Devon lowered his eyes. His chest constricted as he remembered how the same woman had come pleading for his help. He had dismissed her with a cold wave of his hand, eager to rid himself of her presence as quickly as possible. Now he found himself wondering if he could have changed things, if he could have convinced them to choose another path.

He shook his head. There was no point wondering 'what if' now—the deed was done, their fate decided.

On the stage, Quinn moved towards the woman. "Your son killed four innocent Plorsean citizens," he said softly. "Had you brought him to the citadel when his power woke, their lives could have been spared. Instead, you allowed evil into our great city."

The woman stared back at him, undaunted. "We did

what we had to, to protect our son," she hissed. "To keep him away from vile people like—"

Before the woman could finish, Quinn stepped forward and slammed his fist into her stomach. The woman doubled over, the movement pulling the noose tight around her neck. With her arms tied behind her back, she staggered sideways, almost losing her balance. Her mouth opened as she desperately tried to draw breath. Her feet kicked against the wooden stage, and finally found purchase. Gasping, she pushed herself back up. A red streak now marked her throat where the rope had caught her.

Ignoring the woman, Quinn looked out across the crowd. "The Tsar has spoken—"

He broke off as the woman spoke behind him, her voice broken, half a whisper now. "May Antonia protect my son."

Quinn looked back at her, a scowl marking his brow. "The Goddess is dead."

And so is her son, Devon thought sadly, though no one knew what truly became of the Magickers brought before the Tsar.

"The Tsar has spoken," Quinn continued, ignoring the interruption. "All Magickers must be brought to the citadel for the safety of our empire. Those who aid fugitive Magickers, who conceal them from the law, face death. The law is clear. Let it be done."

As he spoke, Quinn lifted his hand, and then dropped it down in a sudden cutting motion. A sharp *crack* rattled across the square as the trapdoors beneath the prisoners gave way, sending the couple plummeting downwards.

Devon quickly averted his eyes, but there was no keeping out the roar of the crowd's approval. All around him, the citizens of Ardath began to cheer. Shaking his head, Devon waited a few minutes, and then made his way through the crowd. There was no need to linger any longer. Normally, he would rather fight a Raptor unarmed than watch a public execution, but when he'd heard about the couple's arrest...

Swallowing, he threaded his way through the crowd, eager to escape the ignominious joy of his fellow citizens. How they could celebrate the death of two loving parents was beyond him. The press of bodies made his passage difficult, but slowly he found his way to the edge of the plaza and slipped into the relative peace of a side alley.

Only then did he let his anger show. A scowl appeared on his lips as he remembered the woman's pleas, her desperate call on the Gods, on their long-lost power to protect her son. He could only shake his head at her faith. The Gods had been gone for over a century now—if they'd ever existed in the first place. They sure as hell weren't going to save the young Magicker.

No, more likely the boy was already dead. The second his magic had manifested, his life had been forfeit, his future stolen. That was the way of things now, ever since the end of the civil war. The outlawing of Magickers had been the Tsar's first decree on his return to Ardath—and had been welcomed by much of the population. The Trolan Magickers had wreaked a dreadful toll on the Plorsean army, and the destruction caused by wild magic was well known nowadays.

Unfortunately, one did not choose to become a Magicker. And those who had surrendered themselves to the citadel had rarely been seen again. A few children had re-emerged as Magickers in the employ of the Tsar, but the others...

Well, no one knew what became of the others.

Forcing the thoughts from his mind, Devon threaded his

way through the darkening alleyways. Above, the light slowly faded from the sky, the sun dropping away to the west. He picked up the pace, his thoughts on the path ahead. After the display in the square, he needed a place to drown his sorrows, a haven where he could escape, and forget the face of the woman as she dropped from the gallows.

Devon sighed in relief as he turned a corner and found himself standing in front of the Firestone Pub. Shaking off his lethargy, he crossed the street and stomped his way up the wooden steps. The door gave a familiar screech as he pushed his way inside. Leaving behind the icy air outside, he crossed to the bar and waved at the bartender.

Behind the bar, Kellian waved back, a clay mug already in hand. It was half-full by the time Devon slumped into the seat across from his friend. Topping off the pint, Kellian sent it sliding across the bar with a grim smile.

"Bad?" he asked.

"Worse than I expected," Devon replied gruffly. He took a long swig of ale before placing the mug back on the bar. Putting several silver shillings on the wooden counter, he looked across at his friend. "Keep 'em coming, would ya?"

Kellian raised an eyebrow. "So long as you don't make trouble, Devon."

Like Quinn, Devon had met Kellian during the war. Unlike Quinn, Kellian had chosen to retire alongside Devon. Now thirty years of age, he was five years Devon's senior, and all the richer for it. Of course, he'd also done a far better job squirreling away his earnings. On his return from Trola, Kellian had traded his sword for an innkeeper's club, and quickly settled into the new life.

Devon, on the other hand, had a habit of spending his shillings as fast as he earned them. To make matters worse, his superiors had not expected the renowned warrior to retire his commission after the war. Plans had been made for him, promotions planned without Devon's knowledge. His announcement had sent shock waves rippling through the army—and caused no small amount of humiliation for several of his superiors. He'd made enemies, but there had been no help for it.

After the carnal house they'd made of Trola, Devon had lost his stomach for war.

"Who do you take me for?" Devon asked, smiling despite himself. "A Lonian?"

Kellian snorted. "Who was that ancestor of yours again? Alan something or other? A Lonian through and through, if I'm not wrong!"

Devon scowled. "Don't remind me."

Scooping up his mug, Devon downed the rest of his ale. Once, tales of the great hammerman had inspired him. Ever since he'd been old enough to lift *kanker*, he'd dreamed of living up to the legend, of carving new tales with the fabled hammer. He'd marched against Trola with dreams of glory in his young head. Instead, he'd found only death and shame.

Silently Kellian refilled his mug. "Sorry," he said softy. "I forget, sometimes."

Devon forced a smile. "It's nothing, old friend. Come on, why don't you join me for a drink? It'll be hours before any customers show after that...display."

Kellian nodded. He had just picked up a fresh mug when the screech of the door announced a new customer. Raising an eyebrow, Devon turned to look at the newcomer. His heart sank as he recognised the golden helm held in the crook of the man's arm.

Royal guard.

A grin stretched across the man's stubbled chin as he saw Devon sitting at the bar. He strode quickly across the room, his boots thumping hard on the wooden floor, and slid onto the stool beside Devon.

"Why, if it isn't the cowardly hero!" Laughter boomed across the bar as the newcomer slapped Devon on the back. "What are we drinking? I've always wanted to meet you."

Scowling at the man, Devon ignored the question—and the insult. He was familiar with the nickname, though few dared say it to his face. Undeterred by Devon's icy glare, the guard waved for Kellian to pour him a pint of ale. Kellian glanced once in question at Devon, but there was little either of them could do to rid themselves of the man. As a royal guard, he had connections of which they could only dream. Silently, Kellian drew another mug from beneath the bar and poured the man his drink.

"Ahhh, that hits the spot!" the guard boomed after he'd slurped down a mouthful of ale. Turning to Devon, he offered his hand. "The name's Anthony. Just came from the plaza. Don't suppose you got a chance to watch the traitors hang?"

Devon stared at the man's hand for a moment before reaching down to shake the pale fingers. Squeezing a little too tightly, Devon couldn't help but take some pleasure watching the man flinch. Anthony's brow hardened as he retrieved his bruised hand, and it was a while before he spoke again.

"Hard to believe a man like you won't use a blade," he said quietly. Reaching down, he drew a dagger from his belt. The steel glinted in the light of the oil lamp as he pointed it at Devon. "No wonder you earned the nickname. I swear, if I was as big as you, I'd be rich!"

Devon turned his amber eyes on the guard. The man

was a full head and shoulders beneath his own six-foot-five, but his slender frame was heavily muscled. He'd moved with the graceful balance of a warrior as he entered the bar, and he held the dagger with the air of a professional. If that wasn't enough to warn Devon of the man's skill, the golden helm resting on the bar left no doubt. Weak men did not get to be guards for the Tsar.

The man was clearly spoiling for a fight, but Devon had made his friend a promise. Letting out a long sigh, he climbed to his feet and looked down at the guard. He placed a hand on the man's back and shook his head.

"If you'd ever used that sword outside the training grounds, you'd understand," Devon said softly.

Turning on his heel, he left the bar before the man could form a response. He moved quickly through the double doors and outside. Just as he reached the bottom of the stairs, the screech of the doors came from behind him.

"I'll not be insulted by the likes of you," called the guard.

Turning, Devon watched the man stride down the steps towards him, his hand on the pommel of his sword. Devon glanced at the blade, then back at the guard's face. His eyes narrowed, his heart beating faster at the thought of a fight. "You draw that, you'd better be ready to use it, Sonny."

Anthony hesitated, his eyes flickering in either direction, but the street was empty. Swallowing, he straightened. "I don't need a blade to beat a coward," he growled.

"Is that so?" Devon asked.

He stepped forward, so that he stood just an inch from the man. Anthony might have had the height and muscle to match most foes, but Devon was no ordinary warrior. He had proven that during the civil war, when men had fallen beneath his hammer like wheat before the scythe. Now unarmed and unarmoured, the power of presence still sent fear slicing through the young guard's bravado.

"Go home, Sonny," he said quietly.

Turning away, he started off down the street. He only made it a couple of steps before the scuffing of leather on stone announced the guard's pursuit. Devon leapt to the side and heard a curse as Anthony stumbled past. His arms windmilled, and screaming, he twisted to give chase.

Devon met him with a right cross to the face. The blow halted the man in his tracks and sent him lurching back. But to Devon's surprise, he did not fall. Staggering sideways, he straightened and came at Devon in a rush. Caught out, Devon caught a blow on his chin before he could register the man's speed. He twisted with the blow, deflecting its power, and slammed a left hook into his opponent's stomach.

Breath hissed between the guard's teeth as he bent in two. Pain throbbing from his cheek, Devon felt the old rush of his anger returning. Blood pounding in his ears, he stepped in and drove two blows in quick succession into his reeling opponent. The man's strength went from him in a rush, but before he could fall Devon caught him beneath the arms.

Anthony's head sagged as Devon lifted him up. "Not so tough now, are you Sonny?" he snapped.

Bone crunched as he smashed his fist into his opponent's chin. Blood dripped from his knuckles, but he no longer cared. A low rumble came from Devon's throat as he lifted the man above his head and hurled him across the street. He landed with a crash in a pile of old pottery, and did not rise.

Teeth bared, Devon watched the man for several seconds before shaking his head. If that was the best the

Tsar had to draw on, it was a good thing the man
magic. Letting out a long breath, he allowed his anger
Guilt rose to replace it. For just a moment, the rush of ba
had overwhelmed him. He had allowed the joy of com
to wash away his common sense, and set the beast free.

Now there would be repercussions. The man was a roya
guard and wouldn't hesitate to make Devon's life a living
nightmare. But that was a worry for tomorrow. Tonight, he wanted nothing more than to sleep. Turning towards home, he started off down the bricked street, before a voice called out behind him.

"*Wait!*"

3

Alana shivered as the giant of a man turned towards her. Blood ran from a cut on his cheek, and his unkept beard and flattened nose gave him a look of such ferocity she almost took a step back in shock. The silence stretched out as his amber eyes watched her, a dark scowl written across his forehead. His massive shoulders were hunched, his hands clenched into fists as he watched her, waiting for her to speak.

Swallowing, Alana forced herself forward. "I know you."

"I don't know you," he replied, his voice gruff and unwelcoming.

"No," she murmured, biting her lip, "but then, I wasn't a hero in the war."

"What's that to you?"

"Is it true you're a sellsword now?" she asked quickly, before the words deserted her.

She had spent the last three days visiting Ardath's various pubs and inns, asking for word of travellers leaving the city, for merchant caravans in need of an extra hand. But with the onset of winter, few dared to venture out into the wilderness at this time of year. A few planned to take ship all the way to Lon, but Alana had neither the coin nor the skill to aid on such a venture.

Desperate, she had turned her search to the poorer quarters of the city. The Firestone Pub was one of the nicer establishments in this area, but as she had turned the corner and started towards it, the two men had staggered outside and begun their fight. She could not recall seeing the legendary hammerman before, but it hadn't taken much to make the connection. Few people in the Three Nations matched the size of the man standing in front of her. And if he was willing to help them…

"No offence, missy, but you don't look like you could afford me," Devon replied, one eyebrow raised.

Heat spread to Alana's cheeks. She'd heard the man was a brute, a soldier who'd do a man's dirty work for a few coins, but she wasn't about to be talked down to. Her cloak rustled as she pulled it back, revealing the hilt of her sabre.

A smile twitched on the giant's lips. "Are you sure you want to threaten me?" He gestured to the man still lying in the pile of broken pottery. "Didn't turn out so well for the last man."

"I'm not a man," Alana growled. She held his gaze for a moment, and then allowed her cloak to settle back into place. "But you're right, I didn't come here to fight."

"What did you come here for?"

"For help." She paused, eyes flickering to the shadows of the street. Biting her lip, she decided to take a chance on the brute. "My brother and I are leaving the city in the morning. I've been trying to find someone to make the voyage with…"

"Not many travellers on the road this time of year," Devon said, chuckling softly.

"I noticed," she snapped. Taking a breath, she continued in a calmer voice. "Maybe you could help us, though."

Devon's laughter boomed across the street. Scratching his beard, he shook his head. "I could," he said, "but like I said, I don't work for free."

"I can pay," Alana said through gritted teeth.

"Really?" The laughter faded away as the giant looked at her with fresh eyes. With her tatty cloak and tangled blonde hair, she knew what he was thinking—that she couldn't possibly have the money for such a journey. "Show me."

The heat returned to Alana's cheeks at being caught in her lie. She lowered her head to hide her blush. "My uncle," she said quickly. "He lives in Lon. You'll get your pay when you deliver us safely to him."

Devon snorted. "I wasn't born yesterday, missy." Shaking his head, he started to turn away.

"Wait!" Alana shouted, anger flaring.

The giant waved a hand. "Goodnight, missy. We're done here."

"They'll come for you now, you know!" she shrieked. Teeth bared, she moved after him. She gestured at the unconscious guard as he glanced back. "That's one of the Tsar's guards. I doubt he'll take too kindly to you assaulting one of them."

A smile twitched on Devon's face. "You think that fool would admit to the Tsar he got knocked on his face by some washed up ex-soldier?"

"If not the Tsar, his friends!" Alana pressed, unwilling to

back down. "You think you can fight a dozen of those brutes?"

"They can try," he grunted.

Alana snorted. "Your arrogance is going to get you killed. Face it, you need to leave the city. Why not make some coin helping us while you're at it?"

For a moment Devon seemed to waver. His amber eyes stared down at her, unblinking, until finally he shook his head. "Sorry, missy," he mumbled. "I'm not going anywhere."

Turning, he strode off down the street without a backwards glance. Alana stared after him, her mind still sluggishly trying to concoct an argument that might persuade the warrior. Only when he turned a corner and disappeared from view did her shoulders slump in defeat.

Swallowing her disappointment, she turned and headed off in the opposite direction. The Firestone looked empty, and after the confrontation with Devon she was in no mood to try and convince anyone else to help them. Exhausted, she threaded her way through the dark streets towards the abandoned building she and her brother had claimed as their own.

She found her brother inside the rundown hovel, struggling to light a fire in the crumbling hearth. He looked up as she entered, his blue eyes brightening as a smile replaced his frustrated frown. Standing, he moved across and pulled her into a hug. Her heart warmed as they embraced, a smile of her own touching her lips.

"Sorry it's so cold in here," he mumbled as they separated. "The wood won't catch."

Alana gave his arm a squeeze. Since his magic's awakening, it had just been the two of them. Everything before that single moment seemed a distant memory now, as though she were viewing her life through another's eyes. She recalled golden days spent on the lake with her brother, and cold winter nights as she wandered the marketplace. There had been pain too, of course; from bruises collected while learning to fight, heartache as her first dog passed away. But that pain seemed distant, false somehow. It could not compare to the agony of their parents' betrayal…

Shivering, she moved towards the fireplace. "Here, let me."

Crouching down, she took up the flint and expertly struck sparks into the wood her brother had placed awkwardly around the debris from the collapsed chimney. A few minutes later she had a small flame blazing amongst the stones. Its orange light sent shadows dancing across the room as she sat back on her haunches and looked at her brother.

"Still no luck?" he asked, reading her mind.

She shook her head. "Almost, but no, no one seems willing to help us." She sighed then, leaning her head back against the brick wall. "I think we should leave tomorrow. The longer we delay, the more dangerous things become."

Her brother nodded. Crossing the room, he rummaged in their meagre pile of supplies and came up with half a loaf of stale bread. Taking his dagger, he stabbed it through the loaf and used the blade to hold it out to the flames.

"I think I can help us get past the guards," he said softly, eyes on the flames.

Alana sat up at that, her eyes widening. "Absolutely not!"

His blue eyes flashed as he looked at her. "I can do it, Alana."

"That's not the point!" she hissed. The heat of the fire

washed across her face as she looked at her brother. "They'd sense your magic the second you tried to use it."

"But we'd be long gone—"

"No," Alana cut him off mid-sentence. Baring her teeth, she pointed a finger at his chest. "Braidon, we don't know the first thing about your power. You don't even know if your magic would *work*, let alone if you could control it."

Braidon stared back, his blue eyes dark with anger. "You could at least let me try," he said. "It's my magic, not yours. You don't know the first thing about what I can do."

Alana leaned towards him. "That's right, I don't," she said softly. Reaching out an arm, she squeezed his shoulder gently. "You could hurt someone, Braidon. Kill someone, even. Then they'd never stop hunting us."

Her brother's mouth opened, but no words came out, and after a moment he closed it again. Lowering his gaze, he shook his head. "But how will we get out without it, Alana?" She heard the fear in his voice now. "I don't want you to hang like those people."

"Hey, that's not going to happen, okay?" She spoke the words softly, keeping her own fear hidden.

She had caught a glimpse of the couple as they were led to the gallows. The woman had been the same one from the stepwell, who had tried to protect her son from the Stalkers. She didn't recognise the man, but it was easy to see his relation to the young Magicker the Stalkers had taken. They had the same hazel eyes.

"How do you know that?" Braidon whispered, a tremble in his voice.

"I just do." She spoke the words with confidence, as though voicing them out loud would make them true. "We'll leave tomorrow. There's no point waiting any longer."

"What about the guards? If they ask too many questions…"

Alana suppressed a shudder. "Let me worry about the guards."

Moving past her brother, she took a moment to examine their tiny quarters. The building had been a stable at some point, and the faint whiff of horses and straw still hung on the air. Fortunately for them, the inn next door had burned down some time ago, leaving the stable empty. The broken fireplace in the corner had probably once been used by the stableboys to keep warm on cold winter nights.

Their meagre possessions lay scattered across the cobbled floor—no more than a few moth-eaten clothes and some scraps of food they'd scavenged from the alleyways behind the market. It wouldn't take them long to pack. They could be away at first light.

Braidon shuffled across the room to stand beside her. Silently he offered the bread he'd heated over the fire. The outside was half-blackened by the flames, but she took it with a grateful smile.

"Thank you," she said, then gestured at the knife in his hand. "Just make sure you have that dagger sharp tomorrow. We may need it."

A fire lit in her brother's eyes at her words. He held out the dagger proudly for her to inspect. She took it with a smile. The blade was still razor sharp. Like her sabre, it was made of fine steel, its value far greater than anything else in their little hovel. She had stolen them as they'd fled, slipping into the darkness of the armoury, all the while terrified they would be caught…

Alana shivered and, reversing the dagger, offered it back to her brother. She reached out and ruffled his hair as he took it. At just a hundred and thirty pounds, Braidon would be outmatched by most grown men, but what he lacked in size, he more than made up for in ferocity. She would feel better with him at her side tomorrow, though she knew if anything went wrong, there was little chance either of them would survive the day.

"Get some sleep," she said softly. "You'll need your strength tomorrow."

"You really think we'll be okay, on the road by ourselves?" Braidon asked.

Alana shrugged and looked away. Her stomach churned as she recalled her conversation with Devon. The man had hardly bothered to consider her offer. He'd taken one look at Alana and dismissed her as a pauper. She clenched her teeth at the memory and forced her anger aside. It didn't matter now—the fool had made his decision. Sure, she didn't *actually* have the coin to pay him, but she hadn't been wrong about the royal guards.

"We'll be fine," she said, though even to her the words sounded weak. Squaring her shoulders, she nodded to the pile of rags that served as her brother's bed. "No more questions, mister. Off to bed with you!"

Braidon scowled at being treated like a toddler, but he went eventually, muttering under his breath as he pulled the blanket around him. Alana smiled, glad the fading light hid her amusement. Devon might have added muscle to their little party, but the giant hammerman was a fool. No, things were better off with just the two of them. Alana had her sabre, and the scars to prove she knew how to use it.

Stretching out before the fire, she stared at the white lines marking the backs of her hand. Her mind drifted through the corridors of her past, memories rising and fading, carrying her off to sleep…

"Again, Alana!" There was anger in her father's voice as he tossed the practice blade.

Reaching up, she plucked the sword from the air. Pain from her bruises radiated down her arm, but she took care to keep it from her face. She straightened and lifted the sword, readying herself.

He attacked without warning, his heavy practice blade flashing for her face. Alana danced back, her own blade leaping to meet the attack. Steel clashed, and she flinched back, the power of the blow almost knocking the sword from her hand. Spinning on her heel, she attempted a riposte, only for a heavy boot to catch her in the chest.

Her lungs emptied as she staggered backwards, still clutching the sword to her side. The scrape of leather on the stone pavings warned Alana of her father's approach. Still gasping for breath, she thrust out with her sword, and felt a satisfying crunch as its blunted tip caught him in the stomach. Groaning, he staggered back. She took the opportunity to suck in a fresh lungful of air.

They circled each other for a moment, wary now. He attacked in a rush, his sword slashing viciously for her head. Alana skipped backwards, her own blade parrying desperately, but now her father seemed to move with superhuman speed. In the dream, she watched in horror as he become a blur.

She screamed as his blade struck her elbow. Agony tore through her senses. Her vision swam as she glanced down, and saw blood gushing from her arm, staining the cobbles. She swayed on her feet, staring at the bloody stump where her hand had been just moments before. Suddenly, her knees gave way. She tumbled to the cobbles, her head ringing as it struck stone.

A face appeared over her, but it was no longer her father's. It was the Stalker from the stepwell, the lieutenant who had captured the boy Magicker. He wore a sad smile on his face, and regret in his almond eyes. His long hair fell around his face as he shook his head.

"Too slow, Alana."

4

The boy stumbled as the guard shoved him from behind. His bare feet slipped on the cold stone steps, and he would have fallen had Quinn not reached out a hand to catch him. He waited until the boy had righted himself, his depleted strength struggling to keep him upright, before shooting the guard a glare. The man quickly looked away, but not before Quinn saw his fear. Nodding, he turned his attention back to the boy.

"Are you okay?" he asked.

Steel manacles encircled the boy's wrists. Chains hung from his ankles, making it difficult for him to walk. Dirt streaked his hollowed-out cheeks, and there was terror in his hazel eyes as he looked up at the guards.

Quinn offered a friendly smile. Crouching beside the boy, he offered his hand. "My name is Quinn, lad," he said softly, "and you don't have to worry anymore, now I'm here. We'll have those chains off you shortly. They're just to keep your magic under control, until we're someplace safe."

When the boy didn't take the offered hand, Quinn let

out a long sigh and stood. Flashing another glare at the guards, he took the boy by the shoulder and led him gently down the corridor. "The gardens are just ahead, lad," he continued, as though this situation were nothing unusual. "We can take your chains off there."

Silently, Quinn cursed the men he'd left in charge of the boy. Many among the Tsar's Stalkers had no sympathy for the young Magickers they caught, and were quick to take retribution for the destruction their captives had caused. With the damage he'd caused in the stepwell, this boy had more than earned the men's wrath.

Quinn had found him locked deep in the bowels of the dungeons, alone but for the rats. He'd screamed and fled to the corner of his cell at Quinn's appearance. No one had gotten a word out of him since. Quinn prayed his men's foolishness hadn't ruined the boy; the loss of another potential Magicker would not please the Tsar—especially not after the recent disappearances.

Shaking his head, Quinn sighed as they stepped through a wide marble doorway and out into the gardens. Beneath his hand he could feel the boy trembling, but as they continued across the manicured grass, the shaking began to slow. The boy blinked, his freckled cheeks wrinkling with confusion.

Quinn allowed himself a smile at the boy's wonder. Here the air was unnaturally warm, heated by the Tsar's magic to protect its inhabitants from the icy winter beyond the citadel's walls. The emerald green lawn spread out around them, dotted with stone courtyards and marble arches, rose bushes and towering oak trees.

Laughter carried through the gardens. Quinn turned and watched as a group of children came running across the grass. Beside him, the boy shrank at the sound, his wonder turning to fear. Quinn cursed again his own men's stupidity. The boy would never learn if he was too terrified to look beyond the edge of his nose. Moving across to him, Quinn placed a hand beneath his chin and forced the tiny face to look at him.

"What do you think, lad?" he asked with a smile. "This will be your home now. Shall we remove those chains?"

The boy nodded and quickly looked away, as though afraid the offer would be rescinded. Taking a key from his pocket, Quinn unlocked the cuffs on the boy's wrists, then moved to his ankles. Metal clattered as the chains tumbled to the ground. Where the chains had been fastened, the boy's skin had been rubbed raw, and Quinn made a silent note to send a healer to check on the boy's health. It wouldn't do for him to collapse in the middle of his lessons.

"Well, would you like to meet your new teacher, lad?" Quinn asked as he stood.

"Teacher?" The boy's head jerked up at the word, the hazel eyes wide. "Wh—what?"

Quinn flashed him a grin. "Of course. A fellow Magicker. How else would you learn to control your magic?"

"Control it?" the boy said, swallowing visibly. "I thought…I thought that wasn't allowed."

"Only without permission from the Tsar," Quinn said, gesturing at the citadel. It stretched up behind them, all glistening marble and towering domes of silver and gold. "Why do you think I brought you here? The Tsar only wants his people to be safe. Wild magic is a deadly thing, but if you are good, and train hard, you can master your power. Then you can use your magic to serve the Tsar."

"Like you?" The boy whispered.

"Like me," Quinn agreed, "and many, many others."

Biting his lip, the boy looked away. For the first time his eyes swept out over the gardens, taking in the vivid green of the grass, the scarlet hue of the roses. Quinn's heart twisted as he saw tears appear in the child's eyes. Following his gaze, he saw the children playing nearby.

"Are they learning, too?" the boy asked, his voice barely more than a murmur.

"Yes, they're Magickers, too. Everyone in this place has been brought here to learn, just like you. We all serve the Tsar."

"And what about my teacher?"

"I'm right here." They looked around as a woman's voice came from across the courtyard.

Quinn forced a smile to his lips as he watched the woman emerge from a nearby archway. Long legs carried her quickly across the grass, her bare feet silent on the soft ground. Scarlet hair tumbled around her shoulders. A plain dress of cream wrapped around her tiny figure, and her green eyes shimmered as she watched them, a teasing smile on her lips.

Wandering across to where they stood, she crouched beside the boy. "My name is Krista. And who might you be, young man?"

"Li…Liam," the boy stammered.

Krista offered her hand. "It's nice to meet you, Liam."

"You're…you're going to teach me magic?" the boy asked as he took her hand.

"I'm going to show you the way." Krista grinned. "The rest will be up to you, Liam. You'll need to be brave. Do you think you can do that?"

With his hand in Krista's grip, basking in her warmth, the boy nodded. "I'd…I'd like to try."

Behind them, Quinn smiled despite himself. Krista had

only just started teaching the children a couple of weeks ago, but he had to admit, she showed promise. Her warmth had won the boy over, where all his shows of kindness had brought only suspicion. She hadn't even needed to use her power. With luck, she would have the boy ready to consciously reach for his magic within a few weeks.

Now, though, it was time for Quinn to take his leave.

Nodding to Krista, he took his leave and turned away. He was just starting towards the doorway when a sharp tingling sensation shot down his spine. Gasping, he stood fixed in place, his fists clenched tight. Beside the boy, Krista rose, suddenly rigid as steel. Her eyes turned towards the north, in the same direction Quinn found his gaze drawn. They stood together in silence, staring at the distant wall, waiting for the last trembles of magic to die away.

"It was close, inside the city," Krista said finally, turning to look at Quinn.

Quinn nodded. "Somewhere north of us. I had best investigate." He glanced across at the teacher, his eyes hard. "Good luck with the boy, Krista. I trust you will prove your worth in this appointment. You know the legacy that came before you."

Krista stared back at him. Her eyes glinted, but Quinn turned away before she could respond. His mind was already elsewhere, feeling out the power he had sensed, seeking its source. Somewhere in the city, another Magicker was at large.

It was his job to bring them to justice.

5

Bang. Bang. Bang.

Devon groaned as the sound of knocking pulled him from his sleep. Rolling over, he lifted his head and swore loudly at the intruder, and then buried his head in his pillow once more.

"Devon, open up!" Kellian's voice carried through the thick wooden door. "We need to talk!"

Devon winced as the banging resumed. He held his hands to his ears, but it did little to stop the drums pounding in his head. He swore again and finally relented. Pulling himself out from beneath the thick blankets, he crossed the room and yanked open the door.

Kellian stood outside, his hand still raised mid-knock. He blinked, then after glancing quickly down the street, stepped inside and closed the door behind him. Still muttering to himself, Devon moved across to the fireplace. The coals from last night were cold, but it only took a few strikes of the flint to get a fresh fire burning in the kindling.

His stomach swirled as he stood and looked at his friend. "There, we have heat. Now, what did you want?"

His friend only shook his head, his eyes venturing around the room. "Anything here you'd like to keep?"

Devon frowned. "Keep?"

He glanced quickly around the room, but there was little to see. Other than the single cot he slept in, there was a small dresser that was half-full of clothes and a plain table with just one chair. The tiny brazier had one dented pot and a pan. His sole possession of value was the chest at the foot of his bed. Made of solid oak, it was held together by steel bolts engraved with his family's insignia—a pair of warhammers crossed at the hafts. Inside were his armour and weaponry from the war. It hadn't been opened for almost five years.

"What are you talking about, Kellian?" he asked, turning back to his friend.

Kellian was busy peering out the tiny window beside the door, but he glanced back at Devon's words.

"The man you fought last night came back this morning. With friends," Kellian said, voice hard. "They were looking for you."

Devon snorted. Moving to the table, he lowered himself into the chair with a groan. "Let them come," he laughed. "Pretty fools, all of them with their golden bonnets. They don't scare me."

"They should!" Kellian snapped.

Something in his friend's tone made Devon look up. "What is it?"

"They're out for blood, Devon," his friend replied quietly. "They woke me by kicking in the front door to the Firestone. By the time I made it downstairs, they'd already smashed half the furniture. I sent them in the wrong direction, but it won't be long before they realise they've been tricked."

"You shouldn't have done that for me," Devon said softly. Standing, he gripped Kellian by the shoulder. "I'm sorry they wrecked the Firestone."

Kellian shook his head. "I don't care about the pub, Devon. But those men, they're not going to stop; at least not while you're close. You need to leave the city."

"A woman told me the same thing last night."

"An intelligent one, by the sounds of it," Kellian muttered. He gestured around the room. "Now, as I said, is there anything in here you're fond of?"

Devon took another moment to look around, but, in the end, he shook his head. His controversial retirement hadn't left him with many commendations, and in the five years since, he had struggled to find work as a sellsword. His refusal to use weapons tended to put off potential employers.

"What about the hammer?" Kellian asked quietly.

A shiver ran through Devon as his eyes were drawn back to the oaken chest. Inside lay not only his chainmail armour and iron half-helm, but the ancient warhammer, *kanker.* He had not touched it since that final day on the fields above Straken. But the weapon had been passed down through his family for generations. Kellian was right, he could not leave it for Anthony and his men to find.

Even so, he hesitated. The thought of lifting the weapon again filled him with trepidation. He recalled the thrill of power he had felt carrying it into battle, the terror in the eyes of his enemies as he scythed through their ranks. And he saw again the pain of the survivors, the agony of men and women as they found the bodies of their loved ones.

An ache began in Devon's chest as the old guilt

returned, but forcing it to the side, he strode across to the chest and flicked it open. Reaching inside, he pulled out the chainmail vest. Its steel links rattled softly as he pulled it over his head and settled it in place. The greaves followed, their iron panels engraved with the same insignia as the chest. The small pouch of silver shillings, all that remained of his wealth, he tied to his belt. Finally, he reached down and lifted the hammer.

"Ready then?" Kellian asked impatiently.

Devon nodded. Looping the warhammer's sheath over his shoulders, he kicked open the door and stepped out into the street. A cold wind swirled across the cobbles as Kellian followed him outside. The boom of the door closing echoed off the narrow walls of the neighbouring buildings.

"What will you do?" Devon asked, turning to face his friend.

"I'll be fine, Devon," Kellian replied. "Just get yourself someplace safe and wait out the winter."

"I'll head for Lon." His various dealings had drawn him to the Lonian capital on more than one occasion. It was a rough, dangerous place, its sprawling streets hosting almost twice the population of Ardath. He had contacts there though, former soldiers he'd fought alongside during the war. His retirement may have made him enemies among the officers, but his heroics on the battlefield had earned him the respect of the common soldiers. With luck, someone would have need of him.

Still he hesitated, looking sidelong at his friend. "Maybe you should join me, Kellian. That guard and his friends won't take too kindly if they discover you misled them."

Kellian grinned at that. "My clientele don't take kindly to those who threaten their local watering hole. It'll take more than a golden helmet to protect them if they venture into the Firestone again."

"Be sure to give them my regards if they do."

Laughing, Kellian extended his hand. "Take care, old friend. I'll see you in the summer."

Devon took Kellian's hand and pulled him into an embrace. "In the summer," he agreed.

Without another word, they separated. Turning, Devon headed off down the street without a backwards glance. His mind was already planning his route through the city. He would head for the northern gates and down to the quays. With only a few silvers to his name, he couldn't afford to book passage down the river to Lon, but it was common for ships departing Ardath to carry passengers across the lake. From there he could walk the Gods Road to Lon.

He had just reached the end of the street when a shout came from behind him. He recoiled as Kellian came racing past him. Devon had time to glimpse a dozen men racing down the street behind his friend before Kellian grabbed him by the arm and dragged him around the corner. The sharp *crack* of arrows striking stone came from the wall beside them.

"Missed me already?" Devon asked as they started to run.

Kellian answered with a string of curses. Ahead, the shadow of an alleyway beckoned and the two of them raced inside. Shouts chased after them. A crash warned Devon they'd entered the alleyway. He leapt a fallen pillar and ducked low. Arrows hissed and sparks flew as they struck the brick walls, but in the darkness Devon and Kellian were little more than shadows. Together they sprinted down a side passage.

"You really know how to make friends, don't you?"

Kellian shouted as they fled through the maze of alleyways that was central Ardath.

Devon's laughter boomed from the walls, drawing their pursuers on. "They say a man…is judged by his enemies," he panted.

His friend didn't deign to reply, and they ran on in silence. In the twisting alleyways, they soon became lost, but the maze was the perfect place to hide, and it wasn't long before all sound of pursuit faded away. Gasping for breath, Devon drew to a stop behind his friend, a grin on his face.

"Decided to rethink that trip to Lon then, old friend?"

Kellian glared back at him. Reaching into his jacket, he drew a dagger and flipped it into the air. His hazel eyes narrowed as it spun. As it started to fall, his hand flashed out and caught it by the blade. Before Devon could react, he drew back his hand, then whipped it forward. The hiss as the throwing knife swept past Devon's face raised the hackles on his neck. It was quickly followed by a *thud*—and a strangled cry.

Turning, Devon raised an eyebrow as he watched a man several feet away slump to the ground. Steel rattled on stone as the sword slipped from his fingers. Glancing around, Devon checked for other pursuers, but the man was alone. He watched in silence as Kellian strode past and retrieved his knife.

"I guess I could use the fresh air," Kellian muttered as he cleaned the blade on the man's shirt. He studied the blade for a moment, before pointing it at Devon's chest. "You've cost me a small fortune, you know."

Devon chuckled lightly. Moving forward, he thumped his friend on the shoulder. The gesture was hard enough to send Kellian staggering sideways. "Ay, but at least you'll have an adventure. Admit it, your talents were wasted as an innkeeper."

His friend only scowled. Grinning, Devon strode past him. "Come on then, we'd best get out of Ardath before they decide to set the city watch on us."

"Just what we need," Kellian muttered, but a moment later the crunch of footsteps on the rubble-strewn ground told Devon he was following.

Together they wound their way through the narrow maze. It was several blocks before Devon found a landmark he recognised, but afterwards they made their way steadily north towards the gates. Finally, they emerged from the shadows into a broad thoroughfare. Picking up the pace, they threaded their way through the crowds leading into marketplace.

Devon swore as the throng jostled them. The marketplace stretched the entire length of Ardath's northern boundary. Despite the wide avenue running alongside the wall, the bustling stalls and vendors made progress difficult. At least their pursuers would have difficulty spotting them amongst the press of bodies. Even so, Devon could feel his anger rising as men staggered across his path. Clenching his fists, he struggled on after Kellian.

Amidst the crowd, it was difficult to gauge their progress. Above, the sun continued its slow climb into the sky. Despite the cold winter winds, sweat dripped down Devon's brow. Only when the shadow of the gate tower fell across them did he know they were close. Looking up, his eyes were drawn to the gleaming spire. The walls facing the city shone with gilded gold, interspersed with mosaics of diamond that depicted effigies of the sun. The northern gates to the city had been dedicated to the Light, the most powerful of the three magical elements. The Earth and Sky were represented on the eastern and western gates, while the south was adorned by inscriptions dedicated to the Tsar—the saviour of the Three Nations.

Devon let out a long breath as the men guarding the gate tunnel came into view. They stood at ease, working their slow way through the line of people waiting to leave the city. Kellian glanced back and flashed him a grin. Together they continued forward, pushing their way through the last of the crowd.

As they stepped out into the open, a shout came from behind them. Turning, Devon looked out over the crowd. His eyes alighted on the familiar face of the guard from the night before. Anthony's left eye was so swollen he looked to be having trouble seeing, and his face was now a mottled purple. If anything, it was an improvement on his looks. He wore the same tunic from the night before, now stained with dirt and blood.

Standing just beyond the crowd, he was separated from Devon by a hundred feet of jostling bodies. With a roar, he drew his sword. His voice carried across the low rumble of the marketplace.

"Devon, you bastard, you're mine now!"

6

Alana's heart sank as she threaded her way through the last of the market stalls and found a line of wagons stretching away from the gates. Sunlight glittered from the golden spire that towered above them, but below they remained in the shadow of the wall. The cold of night still hung in the air, and Alana shivered as she glanced back at her brother. Dust billowed as people and wagons rumbled past on their way to and from the market.

"You have your knife to hand?" Alana asked, leaning in close.

Braidon nodded and patted his waist where a slight bulge beneath his coat was all she could see of his dagger. Alana squeezed his shoulder, offering her reassurance, and then turned and led him to the back of the queue to leave the city. As they walked up, her boot caught a loose brick on the cobbled street, and she stumbled forward into the back of the last man in the line.

"Oi, watch where you're walking, runt," the man snapped as Alana recovered her balance.

Shaking herself, Alana looked up into the man's dark eyes. "Sorry, sir," she said quickly.

He didn't seem any worse for wear, but his brow deepened at her words. The muscles of his jaw clenched as he advanced. One meaty finger jabbed at her chest. "You better watch yourself, girl."

Alana stood her ground. Pushing back her cloak, she rested her hand on the hilt of her sabre. "Is that so?" she asked, her voice hard now. Narrowing her eyes, she stepped closer to the man. "Want to try me?"

She watched the man's Adam's apple bob up and down and grinned. He shook his head and looked away, edging forward to catch up with the rest of the line. Glancing at her brother, Alana winked.

"Never let them push you around," she whispered.

Her brother laughed, and some of the tension left him. Alana wished the same could be said for her. Her eyes travelled down the queue, taking in the silk merchants and spice traders, the bulky woodsmen heading east into the forests, the hunters with their huge bows and fishermen heading down to the lake to begin the day's work. There were almost fifty in all, and while the sun was still low in the sky, at the pace the guards were letting people through it might take them all morning to get away. Shaking her head, Alana closed her eyes and tried to still her racing heart.

"Just the two of ya travelling?" Alana's eyes flew open as a voice spoke from behind them.

Glancing around, she realised a sailor had joined the line behind them. He wore an easy smile on his face, but she swallowed hard, her mind racing. The man had obviously already seen their rucksacks. He knew they were leaving town. Two young travellers alone on the road would be easy prey—if not for him, for someone he might inform.

"We're meeting our uncle on the docks," her brother answered before Alana could think of a response. "He went ahead to make sure everything was ready."

The easy smile didn't change, but Alana thought she caught a flicker of suspicion in the man's eyes. She glanced at his belt, but he seemed to be unarmed. Relaxing a little, she fixed a smile to her face. "We didn't expect the line. Hope he waits for us!"

The man laughed. "It'll move faster once old Bodric finishes his shift. Don't know why they keep 'im on the gates. Man must be blessed by a spell or something."

Alana snorted. "More likely he comes from the right family."

"Ain't that the truth." The sailor scratched at his beard, his eyes looking out over the crowd. "There goes the old fart now. His replacement is usually faster. Shouldn't take too much longer."

His words were quickly proven true as the queue started to move. Alana sneezed as dust kicked up around them. The echo of hooves on stone grew louder as they approached the gate tunnel. Ahead of them, the man Alana had bumped into kept his eyes fixed straight ahead, but she could sense his antagonism. Ever since the attack in the stepwell, the people of Ardath had seemed on edge. Alana would be glad to see the back of the city.

Finally, the man moved forward to the table set up in front of the gates. There a man sat with a great binder of paper, a feather quill gripped in one meaty hand. Two guards in chainmail vests and scarlet cloaks stood behind him, spears at their sides and swords strapped to their waists.

Usually the city guards stood at ease, but today the men

at the gate were jumpy, their eyes alert and weapons gripped tightly. Alana swallowed, lowering her eyes so they wouldn't see her staring. Silently, she sent a prayer to the Goddess to see them safely from the city.

"Name?" Alana was only half listening as the guard at the table took down the traveller's details. Her mind was busy elsewhere, taking in the dark shadows of the gate tunnel, unguarded but for the men around the table. If they moved quickly, she and her brother could be through the gates and out the other side before the guards could react.

Only she couldn't see what waited beyond the tunnel. If the watch had more guards stationed there, they would be caught before they even reached the steps down to the docks. And then there was the matter of securing passage across the lake…

"Next!" Alana blinked and looked up. The man sitting behind the table was staring at her, his eyebrows knitted together in a scowl. "*Next!*" he said again.

Beyond him, the man ahead of them was already disappearing into the darkness of the tunnel, but as she watched him, he flashed a glance back at them. For a second, a grin split his unshaven chin. Then he was gone.

Shaking her head, Alana forced the man from her mind and approached the table. The guard glared up at her, eyes hard. "Name?" he asked in a cold voice.

Alana swallowed. "Margaret and Jon," she lied.

"Where are you heading?"

"Onslow," she lied again. Onslow was halfway to Trola —west through the mountains rather than north along the Gods road. "There's meant to be a ship leaving shortly."

"Always a ship leaving shortly," the guard grunted. He looked in the direction of the gate tunnel, then back at them. His eyes narrowed. "Travelling alone, Margaret and Jon?"

"Our uncle's waiting on the ship," Alana replied quickly.

The guard nodded as he scratched notes in his binder. "What's the name of this ship?" he asked finally.

Alana stood gaping down at the man. His beady eyes were watching her closely. She could see the suspicion on his face. He was asking too many questions, and she wondered suddenly what the man before them had told him. Opening her mouth, she was about to blurt out the first ship name that came to mind when a shout carried across the marketplace.

"Devon, you bastard, you're mine now!"

Alana spun on the spot and stared as the giant from the night before came muscling his way through the crowd. He was armoured now, the steel links of his chainmail glinting as the first rays of sun broke over the top of the wall. Bloodshot eyes glinted from beneath an iron half-helm, and the haft of a warhammer stretched up over his right shoulder.

A second man moved alongside Devon. He stood almost a foot shorter than the giant and was less heavily muscled. Though he wore no sword, he moved with the balanced steps of a fighter. He was older than Devon, the flesh around his eyes crinkled with wisdom. As another shout carried across the marketplace, he skipped quickly around the queue for the gate and headed for the guard sitting at the table.

"Oi, you two, back of the line!" Alana glanced back as the man behind the table stood and pointed at Devon and his friend.

Alana grabbed her brother by the shoulder and stepped aside, moving slowly towards the gate. She watched as

Devon's friend walked up to the table. He was puffing hard, his chest heaving with each intake of breath. Behind the table, the guards bristled. Stepping out into the street, they levelled their spears at the newcomers.

Standing behind the distracted guards, Alana and Braidon continued to edge towards the darkness of the gate tunnel. She watched as Devon moved up beside his friend. The hard amber eyes looked down at the guards with scorn. "Get out of our way."

Steel rattled as the guards hefted their spears.

"Friends, one moment!" Beside Devon, the smaller man finally found his breath. Lifting his arms, he showed his empty hands. "Excuse my friend his rudeness. We only wish to pass through the gates."

"You and your friend aren't going anywhere without waiting in line, Kellian," the guard behind the table growled, eyes flashing with anger. "Now if you'll excuse—"

"I'm afraid we really do need to be going," Kellian interrupted. Another shout came from somewhere in the crowded marketplace. He cast a nervous glance back before continuing, "but I'm sure we can come to a mutually agreeable arrangement."

Before the guard could reply, Kellian's hand disappeared into his tunic and reappeared with a gold *libra*. "One apiece would seem fair, don't you think?" he asked, his eyes flickering to the two spearmen.

In the road, the spearmen wavered, their weapons dropping half an inch. Alana and her brother picked up the pace. The tunnel was just a few steps away now, but she didn't dare make a run for it. The guards were bound to notice any sudden movement. But if Devon and his friend finished their business before they made it into the tunnel…

"One each?" The guard at the table was eyeing the coin greedily.

Still moving backwards, Alana shivered as the air turned cold. She staggered slightly, but glancing around, she breathed a sigh of relief. They had made it into the tunnel. Grabbing her brother by the arm, she turned and pulled him deeper into the darkness. The weight of the wall pressed in around them, the massive blocks of granite hovering overhead. She kept her eyes fixed straight ahead, where she could just make out the glimmer of sunlight on water.

Beside her, Braidon gripped her hand hard. Their footsteps echoed loudly in the darkness. Unable to see where she was placing her feet, Alana pressed her hand to the wall, using the moss-covered stone to steady herself. The wall was only twenty-five feet thick, but the passage seemed to take an age. The light ahead swelled, until it was suddenly all around them.

Alana stumbled to a stop as they stepped back into the open. For a second her vision swam, and a red light stained the world. Looking out beyond the walls, it seemed as though she stood on the edge of a lake of red. Far below, ships bobbed at anchor, their sails pitch-black, their decks packed with warriors. She watched them sail away to the west, her heart soaring with the display of Plorsean power…

"Alana, *Alana!*"

Alana blinked as a voice called her name, and the vision faded. She glanced around and found Braidon standing next to her, his face creased with concern. Turning back to the lake, she saw its waters were the deep blue of midday. They stood at the top of the great stairwell leading down the cliffs to the docks far below. There, several ships waited, but they sported only white sails, not the black sails of war.

Shaking her head, she looked at her brother. "Sorry. Let's go."

She set off down the marble staircase without waiting for a response.

7

Devon caught a glimpse of blonde hair from the corner of his eye as he stepped towards the gates. He turned to look for the owner, but one of the guards moved into his line of sight. Fixing the spearman with a glare, he couldn't help but smile as the man retreated.

Beside him, Kellian was still negotiating with the captain of the watch. Devon glanced around, scanning the crowd for the first sign of their pursuers. The hammer weighed heavily on his back, and he fought a sudden yearning to reach up and lift it clear. Swallowing the temptation, he shook his head and looked at his friend.

"Yes, a gold *libra* for each of you," Kellian was saying, his eyes flickering from one man to another, "and there's another in it for you to split, if you'd be so good as to delay some friends of ours."

The man behind the desk nodded slowly. Devon could almost see the wheels of his mind whirring as he considered the offer. Grinding his teeth, Devon struggled to contain his frustration. A shout came from the marketplace and he checked the crowd again. People were turning towards a commotion behind them: Anthony and the others were drawing close. Devon clenched his fists and fought the urge to begin cracking skulls.

He had not lied to Kellian. He did not fear the royal guard, however many friends the man had brought with him. No, Devon feared what would happen if he faced them, what he might become if he unleashed his rage, and carried the ancient hammer into battle once more. He had lost himself once in Trola, becoming the warrior of dark renown, a man who killed without restraint or mercy. If he gave himself over to that same darkness, Devon wasn't sure he would ever resurface.

Turning, Devon stepped in front of his friend. "Times up. You want the gold or not?" he hissed. A gold *libra* was five times what these men made in a week, and they couldn't wait any longer.

The captain of the watch blanked, his face paling as he realised a small fortune was about to slip between his fingers. Standing, he gestured quickly at the spearmen. "Yes, yes, of course. My apologies, friends. I forgot your paperwork was already filled out yesterday."

Devon smiled grimly as the two men stepped aside. Kellian flicked a golden coin to each of them. Placing a fourth on the table, he nodded back at the crowd. "Our friends should be arriving presently. I trust you'll see they're suitably delayed?"

"Of course," the captain replied with a smile. He quickly pocketed the fourth coin. "A pleasure doing business with the two of you. Happy sailing."

Kellian and Devon moved off without another word. Ahead the gates stood open, the heavy wood reinforced by steel. Engraved into the metal were the faces of animals—

dragons and felines, raptors and great lizards—beasts of old which had fought alongside the forces of Archon. All long dead now.

As they stepped into the cold beneath the wall, the shouts behind them rose to a roar, and Devon looked back in time to see Anthony and his friends charging towards the gates. A smile crossed his face as the guards stepped across their path, spears extended. Their pursuers faltered mid-charge, the elation falling from their faces as the captain barked orders. Normally the royal guard out-ranked those in the city watch, but the Tsar allowed no exception at the city gates. All citizens coming and going from the city had to be registered. Unless of course, you paid the right fee.

Shaking his head, Devon strode down the tunnel after Kellian. With luck, the guards would delay their pursuers long enough for them to find passage across the lake. Beyond the walls, they moved quickly to the stairwell and started down. Five hundred steps were carved from the cliff-face itself, the stone worn smooth by the passage of centuries. Devon took them two at a time, his eyes on the ships waiting below. Ideally, there would be a ship heading for the northern or eastern shores, but with their pursuers not far behind, Devon would settle for the first ship leaving port.

At the bottom of the cliff, Devon took the lead, moving quickly out onto the docks. His eyes scanned the vessels gathered nearby, searching for one looking ready to disembark. A commotion near the end of the wharf drew his attention, and his eyes widened as he saw the blonde woman from the night before arguing with a black-bearded sailor. A tall young boy stood beside her, his dark hair glinting in the sunlight as he watched the woman facing off against the larger man.

"We only want passage to the shore!" the woman's voice carried across to them.

The man, who Devon guessed was the captain of the ship behind them, shook his head. "Only room for folk going all the way to Lon. Can't be wasting space for such a piddling fee."

"But you're leaving now!" the woman growled.

The captain shrugged. His eyes found Devon and Kellian standing nearby. A smile appeared on his face as he waved them over. "How about you, lads? Fancy booking passage to Lon?"

"Depends how much you're asking?" Kellian asked, moving quickly down the wharf to join them.

Beside the captain, the woman's grey eyes widened as she looked up and saw Devon standing there. Her surprise was quickly replaced by anger, though. Her face hardened as she stepped between the captain and Kellian, drawing the sailor's attention back to her.

"We were here first," she hissed.

"Ay, but you can't pay," the captain shot back, "and the price is five in gold, my good man."

Devon's stomach twisted as he thought of how much he was costing his friend, but Kellian was already shaking his head. "Then I'm afraid we cannot pay, either. But did I hear it right, you're about to depart?"

The captain's shoulders sagged, but he nodded. "Ay, as soon as someone fills my last beds for Lon," he said, turning away.

"We'll pay twice the usual ten shillings for you to drop us at the *Scarlet Feline*," Kellian interrupted, "but only if you cast off now."

Pausing mid-stride, the captain looked back at them. "In

a hurry, are you?" he asked, eyes narrowing. "The price is thirty, then."

Beside them, the woman's grey eyes flashed with silent rage. They settled on Devon, and fists clenched, she stepped towards him. Sunlight flashed from the sabre strapped to her waist. "My brother and I need to be on this ship."

Devon shrugged. "So do we."

"Wait your turn," she said.

"Sorry, princess," Devon replied with a grin. "I don't know what to tell you. Sometimes life's not fair."

She made to reach for her sabre, but the boy beside her gripped her arm and tugged her back. "Alana, don't," he said quietly. "Let me try."

"*No!*" Alana spun towards her brother, Devon forgotten, and gripped him by the collar of his jacket. "*Don't you dare!*"

Shaking his head, Devon looked around and saw Kellian had finished negotiating with the captain. He stood beside the gangplank gesturing for Devon to join him. The hammerman moved forward, his eyes drifting over the waiting ship. Paint was flaking from the wooden hull, revealing rot beneath, and there were large patches covering the mainsail. Several men were moving about the ship, while a trapdoor led down to what he guessed were the cramped quarters below deck. A cabin perched precariously at the rear of the vessel, but he presumed it belonged to the captain. Scarlet letters had been painted across the railings, but he could no longer read what they said. Seeing the state of the vessel, Devon was suddenly glad they would only be spending a few hours onboard.

Before he could reach his friend, Alana stepped between them again. "I won't let you leave without us."

Devon laughed again, his voice booming out across the open water. He stood a head and shoulders taller than the young woman. Scratching his beard, he shook his head. "And how do you intend to stop me?"

Her eyes darkened. "You two were in an awful hurry to leave up there by the gates," she said, her voice barely audible above the winter breeze. "That wouldn't have anything to do with last night, would it?"

"What's it to you, princess?" Devon growled.

She took a step closer to him, her grey eyes never leaving his face. "I bet the captain would like to know the kind of men he's carrying. You think you have enough silver to be worth him making enemies of the royal guard?"

Devon stilled, his eyes flickering back to the winding staircase. A steady trickle of people moved calmly up and down the stone steps, but there was no sign of Anthony or his men. His heart thudded in his ears as he looked back at Alana and felt the first stirring of his anger.

"Get out of my way, before I make you."

Alana only raised an eyebrow. Her eyes flickered to the hilt of Devon's hammer, then back to his face. "That's a nice hammer," she said, her voice rich with laughter. "Care to give me a closer look?"

A strained silence stretched out over the dock. Devon's hand twitched, but he made no move to unsheathe his weapon. His body shook with rage as he stepped forward to tower over her. "Step aside," he hissed, "or I'll feed you to the fish."

"Try me," she growled, unflinching.

"Fine."

Devon's hand shot forward to grab her arm, but Alana was faster still. She twisted sideways, and he found only empty air. Before Devon could recover, her fist shot out and slammed into his ribcage. Pain jarred in his chest and gasping, he reared back.

A red haze filled Devon's vision as he roared. Fists clenched, he hurled another punch. This time Alana stood her ground, her arm swinging up to deflect the blow from her body. Even so, the power in Devon's arm was enough to stagger her. Crying out, she retreated a step, and Devon moved in for the kill.

"Devon, enough!" He looked around as Kellian's voice carried down to them. His friend stood at the railings of the ship, his face pale as he made rapid gestures towards the gangplank. Looking around, Devon glimpsed a flash of gold on the staircase. Cursing beneath his breath, he moved towards the gangplank.

Steel rasped on leather as Alana stepped into his path, sabre drawn. "Let's wait around and see what they have to say, shall we?" she asked calmly.

Devon's hand was halfway to the haft of his hammer before he caught himself. His fingers twitched. He could feel the ancient weapon calling to him, urging him to draw it forth. Heat washed across his face as he imagined smashing aside her fragile blade and crushing the life from her tiny body. His heart raced as he imagined the screams, the blood…

Shuddering, Devon violently shook his head. "What do you want?" he asked, looking down into her steely grey eyes.

"Passage to the shore," Alana said quickly. "For me and my brother."

"Captain!" Devon yelled. The captain's face appeared over the railings of the ship. "These two are coming, too. Kellian, pay the man."

Ignoring the two interlopers, Devon strode past them and up the gangplank. He heard the thud of boots on wood behind him but did not glance back. His stomach still roiling with anger, he strode up onto the deck.

Kellian met him at the railing, one eyebrow raised. "You'll bankrupt me by the end of this trip, you know."

Not in the mood to explain, Devon shook his head and stomped past his friend. He heard the rustling of clothes as the two newcomers joined them on the vessel, but kept his gaze fixed on the lake. The sun had just passed its zenith. The winds were beginning to pick up, and far out on the lake he could see flecks of white as waves broke the surface. It would be a rough journey, and silently he hoped Alana suffered from seasickness. At least with the wind behind them, the crossing would only take a few hours.

Shouts came from the dock as the sailors set about casting them off. His stomach lurched as the ship began to pull away, the gentle waves close to the island lifting the ship beneath them. He let out a long sigh, relief rising to wash away his anger. Idly, his mind returned to the confrontation with Alana, and he suddenly wondered why the two were in such a hurry to leave Ardath.

"Men, pull anchor, let's sail!" he heard the captain call from the helm.

The ship gave another lurch, and, looking back, Devon smiled as he saw the docks slowly drifting away. But as they began to turn in the water, a distant horn carried down from the clifftops. Still clenching the railing, Devon stared up at the stone walls of the city. The tiny figure stood there beneath a red flag, a trumpet held to his mouth. As Devon watched, another cry rang out across the water.

"Hold on, boys!" the captain shouted as the horn faded away. Shaking his head, he moved across the deck towards his passengers. "Sorry, folks, looks like we're going to be a little while yet. They're ordering all ships to remain in port."

"We've already set sail," Kellian replied smoothly. "Surely the order does not include us?"

Shrugging, the captain walked away. "Sorry lad, your silver's not worth the risk. Can't go defying the Tsar's orders now, can we? I'm sure it won't take long."

Devon shared a glance with Kellian as a sailor leapt across the widening gap between the ship and the docks. They both knew who it was the guards were after. Above, the golden-helmed men were nearly halfway down the stairwell. There wasn't much time before they reached the docks.

Silently, Kellian slid a hand into his coat. Devon knew he was checking the fastenings on his throwing knives. Closing his eyes, Devon felt the familiar yearning for combat roar in his mind, demanding he draw his hammer, unleash the beast. Fingers trembling, he reached up for the haft…

"Please, captain, I'm sure they don't want us."

Devon's eyes snapped open as Alana's voice carried across the deck. She stood beside the captain, her brother beside her, eyes wide, hands clenched into tiny balls.

Blinking, the captain shook his head, his brow knitting in confusion. "I…no, we have to wait," he said finally.

"Please," Alana persisted. Her fingers tightened on his shoulder. Her brother shuffled closer, the wind swirling in his unkept black hair. "We're in a hurry. Like they said, we've already left the dock."

For a moment, it seemed the man would shout her down. Devon held his breath, waiting for the anger to flare in the man's eyes. Instead, it faded, his shoulders slumping as he waved a hand.

"I guess you're right. And I can't go delaying an entire shipment for some bureaucratic nonsense." Turning to the man on the dock, he waved him back to the ship. "Cast off!"

The sailor frowned, his eyes uncertain, but his hesitation vanished as the captain began bellowing orders. Long poles were extended as the man leapt back to the ship, shoving the shore away and turning to the northeast. Oars slid out from the space below the deck. As they dug down to strike the water, the ship surged forward. Overhead, wood creaked, though the mainsail remained furled.

Devon stood staring at Alana and her brother as they moved to the front of the ship, the relief on their faces palpable. Behind them, the docks shrank from view as they picked up speed. Men stood on the other ships staring after them, but no one tried to call them back. Beyond, Anthony and his friends had finally reached the bottom of the great stairwell. They raced out onto the wharf, arms waving, faces pale with exhaustion. Devon allowed himself a smile as their shouts carried out across the water, made unintelligible by distance.

"Well, she was worth the extra silver," Kellian commented wryly as he re-joined Devon at the railings.

The smile fell from Devon's face as he remembered his confrontation with Alana. His anger stirred, but he forced it away, turning his thoughts to the coming journey.

"I'm glad you think so," he said quietly. "I hope that means you've still got a few shillings tucked up your sleeve. I have all of five left to my name."

"Perfect." Kellian slapped him on the back, his laughter whispering out across the lake. "You'll be paying for our room at the *Scarlet Feline* tonight then. After that ordeal, I'm broke. At least until I can liquidate a few assets in Lon."

Devon groaned, but Kellian was already moving away, his eyes dancing with amusement.

8

It took Quinn four hours to track the lingering taint of magic north through the city. With a squadron of Stalkers at his back and his own magic at the ready, he didn't doubt they would be able to match whoever was behind the outpouring of power; finding them was another matter. Unlike the young Magicker's outburst a week before, this usage had been subtle. It tasted of the Earth, perhaps a healing conducted by some hidden priest.

Only as the day grew old did Quinn begin to suspect something more sinister might be at hand. When they reached the northern gates with still no hint of the Magicker's location, he knew it was no Earth priest they were after. His heart sank as they moved through the gates, following the dwindling scent of power down the stone stairs to the docks.

There, finally, Quinn sensed they were close to the source. Ignoring the stares of sailors and merchants, they made their way through the docks. People and wares packed the heavy wooden planks, hindering their passage.

Quinn cursed aloud as a man staggered into him, shattering his concentration. Spinning on the man, his hand snaked out to catch him by the shirt. The sailor cried out as with a roar, Quinn sent him tumbling over the side. He struck the water with a splash and came up shouting.

Turning away, Quinn continued through the crowd. Now people quickly stepped aside, forming a path for the party of black-cloaked Stalkers. Keeping the smile from his face, Quinn turned his thoughts back to his renegade Magicker. Taking his own power firmly in hand, he used it to reach out from himself, to taste the last traces of magic.

"Here," he said, coming to a sudden stop.

His men halted beside him, their eyes narrowed, scanning the crowd. But Quinn had eyes only for the open water. Beyond the docks, a dozen ships raced across the surface of the lake, their white sails billowing in the afternoon winds. Overhead, dark clouds were gathering, the beginnings of a storm forming over the city. The last traces of Earth magic were fading now, but they had erupted into life somewhere on this dock.

The Magicker had taken passage on a ship. Even now they were winging their way from Ardath, far across the waters, nearing the distant shores. From there, they could go anywhere, threaten any community in the Three Nations.

He swore again, and sensed his own magic rising in response. Taking a deep breath, he allowed his rage a moment's consideration before turning his attention to other matters. He swung back to face his men. "They've taken a ship. Search the docks. Find out if anything unusual happened here four hours ago."

With that, Quinn moved away, heading for the stairwell back to the city. All travellers in and out of Ardath were recorded by the city watch. Whoever had snuck out would have left a trace. He wondered idly if the occurrence was related to the disappearances at the citadel, but quickly dismissed it. It had been a month since the escape. He doubted they could have hidden in Ardath all this time without raising suspicions.

Shaking his head, he moved up the spiralling stairwell. He was puffing by the time he reached the gates, and in no mood for nonsense. The guards were speaking as he walked up, and he slowed to listen to the conversation.

"We 'ave to split it evenly," the spearman standing nearest the gate was saying.

"I don't have to do anything, Jasper." The captain of the watch sat behind his desk, eying the two spearmen guarding the tunnel. "You have your gold libra, don't get greedy now."

Quinn emerged from the tunnel before the spearman had a chance to reply. The guards fell silent at his appearance, their eyes flickering nervously amongst themselves. Fixing an easy smile to his face, Quinn wandered across to where the captain sat behind his desk. The sun was hidden behind storm clouds now, and the space beneath the wall was cold. Placing his hands on the desk, Quinn leaned in close to the captain.

"Si- sir, how can I help you today?" the man managed to stutter.

Quinn answered with a cold smile. "Anything interesting happen here today, captain?" he asked quietly.

The colour drained from the man's face. "No! No, sir!"

"Is that so?" He leaned forward so his face was just an inch from the captain's. "Then why, pray, did I just hear you and your men talking about gold libra?"

A low moan came from the captain's mouth as it opened

and closed. Reaching down, Quinn grabbed him by the collar and dragged him across the table. "If I find out you've aided a Magicker's escape, captain…"

"Ma…Magicker?" The man blinked, then shook his head violently. "Ain't been no Magickers here, I swear!"

Quinn reached down and tore the coin purse from the man's belt. Upending it on the table, he watched as several coppers and two golden libra tumbled onto the table. "Then you'd better start explaining where you came by that gold, captain," he growled.

"It was the coward, Devon, sir! Him and his friend. That's all, I swear it!"

"Devon?" Quinn asked, his grip loosening momentarily on the man's collar. He had fought alongside the man years ago, but hadn't seen him since his shameful retirement. "What has he got to do with my missing Magicker?"

"I don't know anything about a Magicker!" the captain shrieked. "But Devon and his mate, they were in trouble with the royal guard. Paid us to make a quick exit and hold up their buddies. I never knew he had anything to do with a Magicker, I swear!"

Quinn slapped the man hard across the face as he started to ramble. Behind him, he could hear the spearmen edging away, but Quinn kept his attention focused on the captain, sensing he would find his answers there.

"Devon has no magic," he said dangerously. His sabre left its sheath with a hiss. He tossed the captain to the ground, then knelt beside him and placed his blade to the man's neck. "So, tell me why I should believe you?"

"Please, sir!" the guard shrieked, his eyes pressed tightly closed. "I swear I'm telling the truth. Devon and his friend came through, caused a big commotion, that's all I know."

Quinn eyed the man for a moment, waiting to see whether he had anything else to reveal. Finally, he released him and stood, ignoring the pathetic blob of a man as he curled into a ball and started to sob. Moving to the desk, he flicked through the papers, but could find nothing of use. Turning, he walked back through the gate tunnel and out into the dying light of dusk.

Stopping at the railings overlooking the stairwell, Quinn looked out over the harbour. The port was empty now, the last ship just beginning to pull away. From its bearing, he guessed it was making for Trola. His eyes travelled farther out over the lake, taking in the distant glow of white sails. They were racing against time now, their sails at full mast as they sought the safety of the river before the storm caught them.

Closing his eyes, Quinn settled in to wait for his men.

When they finally appeared, they could offer nothing but confirmation of the captain's story. Apparently, several royal guards had come bursting onto the docks around the time Devon had fled. Devon and his friend Kellian had left aboard a ship bound for Lon, though several sailors who'd overheard their conversation with the captain vouched that they'd only paid for passage to the shore.

Quinn shook his head. It didn't make any sense. Devon was a formidable warrior, but he possessed no magic. Nor did his friend, Kellian. Both men were stubborn, borderline treasonous fools, but even they weren't foolish enough to aid a Magicker. The very idea of going up against the Tsar's decree was suicide, and coward or no, Devon was too fond of his own life for that.

Still, something didn't quite add up. Quinn had learnt long ago there was no such thing as coincidences. There was no denying that magic had been used out on the docks. By whom and what for, he had no way of knowing.

But he had a suspicion Devon and Kellian might.

Turning, Quinn looked at his men. "Ready yourselves for the hunt," he said quietly. "We leave as soon as the storm breaks."

9

Alana groaned as she fell back on the bed. Her eyelids fluttered closed, the day's strain finally catching up to her. Outside the wind howled, its violent gusts tearing at the shutters. They had watched the storm building through the afternoon, felt the beginnings of its power as the waves grew around them. By the time they'd reached the shelter of the river, Alana's stomach had been heaving. Even the giant warrior Devon had looked a shade paler, and his friend had been too busy with his head in a bucket to pay them any more attention.

It had been a relief for everyone when the ship finally docked at the *Scarlet Feline*—which turned out to be a riverside inn a league down the river towards Lon. With the rain just starting to fall, Alana had used the money she'd intended for the ferry to purchase a room and meal for herself and Braidon.

Unfortunately, Devon and his friend had also taken a room for a night. With the innkeeper still busy preparing the evening meal, Alana and her brother had retired upstairs.

They would have to return to the serving room soon though—or risk going hungry. She wasn't looking forward to facing the big man's anger.

Thinking of her desperation back on the docks, Alana felt a pang of guilt. She could hardly believe she'd resorted to blackmailing the former soldier. The memory flashed before her eyes, blurred by adrenaline. Already it seemed distant, more a dream than reality. Maybe that was the only way she could accept what she'd done. With the ship about to depart and the guards closing in, blackmail had been her only option. Even so, the act did not sit well with her.

And it had almost been for nothing anyway. Silently Alana sent her thanks to Antonia for the captain's sudden change of heart. If not for his grudging acceptance that they could leave, the royal guards would have boarded the ship. And then...

Alana shivered and forced the thought from her mind.

"You think supper's ready yet?" Her brother's voice came from the other bed.

Her stomach rumbled at the mention of food and she stifled a groan. Through the wooden floorboards she could hear the dim thud of feet downstairs. The inn was empty except for themselves, Devon, and Kellian, which meant the other two were already in the dining room.

"You're really that hungry?" Alana asked, sitting up on the bed and looking at her brother.

Braidon rolled his eyes. "They're not going to bite," he replied with a grin. "It was only a little blackmail."

Alana raised an eyebrow. "And just who taught you your morals, young man?"

Her brother's brow wrinkled, his eyes dropping to the floor. "The same people we ran away from..."

A strained silence stretched out. "Sorry, Braidon," Alana

whispered. Inwardly cursing her thoughtless mouth, she stood and moved across to sit beside him. Rubbing his back, she continued. "We're safe now, though. No one has any idea we're here. We made it. It's all downhill from here."

She smiled as his eyes brightened. "How long will it take us to reach Northland?"

"A long time." Laughing, she stood. "But longer if we travel on empty bellies. Come on, let's get some food.

With Braidon's hand in hers, they left the room. Pausing in the hallway, Alana quickly ducked back inside and picked up her sword belt before bolting the door behind them. With a wave from her, Braidon led the way to the stairway at the end of the corridor. The wooden floorboards squeaked beneath their boots with every step, announcing their approach to those below. The sound of voices ceased as they made their way down the stairs and turned into the dining room.

"Well, well, well, if it isn't the little stowaways!" Devon's booming voice greeted them as they moved towards the bar.

Alana glanced in the giant's direction. He and his friend sat at a table near the hearth, enjoying the warmth of the orange fire burning behind the grate. Two half-empty mugs of ale sat at their table, but Alana guessed it was not their first round. Devon had removed his chainmail and helm, and no longer carried the warhammer on his back. Even so, with his hulking shoulders and matted beard, he was an imposing sight.

Silently, Alana flashed a glare in their direction, but it only brought another boom of laughter from the dark-garbed hammerman. Shaking her head, she looked away, and found the innkeeper waiting for them behind the bar.

"Enjoy your rest?" he asked with a smile as they walked up.

"Very much, thank you," Alana replied, feeling herself relax at the man's easy demeanour.

The innkeeper was easily into his fifties, with greying hair and smile lines that spread across the breadth of his cheeks, but he moved with the vigour of a much younger man. Which was fortunate, since it was only him in the lonely inn.

"Good, good! Well, what can I get my second-best customers for the night?"

Alana laughed: they were his only customers, aside from Devon and Kellian. Most travellers chose to take a ship directly between Lon and Ardath nowadays, rather than risk the landward journey through southern Lonia. Since the losses suffered during the civil war, the Tsar had been forced to cut patrols along the Gods Road, and bandits were no longer as rare as they'd once been. There were even rumours of wandering Baronian tribes making a resurgence.

"What do you have for supper tonight?" Alana asked.

"Got a pot full of traditional curry from Chole, if a bit of spice is to your liking?"

Alana's stomach rumbled her agreement and she nodded quickly.

"Take a seat then, folks," the innkeeper replied. "I'm sure the lads over there would love some civilised company."

Alana laughed. "We're just having a quiet night. Got an early start tomorrow."

"Ay, fair enough. It's a long trip downriver on foot. 'Specially if you're the superstitious sort."

"How so?"

"New in these parts are ya?" the innkeeper questioned. When they nodded, he went on. "The Sitton Forest lies to the south of here. There's some folk who believe it's haunted. Too many travellers go in that don't come out, they reckon. Can't say I've ever paid much attention to the rumours myself. Travelled the entire forest plenty of times, even seen the ruins. I'll admit the place is creepy. Some of the trees even have faces. But I've never encountered any spirits."

"Good to know, I guess," Alana replied, "but I think we've got it covered." She patted the hilt of her sabre with a smile.

"Ay, you look like a capable lass. Ah well, I'll see to that curry. I'll bring you your plates shortly."

"Cheers!" Alana's thanks carried after the innkeeper as he rushed through the double doors behind the bar.

Sharing a grin with her brother, Alana led him across the room to a table in the corner. It was further from the fire than she would have liked on such a cold evening, but she had no wish to be any closer to their fellow guests. Unbuckling her sword belt, she looped it over the back of her chair and sat down opposite her brother.

"What do you think, sis?" Braidon asked.

"Huh?" Alana asked, glancing in his direction. Her gaze had been across the room, where Devon's amber eyes kept flicking them dark glances. Outside, lightning flashed, followed by the rumble of thunder.

"About Sitton forest?" her brother elaborated. "Where have I heard that name before?"

"There used to be a city there, but it was destroyed during Archon's last reign," Alana replied.

Her brother shivered. "Sounds like a place we should avoid."

"He's dead, Braidon. It's been a hundred years since the Gods destroyed him."

"Yeah, but the Gods are gone now," her brother shot back.

Alana sighed. "Yes."

Like most people their age, she was well versed in the tale of the Three Gods and their war with the infamous Archon. A century ago, the mortals Enala, Eric, and Gabriel had wielded the legendary Sword of Light, and worked with the Gods to destroy the dark Magicker. After his fall, the Three Nations had flourished under the rule of the Gods. The only problem was, they'd left. Without their guiding hands, it hadn't taken long for war to return to the Three Nations. Only the emergence of the Tsar fifty years ago had restored peace to the land.

"Where do you think they went?" her brother asked, his voice dropping low.

"I don't know," Alana said simply. "I like to think they're still out there somewhere…watching over us, but they could just as likely be dead. Either way, don't get your hopes up, praying for them to come rescue us."

Her brother's shoulders fell. Instantly, she regretted the harsh words, but there was no taking them back now.

"Here ya are!" Alana looked up as the innkeeper placed two steaming bowls of curry and a plate of rice between them. "Anything else I can get you folks?"

Alana smiled. "I think we're good."

Nodding, the innkeeper moved away. Alana took the chance to inspect the contents of her bowl. The curry was a bright red, thick with ground up herbs and spices. The few chunks of chicken she could see were mostly bone and gristle, but they were more for the flavour, anyway. The dish came from the nearby city of Chole, where for almost a century the land had been plagued by drought. The drought had finally broken with the fall of Archon, but their fiery cuisine remained, remnants of a time when fresh meat was a rare commodity.

Alana's stomach rumbled as she breathed in the rich scent of paprika and turmeric. Almost drooling, she reached for the spoon lying beside her bowl.

"Enjoying your meal, princess?" Alana jumped as Devon's gruff voice came from behind her chair. Metal clattered as the spoon slid from her fingers and jumped across the tabletop. She cursed as her knee struck the table leg.

Gritting her teeth, she turned to find the man towering over them. "I was about to," she growled, "before I was interrupted by a hideous talking donkey."

Devon's mouth dropped at the insult, and his face flushed a mottled red. Fists clenched, he took a step closer and placed his hands on the back of her chair. Alana's heart pounded against her chest as she caught the glint of rage in his amber eyes.

"Excuse me?" he said dangerously.

Alana stared back, brow creased, unflinching. "I said you were a donkey," she replied. When he didn't respond immediately, she added, "A hideous one."

For a second, she thought the giant would explode. His face darkened, turning from red to purple, and he tilted her chair back, its front legs lifting from the floor. Alana tensed, readying herself. Her sabre was trapped behind the chair, closer to Devon than to her, but she inched her right hand towards her table knife.

Then Devon threw back his head and laughed. Alana jumped as the sound echoed from the shutters. Pain shot up her leg as her knee struck the table leg again, but she was too shocked to notice it. She sat staring as the giant hammerman shook his head and wiped tears from his eyes.

"You've got stones, princess," Devon managed finally,

his laughter fading away. "No one's spoken to me like that in years. At least, not to my face."

Despite her fear a few seconds earlier, Alana found herself smiling. "Well, anytime you need a reminder, let me know. I'd be happy to help."

"I bet," Devon said, still chuckling. He nodded to her brother. "How about you, sonny? You as tough as your sister?"

Across the table, Braidon wore a grin as broad as the giant warrior's. "No one's as tough as Alana."

Alana's heart warmed at his praise and she found herself speechless.

"I don't doubt it!" Devon continued, "So, the name's Alana, is it? What's yours, sonny?"

"Braidon," came her brother's reply before Alana could stop him. Inwardly she cursed her foolishness for using their real names in front of people.

"Well, allow me to apologise for my rudeness. It's nice to meet the two of you." He offered his hand. "My name's Devon, though you already knew that. My friend over there's Kellian. You're welcome to join us for a drink, if you'd like?"

Alana smiled at the offer. "Thanks, but we've got an early start tomorrow. We're just going to eat and hit the hay."

Devon nodded, flashing an easy smile. "Fair enough," he replied. "I'd better be getting back to my drinking companion. Perhaps we'll see you on the road." At that, he turned and strode back across to the table where his friend waited.

"Well, that was…strange," Alana said finally.

Braidon shrugged. "Probably realised he'd met his match."

Alana laughed. "I guess so." Her stomach rumbled as she turned her attention back to the food. "Well, we shouldn't let it get cold. Let's eat!"

Later in their room, Alana smiled as the heat of the curry spread through her stomach. Her mind still sluggish with sleep, she moved straight to the bed. Lying down, her eyes fluttered closed, her thoughts drifting. Images flickered before her mind, then faded into the darkness of sleep…

"Alana!"

A smile came to Alana's lips as her brother ran across the shimmering grass. His curly black hair bounced as he ran, falling across his face and forcing him to pause and brush the locks away. She opened her arms and he continued his dash, and she staggered back as he threw himself into her hug.

Laughing, they fell to the grass in a heap. Her brother's giggling echoed from the stone walls as they rolled several feet before finally coming to a stop. Sitting up, Alana brushed grass from his hair.

"Did you miss me?" she asked.

He nodded. "It's been ages, *Alana!"*

"I know, I know. But I have responsibilities now, you know that. I'll try not to be so long next time." She winked at him as she stood, offering her hand.

Braidon took it with a knowing smile and stood. Together they made their way through the gardens, following the broad stretch of wall beside them. Rose bushes were dotted across the lawns, and they were forced to detour several times. Their sweet aroma lingered in the air, drifting on a soft, warm breeze.

"Have you been studying hard?" Alana asked as they finally stepped onto a path.

Her brother wrinkled his nose. "I'm trying, I swear," he replied. "It's just, hard…"

Alana felt a twang in her chest as she looked down at him. "It's not that difficult—" she began.

"Not for you!" Braidon cut her off. "You're the smart one, remember…"

"Hey, it's okay." Alana dropped to one knee beside him. Reaching out, she took his hand and pressed it to her lips. "You'll get there, it just takes practice, okay?"

He eyed her for a moment, his lips pursed tight. "Okay," he said finally. Then he smiled, his eyes dancing. "But first you'll have to catch me!" Spinning on his heel, Braidon took off through the gardens before Alana could grab him.

"Hey, no fair!" Alana laughed, chasing after him. "You get back here, you little brat!"

"Ha!" Her brother glanced back and pulled a face. He ducked around a row of roses, placing the thorny plants between them. "Catch me if you can!"

Alana gave a dramatic sigh, then darted towards him. Her brother's laughter echoed off the high walls, drawing stares from the other occupants of the garden. Laughing to herself, Alana ignored them. It was good to have time with her brother, time to be a child, to run and play again.

Ahead, her brother disappeared behind a line of trees. Picking up the pace, Alana darted to the left. She sprinted along the treeline until she found a gap between the broad trunks, then dashed through, ducking as the branches snapped at her face. Exploding back into the open, she spun in time to catch her brother mid-leap.

"Argh!"

"Gotcha!" Alana cried, a triumphant grin on her face.

Braidon squirmed in her grip, but there was no breaking free. Finally, he gave up, his body going still. Looking up, he extended his lower lip in a pout.

Alana laughed. "I told you there was no escape!"

"How very true."

Alana froze as a cold voice came from behind them. Her heart, already racing from the chase, thumped hard against her chest. Warmth spread to her cheeks as she looked down at her brother. He stood frozen now, eyes fixed over her shoulder, hand gripped tight to hers. Swallowing hard, Alana turned towards the voice.

The world seemed to spin as she moved. A collective groan came from the nearby trees, their branches suddenly becoming twisted and misshapen, their bark stained black. She shrank as they leaned towards her, their branches like limbs, reaching out to grab her. The sky above darkened, the warmth falling away, replaced by a chill breeze that swept through the garden, its touch as sharp as a knife.

Amongst it all stood Quinn, the lieutenant of the Stalkers. He wore the same dark legging and jerkin as that day in the stepwell, only now a chainmail vest covered his torso. Folding his arms, he stared at her, a smile on his face.

Alana's eyes slid down to the longsword at his waist. She clenched her fists, feeling the hopelessness rising within. Empty handed, she moved between the Stalker and her brother.

"What do you want?"

Unfolding his arms, Quinn stepped towards them.

"Such a warm reunion." He shook his head, his eyes boring into Alana's. "I'm sorry to break it up. Are you ready, Alana?"

❧ 10 ❧

Devon looked back as the rumble of galloping hooves approached behind them. Overhead, the remnants of last night's storm still darkened the sky, threatening rain. Open fields spread out around them, obscured by a low haze that had swept in overnight. Squinting, Devon tried to make out the oncoming horsemen. Beside him, Kellian loosened a dagger in its sheath.

The wind swirled, the mists parting to reveal the dark-cloaked riders. Devon breathed a sigh of relief as he saw their helms were of black steel, rather than the gold of the royal guard. Coming to a stop, they watched as the riders closed in on them, their burly steeds moving at pace. Only when they were a few yards away did the men finally pull back on the reins, bringing their horses to a halt.

The rider in the lead reached up and removed his helm. Devon swore beneath his breath as he found the cold brown eyes of his former comrade staring down at him. Silently, he cursed the ale they'd drunk last night. He'd spent his remaining shillings getting roaringly drunk with Kellian in celebration of their newfound 'freedom'. As a result, they'd both slept long past the dawn. The sun had been high in the sky by the time they'd set off down the Gods Road.

The slightest smile touched Quinn's lips. "Devon, so good to see you again."

"Likewise," Devon replied softly.

While they'd fought together during the civil war, things had never been more than professional between the two warriors. Quinn had built himself a fearsome reputation with his blade during the war—and his magic only made him all the more formidable. Yet it had been Devon who'd been promoted to lieutenant, something that seemed to rankle the former Battle Magicker. Devon's rejection of a commission after the war had only added fuel to the man's hostility.

"Kellian, too, I see," Quinn added, looking down at the smaller man. "What brings two former soldiers so far from the capital at such an inhospitable time of year?"

Devon narrowed his eyes as he looked around the gathered horsemen. They had formed up in a semicircle around the two travellers, leaving them only one direction to flee. His fists tightened as he saw several hands resting on the pommels of swords. He returned his gaze to Quinn. The man spoke as though he'd expected to find them out here. Suddenly, Devon wondered whether the royal guard had sent the Stalkers after them. He quickly dismissed the idea —Quinn and his men had no interest in petty squabbles.

"Thought Lon might have better prospects for work," Devon answered. He cleared his throat. "And what brings the legendary Stalkers riding so hard down the Gods Road?"

"Hunting," Quin replied with a grin that sent ice trickling down Devon's spine. The Stalker studied the two men a moment longer, before swinging down from the saddle. He was shorter than Devon by a head, but he carried himself with the authority of a much larger man. Stepping in close, he looked up at Devon. "You wouldn't know anything about that, would you?"

Devon frowned. This time there was no need to fake the expression. "Hunting?" He spread his hands. "Afraid not. I keep myself well clear of anything magic related. Bad for my health."

"The couple we hung a few days back, they came to you for help. Do you deny it?" Quinn replied, his eyes hard and unblinking.

"They did," Devon replied, unsurprised by the man's knowledge. He didn't need to ask how Quinn had come by the information. "I told them they should hand their son in to the Tsar."

Quinn nodded slowly. "Didn't think you needed to share your information with the authorities, though?"

Devon clenched his jaw. "Guess it slipped my mind."

The Stalker jabbed a finger at Devon's chest. "I could put you away for that."

Anger flaring, Devon moved in close to the dark-cloaked man. "Is that so, *lieutenant?*" he asked quietly. His eyes flickered around the ring of horsemen. There were twelve of them, all armed with sabres. His gaze returned to Quinn. "Are you sure you brought enough men for that?"

Quinn didn't flinch, but Devon could see the sudden fear in his eyes. A smile spread across the hammerman's unshaven cheeks. The lieutenant's face turned red and he straightened, a sneer appearing on his lips.

"Did you suddenly find your manhood then?" he laughed, nodding to the hammer on Devon's back. "Or were you intending to hide behind your friend's skirt?"

Iron bands wrapped around Devon's stomach. He bared his teeth, his hand moving unbidden to the haft of his hammer. Quinn's eyes widened, but this time he did not move. Gripping *kanker* more tightly, Devon stared down at the man, feeling the rage burning through him. The moment stretched out, the air taut as a wire. Around them, the other Stalkers watched in silence.

Finally, Devon let out a long breath and released his hammer. He took a step back, adding breathing space between himself and the lieutenant.

"At least I haven't made a living murdering women and children," he muttered.

Quinn bared his teeth, his hand dropping to his sabre. "You'd better show some respect, coward."

"Respect is earned, sonny," Devon replied.

"Earned?" Quinn said dangerously. Now it was his turn to step forward, his hand still wrapped around the hilt of his sabre. "Have I not earned your respect with all my years of service? For the decade I have spent serving our Tsar, protecting our nation from the scourge of wild magic?"

"That couple was no threat to anyone."

"Their son was," Quinn replied, eyes glittering. "Or did you not see what he did at the stepwell?"

"Ay, and what became of him, I wonder? Is he sitting in some dungeon now, or did you kill him yourself, *lieutenant?*"

A smile appeared on Quinn's face. "You don't know what you're talking about, big man," he whispered. "But I digress. Where is the Magicker you're hiding?"

"There is no Magicker," Devon growled. He spread his arms, as if to show he wasn't hiding anyone up his sleeves. "Unless you think I suddenly developed the gift."

Quinn snorted. He stared at Devon for a long moment as though weighing him up, searching for some deceit or trick that would reveal the truth. But for once, Devon had nothing to hide. A smile twitched on his lips as the Stalker finally turned his attention to Kellian.

"And what about you, Kellian?" he snapped.

Kellian laughed. "Still just a simple innkeeper, I'm afraid."

Sneering, Quinn shook his head. "I heard the Firestone burned down. That would make you just a simpleton then, I guess?" Ignoring Kellian's sudden loss of colour, Quinn looked back at Devon. "You had best watch yourself, Devon. Lots of accidents can happen on the road. Would be a shame if something happened to our cowardly hero."

With that, the man turned his back and returned to his horse. Mounting, he placed his fingers to his lips and let out a shrill whistle. The squadron surged forward, the massive horses racing around Kellian and Devon before setting off down the Gods Road at a trot.

When the horsemen had faded back into the fog, Devon shook his head. "What do you think that was all about?"

"I don't know," Kellian replied, his voice hollow, "but they're out for blood. I hope those two kids aren't on the road when they ride past."

THE AFTERNOON FOUND ALANA AND HER BROTHER ON THE road, already half-a-dozen leagues from the *Scarlet Feline.* Alana had spent much of the night imagining the Stalker lieutenant she'd glimpsed in the stepwell chasing her and her brother through the gardens of her dreams. No matter how she tossed and turned, she could not escape him, couldn't keep from returning to that same scene, that same question.

Are you ready, Alana?

No!

How could she ever be ready to face such a man? She was good with a sabre, but the Stalker had access to magic, had been trained since youth to use it. She'd watched Quinn smash aside the young Magicker's feeble flames and knock him unconscious in a matter of moments. What chance did a mere mortal like her stand against him?

Unable to sleep any longer, Alana had risen with the first crow of the rooster and dressed quickly. Waking her brother had been difficult. He hadn't been eager to leave the comfort of his bed, but in the end, she'd forced him, dragging him out from beneath the duvet and dumping him on the floor.

He walked sullenly beside her now, his head down, lips pursed tight. He had hardly said a word all day, but she was just glad they'd gotten away without seeing Devon and his friend again. She'd been afraid they'd offer to join them on the road. She still had her reservations about the man's apparent change of heart, but it was her brother that concerned her more. He was untutored in his power. What if he accidentally revealed it to the two men? Friendly as they now appeared, Alana knew she couldn't trust such a secret to strangers.

As they walked, she scanned the roadside, her eyes travelling out over the rolling farmland in search of danger. Here the land was used for pasture, the bright grass reviving the memory of her dreams. Sheep and cattle dotted the fields, heads down as they grazed. Earlier they'd walked past fields of maize and wheat, their long fronds obscuring her view. Even now a fog covered the ground, and she could only see several dozen yards in either direction. Away to her left she could just make out the towering treeline that marked the banks of the river Lon.

Eventually they would have to cross the river to enter Lonia, but for now Alana was happy to follow the road as far north as they could. They would have to make the crossing themselves—after last night's stay, there was no way they could afford another ferry. But there were bound to be narrow points they could ford.

She paused midstride as dark shapes appeared through the fog ahead. Her heart started to race, but a moment later she let out a sigh as she realised they were only trees. Ahead, the open fields gave way abruptly to the twisted mass of a forest. Beside her, Braidon continued on with his head down, ignorant to their surroundings. Racing to catch up, she gripped him by the arm and nodded at the trees.

"I think that's Sitton Forest," she murmured.

His eyes widened as he looked up and saw the waiting trees. Shadows clung to the earth beneath their twisted trunks. Mould had turned their bark black, giving them an otherworldly look. Where the Gods Road met the trees, it split in two, one heading east around the forest, the other straight through. Small saplings sprouted from the overgrown path leading through the trees, and roots riddled the hard-packed earth.

"Are you sure you want to go through?" her brother asked, his anger apparently forgotten.

The fog seemed to press in around them as they came to a stop at the fork in the road. Alana swallowed, eyeing the trees. The sun remained hidden behind the clouds, but they still had several hours of daylight left. Not so in the forest. Beneath the canopy, darkness reigned. Biting her lip, she looked at her brother.

"I—" She broke off as the sound of hooves pounding earth carried to them.

She spun around, eyes searching the fog for sign of the horsemen. Her heart hammering in her chest, Alana shared a glance with her brother, but there was no telling who approached. The thick fog pressed closer, concealing everything more than a few feet from them.

"The forest!" Alana hissed. Grabbing Braidon by the shirt, she dragged him down the path. "Come on, before they spot us."

An icy breath slid down her back as they staggered down the Gods Road and ducked into the trees on the side of the path. Crouching in the leaf litter, Alana stared back towards the south, seeking out the first sign of the riders. Her breath quickened as she glimpsed shadows through the blanket of grey-white. Blood rushed to her ears, deafening her. She held her breath, trying to still her nerves. Reaching out, she gripped her brother's hand tight.

As the horsemen neared, she began to make out details. They wore dark cloaks and black helms, the markings of the Tsar's Stalkers. Alana crouched lower in the foliage and sent up a desperate prayer to any deity who might be listening. The blood froze in her veins as she recognised the face of the leader; the same face that had haunted her dreams.

Quinn.

His presence could not be a coincidence, surely? Did the Tsar have the power to reach out into her very mind now? Had his power led the Stalkers after them? The thought sent a shiver down to her very soul. Breath held, Alana watched them come, expecting the racing horsemen to plunge straight into the trees after them.

The horsemen slowed as they approached the fork in the road. Alana cursed herself for rushing down the path without taking care to hide their tracks. The light was dim, and she prayed they would not spot any sign left by the two travellers.

Quinn pulled his horse to a stop not twenty feet from where they hid, his eyes fixed to the ground. The other horsemen gathered behind him, their eyes on the forest and surrounding farmland. A frown furrowed Quinn's face as he studied the trail, the gelding jostling beneath him. Its snorts were audible from Alana's hiding place, and she could see foam flecking the coats of their horses. It was clear these men had been riding hard. Closing her eyes, Alana waited for the inevitable shouts of discovery.

She caught the murmur of voices, and looked up again in time to see the lieutenant point his horse down the other trail. "We'll take the ring road. If there's still no sign of this Magicker by the time the paths re-join, half of us will head back through the forest, while the rest recheck the Gods Road."

Without waiting for a response from his men, Quinn kicked his horse. The beast leapt forward, racing down the path away from the forest. Alana let out a breath as the other men followed suit. Slowly, the pounding of hooves faded into the distance. Sitting back on the damp ground, she looked at her brother with a smile.

"Guess we're going through the forest," she panted, her heart still racing.

Braidon said nothing, only nodded, and she read the fear in his eyes. The Stalkers had been so close, that a single movement might have given them away. She could only guess how the hunters had discovered them. The Tsar was said to have power beyond any ordinary Magicker, but surely if he knew their location, the Stalkers would not have ridden past them. She could only assume that meant the riders had no way of magically locating their prey.

Alana had no intention of making the chase any easier for them. From here on out, they would keep off the road. If they walked amongst the trees alongside the path, she was confident they could find their way, and still prevent the riders from taking them by surprise again. It would make for slow going in the gloomy light beneath the canopy, but at least they'd be safe.

Standing, Alana pulled Braidon up with her. "Come on, the faster we move, the more distance we put between us and them."

"Didn't you hear what they said?" Braidon hissed. "They're going to ride back through the forest."

"Yes, but they won't see us," Alana replied with a confidence she didn't feel. "We'll stick to the trees, follow the path from a distance."

She felt her brother trembling as he took her hand. "The trees?" His voice shook as he glanced around.

Alana tried to keep the fear from her face as she followed his gaze. The innkeeper had been right, there was a weirdness to this forest, a wrongness she couldn't quite place. But there was no movement beneath the canopy, no sign of danger—just twisting branches and curling green vines that crawled along the forest floor.

"It's the safest way," she replied finally. "Come on, the faster we move, the sooner we'll put this place behind us."

11

"What do you think?" Kellian asked.

Devon glanced at his friend, one eyebrow raised. "I think I've passed this way a dozen times without a problem," he replied with a grin. "Don't tell me you're getting superstitious in your old age, Kellian?"

Kellian snorted. "I was more concerned about bandits. In those trees, we'd never see them coming."

"What would a bunch of bandits want with a couple of paupers like us?"

"Maybe if you hadn't spent the last of your coin on ale last night, we'd have something for them to steal," Kellian shot back.

Devon laughed, but shook his head. "Come on, the Sitton road is faster."

"Yes, and our old friend's tracks go around. Are you sure you're not just avoiding another encounter?"

"There is that," Devon said, grinning. "Are you spoiling for a fight so soon after the last one?"

Kellian rolled his eyes, but he stepped onto the forest

path without further argument. Chuckling to himself, Devon strode after his friend. To the west, the sun was just beginning to sink behind the trees on the riverbank, while ahead the forest of Sitton lay in darkness. He shivered as they entered the shadows, the temperature plummeting.

"I hope you're right about this place," Kellian muttered as they pressed deeper into the forest.

Darkness clung to the track here. The road was becoming overgrown as the forest reclaimed the hard-packed earth, making the way difficult. Several times Devon cursed as a root tripped him, or he found the soft trunk of a sapling in his path.

"Do me a favour," Kellian said after an hour, "keep that hammer of yours handy."

"You worry too much, old friend," Devon replied in a light-hearted voice, though even as he spoke he reached up and loosened *kanker* in its sheath. "What ever happened to the wily warrior I fought beside in Trola?"

"He got old," Kellian snapped. Devon looked round in surprise, but in the gloom it was difficult to make out his friend's expression. After a moment, Kellian went on in a softer tone. "He grew a brain, stopped taking so many unnecessary risks."

Devon nodded, feeling the weight of responsibility on his shoulders. His friend was right, taking the forest path was an unnecessary danger. It would take at least two days to clear the forest—longer if they lost their way. The road was badly overgrown and it would be easy to wander off the path. That was a long time for any disreputable souls inhabiting the forest to learn of their presence. He and Kellian might not have anything of value, but the bandits wouldn't know that.

Silently he lengthened his stride. "Come on, we can still make good ground before nightfall."

Kellian muttered something beneath his breath, but he picked up the pace. They staggered on for another hour before the darkness became so thick they could barely make out their hands in front of their faces. Several times Devon was struck in the eye by unseen branches, his height for once a disadvantage.

Cursing, he finally staggered to a stop. "This is far enough, I'll not be thrashed half to death by a forest. We'll wait for the light of—"

He broke off as a piercing shriek carried through the trees. A tingle of fear shot down Devon's spine as he swung towards the sound. Hairs stood up on the back of his neck as the cry came again. He glanced at his friend, but Kellian was staring in the same direction, his hand gripped tight around the hilt of a knife.

Kellian looked around as the scream died away. His face was drained of colour. "Someone's in trouble," he said softly.

"How far, do you think?" Devon whispered.

"Close," Kellian replied, "It's difficult to tell in the trees." He looked at Devon, his hazel eyes wrinkled with concern.

Devon's heart was racing at the thought of danger. He glanced back the way they'd come, but the light had died and there was no sign of the path. The scream came again. The hammer weighed heavily on his back. He could feel the burden of its history calling to him, the legends of his ancestors. He thought again of Trola, of the burning cities and bloody streets, and shuddered.

Was he strong enough to wield it once more, and keep to the path of good?

As the scream slowly died away, Devon made up his mind.

"Let's go," he hissed.

He bounded into the trees without waiting for a reply. Leaves and branches crunched beneath his boots as he ran, *kanker* suddenly in hand. He tightened his grip around its wooden haft, drawing reassurance from its weight. A sense of elation filled him as he fought the trees, picturing the battle to come, the spilling of blood and screams of the dying. His breath came faster, his heart pounding like a wagon racing over a rutted street.

Another shriek carried through the trees, loud and piercing, calling him on. The darkness pressed in around them, but Devon no longer struggled with the roots and branches. His feet found their way with sudden accuracy, dancing through the unseen obstacles. He ran on through a tunnel of darkness. He was aware of Kellian's presence beside him, but in that moment, he felt alone with the shadows, at one with the power thumping through his body, the beast writhing within him.

Ahead, the trees opened up, giving way suddenly to a clearing. Movement came from its centre. Lifting his hammer, Devon leapt towards it, mouth open to scream a battle cry…only to stagger to a stop as shapes took form from the darkness.

Alana stood alone in the clearing, grey eyes wild, blond hair a tangled mess. She held her sabre in one hand, the silver blade a blur, darting in and out, striking at the green things that reached for her. For a second, Devon thought they were snakes, only they had no heads, no mouths, no scales. As he watched, one shot out and wrapped a slender tendril around her ankle. The scream came again, one of pure, unbridled rage. Twisting, Alana's sabre flashed down, severing the living vine, allowing her to dance clear.

But already more vines were closing in. Her sabre flashed again as one wrapped around her wrist, but it was clear she was fighting a losing battle. At her feet, her brother lay motionless, wrapped in a seething mass of green. Even as Devon watched, his body jerked, and started to slide away from Alana.

Shouting, Alana leapt after him, her sabre slashing wildly at the vines encasing her brother. Then she staggered, her feet coming up short as several tendrils trapped her legs. Before she could lift her sabre to cut herself free, they jerked violently, sending her crashing to the ground.

"What are you waiting for?" Kellian screamed as he shot past. "Help her!"

Devon shook off his shock and staggered after his friend. Kellian held a dagger in each hand now, their steel blades shimmering as they slashed at the vines around Alana. Beyond, Braidon's body gave another jerk, the tangled vines dragging him across the clearing. Grasping his hammer, Devon charged after the boy.

The thrill of battle boiled in Devon's veins as the weight of the weapon settled into his hands. Roaring, he bounded towards the nearest vines, the ancient hammer sweeping down to crush them. The vines fell back at *kanker's* touch, and he charged on, a war cry on his lips.

Nearby, Alana was back on her feet. She stood back to back with Kellian, her sabre sweeping out to fend off another attack. But the vines had separated them from Braidon. Gritting his teeth, Devon fought his way after the boy.

The blood froze in Devon's chest as his eyes followed the vines to the trees, and he saw what waited there. In the darkness, red eyes glowed from the trunks of the trees. Beneath the eyes, great fissures split the trunks, forming gaping jaws of hardened bark. Alana's cry came from across the clearing as her brother slid inexorably closer to the awful mouths.

Devon flinched as a tendril wrapped around his bicep and he felt the bite of thorns piercing his flesh. *Kanker* swept down, its hardened head catching the vines mid-swing. At its touch, they fell back, their colour fading to black as they dropped to the forest floor. Teeth gritted in rage, Devon forced his way through towards Braidon, fighting to place himself between the boy and the demonic trees.

Behind him he could hear the cries and grunts of Alana and Kellian as they fought for their freedom. Flashing them a glance, his heart lurched in his chest as he saw his friend go down, his feet whipped out from beneath him by writhing vegetation. Alana leapt to defend him, but another vine trapped her sword arm. Cursing, she drew her dagger and sliced at her supernatural assailants, but the steel blades no longer seemed effective.

Torn between his friend and the helpless boy, Devon hesitated. Panic rose in his chest. Around him the vines closed in, forming a writhing wall of green. Tightening his grip on the hammer, he made up his mind. Smashing a path through the vines, he started towards the dark glow of the nearest tree. The red eyes seemed to be watching him, an ancient hatred in their bloody depths. His breath coming in raged gasps, Devon fought his way towards them, driven by instinct now. The vines grew thicker around him, but just a touch from his warhammer was all it took for them to fall back.

With a roar, he reached the demonic tree and raised *kanker* above his head. A high-pitched shriek tore through the clearing, driving shards of pain deep into Devon's skull. The noise seemed to come from all around, but he recognised it for what it was—a last, desperate attempt to halt his attack. Clenching his jaw, he gripped the hammer in both hands and swung.

Vines flashed for his face, wrapping about his neck and torso, but not even the thrashing tendrils could halt his attack now. The great tree seemed to shrink an instant before *kanker* struck, the vile glow dying in the red slits of its eyes. The mouth snapped closed.

A sharp *crack* echoed through the clearing as *kanker* plunged home. The vibration of the blow shook Devon to his core, almost making him drop the hammer. Clenching his teeth, he held on, and lifted the ancient weapon for another swing.

An awful groan came from the tree, but the vines continued to thrash, the terrible tendrils all around him now. Razor-sharp thorns tore at his thighs and he could feel blood dripping down his back, but still he raised the hammer high.

"Die, bastard," Devon growled.

Red light flashed across the clearing as he drove the ancient weapon down into the blazing eyes. The wooden mouth groaned open, and it seemed a pure darkness came rushing out, a cloud of evil that fled away into the forest.

Devon staggered back as a sudden stillness came over the clearing. A wave of exhaustion swept through him, but summoning the last of his strength, he forced himself to look around at the surrounding trees. The other eyes had vanished, plunging the clearing into darkness. His gaze continued around to find Alana and Kellian standing nearby. The boy, Braidon, lay not far from where he stood.

Suddenly *kanker* felt unbearably heavy in his hands.

Devon let the hammer fall. The *thud* as it struck the ground seemed unnaturally loud in the silence. He swayed on his feet, and Kellian quickly stepped forward and offered his shoulder. Cuts marked his friend's arms and face, but he seemed to have fended off the worst of the attack.

Alana gave a strangled cry and ran to her brother. Devon watched as she dropped to her knees beside the boy. He heard a voice sound from far away. Turning, he tried to focus on the face of his friend, but the world was fading now, darkness swirling at the edges of his vision. Relieved, he opened his arms and embraced it like an old friend.

12

"What the hell is that?" Quinn pulled hard on the reins of his horse, bringing the beast to a halt mid-trot.

His men did the same, milling about him as they turned to stare in the direction their lieutenant was looking. Only a few had magic to sense the disturbance radiating from the forest to the west, but they were experienced enough to recognise the look on their lieutenant's face.

Closing his eyes, Quinn allowed the waves of magic to slide through him. They pulsed on the air, dark and unnatural, a power from another time. This was no rogue Magicker, no wild magic. It was something else—dark magic, primal and raw, powerful.

He looked around at his men, sharing glances with the few gifted with magic. He could see the question in their eyes. Something was happening in the forest of Sitton, something against not just the laws of the Tsar, but those of the earth itself. Dark magic was a perversion of the natural world; it was their duty to investigate its sudden appearance.

Yet the detour would mean abandoning their hunt for the rogue Magicker, wherever the renegade had vanished. Quinn still wasn't sure whether they were on the right path. The confrontation with Devon had left him angry and humiliated, and still no closer to finding their quarry. He wished he'd pressed the man more. If he'd managed to goad Devon into drawing his hammer, Quinn would have slain him where he stood. He could have killed him regardless, of course, but it would have shamed Quinn to kill an unarmed man—even one so cowardly as Devon.

Still, with their only lead a dead-end, Quinn had pushed his men onwards in the hope they would stumble upon the rogue Magicker. He had sensed nothing of their prey since leaving the capital, but Quinn's instincts told him they were close to *something.*

Now, though, dark magic was radiating from the forest. Was this something to do with the Magicker, or something else entirely? He had sensed no Earth magic amongst the dark, as he had back in Ardath, but that did not mean their quarry was not involved. He had heard rumours of the forest before; perhaps the Magicker had awoken something in the old ruins.

Quinn shook his head. His gut told him two outpourings of magic in two days could not be coincidence. Swearing under his breath, he turned to his men.

"Vim, take three men," he said, pointing at his deputy. "Continue north along the Gods Road until the roads merge again, then follow the forest road back towards Ardath."

"What about you, sir?" his deputy asked.

"The rest of us will retrace our steps and take the other road. With luck we'll meet tomorrow near the ruins of Sitton."

His deputy nodded and saluted quickly. "Good luck, sir."

Quinn tightened his grip on the reins. A breath of wind stirred around him, picking up dust and lifting it into the air. He smiled as the magic swelled in his chest, feeding strength back to his weary muscles.

"And to you, deputy."

With that, Quinn turned his horse and kicked the tiring beast into a gallop. The roar of hooves chased after him as his eight remaining men followed suit.

13

"How goes your brother's teaching, Alana?" Her father's voice was cold, echoing from the stone walls.

Alana shivered, looking up into his weathered face. "He's… progressing, father."

"Progressing? His birthday is in two months. Will he be ready, or not?" *He spoke the final words in a hard, grating tone that left no doubt such an outcome was not an option.*

She nodded quickly, raising her hands in deference. "He will be ready, I swear it, Father."

"Good." As quickly as it had come, her father's anger vanished. "He will achieve great things, one day. As will you, Alana. When the two of you are ready."

Rising from his chair, he wandered around the dining table and gestured for her to stand. "Come, walk with me, my daughter."

Alana smiled, the weight lifting from her chest as she accepted her father's hand. Together they wandered out into the courtyard. Snow was falling over the roses, but her father led her around the covered walkway, her hand still in his.

"What are your dreams, Alana?" he asked quietly, his eyes on the white frosting covering the garden.

Glancing up at him, Alana frowned. "To make you proud, Father," she replied quickly.

A smile appeared on his bearded face. "Ever the dutiful daughter," he murmured. A light appeared in his blue eyes as he spoke again. "Now, the truth."

Unbidden, the words bubbled up from the depths of Alana's soul. "To be free."

Laughter whispered through the courtyard as her father led her towards the exit. Between the great columns holding up the roof, she glimpsed a shadow approaching. Something inside her screamed a warning, but in the dream, Alana walked on, oblivious. A cold crept through the scene, blurring its edges, as the couple stepped into the doorway leading outside.

Alana staggered to a stop as she found herself staring into Quinn's hard brown eyes.

"Are you ready, Alana?"

"No!" Alana screamed, sitting bolt upright on the forest floor.

Gasping, she stumbled to her feet, hands scrambling in the darkness for her blade.

"Alana, stop, what's wrong?" A voice came from nearby, familiar yet strange.

Steel rasped on leather as she found her sabre and drew it. "Stay back!" she warned, spinning in the voice's direction.

"Alana, stop, it's Kellian!"

Light blazed suddenly in the darkness as someone tossed fuel on the dwindling fire. Flames danced, casting their glow on the man's face. She let out a long sigh as she recognised Devon's friend. Lowering her sabre, she slumped back to the ground, her breath still coming in ragged gasps.

"Are you okay?" Kellian whispered, moving closer.

She shook her head and lifted a palm towards him. "Just give me a second," she panted.

He nodded. Turning away, he crouched beside the fire and stocked it. After a moment, Alana moved across the clearing to sit beside him. She let out a sigh as she felt the fire's heat on her cheeks. Her brother lay nearby, and she reached across to tuck the blanket firmly around him. Brushing a curly lock of black hair from his face, she watched him sleep. His eyes flickered at her touch but did not open. A moan built in her throat, but she pushed it down, willing herself to be strong.

Silently, she cursed her decision to venture off the Gods Road. She had been so confident they could keep in touch with the path, but within half an hour they'd become horribly lost. With the path nowhere in sight, they had stumbled on through the growing darkness. For a moment, Alana had thought them saved when they'd found the clearing. Then the red eyes had appeared in the shadows of the trees, and the vines had come for them, knocking Braidon unconscious before either of them had a chance to fight back. Only pure instinct had saved Alana, her sabre sliding into her hand before she even understood the danger threatening them.

Now, with Devon and Braidon unconscious, she crouched in the same clearing and stared at the silent trees. Alana hadn't left her brother's side since Devon smashed the demonic tree, but afterwards Kellian had ventured close enough to inspect them. Apparently several of the trees lining the clearing had dark faces etched into their bark. She expected them to reawaken at any moment, but there was little they could do if the trees threatened again. Between herself and Kellian, they could barely lift the massive hammerman—let alone her brother.

Instead, Kellian had lit a great fire in the centre of the clearing, and together they had sat down to wait out the night. She must have fallen asleep, because she could already see the first light of morning creeping through the treetops.

Her gaze shifted to Devon's motionless figure. Sleep had softened the rugged features of his face, the furrows in his forehead vanishing, the scowl replaced by a slight smile. Beside his massive shoulders and muscular arms, her brother seemed but a child, precious and fragile. She cursed herself again for ever bringing him to this place.

She flinched as a low groan came from across the clearing. Reaching for her sabre, she made to stand, her eyes going to the trees, before the sound came again. Across the fire, Devon shifted and sat up, his amber eyes blinking in the shadows. His gaze shifted from Kellian to Alana, before returning to his friend.

"We beat the bastards, then?"

Kellian chuckled. He reached down to pick up the warhammer and handed it to Devon. "You beat them, old friend."

"Good." Taking the hammer, Devon placed it beside him and held his hands out to the fire. "No wonder I'm starving. We got anything for breakfast?"

Alana's heart lurched in her chest as another moan came from her brother. She scrambled across to him as he sat up, his brow creased with confusion.

"Alana? Where are we—" He broke off as she smothered him in a hug.

"I'm sorry," she said at last, breaking away. She quickly wiped a tear from her eye. "Are you okay?"

"I'm fine, I think," he replied, rubbing his head where the vine had struck him. "What happened…" He jerked as he looked around and saw the faces on the trees, lit now by the light of day. "The trees!"

"It's okay," Alana said quickly, resting a hand on his shoulder. "They seem to be…asleep," she finished lamely.

"Scared, more like," Devon said gruffly.

"Whatever they are, your breakfast will have to wait," Kellian said, standing. He gestured at the trees. "I don't know about you, but now you're both awake, I'd rather not stick around in this place."

Alana nodded. "Let's get out of here."

There was no telling which direction they'd come from, but Kellian climbed a tree and was able to pick a path northwest towards the river. So long as they kept to that direction they would eventually stumble onto the road. It would take another day to leave the forest by those paths, but with Quinn and his Stalkers behind them, no one was enthusiastic about heading back the way they'd come.

They walked on through the morning in silence, each lost in their own thoughts. When they finally reached the road, the four of them exchanged brief glances, relief etched into their faces. Turning to the north, they continued on, determined to escape the forest as soon as physically possible. Kellian dug into a small pack as they walked, coming up with a few strips of salted jerky. The scraps were passed around without speech. With Alana's meagre supplies lost in the battle with the trees, there wouldn't be any more food until they left the forest.

The day dragged on. The sun rose high above the tree-tops, but its light did not penetrate beneath the canopy. Shadows clung to the path, and when they breathed there was ice in the air. As the sun crept towards the horizon,

Alana's breath began to cloud before her face. Shivering, she pulled her cloak more tightly around her, and marched on.

Only as the light began to fade did Alana glimpse the first traces of the city that had once been Sitton. Fallen stonework, shaped by human hands, appeared amongst the trees. She glimpsed a wall to their left, its surface turned green by moss, then tripped as the path beneath her feet changed to stones, a groove worn into the rock catching her boot. Mounds of broken tiles lay amongst the trees, and as she looked more closely, she realised the path was now threading its way through former buildings, their roofs long gone, their walls crumbling.

"Sitton," she breathed.

Up front, Devon nodded. "All that remains," he murmured, glancing back. "I've come this way before. There's a temple ahead. Its walls are mostly intact, they should offer some protection. We'll camp there for the night."

True to Devon's word, the temple was in better condition than many of the other buildings, though a massive tower had fallen across half the structure, burying everything beneath a mound of stones. The remaining three walls stood strong, offering their ancient protection from the elements. Devon led them to a doorway in one of the walls, its wooden arch long since rotted away.

Alana paused in the doorway as the others moved ahead, her eyes scanning the interior of the temple. There was no sign of broken tiles or roofing material, and she guessed this section must have once been a courtyard within the temple's inner sanctum. Several trees grew in its centre, their long branches stretching high above the height of the walls. She stared at their trunks but could see no sign of the demonic faces.

Allowing herself to follow the others into the temple courtyard, Alana scanned the walls. Moss and lichen covered the stones, but she could just make out the old etchings in their surface—of lightning bolts and spiralling trees. The symbols meant the temple had once been dedicated to Antonia and Jurrien—the Gods of Earth and Sky.

Kellian and Devon moved quickly about the courtyard, gathering branches and kindling for a fire. A tinderbox appeared from Kellian's bag and within minutes they had a fire burning against the far wall of the courtyard. Taking her brother by the hand, they moved across to join them, savouring the warmth on their faces. Silently the four of them sat round the fire, eyes to the flames.

"What were those things?" It was Kellian who finally broke the silence.

Alana shuddered. Her skin crawled where the vines had touched her, their inexorable strength threatening to drag her to her death. She recalled the red eyes, glowing through the dark, the gaping maws opening to greet her. Shivering, she pushed the memory away.

"Nothing I've ever seen," Devon mused, his voice strangely calm. The hammer lay beside him, his hand rested on its haft. "Something evil."

"Really?" Alana snapped. She looked up to find the eyes of the other three on her. Her shoulders slumped and she shook her head. "Sorry. I'm just..." she trailed off, unable to put words to the terror that had lodged in her soul.

"Afraid," Kellian finished for her. His eyes flickered around the fallen temple. "Are we safe here, do you think?"

"I've camped here before," Devon answered, "when I

travelled this way in the past. But those things…who knows how far their darkness reaches."

Beside her, Braidon shuddered. "I barely saw them. They knocked me down before I knew what was happening."

"Count yourself lucky," Kellian murmured. His eyes flickered from Braidon to Alana. "Why did you venture off the path in the first place?"

A shiver swept down Alana's spine as she glimpsed suspicion in the man's eyes. They had been behind them on the Gods Road—that meant they'd seen the Stalkers ride past. Reaching down, Alana took a swig from the water skin, buying herself time.

"We stumbled from the path," she said finally. "It was dark and the path was overgrown. I didn't realise how lost we were until we found that clearing."

"What I don't understand," Devon said quietly, his eyes flickering down to the hammer at his feet. "Is why the vines fell back from *kanker*. Your blades barely cut them, but as soon as *kanker* touched them, they withered away."

The others looked back at him, unable to offer any answers. Alana was about to ask where the hammer had come from when her ears caught the soft whisper of noise from beyond the walls. Goosebumps tingling on her neck, she rose quickly, waving a hand to silence the others. Clutching at her sword hilt, she crept towards the doorway, eyes fixed on the shadows beyond, ears straining.

Crunch.

This time the noise was unmistakable—the sound of a footstep on stone.

✤ 14 ✤

Behind Alana, the others rose, weapons in hand. Gritting her teeth, Alana drew her sabre. At the rasp of steel on leather, all sounds from outside ceased. Cursing softly, Alana slid closer to the temple's entrance.

She lifted her blade as movement flickered in the doorway, preparing to hurl herself at the unknown intruder. Before she had a chance to attack, a hunched figure stepped from the shadows into the light.

Alana blinked, her feet almost tripping over themselves as she pulled herself up short. Soft laughter whispered through the courtyard as the figure took another step towards them. Firelight illuminated the withered folds of a woman's ancient face. Blue eyes glowed in the darkness, and silvery hair hung around her shoulders. Green robes cloaked the woman's ancient body. While she moved at a shuffle, Alana did not miss the glint of a sword hilt at the woman's waist. Taking a hasty step back, she lifted her own blade and pointed it at the old woman.

"Stay back!" Alana cursed inwardly as her voice shook.

The laughter came again, quiet, filled with mirth. "Are you so afraid of an old woman?"

"These are strange times," Kellian said, stepping up beside Alana. "Trust does not come easily. Who are you?"

"A priest."

"What's a priest doing in a place like this?" Devon asked gruffly. He walked forward, *kanker* in hand, firelight reflecting from the steel head.

"Looking for you," the priest replied.

Taking her blade in a two-handed grip, Alana advanced a step on the old woman, until the point rested on her chest. "*Why?*" she hissed.

The blue eyes dropped to the blade, then back to Alana. The smile never left the ancient face. "You fought the *Arbor*," she said quietly. Her eyes turned on Devon. "You killed one."

"What the hell are you talking about?" Devon growled.

"The magic of the black trees clings to you like a cloak." The woman continued as though the giant hammerman had not spoken. "You were fortunate to survive."

"The black trees?" Kellian asked calmly. "That's what you mean by the *Arbor?*"

The woman nodded, turning to face the innkeeper.

"And what do they have to do with you, priest?" he pressed.

"I hunt them," the old priest said simply.

Silence met her answer. Then Devon threw back his head and began to laugh. The booming sound echoed around the courtyard. When it finally faded away, the big man wiped tears from his eyes and looked at the woman. "You hunt them?" he asked. "And how does someone as old as you manage that?"

The old woman had said nothing as the hammerman

laughed, but now a smile of her own spread across her lips. "Like *this*."

Before anyone could react, the woman moved. Short sword suddenly in hand, she lashed out, catching Alana's sabre just above the hilt. The shock of the impact knocked the blade from Alana's hand, then a booted foot lashed out to catch her in the chest. Stumbling backwards, she crashed into Kellian and the two of them went down in a heap.

Cursing, Devon lifted his hammer and swung at the old woman, but she had already slipped below his guard. He froze as the silver steel of her blade touched his throat.

"Do you need another demonstration?" she asked into the sudden silence.

Devon carefully shook his head. "I take your point."

The woman's laughter bubbled forth as she sheathed her blade and wandered across to their fire. She sat down with a low groan, only then glancing back at them. "Well, are you going to stand there all night in the cold, or are you going to join me?"

"Join you?" Alana snapped. Finally managing to disentangle herself from Kellian, she scooped up her sabre and leapt to her feet. "Why don't you try me in a fair fight, you old hag?"

The blue eyes flickered up at Alana. She froze midstride, reading the danger there. "Put away your blade, girl," the woman said, her words like ice. "Before I take it from you."

Alana swallowed, suddenly lost for words. The threat in the woman's eyes was unmistakable, and despite their obvious mismatch, she sensed it would be a mistake to attack. After a long moment, she pushed down her anger and sheathed her sabre.

The smile returned to the woman's face. "Good girl."

She nodded to the log beside her. "Why don't you join me and tell me of the *Arbor* you fought? I would like to hear the tale."

After a moment's hesitation, the four of them shuffled across to join the woman. Embers of rage still burning in her stomach, Alana took the seat across the fire from her. Kellian busied himself with his bag, pulling out a pot and a few stray leaves he'd collected from the jungle. Within a few minutes he had a pot of water bubbling over the fire. Tearing the leaves into smaller pieces, he added them to the pot to make tea.

"There's not much to tell," Alana said shortly. "My brother and I got lost. We stumbled into a clearing, where they attacked us."

"But how did you survive?" The priest asked. She leaned forward, the firelight casting shadows across her wrinkled face.

"We were lucky enough to hear their cries," Kellian answered. "I helped Alana fight off the vines, while Devon destroyed one of the...*Arbor*."

"Yes," the priest mused. "Its death lingers on you still, hammerman."

Devon shrugged. Lifting his hammer, he held it out to the flames. "It was no match for *kanker*."

The woman's eyes widened as they alighted on the hammer. "I know that hammer," she whispered. "Where did you come by it?"

Devon glanced at his friend before answering. "It has been passed down through my family for generations."

A smile appeared on the old woman's face at that. "The bloodline of Alan runs true."

To Alana's surprise, Devon's face darkened at the woman's comment. The hammer slipped from his fingers and struck the cobbles with a sharp crack. Rising, he moved away without speaking, his eyes downcast. He vanished into the trees without a word.

The strange woman stared after him, confusion on her face. She glanced at Kellian. "Did I say something?"

"No, my lady," he replied gently. "Only, his ancestor's deeds have weighed on him his entire life. It is no easy thing, being descended from a hero."

"I am sorry to hear that," the priest murmured.

"It is his demon to battle," Kellian replied. He trailed off a moment, before looking at the old woman again. "I'm afraid we still do not know your name, my lady."

The edges of the woman's eyes crinkled as she laughed. "Forgive my poor manners," she said. "I have not been amongst civilised company for a long time. I go by Tillie."

"It's nice to meet you, Tillie." Braidon, silent until now, finally spoke.

"And you, young man," the priest replied.

"Braidon," he added with a smile, "and this is my sister, Alana. And Kellian and Devon."

"Pardon my interest," Kellian broke in as he took up a piece of bamboo and began cutting it into pieces. "but why have you spent so much time in this forest, Tillie?"

"As I said, I have been hunting the *Arbor.*"

Kellian poured the tea into his makeshift bamboo cups and then offered them around the circle. Alana accepted one with a smile, before taking a sip. The tea tasted of rosehip and mint, and smiling, she took another mouthful.

"But why you?" Kellian asked finally. "I mean no offence, but surely there were younger priests to undertake such a dangerous mission."

Tillie laughed. "You do not pull your blows, young Kellian." She shook her head, considering his words. "Perhaps I did not wish such youthful lives to be risked in such a dangerous task."

"A noble thought," Kellian offered.

Tillie grinned. "I did not say it was true though." She trailed off, her face thoughtful. For a moment, Alana didn't think she was going to speak. When the words finally came, they were soft, filled with sorrow. "There were others once who stood with me against the darkness. I'm the last of them now, though."

"That sounds lonely," Braidon whispered.

Reaching out, Alana gripped his hand, thinking of their own plight, their rush to escape the grip of the Tsar.

As if summoned by her thoughts, the old woman's eyes turned towards her. "And what brings the two of you into this forest, young Alana?"

Alana swallowed, seeing again Quinn's eyes, whispering in her dreams.

Are you ready?

"We're passing through," she said quickly, determinedly keeping the tremor from her voice. She looked around at the ruin of the temple, as though seeing it for the first time. "What happened to this place?"

"Sitton was never a large city, but it once served as a waystation between Lon and Ardath, a safe port for ships to dock and resupply. It was destroyed during the final war between Archon and the Gods, when his demon was hunting the Sword of Light."

Kellian snorted. "That old myth?" he asked, laughter in his voice. "Surely you don't believe the Gods were ever foolish enough to hand their powers over to a mere mortal?"

"Who am I to question history?" the priest replied, her eyes dancing in the firelight. "Even so, there is no question that the God of the Sky met Archon's demon here. The battle shook the very earth, and in the end Sitton was razed to the ground. Empowered by the demon's magic, the forest grew up around the city overnight, spreading for leagues and cutting off the ruins from the rest of the world. Amidst that forest, the *Arbor* took root."

"And you decided to change that?" Braidon spoke in a low voice, his eyes wide.

"I have tried," Tillie replied sadly. "But I fear it has been for naught. The trees are rooted deep. They resist mortal weapons. Fire can hurt them, but only magic has the power to kill the creatures. I have cleared them from the city and the Gods Road, but others still remain, hidden in the depths of the forest."

"You're a Magicker then?" Alana asked, her heart quickening at the thought.

The old woman didn't look up from the flames. "That would make me a renegade from the Tsar, would it not?" she asked, her voice barely audible above the popping of burning wood.

No one spoke for a moment, and quietly Alana let the subject die. Her eyes drifted to where *kanker* lay in the dirt, and her thoughts turned to the question they'd been pondering before the woman appeared. Reaching out, she lifted the weapon and brushed it clean with her hand.

"How did Devon kill the tree, then?" she asked quietly. "He has no magic."

"Alan," Tillie replied. "The man was a mighty warrior, not just because of his strength and courage, but because his hammer was no mortal weapon. He married the daughter of a powerful Magicker. I don't doubt the old man bound his power into the weapon *kanker*, to protect his son-in-law in battle. Though exactly what its nature is, I cannot tell."

"How has Devon carried it for so long then, without coming to the Tsar's attention?"

The priest chuckled dryly. "The Tsar may be a Magicker beyond compare, but even he does not possess all the secrets of magic. The power contained within the hammer is dormant. Other Magickers would not be able to sense it."

Alana nodded, still processing the new information. Before she could reply, a cold voice came from the shadows.

"Thank you, priest, for answering that mystery."

❧ 15 ❧

Devon sat amongst the trees, his mind far away, lost in memories of his past. He could still hear the screams of men as they fell beneath his hammer, smell the stench as their bowels gave way, see the terror in their eyes at the approach of death. For years he had gloried in the triumph of battle, confident in his own invincibility.

Then the war had turned into a slaughter, and doubt had come gnawing into his mind.

Hero?

How could he call himself that, when his hands were stained with the blood of innocents?

Shivering, he clenched his fists, feeling the power in his meaty hands. He had never desired any other trade but war. He was bred for it, as his father and his grandfather had been before him. They had marched in the legendary footsteps of Alan, following Gods and Kings as they fought against the bandits and monsters who still roamed the Three Nations. Devon's grandfather had even joined the

Northland alliance to help cleanse the northern wastelands of Archon's creatures.

Now an evil force had finally shown its face to Devon, and he had faced it down with courage. But he was afraid it had come too late. His soul was already stained, corrupted by the darkness of his past. He didn't deserve to wield *kanker*, wasn't worthy of his ancestor's name.

"Drop your weapons!"

The voice cut through Devon's melancholy, and he looked back to where the firelight glittered between the trees. He frowned as he saw shadows dancing there. Rising from the tree stump, he reached for his hammer, then swore as he remembered he'd left it behind.

Laughter whispered through the trees as Devon took a step towards the campsite.

"Move and you die!" a voice growled.

Devon stilled, but the words had not been directed at him, and after a moment he continued edging towards the camp. Treading carefully between the sticks littering the broken courtyard, he crept towards the fire. Ice slid down his back as he paused at the treeline and looked out at the men surrounding the campfire. The others stood beside the fire with the priest, but now they were surrounded by eight dark-cloaked figures, their swords drawn.

His friends had their hands on their weapons but had not yet drawn them. For a moment he wondered why, until he saw the man leading the intruders. He held one hand stretched out towards Kellian and the others. The tips of his fingers were obscured by a strange haze, and it was a moment before Devon realised the air itself changed there.

His eyes flickered to the man's face, though he knew now who it was.

Quinn!

By the fire, Alana drew her sabre in a rush and charged the lieutenant. But before she could take two steps, there was a roar of air and then a great gale of wind caught Alana in the chest and hurled her back. Tumbling over the ground, she crashed through the campfire, scattering embers across the courtyard. Her brother leapt to her side and brushed her clear of the flames while she struggled to regain her feet.

"Anyone else?" Quinn's icy voice carried across to where Devon hid in the trees.

He ducked lower, praying the shadows would conceal him from the prying eyes of the Stalkers. The company was smaller than he'd last seen it, and he wondered where the rest of Quinn's men were lurking.

"What are you doing here, Quinn?" Kellian said, his voice hard and unyielding.

Quinn ignored the question. He stood motionless, still staring at the woman on the ground. "Alana?" he whispered.

Alana looked up sharply at her name, her eyes widening. She stood quickly and retreated a step, dragging her brother with her. "Stay back, Stalker," she hissed. Her sabre had been lost when the wind struck her, but she drew a dagger and pointed it at the lieutenant's chest.

Almost casually, Quinn flicked a hand. The wind tore at Alana, threatening to knock her flat. Screaming, she drew back her blade and hurled it at the lieutenant, but the wind caught the knife and tossed it far into the trees. Ignoring her warning, Quinn continued towards her. He wore a strange look on his face, his brow creased in a frown, but with the slightest of smiles on his lips.

"It was smart, hiding in the city so long," he whispered,

"but it's over now. You must come back with me, before it's too late."

The look on Alana's face had turned from shock to confusion now. She stared back at the lieutenant, mouth agape, fingers clenched tightly on her brother's cloak. With obvious effort, she bared her teeth, eyes flashing. "We're not going anywhere with you."

The smile left Quinn's lips. "You cannot stop me." He started towards them again, but the priest stepped between them.

"That's far enough, young man." Her voice was soft as a summer breeze, but there was iron in it.

Quinn blinked, as though seeing the priest for the first time. "Who are you, old woman?"

"A priest of the Goddess, Antonia," Tillie replied. "This is her temple still—you are not welcome here."

The Stalker took a moment to look around, his eyebrows raised in disbelief. "This pile of rubble?" He laughed, the sound harsh and mocking. "I did not realise your order had fallen so low, priest." His tone hardened and he took a step towards her. "Now get out of my way, before I make you."

Amongst the trees, Devon's heart sank as he studied the men surrounding the campfire. Anger flared in his chest. Between himself and Kellian, they might have stood a chance—although eight men would have been difficult even for them. But Quinn's magic put the contest out of reach. They were helpless against his power. He turned his gaze on Alana, wondering what Quinn wanted. If he was not mistaken, the lieutenant knew her. If that was true…Devon didn't like to think of the consequences.

Either way, he was better off minding his own business.

He had done his best to avoid drawing the Tsar's attention since his retirement, and he had no wish to break the pattern now. Whatever Alana and her brother had done, this was their fight. The thought of surrendering them to Quinn made his gut squirm, but there was no help for it. Clearing his throat, he stepped from the trees and waved at the Magicker.

"Well met, Quinn," he grunted, walking slowly towards the group standing around the fire.

Several of the men stepped in his direction, but Quinn waved them back when he saw Devon's empty hands. Fixing a smile to his bearded face, Devon strode through the ring of men and held his hands out to the flames.

"Cold night for riding," he said softly. "What brings you and your men into this cursed forest, Quinn?"

Quinn narrowed his eyes. "Dark magic."

Devon nodded. "Might be I know something about that."

"Oh?"

Turning toward the man, Devon nodded. "Ay, I do. Perhaps you'd like to put away your magic, and we can talk like men?"

A dark smile twisted Quinn's lips, but after a moment he lowered his arm.

Nodding, Devon went on. "The priest called them the *Arbor*—demonic trees that feed on human flesh. Something the Stalkers should have dealt with a long time ago, I would have thought."

Quinn's eyes hardened. "What my men and I do is the Tsar's business," he spat. "And the trees might have drawn us here, but I see now it is *you* I have been hunting. Did you really think you could keep a Magicker from the Tsar?"

Devon reeled back at Quinn's words. "What?"

A sneer appeared on Quinn's lips. "Do not play dumb with me, Devon. Now stand aside."

Before Devon could react, a blast of wind caught him in the chest and hurled him backwards over the fire. The breath hissed from his lungs as his bulk struck the ground. Gasping, he hauled himself onto his hand and knees, and began to cough.

He looked up in time to see Kellian leap to the attack, a dagger glinting in each hand. Steel flashed as one flashed towards the Magicker's throat, but a flick of Quinn's wrist sent it whirling away. Before Devon's friend could reach the Stalker, another breath of air sent him hurtling sideways into the priest. The two went down in a pile of thrashing limbs.

Quinn laughed and turned on Alana and her brother.

On the ground, Braidon straightened and lifted himself to his feet. He stood over his sister, blue eyes flashing. Screaming, he threw out his hands at Quinn.

In an instant the courtyard descended into chaos. Light flashed from the boy's hands, and a great, awful howling rent the air. The ring of Quinn's men scattered at the sound, weapons raised to fend off the sudden attack. The very air seemed to vibrate, and with each flash of light, thunder crashed deafeningly. Even Quinn was shaken by the attack. Staggering back, he held up his hands before him. Wind swirled around his body, forming an evanescent shield.

Shocked by the explosion of magic, Devon crouched frozen on the ground, watching in horror as the black-garbed men retreated from the violence of the boy's power, their faces a picture of terror. Quinn retreated to join them, but a loose brick caught his foot and sent him crashing to the ground. Instantly, the howling wind died away.

"*Come on!*" Suddenly Alana was at Devon's side, her eyes wild, hair turning from blonde to black with each flash of light. She shoved *kanker* into his hands and hauled him to his feet. "We have to get out of here!"

Spinning on her heel, she disappeared into the flashing light. He saw her an instant later, grabbing her brother by the waist and heaving him over her shoulder. The flashing light faded away as he collapsed against her, leaving shadows of its presence burning in their eyes. Half blind, Devon stumbled after them, listening as the screams of the Stalkers turned to shouts of confusion.

Without looking back, Alana darted for the broken doorway, her small size belying her strength. The strange old woman followed, and Kellian had already vanished. Around them, the Stalkers were in disarray. Heart hammering in his chest, Devon raced after his friends.

As they emerged from the doorway onto the road, the thunder of horses came from to their right. Devon spun, hefting his hammer, only to find Kellian bearing down on them riding a stolen mount. He held the reins of two more tightly in one hand. Alana leapt forward, pulling herself into the saddle and dragging her brother up with her. Offering his hand, Kellian helped the old woman into his own saddle, while Devon took the reins of the last horse.

He shared a glance with his friend. There was no need for words. The second the Stalkers had walked into that courtyard and found them with the boy, their fate had been sealed.

They were dead men now.

Knowingly or not, they had harboured a Magicker from the Tsar. The Stalkers would hunt them to the ends of the earth to see his justice carried out.

There was no time to linger on that thought now

though, so, kicking his horse, Devon turned it towards the north. Alana gave a shout, her horse leaping beneath her as she led the way. Anger flared in Devon's chest as he followed her. Alana had known, Quinn had said as much. She had led the Stalkers straight to them, and sentenced Devon and Kellian to death alongside her.

16

"They're gone, sir."

Quinn stared at the scout, jaw clenched, fist wrapped tightly around the hilt of his sword. He was still raging at his own foolishness. He, more than anyone, knew how dangerous wild magic could prove to be. His home town of Oaksville still told tales of the boy Magicker who'd all but razed the town to the ground.

Yet he had stood and talked with them, instead of eliminating the threat posed by the boy. It had been a costly mistake.

He sucked in a breath to quell his racing heart, then grated out a response. "How?"

The scout swallowed, his eyes flickering to the other men before returning to the lieutenant. His fingers fiddled absently with the button of his coat. The man was a veteran of five years with the Stalkers, but even he had been shaken by the boy's attack. His magic had come from the Light element—pure and powerful. It was a miracle they'd all survived.

"The horses, sir," he managed finally. "We've rounded up five of them, but three are missing. Seems they managed to steal them in the chaos.

Quinn gritted his teeth. "Which way did they go?"

Silently he cursed himself for allowing Devon to distract him. He had humoured himself, gloating at the man's folly, in the thought of finally bringing the coward to justice. But the boy had always been the true danger.

"North, sir, as far as we can tell in the dark," the scout replied.

Quinn allowed himself to suck in a long breath. If they'd gone north, they were heading straight into the path of Vim and his men. The deputy would be outnumbered, but he trusted his experience. With luck, they could capture Devon and his friends quickly. At the very least, they would slow the fugitives' flight.

Letting out his breath, Quinn's anger flowed away, replaced with a steely resolve. "Good." He glanced around at his other men. They were missing three horses now, and riding double, they would never catch their quarry. He clenched his fists, testing the strength of his magic. It burned in his chest, a deep well of power, only slightly expended by his earlier use. Nodding to himself, he pointed to the three men who'd lost their horses. "You men will return to the capital and report to the Tsar."

"What should we tell him, sir?" the first asked.

"Tell him we've found them."

17

Alana closed her eyes as the horse finally came to a stop. Sliding from the saddle, she stifled a moan, exhaustion weighing on her like a cloak of lead. Patting the horse's neck, she led the beast into the trees, her legs trembling. They had ridden through the night as hard as they dared, praying to the Gods the road remained passable, that no unseen tree root or torn up ground would trip their horses. Somehow, they had made it. Now the sun had begun its slow crawl into the sky, and neither they nor their horses could go any further.

Working by instinct, too tired to process what she was doing, Alana found a low-hanging branch and tied the horse's reins to it. Exhausted by the use of his magic, Braidon had passed out during their flight, and reaching up she lifted him carefully from the saddle. Lying him on the ground nearby, she returned to the horse and dug into the saddlebags, coming up with a blanket. She began to towel down the stead's sweat-soaked rump while doing her best to ignore the sounds of the others as they gathered nearby.

"Do you know what you've done?" Devon snapped finally, impatient, his voice trembling.

Closing her eyes, Alana summoned her last reserves of strength and turned to face the giant warrior. She glimpsed his face, the amber eyes filled with rage, teeth clenched, the muscles on his neck popping, and quickly looked away.

Swallowing, she tried to find her voice. It took several attempts before the words came out. "I'm sorry, I didn't mean…"

"Didn't mean what?" Gravel crunched as Devon stepped towards her. "Didn't mean to see us dead?"

Anger lit in Alana's stomach. "You think we asked for this?" she growled. "You think I wanted any of this?"

"I don't care what you wanted, *princess*," Devon roared. He gestured wildly back the way they'd come. "I don't want anything to do with you and your magic! This isn't my fight. You and your damned brother have nothing to do with me."

"Coward! I thought you were a hero, that your ancestor's deeds meant something to you?"

"A pox on my ancestors," Devon hissed, stepping in close. "I am my own man—and I say you had no right to drag us into this. I knew Quinn once. He's a man of iron. He won't give up until you and your brother are on your knees before the Tsar. I don't know who you are, *princess*, but I want nothing to do with this business."

Alana snorted. "Yes, I wouldn't expect someone like you to care whether we live or die." She shook her head, squaring off against the towering giant. "I never believed the rumours about you, but I see now they were true. You don't have the stomach to fight for what's right.

Devon stared back at her, eyes aflame. "And what is *right*?" he shouted. "The Tsar says your brother is dangerous. We all saw the deaths at the stepwell. We know what wild magic is capable of. Perhaps I should take him back with me. Maybe *that* is the right thing to do."

Alana reached for her sabre, clenching her hand around its hilt. It slid silently into the air. She pointed it at Devon's chest and bared her teeth. "Just you try it," she said.

Devon stared down at her, eyes hard. There was no fear there now, and when he spoke his voice was calm. "Put that toy away, princess, before I take it from you. You may be fierce, but I will crush you in one hand if you ever point that at me again."

"You will not touch my brother," Alana growled, standing her ground.

After a moment, Devon shook his head. "I should take you both back, and beg for a pardon," he rumbled, eyes sad. "But I won't."

Turning away, he walked off into the trees. A tremor swept through Alana, slowly growing until her entire body was shaking. She tried to sheathe her sabre, but her hand was shaking so badly she could not find the sheath, and she dropped it with a curse. Steel rang out as it struck the ground. Silently, she sank to her knees.

Leather scuffed on stone as Kellian crouched beside her and picked up the blade. She looked at him, expecting anger and hatred to match Devon's, but there was only sadness. He took her sword belt and carefully sheathed the blade.

"I'm sorry about Devon," Kellian said finally. Offering his hand, he pulled Alana to her feet and led her across to a fallen tree. "He is...quick to anger."

Alana shook her head. "He's right, I shouldn't have drawn you all into this. I'm sorry, truly."

"I know, Alana, but it is not your fault. You were only doing what any sister would do, protecting your brother."

Hanging her head, Alana fought back tears. "I thought we were safe, once we left Ardath."

"Ay," Kellian's voice drifted off for a moment, then: "I wonder, how did they find us?"

"The *Arbor*." They looked up as the old priest strode across to join them. Lifting a hand, she tossed a strip of beef jerky to each of them. At the sight of food, Braidon finally sat up, blinking back sleep, and then wandered across to join them. "Raided the saddlebags," Tillie said as she offered him a piece, "and to answer your question, innkeeper, the *Arbor's* dark magic must have lured them into the forest."

"But where did the other half of Quinn's men go?" Braidon asked.

A frown appeared on Tillie's face. "There were more?"

Alana and her brother shared a glance. "We counted twelve when they rode past where the road split in two."

"Then the rest must be ahead of us," Kellian ventured. His eyes darted to the road, then back to the others. "Quinn is a canny strategist. If he split his forces, it was to ensure no one escaped. They're likely waiting on the other side of Sitton forest for us. Or heading this way right now."

"There's only four," Braidon said, clenching his fists. "We can take them."

Tillie chuckled. "I admire your spirit, young man," she said softly. "But after your display in my temple, I doubt you have the strength for another round with the Tsar's Stalkers."

Braidon looked at the old woman in question, and she laughed again. "Your magic is not infinite, young Braidon. It came to your aid in the temple, but not without cost. That is why, even now, you are so exhausted."

"I'm fine," Braidon said. He made to stand but stumbled sideways into a tree and fell on his backside.

Alana's laughter rang out through the trees. Braidon scowled at her, but she only shook her head and looked at the priest. "We could still fight our way through," she offered.

"I would prefer to avoid bloodshed," Tillie replied, her voice soft.

Looking into her eyes, Alana caught a glimpse of sorrow in their sapphire depths and quickly turned away. "What other option do we have?"

"We leave the road," the old woman replied simply.

"No!" Alana's head shot up at the suggestion, her heart suddenly racing. "The trees!"

The wrinkles spread across Tillie's face as she smiled. "I know this forest well, my dear. We will not encounter the *Arbor* where I will lead you."

Alana stared back at her, unconvinced. Her heart still hammered painfully against her ribcage.

"It won't be a long journey," Tillie went on as though she hadn't noticed Alana's discomfort. "We only need to reach the river. With horses, the crossing won't be hard, even overloaded as they are. Lonia waits on the other side. Its lands were never touched by the demon's magic. We will be safe there from the *Arbor*."

"And in open farmland," Kellian countered. "How long before Quinn and his men catch us there?"

"That depends on where Alana and her brother intend to flee."

Alana swallowed as three sets of eyes turned to stare at her. She shared a glance with Braidon, caught by a sudden indecision. Dare she tell these strangers the truth? Devon had already threatened to take them back—what if they told the Stalkers their plans? But without them, she knew now their chances of reaching Northland were next to none. Making up her mind, she let out a long breath.

"Northland," she said quietly.

"We heard there were other Magickers there," Braidon added, "ones who fled the Three Nations when the Tsar first outlawed their existence."

"Northland is a long way from here," Kellian mused, "and farmland most of the way."

"Leagues and leagues," Devon said, striding back through the trees.

Alana's head snapped up at his voice, the blood throbbing painfully in her skull. Their eyes met for a moment, but it was Devon who looked away this time.

"It's our only chance," Alana snapped defensively, her own anger stirring at Devon's reappearance. "What else do you suggest we do?"

"Give yourself up," Devon replied matter-of-factly. "Don't expect leniency for yourself now, but at least they might spare your brother."

"Spare him?" she snorted. "You don't seriously believe that?"

Devon shrugged by way of answer. Beside Alana, Kellian shook his head. "He might be right. Now that they're on your trail, they won't stop. They'll catch you long before you can reach Fort Fall. Sooner, if the Tsar sends his demons."

A ball of ice lodged in Alana's throat at the mention of the dark creatures. Unbidden, an image flickered into her mind, of jet-black eyes staring at her from a pale face. She quickly pushed it away. "We'll take our chances, thanks," she said bluntly.

Kellian raised his hands. "We're just discussing options." Moving across to a patch of grass, he sat down. Crossing his legs, he gestured for them to sit. A dagger appeared in his hand, flickering between his fingertips as he waited for them to join him. When no one moved, he sighed and explained. "We took half their horses. I don't think Quinn will have ridden after us at night with such few numbers. He wouldn't want to risk being ambushed before he could summon his magic. And the others have the entire forest to circle. So, we have some time to make a plan."

"I'd rather sleep," Braidon muttered, lying down on the grass beside the innkeeper.

Alana bit her lip, glancing from Kellian to her brother. Even as she stood there, she could feel her eyelids drooping, the soft pull of sleep calling to her. Cursing, she pinched the skin of her palms, forcing herself awake, then moved to sit with Kellian. Devon and Tillie joined them.

"Why are you still with us, priest?" Kellian asked as the woman sat.

The woman laughed. "Where else would I be?"

Flicking a glance in her direction, Alana frowned. She was about to question her further when Devon interrupted.

"The road to Northland crosses two rivers, passes through the Lonian foothills, and dense beech forest south of Fort Fall. Even on horseback, the journey would take weeks. My guess is you have a matter of days before the Stalkers catch you."

Alarm prickled Alana's stomach at the warrior's words. "That's your opinion," she retorted, though the words sounded unconvincing, even to her.

Devon scowled, but before he could reply, Kellian interrupted. "We're not your enemy, Alana," he said softly. His eyes turned on Devon as he continued. "Like it or not, we're all in this together now. Devon speaks the truth. Quinn is an accomplished tracker—he has spent the last five years hunting Magickers. It's unlikely we can evade him for long. He also possesses powerful magic. As terrifying as your brother's ability is, he won't stand a chance against a fully trained Magicker."

"We could take a ship," Devon said suddenly.

Alana's head whipped around at the warrior's words. The hammerman stared back at her. Anger still lurked in the amber depths of his eyes, but it had lost its edge.

"There are captains in Lon who make the occasional trip north with…sensitive cargo," he continued. "I know a few people who could point us in the right direction."

"But we have no money," Alana said, her heart sinking.

Kellian shrugged. "I have a few investments in Lon I've been meaning to settle. It might take a few days, but I believe I could arrange the coin to buy us passage."

"But…" Alana trailed off, struggling to keep the tears from her eyes at the man's kindness.

The innkeeper offered a gentle smile. "It's nothing, Alana," he said, glancing at Devon. "As my friend here has been quick to point out, the quiet life was growing dull."

Alana was about to say something more, but Tillie stood suddenly, her eyes flickering to the road north. "Looks like you were wrong, innkeeper," she said, her voice low. Waving them up, she moved to her horse and grabbed the reins. "Quinn's other party must have ridden through the night!"

Even as Alana stood, she heard the distant rumble of hooves through the trees. Cursing their delay, she grabbed her brother and dragged him upright. Shoving him towards their horse, she looked at the road. There was still no sign of the riders. Amidst the trees, sound carried strangely, and there was no telling how far off they might be. Helping Braidon into the saddle, she stepped up after him and turned the horse to the west.

"Ready?" she hissed, glancing around at the others.

They nodded, eyes fixed on the dense trees. Alana glanced at the old priest as the woman edged her horse into the lead. She bit her lip and surreptitiously checked the surrounding tree trunks for the *Arbor*, but the bark was bare. Within minutes, the road had disappeared from view.

Ahead, Tillie lifted a hand, bringing them to a halt. Alana cursed under her breath, her heart racing. The pounding of hooves had grown to a roar. Closing her eyes, she imagined the men riding hard along the Gods Road, eyes peeled, seeking out sign of their quarry. They had ridden all night in pursuit of them—surely they could not miss the tracks leading off into the woods?

It was a long moment before Alana realised the pounding of hooves had begun to fall away again. Blinking, she looked around, seeing the relief on the faces of her companions. She looked at Tillie, eager for them to continue their flight, but the old woman shook her head, arm still raised. They waited in silence for several more minutes, listening as the last thump of horses' hooves died away.

Only when silence returned to the forest did Tillie lower her hand and smile.

"They won't take long to realise their mistake," she said in a low voice. "Let's ride."

⁂ 18 ⁂

There was no road where they forded the river, but it was hardly needed where they came ashore in Lonia. Sitting atop his horse, Devon glanced back from the muddy shore of the river. The trees of Sitton forest rose above the far banks, casting their shadows across the broad waters. He had travelled through the forest many times since his retirement, but never before had he noticed the malevolence that hung over the trees. The second they had climbed the banks into Lonia, he had felt a weight lift from him, as though a cloud had passed from the sky.

Remembering the terror of the *Arbor*, Devon silently vowed to never step foot in the forest again. Shivering, he urged his horse forward. Kellian had taken the lead now, starting his horse up through the thin trees on the Lonian riverbank and out into the green farmland.

They rode on through the day at an easy pace, taking turns to walk and rest their horses. Devon stayed at the rear, checking their backtrail every so often for signs of pursuit. The horizon behind them remained empty, but he knew it wouldn't be long before Quinn and his men found the trail where they had left the road. At best, Lon was a two-day ride away. Despite their exhaustion, they would have to press on through the day to stand any chance of reaching the Lonian capital before their pursuers.

His eyes drooped as he rode, and he found his mind drifting, the warm haze of sleep settling around him. He clung harder to the saddle horn, struggling to stay awake. Ahead, he could see Kellian talking with Alana. Braidon was asleep in front of her, his young head bobbing with each thump of the horse's hooves. Tillie was taking her turn to walk alongside them.

Devon felt a pang of regret for his angry words. Braidon's sleeping face was one of innocence, a young boy alone in the world but for his sister. Idly he wondered what had happened to the pair's parents, why they had not been the ones to bring them on this journey. He remembered Alana as he had first seen her that night outside Kellian's inn. Her eyes had held a familiar strength, a determination to survive whatever the odds. They reminded Devon of himself, all those years ago when he'd marched off to defend his nation from the Trolans.

He swallowed, forcing the memory from his mind. His eyelids drooped again, the warmth of sleep falling on him, dragging him down.

"You are not what I expected, hammerman." Devon's head snapped up as the old woman's voice spoke from beside him.

Blinking, he looked around and found the priest walking beside him, her blue eyes watching him closely. He shook his head, throwing off his fatigue. "What you expected?"

"Ay," she smiled. "My mother knew your ancestor, Alan.

She fought alongside him at Fort Fall, when the end came for him. She spoke highly of him."

Devon grunted and looked away. "People always do."

Tillie laughed. "You mistake me, Devon," she replied. "I only meant you were right earlier—you are your own man. Alan was a great warrior, no doubt, but, at the end of the day, he was only human, like all the other men and women who stood at Fort Fall." Her voice trailed off, before she added, "Just as you were only human when you marched with the Tsar against Trola."

Silence fell as Devon stared at the horizon. They were moving across open fields now, the distant movement of cattle wandering the paddocks the only signs of movement. Finally, he shook his head.

"It was different. They faced an army they could not defeat, and faced it with courage," he said quietly, clenching his fists. "The Trolans were our equals—until the Tsar trapped their army between his magic and our blades. After that, their nation lay helpless. There was no need for the slaughter that followed."

"Perhaps," Tillie mused. "Or perhaps it prevented more years of conflict. Did you know, before the Gods came, Lonia and Trola were at war for decades? Their battles cost tens of thousands of lives—and turned the land we now know as Plorsea into a wasteland."

"A shame the Gods abandoned us, then," Devon muttered.

Tillie bowed her head, the words leaving her. It was a while before she spoke again. "Perhaps they trusted us to govern our own lives."

"Or perhaps they grew tired of settling our petty disputes," Devon snorted, shaking his head. "It doesn't matter now, though, does it? They're gone. This is the way things are. The Three Nations are a joke—there is only Plorsea now, only the Empire. The Tsar rules us from east to west."

"But not the north," Tillie whispered.

"What is the north but jagged mountains and desolate plains?" he asked. His stomach twisted at the words. "Some exile," he finished bitterly.

"Why not fight instead?" the priest questioned.

"Fight?" Devon's head whipped around at that. "You can't be serious? Quinn alone has twelve men. Even without them, I would be no match for his magic. And that's just one squad of Stalkers. The Tsar has hundreds. Not to mention an army. Oh, and dragons."

Laughter shone in Tillie's eyes. "Did you not just say Alan was a hero because he fought against impossible odds?"

Devon chuckled. "Trying to trap me with my own words, priest?" He shook his head. "Ay, Alan fought the hordes of Archon, knowing he would lose. But he also knew the evil Archon would unleash on his world. Men stood beside him because it was right. Who would stand with me against the Tsar? As you said, there is no right or wrong here. He is evil to Alana and her brother because he seeks to stop their magic. He is a threat to me and Kellian because we inadvertently stood with a Magicker. But to the common people, he is protecting them from the menace of wild magic."

The priest watched him for a long time, her blue eyes seeming to see straight through him. Finally, he shivered and looked away, unable to meet her gaze any longer.

"All that is true," her voice carried over the clip-clop of hooves, "but that is not why you will not fight. Why did you set aside Alan's hammer?"

At its mention, Devon's eyes were drawn to *kanker*. It hung from his saddle horn, bouncing with each stride of his horse. Fear tingled down his spine as he thought of lifting it, of wielding it. Back in the temple, when Alana had handed him the weapon, he'd felt a surge of strength sweep through him. For a moment he'd been tempted to charge Quinn—to end his threat there and then. Bloodlust had flooded through him, and only Alana's cry to flee had turned him aside.

He swallowed, remembering other such moments when he had not stopped, when he had allowed the beast inside him free reign. A lump lodged in his throat as he looked up at the priest.

"I don't deserve to wield it," he whispered.

"Why not?"

Devon shook his head, unable to put the truth into words. "I am afraid of what I might do."

"It is just a hammer, Devon," she replied. "It has power, but there is no darkness in it."

"Ay," Devon murmured, "but there is darkness in me."

The priest said nothing at that, only stared at him, eyes soft, waiting.

Swallowing, Devon went on. "I used *kanker* to do terrible things in Trola," he said. "I will not bring any more shame to my ancestor's name.

"Rubbish." He looked up at the anger in the priest's voice. Her eyes flashed as she continued. "You brought shame to Alan's name when you refused to fight for Alana back in Sitton. You shamed him when you threatened to take two innocents back to those who want them dead."

Devon's own anger flared in answer. "You wouldn't understand—"

"I understand fear when I see it," Tillie hissed. Moving

in close, she gripped his reins, bringing his horse to a stop. Her voice dropped to a whisper. "You are afraid, hammerman. Afraid of yourself, of your own strength, your anger, your life."

Devon's rage died at her words and he looked away, unable to form a response. Silence stretched between them as he stared ahead, watching Alana and Kellian as they rode on. There was still no path, but the fields made for easy riding, and he trusted his friend to navigate them safely through the countryside. Glancing at the sun, he saw it was dropping quickly towards the horizon. Winter was looming closer, and it wouldn't be long before the snow found them. He hoped they had reached the safety of Lon by then.

"You are stronger than you think, hammerman," the priest said finally, her words wriggling their way into Devon's soul. "When next danger threatens, take up the hammer. I fear Alana and her brother cannot survive without it."

At that, she walked away, leaving Devon sitting alone on his horse at the rear of their party. Kicking his horse back into motion, he stared off into the distance, his mind drifting, far away in another time, another place. Only as the setting sun stained the horizon red did he remember to check their backtrail. Glancing over his shoulder, his heart sank as he saw the distant shadow of riders on the open fields.

❧ 19 ❧

"We should ride on," Alana insisted, looking around at the others.

Their exhausted faces stared back at her. Dark shadows ringed their eyes. Her brother was barely on his feet, and his skin had turned an unnatural shade of yellow.

Shaking her head, Tillie stepped forward and placed a hand on her shoulder. "We can go no further today, Alana," she said kindly. "I know you're afraid, but the riders will not reach us tonight."

Alana's heart beat faster at the mention of the Stalkers. Devon had warned them of the riders' presence as the sun was setting, and they had ridden hard through the fading light, desperate to put as much distance between themselves and the hunters as they could. They had reached the second river Devon had mentioned, fording it as the last light slipped away.

They had only been halfway across when darkness found them. Alana shivered at the memory of the black water lapping at her legs, only the power of the horse beneath her keeping her from the cold. Without sight to guide them, they had kept together using the sound of each other's voices. Only when she had felt the thud of her horse's hooves touching solid ground did Alana realise she'd been holding her breath.

Now though, an urgent need to continue was building in her chest. According to Devon, the riders were still at least half a day's ride away—but that lead would be cut down to nothing if the Stalkers rode on through the night.

"We can't let them catch us," she whispered, her eyes flickering to her brother.

"If we press on, the horses won't make it through the night." She looked around as Kellian spoke, and he went on. "They've hardly rested in two days. Another night of riding through the dark and their strength will give out. They need a respite as much as any of us."

Alana clenched her fists, a helpless frustration gnawing at her soul. She wanted to be galloping with her brother across the open fields, to put as much distance between themselves and the hunters as possible. Yet she could not argue with Kellian or Tillie's words—if they continued now, they risked losing everything.

Her shoulders slumped and she nodded quickly. Wordlessly, she moved across to her brother and drew him into her arms. She felt his thin body trembling, the cold and exhaustion wearing him down, and squeezed her eyes closed.

The boom of thunder forced her to look around. She caught a flash of light as lightning forked across the sky to the north. Beside her, Devon swore.

"There's a storm rolling in," he growled. "Come on, I spied a grove of trees before we crossed the river."

A groan came from her brother, and despite her earlier

argument, Alana found herself echoing him. Separating, Alana took up the reins of their horse and lead it after Devon. She could already feel the temperature dropping as the storm raced in from the north. Air burned in her nostrils as she sucked in a breath. Lightning flashed again, followed by an awful crash that seemed to break right above their heads.

A horse screamed, and releasing her brother, Alana gripped the reins in both hands. The horses were the only thing keeping them ahead of the pursuers. They couldn't afford to lose any now.

Eyes rolling in its skull, her mount reared back, almost tearing the reins from her grasp. Alana held on, speaking softly through the violent crackling of the storm. As the thunder fell away, the horse dropped back to all fours. Hearing her voice, it seemed to calm, and with her heart beating wildly in her chest, Alana chased after Devon.

They walked for several minutes, trusting Devon's sense of direction, before finally stumbling across the grove. It was little more than a few trees clustered together in a circle, but their broad trunks and thick canopy would at least keep off the worst of the storm.

Tying her horse to a low-lying branch in the shelter of the trees, Alana stroked her mount's coat. She could feel the poor beast trembling beneath her hands. Its eyes were wide with terror, and its snorting breath revealed its exhaustion. Brushing down its coat, she untacked the saddle and dragged a blanket from the bags to throw over the mount. Finally she turned to the others.

Devon was tending to Kellian's mount, while his friend had set about lighting a fire. He already had a small blaze burning in the centre of the clearing. Though the trees protected them from the worst of the wind, Alana watched as the fire flickered dangerously, threatening to go out. She quickly moved across to the innkeeper and used her body to help shield the flames from the wind. Slowly, Kellian added more wood, building up the flames.

A few minutes later the five of them sat around the warmth of the fire, listening as the power of the storm raged around them. Lightning flashed, casting long shadows between the trees, and Alana shuddered as memories of the *Arbor* returned, their dark tendrils reaching out for her. The crash of thunder drew her back to the present.

Another flash of light came, but this time there was no thunder to follow. Looking around, she saw the terror on her brother's exhausted face. He flinched as a far-off boom rolled across the plains. Light flashed from his palms, flickering and growing before dying away. A moan whispered from Braidon's throat as he clenched his fists tight.

"Braidon, what's going on?" she hissed, shuffling across to him.

He shook his head, his blue eyes wide with terror. She gripped his wrist and felt the rapid pounding of his pulse beneath her fingers. She looked into his eyes, but they were far away. Taking him by the shoulders, she shook him gently, calling his name.

Blinking, Braidon looked around at her. "Alana," he croaked. A shiver went through him. "Alana, *it's inside me.*"

Fear slid down Alana's throat at his words, though she could make no sense of them. Braidon flinched as blue lightning lit the clearing, marked by an awful *boom.* White light shone from her brother's hands, burning their eyes.

"Braidon!" Tillie's voice came from Alana's side as the old woman crouched beside them. "Braidon, you must calm yourself!"

Her brother's terrified eyes turned to the priest. He

opened his mouth to reply, but another crash of thunder drowned out his words. The wind howled, sweeping through the grove, scattering the fire. As Kellian and Devon struggled to save it, Tillie pushed Alana aside and grabbed her brother by the shoulders.

"Braidon, listen to me!" she shouted over the gale. "Your magic seeks to protect you, but you are too weak. If you allow it free rein, its power will consume you."

Braidon stared back at her, his mouth opening and closing, his breath coming in ragged gasps.

"I can help you, Braidon," the old priest yelled over the raging storm. "But you must listen. You must trust me."

A gurgling growl came from deep in Braidon's throat. For a second, his eyes flashed white. Alana blinked, terror clamping a vice around her chest, but when she looked again, her brother's blue eyes were staring back at her.

"How?" he croaked, his voice strained.

Tillie pressed her hand to either side of the boy's face. "Close your eyes, young Braidon," she murmured. "Breathe."

Jaw clenched, Braidon closed his eyes. Alana could see his hands shaking in the flickering light of the fire, the tendons straining on his neck. She crouched nearby, hardly daring to move, a terrible helplessness holding her frozen.

"Take a deep breath, young Braidon," Tillie's voice was gentle, calm despite the crashing thunder.

On the ground, Braidon sucked in a quivering mouthful of air. Light flickered in his hands, seeming to pool in his palms now, growing and shrinking. Beside him, the old priest never took her eyes from Braidon's face.

"Focus on your breath, boy, let it out, that's it, now take another. Listen to my voice."

The light in Braidon's hands flickered again as he

followed the woman's instructions. His throat swelled as he swallowed, his brow furrowing with each boom of thunder. Kellian and Devon had the fire blazing again now, its heat washing through the grove. They moved quickly into the trees in search of more fuel. Her brother's trembling eased as the freezing cold released its icy grip.

"That's it, in and out, think only of your breath. Feel your heart slow, allow yourself to relax, forget the storm, the hunters, the magic. Only your breathing. In and out."

Slowly, the light in Braidon's hands died away, seeping back into his flesh as though it had never been. His eyes remained closed, his breathing deepening, his chest rising and falling with each inhalation. As Alana watched, the tension drained from her brother. His shoulders slumped, and he sagged forward into Tillie's arms.

And slept.

Lowering the boy gently to the ground, Tillie covered him with a blanket before moving back to the fire. Alana checked on her brother before joining her in the warmth.

"What…what was that?" she breathed.

The old woman let out a weary sigh. "Wild magic, young Alana. In his exhausted state, your brother's fear of the storm overwhelmed him, giving life to his magic."

"But what did you do?"

"I only helped to steer him through the storm," Tillie said with her familiar smile. "Among priests of the Earth, it is called meditation, among others, mindfulness. It is the same—a way of controlling our emotions."

"And it helped him control his magic?"

"In a fashion, yes."

"Thank you," Alana said softly, turning her eyes to the fire. "I don't know what I would do if I lost him."

Twigs crunched as Kellian and Devon returned, their

arms laden with firewood. They took in the sleeping boy. "He okay?" Devon asked, his voice gentle, almost kind.

"Sleeping," Alana replied with a weary smile.

The two nodded and took their places on the other side of the fire. Kellian added several branches to the flames. Outside the grove, the rumbling of the storm had moved away, but rain was beginning to fall now. Shivering, Alana hunched closer to the fire, glad for the heavy jacket she'd found in the saddlebags of her stolen horse.

"It's a good thing they already knew where we were," Devon commented wryly as he sat back.

Alana sighed. "I'm sorry for dragging you into this, Devon."

Across the fire, Devon shrugged his massive shoulders. His eyes flickered to Tillie, then back to Alana. "I shouldn't have needed dragging," he said quietly.

An uncomfortable silence settled over the group as they sat there. Beyond the trees, the soft patter of rain grew, becoming a roar as the storm broke over them. Rising, Kellian moved into the shelter of the trees and returned with a pot. Filling it with water from their skins, he placed it over the flames and began adding roots and salted jerky from the saddlebags.

"May as well have something in our stomachs," he muttered.

Alana smiled, just the thought of a hot meal already warming her. She moved around the fire and helped the innkeeper prepare the broth. Devon wandered into the woods and returned a few minutes later with large chunks of bark torn from the trees. Washing them with water, he passed them round. A few minutes later, Kellian announced the stew ready, and they each held out their rounded pieces of bark to receive their portions.

Their stomachs rumbling, they ate quickly, the meagre stew disappearing in minutes. Finally they sat back, their hunger sated.

"At least we're dry," Devon said, stretching his arms with a groan. "Bet Quinn is cursing us tonight."

Kellian chuckled. "No trees on that side of the Jurrien," he said with a grin. "Although I don't think the rain's going to do anything for his temper."

Smiling, Alana shook her head. "You said you knew him?" she asked, looking at Kellian.

"We both did," Devon answered for his friend. "We fought with him against the Trolans. Always was boring as old leather, though."

Alana looked away at that, remembering her dreams, how Quinn had come to her, demanding an answer to his question.

Are you ready?

Always she had felt the familiar terror at his question. His brown eyes unnerved her, robbing her of strength, demanding an answer. Yet in the broken temple, when they'd finally come face to face, it hadn't been terror she'd felt, but warmth—and confusion. Her anger had quickly risen to mask it, but thinking back now, she couldn't help but wonder at it.

That, and the fact he'd known her name.

It could mean only one thing, though she couldn't bring herself to picture it. It meant their parents had given them up, had sent the Stalkers after them. Her heart ached with the knowledge, and she quickly forced the thought from her mind.

Yet as she lay down beside the fire and sought sleep, Alana's mind returned to the confrontation in the temple, to the Stalker's greeting as he stepped towards the fire.

Thinking of Quinn staring at her, she found herself wondering at the strange look he'd worn on his face.

Her thoughts drifted, giving way to the pull of sleep. She fought it at first, knowing what waited for her there, and not waiting to face it. But exhaustion weighed on her, pulling her down. There was no fighting it any longer. Slowly the mists of sleep formed around her mind, the brown eyes of her hunter appearing through the darkness.

And her heart quickened.

QUINN LED HIS MEN TOWARD THE RIVER BANKS AT THE FIRST light of dawn. He had felt the flicker of the boy's magic during the night, but out on the plains at least, such power could do little damage. It had died quickly, without the surging rush of release, and he wondered whether the boy had somehow found a way to control it. The priest, perhaps…

He shook his head and turned his attention back to the path. Ice crunched beneath their horses' feet, and snow lay piled around them as they forced their way towards the river. What had begun as a torrential downpour had turned to heavy snow during the night. The night had been so cold, he and his men had hardly slept. Only by burning the coal in their saddle bags had they survived. Now, as the sun crested the horizon, he welcomed its heat on his face.

His breath misting in the dawn's light, Quinn pressed on, leading his seven remaining men. Vim had met them near the ruins of Sitton around midday, empty handed. Cursing, Quinn had led them back along the Gods Road until they discovered where Devon's party had left the path. Barely more than a deer trail, they had followed their prey to the river and crossed into Lonia. But their horses were tiring by then, and while they'd pressed on hard through the day, they hadn't been able to catch their quarry before the light faded.

Today, though, Devon and the others would not evade them. The boy's magic had not been far, just across the river, and their horses had to be close to exhaustion. They would catch them before the day was done. Then he would finally crush the fool Devon and end his pitiful life.

The ground rose slowly beneath them as they climbed the river bank. The man in the lead drew his horse to a stop at the top of the bank, his eyes flicking back to Quinn. Seeing the worry written on the man's face, Quinn cursed and pressed his horse into a trot. Moving alongside him, he looked out over the river…and swore again.

Brown water lapped at the edges of the riverbanks, rushing past in a swirling torrent, engorged by the night's rain. Massive trees tumbled amongst the flooded waters, and he glimpsed the white body of a sheep as it bobbed to the surface before vanishing back into the murky depths. There would be no crossing the river now, not until the floodwaters receded.

Quinn's eyes continued across to the opposite bank. Snow had covered the lands beyond, where they rose slowly away from the river, up into the foothills of the Lonian mountains. Yesterday the land had been a rich green, but there was only white now, a wasteland barren of life. Except where a lazy curl of black smoke rose from a frozen grove of trees.

As Quinn watched, a dark-garbed figure stepped from the grove leading a horse. He recognised Devon from his size and clenched his fists. The others followed, until all five stood there in the open, taunting him. The soft whisper of their laughter carried on the wind, drifting down to Quinn. The giant figure of Devon raised a hand and waved.

Quinn gritted his teeth. He didn't need to hear the words to know what the hammerman was saying.

Better luck next time, sonny!

Clenching his reins in one gloved hand, Quinn turned to his men.

"Watch the river," he snapped. "We cross as soon as the waters are low enough to ford."

With that, he tugged on his reins, pointing his mount back towards the camp, and kicked the beast into a gallop.

20

Devon swore loudly as a wagon rumbled past on the busy street, its iron-rimmed wheels just inches from his feet. The driver did not so much as glance back as Devon's curses chased after him. Muttering under his breath, Devon pressed on through the crowd, doing his best to keep his head down. He kept watch on the city guard from the corner of his eye. They lined the marketplace, their wary eyes hunting for pickpockets and trouble. He doubted Quinn had managed to send word to Lon so quickly, but it didn't hurt to be careful.

He was close to the port now, and quickly losing patience. This would be the third tavern he'd visited—and there was still no sign of his contact. He had left Alana and her brother in the room they'd rented, while he sought a ship to carry them north. For now, it was best to keep them as far from this business as possible—he doubted there'd be many ship captains willing to help a Magicker.

Around him, the streets of Lon were packed to bursting. He had never liked the city, where people scurried along the rutted streets like flies on a corpse. Long ago, Lon had been the quiet capital of the farming nation, but those days were long gone now. With Lonians fleeing the impoverished countryside, its population was now twice that of Ardath, with half the wealth.

Devon wrinkled his nose as he walked past an alleyway choked with human refuse. He had long since given up walking around the animal dung lying thick in the streets. Amidst the press of humanity, emaciated sheep wandered freely, while stray dogs darted amongst the legs of pedestrians, seeking their next meal. Broken glass and pottery lay discarded in corners, and he saw more than one barefooted beggar with a limp. In another alley, he glimpsed a figure lying in the shadows—either sleeping or dead. No one stopped to check.

Ahead, the streets opened out, the three storey buildings finally giving way to the docks. This was an older section of Lon, its streets at least cobbled, with a raised sidewalk to protect pedestrians from the overburdened wagons rumbling up from the harbour. As the closest remaining city to Northland, Lon was still the centre of trade between the north and south. That alone should have made the city rich —if not for the Tsar's taxes.

At the end of the street, the cobbled road turned to wooden planks where it reached the docks. No longer penned in by the narrow streets, Devon took a deep breath, savouring the sudden tang of salt in the air. A cool breeze blew across his face, carrying with it the stench of rotting fish. Smiling wryly, he shook his head and pressed on.

Out on the harbour, hundreds of ships sat at anchor, while dozens more came and went from the docks lining the city front. Men and women moved quickly across the wharf, unloading wagons and carrying heavy crates up gangplanks onto waiting ships. The neighing of horses mingled with the shouts of men, punctuated by the odd crash as something was dropped. Gulls cawed as they circled overhead, their beady eyes on the lookout for food.

Shouldering his way through the crowd, Devon made his way along the docks until he spotted the inn he had been directed to. He breathed a sigh of relief as he caught a glimpse of the *Black Seagull* and steered his way towards it. Manoeuvring his way around a pile of cages filled with wriggling lobsters, he found himself outside the heavy wooden doors, and pushed his way inside.

Warm air billowed out to greet him, banishing the cold. This close to the coast, the snowstorm had not reached the city, but there was still ice in the air and he was wearing several woollen layers. Stripping off his coat, he hung it beside the door, before looking around to appraise the inn's occupants. It was still early in the afternoon and the bar room was reasonably quiet—although in this case that meant there were only twenty revellers crammed into the tiny tables. His eyes swept the room, seeking out his contact, but he didn't see anyone he recognised. Muttering under his breath, he forced his way to the bar and ordered a pint of ale.

When the bartender returned, Devon handed him several copper *Austral* for the drink and then caught him by the hand. "Don't suppose you've seen a friend of mine? Goes by Julian."

The bartender eyed him closely. "Who's asking?"

"A friend."

The man nodded, eyes still suspicious, and moved away without answering. Shaking his head, Devon gulped down a mouthful of ale and turned to give the patrons of the bar another look-over. Most of the men were sailors, their beards long and grizzled, faces tanned by the constant sun. They would be enjoying their brief time ashore before their next voyage. More than a few women sat amongst them, looking just as rough, their hair dry and split, heavy knives on their belts. Devon grinned as he saw one sailor get too friendly, only to have his head slammed into the table top. The men around him boomed with laughter as one of the bar's minders quickly dragged the man outside.

"Sailors," Devon muttered, turning back to his drink.

"I know a ship in need of some muscle, if you're looking to join the lifestyle, Devon," a man said with a laugh as he sat on the neighbouring stool.

Unlike the sailors in the bar, the man's beard was neatly trimmed, though a few grey hairs had appeared amongst the black. His hair remained the same jet-black as during the war, but it was starting to recede at the brow. Wrinkles had appeared around his hazel eyes. He wore a clean white tunic and sleek black pants, along with a slim rapier strapped at his waist.

Devon flashed Julian a grin. "I've no taste for the sea, old friend."

"No, now that you mention it, I seem to recall you growing rather green on that last voyage."

Devon snorted. "Not sure how, since you spent most of your time huddling below deck."

Julian held up his hands, the ale sloshing from his mug. "What can I say? One must know his strengths! I never had your talent with death, Devon."

"Ay," Devon replied, his amusement falling from him like water. "Few do."

An awkward silence followed, punctuated by a man's yell as one of the fisherwomen hurled him across a table.

"So, what brings you to Lon, old friend?" Julian asked finally. "Not like you to be skulking around these parts."

"Business," Devon replied with a grunt. "Got a client who needs a ride."

"I see." Julian's eyes narrowed. "Nothing to do with that spot of trouble you got yourself into in Ardath, then? Heard you've got a bit of a bounty on your head."

Devon tensed at his friend's words, his heart beating faster. "What did you hear?"

Julian raised an eyebrow. "So serious, Devon? Didn't think a few royal guards would worry you overly much."

Devon let out a long breath and forced himself to smile. "Oh, it's not that greenboy and his friends who worry me. It's the bloody bounty on my head!"

"The bounty?" his friend guffawed. "Well, you need not worry about that. The fool put out a bounty alright, but it's hardly worth the paper it's written on. Half a gold *libra*, if you can believe that? And he wants you alive! Not a hunter in the Three Nations foolish enough to take on a legend like you for such a piddling sum."

Devon feigned anger. "It's almost insulting," he replied. Knocking back his ale, he hailed the bartender for another. He turned back to his friend and went on. "I've half a mind to go back and hit him again."

Julian grinned. "So, these clients of yours, where are they headed?"

"Northland."

Sitting back in his chair, Julian eyed Devon. "Sounds like a dangerous client." He paused. Licking his fat lips, he eyed Devon, as though seeing him for the first time. "Are you sure these are clients you want to get in bed with, Devon?"

Devon stared back, jaw clenched. "Do you have a ship or not, Julian?"

Julian was silent for a moment longer, before offering a quick nod. "It just so happens the *Songbird* is sailing on the morning tide. She's a Northland ship, heading for Duskenville. How many passengers we talking?"

"Five," Devon replied. Duskenville was the closest Northland port. Nestled at the foot of the coastal cliffs, the colourful town was only a few days' sailing from Lon.

"You wouldn't be one of those five, would you?"

"Could be I am," Devon said with a shrug. "Let's just say my recent troubles have opened my eyes to new adventures."

"It'll be costly," Julian shot back, eyes alight.

"My clients can pay," Devon replied with an easy grin.

Julian raised an eyebrow. "I should hope so." There was open scepticism in his voice.

Devon laughed. "What, you don't trust me, old friend?"

Julian relaxed at Devon's laughter. He shook his head. "Forgive an aging man his distrust. Course I trust you!" He trailed off, then added quickly, "Only, you do still owe me a gold *libra* for that business back in Coral."

"You do have a long memory, don't you?" Devon muttered. "Well, you can add that to the tab for our passage tomorrow. I take it ten *libra* per passenger is still the going rate?"

"Ten!" Julian exclaimed, spilling more of his ale. "You have been gone a while. The price is now twenty!"

"Ha! You haven't changed a bit, have you, Julian? It can't be more than twelve."

The exchange continued for a few more minutes before Devon finally settled on fifteen gold apiece. He winced at the cost, though he had no doubt Kellian would have the coin. At least they'd managed to get a decent price for the horses they'd taken from the Stalkers. Their branding meant they'd been forced to sell them on the black market, but they'd still been able to use the profits to pay for their lodging and supplies.

He spent another hour talking with Julian, going over details for the journey, which eventually turned to tales of one another's exploits during the war. Despite his regrets, Devon felt a touch of nostalgia as Julian regaled him of his heroics during their march through the Branei Pass into Trola. Those had been the early days of the war, simpler times when the Trolans had been evil aggressors, the Plorsean army the noble defenders of the innocent.

Finally, Devon knocked back his ale and stood. Bidding his old friend farewell, he promised to meet at the fourth dock the next morning at daybreak. There was plenty more to do before the day ended, and outside he could already see the light beginning to fade. He threaded his way through the crowd and claimed his coat from the rack, before stepping back out into the cold.

21

Alana shivered as she stepped back from the window and slammed the shutters closed. The sky was thick with clouds, the air untouched by the sun's heat. Inside their room was little better. The ceiling was thick with mould and its only window faced north, allowing in a thin breath of cold whenever the wind blew. There had been no other lodging available though, and it was better than sleeping in the gutters.

Earlier, Kellian had headed out to collect his funds from a local merchant. Devon was organising them a ship for Northland, leaving Alana and her brother to stew in the tiny room with the old priest.

She was sitting now in a chair before the fire, her blue eyes distant. Braidon sat in the opposite chair, his knees pulled up to his chest, his face still lined with exhaustion. They had ridden hard through the Lonian foothills yesterday, reaching the city only as the last light was fading from the sky. It had taken all her brother's strength just to make it up the stairs to their room. Food and a full night's sleep had done them all good, but it would be days before Braidon was fully recovered.

The room consisted of a fireplace, a wooden table and stools, the two chairs near the fire, and three beds—Devon and Kellian were bunked next door. Taking a stool from the table, Alana dragged it across the moth-eaten carpet and joined the others at the fireplace.

Her brother smiled and held out a plate of chocolate biscuits. Seating herself, Alana took one with a smile.

"Do you think they'll be back soon?" Braidon asked quietly.

"Patience, young one," Tillie answered for Alana. "They will be back when they're done—and not a moment sooner."

Alana wondered for a moment whether she'd made the wrong decision in trusting the men. At this moment they could be fetching the city watch, or a squadron of Stalkers, while she and her brother sat here in blissful ignorance. Even now the hunters might be closing around them. Shivering, she shook her head to rid herself of the thought, and turned to the priest.

"Tillie, during the storm you told me my brother's magic could be controlled by…what did you call it, meditation?"

The priest nodded, her eyes dancing. "Of course. Meditation is how Magickers have controlled their power for centuries."

Alana shared a glance with her brother. "Can you teach him?"

"I could, if he wished to learn," Tillie replied, turning her eyes to Braidon.

Her brother nodded quickly, his blue eyes alive with excitement. "Yes, please!"

The old woman laughed. "Very well, would you like to start now?"

Braidon nodded. Moving from her chair, Tillie seated herself on the rug before the fire and nodded for Braidon to join her. Then her eyes looked up at Alana. "You may join us if you wish, Alana."

Alana blinked. "It's not just for Magickers?"

"Or course not. Anyone can take part—though only with dedication and practice can you truly master the art."

Alana looked from the priest to her brother and then joined them on the rug. Copying the old woman, she folded her legs beneath her, then looked to Tillie in question.

"Do we have to sit like this?" her brother asked suddenly, already wriggling.

Alana sighed—her brother had never been good at sitting still. No wonder he had never excelled in his studies…

"You may sit however you wish, young Braidon, but…" Tillie trailed off as Braidon quickly flopped onto his side. Shaking her head, Tillie continued with an amused smile. "But sitting with your legs crossed will prove most comfortable over long periods, I assure you."

Alana's backside was already aching but she kept her mouth shut, trusting the old woman was right. "Okay then," she said, glancing at her brother. "Should we give this meditation thing a go?"

Braidon rolled his eyes. "It's only breathing, how hard can it be?" He let out a long breath. "But I suppose I'll give it a go."

"Very good," Tillie replied. "But first, what do you know of your power, young Braidon?"

Her brother shrugged. "Not much. That was only the second time its appeared. The first was…on my birthday."

Tillie nodded. "Yes, magic always awakens on the anniversary of a birth. That is why we sometimes call it the Gift."

Braidon looked away at that. "Some gift," he muttered.

"Perhaps not now, but I have seen Magickers do wonderful, incredible things." She paused, her eyes taking on a distant look. "How else do you think the drought around Chole was broken?"

"That drought was created by magic in the first place, wasn't it?" Alana cut in.

"Dark magic," Tillie replied, "is an altogether different beast."

"How so?" Braidon questioned.

Tillie sighed. "Dark magic sits outside the natural order of our world. It is capable of incredible feats, but always there is corruption, a perversion of the wielder's original intent."

"What makes my magic different then?"

"Your magic stems from one of the Three Elements, and so operates within the natural world. A true Magicker can manipulate part or the entirety of one Element, but never more than that. For instance, your magic, while I don't yet understand all of its nature, comes from the Light. Your power may be able to manipulate fire, or light, or magic itself, but you will never control the weather, nor speak with plants, since those abilities come under the Elements of Earth and Sky."

"So his power could start a fire once he gets control of it?" Alana asked, her curiosity growing.

Tillie smiled. "Perhaps. As I said, from the brief display back in Sitton, I couldn't discern Braidon's true power – only that it came from the Light. Now, enough of this! The others will return soon, so if you want to practice, young

Braidon, we had best start. To begin, we must close our eyes."

Alana nodded, remembering the old woman's instructions from the night in the grove, and did as she was bid. Idly, she wondered how ridiculous they must look, the three of them sitting cross-legged on the floor in front of the fire. She hoped Devon and Kellian did not return while they sat there.

"Now, we begin by exhaling until our lungs are completely empty," the old priest said. "When you can breathe out no longer, inhale, and allow the air to fill your chest."

Alana did as she was told, exhaling until the longing for air grew too much, and she was forced to suck in a fresh breath. Across from her, she could hear her brother giggling as he did the same, and struggled to keep from laughing herself.

"Keep your mind focused on your breath," Tillie continued, ignoring the laughter. "It may feel strange at first, uncomfortable or, yes, amusing, but trust me. There is purpose in this madness."

Smiling to herself, Alana continued the exercise. For a while she concentrated on the rise and fall of her chest, the swelling of her stomach with each inhalation. But after a time, she noticed her mind drifting, her thoughts turning to the *Arbor*, to Quinn and Devon, to their voyage across the lake…

"Your mind will drift," Tillie's voice cut through her thoughts. "It is to be expected. When it does, allow yourself to examine what distracted you, then turn your mind back to the breath."

Alana shivered, turning her thoughts inwards once more.

In, out. In, out. In, out.

Her mind flickered, centring in on the mindless process of her breathing. Other thoughts continued to press against her, but as each rose into the darkness of her mind, she took it firmly in hand, considered it for a moment, then sent it spinning back out into the void. To her surprise, the exercise came naturally to her, and she found the chaos fading away, the cacophony of ideas and worries becoming but a drop in the infinity of her mind.

Finally, only one sensation remained to her—the strongest one of all.

Fear.

Fear that she would be captured, that her brother would be taken from her, that he would disappear into the bowels of the Tsar's citadel and never be seen again.

Fear that she would fail.

Taking another rhythmic breath, Alana allowed the emotion to fill her, to rise to the surface. Her body shook, the hairs standing up on her arms as she saw again the step-well, the Stalkers racing down the steps, dragging away the boy. Then the circle of trees, the vines encasing her brother, the twisted mouths opening to snatch him away. And, finally, the eyes of Quinn as he stepped into the firelight, magic at the ready.

Trembling, Alana scrunched her eyes tighter, her body taut with the power of her fear. Time passed, unknown, uncountable, as she sought to release the feeling, to allow it to pass from her. Finally, she shuddered, her shoulders slumping as the tension rushed from her. Her breathing relaxed into the gentle rhythm of sleep—but she was not asleep.

Opening her eyes, Alana found herself adrift on a sea of darkness. Watching the infinite black, Alana knew she should be panicked, that she should fear the eternity around her, but she felt only peace.

Slowly she drifted, alive but not alive, free but still trapped. For the longest time she was alone. Then, like a fire igniting in a cold room, she became aware of something else. She turned amidst the black and found a distant source of light. It glowed scarlet through the darkness, calling to her.

Unbidden, her ethereal body shot towards it, and she watched the light grow, swelling until it became an angry ball of red and orange. Emotion pulsed from it—fear and anger, jealousy and love, all tangled together in an endless puzzle. And within, she could sense something else, something different, something hidden.

Drawing closer, Alana allowed her mind to flow through the knot, seeking out its puzzle. It called to her, begging her to solve it. A tingle of energy swept through her as it touched her mind, and somewhere deep within a voice called a warning. Retreating, she waited, a speck of light drifting in the void.

When nothing happened, Alana approached again. Her mind circled the knot, picking at its tangles, pulling threads. It began to spin, slowly at first, then more quickly as it unravelled. Lines red and orange spun off into the void, shooting stars lighting the facets of her mind.

Unease rose within her as she watched the knot shrink, as though with its release, she had lost the peace she'd found in the void. Fear returned, piercing her spirit, filling her with sudden terror.

She retreated from the knot, allowing her work to cease, and alarm tingled in her soul. The knot was almost gone now—only a tiny ball of flaming red remained. She was so close to discovering what lay at its core. She could still sense it calling to her, its secrets just beyond her reach.

Resisting its call, Alana pulled away. Rage washed over her, as though some other's emotions now possessed her. She shrank from it, racing away, darting through the darkness, up towards the light that appeared far above…

Alana awoke with a gasp. Trembling, she opened her eyes and found herself still sitting on the floor before the fire. Braidon and Tillie sat unmoving, their eyes closed, the soft whisper of breath the only sign of life. Looking around, Alana saw the lamp in the corner had burned low, and the light outside was fading into dusk.

Hours had passed.

Her gaze was drawn to Braidon. He almost looked asleep, but as Alana leaned in, she saw his eyelids flickering. She smiled, remembering Tillie's warning that only the experienced could master her drill. Apparently her brother had taken to it far faster than the old woman had expected.

Looking back at her brother's face, anxiety touched her. In the darkness of her mind, she had sensed a danger, an unknown threat the old woman had not mentioned. Now she saw a shadow cross her brother's face, the slightest tremor to his lips, a twitch on his brow. She leaned closer, and saw his hands were shaking. Reaching out, she touched a finger to his wrist. His pulse was weak and erratic, his skin clammy to the touch.

"Braidon," she called, tugging at his arm. "Braidon, wake up!"

When her brother didn't stir, she gripped him by the shoulder and shook him. His head lolled on his shoulders and slumped to the side, his eyes still closed. She caught him by the waist and pulled him upright. A low whisper came from his lips as she turned his face to look at her.

"*Braidon!*" she screamed, her voice echoing through the room.

Beside her, Tillie jerked to wakefulness. Blinking, she looked around, frowning when she saw Alana with Braidon.

"What's going on, Alana?" she asked.

"He won't wake," Alana growled, turning on her. "You did this!"

Tillie shook her head, the light coming back to her eyes. "I did nothing." She leaned closer, staring at Braidon's face. "You both fell asleep. I took the chance to refresh my spirit."

"I did not fall asleep!" Alana snapped. "Does it *look* like he's sleeping?"

The old woman's frown deepened as she looked from Alana to her brother. "He could not have advanced this quickly. Even the finest students take a few attempts to delve into their subconscious."

"What does that *mean?*" Alana hissed, grabbing the old woman by the wrist.

Ignoring her, the priest leaned closer, inspecting Braidon's face. Shaking her hand free of Alana's grip, she pressed her hands to Braidon's cheeks. "Braidon," the old woman called, her voice soft. "Come back."

Alana sat with breath held, watching the old woman closely. Her heart was pounding in her chest. While she did not understand what was happening, she sensed something was wrong. She recalled the rage she'd felt, the fear and anger tangled up at the centre of her soul, and felt a sense of impending doom.

"What's wrong with him, Tillie?" Her voice was tinged with desperation now.

Tillie shook her head and waved her back. "*Braidon!*" she called, more urgently now. "Come back, before it's too late."

"Too late?" Alana shrieked, her chest tightening.

In a rush of panic, she shoved the priest aside and took her brother's arms in hers.

"Braidon!" she called, then again in her head, *Braidon, Braidon, Braidon!*

Her cheeks flushed, heat rushing to her face. It spread

down her neck, a warmth that lit her body aflame. It swirled in her mind as she called her brother's name again and again, fear giving rise to desperation, desperation to panic. As the heat reached her hands, she felt her ears *pop*, and suddenly the heat was gone.

Exhaustion swept through Alana like an incoming tide. Slumping back on her heels, she gasped in a breath of air and released her brother. Closing her eyes, she fought back tears.

"Alana?"

Her eyes snapped open as her brother croaked her name. Across from her, Braidon sat blinking, his blue eyes streaked with red. Her heart leapt as he yawned and stretched his arms. "What's going on? We done?"

Ignoring his question, Alana threw herself forward and wrapped him in her arms. "You scared the Goddess out of me!"

Braidon cried out in protest, but it was several minutes before he managed to disentangle himself from her. He sat back, confusion written across his youthful face.

"What's got you so worked up?" he questioned. "I was just napping."

"You were not asleep, young Braidon," Tillie's voice cut in. "You were meditating."

Braidon snorted. "Felt a lot like sleep to me." He shook his head and yawned again. "Although I'll admit I had some strange dreams."

Silently, Alana reached out and hugged him again. He flashed her another smile, though there was doubt in his eyes now. A long silence stretched out. Braidon broke it suddenly with a yawn. His eyes flickered from Alana to Tillie.

"Err, if we are done, you don't mind if I take an actual nap, do you?" he asked.

Alana forced a laugh and nodded. Rising, Braidon crossed quickly to his bed and dragged himself under the covers. Within minutes his soft snores filled the room. Alana watched him for a moment, reassuring herself he was okay, before turning her eyes back to the priest.

"What happened to him?" she asked, voice hard. "He was in danger, wasn't he?"

Tillie was eying her closely now, a slight frown on her forehead. "Where did you say the two of you came from?" she asked, ignoring Alana's question.

Anger flared in Alana's chest at the woman's impertinence. She caught the priest by the front of her olive-green robes.

"*I asked you what happened to my brother!*" She ground out through clenched teeth.

The old woman stared back at her, eyes hard. "Release me," she commanded.

Despite herself, Alana did so, but she refused to drop the matter. "It was his magic, wasn't it?"

After a long pause, Tillie nodded. "He shouldn't have been able to go so far so quickly, especially in his exhausted state. That's why I thought he was merely asleep. It was fortunate he didn't manage to reach his magic before we could call him back."

"What would have happened then?"

"The consequences would have been...severe."

Alana's lips drew back in a snarl. "What do you mean, 'severe'?"

There was no humour on the old woman's face now. "He would have been lost…" Her voice trailed off. Alana was about to press further when she continued. "Do you know the story of the demon who destroyed Sitton?"

Alana opened her mouth and then closed it again, surprised by the sudden change of topic. Wordlessly, she shook her head.

"That demon was once a great man, descended from the line of Trolan kings who had ruled over the west for centuries. His name was Thomas, and he was a powerful Magicker."

A tremor went down Alana's spine at the woman's words. She knew the tales of Thomas—of the ancient king who had stood with the Gods against Archon. A myth, surely? Yet she sensed there was more to the old woman's story. Swallowing, she asked the question burning on her lips. "How did he become a demon?"

"His magic took him."

"Took him?" Alana could not keep the fear from her voice. "What do you mean?"

Tillie sighed. "Magic is not an inert force—it lives! Lives to fight, to make war, to break free. A Magicker is forever at war with the force inside them. Each time they touch it, they risk losing themselves in its power. Once lost, they become what we know as demons, drowned by their own magic, taken over by its energies."

"And…my brother…" Bile rose in Alana's throat as she stumbled to her feet. "How could you not have told us?"

The priest rose quickly beside her. "It is not something you speak of during ones first attempt at meditation," she snapped. "The fear would make the exercise impossible."

"You're telling me he might never have woken up?" Alana shrieked, hardly hearing the woman's words.

"Calm yourself, Alana," the priest snapped suddenly, her eyes flashing. She caught Alana by the wrist and dragged her forward. Alana swallowed as her gaze was caught by the crystal blue eyes. "Your brother is stronger than you know, girl," the old woman continued, "but he will never be able to grow if you continue to smother him."

Alana tore herself free, anger giving her strength. "Smother him?" she gasped. "I'm *protecting* him!"

The cold eyes stared back at her, unblinking. "So you say." The woman strode after her. "Who are you, Alana? Where did you come from?"

"None of your goddamn business!" Alana said, baring her teeth. She pointed a finger at the woman's chest. "And if you so much as touch my brother again, I'll kill you!"

She swung towards the door, but her brother's voice called her back. "Alana, no." Freezing midstride, Alana turned back to see Braidon sitting up in his bed. His eyes caught hers, holding her in place as he continued to speak. "She's right," he whispered. "This power is inside me, whether we like it or not. I can't ignore it. I don't want to hurt anybody. If she can teach me to control it, that's a risk I'm willing to take."

Alana swallowed. "But it might kill you."

Braidon's eyes flashed. "It can try," he said, his voice like iron now.

Crossing the room, Alana buried herself in his arms once more. "I don't want to lose you," she sobbed into his shoulder.

His soft hands stroked her hair as they held each other. "You won't, sis," he whispered. "Trust me."

A spasm racked Alana's chest as she nodded, aware her tears were soaking her brother's shirt. "Okay," she croaked finally. Lifting her head, she looked into his eyes. "Okay, I trust you, Braidon. But you have to be careful, okay?"

He nodded, a crooked smile on his face. "I'll be fine,

sis." He winked. "Remember what happened with the Stalkers."

Alana smiled, stroking a hand through his soft hair. "That was instinct," she murmured. "Just be careful when it's the real thing. We don't even know what your power *does*, remember?"

Braidon sighed. "Okay, Alana, but only because I'm afraid you'll have another tantrum if I don't."

"That wasn't a tantrum!"

Her brother snorted, humour dancing in his eyes. "Sure. So, you weren't going to slam the door on your way out?"

Scowling, Alana shoved him back on the bed. "I take it back, go ahead and use that magic of yours. Don't think it'll protect you from *me*, though."

Laughter spread around the room as Alana sat on the other bed. She didn't look at the old priest—her anger at the woman's omission was still fresh, and Alana wasn't sure whether she could keep the rage from her words. Before their laughter could fade into awkward silence, the door to the hallway banged open.

Spinning around to face the newcomer, Alana relaxed when she saw Devon step into the room. Water dripped from his jacket as he pushed the door closed behind him.

"Bloody rain," he muttered, glancing around the room. One bushy eyebrow lifted as he saw the tears on Alana's cheeks. "Am I interrupting something?"

Alana quickly wiped the last of her tears away and shook her head. "No," she replied, more sharply than she intended. Silently, she cursed herself for allowing the warrior to see her weakness. "What kept you so long? Did you find a ship?" she asked, more harshly than she intended.

Shaking his head, Devon moved to the spare seat by the fire and lowered himself into the chair with a groan. He held out his hands to the blaze, allowing its warmth to wash over him. "You could show a little gratitude, you know," he said gruffly. "I've been out all day in the cold searching for this ship. And poor old Kellian, who knows how many strings he's having to pull to get to his funds on such short notice."

Heat flushed to Alana's cheeks at his admonishment. Her eyes dropped to the ground. "Sorry," she muttered. "I do appreciate it, I swear. It's just...been a stressful afternoon."

Devon chuckled. "Getting a little restless in this little room?" He waved a hand. "You can relax, I found a ship that leaves tomorrow at first light."

Alana's heart lifted at the news, then sank as she realised Kellian still had not returned. "If Kellian gets the gold."

"Oh, he will," Devon grinned. "He's a good man in a pinch, don't worry about him. He'll come through. Now, what's say we get some supper? We've some time to wait yet before he returns, I think."

The loud rumble of Alana's stomach was all the answer he needed.

22

Quinn sighed as he lowered himself down into the chair behind the mahogany desk. It had been a long and drawn out night, filled with urgent meetings and the furious scribbling of messages. The morning was already approaching, and he still had not slept. His back ached from the hard days of riding, and his heart was weary with failure.

When the river had finally receded, he and his men had spent a day and a night racing across the Lonian plains, following the fading tracks of their quarry. He'd thought they'd continue heading north, but instead the party had veered east towards the Lonian capital.

Now Devon and his friends had vanished into the human cesspool otherwise known as Lon. Quinn's men were scouring the city, checking in with contacts and informing the city guard, but amidst Lon's slums and backstreets, it would not be hard for the Magicker to disappear. Despite their best efforts, they might be forced to wait for another outburst of the boy's magic.

In the meantime, he and his men would keep a low profile, so as not to alert Devon of their presence. If they were lucky, the giant warrior or his friend, Kellian, would slip up and reveal his presence. Quinn knew the men well—neither was suited to a life of poverty and anonymity.

No, the more he considered it, the less he thought it likely the two would seek to remain in the city. And if they left its crowded streets, there was only one other place they could turn to—Northland.

With the Trolan revolt, the Tsar's plans to conquer the independent state had been put on hold, but it would not be long before his eyes turned north once more. It was well known that the northern state still allowed Magickers the freedom to wander its streets. This could not be allowed to continue—lest they return to the Three Nations unknown and continue the spread of wild magic.

Quinn had several contacts on the docks. He had sent out messages to them but had yet to hear back. The delay was frustrating, but there was little he could do now but wait.

Reaching into the drawer of his desk, he took out an old bottle of whiskey. It had been almost a year since his last visit to Lon, and he was pleased to see its contents remained untouched. Pouring himself a glass, he took a sip, savouring the fire as he swallowed.

He looked up as a knock came from the door. Glancing out the window, he saw the distant glow of the rising sun on the horizon and sighed. Exhausted, he lit another candle, but as he moved to open the door it swung inwards. He was about to bark a reprimand to whichever servant dared let themselves into his office, when a figure stepped into the room.

Swallowing, Quinn took a step backwards. The intruder

followed him, the very air seeming to blacken with its approach. A dark cloak swathed the small body, its hood casting the pale face in shadow. But there was no hiding from the pitch-black eyes as they gazed around the room.

Quinn. The demon's voice slithered through his mind like a snake.

Knees shaking, Quinn managed to reach out and grip the edge of his desk for support. With the demon's presence, all warmth seemed to have been sucked from the room. Terror gnawed at his stomach, but he straightened, drawing on reserves of strength he hardly knew he had. Walking around the desk, he lowered himself into his seat.

The figure followed him, gliding across the room as though it no longer had need for its feet. It was small in stature, barely coming up to his shoulders, but that only added to its terror. Darkness swept before it like a wave, the candles sputtering, the lanterns dimming to little more than pinpricks.

"What are you doing here, demon?" Quinn asked, struggling to keep the fear from his voice. "I did not send for you."

The Tsar sent me, the creature hissed. *He is…disappointed with you.*

Quinn gritted his teeth. "I will have them shortly."

Laughter bubbled through the room, sending icicles dripping down Quinn's spine. *She has evaded you again and again…*

"The boy surprised us."

A mistake that was…beneath you, came the demon's reply. Its head bent horribly sideways, as though to inspect him. *Perhaps age has dulled your instincts.*

"No," Quinn growled, anger pushing back the fear. He

stood, hands gripped around his desk. "I will have them soon."

They have all of Lon to hide in.

"They won't stay," Quinn shot back. "They'll try and flee to Northland. When they do, I'll be waiting for them."

So sure of yourself, the demon laughed again. *Yet they evaded you at the temple of the Goddess, slipped through your fingers by the river.*

"Luck!" Quinn said, trying to keep his desperation from showing.

Perhaps… the demon hissed. *Perhaps you* want *them to escape.*

"Never," Quinn whispered, his face paling. His fingers twitched as the demon moved closer. He felt his magic beginning to stir and pressed it down. "I am loyal to the Tsar."

Pray that is true, Quinn. The demon stood in front of him now. Before he could move, pale fingers shot out and pressed into his forehead.

Colours swirled across Quinn's vision, flashing to black. Slowly the darkness faded, and he found himself in a windowless cell, his hands chained to the wall, his body naked to the freezing cold. A shadow moved towards him, blade extended. White-hot agony burned in his side as the blade bit him, driving through his kidney, stealing his breath.

Even as the physical pain tore at him, he felt something else, another force, a dark violation as something cold and terrible slid into his body. The pain fled as ice spread through his veins, then returned a thousand-fold as talons lashed at his insides, tearing him asunder. An awful darkness ripped into his mind, harrying his spirit. Opening his mouth, Quinn made to scream…

And found himself back at his desk. His brow soaked with a cold sweat, his breath coming in ragged gasps, he threw himself back from the demon. His boots scraped loudly on the stone floor as he stood.

"They will not escape," he wheezed. "I swear it."

Very good, came the demon's reply. Its laughter whispered through the room.

Quinn nodded, struggling to calm his racing heart. "Perhaps you could help us."

He clenched his fists, hating himself for showing such weakness. But if the Tsar had sent the demon, it meant Quinn was at terrible risk. One more mistake, one more loss, and the vision the creature had shown him would soon become a reality.

As much as Quinn hated the dark creatures, its presence would ensure success. Few Magickers could withstand their power. A mortal like Devon would be swept away like sand before the tide.

Of course, the demon said, a sly smile spreading across its face.

Before Quinn could reply, another knock came from the door. Beside him, the demon vanished without a sound, though he didn't doubt it remained close. Quinn shivered, and called out for the newcomer to enter.

One of his men stepped inside, his eyebrows raised as he looked around the empty room. "I thought I heard voices…" He trailed off as Quinn waved a hand.

"You have something for me, Kaylib?"

His man blinked, looking as though he'd momentarily forgotten why he was there. He stared blankly at Quinn, then nodded quickly and cleared his throat. "Ye…yes, sir! We…it appears we may have a lead on our prey, sir."

23

Devon sucked in a lungful of air, savouring the fresh taste of salt on the wind. Overhead, the familiar gulls circled, their harsh cries mingling with the gentle creak of the ship as it rocked against its berth. Shifting his feet, he leaned over the railing and looked down at the docks, checking the progress of the sailors as they prepared to depart.

As far as he could tell, things were running to schedule. The five of them had arrived just before sunrise, having left the inn early to avoid being seen by morning commuters making their way to work. The crew of the *Songbird* was just beginning their preparations when the party arrived on the docks to board.

Now those preparations were almost complete, with only a few crates of supplies left to be brought aboard. From what Devon had seen so far, the ship was mostly transporting silks and spices to the northern port. No doubt they would fetch a high price, though buyers might be in short supply in the developing nation.

Shaking his head, Devon checked on the others. Alana and Braidon stood at the bow with the priest, their eyes on the harbour. He could read Alana's impatience by the way she stood at the railing, her shoulders tight, one hand resting on the pommel of her sabre. He couldn't blame her. They were exposed out here on the docks. He had heard no word of Stalkers entering the city, but that meant little if Quinn and his men were keeping a low profile. If they were recognised before the *Songbird* set sail, they would be trapped on the ship with nowhere to go.

His eyes travelled to the other end of the ship, where a lantern burned in the window of the captain's quarters. Kellian was there now, settling their bill with Julian and the captain. The night before he had brought back a small fortune in gold, and not for the first time, Devon found himself cursing his wasteful youth. If he'd set aside more of his salary while he'd been in the army, he might have avoided this mess altogether.

Devon cursed as he returned his gaze to the docks in time to watch two sailors drop a crate. The box shattered on impact, scattering clay jars across the wooden boards. Several cracked open, sending red spices flying as the men raced to save the remaining jars. Beyond the chaos, all progress loading the ship came to a halt as the other sailors waited for the men to clear the way.

Grating his teeth, Devon forced himself to take another breath. His heart was pounding against his chest, his nerves more than a little raw. He shook his head, trying to relax. The sun was still low on the horizon, and they would be away soon enough.

At the thought, the door to the captain's cabin banged open, and he turned to see Julian approaching. Forcing a smile to his lips, he waved a greeting.

"Still get that unsettled stomach, ay, Devon?" Julian's laughter rang out across the docks as his friend joined him at the railing.

Devon flashed the man a scowl. He'd never liked sailing. During the civil war, he'd been on more than his fair share of ships, but his stomach had never grown used to the rocking motion of the sea. "Nothing wrong with my stomach," he muttered. "It's the ocean that makes me sick. It's unnatural, floating all the way out there with nothing but a few planks of wood to keep you from a watery grave."

Julian grinned and patted the railing. "I wouldn't worry, old friend. The *Songbird's* one of mine. I trust her more than I'd trust my wife."

"I thought your wife ran off with half your fortune?"

"Hardly!" Julian exclaimed. His eyes flickered furtively at Devon and he forced a grin. "It was a few gold bars and my favourite horse. Hardly half!"

Devon chuckled, slapping his friend on the back. "The single life suits you better." He turned his eyes back to the dock. The men had finally cleared the spilled jars and loading had resumed. "Are you joining us on this voyage? We should be away shortly, I hope?"

"Ever the impatient one, Devon!" Julian laughed.

A grin spread across Devon's cheeks. "If I'd known this was your ship, Julian, I would have waited until noon to show up. Once upon a time you couldn't leave port less than two days late."

Julian snorted. "Like I told my lieutenant at the time, conditions weren't right to sail."

"Tell that to the twenty other captains who arrived on time," Devon replied.

"Reckless souls, all of them!" Julian said, then the smile fell from his face. "Thankfully those days are past. I wasn't made to captain ships. My instinct for self-preservation is far too strong."

"You seemed to have found your calling," Devon murmured, eyeing his suddenly sombre friend.

Julian nodded, his eyes on the men below. "It's been a hard year, Devon," he said. "Business has been slow. I've had to make sacrifices."

Devon sighed. "Things will improve."

"I can only hope so." Shaking his head, Julian looked up at Devon and forced a smile. "It's been good seeing you again, old friend. I had best be going, though. Wouldn't want to get in the way." He paused a moment. "You sure you and Kellian don't want to reconsider this journey? It's going to be a cold winter in Northland."

"Sorry, old friend, but our minds are made up!" Devon replied, offering his hand.

Julian gripped his palm. "Until next time then, old friend."

"Until next time," Devon replied.

Devon watched as he turned and wandered down the gangplank, wondering at the sudden change in his friend's mood. The former ship captain paused on the docks, shouting a few words to the men there before continuing through the crowd. The remaining sailors moved quickly up the gangplank, carrying the last of the crates with them.

His eyes continued on across the docks. The crowds were building as the sun lifted higher in the sky, and other ships were beginning to pull away from the docks now, readying themselves to set sail on the high tide. He caught a last glimpse of his friend's red cloak through the press of bodies, then he was gone.

Devon was about to look away when something else caught his attention. He frowned, staring into the crowd.

His stomach swirled as he caught sight of a black-cloaked figure, then another. Swallowing, he clamped his hands around the railing and licked his lips. Silently, he prayed to the Storm God he was wrong.

Boots thudded on the wooden boards as Alana appeared beside him. "I thought we were leaving?" she asked, leaning against the railing.

"We're meant to be," Devon muttered, his eyes never leaving the crowd.

The dark-cloaked figures had come together now, their long strides eating up the distance to the *Songbird.* Fear clawed its way up Devon's throat as he recognised the figure in the forefront. It was Quinn. He and his Stalkers would be on them in minutes.

Out on the docks, people were moving quickly about their business, filing between fish stalls and weaving their way between ships. Their presence was hindering Quinn and his men, but it would not delay them long. Already people were noticing the Stalkers and falling back, flinching away from the advancing black tide, almost fleeing in their eagerness to avoid them.

Beside him, Alana cursed as she saw Quinn and his men. Ignoring her, Devon turned from the railing and strode across the deck. Kellian and the captain were in conversation beside the cabin, and he made straight for them. Kellian looked up at his approach, but Devon had eyes only for the captain.

"We need to leave," he said shortly.

The captain looked around, seeing the last of his men had just come aboard. "Looks like we're ready to sail, just let me go sign the log book and we can be off."

"No." Devon caught the man by the wrist as he made towards the gangplank. "We need to leave *now.*"

Shaking his head, the captain tore his arm loose and fixed Devon with a glare. "Listen, young man, I understand your journey is somewhat…urgent, but I cannot simply depart without the proper paperwork."

"You can and you will," Devon snapped, grabbing the man by the front of his shirt. With his other hand, he pointed out at the crowd. "See those men? They're Stalkers. They're here for *us*, and anyone caught helping us. So, unless you fancy spending the rest of your wretched life in a Lonian dungeon, you'd best get this ship moving!"

The man's eyes flickered out across the docks, alighting on Quinn and his men. He swallowed, his eyes turning back to Devon.

"Don't even think about giving us up," Devon growled. Reaching up, he unsheathed his hammer and hefted it. "You wouldn't live to see the reward."

The man swallowed again, eyes wide, mouth gasping. Finally, he gave a curt nod. Devon released him but followed closely as the man marched around the deck screaming orders to his crew. Across the ship, men leapt into action, throwing off mooring lines and raising the anchor. Overhead, cloth rasped as the sails unfurled.

"That won't work," Devon said quickly, grabbing the man by the arm. He pointed at the rows of oars below the deck. "They have wind magic. Your men will need to row."

The captain nodded quickly and began shouting fresh orders. Devon's stomach lurched uncomfortably as the ship started to move. Freed of its restraints, it rocked gently beneath them and began to drift away from the docks. Still a hundred yards away, Quinn and his men redoubled their efforts to reach them.

"You think Julian betrayed us?" Kellian asked, coming alongside him.

Devon nodded. "He was jumpy," he said softly, keeping the hurt from his voice. "I should have guessed. He must have sent someone to fetch Quinn."

Steel rasped on leather as Alana drew her sabre. She didn't speak, just stared out over the crowd, watching as the Stalkers advanced. From below the deck came the thump of oars being shipped. Behind them, the captain stood at the tiller, slowly turning the ship away from the dock. As Devon had predicted, the sails hung limp above them. The wind had died away to nothing.

A foot opened between the ship and the dock, then a yard, then more. As the gap widened, Devon's panic began to ease, his heartbeat slowing. His eyes followed Quinn and his men, but he could see now they weren't going to arrive in time. Slowly, the ship drifted away from the dock and turned towards the open sea.

"Devon!" A voice carried to them on a sudden breath of wind.

Devon turned back, his spine tingling as he saw Quinn had come to a stop. The Stalker's words carried to them across the open water. "Turn back now, or die."

Grinning, Devon stepped up to the railing and laughed. The sound boomed out as he lifted *kanker* above his head and shouted. "Come and get me, sonny!"

With that, he turned away, his anxiety melting like ice before a flame. Quinn and his Stalkers had almost had them again, but it seemed luck remained on their side. Julian had betrayed them, but his strange manner at the end had been enough to alert Devon in time. He breathed out a long sigh, a smile touching his lips.

"That was too close," he said, looking at the others.

Just close enough, an ice-cold voice replied, whispering through their minds.

24

Just close enough.

Alana spun away from the rail as a dark voice whispered through her thoughts. Her gaze swept the deck, passing over crew and captain to settle on the figure of a boy sitting on the port railing. Swathed all in black, he sat on the railing with legs crossed, hands clenched before him. A hood hid his face, but as the *Songbird's* passengers looked on, pale hands reached up and pulled it down.

The jet-black eyes swept the ship before settling on Alana. She knew instinctively what it was, that this was a demon sent by the Tsar to bring them back.

Alana, the voice came again, drilling its way down into her consciousness. *How good to see you.*

The voice was shocking, like a cold breeze on a summer's day. Fear tied Alana's stomach in knots as she staggered back from the creature. She grabbed her brother by the wrist, pulling him close. Dragging him with her, she retreated towards the gap in the railing where the gangplank had been.

"Stop."

Alana groaned as the demon spoke out loud, the command bringing her feet to a sudden halt. She stood trembling, her brother's wrist locked in her iron grip, and watched as the creature slowly climbed from its perch. As it moved, its cloak swept out, revealing the dark hilt of a sword at its waist. A smile twitched on its pale face as the black eyes swept the sailors crowding the deck. At its voice, all movement had ceased.

The creature's awful laughter rent the air. Alana gritted her teeth as it turned back to her. "You have led Quinn a merry chase, Alana," it whispered, dark eyes flashing. "But it is over now."

A terrible sob tore from Alana's lips. She could feel her brother trembling in her hold. Alana looked across the deck, seeking help, but as she looked on the faces of Devon and Kellian, their eyes fell away.

"Come to me."

She gasped as her foot took an involuntary step forward. A low keening came from the back of her throat. She tried to release Braidon as her legs marched her towards the creature, but her hand had become a vice around his arm. He cried out as Alana dragged him with her. Their eyes met, and she wept at the horror she saw in his face. Tears streaming down her cheeks, Alana swung back to the demon.

"Please," she whispered, staring into the merciless face of the creature. There was no sign of life in its pitch-black eyes, no compassion on which to draw—only darkness.

Alana suddenly realised that a great hush had come over the ship. The cries of the gulls had fallen away, the distant shouts of street vendors were silenced. Only the gentle creaking of the ship beneath them remained.

She watched in open terror as the demon strode forward. It moved with a strange grace, its boots making no sound as it trod across the wooden planks. A chill breeze wrapped around Alana as it approached, as though its presence sucked the very life from the air. A thin white hand reached out, stretching towards her. She closed her eyes, waiting for its touch, knowing it would be the last thing she ever felt…

"No."

The voice was gruff, almost shaking, but with an iron in it that brooked no argument. Alana's eyes snapped open. She stared as Devon strode across the deck, placing himself between them and the demon. His amber eyes flickered in her direction, shining with fear, but, nonetheless, he turned and faced the demon. He held *kanker* gripped tightly in one hand.

Awful laughter whispered over the ship as the demon looked at the giant hammerman.

You are in my way, mortal.

The muscles along Devon's back rippled as he straightened. "You're not taking her anywhere, demon."

DEVON HARDLY KNEW WHAT HE WAS DOING.

A moment ago, he'd been standing beside the railing, staring at the dark creature that had appeared in their midst. As the black eyes had fallen on him, he'd frozen, memories rising up from his past. Demons had been the Tsar's secret weapon during the civil war, the reinforcements sent in to sweep away the enemy when all else failed. He had watched creatures such as this one toss full-grown men around like ragdolls, had seen their dark magic tear buildings to pieces. Now one was standing on their ship, and there was nothing anyone could do to stop it. A glance at Braidon was all it took to see the boy was exhausted, his youthful energies spent from the hard ride across southern Lonia. Without magic, they didn't stand a chance against the creature's power.

Then the demon's voice had whispered across the ship, calling Alana to it. Her eyes had flickered in Devon's direction, but he'd quickly looked away, *kanker* suddenly heavy in his hand as shame welled inside him. Yet even the legendary weapon could not aid him against such a creature. No mortal in recent memory had ever stood against a demon and lived.

But as Alana had continued towards the demon, Devon's gaze had caught in the crystal blue eyes of Tillie, and her words from the road had come rushing back.

You are stronger than you think, hammerman.

And Devon had suddenly found himself moving forward, stepping between Alana and the creature, *kanker* held at the ready.

"No," he heard himself saying. "You're not taking her anywhere, demon."

Now, as the awful eyes looked up at him, it was all Devon could do to keep himself upright. They bored into him, piercing his soul, robbing him of strength. He gripped the haft of *kanker* harder, willing himself to defy the creature, to stand strong. A shudder went through him as it laughed again.

"Devon," came Alana's voice from behind him. "Don't."

He ignored her. Breath held, he glared down at the demon, every muscle in his body taut, ready to do battle. He forced himself to move, to take another step towards the creature. It watched him come, a smile on its ghostly face. Slowly, it unfolded its hands and shook its head.

Do not be a fool, hammerman.

Devon gritted his teeth as the awful voice spoke in his mind. "Get off my ship," he growled, drawing on his anger.

The demon's eyes flashed, and, despite himself, Devon found himself retreating a step. The dark laughter chased after him, sliding its way inside him. His legs shook, but with an effort of will, he forced himself to stop, to stand his ground.

Very well.

Grinning, the creature reached down and drew its sword. The black blade glinted in the sunlight as it slid free, gripped in a paperwhite hand. Lifting it high, the demon laughed, and a darkness pulsed from the weapon, stretching out to encircle the creature.

From somewhere deep within, Devon found the courage to speak. "A pretty trick, demon," he laughed. Hefting his hammer, he started towards it.

For a second, a flicker passed across the creature's face. The brow of the boy it had once been creased. A low hiss came from the awful mouth as it pointed the blade at Devon.

Die!

The shadows swirling around the blade crackled, gathering on its iron tip. A *boom* sounded across the ship, and then the darkness rushed from the sword towards Devon.

Watching it come, he found himself smiling. The fear had fled now, the doubt of the last five years vanishing like mist before the dawn. Gripping the weapon of his ancestor, he lifted it high and screamed a battle cry. The dark magic rushed onwards and crashed into the steel head of the hammer.

Another *boom* rang out, sending gulls screaming in flight. Across the deck, men were thrown from their feet. Devon stumbled back, still waiting for the pain, for the rush as his life was swept away.

Instead, there was only a strange, drawn out silence.

Blinking, Devon shook his head and straightened. He glanced down at his body, expecting to see a tangled mess, but he remained whole. Not even the stained fabric of his brown tunic had been touched by the creature's power. His eyes turned to *kanker.* The weapon glinted in the morning sun, but the ancient runes on its head glowed with a light all of their own, although it was already fading.

Devon smiled as he looked back at the demon. Around him, the occupants of the ship were picking themselves up and staring with wonder at the giant warrior standing against the demon.

The demon still stood with its arm outstretched, sword extended, a look of pure bewilderment written across its ghostly face. It was clearly as shocked to see Devon still standing as he was himself.

Devon's laughter rung out across the deck as he pointed *kanker* at the demon.

"Now *you* die, demon."

Still cackling, he advanced on the creature. The demon blinked, drawing back its sword and straightening. For a moment it stared at the oncoming warrior, before pointing the blade again. The shadows gathered once more. With a scream from the demon, they sliced across the deck towards him.

This time, Devon did not so much as break stride. With a contemptuous swing of *kanker*, he sent the darkness swirling off into the harbour. The water hissed and boiled where it struck, and pure hatred twisted the demon's face.

With a roar, he charged.

For a moment the demon's hatred gave way to fear. It staggered back, the dark cloak rustling around it, the sword extended uselessly before it. Devon closed the gap, his powerful shoulders directing the hammer down at his foe's head.

Sparks flashed as the demon recovered and raised its blade. Moving with impossible speed, it twisted in place, its own sword arcing back out to slash at Devon's ribs. He leapt backwards, cursing softly as he felt the tip slice through his shirt. Not wanting to draw attention to themselves, he had neglected to put on his mail-shirt before boarding the ship.

The demon growled, chasing after him with eyes of dark fire, its tiny figure belying its awesome strength. *Kanker* leapt to meet it, the ancient hammer shining like gold as it deflected another blow from the black blade. Vibrations shuddered down Devon's arm as their weapons met, but he held tight to the hammer's haft, and swung it back at the creature's face.

Spinning, it ducked the blow. A grin spread across its face as its blade lanced for Devon's stomach, too close to avoid. Dropping *kanker,* Devon's arm swept down and caught the creature by the wrist, halting the attack. The demon's eyes widened as he lifted the thing from the ground and hurled it at the mast.

A dark cackling carried across the ship as the creature twisted, landing easily on one foot. Its blade flashed up, black energies crawling along its length to surge at Devon, but he had already recovered *kanker* and batted the attack aside.

Steel rang as they came together again. Devon grunted, the demon's speed and strength forcing him back, only raw instinct keeping him alive. The creature's movements grew more frenzied, its arms becoming a blur, and twice he felt the lick of its blade on his flesh. There were no words now, only silence as the two combatants tore at each other.

The initial thrill of combat faded, and Devon felt his energies tiring, his body unused to the rigours of armed combat. Still he fought on, driven by a primal need to conquer the enemy before him, to best the creature who dared challenge him. Swinging his hammer, he roared, fighting his way back against the demon's blistering assault.

Devon saw something cross the creature's eyes as he pressed forward. The black blade still moved with unnatural speed, flicking out to turn aside his blows, but there was a hesitation now, a doubt before each movement. This was a beast unused to defiance. Its enemies fell to its power like trees before the storm, devoured by its magic.

Yet now a mortal man stood against it, unyielding, and Devon could sense its doubt.

Snarling, the creature pressed forward again, but Devon began to laugh. He swept his hammer down, blocking a disembowelling cut.

"Is that all, demon?" Devon's mirth boomed out across the waters.

The demon's face twisted and a screech tore from its throat. The air grew cold, and it seemed the very light was being sucked from the world about it. Yet where Devon stood, *kanker* in hand, the sun shone brightly, setting the runes of his hammer aglow. Screaming, the demon hurled itself forward.

Devon met the creature's charge with a scream of his own, *kanker* rising to block its desperate attack. Once, twice, three times their weapons met. Then, with a shriek of breaking metal and boom of sundered energies, the black blade shattered. Bellowing his triumph, Devon drove forward and brought the ancient hammer down on the creature's skull.

A white brilliance flashed across the ship, and with a sharp suddenness, light and sound and life were restored to the world. A gull cawed, circling overhead, and the sun shone brightly across the watchers on the *Songbird.* Wind blasted into the sails, sending the ship surging forwards.

Drawing back his hammer, Devon watched as the creature collapsed face first onto the deck. A whisper went through the crew and, looking around, he saw the fear in their eyes. Ignoring them, Devon dropped *kanker* and strode across to the creature. Lifting the frail body above his head, he carried it to the railing. In the distance, he could see the Stalkers gathered on the docks, watching the *Songbird's* retreat.

With a great heave of his shoulders, Devon hurled the body of the demon over the side. It struck the waters with a crash and vanished beneath the surface without a sound, as though it had never been.

25

Quinn stood on the deck of the *Ice Queen* and looked out over the empty waters, seeking sign of the missing ship. The air was crisp and cool, the sun sinking towards the western coastline. Wind crackled around him, called by his magic, filling the sails to drive them on through the silent waters. Yet still a cold dread clenched around his heart.

Devon had killed the demon. It shouldn't have been possible, but he had seen it himself. He had watched in disbelief as the giant hammerman turned aside the creature's dark magic and fought off its frenzied attacks. The shock of the final blow had caused him to stagger back in horror. In silence, Quinn had stared as Devon carried the body to the side of the ship and hurled it out into the harbour.

His message had been clear: *come after us and die.*

Yet, here he was.

Quinn shivered again, forcing the doubt from his mind.

The man might have found a way to counter the creature's power, but Quinn still had the weight of numbers on his side. He had brought another company of Stalkers with him from Lon. Their sixteen men would be more than enough to kill Devon. The man was a fearsome warrior, but he was not invincible.

If only he could convince his men of that. Already he had caught them speaking in hushed whispers of the giant warrior, about his exploits in Trola and his battle with the demon. Enraged, Quinn had ordered any man caught spreading rumours about the hammerman be lashed. All his life it seemed he had been standing in the shadow of the man. In Trola, Devon had been promoted to lieutenant ahead of Quinn, despite his common upbringing and lack of magic. When the fool had rescinded his commission and quit, Quinn's hatred had only grown, seeing it as an attack on everything in which he had ever believed.

It galled him now to find himself still standing in that same shadow. Worse yet, Alana stood with the man.

He gritted his teeth, turning his mind to other pursuits. Leaving the railing, he strode across the deck to where the captain stood at the helm. The man's nervous eyes flickered in Quinn's direction as he approached. He hadn't wanted to set sail after the escapees, but Quinn hadn't given him a choice, commandeering his ship and crew in the name of the Tsar. To refuse would have meant death.

Unfortunately, the *Ice Queen* had proven a poor choice. Despite full sails, it was sluggish in the water, and Quinn guessed it had been a long time since the hull had been scraped clean of barnacles. Silently, he cursed the captain for a fool.

"How goes our progress?" he asked out loud.

"With your magic, we'll catch them, my lord," the captain replied, an edge to his voice.

Supressing his anger, Quinn shook his head. "We had better, captain," he said dangerously. "It'll be your head if we don't."

With that, he wandered across the deck to where the captain's cabin waited. His soul was weary, the strain of using his magic draining him. Yet he could not release it—without his power, the ship would slow to a creep.

Pulling open the cabin door, he moved inside and slumped onto the captain's bed. Leaning his head back against the wall, he struggled to keep his eyes open. Magic still poured from him, drawing wind into the sails, but as he looked inside, he saw his pool of power shrinking. It would only last a few more hours.

They would not catch Devon's ship before then.

Defeat settled on his shoulders like a blanket. His heart ached, and he wondered how long it would be before the Tsar came for him. Despite all his faithful years of service, this failure would cost him everything.

If only Julian's informant had come sooner, he might have caught them before the ship departed. If only there had been another ship ready to leave the instant the *Songbird* had escaped. If only he'd had the power to strike the ship down with lightning.

Instead, he'd been forced to watch, helpless, as the *Songbird* carried his prey beyond reach. He had robbed the wind from their sails, even tried to force them back with his powers, but the rowers aboard were strong, and he was not strong enough to overcome all of them.

Now he found himself aboard another ship, leagues behind his quarry, praying to long dead Gods to bring them within his reach.

Hours crept past as Quinn tracked his magic's slow decline, until it was nothing more than a blue spark in the darkness of his mind. Outside, night had fallen over the ship, but still they sailed on. He sighed as he heard the sails overhead flapping, then fall silent as the last breath of wind left them. Curses whispered through the wooden walls as the captain shouted for the few sailors he could spare to take to their oars.

Closing his eyes, Quinn lay back on the bed as the ship rocked beneath him. The rowers would soon tire. Devon and his wards had slipped through his fingers again. Within days, they would disappear forever into the vast expanse of Northland. And he would feel the Tsar's wrath.

He fought against the pull of sleep, dreading what would find him there, but it was insistent, his exhaustion beyond his will to resist. Slowly the darkness wrapped around him, drawing him down into nothingness…

When Quinn woke, the gloom was still all around, but he was no longer alone. A man moved through the shadows, his aura flickering with multicoloured hues, drawing closer. Quinn shuddered as he looked on the figure and felt the fiery blue eyes of the Tsar pierce him.

"You have lost them." The voice rang with power.

Quinn bowed his head. "The demon failed."

"You failed," *boomed the voice.*

Shuddering, Quinn drew back, but bands of fire swept out to wrap around him. He screamed as the flames burned into his spirit. He reached for his magic, but the power was gone, consumed by his futile pursuit of Devon.

"For years I have watched you." The Tsar's voice was soft now. "Nurtured you, made you one of my most trusted servants. And how have you repaid me?"

"I am sorry, your majesty," Quinn croaked, forcing back a scream.

Bowing his head, he began to beg. "Please, they have not escaped me yet. I can catch them!"

"You cannot," came the Tsar's reply. "Your weakness has betrayed you."

Anger gave Quinn strength. Summoning his courage, he looked into the Tsar's burning eyes. "No!" he growled. "They shall not escape me, not while I still breathe."

The form of the Tsar flared, the spiralling colours of his form shifting. A smile appeared on his ethereal lips. "Your spirit remains, Quinn," he spoke quietly. "Perhaps you might yet serve me."

"Anything, your majesty," Quinn whispered as the flames binding him died away.

A long silence stretched out as the Tsar studied him. Colours spun and grew amidst his form, red and green and white and blue, plus a thousand others unnamed. Quinn found himself drawn to them, a part of himself yearning to join the swirling display.

"Feshibe and her children have been sent to intercept them," the Tsar said at last.

Quinn's spirit flickered at the mention of the beast's name. His heart twisted. The creatures would bring death to everyone aboard the Songbird. *Alana's face rose into his thoughts.*

"She has had her chance." There was regret in the Tsar's voice now. "I can spare her no longer. She will die with the others. Only the boy must survive. You will retrieve him for me."

"If she dies, we cannot reverse—" Quinn tried to argue, but the Tsar waved a hand and his voice faded away.

"So be it," the man's words whispered through the void. "Bring me the boy. His power intrigues me."

Quinn swallowed. "The beasts, they will bring him to me?"

Laughter sent a tremor through Quinn's soul. "No, you must find him," came the Tsar's reply. "Scour the coast. You will find the boy there."

Quinn bowed. "Yes, your majesty."

With his words, the darkness shook, the vision of the Tsar fading away. Quinn lingered there a moment longer, wondering at his ruler's words, and the death now winging its way towards his quarry. There would be no stopping the beasts when they came to them. No magic or hammer would turn them aside.

Alana would die alongside Devon and Kellian.

26

Alana sat on the bow of the ship, staring out over the open ocean, to where the coastline flickered in the distance. The burning globe of the sun was just beginning to disappear behind the scraggly trees. A cool breeze blew across her neck as darkness slowly crept over the ship and the last calls of the seabirds faded away.

Safe.

She could hardly bring herself to believe it. For hours she had been watching to the south, waiting for sails to appear, for the first signs of the pursuit that would drag them back to the capital. But the seas had remained empty, and, bit by bit, hope crept unbidden into her heart.

Freedom.

It seemed such a strange word to her, after so long spent in the darkness. It was so close now; she could taste it in the salty air, feel it in the cold wind, smell it in the fishy tang of the cargo hold.

"How long will it be?" her brother asked, coming to sit alongside her.

Alana shook her head. The wind was weak, and the captain was using the rowers below sparingly. From Lon to Duskenville was a journey of many leagues, and it could take days to reach the northern city. Even so, a smile crept to her lips as she looked at her brother.

"As long as it takes," she said. "They won't catch us now, Braidon."

Her brother nodded solemnly, his eyes trailing out to where the last red of the sunset was fading to black. "Why did he fight the demon?"

"I don't know," Alana whispered, remembering Devon's amber eyes as he faced the creature.

Her thoughts drifted, recalling the battle between hammerman and demon. Trapped by the demon's power, she and her brother had stood on the brink of defeat, staring into the black eyes of death. Had it not been for Devon, they would both be sitting in the Tsar's dungeons by now.

Instead, they were free.

She saw him now, sitting on the deck with his back pressed up against a barrel. His eyes were distant, their amber depths catching the last glint of the dying sun.

How had he done it? The ancient warhammer lay at his side, his hand resting on its haft. Tillie had said the weapon had magic, but none of them had guessed it possessed the strength to turn aside the demon's power. More so, Devon had matched the creature's superhuman strength, blow for blow. She had never seen the like.

"You going to sit there all night staring, princess?" Devon's voice called across to her.

Alana jumped, while at her side Braidon laughed. She flashed a scowl in his direction. Devon hadn't moved from his perch, but she saw the hint of his smile on his lips.

"Who says I was staring?" she shot back.

"You were, sis, I saw it," her brother cut in. His mouth snapped closed as her grey eyes turned on him.

Devon stood and sheathed *kanker* on his back, then walked across the gently pitching deck towards them. As he moved, several sailors cast angry glares at his back. The entire crew now knew they'd been tricked into safeguarding a Magicker from the Tsar. Most were from Northland, beyond the southern ruler's influence, but the ship's name would need to be changed if they ever wished to trade with the Three Nations again.

Devon ignored them. Silently, he lowered himself down beside Alana and trailed his legs out over the side of the ship.

"You think they'll get us to Duskenville?" Alana asked suddenly, her gut churning at the thought of failure.

"They'd better," Devon replied loudly. Reaching up, he tapped the haft of his hammer. "Or they'll soon learn what a kiss from old *kanker* feels like."

Alana shuddered despite herself. In the moment Devon had faced off against the demon, he'd been as fearsome as any God, his eyes burning, his face impassive, his shoulders rippling with power. Such had been his ferocity, even the demon seemed to shrink before him. Sitting there now, his massive arms pressed against hers, Alana couldn't help but shiver, fear and admiration welling within her.

"How did you do it?" she asked, more to distract herself from his nearness than seeking an answer.

"Do what?" Devon asked. Leaning forward, he stared down at the racing waters, his eyes hidden by shadow.

Beside Alana, Braidon stood suddenly and wandered away. She stared after him, frowning as he approached

Tillie and Kellian at the other railing, before returning her gaze to the hammerman.

"Umm." She bit her lip, struggling to put words to her question. "How did you face it? How did you *beat* it?"

The big warrior laughed, the sound gentle, almost mocking. "The same way I always have."

"Oh?"

Devon scratched his beard, the amber eyes flickering in her direction. "I didn't think."

Alana raised an eyebrow. "That sounds more like a way of getting yourself killed."

"Ay, Kellian used to say the same thing, during the war." His face darkened and he looked away. "But it's the truth. Other men, they worry about what will happen if they fail, about dying, or being wounded, about their family and friends and comrades around them. For me, once I pick up the hammer, there's none of that. There's only myself and the enemy."

His words sent a shiver down Alana's spine. "But it was a demon," she countered. "It was faster and stronger than you. How could it have lost?"

"Doubt," Devon replied simply. "I could see it in the thing's eyes. Its magic had never failed it before today. Sure, it had fought other men with its sword, but that was only ever a game. Today it had no choice, it was *forced* to cross arms with me. That unnerved it, sowed the slightest seeds of doubt in its mind."

"And then you laughed at it..." Alana murmured.

Devon smiled.

"It lost control," Alana continued for him, "grew reckless."

A gentle silence fell between them. Alana closed her eyes, feeling the heat of him pressed against her. A smile tugged at her lips. In that moment, she felt safer than at any other time in recent memory.

"Thank you," she whispered suddenly, "for protecting us."

A giant hand settled around her own. "Anytime, Alana."

She nodded, leaning her head against his shoulder. Her thoughts wandered as she sat there, and after a while she found herself drifting off to sleep, the exhaustion of the past few days returning to claim her.

This time, when she dreamed, Alana found herself a silent observer, a ghost standing amidst the green gardens of the past. She watched in silence as her brother ran through the roses, surrounded by other children, their youthful faces relaxed and smiling.

But as she drifted closer, she found one who did not smile or run with the others, who stood in silence, his face turned away, watching the others play. She circled him, her heart hammering hard in her chest as the boy's face came into view.

The demon stared back at her, his eyes the brightest shade of green…

Suddenly, darkness fell across the garden, a great shadow plunging the roses into black.

And Alana woke…

Sitting up on the ship, Alana glanced around quickly, surprised to find herself in the small cabin they'd taken over from the captain. Her heart raced as she looked for the others, and found Devon, Kellian, Braidon and Tillie sleeping close by. She breathed out a sigh of relief, touching a hand to her heart.

Closing her eyes, she sought sleep once more, but now it would not come. She tossed and turned for a time, struggling to forget the dream, and the dark cloud that had covered the garden. Finally, she surrendered to her wakefulness. Rising, she clipped her sword to her belt and moved outside, leaving the others to their sleep.

Overhead, the night was crisp and clear, the stars shining in the sky. A half-moon was slowly rising. The air was calm, the sails furled, leaving the ocean around them as still as glass. Standing at the railing, it seemed to Alana as though they sailed through the sky itself, their boat becoming a bird to soar through the stars.

At that moment, she saw something flicker across the moon. She frowned, squinting her eyes to search the night sky. Had it been a bird? It had seemed too big for that, as though some great hand had covered the moon for half an instant.

As she stared up at the sky, she heard the door to the cabin squeak behind her.

"Alana?" Devon's voice carried across the deck.

She turned towards him, raising a hand to silence him, then pointing at the sky. He glanced from her to the stars. Her heart eased as she saw he had *kanker* strapped over his shoulder. Whatever might be out there, she was confident they could face it with the ancient weapon on their side.

Devon moved towards her, his eyes on the sky now. Before he could reach her, the shadow passed across the moon once more. He came to a stop and reached for the haft of *kanker.*

As his hand gripped the weapon, an ear-splitting roar pierced the night. Alana's heart froze in her chest as she swung towards the sound, hand fumbling for her sword. Around them, the sailors asleep on the deck came alive, scrambling from their hammocks. The door to the cabin slammed open as the others emerged onto the deck.

"What is it?" Kellian called.

Devon had joined her at the railing now, his amber eyes

fixed on the stars. "Nothing good," he muttered, though Kellian would not have heard his words.

Alana shivered. She opened her mouth, and then closed it again. With her second glance, she had recognised what it was, the death that hovered overhead, but the knowledge would do them no good. Whatever magic her brother might possess, whatever power Devon's hammer had imbued in its steel head, they could not fight this beast. It would kill them all.

Dragon.

The word was on her lips as the first flames blossomed. An angry red flashed across the sky, blotting out the stars. By its light, they saw the beast's head illuminated against the sails. Blood red scales rippled across the massive body as it dove towards them, jaws wide, flames building in the black void of its mouth. Teeth glinted in the moonlight, each the size of her brother's dagger. The great wings spread out to either side of it, crackling in the wind as it rushed towards them. A long tail slithered out behind it as the golden globes of its eyes slid across the deck to find them.

"*Dragon!*"

The cry went up from the crew, then the men were hurling themselves overboard. Alana shivered, readying herself to follow. In the darkness she could not tell which direction the shore was, or how far, but it was better than remaining on the ship to burn.

"Get down!" Devon crashed into her as the dragon swept past.

His weight pressed her down against the deck as a wave of heat engulfed the ship. A *whoosh* came from the mast as the wood went up in flames, and overhead the sails turned to ash. Screams came from the crew who remained on the ship as their clothes caught fire. One staggered sideways into the railing and tumbled overboard, the flames dying as he struck the sea. Others crumpled to the deck, overwhelmed by heat and smoke.

Light flashed, brilliant and blinding. Shielding her eyes, Alana saw her brother standing outside the cabin, arms extended. Power crackled as he pointed at the dragon. Light shot upwards to meet the beast. Its roar washed over the ship as it seemed to freeze in the middle of the sky. But as the light struck its scarlet scales, the magic shattered, spiralling outwards into the night. With a roar, the dragon twisted and came at them again.

The great wings swept down, sending them reeling in a blast of wind. The flames leapt higher, fed by the fresh air, and in seconds the entire ship was ablaze. There was nowhere left to go but over the side.

Alana staggered to her feet. Flames separated her from Braidon and the others. Choking on the smoke, she waved a hand and screamed over the crackling of burning wood. "Make for the shore!"

She couldn't tell if they'd heard her, but Kellian waved back and then grabbed Braidon and Tillie by the hand. Turning, they staggered to the railing and disappeared over the side.

Alana was about to follow them when she remembered Devon. She searched the flickering shadows for him. The flames hissed, leaping through the rigging overhead, and a great groan came from the mast. If it fell, it would drag the entire ship down with it. Another roar came from the sky as the dragon turned for another pass.

Glimpsing movement nearby, she found Devon on his knees, blood streaming from a cut on his forehead. She rushed to his side, dropping to a crouch beside him and offering her shoulder. Wordlessly, she heaved him to his feet.

The hammer was still sheathed on his back and, gritting her teeth, she began to half-carry him towards the side of the ship.

As they reached the railing, a rush of wind came from overhead, and, looking up, Alana saw the dragon heading straight for them. The great jaws opened, flames blossoming. Without thinking, she dove forward, dragging Devon with her.

Ice swallowed Alana as they struck the dark waters. She gasped at the sudden cold, her breath rushing out as salty water filled her mouth. Choking, she thrashed, kicking out. Breaking the surface, she coughed out water and sucked in a breath. She looked around, searching for Devon, but there was no sign of him. Cursing, she sucked in another lungful of air, and dove back into the depths.

Forcing her eyes open, Alana squinted through the black water. Lit by the flames overhead, she glimpsed Devon below. Eyes closed, the hammer strapped to his back, he was sinking slowly into the abyss. Diving down, she slid his arm over her shoulder and began to kick.

The man's giant bulk slowed her, the weight of the hammer fighting her. Alana clung on, determined to save him. Her sabre, still strapped to her waist, slowed her ascent, but there was no time now to stop and remove it. Above, she could see the surface glowing, the flames of the burning ship calling her upwards.

She gasped as they burst through the surface. The sudden heat of the flames burned her lungs, but she sucked in the breaths as though the air were fine wine. Finally, she turned her attention to Devon. He was still breathing, but his eyes refused to open. A dead weight beside her, she could barely keep his head above the surface.

Somewhere overhead, the dragon's roar came again.

She sensed its eyes scanning the waters. Grabbing Devon by the back of his shirt, she began to kick away from the burning ship. With Devon lying on his back, the air in his lungs would keep him afloat, leaving her the hard work of moving them towards the shore.

Or so she hoped.

Slowly, the flames faded behind them, and with it, the screams of the dragon. She prayed it would be gone by dawn. On land the creatures could smell a human from a league away, but their vision was poor in the darkness. With the smoke and ocean all around, it was unlikely the beast would find them now.

When a partially scorched board from the ship bumped against them, Alana snatched at it desperately. Exhaustion weighing on her, she helped Devon grip one side of the board. He was half-conscious now, and it was large enough to keep them both afloat, for a time. Together, the two of them clung to the wooden raft and allowed the cold ocean currents to carry them where they would.

27

Devon woke to the sound of waves crashing on a rocky shore. Moments later, the pounding in his head struck him, sounding through the darkness like a hammer on a gong. Groaning, he rolled onto his side, the contents of his stomach churning. In a rush, he vomited onto the smooth gravel, the taste burning in his throat.

When he was done, he lay back, gasping at the cold air. Dark clouds rolled across the sky, and he shivered as a wave washed up the beach to soak his leg. Looking around, he found Alana lying next to him, her eyes closed, the sabre still strapped to her waist. He stared at her a moment, breath held, until he saw the gentle rise and fall of her chest. Taking a moment to gather his strength, he watched the waves as they lapped gently at his boots. Finally, he stood and, lifting Alana in his arms, he began to make his slow way up the beach.

The gravel shifted beneath his boots, making him stumble, but he did not fall. Shifting Alana to his shoulder, he looked up at the low cliff ahead of him. Its face was crumbling away, leaving piles of gravel around its base, but it was still too high for him to scale. If he tried, he would likely bring half the cliff down on the two of them.

Looking along the beach, he saw a thin gleam of water threading its way down towards the ocean. He moved towards it, knowing the creek would have carved a path through the gravel cliff and hoping he could follow it up into the forest beyond.

By the time he reached the break in the cliffs, he was panting hard. His clothes were heavy with sea water, and Alana still hadn't woken. The warhammer strapped to his back only made matters worse. Shaking his head, he looked up at the cliffs. The creek was little more than a trickle, but his guess had been correct, and the water had cut a narrow slit through the cliff-face. Soft sand and gravel had given way on either side, forming a ramp for the water to trickle its way down. Wooden debris from the trees further upstream had lodged in the little gorge.

Glancing back out over the ocean, Devon scanned the skies, but they remained empty. He breathed a sigh of relief—he had no wish to go up against the creature again. A shudder went through him as an image of the dragon flickered into his mind, its blood-red scales glowing in the light of its flames. Shaking his head, he turned his thoughts back to escaping the beach.

The ground over which the creek ran looked soft and unstable, but the broken trees and branches lining the stones offered a better path. Taking a firmer grip on Alana, he started up the trail.

He was halfway up the ramp of wooden detritus when Alana suddenly began to thrash in his hands. A sharp shriek echoed off the gravel walls. Cursing, he tried to set her down, only to catch an elbow in the face. The blow knocked him backwards, sending them both crashing into the creek bed. The stones crumbled beneath him and he began to slide. His hand shot out and wrapped around a fallen tree branch, the other snatching at Alana before she tumbled away.

"Alana?" he panted, lying back on the shifting stones.

Alana didn't reply, and he saw that her eyes remained closed, her eyelids fluttering with untold dreams. A low muttering came from her lips, but he couldn't make out the words. Devon swore and pulled them both back onto the broad branch of the fallen tree.

Taking a moment to catch his breath, Devon sat up and looked down the gully towards the sea. They could be anywhere in Lonia now—or in Northland, for that matter. He had no way of telling which until he had a better look at their surroundings.

His heart twitched as he thought of Kellian and the others. There had been no sign of anyone on the beach—not even the crew. He tried to think back to the ship, whether anyone else had made it off, but his memories were foggy. Only the image of the dragon remained crisp in his mind. Shaking off his melancholy, Devon stood, dragging Alana up with him.

There was nothing he could do for the others now. If they survived, they would head north. If not…he shook his head and pushed the thought away.

At the top of the gully, he found himself amongst the trees of a youthful forest. Looking around, he glimpsed larch and juniper trees; all species among the first to colonise barren land. Spotting a few oak and hickory trees, newcomers which only grew beneath the shade of older trees, he guessed the forest was probably fifty years old.

That, along with the gravel cliffs, told him they were still south of Fort Fall – still within the realm of the Tsar.

His eyes turned eastward to the ocean. The waters and sky remained empty, but there was no telling how long this would last. They needed to get going before someone or something came looking for them. Settling Alana on his shoulders, he started off towards the north, keeping the treeline in sight but never venturing too close. If the dragon was nearby, he had no wish to be spotted by the beast.

Devon's thoughts drifted as he walked, turning to Kellian. Had his recklessness finally gotten his friend killed? He thought back to the night at his friend's inn, when he'd insulted the royal guard and left him unconscious in a pile of garbage. If only he'd left things alone, they would still be in Ardath now, beyond the Tsar's knowledge.

Instead, he was carrying a fugitive through an unknown forest, his friend lost, probably dead. Stalkers and demons and dragons were hunting them, and there was little sign of hope. The odds were impossible, the challenge unassailable.

Despite himself, Devon found himself grinning as he walked. He remembered the look in the demon's eyes as he struck it down.

The stuff legends are made of!

Late in the afternoon, the trees finally began to thin, the taller trunks giving way to scraggly bushes of mulberry that offered little shelter. Devon continued casting glances at the eastern horizon, but it seemed the beast had given up for the moment. He wondered if that meant Braidon had been captured.

His heart sank at the thought of the boy, the weight of Alana pressing down on him. Imagining Alana's face when he told her the boy had been lost sent a shiver down his spine. He would rather fight ten demons than face the young woman's anger again. She would not be stopped, not by anyone. If the boy had been taken, she would turn around and march straight back to Ardath and demand his return. Silently, he prayed to the Storm God, Jurrien, that the boy was safe.

As the last of the trees fell behind, Devon's eyes were drawn out across the plains. Ahead, the coast twisted inwards on itself, the cliffs growing into the towering expanse of The Gap. There, lifting above the granite cliffs, were the immense walls of the greatest fortress ever constructed.

Fort Fall.

For more than five hundred years the fortress had stood in defiance of the north, the first and last bastion of the Three Nations against the ragged wasteland. In all that time, it had fallen only once, when the dark Magicker Archon had used his power to sweep the defenders from the walls. Eventually the Gods had defeated him, but even with their powers, they had only been able to banish him to the wasteland.

A hundred years later, he had returned. Only this time, Fort Fall had held, the courage of men prevailing, restoring the power of the Gods and casting down the dark Magicker.

Afterwards, the Gods had brought peace between the Three Nations and Northland. With peace had come trade and prosperity, and soon the borders had opened. Then there had been no more need for the great fortress.

Now Fort Fall stood empty, the gates torn asunder, the ancient walls unguarded but for the ghosts of long-dead warriors.

Looking at it now, Devon shuddered, the tales of his ancestor rising up from his childhood. His hand drifted to the haft of his hammer. It was on those walls where the legends of his ancestor had come to an end, as Alan stood in defiance of the dark Magicker's power. Already a legend amongst the Lonians, his strength faded with age, Alan had stood with *kanker* in hand and fought the enemy until his dying breath.

It was said he had fallen on the first wall, holding it with a handful of men against the dark Magicker's beasts, allowing the bulk of the army to retreat to the second wall. His sacrifice had saved hundreds of lives, keeping the defenders from being overtaken by Archon's vile beasts.

Devon's heart twitched as he thought of his own deeds, of the hundreds of souls who had fallen beneath the same hammer his ancestor had wielded in defence of the Three Nations.

In his arms, Alana twitched and moaned. A shiver went through her, and, touching a hand to her forehead, Devon cursed as he realised she had grown cold. Knowing where he was by Fort Fall's proximity, he set off across the open landscape.

He found the pools a few minutes later, their crystal-clear waters untouched by the darkness that had once come creeping into the land. Setting Alana down, he pulled off his jerkin and covered her with it. Quickly, he set about collecting dry wood for a fire.

28

Stones crunched as the *Ice Queen* ground its way up the beach, the wooden boards quivering beneath Quinn's feet before coming to a halt. Without waiting for a gangplank to be lowered, Quinn moved to the bow and leapt down onto the gravel shore. The loose stones slid beneath his feet as he landed, but he quickly straightened and looked around.

The burnt and blackened remains of the *Songbird* lay scattered along the beach, interspersed here and there by silent corpses. He walked away from the *Ice Queen* while his men disembarked, his eyes scanning the wreckage for signs of life. Here and there he found injured sailors, their chests still rising with the breath of life. Those who were unconscious, he killed quickly. Those who were awake he questioned, but none had seen what had become of the Stalker's prey, and they soon followed their comrades. Beyond the wreckage, three red specks circled on the horizon.

The sun rose higher in the sky as he continued along the coast. His heart sank as the amount of debris from the sunken ship grew thinner. He could hear the crunch of his Stalker's footsteps as they spread out behind him, but he ignored them. His movements became more frantic as the wreckage finally came to an end, and he looked out over empty gravel.

"Where are they?" he muttered into the wind.

Unable to turn back emptyhanded, Quinn marched on, his hopes fading with each footstep. In the distance, the red specks grew larger as the dragons approached. His stomach coiled into knots at the sight, and he picked up his pace, desperate for some sign, some hint Devon and his party had survived.

His eyes scanning the coastal cliffs, Quinn almost tripped over an indentation in the gravel shore. Stumbling, he cursed and righted himself. He was about to press on when he noticed the slight depressions of footsteps leading away from him. Looking down, he saw now the hollow beneath his feet matched the shape of a large man.

Devon.

A smile tugged at his cheeks as his eyes followed the footsteps to where they led up a break in the cliffs. So the big warrior had survived. If that was true, there was hope that Alana and her brother might also live. Glancing back, he found the eyes of his men watching him.

"They're alive," he said softly.

Before he could continue, a sharp *crack* came from above them, and a shadow fell across their company. Quinn caught a flash of red scales and the stench of rotting meat, before the dragon crashed down. The force of its impact sent gravel flying, and he quickly turned away as the hard stones pelted him.

The humans live?

Quinn shuddered as the dragon's words reverberated

through his mind. There was a madness to its voice, a terrible hate for the creatures standing before it. For centuries the Red Dragons had loathed mankind, slaughtering any who ventured into their territory. Only the Tsar's power kept the creatures in check.

Swallowing, Quinn looked up into the beast's golden eyes. The scarlet scales shone in the morning sun, the muscles beneath rippling with pent up power.

"It seems that way," he said, struggling to keep fear from his voice.

Where? The dragon growled, its great talons tearing up the gravel in emphasis of its question.

"We will find them," Quinn replied quickly. "You and your…offspring, should remain here."

No. The great head leaned closer, its breath like the bellows of a furnace. *We shall follow you, Stalker.*

Suppressing his anger, Quinn blew out his cheeks and nodded. "At a distance," he countered. "So you do not give away our position."

The golden eyes stared down at him for a long moment, as though appraising him. The slits of the beast's nostrils widened as it sucked in a breath.

Your magic is diminished, Stalker, the dragon replied finally. Turning, it moved away along the beach. *Call us when you fail.*

Quinn gritted his teeth as the beast spread its wings and leapt into the air. Dust swirled across the stones as the great wings beat down, hurling it into the sky. Fists clenched, he turned back to his men and saw the disdain in their eyes. Cursing inwardly, he straightened.

"What are you standing there for?" he snapped. "Get moving! Devon cannot be allowed to reach Fort Fall!"

29

Alana woke to the crackling of fire and the acrid smell of smoke. Wrinkling her nose, she lay still, eyes closed and mind racing as she tried to recall how she'd come to be there. The memories returned slowly, images swimming past her eyes before receding back into the fog of her past. She saw a garden, its leaves and flowers strangely aglow, the colours over-bright, then a ship at sea, its sails full and oars pounding the smooth waters. Drawing closer to the ship, Alana saw herself with Devon on the bow. Darkness fell, and her eyes slid closed, fading into sleep.

The image drifted away, then snapped back into sharp focus—only now the ship was ablaze, the mast burning, the flames creeping closer. And overhead…

With a scream, Alana jerked upright, her arms thrashing to escape the flames. Her eyes shot open, taking in the fire dancing in the darkness. She scrambled backwards, her hands digging like claws into the soft earth.

"Alana, stop!" Devon's voice called through the black.

Her eyes swept up and found the hammerman

standing nearby, his brow furrowed with concern. She shuddered, her heart still pounding. Slowly, she looked around, taking in the small blaze of the campfire and the stars overhead. A few yards away she saw the glint of water in the firelight.

"Devon?" she gasped, her throat feeling like she'd swallowed sand. "Where are we?"

Devon moved across to where she lay and lowered himself down onto a log beside the fire. "A day's walk from Northland."

Alana nodded. Placing a hand on her chest, she willed her heart to slow. A few more breaths and she finally started to calm. She fixed her eyes on Devon.

"Where's my brother?"

"I don't know," Devon replied, looking away. "The others...I'm not sure if they made it off the ship."

A lump lodged in Alana's throat, robbing her of words. She swallowed. "No," she croaked.

Something about his words seemed wrong. Sitting up on her knees, she closed her eyes and saw the dragon again, its scarlet scales flashing in the night sky.

A dragon!

The memory sent a shiver through her soul. Only the Tsar himself could have sent such a creature. Why was the man so determined to stop them from escaping? Her stomach chilled at the thought of what he would send against them next.

Gritting her teeth, she forced her fear aside and concentrated on the memory. She saw again the dragon flashing from the sky, felt the impact as Devon tackled her from the path of its flames. She was about to speak, to thank him for saving her, when the sight of Kellian, Tillie, and Braidon diving over the railing emerged from the fog.

"They made it off the ship," she said as relief flooded her.

"You're sure? All I can remember when I think back is the dragon," Devon replied. He lifted a hand to his forehead. "Do you know how I struck my head?"

"Nope," Alana replied straight-faced, deciding the hammerman didn't need anything else on her. "Probably something fell from the rigging. I had to drag you off the ship and halfway to shore."

He raised an eyebrow. "Really?" he murmured.

Alana laughed. "Anytime, big man," she shot back, then added, "Well, maybe lose some weight first."

Devon snorted. Unstrapping *kanker* from his shoulders, he placed the hammer beside him and stretched his legs out towards the fire. His amber eyes did not look at her, but she could see his hands were trembling.

"What do we do now?" she asked, changing the subject.

"Now?" he sighed. "Now we cross into Northland. We'll be safer there. If the others survived, they'll be heading in the same direction."

Gathering herself, Alana started to rise. Her legs ached as though she'd been running all day, but she managed to stumble to her feet. Devon stared up at her, open astonishment on his face, and then he started to laugh.

"Princess, I've been carrying you all day. I'm not going anywhere tonight unless you're returning the favour!"

Alana stood looking down at him, as though considering the idea. In truth, she was shocked at the pain radiating through her body, and, despite her need to find her brother, she knew she wouldn't make it far either. At least not without risk. After a moment, she sighed and sat back down.

"Alright, big man," she said with a grin. "You'd better be able keep up tomorrow, though."

Amusement danced in Devon's amber eyes. "Without your dead weight, princess, I could walk all day!"

Laughter bubbled up from Alana's chest, joined a moment later by Devon's. The sound whispered out into the darkness, light and filled with an unknown joy. When it finally died away, they sat in a companionable silence for a while.

"I'm glad I met you, you know," Devon said after a while, his eyes on the flames.

Alana smiled. "Me, too."

She lay back, staring up at the stars glistening in the night sky. They weren't half as bright in Ardath, where the lanterns dimmed your vision and masked the night's beauty. Here, though, their number seemed infinite, a million, million tiny pinpricks of light. Her eyes slowly drifted closed, her mind strangely at ease despite her brother's absence. With Devon at her side, she felt safe, as though no harm could come to her and no task was too great.

Tomorrow they would enter Northland and find her brother. Tonight, she could rest.

A soft curse from nearby pulled Alana back from the brink of sleep. Sitting up, she found Devon standing, pulling off his jerkin. His amber eyes saw her looking and she could have sworn his face reddened in the darkness.

"Sorry," he murmured, "it's the salt, itches like the devil. I'm going for a swim."

Alana raised an eyebrow as he stripped down to his undergarments. "You're going to freeze!" Beyond the heat of the fire, a frost was beginning to gather on the grass.

"Probably!" Devon muttered.

He moved towards the glimmering pool, muscles rippling along his shoulders and arms. The fire lit his skin, showing long white scars where swords and axes had cut him. She shivered, remembering the man he had once been, the tales told about his bloody conquest over the Trolans. The way the bards put it, Devon had won most of his battles single-handedly.

The splash of his body hitting the water sent waves sliding out across the icy pool. Alana shook her head as he surfaced and began to curse. Laughing softly to herself, she lay back down and closed her eyes.

But as she lay there, she now felt the itching Devon had described, the dry rubbing of her clothes against her skin, an irritation on her scalp. She gritted her teeth, trying to ignore it but knowing it was useless. Now he had pointed it out, the sensation had become unbearable. Swearing, she sat up and began to strip down.

"Don't look!" she shouted as she made her way to the pool in nothing but her underclothes.

"What sort of gentleman would I be if I looked?" Devon laughed, his eyes glittering as he watched her approach.

Alana snorted. "Rogue!" Gathering herself, she leapt out over his head.

Arms raised, she slid into the water like a knife through butter. The cold engulfed her, but after the heat by the fire, it was a refreshing change. Surfacing, she swam across the pool with smooth strokes of her arms. Growing up in the lake city of Ardath, she had always loved to swim. The pool was not wide, and it wasn't long before her hand struck the stone edge on the other side. She turned and swam back to where Devon waited.

"You swim well," he murmured.

Smiling, she flicked back her head, her long hair sending water spraying across the pool. "The best," she agreed with a grin.

Now they were away from the fire, Alana's eyes were adjusting to the moonlight. She saw the pool in which they floated was one of several. Their shining waters were clustered closely together, separated by thin lips of rock. The ground lifted gradually away from them, the pools forming a staircase in the rocks that lead up towards a distant line of trees.

"What is this place?" she whispered.

"An old iron sand mine," Devon replied. He moved alongside her, sending water rippling outwards. "The pools formed around where they dug the sand down to the bedrock."

She nodded, turning her eyes on him. "How did you know it was here?"

Devon smiled. "I know many things, princess." He floated closer to her. "I have travelled much of the Three Nations in my twenty-three years."

Inexplicably, Alana's heart beat faster as he neared. She swallowed, her throat suddenly dry. Her hands moved by memory, keeping her afloat, but as they swept out once more, they bumped into Devon's chest. Before they could move away, his hands caught hers by the wrist. He lifted her, and she realised he was tall enough to stand above the water.

A shudder swept through Alana as she looked into his amber eyes. They stared back at her with a burning intensity. Her lips parted, and she found herself leaning towards him, her own eyes fluttering closed.

Alana jumped as something small and sharp struck her foot. In the same instant, Devon cursed, jerking away from her. The movement sent water splashing across the pool and crashing over the rocky lip. They glanced at each other, and then down at their feet. In the feeble light of the moon, Alana could just make out the fish circling her legs.

She yelped again as one darted in and bit her heel. Her flesh crawled and, suppressing a scream, she struck out for the edge of the pool. In her mind she pictured the fish following her, their tiny mouths poised to strike, ready to strip the flesh from her bones, to tear her to pieces.

Reaching the end of the pool, Alana threw out an arm and grabbed at the rocky lip. As she hauled herself up, she twisted, looking around for Devon, terrified the fish had already taken him…

And found him still standing in the middle of the pool, a broad grin on his bearded face. His laughter boomed out through the night.

Alana stared at him a moment, mouth agape. Before she could question him, she felt another sharp twinge in her leg, and she scrambled quickly out of the water. Sitting on the stone lip, she glared across at Devon.

"What the *hell?*" she shrieked.

Devon's laughter trailed away as he shook his head. "They're called Doctor Fish," he called across to her. "They're harmless."

"They don't *feel* harmless!"

He chuckled again. "They're just eating the dead skin, princess. Don't be such a coward!"

Alana gritted her teeth and glared at the big man. "I am not a coward."

"Then come back in," he replied with a grin. "The water's warmer than out there!"

At his words, a cold wind swept across the pool, raising goosebumps on Alana's flesh. She shivered, eyeing the eerie waters, and then slowly lowered herself back in. The water was still cold, but she would brave the fish for a few minutes more, if only to prove Devon wrong.

He swam across to her, but her glare kept him at bay. She floated there a while, her breath ragged, her body tensed with expectation.

Her sudden movements had spooked the fish, and they took a while to return. When they did, Alana almost leapt straight back out of the pool at the first creature's bite. But Devon was watching her, and she was determined not to show her fear. Teeth clenched, she scowled at him, seeing the laughter in his eyes. She did not so much as flinch as the next fish struck.

Bit by bit, the fish grew bolder, until she had several of the tiny creatures nibbling at the soft flesh of her feet. The creatures continued up her legs, some biting hard and fast, others almost gently as they set about their meal.

Biting her lip, Alana fought to keep from crying out. Several of the fish had found the sensitive flesh on the bottoms of her feet. She felt laughter bubbling up from her chest as the sensation began to tickle. Eyes watering, she looked at Devon.

"This is *weird*," she gasped.

He nodded, face twitching, and she realised he was struggling to hold back his laughter. Snorting, Alana splashed a wave of water into his face. The suddenness of her attack sent him stumbling back. The slick rocks slipped under his feet and he vanished beneath the surface, reappearing an instant later, coughing and spluttering.

"Idiot," Alana said, grinning. The fish had scattered at her movement, and, swimming back to the edge, she hauled herself out. Quickly she used her clothes to towel herself down and then slipped back into them. She glanced back as Devon swam up. "You'll pay for that, you know."

Devon's eyes danced. "I look forward to it."

Straightening, Alana's stomach rumbled and her eyes turned to the distant trees. A smile crossed her face.

"Wait here," she said. She wandered away before he had a chance to respond.

30

The fire was burning low by the time Alana returned. Devon threw off the dregs of sleep and sat up. Picking up a stick, he quickly stirred the flames back to life. Adding wood, he surreptitiously studied Alana as she wandered up to the camp. Back in the pool, for half a moment it had seemed there was something between them. He recalled the thumping of blood in his ears as they drifted together, eyes locked, her skin beneath his fingers.

Alana wore the same smile she'd left with, only now she carried the carcass of a hare in one hand. Devon raised an eyebrow in question as she tossed it down in front of him.

"I caught it, so you get to cook," she said with a grin.

Unable to keep the admiration from his face, Devon wordlessly picked up the pitiful creature. Away in the darkness, crickets chirped as Alana took a seat nearby. Taking a hunting knife from his belt, he set about skinning it.

"How did you manage to kill it?" he asked as he worked.

"We used to hunt them in the fields around the lake when I was younger," she said by way of an answer. When

Devon only shook his head, she added. "I hit it with a stone."

"Impressive," he murmured. His stomach rumbled and Alana laughed. "I never was much of a woodsman," Devon admitted.

"Really?" Her grey eyes studied him closely. "You always seem so…capable."

Devon smiled despite himself. "I'm capable in one thing only, Alana," he murmured, touching the haft of *kanker.*

The conversation trailed off, and Devon busied himself with his task. The skin removed, he gutted the little hare, then quickly set up a spit from a few thicker pieces of wood. Placing the spit with carcass attached over the fire, he stoked the flames.

"Will it take long?" Alana asked, her eyes aglow with hunger.

"Long enough," Devon said, sitting back. He looked across at her, recalling her lithe frame as she dove over him into the pool. "Alana," he said suddenly, "what will you do if Braidon has been taken?"

She sat in silence for a long while, staring into the flames. When she finally answered, her voice was soft, distant. "I'll go back and find him."

"They'll kill you." Devon said the words without judgement.

Alana nodded. "Probably."

Devon shivered as he watched her. His earlier thoughts had been right; there was no give in the young woman sitting before him.

To his surprise, he found himself speaking. "You wouldn't be alone." She looked up at that, her grey eyes wide, and he went on. "I'll walk beside you."

Alana stared across at him, and for a second Devon

thought he glimpsed tears in her eyes. She quickly looked away. "You don't have to do that."

"I know," Devon chuckled, thinking back to the fiery woman he'd met on the streets of Ardath. "Truth is, my life before was empty. I had nothing to live for, no purpose. I lost myself back in the war, and I've been trying to find my way ever since."

"And my destroying your life changed that?"

Devon grinned. "In a way," he replied. "Maybe it was Kellian's words, or that woman Tillie's, or maybe just being around you and your brother, but I feel like my old self again. Thank you for that."

"You're a strange man, Devon," Alana said. "You thank me for destroying your life, but not for saving it!"

Laughter roared up from Devon's chest. "Ha! I figured you owed me that one!"

"I see!" A smile danced on Alana's face. She edged closer, her eyes on the rabbit. Devon quickly reached out and turned it before it could burn. "How much longer, you think?" she asked.

"Hungry critter, aren't you?" Devon took up his dagger and sliced a cut down the rabbit. The meat beneath was beginning to darken. "Soon, princess," he teased.

She punched him in the arm. "Why do you keep calling me that?"

Devon sat back and looked at her. "I have trouble remembering people's names sometimes," he admitted.

"So you gave me the nickname princess?" she asked. "Do you think I'm too weak to look after myself?"

Laughing, Devon shook his head. "The opposite," he replied. "You're the fiercest woman I've ever met."

"So why?"

Devon grinned. "Because of the fire in your eyes when I say it."

She hit him again, but this time Devon reached out and caught her by the wrist before she could retreat. Their eyes met, and she did not pull away. He leaned towards her, his heart pounding in his ears.

"It's burning!" Alana said suddenly, jumping up and snatching the hare from the flames.

Cursing inwardly, Devon helped her set it down. Fat bubbled from the roasting meat, and in a few places the flesh had blackened.

"You aren't much of a cook, either, you know?" Alana said, her eyes dancing.

Devon muttered something choice under his breath. Ignoring her, he took up his knife and went to work on the hare. It was difficult with the meat still scorching hot, but from the look in Alana's eyes, she wasn't going to wait until it cooled.

Silently he cut a slice of meat and offered it to Alana on the blade. She raised an eyebrow, and he grinned at her.

"Ladies first," Devon said.

Alana's lips twitched as she took the morsel from his knife. "Such a gentleman," she said, before sinking her teeth into the chunk of hot meat.

A dribble of juice ran down her chin as she chewed, and Devon chuckled. "I take it back," he said. "Kellian is more of a lady than you!"

"No one's perfect." Alana winked, still chewing on her mouthful.

A comfortable silence fell across the campfire as they ate. Cutting a slice for himself, Devon sat back, savouring the rich flavour of the fresh meat. It could have used a bit of seasoning, but Kellian was the innkeeper and cook. They'd be lucky if Devon managed not to poison them with the skinny hare.

"Why did you leave the army?" Alana asked into the silence.

Devon froze mid-bite. He swallowed slowly and turned to look at her, finding her grey eyes on his hammer. He glanced down at *kanker*, its steel head glistening in the firelight. His thoughts drifted, returning to the dark days in Trola. He shuddered.

"I didn't like what I'd become," he murmured.

"A soldier?"

"A killer," he replied, a shadow passing across his soul. Reaching down, he hefted *kanker.* "A murderer. An ender of life."

"You fought to protect us from the Trolan invaders," Alana replied, though when he looked at her he could see the doubt in her eyes.

"That's how it began," Devon murmured, his mind distant, his thoughts on a place far away, a past long ago. "Not how it ended."

"You mean the conquest?" she pressed.

Devon's fist tightened around *kanker.* "It was no conquest. It was a slaughter."

Alana fell silent, her eyes on the fire. "It ended the war."

"It did," Devon replied. "Because there was no one left to threaten the Tsar."

"Or our people," Alana added.

Silence fell again, but Devon knew it was not an end to Alana's questions. He squeezed his eyes closed, waiting for it to come, for the question to be asked.

"Why did you give up your hammer?" Alana whispered. "You had the Tsar's favour, the love of the people. You could have been rich."

Devon sucked in a breath, gathering his courage. Only Kellian knew the truth, knew of things he'd done when the bloodlust was on him. "Because I liked it," he whispered. He saw her eyes come up, the question on her lips, and continued before she could speak. "Because I enjoyed it. I lived for the thrill of battle, for the destruction and the slaughter, for the sight of life fading from an enemy's eyes."

"You have the warrior's spirit—" Alana began, but he cut her off.

"I killed all who came before me. Men, yes. Women, too. Old men and boys barely out of childhood. It didn't matter who they were, only that they stood in my way." He paused. "I killed a child once. He ran at me with a spear, and I didn't even think." Reaching down, he lifted *kanker* and held it up before the firelight. "My ancestors wielded this hammer to defend the innocent, to protect the Three Nations from darkness. Now it's stained by my evil. If my ancestors could see me now, they would spit at my feet."

Devon drew in a great, shuddering breath, and let the hammer fall. It struck the ground with a thud. Silence fell, strained and awful, but he kept his eyes fixed to the ground, terrified to look up and see the judgement on Alana's face. But as time stretched out, he knew he could hide from his past no longer. Clenching his jaw, he forced himself to look at her.

She stared back, lips parted, her grey eyes sad. For a moment it seemed she would speak, then her mouth closed again, her jaw tightening. She bit her lip and looked away.

Shame swelled in Devon's chest as he returned his gaze to the fire. He wanted to defend himself, to explain how it had been, how when the bloodlust took him he had no control. But the words would not come. In his heart, he knew what he'd done could never be forgiven. Never mind that he'd been following orders, that the Tsar had commanded all who stood against them be swept away.

Darkness descended on the campsite as the fire burned down. Devon's stomach was warm now, filled with the meal of half-burnt hare, but his spirit was low. Across from him, Alana sat staring off into the distance, refusing to meet his gaze.

Silently, Devon settled himself down on the ground. His body was exhausted, refreshed by the swim, but aching from the long day's march. He needed to sleep, but even as he closed his eyes, he knew it would not come. Letting out a sigh, he settled in for a long, cold night.

31

Alana walked across the open ground in silence, her heart heavy, her thoughts far away, dreaming of a war she could hardly remember. How many men and women had marched with Devon into the mountains of Trola? How many others had stained their hands with the blood of innocents? Had they all succumbed to the same bloodlust as Devon?

Staring at his broad back now, she realised it didn't matter. A thousand others could have admitted to the same foul deeds as the hammerman and it wouldn't change things for her. Whatever those other soldiers had done, in the past few days she had come to see Devon as a man above others, a warrior beyond repute. From the moment he had charged the *Arbor*, to the day he'd faced the demon and won, he'd become a hero in her eyes.

She heard again his words, the terrible admission that had brought her image of him crumbling down, and suppressed a moan. His past should not have mattered, not after everything he'd done to protect her and her brother; yet it did.

Her eyes dropped to the ground as Devon checked their backtrail, and a pang of guilt touched her. She could sense the hammerman's pain. Last night in the pool, for the briefest of moments, she had felt something growing between them, something she hadn't dared to put into words. A warmth in her chest, a smile that came to her lips when she was in his presence.

That feeling had died like flames in the rain. The warmth was gone, her face fixed in a frown, her eyes set on the distant fortress.

"That's not good."

Alana looked up as Devon spoke, his first words since the night before. His eyes were still studying their backtrail. Alana glanced around and swore as she saw the men emerging from the distant woods. Garbed all in black, there was no mistaking the band of Stalkers. She counted them silently as they moved into the open, settling finally on sixteen.

"They're a league off," she said, swinging back to Devon.

"Quinn must have taken a ship and followed us," he muttered, looking from the Stalkers to Fort Fall. "They move fast, even on foot. We'll be hard pressed to outrun them."

"We'd better get moving then," Alana replied, pushing her way past him.

She studied the fortress looming in the distance. The grey walls towered above the ocean cliffs. Sitting astride the narrow patch of land known as The Gap, it marked the border between the northern and southern continents. But with its garrison disbanded and its gates long since rotted away, the ancient fortress would offer them little protection from the Stalkers.

They raced on through the morning, the cold wind blowing harder as the land narrowed. She glimpsed the sea to their west now, its blue waters a mirror of those to their east. Storm clouds were forming in the distance, and she prayed they would come soon. Rain would wash away their tracks, giving them a chance to lose Quinn and his men in the lands beyond the fortress.

As they drew closer to Fort Fall, the last of the vegetation vanished, the earth becoming barren beneath their feet. The ground turned to a soft red sand, sinking beneath each footstep and slowing their progress. Narrow gorges crisscrossed the wasteland, barring their path in places. Devon took the lead once more, guiding them through the maze of gullies.

They ran on, boots slipping in the soft sand, eyes wary for loose rocks. Every few minutes, Alana cast a glance over her shoulder, checking on their pursuers' progress. Despite their speed, Quinn and his men kept pace with them, then, as the day dragged on, began to close the gap.

Muscles burning, Alana gritted her teeth and forced herself on. Exhaustion weighed on her shoulders. The loose sand dragged at her feet, draining her strength with each laboured step. Time slipped by, her strides growing shorter. Ahead, the towering walls and spires of Fort Fall seemed no closer.

Bit by bit, they fought their way across the northern desert of Lonia.

Dusk found them nearing the walls, legs weary and backs bowed by the weight of their exhaustion. Walking with her head down, Alana almost slammed into Devon's back as he staggered to a stop. Blinking in the red light, she looked around, surprised to find the empty arch of the gates just a few dozen yards away. Beneath the granite blocks of the wall, the shadows of the gate tunnel beckoned.

She frowned at Devon. He stood over her, his eyes fixed in the direction from which they had come.

"What are you doing?" she snapped, exhaustion making her impatient. "The gates are right there!"

He nodded. "Yes," he murmured. "Almost there."

Devon turned and moved across the open ground towards the tunnel. After a moment, she followed him, still wondering why he had stopped. Then the shadow of the wall fell over them, and she looked up at the massive structure. They were approaching the southern wall of the fortress, which only stood fifty feet high and was attached to the inner citadel. Towers rose to the east and west, their marble ramparts looking out over sheer cliffs that dropped down into the hungry oceans.

A cold breeze blew across Alana's neck as she found herself at the mouth of the tunnel. Darkness opened out before her, beckoning. She shivered as something moved in the gloom, before her eyes adjusted and she realised it was only Devon. A frown formed on her lips as she saw he had drawn *kanker* from its sheath.

"What are you doing?" she whispered, glancing behind her. Beyond the gates, the ground lifted slightly, cutting off her view of the Stalkers, but they couldn't be far now.

"Go, Alana," he said quietly.

"What are you talking about?"

"We'll never outrun them," he replied. "Not unless I slow them down."

"No!" Alana's heart lurched in her chest as she stepped towards him. "Devon…you don't have to do this."

"I do," he whispered, still not meeting her eyes.

A lump lodged in Alana's throat as she looked at him. The warmth came flooding back, wrapping her chest in tendrils of heat. Silently, she cursed herself a fool for judging him, for thinking less of the man who'd saved her from a demon. Tears welled in her eyes as she shook her head, but the words would not come.

Swallowing, Alana stepped forward and placed a hand on his shoulder. "Please don't do this," she croaked.

Devon didn't move, but his eyes flickered down at her. Grief radiated from their amber depths, mingling with the shame and guilt written on his bearded face. A smile touched his lips as their eyes met. Transferring his hammer to his left hand, he reached out and wiped a tear from Alana's cheek.

"Go, princess," he murmured. "I'll hold them as long as I can."

Alana nodded, choking on a grief all her own. Blinking back tears, she stumbled past him, and onwards into the darkness.

32

Devon let out a long breath as the crunch of Alana's footsteps faded into silence. His heart ached with the parting, but for one reason or another, he knew he had made the right decision. Together, they would never have escaped Quinn and his men. There were too many of them to fight and win, no matter their strength or courage. But here beneath the wall, he might delay them long enough for Alana to escape.

Where he stood, the tunnel curved inwards to its narrowest point, the design intended to funnel attackers onto the defenders' spears. It was still three-men wide, but with his hammer in hand, Devon was confident he could prevent the Stalkers from encircling him. With luck, they would pay a heavy toll to gain entry to the fortress.

His heart twitched as his thoughts turned to the night before, and he saw again the accusation in Alana's eyes. She'd been disgusted by his admission, but he could hardly blame her—he'd felt the same self-loathing every day for the past five years.

But this was his chance at redemption. Closing his eyes, he pictured the beast inside him, the awful bear chained at his core. The creature represented everything he hated about himself—all his rage and bloodlust tangled into one awful monster. For half a decade he had kept it shackled, hiding it from the light. He would need it now, though, if he was to stand any chance of holding back the tide of dark-cloaked warriors.

It wasn't long before the first man appeared over the lip of the hill leading up to the fortress. The others quickly followed, their long shadows stretching out across the plain towards him. He counted them as they approached, though he already knew their number.

Sixteen.

Each was heavily armoured, their torsos covered by glimmering chainmail, with iron greaves and gauntlets to protect their arms and legs. They glittered prettily in the fading light and Devon couldn't help but grin. They would kill him in the end, but their armour would not protect them from *kanker.* The warhammer had been created to kill men in armour. A sense of harmony settled on his soul as he gripped the weapon tighter.

Inside, the beast growled, tasting freedom.

The Stalkers slowed as they approached the tunnel, their hands dropping to their sword-hilts as they saw the man waiting for them. Devon's grin faded as he recognised their leader—Quinn. The man's brown eyes swept over him, studying the empty tunnel before returning to Devon. A smile appeared on the lieutenant's face as he drew to a stop.

"All alone, Devon?" His voice echoed through the shadows.

"I thought I'd stay behind to greet you and your

friends," Devon replied gruffly. He brought *kanker* up, pointing it at the man's chest.

Quinn's soft laughter echoed through the tunnel. "Come now, Devon," he said finally. "Do you really want to die here?"

Devon rolled his shoulders, his neck cracking loudly in the silence that followed. "Seems as good a place as any."

Anger replaced mirth on the lieutenant's face. "So be it."

The man's arm snapped out. A great roaring came from beyond the tunnel, and a rush of air struck the lieutenant, sending his cloak whirling about his body. Sand lifted from the ground to join the conflagration. It hovered there only an instant, and then came rushing down the tunnel towards Devon.

He met it with a roar, swinging his hammer in defiance. The ancient weapon struck the whirling gusts and a sharp hiss whispered through the tunnel. As quickly as they'd appeared, the winds died away, sucked into the shining head of *kanker*.

In the mouth of the tunnel, Quinn swayed on his feet for a second, arm still outstretched, teeth bared.

Devon's laughter boomed in the darkness. "You always were a coward, Quinn," he said, taking a step towards the waiting Stalkers. "No wonder they passed you over for promotion so many times."

"How dare you?" the Magicker growled.

"I have *earned* the right to dare, coward," Devon spat. "While you cower behind your magic, I meet my enemies face to face, man to man. You think yourself a warrior? Prove it!"

He watched as the lines on Quinn's face tightened, saw the uncertainty in his former comrade's eyes as he glanced at his men. Baring his teeth, Quinn drew his sabre and started towards Devon.

"Very well," he said quietly. There was no trace of fear in his voice now. "Come then, Devon. Let us discover once and for all who's the better man."

His sabre cut the air as he moved forward, his boots shifting carefully on the packed sand beneath the wall. Devon grinned in response, widening his stance and hefting *kanker.* He stood almost a head over the Stalker, and the long haft of his hammer gave him more reach than the man's sabre. Still, despite his mocking words, he had seen Quinn fight during the war. The man was a deadly swordsman.

"Let's see if the legend bleeds," Quinn hissed.

He darted in, sabre flashing for Devon's face. Standing his ground, Devon raised *kanker* to block the blow. The clash of steel rang loudly in the passageway. Devon shivered as the beast in his soul shook free its bonds and roared. Unleashing a roar of his own, Devon charged, his hammer swinging out at his opponent's chest.

Quinn danced back, his feet moving lightly to carry him clear. Devon gave chase, seeking to close the gap, but the sabre danced out once more, almost impaling him on its silver tip. His feet sliding on the uneven ground, Devon was forced to retreat as Quinn went on the offensive, his blade slashing out again and again.

Teeth clenched, Devon fended off each blow, studying his opponent's actions, waiting for the right moment to counter. But Quinn moved in perfect balance, his feet shifting in constant movement, his blade never still.

Devon was breathing heavily when they finally separated. Eyes fixed on Quinn, he sucked in a great gulp of air, struggling against his exhaustion. Across from him, the Stalker chuckled, rolling his head on his shoulders.

"Need a break, Devon?" he asked.

Devon lifted *kanker* and charged again, a battle cry on his lips. Sparks flew as Quinn's sabre deflected the blow sideways. Then Quinn surged forwards, his blade lancing out. Devon swayed to the side, unable to bring *kanker* up in time to deflect the attack. Pain rippled through his arm as the sword sliced his skin.

Kicking out, Devon's boot caught Quinn in the chest and sent the smaller man staggering back. Devon chased after him, but the lieutenant recovered quickly, his blade hissing out, almost catching the hammerman mid-charge.

Leaping sideways, Devon narrowed his eyes, studying his former comrade as they circled one another. Blood dripped down his left arm, but a quick glance told him the wound wasn't deep. Quinn closed on him, his eyes hard, sabre poised at the ready. A slight sheen of sweat showed on his forehead, but otherwise the lieutenant looked as fresh as when the fight began.

Quinn came at him in a rush now, his sabre hissing out, fast as lightning, and it was all Devon could do to catch the blows on *kanker's* shining head. He was forced back a step, then another. Around him the walls of the tunnel widened. His eyes flickered to the other Stalkers and he saw several of them beginning to edge forwards.

Sucking in a breath, Devon straightened. He brought up his hammer to deflect another blow, and then struck out at the lieutenant's head. Quinn ducked, but the riposte halted his momentum. Muscles straining, Devon surged forward, forcing his opponent to retreat. Anger fed strength to his weary limbs. He was Devon, hero of Plorsea, slayer of demons. He would not be defeated by a mere mortal.

Laughter echoed through the tunnel as Devon swung the ancient hammer. A madness took him then. Blood pounded in his ears, drowning out the clash of steel and gasping of breath, until there was only the roar of his inner beast. He grinned as he saw the change come over Quinn's face. With each attack, his confidence seemed to shrivel. Fear shone in the man's eyes as he was forced back, each swing of Devon's hammer drawing closer to finding its mark.

Then the Stalker slipped, his feet tripping over a crack in the earth, and he went down. Screaming his triumph, Devon lifted *kanker,* ready to crush the man's skull with one final blow.

Before it could land, a sharp pain tore through Devon's shoulder, sending him reeling backwards. He gasped, clutching the hammer to his side as the strength fled his arm. Swaying, he glanced at his shoulder and saw the crossbow bolt sticking from his flesh. He turned and found the archer standing amidst the other Stalkers. The *click-clack* as he rewound his crossbow echoed loudly in the tunnel.

Rage swept through Devon as he turned his gaze on Quinn. The lieutenant had recovered and was standing nearby, a grim smile on his face.

"Coward," Devon hissed.

Quinn's face twitched, the smile faltering for half a second before falling back into place. "This is war, Devon. There is no honour in death."

"No," Devon said. Gathering his courage, he straightened, switching *kanker* to his left hand. "So come and die."

Quinn's laughter chased him down the tunnel. "Such bravery." He shook his head. "Your skills are wasted here, Devon. A shame your legend must end this way, in disgrace and death."

Devon bared his teeth but said nothing. Agony radiated from his shoulder, and it took all his willpower not to give voice to the pain. He could feel the wound pulsing, his strength fleeing with every ounce of blood trickling down his side. Beyond Quinn, the crossbowman raised his weapon again, but the lieutenant waved him down.

"No," Quinn whispered, "he's mine."

Despite the pain, Devon found himself smiling. He licked his lips, his eyes flickering to the other Stalkers, then back to Quinn. Smiling, the man darted forward. Devon growled and tried to meet the man's charge, but his movements were sluggish now. He stumbled, and Quinn slipped past, his sabre flashing out.

A scream tore from Devon as the sabre slashed through his hamstring. His legs gave way and he found himself suddenly on his knees. *Kanker* slipped from his hand, pain stealing away the last of his strength. Swaying, he looked up at Quinn. Silently, the lieutenant placed his blade to Devon's neck.

"Any last words, Devon?"

33

Alana fled through the shadows of the citadel, blood pounding, breath coming in ragged gasps. From behind her she could hear the ring of steel as blades met, and knew Devon still stood. Her heart screamed for her to turn back, but she ran on, driven by her friend's final command. Her eyes swept the gloom, finding a corridor to her right. She took it, not knowing where it led, only that she had to keep moving.

The gate tunnel had led into the unlit hallways of Fort Fall's citadel. Without a torch to light the way, she'd been forced to stumble blindly through the endless courtyards and receiving rooms, finding her way by instinct and guesswork. But now the last glow of sunlight had dropped behind the outer walls, and Alana feared she would never find her way to the northern battlements.

Panic rising, she forced herself to breathe, to stop and think. Standing alone in the darkness, she closed her eyes, struggling to overcome the terror rising in her chest. How long could Devon hold the men at the gates? How long did she have before they came stalking through the corridors, hunting her with torches, their swords poised to strike her down?

She cursed loudly, forcing the thoughts from her mind. Swinging around, she squinted through the gloom. She stood at another fork in the corridor. Her eyes flickered from left to right, struggling to choose which way to take. Then she frowned, ice forming in her chest as something flickered in the left corridor. The movement came again, a sudden glow lighting the shadows, coming closer.

As quietly as she could, Alana drew her sabre and started towards the light. If the Stalkers were ahead of her, there would be no escaping them now, but at least she could take a few with her. Creeping forward, she held her blade low, ready to slam it into the chest of the first man she saw.

The light at the end of the corridor grew brighter as she approached the corner. She could hear the soft padding of footsteps, the crackling of the torch, the whisper of voices, and knew her hunters were just out of sight. Taking a breath, she gathered herself, and sprang…

"Alana!"

Alana froze, sabre poised to strike, as her brother's voice echoed through the corridors. He stood standing in the middle of the hallway, torch in one hand, knife in the other. Eyes wide, he stared back at her, his mouth agape.

With a half-choked cry, Alana dropped her blade and threw herself at Braidon. He yelped as she swept him off his feet, and then he was hugging her back, his thin arms tight around her waist, his head buried in her shoulder.

"I thought I'd lost you!" she managed at last, placing him back down. Holding him at arm's length, she looked down at him, checking him for injuries. "Are you okay?"

He nodded, though by the light of the torch she could see he was pale, his eyes ringed by shadows. "We're okay."

For the first time, Alana noticed Kellian standing a few steps further along the corridor. He looked as worn out as she felt, his clothes torn, his face streaked with dirt. He held a hunting knife in one hand, a dagger in the other.

"Devon?" Kellian asked as he moved forward.

Alana swallowed. "At the gates," she whispered. "Holding off the Stalkers. Where's Tillie?"

"Disappeared when we got here. Don't know where she went. How many does Devon face?" Kellian asked.

"Sixteen, including Quinn."

Kellian nodded. "Take your brother."

"What about you?"

A smile spread across the innkeeper's face as he drew a second dagger from his shirt. "I never did like Quinn." At that, he stepped past Alana, heading in the direction from which she'd come.

Alana stared after him for a moment, and then dropped to her knees beside Braidon. "Go find Tillie," she whispered, squeezing his shoulder. "I'll see you soon."

Braidon's eyes flashed as he shook his head. "I'm not going anywhere, sis," he growled. Before she could argue, he slid past her and started after Kellian.

Alana opened her mouth and closed it again, her throat suddenly dry. For a moment, she wanted to scream and rage, but the words died on her lips as she watched Braidon walk away into the darkness. Tears welled in her eyes, her heart swelling with pride. Wordlessly, she followed the bobbing light of her brother's torch.

Quinn grinned as the giant warrior closed his eyes. Hamstrung and on his knees, there was nowhere the man could go, and he knew it. Heart hammering in his chest, Quinn lifted his sabre, preparing to deliver the final blow, and put an end to the man's legend.

Before the blow could fall, he glimpsed a flicker of light from the corner of his eye. Something flashed from the shadows, catching the hilt of his sabre and tearing it from his grasp. The clang of steel on rock echoed around him as he gasped, staring dumbly at his fallen blade.

At his feet, Devon's amber eyes snapped open, alighting on Quinn's fallen weapon. A throwing knife lay alongside it. With a roar, the giant warrior threw himself at the blade. But Quinn was on his feet and he dove for the weapon, reaching it mere moments before his foe. Sweeping it up, he spun, and caught the glint of another blade as it sped from the shadows. The sabre swept up, and the knife clattered harmlessly to the ground.

Kellian came racing from the darkness, a knife in each hand, and hurled himself at Quinn. Still reeling from the sudden attack, Quinn was forced back, his sabre flashing out to deflect the two shorter blades. Gritting his teeth, he absorbed the fury of the man's attack, and gathered himself to strike back.

Then Alana was there, her blade flashing out, and cursing, Quinn was forced back another step. Blood pounded in his ears as he retreated, the sudden rush of fear taking hold of his heart.

"What are you waiting for?" he screamed to his men. "Help me!"

The cries of his Stalkers as they charged gave him strength, and he straightened, fending off a blow from Alana and replying with a riposte that almost speared the old innkeeper through the chest. A second later, his men were alongside him. The weight of their numbers forced the two backwards to where the tunnel narrowed and Devon still sat crouched on one knee.

"Stop!" Quinn shouted, waving his men to stand back. In front of him, Alana and Kellian paused, their eyes hesitant, weapons still raised. Lowering his sabre, Quinn took a step forward. "There's no need for this, Alana. Come with me, and I will let your friends live."

She was tempted, he saw it in her grey eyes, but beside her Kellian only sneered. "Don't listen to him, Alana, the man's a snake if ever I saw one."

Behind them, Devon groaned, and drew slowly to his feet. With *kanker* clutched in one hand, he staggered forward to join them. "He's right, Alana. Don't give up your life for us."

Alana swallowed, looking from the men to Quinn. Sensing she was wavering, he spread his arms, sabre held flat. "There are no other options, Alana," he said. Movement came from the tunnel behind them. Looking up, Quinn saw Braidon approaching. "Ah, your brother survived as well." He turned back to Alana. "I give you my word, he will not be harmed, but you must give yourselves up."

For a moment, it seemed she would agree. Her eyes flickered back to her brother, and her head bowed. The blade quivered in her hand. He licked his lips and remained silent, allowing the weight of doubt to work its way into her mind.

"No." Quinn's head whipped up as Braidon spoke from behind the others. He walked slowly forward, blue eyes hard, fists clenched, teeth bared. "Why don't *you* give up, Quinn, and I'll promise not to kill you," he growled.

Quinn allowed himself a smile. "Young Braidon, your power may be great, but do not think an untrained Magicker can match me!" He pointed at the boy to emphasis his words.

Delving down into his consciousness, he sought out his magic, determined to smash aside the boy's resistance. He fell away into the darkness, his mind probing out, searching for the flicker of blue. It appeared as a flash of light, brilliant and shining, but as he approached, his spirit sank. His stomach clenched as he looked on the tiny pool of magic, all that remained of his power now. The long chase and the brief fight with Devon had used up what little he had left.

"Give up, boy. Don't make me hurt you," he bluffed.

A smile twitched on Braidon's face. He pointed at Quinn's chest. "No."

With a boom and a flash of blue, lightning appeared in the palm of the boy's hand. Screaming, he threw out his arm. Blue fire arced towards the Stalkers, and struck their feet with a crash of thunder.

34

Alana screamed as lightning went crackling over her head and struck the feet of the Stalkers. Light flashed, blinding her, and she staggered back, one hand raised to shield her eyes. Her ears rang with the crash of thunder. Forcing open her eyes, she watched as the Stalkers fell back, panic spreading through their ranks.

The stench of burning filled the air as blue light drove the shadows from the tunnel. Movement came from alongside her as Braidon strode forward, eyes aglow, hands still outstretched as he hurled his power at their hunters. Beside her, Devon and Kellian stood frozen, locked in the grip of her brother's power.

Alana shivered as she watched Braidon advancing on the Stalkers. Lightning flashed from his hands, sizzling through their ranks, sending the men reeling. Several turned and fled, their screams like whispers before the boom of thunder. Others threw themselves to the ground, desperate to avoid the awful power flashing around them.

As Alana watched, a bolt struck one of the Stalkers in

the back, igniting a booming *crash.* She blinked, staring as the man continued his flight from the tunnel. Another was hit, his clothes turning black, but he did not go down. The roar and smell of burning was all around, but now Alana realised not a single Stalker had fallen.

Her eyes flickered to her brother as the truth came to her.

It's an illusion!

Beyond her brother, a few of the Stalkers were coming to the same realisation. They hovered near the walls of the tunnel, eyes still wary, but growing in confidence with each crash of thunder. In the centre of the tunnel, Quinn dragged himself to his feet. Knowledge shined in his brown eyes as he looked around. He pointed at Braidon and screamed an order. A man beside him straightened, lifting a crossbow to his shoulder.

"No!" Alana screamed. She started forward, even as the crossbow *twanged.*

Time seemed to slow as she moved towards her brother. She watched as the bolt sliced across the open space, its steel tip flashing with the glow of the illusory lightning. Stretching out a hand, she strained to throw herself between Braidon and the archer. But she was too far away.

The bolt shrieked home, burying itself in the soft flesh of her brother's stomach.

In an instant, the lightning vanished. The light flickered and died, plunging the tunnel back into shadow. Silence fell around them, absolute and terrible. In the gloom, she watched her brother fall, heard his low moan as he collapsed, the thud as his body struck the ground.

Alana staggered to a stop, a sob tearing up from deep inside her. Grief washed over her, threatening to tear her heart to pieces. But, as her eyes swept up and saw Quinn watching her, rage rose to drown her sorrow and clenching her sabre tightly, she advanced on the Stalker.

"Alana..." he whispered as she approached.

The hiss of her blade answered him. Steel clashed as he blocked the blow and retreated. Teeth bared, Alana lashed out with her blade again, rage driving her on. This time Quinn moved too slowly, a gash appearing on his arm as her sabre sliced beneath his guard. He cried out, falling back, but there was no escaping her fury.

"Alana!" he screamed, fear showing in his eyes.

"*How do you know my name?*" Alana shrieked back, the crash of steel ringing in her ears.

Around them the Stalkers began to regather. They edged closer, coming at her from all sides. She paid them no attention; she had eyes only for Quinn now. He had given the order, had seen her brother cut down.

Quinn did not answer her. He stumbled back, but her sabre caught him again, opening a cut across his chest. Cursing, he swung out with his blade. Alana threw herself back, almost taken by surprise. Space opened between them, and Quinn retreated another step to widen the gap.

"How do I know your name?" he hissed, wheezing for breath. "I know everything there is to know about you, Alana! Where you come from, who you are. Can you say the same thing about yourself?"

Alana paused as his words struck home. She frowned, her thoughts drifting backwards in time, through their long flight across the Three Nations, to the day she had woken beside the stepwell. Her frown deepened as she sought the memories beyond that day, but was met by a dense fog, a sudden darkness. Blood pounded in her ears as she shook her head.

"What have you done to me?" she gasped.

"What have you done to yourself?" Quinn shot back.

Alana's rage came rushing back as she looked at him. "Give me back my memories!" she screamed, hurling herself forward.

This time Quinn met her blade to blade, blow for blow. The words died away as they attacked one another, swords flashing. Death circled them like a vulture overhead; one slip, one mistake, and it would find them with the icy tip of a sword. Alana gasped as Quinn's blade sliced her forehead, but she countered with a riposte that came within a feather's breadth of his throat.

"Stop this, Alana!" Quinn attacked again, forcing her to retreat. "I only want to help you!"

"I don't know you!" Alana fought back, stabbing out for his groin.

But Alana's strength was fading now, her movements slowing, and Quinn dodged her attack easily. She still had not recovered from the long swim from the burning ship, or the flight across the wasteland. Sabre flashing, Quinn pressed the advantage.

Behind her, Alana heard the ring of steel as the other Stalkers engaged with Devon and Kellian, but, at a wave from Quinn, none came near her.

"She's mine," he said, his voice low.

Alana's eyes narrowed as rage fed strength to her tiring limbs. Gripping her sabre in two hands, she attacked with renewed fury. But he blocked each blow easily now, retreating slowly down the tunnel, a sad smile on his face. Screaming, Alana hurled herself at him.

"Fight back!"

Her arms aching from the shock of connecting blades, Alana leapt sideways, seeking to take him by surprise. Her blade licked out, lancing for his ribs, but he twisted at the last moment and she cut only empty air. His sabre slashed down with sudden violence, connecting with hers near the hilt. The shock of its impact drove the weapon from her hands.

Alana gasped, but recovering quickly, she kicked out. The blow caught Quinn in the chest and sent him wheeling backwards. Diving for her sabre, Alana swept it up and spun in time to deflect a blow from Quinn. Sparks leapt as their blades met.

Behind her, she glimpsed Devon and Kellian staggering back. Her eyes widened as she saw Devon had her brother slung over one shoulder. A sudden hope surged in her chest. Did her brother live? But a dozen Stalkers still stood, and, alone, Kellian could not hold them off. The weight of their numbers was forcing him back to where the tunnel opened out.

Quinn's gasped as she swung on him and renewed her assault. Filled with righteous fury, her sabre became a blur, drawing closer and closer to his flesh. A dagger appeared in his other hand as he fought desperately to defend himself.

But her strength did not last, her legs beginning to shake, and she sensed the end was growing close. Pain flared in her arm as his blade caught her, opening a shallow cut. Hope fading, she staggered back a step.

"Give up, Alana," Quinn murmured. "You're better than this."

"Never," she grated.

She renewed her attack, but he parried her easily and riposted, forcing her back. Panting, she dropped her sabre arm to her side, the last of her hope fading away. "Just kill me!" she spat, holding back tears. "I won't let you take me back!" The words bubbled up from her chest.

Quinn watched her, his eyes sad. "You know I must."

Alana shook her head, though somehow, she knew he spoke the truth. Lifting her blade, she launched a last, desperate attack. His sabre flashed out, quick as a viper, and smashed the blade from her hands. It struck the stones with a crash of steel. A shiver ran through Alana as she looked up and found him standing over her.

"Kill me," she repeated, begging now.

Quinn shook his head. "I'm sorry."

Before Alana could move, his arm flashed out, the hilt of his sword descending on her head. A sharp *crack* echoed in her ears, followed by a flash of red.

Then everything went black.

35

"Alana!" Devon screamed as she collapsed at Quinn's feet.

He staggered forward, but pain shot up his leg and a wall of men moved to bar his path. Gritting his teeth, he hefted *kanker* and made to lower Braidon to the ground.

"No." Kellian's hand grasped Devon firmly by the arm and pulled him back.

In front of them, the Stalkers edged forward, swords held at the ready, their eyes filled with loathing. Despite his injuries, Devon had downed several with his hammer, Kellian two more. But now they'd been forced back to where the tunnel widened, the Stalkers threatened to encircle and overwhelm them. Their only chance was to keep retreating.

Devon's anger flared as his eyes swept across to where Quinn stood. He watched with teeth clenched as the man crouched down and lifted Alana into his arms. Turning, he walked away down the tunnel. For a moment, Devon thought he was sparing them; then his words carried back to the Stalkers facing them.

"Kill Devon and Kellian. Bring me the boy, if he lives."

"Come and get him!" Devon bellowed, but he knew the threat was an empty one. He could barely stand with the boy's weight on his shoulder.

One of the Stalkers leapt towards them, sword extended. Kellian parried with a flick of his dagger, then buried his second blade in the man's eye. Screaming, the man reared back, tearing the weapon from Kellian's grip. His comrades charged forwards, but the man staggered blindly to the side and sent two more crashing to the ground with him.

"That's far enough!" rang out a voice from the tunnel.

Devon froze where he stood and cast a glance over his shoulder. The voice had been softly spoken, barely audible above the pounding of his own heart, yet it carried with it a ring of power. At the other end of the tunnel, Quinn stopped and swung back towards them. The other Stalkers exchanged looks.

Turning, he stared as the demure figure of Tillie walked from the shadows, stepping past Devon and Kellian and advancing on the men. She held the familiar short sword in her right hand—and fire in her left.

"Who are you, woman?" Quinn's voice came from the end of the tunnel. "How dare you use magic in the Tsar's lands?"

"How dare I?" Tillie laughed. "By the power of Antonia, I defy your false god!"

The colour drained from Quinn's face. Even from a distance, Devon could see the man's fear as he looked at the flames crackling in the priest's hand. As the Stalkers hesitated, the old woman flashed a glance over her shoulder, a smile on her lips.

"Sorry I'm late, boys," she said in response to their stares. "I was finding us a ride."

With that, she turned back to the Stalkers. The fire in her hand roared, doubling in size, and the men stumbled back. Beyond them, the last of the colour fled from Quinn's face.

"Stop her!" he yelled, then turned and fled, Alana still draped over one shoulder.

The remaining Stalkers hesitated, looking from one another back to the old Magicker. But they were soldiers still, well trained and professional. For the past five years they had spent their days hunting down rogue Magickers, trapping them and dragging them back to the Tsar's dungeons. Overcoming his fear, one unleashed a battle cry, and the spell broke. Together, the men charged.

And died.

Devon stared as Tillie carved through the warriors, her sword little more than a blur, flames dancing out to engulf men in its blazing light. A man ran at her screaming, and staggered back, choking on his own blood. Two tried to encircle her, but the old woman only spun on her heel and sent flames rushing out to swallow them. Acrid smoke stung Devon's eyes as he retreated from the battle. One by one, the priest cut the Stalkers down, until none remained to face her.

Gaping, Devon watched as the old priest came to a stop, her shoulders heaving, a thin sheen of sweat on her forehead. Glancing back at them, she waved her sword towards the citadel.

"Get back to the courtyard beyond the gate," she ordered. "Dahniul is waiting for you."

Before Devon could ask who or what Dahniul was, the woman turned and started down the tunnel after Quinn and Alana.

QUINN'S HEART POUNDED HARD IN HIS CHEST AS HE RACED out onto the open plains before the gates of Fort Fall. Alana weighed heavily on his back, but he did not set her down. If he lost her too, there would be no more chances for redemption. The Tsar would see him locked away, his soul torn from his body, his mind destroyed. No, better he face death than succumb to that fate.

Sprinting across the barren land, he scanned the skies, searching for the dragons he knew were lurking nearby. An explosion echoed from the tunnel behind him. He watched the light flickering within the darkness. His men didn't stand a chance against the woman, but if they could hold her long enough, he at least might escape.

He turned away from the fortress and continued his flight. Silently, Quinn cursed his recklessness, using up so much of his magic filling the ship's sails. He'd barely recovered enough power to strike at Devon, but the man's cursed hammer had turned away the attack as easily as it had the demon's dark magic. Now a powerful Magicker had shown herself, and he had nothing left with which to fight her.

"Give her up, Quinn!" The old woman's voice chased after him.

He glanced back, seeing her standing in the gate tunnel. Flames gathered in an outstretched hand, and then rushed towards him. Quinn threw himself to the side as the conflagration struck the sand where he'd been, showering him with molten glass. The unconscious Alana tumbled from his shoulder, her head lolling against her shoulders like a ragdoll's.

Leaping to his feet, he hauled her up, but another blast of flame struck the ground before he could go further. He staggered to a stop, turning to face the old woman. She walked slowly towards him, her eyes flashing an angry red, power flickering in the palm of her hand.

Quinn swallowed hard. Where had this woman come from? She was certainly not a priest, not from the Earth Temple, at least. Had one of the Trolan Magickers escaped during the war, and bided her time for all these years?

"Drop her, Stalker!" Her command rang off the castle walls.

"Never," Quinn growled.

Fire was building in the palm of her hand, but with Alana in his arms, he knew she couldn't risk another attack. Quinn thought quickly, seeking an escape. She was still some fifty yards distant, but she was moving slowly, her aging frame betraying her. He started to back away, matching her stride for stride.

"You think you can escape me?" Her voice chased after him, harsh and mocking.

Quinn shook his head but didn't reply. From the corner of his eyes, he caught the glint of three specks on the horizon. He smiled, keeping the relief from his face.

"Who says I wish to escape you, my lady?" he asked.

A frown appeared on the woman's face. She spun towards the horizon, spying the specks of red hovering to the south. They were already growing larger. Returning to Quinn, she pointed a finger.

"Give her up, Quinn," she hissed. "Now!"

It was Quinn's turn to grin now. "You know what

approaches, stranger. Even your magic cannot defy three Red Dragons. Perhaps it is you who should give up?"

The woman bared her teeth, rage showing on her face. She took a step towards him, her flames crackling, but Quinn pulled Alana's unconscious body in front of his chest, forming a human shield.

"Go ahead!" He laughed as the woman lowered her hand.

"You truly are a coward," she hissed.

A tremor went through her, and for a moment it seemed she would attack him, regardless of Alana. He pulled her closer against his body and held his sabre to her throat. "One more move, and she dies," he snapped.

Slowly, the fire died in the woman's hand. Her eyes shimmered, returning to a crystal blue. She stared at him a moment longer, fists clenched, then she sheathed her sword and swung away. Moving quickly, she retreated to the gate tunnel and vanished into the darkness beyond.

Quinn allowed himself a long breath out, his shoulders slumping in sudden relief. He watched the shadows of the gate a moment longer, then turned to watch the southern horizon.

36

Agony tore at Devon's leg as he staggered after Kellian. His friend had sheathed his knives and taken the boy, but still Devon struggled to keep up. With each step he could feel the crossbow bolt grating against his collarbone. Fire radiated from the wound in his shoulder, but he still held *kanker* clenched in one hand. With sheer bloody-minded determination, he stumbled on.

Ahead, the darkness receded, giving way to the courtyard beyond the gates. His heart pounded hard in his chest as he moved out into the dying shadows, joining Kellian in the cobbled centre. With Braidon slumped over one shoulder, his friend had drawn to a stop and was looking back the way from which they'd come. Following his gaze, Devon's stomach clenched as he saw the silhouette of the old woman approaching.

Alone.

"Alana," Devon murmured. Without thinking, he stepped towards the tunnel, but a hand from Kellian held him back. Devon swung on him. "We can't just leave her with him!"

"We must," Kellian replied softly. He nodded to the boy. "Her brother lives. She would want us to save him—you know that!"

Devon swallowed, words abandoning him. The last of his strength fled into the void and he slumped against his friend. Kellian staggered but held him tight, supporting his weight. Eyes tearing up, Devon looked away, his gaze drifting upwards.

He frowned as a shadow swept across the sky. The hairs on his neck stood on end as, moments later, a roar echoed through the courtyard. Kellian tensed beneath him, and, gritting his teeth, Devon forced himself to take his own weight. Bile rose in his throat as his head swam, but he growled in defiance and hefted *kanker* above his head.

"Come on, dragon, come and get us!" he screamed at the sky.

A roar from above answered him, followed by the rush of wind and a violent crash as the beast came barrelling down into the courtyard. The ground shook beneath their feet as it struck, causing Devon to stagger and fall to his knees. The courage went rushing from him as he stared up at the beast.

The dragon towered over them, its jaws like an open doorway, stretching wide to swallow them. Giant claws sliced through the cobbled ground like it was butter. The scales glowed golden in the last rays of sunlight. Its massive tail lashed out, smashing through a cluster of pillars and causing a low roof to topple inwards. The great blue eyes blinked as the long neck twisted around to inspect the damage.

Sorry.

Devon blinked as the voice spoke in his mind. He stared up at the creature, taking it in, struggling to comprehend. It was far larger than the dragons he'd seen in the Tsar's thrall. His fear slowly trickled away, replaced by awe. Pulling himself back to his feet, he shook his head, unable to believe what he was seeing.

Its scales were *golden*.

The Gold Dragons had fought alongside the Three Nations against Archon, and been wiped out during the final conflict. Yet here one stood, its head lifted high, its glistening blue eyes staring down at them with unmistakable intelligence.

Looking into those eyes, Devon suddenly realised it had been speaking to them. He glanced at the ruined pillars, then back at the dragon. He waved one shaking hand.

"It's nothing..." he hesitated, trying to remember the name the priest had used. "Dahniul?"

A low rumble came from the dragon's chest. *Very well.* There was a pause as the blue eyes flickered to the tunnel. *You must be quick, if we wish to survive.*

Beside Devon, Kellian still stood staring at the dragon, his face frozen with fear. Devon nodded for him, and the beast crouched down, offering a forearm. Gripping his friend by the arm, Devon dragged him towards the creature.

"What are you doing?" Kellian gasped, coming back to life.

"Gold Dragons are *allies*, remember?" he replied. "We're going to ride him!"

"Are you insane?" Kellian yelled, but some of the fear had gone from his eyes and his resistance ceased.

Together, they made it to the dragon's side. Even

crouched, it was twice the height of a horse, and they were forced to use its forearm to climb up. With Kellian's help, they managed to get the unconscious Braidon on the dragon's back. Devon followed him, only the adrenaline thumping through his veins keeping him upright. Scrambling up, he glanced back and grimaced at the trail of blood he'd left on the golden scales.

Reaching down with his good arm, he helped Kellian up behind him. His friend's face was pale and he settled into place without a word. They had both seen what these creatures were capable of, had watched as the Tsar's Red Dragons burned entire fields of men alive.

"Now what?" Kellian yelled, his voice several octaves higher than usual.

The dragon shifted beneath them, its great head turning back towards the tunnel. Shadows flickered in the darkness as the green robes of the old priest appeared. Tillie was limping now, moving slowly. The dragon lowered its head to meet her, and Devon sensed words pass between them.

A second later, Tillie appeared. Her face was dark, her lips drawn tight. Her blue eyes flashed back at them as she sat in front of Devon.

"You have Braidon?"

Devon sat frozen by the power in her gaze, but Kellian's voice came from behind him. "We have him."

"Then go, Dahniul!" Tillie shouted.

Dahniul crouched, and leapt into the sky with a roar. Devon gasped as his stomach fell away. The air crackled as the great wings swept down, sending dust swirling across the courtyard. Below, the walls shrank as they lifted higher, unveiling the great expanse of the fortress beneath them. Devon glimpsed a dark-cloaked figure standing beyond the gates, looking up at them. A body lay on the ground beside him.

"Can't you help her?" Devon screamed, his heart aching as he looked down at Alana.

But the dragon was already turning beneath them, its giant wings beating hard, heading north.

Tillie did not look back, but her words carried to him over the rushing wind. "I'm sorry," she said, her voice sad. "I tried, but even Dahniul cannot fight three." With her words, she pointed to the south.

His hope falling away, Devon twisted to look at the horizon, where three scarlet specks hung in the air. They grew larger as he watched, the great beasts rushing across the sky, trying to cut off their escape.

As though in response, Dahniul unleashed an awesome roar. It rose higher in the sky, until it seemed the air itself would turn to ice around them. Trembling with the cold, Devon's thoughts fell away as he concentrated all his energy into just hanging on. Through the clouds below, a desert was flashing past, a myriad of rocky escarpments and rolling dunes. They began to lift, growing and stretching, becoming rolling hills, then jagged mountains that reached up towards them. His gaze travelled on, the white-capped peaks rushing closer.

Devon glanced back and saw the Red Dragons had fallen far behind. Their smaller wings couldn't keep pace with Dahniul, and now they were little more than specks on the horizon again. They would soon lose them in the mountains.

Despair welled in Devon's heart he looked at the distant fortress. Fort Fall was just a black dot in the narrow neck of land that was The Gap now, its giant ramparts and spiralling towers reduced to miniature. Somewhere beyond, Alana lay unconscious, imprisoned by the vile lieutenant of the Stalkers. Closing his eyes, he sought to stem the pain, to assure himself they'd made the right decision. Alana would have wanted them to escape with her brother.

It was no good, and he found himself falling into the familiar trappings of guilt. If only he'd fought harder, had killed Quinn before the archer could stop him. If only he'd stayed, tried to save her. But he hadn't, and now the fiery young woman was gone.

Devon remembered her words around the campfire then, the spark in her eyes as she told him she would go back for her brother. A sudden resolve came over him, a soft determination that cut through his pain and despair. He knew what he had to do.

He would regain his strength and march south. With an army or by himself, it didn't matter. One way or another, he would free her from the dark clutches of the Tsar. He just prayed to the Gods Alana would survive that long.

Beneath them, the dragon drifted lower as they entered the clouds that clung to the mountains. Water formed on Devon's beard, but he wiped it away, his eyes turning to the woman riding in front of him. He thought back to their first meeting in Sitton Forest. Where had she come from, this powerful Magicker? Why had she travelled with them all this time, helped them, saved them?

As though sensing his thoughts, the old woman stood suddenly. Balancing precariously on the dragon's neck, she turned and sat down once more. Now she was facing them, Devon could see her eyes were blue again, their sapphire depths clear and piercing. He swallowed as she looked at him, remembering how she had carved through the Stalkers like they were amateurs, not accomplished swordsmen.

The question came to his lips unbidden, slipping out before he could catch himself. "Who *are* you?"

A smile appeared on her aged face, the wrinkles seeming to vanish for a moment, so it seemed a much younger woman sat before them. Her eyes danced as she spoke.

"My name is Enala," she said, "and I was sent by the Goddess to find you."

EPILOGUE

Consciousness came slowly to Alana. It began with the faint tug of wind in her hair, the awareness of a cushioned mattress beneath her, the warmth of the air in her nostrils. Light seeped through her eyelids, shaking away the last dregs of sleep. A frown creased her forehead as an unknown fear touched her, and she sought to return to her dreams.

An image floated through her mind, of a man with black hair streaked with blonde, and brown, piercing eyes. He stood over her, sword poised, the blade glistening as he prepared to strike.

A scream tore from Alana's throat as she jerked upright, throwing off a heavy blanket and scrambling to escape. She yelled again as she tumbled sideways and fell from the bed. Stars flashed across her vision as her head struck something hard, followed by the thud of her body hitting the floor. Groaning, she struggled up, sanity creeping back into her thoughts.

Alana took in her surroundings, her confusion mounting. The bed on which she'd lain was massive, its heavy duvet thrown back, the silken sheets still tangled around her legs. Four columns at the corners of the bed held up a rich oaken panel and velvet curtains. The curtains were a vibrant red and sported embroideries of great dragons and shining knights in their plated armour.

Jerking back the curtains, Alana checked to see if anyone else was hiding in the bed, but it was empty. Shocked with the strangeness of it all, she looked around the empty room, hardly able to believe the riches surrounding her. Woollen carpets covered the floor, spilling out across the room like discarded afterthoughts. A meticulous mural had been painted on the far wall, showing a group of mounted nobles in a hunt. At one end of the wall, the men were gathered with bows raised, arrows already in flight, while at the other, an enormous feline fled their party. Shivering, Alana studied the faces, but there were too many to recognise any.

Alana rubbed her head where a bruise was starting to swell, and swore at the bedside table she'd struck it on. She stood and kicked it on its side. Realising suddenly that she was naked, her eyes alighted on a trunk at the foot of the bed. She moved cautiously towards it and flicked it open with a toe, fearful this was all some trap her captors were waiting to spring.

Nothing happened and, looking inside, she found a set of leather riding pants and a black jerkin with studded steel on its wrists. A couple of dresses lay beneath them, but otherwise the contents could have been mistaken for a man's wardrobe. Hesitantly, she pulled on the clothes she'd chosen, feeling sick as they slid comfortably around her small frame. Somehow, she knew everything within the trunk would fit her perfectly.

Sucking in a breath, she turned, taking in the rest of the room. Beside the bed, two sofas had been arranged around a granite fireplace. Behind the steel mesh, glowing coals still burned, warming the room. Past the sofas was a massive archway, and beyond that she glimpsed the grey light of a cloudy sky. On the other side of the room was a massive set of mahogany doors. Guessing they would be locked, Alana chose the archway.

A cold wind blew across to meet her as she started towards it. Noticing a heavy down jacket discarded on one of the sofas, she paused to pull it on. If she was going to escape, it wouldn't be to end up freezing to death in the wilderness. Without any idea where she was, she moved to the archway and stepped outside.

Alana's heart fell into her stomach as she found herself on a marble balcony, looking out across a shimmering garden and spiralling towers. Hope curdled in her chest. Beyond the towers, she could see the familiar red rooftops and shining blue lake of Ardath. Quinn had dragged her right back to where she'd started. Worst of all, she was now trapped in the citadel, at the very centre of the Tsar's power. There would be no escaping this place.

Looking out over the balcony, Alana stared down at the six-storey drop to the stone paving below. She gripped the marble railing tight, gathering her courage. The walls on either side of her were smooth, unassailable, but if she just climbed onto the railing…

The slam of the outside door opening made her turn. Forcing the despair from her face, Alana turned and watched as Quinn paused in the doorway, a smile on his face. Seeing her awake and standing on the balcony, his smile grew and he stepped into the room. He carried a sheathed sword in one hand, and wore another at his waist.

"Awake at last, I see!" he said brightly, moving towards her.

"Stay away from me," Alana growled. She shrank back, until the railing of the balcony brought her up short.

He paused, a frown replacing the smile. "You still do not remember me? I thought the room…" he shook his head, waving a hand. "I apologise. Here, take your sword, if it makes you feel better."

He tossed the sword across the room. Alana watched it twist through the air as though it were a snake. It made a soft thud as it landed on the carpet. She stood for a moment, still staring at it, before darting back into the room and snatching it up. Leather scraped on steel as she drew it and advanced on him, blade raised.

Quinn didn't move, but his smile returned. "Magic or no, you have lost none of your fire, Alana." He shook his head. "But my power has returned. You cannot defeat me with that."

As though to emphasise his words, a soft breeze whirled across the room from the balcony, touching Alana's cheeks. She stared at him for a moment longer, teeth bared, and then lowered her sword. Still holding it tightly in one hand, she glared at him.

"What have you done with my brother?"

His face tightened. "I am afraid your friends took him. I do not know if he survived without our healers' aid." He shook his head. "I am sorry for what my man did. He has been…dealt with."

Alana's heart fluttered at the thought of her brother free. For the first time since awakening, a smile touched her lips. She stared at the hunter, defiant.

"What do you want with me, Quinn?"

"You truly do not know?"

She shook her head, lips pursed. "I only know you tried to kill me."

"That…was not me. The Tsar was…desperate not to allow you to escape his realm."

Alana laughed, the sound echoing off the stone walls. "The Tsar, desperate?" she shook her head. "What are my brother and I to the ruler of the Three Nations?"

Quinn sighed. "Let us find out, shall we?" He stepped aside, waving a hand at the open doors through which he'd entered.

Alana narrowed her eyes. Hesitantly, she stepped around him, and saw two guards standing in the corridor, waiting for them. Gripping her sword tightly in one hand, she considered charging them. Perhaps she could slay one and then flee before Quinn could react…

"Coming?" Quinn asked lightly, stepping past her.

Watching him join the guards in the corridor, her shoulders slumped. He would not let her escape. Even if she could slip past the guards and Quinn's magic, the citadel was full of armed men. It wouldn't be long before they all came hunting her. No, no one could escape this place without the Tsar's leave.

"Would you like to come willingly, or be dragged before the Tsar in chains?" Quinn asked, his voice still light, as though discussing tomorrow's weather.

Alana flashed him a glare, but she gave a curt nod. Ignoring the three men, she stepped out into the corridor.

"Which way?" she all but spat.

Chuckling to himself, Quinn moved around her and took the corridor to the right. The guards fell into place either side of Alana as they started off. They looked at ease, as though Alana posed no more danger than a child. She grated her teeth. Was that why Quinn had returned her sword? Did they truly consider her so little a threat?

Moving through the long corridors, Alana studied her surroundings, seeking potential escape routes. At every branch in the passageway, a pair of guards stood in full armour, equipped with spears and short swords and daggers. It would have taken an army to escape through the halls they walked along.

When they finally reached the throne room, Alana could hardly bring herself to step through the golden doors. She knew Quinn was marching her to her death, that she would likely never leave this place again. Perhaps the Tsar had invited all his nobles and courtiers to attend her execution, to remind his followers of his power, of what became of those who defied him.

Yet, as Alana stepped inside, she was surprised to find the throne room almost empty. Open space stretched out from her, marked only by the scarlet carpet leading up to a raised dais. A dozen guards stood there, the bulk of their armour shielding the throne from view. On either wall were enormous silken tapestries, each depicting a scene from the second battle of Fort Fall, when the men and women of the Three Nations had made their last stand against Archon.

In the tapestry to the right, she glimpsed a giant figure standing atop the walls, a familiar hammer in hand. Her heart ached as she thought of Devon, Kellian, and her brother. Silently, she prayed Quinn had spoken the truth, that they lived.

Movement drew her gaze back to the raised dais. The ring of guards shifted, parting slowly to reveal the throne behind them. A tremor went through Alana as her eyes alighted on the man who sat there. Slowly, he pulled himself to his feet.

The Tsar was not a large man, standing only a few inches taller than Alana, but about him he carried an undeniable power, a sense of invincibility that could not be denied. His jet-black hair had been slicked back close to his skull, and while there were streaks of grey there, his face was unmarked by the passage of time. His eyes flickered down, catching her in an ancient stare.

Alana froze, her body suddenly quivering, as if struck by an invisible bolt of electricity. Her mind ground to a halt. It felt as though, with a single glance, she had surrendered all control of her body to the man on the throne. Unbidden, her legs started down the red carpet, past Quinn and the guards, across the empty room. The blue eyes followed her every step as she approached the dais. Only at the stairs did she finally stumble to a stop. With a half-choked cry, she fell to her knees.

Chainmail rattled as Quinn joined her, bowing low. "Your majesty, I have returned her."

Returned?

Movement came from the dais, and Alana watched as the Tsar started down the marble stairs. A shiver swept through her, an awful terror rising in her throat. Yet she remained on her knees, unable to move, trapped in the cold gaze. Looking into their eerie blue, Alana imagined herself in the grips of some ancient power, her mortal strength nothing before the man's might. She felt death staring back from them.

And still Alana could not look away.

She knelt, frozen, as he walked down the steps and approached her. So close, she could feel the power radiating from his body. It seemed to ripple the very air around him, to distort the essence of reality. It reached out for her, and Alana gasped as she felt something inside her respond.

Opening her mouth, she tried to scream, but no sound came out. Fire sprang to life in her chest, swirling, writhing, reaching out for the power emanating from the Tsar.

As quickly as it had appeared, the pain vanished. Tears streaming down her face, gasping at the sudden release, Alana looked up and found the Tsar standing over her.

Wordlessly, the Tsar reached out a hand. His skin was warm to the touch as he wiped the tears from her cheeks. Alana shivered, unable to move, struck now by the unexpected kindness of the gesture. His touch was soft, almost familiar, as though this scene had played out many times between them.

A smile touched his lips, transforming his face. Gone was the coldness, the silent judgement, the executioner. In his place was a friend, a comrade, a hero. Silently, his warm hand cupped Alana's cheek and drew her to her feet.

"My daughter," his words echoed in the silence of the throne room. "Welcome home."

HERE ENDS BOOK ONE OF
THE LEGEND OF THE GODS
The story continues in…
Shield of Winter

ENJOYED THIS NOVEL? **FOR FREE BOOKS AND NEWS ON THE upcoming books,** don't forget to join Aaron's VIP group by following the link below!

http://www.aaronhodges.co.nz/newsletter-signup/

NEW YORK TIMES BESTSELLING AUTHOR

AARON HODGES

SHIELD OF WINTER

LEGEND OF THE GODS BOOK TWO

PROLOGUE

Betran coughed as a whiff of smoke drifted towards him from the fireplace. Leaning sideways on his stool, he hacked up a gob of phlegm and spat it on the mudbrick floor, then took another swig of ale to wash away the acrid taste of the coal fumes. The mood in the tavern was sombre, the low curved ceiling seeming to mute what little conversation there was to be had. Not that Betran was in any mood to talk with his fellow Trolans.

Catching the eye of the man behind the counter, he raised a finger and pointed at his empty mug. The bartender narrowed his eyes, but after a moment's hesitation swept up the mug and wandered over to the kegs lining the wall behind the bar.

Golden ale streamed from the keg while Betran allowed his gaze to roam around the room. The hour was growing late, and the few customers in the underground tavern were finally beginning to disperse. The poorly constructed tables were almost empty, leaving only a few men sitting at the bar.

Most of them were known to Betran, except for the man seated two stools down from him.

His chest tightened as he stared at the stranger. Even seated, he was the largest man Betran had ever seen. Barrel-chested with arms like tree trunks, he seemed to radiate a power all of his own. He had been sitting in the gloomy tavern for over an hour now, downing tankard after tankard of the innkeeper's finer ale. Betran had caught a glint of gold the last time the man had reached for his belt purse, and had been watching him ever since.

Swallowing, he looked away as the man caught the attention of a barmaid and waved for another drink. She flashed him a smile as he slipped a silver shilling into her palm. It wasn't long before she returned, the tankard almost overflowing.

A few moments later, the bartender finally came back with Betran's own mug. Scowling, he reached out to take it, but the man lifted the drink out of reach.

"Ya got the coin for it, Betran?" he asked, his voice gruff from the days spent in the smoky tavern.

Betran's stomach twisted with anger as he glared at the man. He was well known here—had grown up just down the road in old Kalgan, before the Tsar had burned everything above ground-level to ash. Only a few thousand survivors lived amongst the ruins now, making do with what they could as they slowly rebuilt the former jewel of Trola. Normally, locals were only asked to settle their bill at the end of the night.

But then, Betran shouldn't have been surprised. It had been months now since he and the other labourers had finished restoring the bathhouse, and with no new prospects on the horizon, Betran was quickly growing desperate.

Word had obviously gotten around he had little coin left to spare.

Gritting his teeth, Betran reached into his purse and slammed a silver shilling down on the bench. "Good enough for you?" he snapped.

The innkeeper only smiled and swept the coin into his pocket. "Good for now." He placed the tankard in front of Betran and moved away.

Muttering under his breath, Betran lifted the tankard and gulped down a mouthful of the cool liquid. His eyes flickered back to the stranger. He was already halfway through the new drink, making it his eighth in less than two hours. Betran had known strong men to slide unconscious beneath a table with less, yet the man still seemed alert. Only a slight swaying on his stool suggested the ale was taking effect.

Betran shivered as the man looked around, the amber eyes seeming to stare straight through him. He quickly looked away, fixing his eyes on his tankard of ale. When he finally looked back up, the man had returned to his drink.

Unconsciously, Betran dropped his hand to the knife on his belt. It would take only moments to follow the man into some darkened alleyway and drive the blade through his back. No one would miss the stranger—or the purse on his belt. Even a single gold Libra would be enough to feed Betran's family for a month, and from what he'd glimpsed, the stranger had far more than that.

How did it come to this?

A sick feeling settled in Betran's stomach as he contemplated his victim. Six years ago, he'd been an officer in the Trolan army, marching to glory against the Plorseans, determined to liberate his nation from the tyranny of the Tsar.

But within the year, his dreams had turned to ash, scattered to the winds along with the remnants of the Trolan army.

He had only survived because his cohort had been cut off from Kalgan while out on a scouting trip. Harried by marauding bands of Plorsean soldiers, they'd retreated into the mountains and watched from afar as the city fell.

Now, six years later, Trola was a shadow of its former glory. Kalgan was slowly being rebuilt, but elsewhere the fields lay untended, towns and villages empty of life. Even here, much of the city remained underground, its former cellars and basements converted to taverns and homes, as though Kalgan's occupants feared reprisal if they showed their heads above ground. But even the darkness could not hide them from the Tsar's taxes; as things stood, an entire generation was hovering on the brink of starvation.

Thinking of his wife and child back home, Betran sucked in a breath, steeling himself for the task to come. He clenched his fists, seeking to calm the trembling in his hands. Petra and his son, Onur, were relying on him. He had come here to drown his despair in ale, but now that an opportunity had shown itself, he could not allow it to pass him by.

Courage, Betran.

The thought made his heart beat faster. He'd been a brave man once, before the weight of poverty had dragged him down. What his former self would think of him now, he could only guess. Would he understand the desperation, the despair that had driven him to this point? Or would he despise the filthy man who sat silently at a tavern, contemplating theft and murder?

His hands were shaking again. Clenching the hilt of his dagger, he ran his mind over the plan. There was no doubt the stranger was a fighter—and while he didn't seem to be carrying a weapon, Betran had no desire to risk a direct confrontation. No, he would wait for the giant to leave and follow him, then strike when the moment was right.

You are not a murderer, Betran.

The thought came to him unbidden, but he pushed it aside. Thoughts of honour and morality in Trola had died along with its freedom. Few could afford such luxuries now. The city had become a place of corruption, where the strong ruled and the weak were used and discarded at will.

Betran tensed as the stranger pushed back his stool and stood. Slamming a handful of shillings on the bar top, he swayed on his feet, then bid the barmaid goodbye and headed for the door.

For a moment Betran hesitated. Then he stood and started after the man.

As the giant strode towards the worn stone steps leading up to the street, a bang came from the door above. The sound of raised voices echoed down into the tavern. Betran froze as a group of middle-aged men came thumping down the stairwell. They stopped as they reached the bottom and found themselves face-to-face with the giant. A long silence stretched out as the five newcomers stared at the stranger.

"You going to stand there all day, sonny, or are you going to get out of my way?" the stranger asked suddenly.

Betran winced as he heard the man's Plorsean accent. Until now, the stranger had only spoken in hushed tones, his origins disguised by the other noises in the tavern. The faces of the newcomers darkened as the one barring the way dropped a hand to the knife on his belt.

"Plorsean, are ya?" His eyes narrowed. "You look familiar."

The giant stood in silence and returned the man's stare. The other newcomers fanned out as the ringleader continued. "Yes, I do know you. You're the Butcher of Kalgan. I heard you were dead."

"Apparently not." The giant's words were softly spoken, but they reverberated through the tavern.

Betran retreated a step, the ale in his stomach curdling with sudden fear. Even the ringleader swallowed, but a glance at his friends seemed to restore some of his courage. Advancing a step, he forced a grin. "You're a wanted man, butcher," he growled. "Though most in these parts would kill you for free."

"They're welcome to try," the giant replied.

"Might be we will," snapped the man, drawing his dagger.

In that moment, the giant surged forward. One hand flashed out, blocking the dagger's thrust, the other snapping out to catch the ringleader in the jaw. A sharp *crack* echoed from the low ceiling as the man collapsed. He struck the floor with an audible thud, and did not rise again.

Straightening, the giant swept his gaze over the remaining men. "You know my name. If any of you wish to stop me, you're welcome to try. One way or another, I'll be leaving through that door."

The men around the stranger wavered, their eyes wide, faces pale. Silently, the man started forward. His attackers exchanged glances. The man had almost reached the stairs when Betran saw the change come over them. With the giant's back exposed, one man drew his dagger and leapt. The others followed, weapons in hand.

As the first reached the stranger, he raised his dagger to strike. Before the blow could fall, the giant spun, his fist flashing out to catch his attacker in the face. The Trolan staggered back into two of his fellows, slowing their charge. The final man leapt past them, dagger held low.

Roaring, the giant swung to meet his attacker. His hands swept down and caught the knifeman by the wrist. Before the assailant could tear himself free, he was dragged forward into a crunching headbutt. Betran winced as the man dropped without a sound. His dagger slid across the floor, coming to a rest at Betran's feet.

Beyond, the remaining three had recovered, but the giant was already closing on them. Stepping in close, he caught two by the head and slammed them together with a sickening *thud*. As he released them, their legs crumpled beneath them, and they slid to the ground.

The last man, realising he was alone, tried to flee up the stairs, but the giant caught him by the collar. He cried out as he was hauled back, trying to bring his dagger to bear. The giant punched him square in the forehead, and the weapon slid from his suddenly limp fingers.

Grunting, the stranger released the man, allowing him to tumble to the floor alongside his comrades. Silently his gaze studied the room. Betran shuddered as the amber eyes settled on him.

"What about you?" the giant growled.

His mouth suddenly dry, Betran jerked his head sideways. "No…no I'm good," he stuttered. The giant stared back, seeming to see right through him. Betran glanced at the dagger lying at his feet. He quickly kicked it away, then drew his own blade from his belt and tossed it aside. Raising his hands, he nodded at the discarded weapons. "See?"

To his surprise, the stranger chuckled. Moans came from the fallen men as he walked past them and slapped a hand down on Betran's shoulder. "That's good to hear!" he boomed. "I was meant to be keeping a low profile. The name's Devon."

"I know who you are," Betran said, staring up into the

man's grizzled face. "My name is Betran. You killed my brother in the battle for Branei Pass."

For half a second, a look of pain crossed the giant's face. Then it was gone. "I'm sorry to hear that," Devon said, shaking his head. "There's a lot I regret, from my past. But that's life I suppose. Can't change what's been—only what's to come!"

Betran found himself nodding. "I can believe that," he lamented, thinking of their king's foolhardy march into Plorsea. "There's plenty I regret too."

Devon nodded. "The curse of old age," he said with a grin. He studied the fallen men for a moment. "Don't think they'll be going anywhere for a while. Still, it won't take long now for word to spread I'm in town. Don't suppose you know where I can find someone by the name of Godrin."

A lump lodged in Betran's throat at the mention of the name. Godrin was a former soldier turned crime lord, who'd all but taken over the impoverished city. He had built a reputation for himself during the war as a competent General, and been one of the few to survive the city's fall. His cohort had mostly avoided the final battle and subsequent purge of the army, though there were conflicting rumours about how Godrin had accomplished this.

All anyone knew for sure was that, in the aftermath of the war, Godrin had used his cohort to take control of a section of the city. His territory had only expanded since then. Those under his sway were forced to pay for protection, only adding to the burden imposed on the citizens by the Tsar's taxes.

Godrin was not a man Betran wanted to cross. And if the Butcher of Kalgan was looking for him…

"Why would you be looking for a man like Godrin?" he asked softly.

"I was told he might help me solve a problem."

Betran eyed the man. He sensed if he refused, Devon would become angry again. Yet if Betran took him to Godrin, and Devon killed him, Betran's life would no doubt be at risk from Godrin's conspirators. Biting his lip, he opened his mouth, then closed it again, unable to come to a decision.

Grinning, Devon reached into his belt purse. His hand emerged with a Gold Libra, which he flicked into the air. Jumping in shock, Betran caught the coin before he knew what he was doing. Speechless, he looked from Devon to the coin.

"For the bother," the giant said quietly. "There's another in it for you if you take me to Godrin. I swear, I'm not looking for trouble."

Betran hardly heard Devon's words. He stared down at the coin, his eyes misting, and he quickly blinked back the tears. The coin would get his family through the rest of winter. With the coming of spring, the long task of rebuilding the city would resume and he would have work again. Biting back the emotion swelling in his throat, Betran found himself nodding.

"I'll take you," he said quietly.

Pocketing the coin, he waved at the bartender, who glared back at them, clearly upset about the unconscious patrons lying on his floor. Remembering the man's earlier discourtesy, Betran only grinned and turned away.

Stepping over the failed attackers, he walked towards the stairwell, then cursed as the thud of the door above echoed down to them. A slender stranger appeared on the stairs above. He wore tight-fitting black leggings and a sheepskin jerkin, matched with a fine woollen cloak. His cheeks were clean-shaven, and as he reached up and pulled back his hood, Betran saw there was some grey in his short black hair. His hazel eyes studied the tavern, lingering on the unconscious men, before turning on Devon.

"Kellian, about time you showed up!" Devon boomed from behind Betran.

The newcomer shook his head, a weary look passing across his face. "Yes…well, I see you've been making friends as usual."

Chuckling, Devon took Betran by the shoulder and gave him a friendly push towards the stairs. "Had to do something to pass the time. But you're in luck: while you were busy sleeping, I found someone to take us to Godrin."

"Oh, joy," the newcomer muttered, turning to push open the door.

Betran and Devon joined him, and together they walked out into the streets of Kalgan.

❧ I ❧

Alana lay on the soft feather mattress and stared up at the panelled ceiling of the canopy bed. A mosaic of gold, silver, and precious gems had been set into the mahogany, depicting a creek running through a wooded valley—but in the past few weeks, Alana had spent so much time lying there she hardly noticed it anymore. Her thoughts were far away, lost in another life, in the sporadic images flickering through her mind.

Images of her father and mother, of her brother, of friends and people she'd once known.

Or so she had believed.

She knew now those memories were lies, a fabrication, some foul construction cast over her mind.

A tremor ran through Alana as she choked back a sob. Forcing her eyes closed, she sought the escape of sleep, though she knew it would not come. How long had she lain in this room now, staring into space, sleeping in fits and bursts amidst the silk sheets? A week? Two?

She no longer had the will to care—how could she, when everything she'd ever known was a lie?

Despite her best efforts, a tear streaked across her cheek as she recalled the words of the Tsar.

My daughter, welcome home…

From the start, she had tried to deny it, to fight and rage against the man. Yet even in those first few moments, his words had rung with truth, sending vibrations down to the very core of her being. In that instant, the hazy memories of her past had shattered, revealing the gaping hole where a lifetime of memories should have been. The truth had left her stumbling through the ruins of her mind, struggling to piece the fragments back together, to answer the one, impossible question.

Who am I?

The question had haunted her through the days and nights, stalking her through every waking hour, following her even into the sanctuary of her dreams. Always the answer seemed to shimmer just out of sight. She could not grasp it, could not quite bring it into focus. Finally she had given up, surrendering to the icy grips of despair.

A sob tore from Alana's chest as she felt the familiar pain. She couldn't go on like this, empty and alone. She was a phantom, an illusion, some dream made real by an unknown power.

Silently, she rose from the bed. The massive room stretched out around her, its furnishings of gold and silver speaking of a wealth she could only ever have dreamed of when living on the streets. Except she knew now that wasn't true. This had been her room since birth, her sanctuary, the one place she should have known before any other. Yet even now she felt only a cold indifference for it.

She stared at the painting on the far wall, of the nobles

on the hunt, their bows taut, arrows ready to fly. When Alana had first woken after her capture, she had hardly glanced at the artwork, but on returning to the room, she'd found herself drawn to it. Studying it now, her eyes were pulled as always to the woman standing amidst the hunters. Blonde hair fluttered in an imaginary wind as the woman held her sabre high, a cry on her crimson lips. Her stone-grey eyes seemed to stare down at Alana, an accusation in their murky depths, a perfect reflection of her own.

Thief!

Alana's stomach churned and she looked away, unable to gaze on her own likeness a moment longer. Heart pounding, she crossed the soft carpets, brushed aside the drapes, and stepped out onto the marble balcony. She paused as the wind struck her, its icy touch robbing her of breath. Tears cold on her cheeks, she stood there a moment, sucking in great gulps of air, struggling to lift her soul free of the despair that gripped it.

Beyond the balcony, the rooftops of the citadel stretched out around her, the slate tiles and twisting crenulations falling slowly away to the city of Ardath. A thin haze clung to the city, but through it she could just make out the red-brick walls of the merchant quarter. The distant ring of bells carried from the three-pronged spires of the temple. Slowly the ringing faded, and was replaced by the sounds of the waking city.

A lump rose in Alana's throat as she listened to the shouting voices and clip-clopping of hooves on the brick streets. Down amongst the people was where she belonged, amidst the chaos and the noise. Not up here, surrounded by stone, amidst the trappings of the Tsar's power.

She stood at the marble railing and looked into the courtyard six storeys below. Basalt and limestone cobbles wound outwards from the central fountain in a spiral pattern, and small shrubs grew around the edges of the courtyard.

A sudden resolve came over Alana, and carefully she climbed up onto the railing of her balcony. The wind swirled around her, threatening to drag her to her death. Her stomach plummeted into her boots as she looked down and saw how far it was to the ground. A sudden weakness took her. Her legs shook as she crouched down and gripped the railing with both hands. Struggling for breath, she clenched her eyes closed.

What are you doing?

Alana shivered. She didn't know the answer. The wind caught in her bedclothes and her heart lurched as she wavered on the edge.

"What are you afraid of?" she heard herself ask. "You don't exist, Alana."

Tears burned in her eyes, but releasing the rail she straightened. Her throat contracted as she looked down into the courtyard. The spiral pattern seemed to be spinning, and she wavered on the edge, the edges of her vision turning dark. Fists clenched tight, she sucked in another breath. Her heart beat slowed, and her fear receded, giving way to the awful emptiness.

"*Alana!*" a voice yelled from behind her. Over her shoulder, Alana saw Quinn appear in the alcove. Eyes wide, he stood frozen to the spot, hand outstretched. "What are you doing?"

"I'm sorry," Alana whispered, tears blurring her vision.

Before he could stop her, she closed her eyes and allowed herself to topple backwards.

Her stomach lurched as she began to fall, and the wind howled in her ears. Air rushed around her as she screamed, the breath catching in her throat. She kept her eyes closed tight, waiting for the *thud*, the final flash of light as she struck hard stone, for her life to go howling into the void.

The shrieking of the wind seemed to grow louder. It whirled around her, catching at her clothes, clawing at her hair, and somehow the sense of falling began to slow. Time stretched out, until unable to resist any longer, Alana opened her eyes. She gasped as she found herself hovering just a few feet above the cobblestones. Terrified, she thrashed against the wind that still buffeted her. Abruptly the vortex suspending her mid-air dissipated, and she fell the last few inches to the ground.

Air rushed from her lungs as she struck the cobbles. Gasping, she rolled onto her side and clutched her stomach, her lungs straining for breath. She was still struggling to breathe when Quinn dropped from the heavens, his cloak whipping around him as gusts of wind, summoned by his Sky magic, slowed his fall.

He blinked as he touched down, flicking a glance back at the tower. "Well, that's a new trick..." he muttered. Shaking his head, he crouched beside her. "Alana, are you okay?"

Alana cursed as she finally caught her breath. Pushing him away, she pulled herself to her feet. "Why did you save me?" she shrieked, shoving him hard in the chest.

He stared back at her. "You don't know what you're doing, Alana," he replied. "This isn't you."

"I know that!" she yelled, swinging on him. She jabbed a finger at his face. "How do you think it feels, finding out that everything you've ever known is a lie? That everything I am is some...some construct?"

Reeling back, Quinn held up his hands in supplication. Her words trailed off as she sucked in a breath. Her chest still ached from the fall and her heart was racing, the panic building within her. Wheezing, she staggered, her legs beginning to tremble. Alana slumped back to the ground and drew her knees up against her chest.

Seating himself beside her, Quinn placed a tentative hand on her back. Alana flinched, but this time she did not pull away. In that instant, her hatred and fear of Quinn seemed small beside the desolation within.

"Just breathe," he murmured, rubbing her back. The silence stretched out, but when he finally spoke again, his voice was soft, reassuring. "I'm sorry. I should have come sooner. Your fath– the Tsar, he thought it best to give you your space."

"Why is this happening to me?" she croaked, trying to keep herself from sobbing.

"It is…difficult to explain," Quinn said. "But I'm here now. Maybe I can help."

Alana closed her eyes, still struggling to control her breathing. Quinn's hand moved across her back in slow circles, his warmth and presence strangely comforting. The thought gave her pause. This was the man who had hunted her and her brother across the Three Nations. She had fought with every ounce of her strength to escape him, yet he had just saved her life with his magic. Sitting with him now in the quiet of the courtyard felt strangely warming, and she shivered at the familiarity of it.

"Are you okay, Alana?" he asked into the silence.

Shaking her head, Alana glanced at him. The sight still set her heart racing, but she fought the instinct to run. "Quinn…please…help me?"

He nodded. His hand slid beneath her arm and he pulled her up. "Come with me."

Alana obeyed, taking his shoulder for support. She felt

strangely exhausted, as though her plunge from the balcony had stolen away the last of her strength. If not for Quinn, Alana wasn't sure she could have made it back inside, let alone up the long stairway to her room.

Still in her nightclothes, she allowed herself to be led through the winding corridors and endless courtyards of the citadel. There were fewer guards now than on the first day she'd woken, though she hadn't bothered to ask anyone where they'd gone. Those they did pass kept their eyes fixed straight ahead. Even so, Alana's cheeks warmed with embarrassment. The silk nightgowns she'd found in her clothes trunk barely went down past her waist. In the life she could remember, Alana would never have worn such tight-fitting bedclothes, but here there'd been little else to choose from.

Alana's thoughts were jerked back to the present as warm air touched her cheek. Blinking, she looked around, surprised to find herself in a sprawling lawn and garden. Beyond the short-cropped grass and twisting rosebushes, the outer walls of the citadel towered overhead, the dull grey stone standing out in sharp contrast to the vibrant colours below.

Pathways of red sandstone and blue marble twisted away from where they stood, threading their way through the green lawns and passing beneath archways of flowering vines. Despite the icy winds of winter beyond the citadel walls, the air here carried with it the touch of summer. The trees dotting the gardens were in full blossom, the reds and yellows and blues of their flowers seemingly aglow with magic.

Despite the warmth, Alana found herself shivering. She knew this garden, had seen it in the dreams that had plagued her during her flight across the Three Nations. She had seen herself and her brother here, running across the lawns, playing in the distant trees.

"I know this place," she whispered.

Quinn smiled. "That's good." Taking her hand, he led her onto the lawn.

Alana was barefoot, but the grass was soft beneath her feet. Closing her eyes, she savoured the touch of sunlight on her skin, the warmth of the air, the distant chatter of laughter. Looking around, she sought the source. To her wonder, a troupe of children came running across the grass, closely followed by a woman in a sunflower yellow dress. Scarlet hair bobbed as she ran, her pale skin aglow with the morning sun. She wore no jewellery except for a pair of emerald studded silver bracelets, and there was a smile on her face as she watched the children.

The smile fell from the woman's lips as she saw them. Leaving the children to their play, she wandered over. Alana started to speak, but before she could get a word out, the woman swung on Quinn.

"She shouldn't be here," the woman hissed, her voice taut with anger.

Quinn's eyes flashed and he stepped forward, placing himself between Alana and the woman. "Afraid of an audience, Krista?" he asked coolly.

She glared at him, eyes narrowed. "Never," she snapped, "but the children do not need the distraction. The boy, Liam, is taking his examination this week."

"We will not interfere, Krista," Quinn said with a smile. "Now, I suggest you get back to your charges. They seem to have wandered off."

Krista glanced around and swore when she saw the children disappearing through an archway. She took off without another word.

Chuckling, Quinn turned back to Alana. "You'll have to excuse Krista."

Alana hardly heard him. One of the children had caught her attention. She started after them, eyes narrowed, trying to catch another glimpse of the boy. She could have sworn she recognised him. The breath caught in her throat as the boy she'd spotted glanced back. For a moment he stared at her, a frown on his young face, then he turned and disappeared through the arch.

"That was the boy from the stepwell," she whispered.

Quinn rested his hand on her shoulder. "His name is Liam."

Alana shook her head, tears welling in her eyes. "What is this?"

"The truth," Quinn murmured.

Her breath coming in ragged gasps, Alana looked into Quinn's eyes, seeking some sign of deception. He stared back at her, his face soft now, his forehead creased with concern. Gone was the steely glint of the Stalker who had chased her across the Three Nations. From the depths of her memories, she heard again the question in her dreams.

Are you ready, Alana?

She closed her eyes. For weeks she had fought the truth, clinging to the belief the Tsar and his people were evil. According to his laws, all Magickers were to be brought to the citadel. Once taken into custody, they were never seen again. The day her brother's magic had woken, she had *known* they had to flee, or face death. But now…now everything was wrong.

The boy she'd seen was the same one Quinn had arrested in the stepwell so many weeks ago. He should have been dead, and yet here he was, healthy and alive, happy…

A sob tore from her lips as the last of her resistance crumbled. "Why is this happening to me?"

"Your magic," Quinn said.

"*My*...magic?" Alana whispered. Her mouth opened and closed as she struggled to find the words to reply. "My...no...that's not possible."

Clutching her chest, she staggered back, struggling to keep herself upright. Before she could fall, Quinn grasped her firmly by the shoulder.

"It's the truth, Alana," he said as she steadied herself. Taking her hands in his, he held them tight. "You have the power to alter minds."

Silently, Alana shook her head. Her hands slipped from his grip as she sank to her knees. Wrapping her arms around her chest, she locked eyes with Quinn, silently beseeching him to take back the words.

Instead, he knelt beside her, unblinking. "We believe that, somehow, your magic went wrong," he continued inexorably, "that you lost control, and wiped away the memories of yourself and your brother. Your power must have imprinted another...reality over your own consciousness."

"How is that possible?" Alana croaked.

"I don't know," Quinn murmured. "I have never seen you lose control before. All I can tell you is that you disappeared with your brother on his sixteenth birthday. We searched for you, locked the city gates and sent out men to search the streets. But for weeks, there was no sign of either of you. Not even your father, with all his power, could find you."

"It wasn't until I sensed Earth magic near the northern gates that we picked up your trail. I didn't know it was you though, not until that night in Sitton Forest."

Alana closed her eyes, struggling to comprehend, to

make sense of this new reality. She thought back to their escape from the city. A cold breeze blew across her neck as she recalled her conversation with the ship captain, how he'd suddenly changed his mind and allowed them to depart.

"How…how can…" she trailed off, fighting back tears.

"I'm sorry this happened to you, Alana," Quinn said. He paused, taking a breath. "But…you were happy here once. You had a place, a role in this world."

Tears welled in Alana's eyes. "I don't remember…"

Quinn smiled. "Then let me show you," he whispered, offering his hand.

Trembling, Alana stared at him a moment. Fear spread through her chest as she wondered what fresh revelations Quinn had in store for her. It seemed that every word from his mouth further unwound her sense of self, making a lie of everything she believed in. A yearning rose within her, to flee back to her room, to hide beneath the blankets and block out the world.

Yet there was no running from this truth. She could hide no longer. Swallowing back her terror, Alana reached out and took his hand.

2

Devon fell in with Kellian as they left the tavern. He was aware of his friend's irritation, but couldn't help but grin as he caught the man's eye. After all, the unconscious men in the tavern were hardly his fault. Knowing it would be recognised, Devon had left his warhammer *kanker* at the inn, but in the end it hadn't mattered: as much as he'd wanted to lay low, Kalgan was a small place nowadays, and his reputation amongst the survivors of the war was well-earned. Whether they succeeded in finding Enala's contact tonight or not, they would have to leave the city by morning, or risk being hunted down by a mob of vengeful townsfolk.

Thinking back to the wily old priest, Devon found himself wishing Enala had joined them on this quest. Recalling that last day in the gate tunnel of Fort Fall still filled him with awe. With fire and sword in hand, Enala had sliced into the Stalkers like a scythe through the wheat fields of northern Lonia. Only the arrival of the Tsar's Red Dragons had prevented her victory. As it was, they'd been forced to flee on the back of a Gold Dragon the old woman had summoned.

Devon would never forget that wild flight; yet as they'd soared high above the mountains, it had been sorrow, not joy, that had filled his heart. They had escaped, but Alana had been left behind, trapped in the vile clutches of the Stalker lieutenant, Quinn.

His heart twitched at the thought of Alana, of what she must now be suffering for his failure. If only he'd managed to kill Quinn, things might have ended differently. Instead, a crossbow bolt had torn through his shoulder, all but incapacitating him. The wound would normally have taken months to heal, but after their escape, Enala had directed the dragon to a temple high in the Northland mountains. There, they had discovered an order of priests dedicated to the Goddess, Antonia. Several of the men and women there had possessed the healing magic of the Earth, and had quickly set about tending to the wounds of their visitors.

The hairs on Devon's neck stood on end as he recalled the soft green light that had seeped from the hands of the priests. His pain had fled at its touch, his wounds stitching themselves together before his eyes. Within minutes he'd been whole, without so much as a scar to remind him of the desperate battle in Fort Fall.

The healers had taken more time with Alana's brother, Braidon. The wound in his stomach had been deep, and the boy was barely clinging to life when the priests reached him. Hands raised, three priests had gathered in a circle, their power forming a glowing dome of green around the boy. For hours they had stood thus, unmoving, their eyes closed and brows creased, features like stone.

Devon's worry had reached a fever pitch by the time they finally lowered their hands. Shuffling forward, he'd barely dared to breathe as he searched for signs of life in the young man. Only as the last of the green light faded away did he glimpse the gentle rise and fall of Braidon's chest, and that the wound in his stomach had vanished.

Even now, Devon could hardly believe he'd witnessed such a miracle. During the war, he'd watched the Tsar's Magickers decimate the Trolan army with their power. Yet there were few healers amidst their ranks, and their powers were never wasted on regular soldiers. Thinking of friends he'd lost to lesser wounds than the one Braidon had taken, Devon felt the familiar anger stirring.

After the temple, Enala and her Gold Dragon, Dahniul, had flown them further into the mountains, to the hidden city of Erachill. It was there Devon had announced his decision to return to the Three Nations, and save Alana from the clutches of the Tsar.

To his surprise, Enala had readily agreed, though she had left it up to Dahniul to decide whether the dragon would carry them. He could still remember the dragon's soft voice in his mind, after asking why he would risk such a quest. Devon's response had been simple and to the point.

Because I do not desert my friends.

A rumble had come from deep in the dragon's chest, and Devon had felt an odd warmth spreading through his mind, even before the reply came.

Then I will take you.

Afterwards, Kellian had been quick to announce he would be coming as well, hopeless though their mission seemed. Devon had tried to dissuade his friend, but there was no changing the man's mind once it was made up, and two days later they'd left the mountain fortress on dragon back.

Enala had joined them for that first length of the journey, directing Dahniul south and west across Northland until they reached the northern coast of Trola. The dragon had landed near the ruins of Straken. There, priest and dragon had bid them farewell.

"The Tsar will sense me if I journey further with you, my friends," Enala had told them. "Now he knows I live, he will be searching for me. He won't be taken by surprise again, and even I don't have the power to fight the creatures he will send."

So Enala and Dahniul had bid their farewells and soared back into the northern skies, to Erachill and the boy they'd left behind.

Devon found himself smiling as he thought of Braidon. The boy had wanted to come as well, to help save his sister, but he'd found the rest of the party aligned against him. No one wanted to face Alana's wrath if she discovered they'd allowed her brother to return to the Three Nations. As it was, it was a relief to know Braidon remained in Northland, safe beyond the reach of the Tsar.

"Master that power of yours, Braidon," Devon had told him. "Then we'll see."

He wondered how Braidon's training was progressing beneath Enala's watchful eye. Bright as he was, the boy seemed to be struggling in the days before Devon and Kellian had left. The loss of Braidon's sister had left him despondent. His eyes were often distant, his mind far away in another world. Devon prayed to the Gods he could find a way to save Alana and reunite the two siblings.

"We're close." Betran's voice from the road ahead snapped Devon back to the present.

Looking around, he shivered. The streets were dark, most of the buildings just crumbling remnants of the ancient structures which had once decorated the Trolan city.

Here and there lights flickered, the dim lanterns of the few residents piercing the gloom. Above, the sky was black, the stars hidden by clouds. Even so, he could sense Kellian's tension beside him.

"Where are we heading?" Kellian asked, keeping his voice low.

"The bathhouses," Betran replied. When Kellian muttered something choice, the man shrugged and replied, "Can't rebuild a civilisation without bathhouses."

Devon chuckled, but Kellian caught him by the arm and pulled him back as Betran moved on. "Are you sure we can trust this man?" he hissed.

"Probably a bit late to be asking that now," Devon replied with a grin. When Kellian only glared at him, he elaborated. "If he'd wanted trouble, he would have already taken us down some darkened alley and had his friends waylay us. Now come on, if I smell half as bad as you, we're both in need of a bath."

He continued down the street to where Betran now stood beneath a bright cluster of lanterns. Kellian grumbled something unintelligible behind his back, but a moment later his friend's footsteps followed after him. As they approached the building, a wooden door swung open and a burly man stepped out into the street. Folding his arms, he studied the three of them, then settled his gaze on the Trolan.

"What's this, Betran?" he rumbled. "Last I heard you couldn't afford a barber, let alone a bath." The man waved a hand in front of his face to emphasise his words. "Certainly smells like it."

Betran bristled, but Kellian stepped forward briskly before their companion could find the words to respond.

"Betran here was just showing us the way. We're new in town."

Taking a breath, Betran collected himself. "They're here to see Godrin."

The doorman narrowed his eyes. "He's not taking visitors."

"We're friends," Kellian said quickly, then in a voice no louder than a whisper: "Enala sent us."

For a second it seemed the doorman had not heard. He stood still as a statue, the muscles of his neck and shoulders bulging. Devon tensed, readying himself for a fight, but before he could move the guard silently turned and stepped back into the establishment. Leaping forward, Devon jammed his foot into the doorway to keep the man from locking them out.

Inside the bathhouse, the guard glanced back and raised an eyebrow. "Are you going to stand in the doorway all night, or are you going to come inside?"

Devon blinked. Beneath his beard, he felt his cheeks grow warm. Giving a gruff nod, he stepped through the doorway, followed closely by Betran and Kellian. Inside they waited as the door was closed and bolted behind them, then followed the guard down a long corridor leading into the earth.

The temperature rose as the corridor ended abruptly, giving way to a circular chamber with a domed ceiling. On the other side of the chamber was another stone corridor, but elsewhere wooden booths lined the room. Most had their doors closed, but the guard gestured to one that still stood open.

"Cloaks, clothes and boots in there, please. You'll find towels and slippers inside," he said.

Grinning, Devon shared a glance with Kellian and Betran. "Right boys, who's first?"

"I'll wait out here," Betran said quickly, his eyes flickering nervously towards the exit.

Devon couldn't fault him for his worries—no doubt he'd get the blame if things went wrong with Godrin. He was about to agree with the Trolan, when the guard spoke again.

"You'll join your friends, Betran," he said in a tone that brooked no argument.

A strained silence followed. Feeling the tension rising, Devon glanced at the guard, then shrugged. "Well, we'd best get to it boys!" Grinning, he stepped into the booth.

After a moment's hesitation the others followed. The small wooden room sported a single bench and hooks for their clothing, but it was clearly designed for two occupants at the most. A lot of grunting and shuffling followed as they fought to remove their clothes in the cramped quarters, before quickly wrapping towels around their waists to hide themselves.

Finally, they stepped back out into the stone chamber and locked the door behind them. Entrusting the key to Kellian, Devon looked around for the guard, feeling more than a little exposed with only a towel to cover him. It wasn't the being naked that bothered him, so much as the sudden sense of vulnerability. It was one thing to walk into danger unarmed—it was something else entirely to do so without even a thread of clothing on his back.

The guard appeared from the corridor that presumably led deeper into the bathhouse, his expression still unreadable.

"Ready?" he asked, his voice echoing off the stone ceiling.

Devon nodded, and the man turned on his heel without another word. They followed him a short way down the corridor, until he stopped in front of a heavy metal door. He undid the latch and heaved it open. A cloud of steam billowed out, and the guard gestured them inside.

One by one they ducked through the door and entered the sauna. Through the steam, Devon glimpsed a circular stone bench in the centre of the room. Several men lounged there, laying with their backs to the stone or sitting in silent contemplation. Around the edges of the chamber were more ledges, along with stone bowls and steel faucets. Sweat dripped from Devon's forehead as the hot air swamped him.

As they moved further inside, the guard's voice came from behind them. "Cross the room and go into the next chamber. You'll find a thermal pool. Godrin is waiting for you there."

An ominous screech came from behind them as the door swung closed, followed by the muffled *click* of the latch being locked. Despite the heat, a chill slid down Devon's spine. Doing his best to ignore it, he straightened his shoulders and walked around the stone bench in the centre of the room, taking care not to trip over any outstretched limbs.

The doorway took shape from the steam as he approached the far side of the chamber. Sweat trickled down his brow as he stepped through, eager to leave behind the scrutiny of the half-naked men. The walls narrowed around him as he entered a corridor, then widened again into a secondary chamber. Here, the ground ended abruptly in the clear waters of a steaming pool. It was difficult to see more than a few feet into the rippling waters. As he came to a stop a voice called out to them in a Trolan twang.

"Devon, Kellian, how pleasant of you to join me. I heard you were dead."

"I've been hearing that a lot," Devon replied with a grunt.

Laughter carried across the water. "Come, join me. You must be weary after your travels."

Devon shrugged, and removing his towel, stepped into the water. He winced as the heat engulfed his leg, reminding him of the blows he'd taken in the bar, and he paused. Kellian stepped past, a weary smile on his face. Walking down the steps into the bath, he sank beneath the surface, only to reappear a few seconds later. Silently he raised an eyebrow at Devon.

Muttering under his breath, Devon steeled himself and followed his friend into the scalding water. A splash came from behind him as Betran did the same, and together they walked forward until they were submerged up to their waists. Slowly the heat became more bearable, and Devon found the aches in his muscles beginning to fade.

Kellian had already disappeared into the steam, and gritting his teeth, Devon chased after his friend. Back in Ardath, Kellian had been wealthy enough to afford luxuries such as the bathhouses. Devon usually had to make do with washing himself in the pig trough nearest the *Firestone.* Ahead, Kellian reappeared, but he was no longer alone.

Lounging on the other side of the pool was a man almost as large as Devon himself. He sat with the water up to his chest, bulging arms stretched out on either side of him, an amused smile on his clean-shaven face. Muscles along his shoulders rippled as he lowered his arms and stood, his hawk-like brown eyes studying them intently. Devon shivered as they settled on him.

"Well, if it isn't the Butcher of Kalgan," the stranger said softly.

"I take it you're Godrin."

The man nodded. "I hear you have a message for me from Enala. You had better hope it's important. Your life depends on it."

Devon glanced around them, but the steam hid the rest of the room from view. As far as he could see, they were alone. Even so, the hairs on the back of his neck tingled, and his heart beat quickened.

Forcing a bravado he didn't quite feel, Devon smirked. "Sorry to disappoint you, but we're the message."

Godrin's brow deepened as he looked from Devon to Kellian. "You'd best explain," he said. As he spoke, he raised a hand. Movement came from behind him as two men stepped forward, crossbows in hand. "Or I'll be sending you back to Enala in pieces."

3

For Braidon, the weeks since the final confrontation at Fort Fall had dragged by with excruciating slowness. Each day he waited for news of his sister, for word of her public torture and execution at the hands of the Tsar. With each passing hour he could feel his anxiety rising, the strain of expectation slowly tearing him apart. His nights were spent tossing and turning, his thoughts consumed by the awful things the Stalkers might be doing to Alana.

Yet still there was nothing, not a single whisper of her fate. It was as though she had vanished off the face of the continent.

Often Braidon would find his thoughts drawn back to the last battle, to what he might have done differently to save Alana from the Stalkers. But those final moments were little more than a blur now. From the moment the crossbow bolt had torn through his stomach, he could recall only glimpses, of Quinn laughing and Alana crying out in agony, of flames burning in the darkness, and a golden dragon soaring through icy skies.

Only when the warming light of the healers had touched him did the memories resume, drawing him back to the agony of a reality without his sister. He had woken with a cry in the quiet sanctuary of an Earth Temple. For a moment he'd thought himself back in Sitton Forest, in the ruins of Antonia's temple. But as his vision cleared and he saw the light fading from the hands of the priests surrounding him, he'd realised the truth.

He was no longer in the Three Nations, no longer under the influence of the Tsar. He was finally free.

And Alana had given her life to make it so.

Exhaustion had taken him then, and he'd faded back into the darkness. When he'd woken next, he'd found himself here, in the strange city known as Erachill. Hidden deep in the mountains of Northland, it was difficult to know where the city itself ended and the original caves began. Even now, as he wandered down the winding corridors of the city, he could only wonder at the centuries of toil it must have taken to construct such a place.

Ahead the light was growing, the flickering lanterns giving way to natural sunlight. He breathed a sigh as he stepped out into the open, his chest swelling with relief to have open space around him. Above the cliffs stretched up a hundred feet, the worn granite pockmarked by dozens of caves identical to the one from which he'd just emerged. Around each opening, blocks of marble formed great facades of polished white, each engraved with runes and glyphs depicting the rooms hidden within. Great staircases had been carved into the cliff-face, winding their way up between the caves without so much as a banister for safety.

Shivering, Braidon turned his gaze to the distant flood-plains of Northland. They fell away below him, the rocky slopes of the mountain giving way to open ground. With winter now gripping the continent, snow blanketed the land as far as the eye could see, broken only by the occasional rocky outcrop. Above the mountains the sky was grey and beginning to darken, the heavy clouds promising the approach of yet another winter storm.

Hoping there was still time before it struck, Braidon set out across the rocky slopes, taking care to avoid patches of ice as he searched for the flash of green robes that would reveal his mentor's location. The mountain winds had already blown the slope clear of snow, but the going was precarious, and it was a few minutes before he finally saw her. She was in her favourite spot, seated atop a ledge with her legs hanging out over the five-hundred-foot drop. Swallowing hard, Braidon picked his way towards her, coming to a stop when he was still a few feet from the edge.

"You're late, boy," Enala said without looking up.

"Sorry, Enala, I…was distracted."

She glanced back at him, her eyes creased with sadness. "You were thinking of your sister." When he didn't reply, she went on. "Devon and Kellian will bring her back, Braidon. You must have faith."

"Faith?" he asked. His eyes burned, but remembering his sister's strength, he refused to show his weakness. "They don't even have magic. What chance do they have against the Tsar?"

"They saved you…"

"*You* saved me, Enala," he snapped. Taking a breath, he tried to quill his sudden anger. Shaking, he crouched down on his haunches and looked across at her. "Maybe if you'd gone with them…"

Enala shook her head. Her wrinkles seemed to have deepened since she'd returned from Trola, and her sapphire eyes were weary when she looked at him. "He knows I live now, young Braidon. He will be searching for me. If I went with them, it would not take long for him to find me. Then my powers would matter little."

Despair swelling in his chest, Braidon looked away. A strained silence fell between them as Braidon looked out over the plains, where the soft flickering of lightning burned in the distant clouds.

"Shall we begin then?" he said abruptly.

The old priest looked at him closely. "Are you sure–"

"I'm fine," he snapped, cutting her off. "The sooner I master my useless power, the sooner I can be rid of this place."

Enala pursed her lips, but he turned away, unable to bear her pity. He heard her sigh. "Very well. You know the process. I will observe you while…"

"Fine," Braidon grunted.

Seating himself, he crossed his legs and closed his eyes, doing his best to force thoughts of the old woman and his sister from his mind. His lungs swelled as he sucked in a breath, then exhaled. Concentrating on his breathing, he sought the peace of mindfulness, to escape the pull of his body, the lure of emotion, the strain of his memories.

Yet even as he did so, he felt the chaos pressing back, the past rising up to haunt him. A pang came from his stomach, and his hand drifted unconsciously to where the crossbow bolt had struck him. Not a mark remained, but amidst the darkness, the memory felt fresh, an almost tangible thing, piercing his consciousness.

He shuddered, but with an effort of will, released the memory. It drifted back out into the void as he forced his mind back to his breath.

In, out. In, out.

The darkness swirled as more memories rose to assail

him. He saw again their arrival on the back of Dahniul, felt the thrill of flight and the wonder of the beast's power. Thought to be extinct in the Three Nations, a few dragons had apparently survived in the wild lands of the north, descended from those that had fought alongside mankind against the dark Magicker Archon a hundred years prior. Bound by an ancient treaty between the Gold Dragons and the king of Trola, the creatures only allowed royal descendants to ride them. Fortunately for Braidon and his friends, Enala was such a descendent—perhaps even the last one left living.

Realising he'd been distracted again, Braidon tore his thoughts away from the noble beasts. It did not take long, though, for his undisciplined mind to wander again, and he found himself thinking of the escort that had met them as they'd landed beneath the cliffs of Erachill. Armed soldiers had marched out to surround them, before leading them deep into the bowels of the city. Enala they had treated with reverence, but Braidon and the others they had looked on with anger and suspicion.

Then the Queen had come, with her steely green eyes and a crown of twisted iron upon her head. Grey had streaked her auburn hair, but she carried about her such an authority few would dare challenge her.

Braidon shivered at the memory, and releasing it, plunged deeper into his subconscious. Something was flickering in the darkness now, a white light that seemed to radiate from all around. The sight of it sent a shiver through his spirit and he pulled back. An image formed in his mind, of his sister, a smile on her face, her eyes dancing with amusement.

Alana.

Pain sliced through him at the thought of her. He shuddered as memories flashed by, and he watched again her desperate battle against Quinn. He'd tried to save her, had tried to use his magic to drive back the Stalkers. Only then had he learned the truth: his magic was a sham, no more than a fancy trick with the light to create illusions, harmless.

Braidon fled into the darkness, seeking now not inner calm, but to escape the memories, to forget that final glimpse of Alana as she was dragged away by the Tsar's Stalkers.

And in the darkness, the white light grew. Only when Braidon finally recovered his senses did he realise it was all around him, brilliant and shining, hemming him in. Terror filled his soul as he realised he was lost, trapped amidst the swirling powers of his magic. If it engulfed him, he would be lost.

He spun, searching the white, seeking the darkness. A speck appeared far above, impossibly distant, unreachable. Gathering himself, he raced towards it. The light swirled, circling and drawing nearer. Claws reached out to tear at him, and he screamed as the icy hooks dragged him back. His flight faltered, and he watched with despair as the light folded in on itself, gathering all around, twisting and changing, until the great shining form of a Feline rose before him.

Braidon opened his spirit mouth to scream as the Feline loomed. The creature took a step towards him, jaws agape, teeth reaching out to tear him asunder, to hurl his soul into the void. Should it succeed, he would be consumed, his body reduced to an empty husk to be controlled by his magic. He would become a demon.

With a roar, the beast leapt…

…only for a shining red inferno to spring into life between them. As the Feline struck the blaze, it screamed, the white light flickering and falling back, the creature shrinking as it retreated.

And then Braidon was back in the real world, his cries echoing off the nearby cliffs as he threw himself back from the awful fangs…

"Braidon, calm yourself!" He froze as a steely hand gripped him by the wrist.

Blinking, he found Enala sitting alongside him. His terror fled, replaced by the sickening despair of failure. Tearing his arm from the old woman's grip, he stood abruptly and swung away. A loose stone lay nearby and he lashed out at it with his boot, sending it soaring out over the ledge.

"*Damnit!*" he screamed.

"Braidon, stop, you're okay–"

"I'm *not* okay," he snapped, turning on Enala, "I'll never be okay, not with this…this *thing* inside me."

"It is a part of you, Braidon," Enala replied, "and you were closer that time."

The anger left Braidon in a rush. His shoulders slumped as he lowered his gaze to the ground. They had been at this for two weeks now, but still he felt no closer to mastering the magic within him. Whatever Enala said, he continued to fail at the final step. When his magic appeared before him, his courage would fail and he would flee into the darkness until Enala intervened. One day, he knew the creature would catch him…

"Fear is its only weapon, Braidon." Enala's voice cut across his thoughts.

"What's the point, Enala?" he asked bitterly. "Why does it even matter? Everything I do is just an illusion!"

"There is always a point, Braidon. There is no *just* when it comes to magic." She sighed, her eyes taking on a faraway look. "I knew a Magicker once, with powers like yours. She could manipulate the light to conceal herself, become invisible. I've never met anyone as brave."

"Who was she?"

Enala grinned. "A Baronian thug who tried to kill me on more than one occasion."

Braidon's head jerked up. "What?"

Enala smiled. "Life isn't always as simple as it seems, young Braidon."

Still confused, he shook his head. "What happened to her?"

"She gave up her life to save us from Archon's demon."

Braidon was lost for words. He swallowed, staring into the aged face of the woman standing opposite him. The years had turned her hair white and wrinkled the once youthful face, but her eyes shone with power and an ancient wisdom. Even so, it was easy to forget the things she had seen, the dangers she had faced in her long life.

"How have you lived so long, Enala?" he asked suddenly, the question slipping out before he could bite his tongue.

Enala's laughter bubbled across the clifftop. Gently, she eased herself back to the rocky ground and gestured for Braidon to join her. They sat in silence for a moment, looking out at the approaching storm. It was a long time before Enala answered, and a cramp was beginning to form in Braidon's leg when she finally spoke.

"Truthfully, I don't really know why I have lived this long. It was the same for my brother. He told me once that it happens for one in a thousand Magickers, that occasionally the magic will grant its wielder extended life. Or perhaps it came from our…interaction with the Gods. Although for Gabriel…" She trailed off.

For a second Braidon thought he glimpsed tears in her eyes, but she looked away before they could fall.

"Enala?" he said. Leaning forward, he placed a hand on her shoulder. "Are you okay?"

Enala smiled, all trace of tears vanished. "Do not concern yourself with the sorrows of an old woman, young Braidon," she said. "There is so much behind me now, Gabriel seems little more than the memory of another woman at times."

Braidon swallowed, not understanding, but hearing the grief behind her words. Sensing this was not a topic the old woman wished to speak of, he changed the subject.

"What was she like? Antonia?" he asked, remembering the legends. "You met her?"

Enala chuckled. "'Met' would be putting it lightly."

"And were the legends true? Was she really as powerful as they say?"

"She is an enigma," Enala replied, her wrinkles deepening as she smiled.

"Is?" Braidon asked, a tingle running down his spine. He sat up, suddenly alert. "She's gone though, isn't she?"

"Her body, yes. Like all the Gods, she gave up her physical form after the battle with Archon," she answered. "But they never truly left us."

"What do you mean?"

"The Gods existed long before our priests devised a way to channel their spirits and power into physical form," Enala replied, "and they exist still. Their spirits are all around us: in the light of a sunset, in the earth beneath our feet, in the wind and the rain and clouds. They are the spirits of the land, the balance to our world. The source of all magic."

Braidon clenched his jaw as he realised what she was saying. “But they cannot help us.”

Enala threw back her head and laughed. “You are an insightful student, young Braidon, I will give you that.” Her eyes danced. “But still not entirely correct. Even in spirit, the Gods are not impotent. It was Antonia, after all, who sent me to find you.”

“Antonia? Truly? How is that possible?”

“Let us just say, the Gods are inside some of us, more than others.”

Braidon frowned. Sensing he would get no more information on the subject, he changed tactics. “But why would she care about me and my sister in the first place?”

Enala sighed. “I do not know the answer to that,” she replied. Her eyes grew distant as she looked out over the plains of Northland. “But I have a feeling we will find out before the end. Now come, we’d best return to the city. The storm is almost upon us.”

She stood and started off towards the cliffs of Erachill, leaving Braidon to scramble to his feet and chase after her, a dozen questions still clambering within his mind for answers.

4

Alana followed Quinn through the corridors of the citadel, fully dressed now, her sword thumping gently against her side. The blade made her feel more at ease, though she knew it would be pointless attempting to flee. The guards no longer tailed her, but there were eyes everywhere, and she doubted she'd make it as far as the gates before someone stopped her.

Regardless, she could not run, not while a million questions still filled her mind. She caught a glimpse of herself in the shining breastplate of a nearby guard. The hackles rose on her neck as she saw the cool eyes staring back at her. She quickly turned away. Even her own reflection seemed foreign to her now.

Who are you?

Casting aside the question, she looked up in time to see Quinn push open two double doors and make his way into a large hall packed with long wooden tables. Men and women were walking along the rows between the tables, and along the far wall cooks were serving food over a steel counter. Following Quinn into the dining room, several of the occupants looked up at their approach. Whispers spread around the room, giving way to a hushed silence.

Alana clenched her jaw as she felt the eyes of everyone on her. She glanced at Quinn, her mouth suddenly dry. "They know me?" she hissed beneath her breath.

"Of course," Quinn replied. "You were their teacher."

"Their…teacher?" Alana stuttered. A sudden laughter bubbled up from her chest, emerging as a half-muted snort. Struggling to control herself, she gasped the next words. "What did I *teach?*"

"Magic," Quinn said.

"Oh…" Alana trailed off. She opened her mouth, then closed it again, lost for words, struggling to comprehend what Quinn was saying. The men and women in the room were staring back at her with a mixture of awe and surprise, their silence absolute. Most wore ordinary clothing, though a few sported the red cloaks of soldiers.

Beside her, Quinn was still speaking. "Your father placed you in charge of the young Magickers. You taught them how to reach their magic, trained them to be strong enough to master it."

Alana tore herself free of her shock. "Taught them to use it? I didn't even know I had magic until an hour ago!"

"That's not true, Alana. Deep down, you know that. Look around you, this is the truth. This is who you were—and will be again!"

Shaking her head, Alana stumbled back a step. Chest tight, she wanted to scream, to tell him leave her alone, to stop with his lies, but before she could speak, a tentative voice came from behind her.

"Alana?"

Heart racing, she swung towards the voice, reaching for her sword hilt. Behind her, the young man who'd spoken jumped back. Raising his hands, he gaped at her, eyes locked to the half-drawn sword.

"Who…who are you?" she gasped.

The young man blinked and glanced over her shoulder at Quinn. His plain face was heavily tanned, and long black hair tumbled down around his shoulders. He was dressed for the cold in a plain white tunic of homespun wool and heavy black pants. Alana was sure she'd never seen him in her life.

"My apologies, young Bodrum," Quinn said, stepping up alongside her. "Alana's magic has…backfired. She has—temporarily—lost her memories. I brought her here to see if her old students could help jog them."

"Oh!" The young man turned to Alana, his mouth hanging open. Then he seemed to remember himself, and clamping his jaw shut, offered his hand. "My apologies, princess! My name is Bodrum, you were my teacher a few years back. You…taught me to master my magic over the Earth."

Still struggling to contain her own shock, Alana stared at his outstretched hand for a second too long, noticing he wore the same silver and emerald bracelets as the teacher she'd met in the gardens. Finally, she reached out and took his hand.

"It's nice to…meet you?" she said.

A grin appeared on his face. "It's good…to see you again," he said. "I…never got to thank you for your help. I did not appreciate your teaching at the time, but you…you gave me the strength I needed to survive."

Alana smiled despite herself. "I'm glad I could help you, Bodrum."

Nodding, the young man walked away. Alana made to speak with Quinn, but before she could get a word out, a young woman appeared. She smiled, words tumbling from her mouth so quickly Alana struggled to keep up. She was saying something about how long it had been since Alana had last been around the citadel, and how good it was to see her again. Alana noticed she seemed nervous, her eyes constantly flickering to Quinn, her hands deep in her pockets.

Alana hardly managed a "hello" before the woman darted off again. Another student quickly moved in to take her place. Before Alana knew it, she was stammering through explanation after explanation, even as more students gathered around to await their turn. They were all studiously polite, keeping their distance, bowing and curtseying, speaking in respectful tones and never questioning how she could have lost control of her power.

As the crowd finally started to thin, Alana found herself feeling unexpectedly alone. While every student had offered her their thanks, there was a stiffness about the way they approached her, as though they were speaking out of obligation rather than gratitude. All kept a respectful distance, offering token apologies when they discovered her predicament.

When the last of them had left, Alana could only shake her head in confusion. Their thanks had at first lifted her, yet she found herself wondering why none of them had seemed anything more than just students to her. Had she not befriended any of them, not inspired anything but respect and professional courtesy?

Hugging her arms to her chest, she turned and found Quinn watching her.

"Are you okay?" he asked.

She scowled, growing irritated by his constant concern. "I'm fine," she snapped.

He nodded, though she could see in his eyes he did not believe her. Even so, he dropped the subject and taking her arm, led her across the room to an empty table. As they seated themselves he waved to a nearby servant, sending the man scurrying across the room in search of food. A tray of roasted lamb and stewed vegetables appeared a few minutes later, followed by two tankards of ale.

"Your favourite…once," Quinn said, gesturing to the food and drink.

"I guess some things don't change." The tankard was halfway to Alana's lips when she glanced up and found Quinn watching her. A familiar flash of anger reared inside her, but remembering his earlier kindness, she pressed it down.

Hesitantly, she tilted her tankard in his direction. "Cheers."

Quinn smiled and lifting his own drink, clinked it against hers. "Cheers."

Meeting his eyes, Alana took a long swig of the bitter ale, enjoying the cool liquid in the heat of the dining hall.

"What do you think?" Quinn asked.

"It's good," Alana replied, though she knew he wasn't talking about the ale. When he only raised an eyebrow, she sighed and went on. "I don't know what to think of all this, Quinn. I'm…sorry I've been so hard on you. I know you're only trying to help but…it's just all so overwhelming."

"I know…" he began, but she raised a hand and he trailed off.

"You have to understand, just a few days ago I thought all the Magickers…captured by the Tsar were dead. And now it turns out I was *teaching* them?"

Quinn laughed at that. "Yes, I guess I can see how that would be confusing."

Alana shook her head. "I don't understand though: why haven't the people been told what happens here? About what happens to the Magickers who are brought to the citadel?"

"Because they cannot know their children live." Alana made to speak, but at a look from Quinn, closed her mouth again. After a moment he went on. "It is one of the reasons they are brought here. Once, before the Tsar, magic was ungoverned. It was chaos. Wild magic was free to wreak havoc across the Three Nations, taking lives at random. There is a legend in my hometown, about a boy who once levelled our town and brought its community to its knees. Such power cannot go unchecked."

"Yes, but that doesn't explain why you allow–"

"Please, let me finish, Alana," Quinn interrupted her. She saw the pain behind his eyes. Gritting her teeth, she nodded, and he continued. "As I was saying, before the Tsar, people with magic were free to exploit their powers, to take advantage of the powerless, to destroy the lives of others, usually without repercussions."

"The Tsar's rule has changed that. After he was crowned, he passed laws to protect the people from exploitation by Magickers. Those who used their powers to harm others were brought before his judgement, while the benevolent were allowed their freedom. It worked for a while—until a General overthrew the Trolan king and led an uprising against the Empire. Hundreds of Magickers stood with him. Their powers enacted a terrible price, and while ultimately the rebellion failed, their treachery convinced the Tsar that the price of free magic was too great."

"And so magic was outlawed. Those Magickers known to the crown were brought here and offered a choice: imprisonment, or service to the Tsar. So it has continued with every new Magicker we discover."

"But that doesn't explain why the people can't know what happens to the Magickers you capture!"

Quinn sighed. "They cannot know, because the children cannot know of their lives before this place."

"What..." Alana trailed off as realisation struck her, her stomach curdling. She stared at Quinn, open-mouthed. "I wiped their memories," she breathed.

"Yes," Quinn said solemnly. "The children are made to forget their past, so they will never be tempted to use their magic to benefit their former families."

"No wonder you wanted me back so badly," she croaked, the words catching in her throat.

Quinn reached across the table and placed his hand on hers, but she flinched away. He looked at her, a frown on his lips. "It's more than that and you know it, Alana," he said. "Your father loves you, and your brother too. He would do anything to protect you."

"Oh?" Alana snapped, on her feet now. "Is that why he sent his dragons? Can you honestly say he wasn't trying to kill us with those beasts?"

"He was...desperate. He thought you were lost to him."

Alana swallowed. "So he ordered us killed, rather than let us escape."

"No...he only wished to stop you," Quinn said quickly. "He would never have seen you harmed, Alana."

Alana stared down at him, trying to judge the truth behind his words. She could still remember her terror as the scarlet creature dropped from the sky, still recall the searing heat of its flames, the stench of rotting meat and burning ash. Looking at Quinn now, seeing the pain in his eyes, Alana knew he would never have sent such creatures to kill her. Yet her own father had. Or was Quinn telling the truth? Had the dragons only ever been meant to stop them?

The anger left her in a rush as she slumped back into her chair. She stared at her food for a moment, the roast lamb and vegetables still untouched. Absently, she picked up a fork and began to push them around the plate. Memories swam before her eyes, of Quinn and Devon, her brother and Kellian. The faces of her students followed, one by one, and she felt the weight of guilt on her shoulders. She had stolen their families from them, robbed them of their pasts.

Who are you?

Yet even as the question rang in her mind, she found herself looking around the dining hall, watching the other Magickers as they sat together. Many wore smiles on their faces, and most seemed at peace, content with their place in life. She shivered, wondering if they could sense the hole in their lives, the abyss she had left within them. Or had her spell been a gift to them? Had her magic released them from the pain of loss, of being separated from their parents forever?

Across from her, concern lurked in Quinn's eyes. In a flash of intuition, she realised the compassion he'd shown her today had been far more than that of a servant. With the students, she had wondered why none of them had seemed to really know her, why they had been distant, indifferent to her loss. Now, as she looked at Quinn, she realised he had been the only one to show her true kindness since arriving in this cold palace. And she knew there was something more between them, something he had not yet revealed.

The question came unbidden to her lips before she could stop herself. "Who are you to me, Quinn?"

He smiled then, his eyes alight. "I am *your* teacher, Alana."

5

"Well, I'm waiting." Godrin stood with his arms crossed, eyes glowering as he watched them.

Devon studied the crossbow men standing behind the hulking crime lord, trying to judge the distance between them. On flat ground he might have risked charging Godrin, but waist-deep in the bath, there was no way he would be fast enough. Letting out a long breath, he smiled at the mobster.

"Really, is this any way to treat friends?" Kellian spoke before Devon could. Moving in front of the others, he gestured to the archers, who quickly redirected their crossbows at him.

"Friends?" Godrin spat the word like he'd swallowed poison. "Do you know how many of my countrymen lost their lives to his hammer, Kellian? To *your* blades, for that matter?"

"Eighty-six," Devon interrupted. "Now ask how many friends I lost to Trolan swords."

Godrin sneered. "They got what they deserved, as will

you. If this is all the Butcher of Kalgan has to say for himself…"

"My friend, please, do not be so hasty!" Kellian cut in. Holding up his hands, he continued smoothly. "We did not come here to rehash the past, though no doubt we could debate for hours who was responsible for the war. No, we came to talk of the future, of a chance for Trola to regain its former glory."

The man froze at Kellian's words, his eyes narrowing. "And how exactly do two Plorsean rebels propose to accomplish such a task?"

"By bringing down the Tsar, and the Empire with him."

"Ha! You must think me a fool, Kellian. Do you think you can tempt Trola into a war it cannot possibly hope to win? We would be crushed in the first battle. And then where would my people be? The Tsar would slaughter or enslave the survivors. Trola would truly be doomed."

"I took you for an intelligent man, Godrin. Can you not see that Trola is doomed regardless? You hardly have the people to till the fields or man your ships, and any progress you make is crippled by the Tsar's taxes. How long before your people starve? Two years? Three?"

"We are Trolans. We will survive."

"You will die as paupers in your own country," Kellian snapped. He paused, and a sly smile spread across his lips. "Or you can join us, and fight for your freedom."

"I will not drag my people into another war."

"Who said anything about a war?" Kellian retorted.

"How else do you intend to free us from the Empire?"

"By assassinating the Tsar. Without his magic, without the dragons and demons, the Empire would be sundered. Trola and Lonia could be free once more. Northland would support you, send aid to your freedom fighters, as your nations once did for them."

Godrin stared at them, lips pursed, expression unreadable. Then he began to laugh, softly at first but quickly growing louder, until the sound of his mirth echoed from the stone walls. "Assassinate the Tsar?" he gasped. "A brilliant plan—if not for, how did you put it, the magic, demons and dragons that protect him!"

"Enala believes there is a way to defeat him—if we can get close enough to the man."

"Then the old woman has finally lost her mind," Godrin snapped, the laughter dying in his throat, "and anyone mad enough to believe her is a fool."

"Fools we might be," Devon said, wading up alongside Kellian, "but at least we're not cowards, wallowing in the former glory of a fallen city."

"What did you say to me?" Godrin hissed, lurching forward. Behind him, the archers raised their crossbows. The steel points of the loaded bolts glittered in the lantern light.

Ignoring the weapons pointed at his chest, Devon laughed. "You heard me! I called you a coward, Godrin. You're nothing but a washed-up commander, using your power to prey on the same people you claim to care about, to terrorize the same citizens who once looked to you for protection. You call me a butcher, but at least I never betrayed my own people!"

"Terrorize…betray…" A vein bulged on Godrin's forehead as he sputtered out the words. "How…dare…you?"

Devon took another step forward, his voice dropping to a whisper. "Tell me, Godrin, how did you survive the battle for Kalgan? I know for a *fact* the Tsar burned everyone in the city to death. So how did an entire *cohort* survive?"

Baring his teeth, Godrin stepped forward, so that he stood eye-to-eye with Devon. "We ran," he spat. "I told the King the war was lost, that we had no choice but to surrender ourselves to the Tsar's mercy. He refused. So I took my cohort, along with any citizens who would follow us, and commandeered a ship. The city fell two days later, but we were already gone."

"So you left your comrades to die?"

"Yes," Godrin said quietly, his eyes flashing, "and I would do it again. Because of me, there is still order in Kalgan. Without my men, the city would still be a wasteland, a battlefield to be fought over by the survivors."

"Or you might have tipped the balance for Kalgan, saved the city from destruction."

"Do not mock me, Devon," Godrin replied. "We were both there. You know there was never a chance. The Tsar had already destroyed most of our forces in the Brunei Pass. The city was doomed from the moment the Tsar marched across the border."

A strained silence fell across the baths then, as the two warriors stared at one another. Devon was close enough to reach Godrin now. One quick rush, and he could use the man as a shield against the archers, giving his friends a chance to flee. But he made no move to attack. Instead, he reached out and placed a hand on the man's shoulder.

"I cannot change the past, my friend," he said, "but for what it's worth, I am sorry for what became of your people, and the part I played in it. It is a regret I will carry with me forever."

Godrin bowed his head, and Devon felt a shudder go through the former soldier. "Why are you here, butcher?" he whispered at the steaming waters. "And do not entertain me with tales of freedom and toppling empires."

Sucking in a breath, Devon glanced at Kellian. His friend shook his head, but when Devon returned his gaze to the Trolan warrior, the lie he had planned turned to dust on his tongue. "To rescue a…friend," he said instead.

Chuckling, the man straightened. "And for this friend you would go against the might of the Tsar?"

Devon grinned. "What's the point of being friends if you wouldn't walk through hell for one another?"

Godrin stared at him for a moment, the hate still lurking behind his eyes. Taking a breath, Devon moved alongside the man and sat on the stone bench running the length of the pool, exposing his back to the archers.

"You are a strange man, butcher," the former General said.

"If we are to be friends, I would prefer to be called Devon," he replied.

"Devon…" Godrin said, a pained look on his face. He shook his head. "I'm beginning to regret entertaining this meeting. I should have had my guards cut your throats and toss you in the harbour."

"And doomed your people to a slow extinction," Kellian interrupted.

"Perhaps, but they still would have thanked me for it." He started to laugh. "As it is, if word gets out you left my bathhouse alive, my own days will be numbered."

"Then you're not going to kill us?" Quiet until now, Betran burst into life. "Thank you, sir!"

Godrin stared at the young man for a moment, his eyes dark. "Betran." He said the man's name like a curse. "Don't think I've forgotten your part in this."

Betran shrank before the former General's gaze, retreating into the pool until he almost vanished into the steam. Shaking his head, Godrin turned his attention back to Devon and Kellian.

Kellian spread his hands. "You didn't answer the man's question."

"And you have not told me how you plan to rescue this friend of yours. Or how you think you can kill the Tsar."

"He is not the all-knowing, all-powerful immortal he would have you believe, Godrin," Kellian insisted.

"No?" Godrin asked.

"No," Kellian replied, "because we're still here. He sentenced the two of us to death, sent his Stalkers and demons and dragons to hunt us down, and yet here we are. Is that not enough to make you curious?"

Godrin stared at the two of them a long while, his hands trailing in the waters to either side of him, as though weighing up their fates. Devon's patience finally snapped.

"Look, sonny," he growled. Pushing himself to his feet, he climbed from the pool. The archers bristled, the crossbows rattling in their grip. Contemptuously he turned his back on them and glared down at the crime lord. "It's been a long night and my bed is calling. If you're going to try and kill us, get it over with. But I promise you, I don't die easily." He turned and glared at the two bowmen. They took a collective step back.

"You're a bold man, Devon," Godrin growled.

"Bold? Not really." Devon laughed, the sound booming from the stone walls. "Reckless, maybe. A few weeks ago I thought my time had finally come, but Alana and her brother saved me. I owe her for that. Now, are you going to help us, or not?"

Godrin's face was grim, his eyes hard, but suddenly his face split, and he threw back his head and laughed. "By the Three Gods, I think I could have liked you, Devon. If you hadn't marched with an army into my country and slaughtered my people, we might have been friends. As it is, I think that I will help you. You're right, the Tsar is not immortal. It's time we proved it. I'll march with you to Ardath. I have contacts there, might be they know a way into the citadel."

"We'll be glad for the company," Devon replied. He glanced behind him at the bowmen, who had finally lowered their weapons. "Hope you'll be leaving your friends behind, though."

Climbing from the water, Godrin offered his hand, which Devon took in his meaty grip. "What was your plan if I'd refused?"

"Kill you, and anyone else that got in my way. March up to the gates of the citadel and demand Alana's return." Devon shrugged. "I like to keep things simple."

Godrin blinked, his eyes showing surprise for the first time. Twisting, he looked down at Kellian, who was still in the pool with Betran. "He's not serious?"

Kellian smiled. "Devon is the most stubborn man I've ever met." Climbing from the bath, he joined them. "Luckily for him, he usually has the strength to back up his words."

Shaking his head, the Trolan looked from Kellian to Devon.

Devon grinned. "Admittedly, General, I'm hoping you have a better plan."

6

Quinn paused outside the giant oak doors to the throne room and took a moment to collect himself. The day had been long and strained, beginning with Alana's precipitous plunge from the balcony. Remembering her tumbling backwards over the railing, he suppressed a shudder. In that instant he had thought her lost, but unexpectedly, his magic had come to her rescue. As his heart had lurched in his chest, his magic had rushed from him, drawing in the air currents and wrapping them around Alana.

It was an ability he had not known he'd possessed, though he had heard rumours of Storm Magickers who could fly with the winds. Either way, it had saved Alana, and by extension himself. He shuddered, imagining the Tsar's rage if his daughter had succeeded in taking her own life. No, had Alana died, Quinn's life would have been forfeit—and it would not have been an easy death.

Still, it had worked out in the end. The shock of her near-death experience seemed to have snapped Alana out of her depression—at least long enough for Quinn to talk with her. Reticent as she was, it was difficult to tell whether he'd succeeded in getting through, but she had at least seemed calmer when he'd left her.

He smiled then, remembering their fiery argument in the dining hall. However much Alana fought against it, he could see much of his former student in the young woman. As they'd spoken he'd caught glimpses of the Alana he'd known—of her calculating mind and dogged determination to hunt out the truth. And at the end, the fire in her eyes when she'd accused the Tsar of trying to kill her…he could have been looking into the past, when they'd spent long afternoons arguing over the best methods of tutoring young Magickers.

Letting out a long breath, Quinn pulled himself back to the present. He nodded to the royal guards stationed outside, and one pushed open the doors. Squaring his shoulders, Quinn marched after him, while inside the throne room the guard announced his arrival.

"Your majesty, Lieutenant Quinn has arrived."

Beyond the doors, the throne room was empty but for the ring of guards surrounding the dais. Ignoring the man who'd announced him, Quinn strode across the room, his footsteps muffled by the line of red carpet leading up to the throne. The guards at the base of the dais parted as he approached. Striding up the steps, he dropped to one knee.

"Lieutenant, Krista tells me you have been showing my daughter her former pupils." The Tsar's voice came from the throne, soft and dangerous.

His mouth dry, Quinn swallowed. "She was…upset. I thought it best to show her some of her former life."

"Did I not tell you she was to be left alone?"

Quinn climbed to his feet. He stared into the Tsar's

crystal blue eyes, seeking some hint of emotion, but the man's expression remained unreadable. Though not a tall man, the Tsar was powerfully built. His jet-black hair was streaked with grey, but he showed no other outward sign of aging. He had first been crowned King of Plorsea some fifty years ago, yet he looked no older than forty, and not for the first time, Quinn found himself wondering at the man's true age.

"With respect, sir," Quinn began, clearing his throat, "if I had not acted, she would now be dead."

The Tsar did not move, but Quinn thought he detected a slight tremor to the man's brow. "Explain."

"She…threw herself from the balcony," Quinn said in a rush. "I was just in time to catch her with my magic. But afterwards, I thought it best to…take precautions as to her state of mind. I showed her the gardens and children, then took her to the Magicker's quarters, introduced her to some of her former students. She…seemed to…take the new… information well." He stammered to a stop beneath the withering glare of the Tsar.

A strained silence hung in the air, and Quinn found himself shrinking before the man on the throne, as though his very essence was being drawn from him. Clenching his jaw, he forced himself to look into the icy eyes.

"You overstep yourself, Lieutenant," the Tsar said. He paused, and a smile spread across his face. "But you have done well. Again, I find myself in your debt."

Quinn bowed his head. "It was my pleasure, sir," he said. "You know I have always been…fond…of your daughter."

A soft chuckle echoed from the tall marble walls. "If she can be saved, perhaps she will finally return the affection."

Heat spread across Quinn's cheeks, and clearing his

throat, he changed the subject. "What about your son? Have you heard anything from the Queen?"

"My spies tell me he lives," the Tsar replied, "but my emissary has not yet reached their capital."

"He will be returned," Quinn said. "She will not dare risking war for a single boy."

"No, though she would dearly love to defy me." The Tsar chuckled. "How are preparations proceeding for the invasion?"

"You have a force of ten thousand foot soldiers and two thousand cavalry gathering on the northern shores of the lake. Half the guard have already been shifted into their wartime regiments. In addition, you have a force of almost a hundred Magickers trained in warfare, and a dozen demons at your command. As you know, only three Red Dragons remain under your control. They have not fared well in captivity."

The Tsar waved a hand. "Should we need more, I will fetch them from Dragon Country," he growled, though his smile did not waver. "So we are ready to march?"

Quinn hesitated. "Within the week, I think," he said. "Your generals tell me they still need time to organise provisions, and restore war time discipline to the troops."

"No matter," the Tsar replied, "it gives us time to secure the release of my son. Once he has been returned, Northland will fall, and there will be nowhere left for the treacherous Magickers to flee."

"What of the priest who attacked me? If the Queen has more Magickers of such power–"

"There are no more like her," the Tsar said, cutting him off. He rose to his feet. "And I will see her dead before the end. Now be gone, Quinn. After her…adventures today, perhaps it's time I visited my daughter."

7

Alana paced across her room, her thoughts far away, lingering on memories that hovered just beyond reach. Fog swamped her, but through it she could sense the truth, taunting her with its unseen knowledge. Without it, she felt helpless, forced to trust Quinn's words. And trust had never come easily for her.

Or had it?

Confused and frustrated, she slumped down onto a velvet sofa.

"It's impossible," she murmured to the empty room.

Anger flared in her then, feeding strength to her weary body. Determined, she sat up, seeking another way. Quinn had told her that only she could unlock the secrets of her mind, but without her power she had no way of doing so. She gritted her teeth at the impossibility of the task set before her.

Yet she knew there had to be a way.

Then she remembered the ancient Tillie, and how she'd begun teaching Braidon meditation to control his power.

Alana had attempted it herself, and found herself surprisingly adept at the exercise. An image flared in her mind, of the angry ball of red she'd discovered within while in the trance. She shivered, imagining it inside her, its twisting tendrils tied in unending knots, and the secret hidden within.

Could that be where she'd hidden her memories?

Alana sucked in a breath. Meditation was dangerous for those with magic—she had seen as much with her brother. Tillie had warned them what happened to those who lost control, that magic could overwhelm its user and take control. But what other choice did she have but to try? There was no other way—she had to find what lay hidden within that ball of light.

Besides, she knew now how she'd mastered the exercise so quickly, why her brother had progressed much faster than Tillie had expected: they had done it before, in another life. When they'd entered the trance, their subconsciousness had taken over, propelling them into the depths of their minds as they had apparently done so many times before.

Lowering herself to the floor, Alana closed her eyes. She focused on the rise and fall of her chest, the soft whistle of each inhalation, the thumping of blood through her veins. Memories drifted in and out of focus: of Devon, *kanker* in hand, as he fought the demon; then his face in the darkness, as they spoke of their past, and future, on the plains south of Fort Fall; and finally, the racing of her heart as his arms wrapped around her in the midnight pools.

Alana released her breath. The air slowly emptied from her lungs, and with it the thoughts of Devon drifted away. Darkness swelled, before her brother's smiling face shimmered into view. Terror gnawed at her stomach as she watched him fall, a crossbow bolt in his stomach. Quinn insisted he still lived, that the wound had not been fatal, and had been healed. Despite her mistrust, she clung to that hope. The thought of her brother free gave her strength.

Concentrating, she turned her thoughts back to her breath, imagining the air flowing through her, filling her chest and arms, her legs and head. Strength flowed into her weary body, swirling and growing, even as her consciousness expanded. Beyond herself, she sensed tremors of power twisting on the air. Instinctively she knew it was the workings of other Magickers within the citadel.

Her curiosity was piqued, but there would be time for that later. Turning from the vibrations, she forced her mind inwards, and suddenly found herself floating amidst an infinite darkness.

Alana shivered as she looked around, utterly alone amidst the black. Not a spark shone amidst the dark, not a star or candle to light the way—until she turned and saw the distant spark of red.

The sight did nothing to quell her fear. Instead it grew, swelling until it was all she could manage not to go fleeing back to the confines of her body.

Are you ready, Alana?

Quinn's words echoed through the void, and she saw again the way he'd looked at her in the dining hall.

I was your teacher, Alana.

His words had rung true, yet she sensed there was more, something he had not revealed. A part of her yearned to scream at him, to demand the answers he continued to withhold. Yet she knew now the only way she'd ever unravel the lies and half-truths was to restore her memories.

To do that, she would need to face the terror within.

Releasing a breath, Alana concentrated on the speck of red. Fear still clung to her soul, but gathering herself, she drove towards it, racing through the darkness like a fish through an endless ocean. The light appeared before her, growing larger, clearer, until it loomed like a sun, flickering from red to orange to raging blue.

She hovered before it, sensing the emotions radiating out from the tangled knots, the hidden thing lurking within. She touched her spirit hand to a thread. A wave of hatred swept through her. For a second Alana thought she would drown in it, but closing her eyes, she allowed it to wash over her. Slowly it dissipated, like a wave crashing on a sandy shore.

As the hatred faded, Alana took hold of another string and sent it whirling out into the darkness. This time it was fear that touched her, piercing her core, adding fuel to her mounting terror. She clenched her teeth and fought on, turning the ball with her mind, determined to unwrap the convoluted emotions and reveal the mystery inside.

Time passed, and the ball grew smaller, spinning faster. Flecks of light shot off into the darkness, where they drifted like stars, flashing red and orange before finally vanishing as though they'd never been.

Finally, she sensed the end was near. Only a few strands remained now, though when she reached out to pull them clear, she felt a new wave of terror strike her. More powerful than anything that had come before, it overwhelmed her. With a scream, her spirit turned in the darkness, preparing to flee.

Are you ready, Alana?

The question came again—and this time, she found her answer.

Yes!

Crying out in triumph, Alana pulled the last strands clear.

The red bindings went flashing out into the void, and a new light bathed Alana. In that second, Alana knew she'd made a terrible mistake. It was not her memories hidden amidst the tangled emotions, nor the woman she'd once been; it was the magic that had stolen them away.

Now it reared up before her, its glow not the red or orange or blue of her emotions, but the deepest green of the Earth. Terror froze Alana in place as the magic reared back on itself, twisting and morphing, its cries of release echoing through the darkness.

Alana watched as a dread Feline took shape, its giant maw open wide, its claws stretching out to engulf her tiny spirit. Pain sliced through Alana at their touch, unlike anything she'd ever experienced. She opened her mouth to scream, but in the void her cries went unheard. Agony engulfed her, driving away her strength, crushing her spirit. She found herself falling, even as the beast rose, tearing her soul from her body and flinging her into the darkness.

Back in her room, Alana's eyes flickered open, but it was no longer Alana who looked out. A soft glow bathed the carpets as the grey of her irises gave way to green. As though by a will of its own, her head turned, the magic within gazing out at its surroundings. An awful smile touched her lips, and laughter whispered from her throat.

Slowly, tentatively, her body stood, the magic in control now. Finding its balance, it strode to the outer doors and threw them open. Two men stood guard outside. Their eyes widened at her appearance, the green glow of her eyes lighting the corridor.

"Princess?" one asked.

The magic did not reply, but stepped in close and placed a hand to the man's chest. At its touch, his eyes glazed over, and before his companion could react he drew his sword and drove it into his comrade's chest. Crying out, the dying man fell back, clawing at the bloody wound.

The magic laughed as the guard died, his screams echoing loudly in the narrow corridor. Then the magic turned its gaze on the other. Immediately, the man reversed his blade and drove it into his own stomach.

Elation swept through Alana's body as the magic started down the corridor. Within, its power was spreading, harrying the spirit of the girl who'd dared command it. Power burned through the girl's veins, magic joining with blood. Within, it could feel the girl's strength fading, the flames closing on her spirit.

In the corridor, two men came running, drawn by the screams of their fellow guards. Seeing their princess, they staggered to a stop, mouths wide as they stared at the dead men behind her.

A touch to their chests, and the two began to hack at each other with their swords. They died screaming as the magic continued on, its power growing, spreading out beyond its mortal host. When the next men came into view, it no longer needed to touch them. One look into the girl's emerald eyes, and they turned and leapt on the guards who came close behind them.

"*Alana!*"

The magic spun as a voice came from behind it. A man stood in the corridor, a glowing sword in one hand, his face hard as granite.

"Alana!" he called again.

Somewhere deep within, Alana heard her name echo through the void. Turning, she saw a blinding light shining in the darkness. At its touch, her fear fell away, and she saw the awful green retreat. She shuddered, clinging to it like a lifeline in stormy seas. Her name came again, echoing through her consciousness, feeding her strength. She clambered upwards, fighting back the claws and teeth of the awful Feline.

In the hallway, the man advanced, glowing sword held tightly in one hand. It flashed once, then again, the glowing green of Alana's magic falling back before it. His jaw was set, his blue eyes flashing with untold power. Yet still the green light shone from Alana's eyes.

"Alana!" he called again, despair in his voice now. "Come back to me!"

Within, Alana heard the call. Gathering her strength, she tore herself free of the last bindings trapping her in the dark. With a scream, she shot towards the white, as the beast roared its frustration. The green flickered around her, its grip on her body loosening. She could hear her name echoing from all around her now, and she followed it like a beacon, reaching out, grasping it with all her strength…

Alana gasped as she found herself suddenly back in her own body. Shuddering, she staggered sideways into a wall. The strength went from her legs and she slid to the floor, her eyes falling on the bloodstained carpets, on the broken bodies lying nearby. Her throat contracted as she struggled to breathe. Slowly, she toppled sideways to the floor, unable to even lift a hand.

Staring up at the gold inlaid ceiling, Alana groaned as agony spread through her limbs. Darkness swirled at the edges of her vision, as from somewhere nearby she heard her name called once more.

Teeth clenched, she fought to remain conscious. Overhead, the face of the Tsar appeared, his brow creased in concern. "Alana," he said, his voice shaking. "You're back. You're safe."

Alana tried to reply, to ask what had happened to her,

but her mouth would not open. The pain spread as her muscles cramped. Her vision turned to red, and she would have screamed, had any part of her body been able to move.

"Be calm," the Tsar said, sounding calmer himself now. Reaching down, he gently closed her eyelids. "You're safe now. Sleep."

At his words, a soft white swirled in Alana's mind. The pain faded and the darkness rose to claim her. This time, she surrendered to it without a fight.

8

Braidon shivered as he followed Enala out into the shimmering light of dawn. Blinking, it was several moments before the world clicked back into focus. The air outside was crisp and cold, and he found himself standing in a narrow box canyon, stretching only a few hundred feet in either direction. Behind them, the familiar stairs wound their way up the granite cliff-face to the other tunnels.

On the cliff facing them, however, there was only one opening, though it was as large as all the others combined. Huge marble columns lined the entrance, supporting the intricately carved façade. Three small ledges had been cut into the stone surrounding the cave mouth, each supporting a statue of blue marble. In the centre stood a towering man, hair long and eyes distant. Another man stood alongside him, while on the right stood a woman, her face strangely familiar.

Braidon frowned, studying the statue, trying to place the woman. But Enala was already disappearing into the cave mouth, and shaking himself free of his curiosity, Braidon followed her.

Inside, he paused again, though the darkness wasn't as great as he'd expected. A thousand candles sparkled within, and he couldn't help but marvel at the size of the cavern he found himself in. A scarlet carpet stretched down the centre of the polished stone floors, terminating some fifty feet away in three large alters.

On either side of the cavern, the rows of stone columns from outside continued, holding up the vaulted ceiling, where an artwork of stunning scale had been painted. At the end of the room he recognised the three figures from the statues outside. Here though, they were bathed in light—green and blue and white—and he realised now they were depictions of the Three Gods. Light flew from their outstretched hands, over hordes of painted men, women, and monsters, to strike a singular figure depicted above the entranceway.

Braidon swallowed as he looked on the likeness of Archon. Black magic swathed his slim body, his pale face and dark eyes looking across at the Gods, alight with hatred. Averting his eyes, Braidon looked around the rest of the room, glimpsing tiny alcoves and other statues. Rugs covered the stone floor, and here, men and women knelt in silence, their eyes fixed to the altars at the front of the room.

"What is this place?" he found himself asking.

"A shrine to the Three Gods," came Enala's reply. "After the fall of Archon, the Northerners had it built here, at what was once the heart of his power, to celebrate their freedom."

"I thought the people of Northland fought *for* Archon."

"They did," Enala said sadly. "But not all did so willingly. Though they were descendants of the banished, the people here were never the true enemy. They only wanted what was best for their families, for an escape from the vile creatures that stalked their land, from the wasteland that was this nation."

"It doesn't look like such a wasteland now."

Enala smiled. "Before the Gods departed, they spent much of their time in Northland, healing the land of Archon's magic, driving the monsters back into their holes. After their...disappearance, the kings and queens of the Three Nations continued their work."

"That was how they built Erachill?"

"No. Erachill has always been here, though it was hidden from the peoples of the Three Nations for centuries. Even now, few know of its existence, since most trade with the Three Nations is conducted on the coast. It is the final bastion of the northern people, carved from the mountains where their ancestors first took refuge from the beasts."

Braidon shivered, thinking of the terror the people must have felt then, forging a new life for themselves in the barren lands. From what he'd seen there was little fertile land even now, with much of the northern continent full of towering mountains and harsh steppes.

"Take off your shoes." Enala said, pointing to his boots, then to a pile of shoes beside the entranceway.

Noticing she'd already removed hers, Braidon quickly followed suit. With that done, Enala led him across the room to a quiet rug in front of one of the altars. Sitting beside her, Braidon glanced at the altar, noticing the vines and strange creatures carved into the stone.

"Why is the temple dedicated to all three of them?" he asked, nodding at the Three Gods depicted overhead.

"Why not?" Enala smiled. "The Northerners saw the truth at the final battle of Fort Fall. Separate, the Gods could do little to halt Archon's reign—it was only when they came together that he was defeated."

"What really happened back then?" Braidon asked, still studying the mural on the ceiling. "There are so many tales now, no one seems to know the truth. I thought it was you and your brother who destroyed Archon, with swords the Gods had imbued with their powers."

Chuckling, Enala shook her head. "Perhaps it seemed that way to some," she replied, "but no, we played little part in the end. It was the Gods themselves who cast Archon into the earth, finally destroying him."

"And what about you, Enala? How did you come to be here? You were a legend, a hero amongst our people. But you and your brother, you disappeared."

Enala sighed. "After we…returned, my brother and I were supposed to be the heirs to the Trolan throne. But after everything we'd been through, we didn't want it. Eric left with Inken for southern Plorsea. I married my love, Gabriel, and eventually followed them. Together, the four of us made our home in a forest far from the outside world, and for a time, we were happy. Sometimes a king, queen or council would send emissaries, asking for our help with some problem or another, but for the most part we kept to ourselves. They were good years. It wasn't until my thirtieth birthday that I began to realise something was different. That Gabriel was aging, while I was not."

Braidon watched the lines on Enala's face deepen, her eyes beginning to shimmer. He said nothing, but reached out and squeezed her wrinkled arm. She nodded, a smile brightening her face, and went on.

"He was nearing sixty when his heart gave out. By then, I only looked like a woman in her thirties. After his death, our home was no longer the same, and I returned to civilisation, but there was almost no one left who remembered me. I was a remnant, a relic from a time long since passed, when Gods and Archon strode the land. So I left, took my sorrows and wandered the lands beyond the Three Nations."

"Did you not have children?" Braidon asked.

"We had a son, a year after Inken and Eric gave birth to a boy of their own. They were fast friends, but I learned long ago a life of isolation is not for the young. They left when they were still in their teens, and forged lives of their own. By the time I returned…I thought it best not to interfere with what they had built for themselves."

"And so you came to Northland?"

"Eventually. It was here that I finally found a people who had need of my…skills. I made a new life for myself in the northern wilderness, slaying creatures and helping to make the land safe. With other Magickers, we finished the work the Gods had started, lifting curses from the land, bringing rain and prosperity."

"While the Tsar conquered the Three Nations," Braidon murmured.

"Yes." At his words, Enala's eyes had taken on a haunted look. She grew very still, and when she spoke, her voice was little more than a whisper. "He wasn't always like that, you know. The leaders of the Three Nations raised him up as a peace bringer, to unite their troubled peoples. The laws he passed seemed just, placing limits on how magic could be used, on the harm it was capable of."

"But he changed?"

"Perhaps," Enala replied, "or perhaps we only saw the truth too late. He always hated magic. I wonder now, whether those early days were part of some greater plan."

"Why does he hate magic?" Braidon whispered. "He is a Magicker himself."

"No," Enala replied, "he was not born with the gift."

"But…that's not possible. The Tsar is the most powerful Magicker in the Three Nations!"

"Yes. But he found another way..."

Braidon sat in stunned silence for a moment. "How?" he finally managed to gasp.

Enala did not answer immediately. She sat looking up at the painting of the Gods, the lines on her face making her look all of her hundred plus years. When she finally spoke, Braidon jumped, his heart beginning to race.

"He came to me once, in happier days, before Gabriel had passed. He wanted to know more about our tale, about what had truly happened during the days of Archon. He asked me what became of the old king of Trola, whose magic had been devoured by Archon's curse."

"What are you talking about, Enala? Which king?"

"King Jonathan," she murmured. "The traitor king, who would have doomed us all to regain his magic. He tried to steal mine, took me to Witchcliffe and tried to rip it from my dying body. Eric stopped him."

Braidon swallowed. A pit had opened up in his stomach, but he forced himself to ask the question. "What does any of this have to do with the Tsar?"

Enala's ancient eyes turned on him, and he saw the pain there, the weight of regret. "The Tsar was not born of magic. All the power he has, he tore it from the broken shells of other Magickers."

A terrible silence fell over the temple. Looking around, Braidon saw the other worshipers had vanished, leaving them alone in the great hall. He shivered, his breath coming in ragged bursts as he thought of all those Magickers who'd been taken before the Tsar. Had he truly murdered them all to feed on their magic?

But if that was the truth…

"Why did no one stop him?" The question tore from his lips, echoing loudly in the hall, growing louder, until it seemed an accusation, hurled into the face of the woman who'd saved him.

"They tried," Enala whispered, "but it was already too late. My brother was the last to face him. Had I known what he intended to do, we could have faced him together. Instead, Eric stood alone against the darkness of the Tsar."

"What happened to him?" Braidon breathed.

"He died."

9

Devon's teeth rattled in his skull as the horse trotted along beneath him, its two-beat gait sending vibrations up his spine. He'd never been much of a rider, and a dull ache was already growing in the small of his back. Resettling himself in the saddle, he eased back on the reins, slowing the beast to a walk.

Three days had passed since the meeting in the bathhouse, and now the mountains of the Brunei Pass stretched high above them, their white-capped peaks glistening in the afternoon sun. Away to his right, the Onslow River raced past, its white waters surging over unseen rocks and boulders. The land around them was barren but for a few scraggly bushes, the cliffs to either side stretching up over five hundred feet. Any army passing between Trola and Plorsea had to venture through this gorge—and many thousands had died over the centuries in battle for its possession.

Now though, it belonged to the Tsar and the Empire, the old borders drawn between the Three Nations little more than remnants of a time long passed.

Devon sighed as the riders in the lead picked up the pace. Urging his horse after them, he thought of the road ahead. The last time he'd passed this way had been at the end of the war, when the triumphant Plorsean army had marched home. It had been a stark contrast to his first passage through, when every inch of ground had been paid for in the blood of fallen soldiers.

Looking at the land now, he could almost hear the screams, smell the blood, see the anguish on the faces of the dying. Shivering, he realised his hand was clenched around *kanker.* The great warhammer rested on his pommel, the runes carved into its steel head shining in the afternoon sun. Its elm haft was smooth in his hand, comforting, but he forced himself to release it. Their Trolan companions were hostile enough as it was, without him brandishing the weapon that had killed so many of their comrades.

He turned his gaze back to the horsemen riding ahead of him. Despite Devon's suggestion, Godrin had brought along five of his own men. They said little, other than to voice their disgust at riding with Plorsean soldiers. Devon couldn't blame them, but he'd seen the hurt in Kellian's eyes. The man was used to being liked—it was part of the reason he'd opened an inn after his retirement—and their hatred did not sit well with him.

Devon smiled as he watched his friend. Kellian was riding between Godrin and the young Trolan, Betran. After their meeting in the bathhouse, when the crime lord had told them of the men he'd be bringing with him, Devon had offered the man another Gold Libra to accompany them as far as Ardath. Despite the loss of his brother during the war, the young man had proven more than trustworthy, and Devon had a feeling another loyal sword wouldn't go amiss on the long journey to Ardath.

Ahead, Kellian looked back. They shared a glance, and his friend pulled back on his reins and rode back to join him. Devon kicked his horse forward and they fell in step together, a dozen paces behind the Trolans.

"I don't like it," Kellian said, his words muffled by the *click* of steel-shod hooves on rock. "I don't trust Godrin, certainly not his men. He could be leading us into a trap."

"If he'd wanted us dead, he'd have killed us back in the bathhouse, old friend," Devon replied reasonably. "Besides, if he plans to betray us, he should have brought more men." He rested his hand on *kanker* with a grim smile.

Kellian rolled his eyes. "You're growing arrogant in your old age, Devon," he snorted. "Even with Betran, we're still outnumbered two to one."

"We faced worse odds in Fort Fall," Devon said.

"And if not for Enala, we would have died," Kellian snapped. "Anyway, he doesn't need to fight us. We're riding for Ardath—if he wishes, he could deliver us straight into the Tsar's hands. Did you think of that?"

Devon shrugged. "It crossed my mind. But I don't see what other choice we have. Without his contacts, we have no way of reaching the citadel, let alone getting inside. Our faces are known in Ardath, we wouldn't make it through the gates without being spotted."

"I have contacts of my own," Kellian growled, but when Devon raised an eyebrow, he only shook his head. "You're right, though, they couldn't get us through the gates—maybe into the citadel if we were lucky. But I still don't like it."

"Enala trusts him, remember," Devon added. "If Godrin had betrayed her, the Tsar would have known she was alive before Fort Fall."

Kellian sighed. "You're right, of course. Still, it just

seems wrong, trusting the Trolans. What reason do they have to help us?"

"Freedom," Devon murmured, his eyes sweeping out over the canyon. They fell silent for a moment, remembering the final battle, the surging of men and horses, the crackling of magic and the clash of steel.

"Remember when the Trolan's broke?" Kellian asked suddenly. Devon nodded, and Kellian went on. "I thought it was done then, that the Tsar would sue for peace with Trola, and we'd return home."

"If only."

Kellian chuckled. "If only. Now there's the two most useless words, if ever I heard them. If only he'd sued for peace. If only we'd defied him. If only the Gods would return."

"You're in a cheerful mood this evening," Devon said dryly. He trailed off, his mind turning to Kellian's last statement. "You ever wonder what happened to them?" he asked finally.

"The Gods?" Kellian replied. He shrugged. "Probably got tired of settling our childish bickering."

Devon's laughter echoed from the cliffs. At last he shook his head, his mirth dying away. "Perhaps they'll return when the Three Nations are finally at peace. Either way, we're on our own now. Not much point dwelling on the past."

"I disagree," his friend said. "There is *every* point wondering about the past, about the way the world has changed since the departure of the Gods. They say the days before Archon were a golden age, that the Gods ruled over the Three Nations as though we were all one people."

"Ay, and now we have the Tsar."

"He is the most powerful Magicker the world has seen since Archon," Kellian agreed. "But many would consider him a force for good. Has there not, largely, been peace since he united the Three Nations?"

"Until the civil war," Devon grunted.

"Ay, we have seen the darkness he wields over men and women. But remember, back in Plorsea, he is still seen as the saviour, the man that prevented a Trolan army from marching on our homeland. The atrocities we committed in his name took place far away. They are nothing but tales and rumours to them, easily forgiven. Especially when seen through the lens of peace."

Devon fell silent, his heart heavy with remembered guilt. "I will not forget them, nor forgive myself for what I did."

"Nor I," Kellian said, "but how do we make them see? And even if we win, without the Gods, how do we prevent another such tyrant coming to power?"

"We fight," Devon said, resting his hand easily on the head of his hammer. "Whether we can win or not doesn't matter, so long as we make a stand. You said 'if only' is nothing but useless words. I agree. But when we marched on Trola, when we sacked their cities and slaughtered their inhabitants, I knew it was wrong. If only I'd made a stand then, perhaps my soul would be clean. But I did not, and while I cannot change it, I will never allow myself to fall in with such evil again. I will stand against the Tsar, even if it means my death."

"I will be with you, Devon," Kellian said, his eyes shining in the dying light. "To the end."

Silence fell at their words, so that the only sounds in the valley were the distant echoes of falling stones and the *clip-clop* of their mounts. Above, the sun disappeared behind the line of the cliffs, plunging them into shadow. They were high in the mountains now, and without the sun the temperature fell rapidly. Shivering, Devon pulled his woollen cloak tighter about himself. Ahead, the ground was still clear of snow, but despite the dry winter, the pass at the end of the valley was likely to be frozen over.

"I'd prefer to live though," Kellian added suddenly.

Devon saw his friend's face split into a grin. He raised an eyebrow. "You have a plan?"

"Call it a backup plan," Kellian said lightly. "In case *kanker* isn't as powerful as we hope."

Devon looked at the fabled hammer, his stomach tightening. He hadn't told Kellian, but Enala had come to him before they'd left. As though able to read his mind, she'd asked if he planned to use the hammer on the Tsar. When he'd nodded, she'd sighed, and told him there was little chance that such an attack would succeed. The Tsar's powers were too great—but there was no need for the others to know that.

Forcing a smile to his lips, Devon chuckled. "Only time will tell, old friend. But *kanker* has yet to see an enemy it could not best."

"You as well, Devon," Kellian added. His smile grew, and Devon felt a pinch of guilt at the deception.

Shaking it off, Devon pointed at the way ahead. "I'd say we have another three days until we reach Ardath. Want to fill me in on this plan of yours?"

"No," his friend replied, brushing a strand of black hair from his face. After the long weeks on the run, his usually well-trimmed hair now stretched halfway down his neck. "Not this time. I wouldn't want to spoil it for you."

"Ha! Well, I'm sure we won't need it. Godrin has a plan…"

"Which he also won't share," Kellian replied, his face hardening. "Whatever you say, I don't trust him..."

"And we've come full-circle," Devon cried, throwing his

arms in the air with a dramatic flourish. Kellian scowled, but Devon only laughed and kicked his horse into a trot. "I'll leave you to your worries, Kellian. At this point, even the Trolans sound like better company than you!"

"Fine, but send Betran back, will you?" Kellian's voice carried after him.

Devon raised a hand to show he had heard, then directed his horse forward to where the six Trolans were riding close to the river. The men's faces darkened as he approached. He grinned, knowing each of them would rather drive a dagger through his back than fight alongside him. But then, in his short life he'd seen his fair share of friends become enemies. He saw no reason why the reverse could not happen as well.

"Betran!" he shouted as he rode up. "Kellian would like to speak with you!"

The young Trolan raised an eyebrow. "Why?"

"Didn't ask, sonny. But I'm all out of coin, so if you want your pay you'd best get down there quick."

Betran nodded, a smile on his face despite Devon's sardonic words. "He get sick of your company, big man?"

Devon laughed. "I may be broke, sonny, but I can still give you a thrashing. Now get out of here, before I pull you off that horse and teach you some manners!"

Chuckling, the Trolan tugged on the reins, turning his horse to the side of the trail to wait for Kellian to catch up. The others rode on, Godrin in the lead. Devon pulled his horse alongside the crime lord.

"So how's that plan coming along, Godrin?"

"None of your business," he snapped.

A strained silence fell across the group as they continued up the mountain trail. The sky was growing darker with each passing minute, the air colder, yet no one suggested they stop and set up camp. The men stared straight ahead, their eyes steadfastly fixed to the distant peaks. With a sigh, Devon turned his gaze to the path, and let the silence deepen.

Well, maybe not these enemies.

❧ 10 ☙

Pain dragged Alana back from the darkness. Opening her eyes, she clenched her fists and moaned, feeling the burning of her muscles in every inch of her body. It was as though she'd swum the length of Lake Ardath and returned without rest. A tremor shook her as she tried to sit up. Cramp tore into her forearms, and she collapsed back to the sheets, a scream on her lips.

Movement came from nearby and the curtains around her bed were pulled back. She flinched as the Tsar appeared at her bedside. Her stomach turned to ice, before an image flickered into her mind—of a man standing before her, glowing sword in hand, calling her back from…

Alana cried out as she sensed her magic stirring. Clutching her arms around her, she fell back on the bed, her heart thudding hard against her chest. She shook her head, feeling the glowing green beast as it slowly lifted from its slumber.

No, no, no!

"Alana!" the cool voice of the Tsar sliced through her

panic. His eyes trapped her gaze as he gripped her arm. "Take a deep breath. Calm yourself!"

Still struggling for breath, Alana found herself obeying his orders without question. Exhaling, her lips quivered as she sensed the magic roiling inside her. Tears welled in her eyes, but she took another breath, seeking to calm her racing heart.

"It cannot harm you unless you touch it," the Tsar said softly, seating himself on the bed beside her. "It wants you to panic."

Alana shook her head, her fear rising once more. "It took control…"

"But you took it back!" The Tsar growled. "Even without your memories, you are my daughter still."

For the first time, she noticed the crinkles around his eyes, the warmth in his smile. Impulsively, she reached out and gripped his hand. "Thank you for saving me."

"I am your father," he said simply.

His words shook her, but this time she did not look away. "It's really true?"

He nodded, and she closed her eyes, the last of her doubt crumbling away. A fresh resolve rose within her, a need to discover the rest of the truth. But she knew now she could never do it alone—the magic would destroy her. It was like a caged animal, waiting for its moment to strike.

She looked up into the face of the Tsar—of her father. "Will you help me find myself?" she asked. "I…I can't do it alone."

The Tsar watched her for a long while, his face impassive, eyes unreadable. Finally, he nodded. "I will do what I can."

"Thank you," Alana whispered. She hesitated, still feeling the power swirling in her chest, the awful ache of her body. "Can it be now?" she added. "I can…feel it, seeking a way back. I'm afraid…"

The Tsar squeezed her fingers. "Of course. Come, let us sit on the sofa. It will be more comfortable—and more seemly."

Alana nodded and pulled herself from the bed. As her legs took her weight, the muscles knotted and screaming, she fell against the Tsar. His powerful arms went around her waist, lifting her back up, and with his help she made it to the couch. He lowered her down and sat beside her, his eyes touched with concern.

"You are sure you wish to do this now?"

"Yes," she insisted, biting back a moan. Her hands were locked in claws, her forearms aflame. "It has to be now."

"Very well." He held out his palms. "Take my hands, and we will face the beast together."

A shudder ran down Alana's spine as the image of the green Feline formed in her mind. "I…I don't know if I can!" The words tumbled from her in a rush. Tears formed in her eyes, but she blinked them back.

"I will be beside you." The Tsar's voice was calm, powerful, and she found herself drawing strength from it.

Taking a deep, shuddering breath, Alana nodded. "Okay."

Before she could lose her nerve, she closed her eyes and began to breathe rhythmically. As she meditated, the Tsar took her hands in his own. Warmth spread from her fingertips and along her arms, expanding to wrap around her chest. At its touch, the fear left her. Anger rose to replace it, a rage at her own weakness, at her failing to master the power within her.

She was Alana, and she feared nothing!

The tangled threads of emotion were gone now, torn

asunder by her meddling. Without the cage to bind it, her magic was free, its green fire flickering amidst the void. It rose before her, the Feline taking shape as an awful roar shook her consciousness, sending cracks through her newfound courage.

Fire burning in her heart, Alana faced the beast. It padded towards her, its claws spread, extending to grasp her. But now she felt no fear, no terror of approaching death. Only anger that this creature should think her prey.

As the beast approached, it started to shrink, each step seeming to take from its power. When it finally reached her, the Feline was no longer a monster, but a kitten, tiny and impotent. Smiling at its weakness, Alana reached down and lifted it into her arms…

In a blinding flash, the world around Alana exploded. She found herself hurtled back, her consciousness sent tumbling through the void. Images flashed amidst the darkness, and she perceived a thousand, thousand memories in the blink of an eye, each at once familiar and strange to her.

Alana saw herself, standing on the banks of the lake and hurling herself into the freezing waters, her strong strokes as she swam the circumference of the island Ardath. Then she became a young girl, sitting in a courtyard with Quinn, seeking the pathways to her magic. The images changed again, and she found herself watching the familiar dream as she fought her father, the clash of steel blades, then the pain as the Tsar's sword flashed down, slicing through the flesh and bone of her arm. Her consciousness had fled, only to return hours later, her severed limb whole once more.

The memories continued, becoming a flood that threatened to wash her away. She saw herself with the Magicker children, shouting orders, batting at them with cane and magic, sending them sprinting through the gardens until they collapsed from exhaustion. She took a cold delight from their pain, remembering the years she'd suffered at the hands of her father.

Dark emotions assailed her, and Alana felt herself sinking, her sense of self overwhelmed. Within, another consciousness was stirring, a woman at once her, and yet wholly different. Alana cried out as the woman rose, fed by the memories. Desperately, she sought something, anything that might anchor her to the person she knew herself to be.

A moonlit image flickered into view, of the night she had spent with Devon in the pools beneath Fort Fall. She clung to it, to the feel of his hands around her wrists, the desire in his eyes, the rush of blood to her head.

Then the image of a woman flashed into view, red-haired and brown-eyed. She stroked Alana's cheek.

I love you, my daughter.

The image changed again, and she saw the woman that was her mother dying in her bed, blood staining the satin sheets. Silence fell over the room as the midwives stood back. Then a piercing scream echoed from the walls, her new-born brother crying out for life.

Grief and love swirled through Alana, and her grip on the memory of Devon faltered—then was swept away. With a cry, Alana found herself sinking, falling, drowning in the memories of another life.

Yet still they continued, each flickering recollection filling in another piece of the jigsaw. Bit by bit, the true Alana reasserted herself, taking form from the darkness, restored by her power. The green light of her magic began to rise, but almost by instinct, she reached out and crushed it down. The magic was not her master, but a slave to be used as she saw fit.

Finally, the rush of memories slowed, and as the last of them snapped back into place, she was complete.

When Alana opened her eyes again, she was no longer the renegade who had fled the capital with Devon and Kellian, but the Daughter of the Tsar, the warrior, the Magicker. A smile spread across her face as she found her father seated beside her.

"Father," Alana said, pulling herself up on the sofa. "Thank you for your help."

His face remained impassive. "Has my daughter returned to me?"

Alana's smile faded, and brow creasing, she turned her eyes inwards. For a moment there was nothing—then with a jagged flash of images, she felt that other self. The girl's cries echoed blindly in the darkness of her consciousness, desperate, despairing. Disgust welled in Alana as she studied the pitiful creature she had become without her memories. Shivering, she tried to recall how her power had been set free but to her surprise, she found that memory still lost to her.

Devon? Kellian? Help me!

Laughter came to Alana's lips as the girl's voice carried up from the void. Summoning her magic, its power still weakened by the girl's stupidity, Alana sent bands of fire down to wrap around her counterpart. A single scream echoed through her mind, followed by a deathly silence as the girl succumbed to her imprisonment.

Opening her eyes, she looked at the Tsar. "I am here, father."

Jaw clenched, the Tsar nodded. "I am glad," he said softly, "for we have much to discuss."

Alana nodded, the girl's memories of the last few weeks

surfacing. "We have a new enemy. The woman, Tillie. Who is she, truly?"

"An old enemy, from before your time," the Tsar replied.

Reaching out a hand, he drew her to her feet. Alana swore as pain shot through her legs, and again she cursed the foolish girl who had taken control of her body. Pushing aside her father's hand, she straightened, embracing the pain, becoming one with it.

"I thought all your enemies were dead."

"So did I," her father said, "but I should have known she would not go quietly to her death. I fear her hand is behind much of the strife we have suffered this last decade. You know her true name."

Alana eyed her father, thinking quickly, running over the list of those who'd stood against her father through the years. He had told her of them all: Caelin and May, Nikola and Darien, Eric and…

Realisation came to her in a rush. There was one woman whose end her father had never spoken of, though she should have been long dead by now. Frowning, she thought back to the woman she'd known as Tillie. The old woman had spoken of times, of people that she could not possibly have known.

Not unless…

"It was Enala," she said, looking into her father's eyes.

"Yes," her father replied, "somehow, she has returned from the dead to defy me."

A third voice echoed from across the room. "Then we will find a way to make her pay."

11

"Then we will find a way to make her pay," Quinn heard himself say.

On the sofa, Alana and the Tsar looked up, their eyes widening as he entered the room. Their surprise was short-lived though, and smiling, Alana rose to greet him.

Quinn had been across the lake checking on preparations for the army, and had only heard of Alana's attack on his return to the city. Fearing the worst, he'd headed straight for her residence, and had overheard the end of their conversation while he'd approached the open door.

"Teacher," Alana said, laughter in her eyes as she placed a hand on his chest. "Thank you for rescuing me."

A lump lodged in Quinn's throat as he felt the warmth of her fingers through his woollen shirt. He stared down at her in stunned silence, and she laughed out loud. Lowering herself down on the sofa opposite her father, she gestured for Quinn to sit.

"You...have returned?" he said, finally finding his words as he sat alongside her.

"I have, thanks to you, *teacher*." She said the last word playfully, even as her hand drifted down to rest on his thigh.

Quinn shifted on the couch, suddenly uncomfortable. He did his best to ignore Alana's close proximity, the sweet cinnamon scent of her hair, the warmth of her hand…

"You said it was Enala?" he all but shouted. "How can that be? She must be well over a century old by now."

"The woman worked with the Gods to destroy Archon," the Tsar replied. "Who knows what secrets she discovered? She disappeared when I was first coming to power. I always thought she would return to defy me, but even I had long thought her dead. Her reappearance is concerning, though it may also prove to be an opportunity."

"How so, father?" Alana asked, sitting up.

"Her knowledge after a century of life must be vast. She may hold the key to unlock the final secrets of magic."

Quinn's chest tightened as he remembered facing off against the ancient priest. "She bided her time well," he mused. "I sensed no magic from her in Sitton Forest, nor on the docks of Lon. Not until she attacked my men at Fort Fall. By then, my own magic was too weak to fight her." He cursed. "I should have saved my strength…"

"Nonsense," the Tsar growled. Quinn looked up at the man's tone. "Had you not used your magic to power the sails of your ship, you would never have reached Fort Fall in time to save my daughter. Besides, if you'd fought Enala, she would have destroyed you, magic or no."

"I have bested fire Magickers before," Quinn argued.

"Not *this* fire Magicker," the Tsar said. "You think you have the knowledge to outsmart a woman who has lived for over one hundred years? Especially after she spent most of them fighting demons and dragons and Magickers far more dangerous than yourself!"

His mouth dry, Quinn shook his head. Alana laughed, and her hand trailed lightly over the fabric of his leggings. "Do not look so sad, teacher," she said. "You saved my life, after all."

"Yes, Quinn, you did well, despite the odds. Enala must have known I'd have sensed her if she'd used her magic sooner—and indeed I did. Sadly, even Fishibe and her kin could not reach you in time to save my son from their clutches."

"Does he truly still live?" Alana asked quickly.

Quinn saw the concern in her eyes. Her teasing momentarily forgotten, he reached out an arm and hugged her to him. "He lives," he replied. "We received word from our spies in Erachill—he was healed at an Earth Temple not long after our…fight."

He felt Alana relax, the worry falling from her face. "That is a relief." Her eyes hardened. "Did the Stalker who shot him survive the battle?"

A chill spread through Quinn's stomach at the look on her face. In the chaos, he had shouted an order without thinking, and one of his men had loosed a crossbow bolt at the boy. Fortunately though…

"No," he said quickly. "Enala…killed them all."

"A shame," Alana said with a sigh. "I would have liked to hear his screams as he died. I hope the witch took her time with him."

"I…" Quinn began, then decided it was best to remain silent.

"Yes, if it comes to moving against the Queen to get him back, your Stalkers had best retain their discipline this time. I won't see my children harmed." Quinn gritted his teeth at the man's hypocrisy after ordering Fishibe and her kin after Alana. Smiling, the Tsar went on. "And what of you, my daughter? Do you remember…why your magic took your memories?"

Beside him, Alana sighed. "No," she said, "I have searched my mind, but there is still a mist over the months before I woke in the stepwell. I cannot remember how it happened, or what Braidon and I did in the first few weeks after we vanished."

The Tsar waved a hand. "No matter. They will return, or they won't. What matters is you are yourself again. We will need all our strength in the coming months."

"What of Devon and Kellian?" Quinn asked. He felt Alana tense at the mention of her former companions and glanced sidelong at her, but she was staring at the Tsar and he couldn't tell what she might be thinking.

"They have left Northland and flown to Trola on the Gold Dragon. Enala only followed them as far as our northern shores before returning to Erachill. The two are entirely untalented, however, and I was unable to track them from there. But I believe they are heading here, to rescue you, Alana."

"It seems my…other self, worked quite the spell on the hammerman," Alana said, smirking. "More fool on him. I take it appropriate measures have been put in place to stop them?"

"Even better. My magic may have lost them, but I received word last night they have encountered one of our agents in Trola. A team of Stalkers has been sent to welcome them back to the Three Nations."

Quinn's head jerked up at that. "They have? Why was I not told?" he said, a little too sharply.

The Tsar held Quinn's gaze for a long moment, the sapphire eyes boring into him. Finally, he swallowed and looked away. A dry chuckle came from the Tsar. "After your…recent battles with the hammerman, I thought it best to send Darnell's pack."

"Darnell?" Quinn growled. "You think her Stalkers have the skill to take on a warrior like Devon?"

"They had better," the Tsar replied, his voice like ice, "or they'd best die trying."

Sensing the conversation had come to an end, Quinn swallowed back his anger and nodded. "You know best, my liege," he said stiffly.

"I do," the Tsar replied, "and you'd do well not to forget it."

Silence fell over the room, and a chill spread through Quinn's stomach. Suddenly the Tsar laughed, a grin appearing on his face. "Besides, after everything the two of you have shared, I doubt you would have brought him back alive, Quinn." His voice hardened, the smile falling from his lips. "And I would rather like to meet the man who thought he could steal my children from me."

Despite himself, Quinn shivered at the glitter he saw in the Tsar's eyes. Since the hammerman had first joined the army, he and Quinn had shared a mutual rivalry. And despite his magic, Quinn had far too often found himself finishing second-best to the giant warrior. Even while hunting him, Quinn had always been a step behind. Now though, no force in the Three Nations would compel him to switch places with the hammerman.

On the opposite sofa, the Tsar let out a long sigh and climbed to his feet. "Well, I have kept you long enough, my daughter," he said, brushing the greying locks of his hair from his face. "There is much to be done and my attention is needed elsewhere. I will leave you in the tender care of your teacher."

With that, he turned his back and left, the heavy doors

swinging shut behind him. Alone now with Alana, Quinn swallowed as he found her staring at him. Looking into her eyes, he sought the girl he remembered, the one he had sat with for so many long evenings, who'd he'd trained and taught to use her powers.

"Is it truly you, Alana?" he asked quietly.

"Almost," she whispered.

12

Sitting on the couch facing Quinn, Alana had never experienced such turmoil. All her life she'd known exactly who and what she was—the Daughter of the Tsar, born to rule the Three Nations. Her father's enemies were legion, and as his oldest child, one day they would be her enemies too. Weakness had never been an option.

Yet as she'd sat listening to her father discuss his plans for Devon and Kellian, she'd felt that other side of her stirring. A lead weight had settled in her stomach as they spoke of the capture of her former companions, her heartbeat quickening. She knew her father well, and it was unlikely either would be treated to a quick death.

They are nothing to you! she told herself.

They are important to me! another voice echoed from the depths of her soul.

Gritting her teeth, she turned her eyes inwards, finding the shivering consciousness of her other self hovering in the void of her mind. The spirit of the girl flinched back from her, but too slowly, and Alana's magic swept out to encircle her.

You are nothing! she growled, watching in satisfaction as her magic dragged the other girl back down into the darkness.

The confusion went with the girl, and opening her eyes, she smiled at Quinn. His eyes were locked on her. The intensity in his gaze made the breath catch in her throat.

"Is it truly you, Alana?" he asked.

Somewhere far away she could still hear a voice crying out, and for an instant the scraggly face of Devon drifted across her thoughts. Her rage flared and she tore the image away, hurling it into the abyss along with the foolish girl. Licking her lips, she looked across at Quinn.

"Almost," she whispered, brushing a strand of hair from his face.

His eyes closed at her touch, but she paused, noticing the blood on the sleeve of her white cotton shirt. Realising she was still wearing the same clothes from when her magic had taken control, she cursed and stood. Quinn's eyes snapped back open, but ignoring him now, she crossed to the trunk at the foot of her bed and pulled it open. She picked out a woollen jerkin and brown leather pants, and tossed them on the bed.

"I'm glad you're back, Alana," Quinn said, coming up behind her and placing his hands on her shoulders.

She smiled, enjoying the warmth of his touch, but shrugged him off. Turning, she looked up at him. "It seems I am in your debt yet again, teacher," she murmured. She drew circles on his chest with her finger, a sly smile coming to her lips. "How can I ever repay you?"

Quinn swallowed visibly, and she felt him trembling at her touch. When he said nothing, she laughed and took a step back. Slowly she began to unbutton her bloodstained shirt. His eyes widened.

"Alana, what are you doing?"

Alana's smile broadened. Deep in her mind, she could hear the voice screaming again, and felt a slight stirring in her stomach, as though a part of her recoiled at the thought of Quinn's touch. But it was weak, already fading. With a sense of triumph, she unclipped the last button and pulled off her shirt, tossing it to the floor.

Quinn stood open-mouthed before her, his eyes wide, drinking her in. Seven years her senior, Quinn had been like an older brother to her when she was young, having come to the citadel when he was a boy to dedicate himself to the Tsar's service. He had taught her to climb and fight, to wield her magic against her enemies. Many were the bruises she'd sported from sparring with him, yet it had been Quinn who had given her the strength to withstand her father's private lessons.

She had never thought of him as more than a mentor, even as she'd noticed his feelings changing as she'd grown older. A new light had come into his eyes, a fire that had driven him to chase her across the Three Nations and restore her to life. Thinking of that fire now, viewed through the memories of her…softer self, Alana felt a lust of her own.

More than that though, she wanted to restore her sense of self, to mark a line in the sand. Watching the flickering memories of the other Alana, she sensed the growing love she'd felt for the hammerman, Devon. It was a strange, distant sensation, and one she had never experienced before. She didn't like it, didn't like the way it stole away her control, as though her destiny was no longer her own.

But she knew how to kill it, knew how to crush the last hopes of her other self.

Half-naked now, Alana smiled up at Quinn, her eyelashes fluttering. "Do you not like what you see…teacher?"

There was naked lust in Quinn's eyes as he looked on her, yet still he hesitated. "Alana…" he murmured, "what is this?"

Alana reached out and grabbed Quinn by the collar of his shirt, pulling him close. He had stopped shaking now, but a soft moan whispered from his throat as she moved against him. Standing on her tiptoes, she pressed her lips to his ear.

"You have always wanted me," she whispered, her breath hot. "I see it now, watching my memories afresh, the burning in your eyes."

"I…I…" Quinn's words fell away as Alana's fingers trailed down his front, plucking at his buttons as they went. He stiffened as she slid her hands inside his shirt, playing with the hair on his chest.

"You brought me back, *Quinn*," Alana continued. "Saved me, stopped me from betraying everything we've worked for. How can I ever repay you?"

"Alana…"

"I think I know how to start."

Her lips moved from his ear to his neck, and she nipped at his flesh, savouring the groan that rumbled up from his chest. Suddenly his arms were around her waist, drawing her in, gripping her tight. Feeling the warmth of his chest against her, she yanked his shirt open, tearing the remaining buttons clear. He released her then, dragging it from his shoulders and hurling it across the room.

Stepping back, Alana took a moment to savour his

naked chest, her eyes lingering on his hulking shoulders, his chest, his arms. Then he was stepping in close again, leaning down, and she was lifting her mouth to meet his, and they were kissing. His hands pulled at hair, drawing her in deeper, and her tongue darted out, tasting, teasing. She shuddered as he cupped her breast, and groaned, feeling him harden against her. Gasping, she kissed him back, her lust rising with a fierce, violent need.

Suddenly an awful horror swept through her, a swirling disgust, and then Devon's face exploded in her mind. She cried out, thrusting Quinn back from her as she staggered across the room. The strength went from her legs and she slid to the ground, the pain flaring as she felt again the cramping muscles of her weary body. Within, she sensed the other part of her rising, her revulsion sweeping out, filling her.

"Alana, are you okay?" Quinn shouted, his voice slicing through her thoughts.

"*Get out!*" Alana shrieked, hardly hearing him. Her power roared, chasing the girl back into the darkness.

She gasped as the girl's emotions fled, leaving her feeling strangely, sickeningly alone. Tears stung her eyes and she quickly blinked them back. Shaking her head, she looked up and saw Quinn standing over her, bare-chested with open shock written across his face.

Rising, Alana shook her head, dismissing the last traces of the girl from her thoughts, and then stepped towards him. He retreated, lifting his hands as though to fend her off. "Alana, what was that?"

"Nothing." She scowled. "Just the witch that took my body. She's gone now."

Before he could slip clear, she darted forward, catching him by the wrist. With a tug, she pulled him forward, so that they stood close together once more, mere inches separating them. But she could see the hesitation in his eyes now, the rejection on his lips. She gripped him tighter, her mind turning inwards. Her magic was still weak, but she allowed a trickle to touch him, muting his fears.

Quinn shivered, his eyes glazing for a moment, before he blinked, a grin coming to his face. Lifting a hand, he brushed a lock of blonde hair from her face. She could feel his desire, his need to take her, and savoured in it. With a sense of euphoria, she leaned up and pressed her lips to his, and felt the last of his barriers give way.

Locked together, they stumbled backwards across the room, until she felt the wall pressed up against her back. She gasped as Quinn moved his mouth to her neck, and felt the soft bite of his teeth. Her fingers tightened in his hair, and she drank in the pain she sensed in him. Then he paused, pulling back for a moment. She was surprised to see the concern in his eyes once more.

"Are you sure you're okay?" he murmured.

Alana only laughed. Gripping him tight, she pushed him backwards. He retreated, though this time she did not release him. She directed him towards the bed, waiting until he was close, then shoved him hard in the chest. He toppled backwards onto the soft mattress.

"Not yet," she said, as she joined him.

Straddling him, she began to unbuckle his belt.

13

"*Damnit!*"

Surging to his feet, Braidon stumbled and tripped over the candles scattered about the room. Two toppled to the floor and flickered out on the cold stone. Cursing again, he crouched and righted them, though his hands were shaking and it took two attempts to fit them back into their copper holders.

"You must have patience, young Braidon," Enala said, her voice carrying across from where she still sat cross-legged on the floor.

He swung on her, teeth bared, angry words tumbling from him in a rush. "I've *been* patient!" he snapped, "but I can't do it, it's too much, it's…impossible!"

Enala's expression was untouched by his screams, her eyes shining in the candlelight. "It is not impossible," she answered, rising to her feet. "Remember back in Lonia, when your magic was threatening to take control? You mastered it then, found the peace to turn it back. You can do so again."

"That was different," Braidon growled. "I hardly knew what I was doing. I didn't know there was some...*demon* inside me, waiting to tear me apart."

"It is *nothing* to you, Braidon," Enala replied. "Why can you not see that? Only your fear makes it real."

Braidon turned away, bitterness rising in his throat. All his life he'd lived in his sister's shadow. She was the strong one, the warrior, their father's favourite. Then had come his magic's emergence, flickering into life on his sixteenth birthday, and everything had changed. His memories of that day were strangely blurred, indistinct, but he could remember feeling pride as his power came to life. Even the threat of persecution could not change the fact he finally possessed something his sister did not.

But even that had been a lie. The battle in Fort Fall had shown him the truth of things, had revealed the lie that was his magic. His power accounted to little more than circus tricks, illusions to fool the senses, ultimately worthless.

Braidon had thought to use his power to save his sister in Fort Fall. Instead, as always, she had been the one to save him. And she had been stolen for it. Even now, the knowledge ate at him.

Looking at Enala, he felt lost. "I can't do it."

For a moment he glimpsed disappointment in the priest's face. She quickly masked it with a shake of her head. There was a long pause, and then she smiled, the wrinkles falling from her cheeks. "We shall see, young Braidon. But for now, I think it best we take a break. Come, it is past time I showed you more of the city."

Braidon had little desire to do anything but curl up in his bed and hide away from the world, but Enala was already moving away, and he had little choice but to follow her. Together they wandered from the stone chamber that served as their meditation room, out into the long corridors of the mountain city. The ground was smooth beneath their feet, seamless, as though the rock itself had been shaped by some immortal hand.

Enala led him deeper into the city, along pathways Braidon had never seen before. Those they encountered as they walked payed them little attention, though a few stopped to greet Enala. It was clear she was well-known here, a legend amongst the residents. Slowly the crowds grew denser, until at last they emerged into a grand cavern some three-hundred-feet wide. Two-hundred-foot walls towered over them, ending abruptly in open sky.

Braidon struggled to hide his shock. Before him was a marketplace that would rival even the bustling bazaars of Ardath and Lon. Alcoves cut into the walls boasted dozens of stalls, while others had been set up in rows spanning half the cavern. Their vendors lounged in hammocks behind the counters, many dozing as they waited for customers to find them.

Men and women thronged the alleyways between the stalls, pausing to purchase fresh bread and produce, meat and fish. Braidon could hardly believe the wealth of goods on hand. Amongst the stalls in sight, he could see blankets of Lonian wool, wooden furniture boasting of Trolan origin, even incense and spices from the south of Plorsea. Until now, he'd thought Northland to still be a poor nation, its development hindered by the centuries of strife under Archon's rule. Never had he thought to see goods from his homeland so far north—yet now he could only marvel at the industry of it all.

"This way," Enala called. Blinking, he found her waving from across the way.

Following her, they moved away from the market stalls

and out into the open. The sky was bright and clear, and Braidon smiled as the sun's rays touched him. The air was cool, but within the cavern they were protected from the winter winds. The ground sloped downwards, until it disappeared into the waters of a natural spring. Braidon was surprised to see a dozen children floating in the water, their youthful voices echoing loudly from the sheer cliffs.

"Aren't they freezing?" he asked.

Enala laughed. "I think you'll find the water quite pleasant. The spring is fed from deep inside the earth, where the natural fires keep it an agreeable temperature all year round."

They had reached the edge of the pool now, and crouching down, Braidon ran his hand through the water to confirm the priest's words. While not hot, it was a great deal warmer than the air outside the city. Straightening, he joined Enala where she had seated herself on the rocky shore.

"They're like you, you know," she said softly.

Braidon followed her gaze out to where the children were playing. He frowned. "What do you mean?"

"Most of them are Magickers, or the children of Magickers. All of them came here from the Three Nations to escape persecution by the Tsar. The Queen takes them in, gives them a home, helps them to master their powers."

Braidon looked at the children with fresh eyes. There was a dozen in total, the oldest around eighteen, the youngest maybe ten. All wore broad smiles as they tossed a leather ball between them. There was a great splash as one of the older boys dove, catching the ball and then plunging beneath the water. Laughter followed as he surfaced spluttering.

Braidon grinned at the sight. Then a sadness crept over

him, his thoughts turning to his own lonely childhood. For as long as he could remember, Alana had been his only companion, though she had often been…away with their father. He couldn't recall ever playing with other children like this, though why…he could not remember.

"Would you like to join them?" Enala asked.

A lump formed in Braidon's throat. Suddenly his heart was racing, his shoulders tense with anxiety at the thought of introducing himself to so many new faces. He clenched his fists against the stone, his eyes flickering between Enala and the crystal waters.

"I…" he started, but before he could complete the thought, a voice shouted from behind them.

"*Enala!*"

Braidon jumped, swinging towards the newcomer, his hands forming fists to fend off an attack. He lowered them again when he realised there was no one close by. A moment later, he spotted the speaker, still some fifty feet away, but closing in fast. It was a woman. Two men in chainmail shadowed her, swords sheathed at their sides. Braidon swallowed hard as he recognised the woman from his first night in the city. She wasn't wearing the iron crown, but there was no mistaking the aura of authority she carried.

Beside him, Enala calmly rose to her feet as the Queen reached them. "Your majesty," she said, "what brings you to the bazaar?"

The woman came to a stop before them, her green eyes flickering from Enala to Braidon. "Take him," she snapped, gesturing at the men behind her.

Braidon cried out as the men surged forward. Taken by surprise, he had no chance to resist. The first struck him hard in the stomach, driving the wind from his lungs and dropping him to his knees. The second man stepped in, grabbing his arms and pinning them behind his back.

Gasping, Braidon swayed in the man's grip. An awful heat spread through his chest, his magic stirring, rising through the depths of his consciousness. Fear flared inside him, but it was too late to cool the flickering glow, and he felt a rush as the power flowed from him.

Blinding light flashed across the cavern and a great *boom* echoed from the cliffs, igniting screams from nearby. A shout came from behind him as the hand holding Braidon loosened. Anger took him then, and he surged backwards against his attacker. The sudden movement sent the man stumbling. As his hands came free, Braidon spun and slammed his fist into the man's stomach.

Lights were still flashing around them, appearing overhead and rushing away, sizzling through the air like fireworks. Nearby, the marketplace had descended into chaos as people rushed to and fro, unaware the light show was nothing more than an illusion. Even the Queen had retreated, her hands raised over her face to protect her eyes.

But now the other guard had found his courage. Drawing his sword, he advanced on Braidon with murder in his eyes.

Before the man could reach him, Enala stepped between them, her eyes burning red.

"*Stop this!*" Her words rang out, slicing through the chaos.

The guard froze at her command, his eyes suddenly fearful, and Braidon saw that Enala's hands were aflame. Beyond her, citizens were stumbling around the bazaar, their faces twisted in terror. Shame filled him then, his anger dying away. The light went with it, and silence fell once more over the cavern.

Weariness swept through Braidon. Sinking to his knees, he watched as the Queen straightened, her hands falling to her side. He swallowed as their eyes met, and the strength of her rage washed over him.

"Take. Him," she spat, pointing a trembling finger at Braidon.

Her men hesitated, still shocked by the sudden display of magic, and Enala quickly barred their way.

"What is the meaning of this, Merydith?" she growled. The fire in her hands had died away, but now her eyes shone with a rage to match the Queen's.

"Get out of my way, Enala," the Queen snapped. "This does not concern you."

"The boy is under my protection," Enala replied, her voice trembling. "And you will answer to me if you wish to harm him."

"Harm him?" came the Queen's reply. "The boy may have brought about the destruction of my kingdom—and you worry about my *harming him?*"

Braidon could only look in confusion from the Queen to Enala. Her words made no sense to him. Surely she couldn't mean the Tsar intended to invade Northland because Enala had given him refuge?

"What are you talking about, Merydith?" Enala asked, the anger falling from her voice.

The Queen sucked in a breath, her hands shaking. "The boy is not who he would have us believe, Enala," she said softly.

"What?" Braidon gaped, but the two women ignored him.

"What do you mean?" Enala asked for him. "Who could he be that the Tsar would threaten war with us?"

The Queen closed her eyes, a pained look coming over

her face. "His emissaries just arrived. Unless we return him, they claim the Three Nations will march north with all their strength. They're claiming we have kidnapped the Tsar's only son."

Braidon's mouth dropped open. The colour slowly drained from Enala's face, her skin turning a paled grey. The old woman swayed on her feet, and it seemed as though she had aged ten years in a matter of heartbeats. Reaching out, she gripped the Queen's arm.

"What did you say?"

The Queen stared at Enala, her frown softening. Then she looked across at Braidon, and he saw the hate lurking behind her eyes. "I'm saying Braidon is the Tsar's son, Enala. I'm saying he has betrayed us all."

☙ 14 ❧

That evening Devon and Kellian made camp beneath the cliffs, taking advantage of a small crag to shelter them from the cold winds sweeping down the valley. As darkness fell, they lit a fire against the cliff-face, so that its heat would be reflected back on them.

After eating a meagre stew of toughened beef and tubers, Devon wandered away from the others. His mind was distant and he was in no mood for company. Seating himself on a boulder some distance from the camp, he stared out over the moonlit valley. Images rose from the vaults of his memory. It had been here, in this valley, that he'd first tasted glory.

In those early days, victory had been far from assured, flitting above the heads of the armies like a firefly, always just out of reach. The Plorseans had battled for every inch of ground, forcing the Trolans back with nothing but sheer bloody-minded determination. Devon had stood at the front, his hammer rising and falling like death itself, smashing his way through the Trolan line, a giant amongst men.

Back then, there had been no doubt in his mind of the Tsar's righteousness, of Plorsea's right to govern the Three Nations. But that had been before the destruction of Kalgan, before the razing of cities and the slaughter of innocent civilians. Before he'd brought shame to his ancestors.

Now, looking out over the former battlefield, he felt only sadness. In the moonlight, the boulders lining the valley shone a ghostly white. He could almost imagine them to be the souls of fallen men, doomed to wander these faraway mountains, forever in search of home.

"I hear them too."

Devon jumped as a voice spoke from behind him. Betran appeared in the moonlight, his eyes distant as he looked out over the valley. Devon was surprised he hadn't heard the little man approaching, and he felt a flicker of irritation at the intrusion on his solitude. It faded as he untangled the Trolan's words.

"Hear who?" he asked.

"The ghosts," Betran shivered. "How many lives have been lost here, in this pass, do you think? How many generations of young men and women have marched to their deaths, their lives lost to the futility of war?"

"They say twenty thousand met here, when the Tsar marched against your…people."

"Ay," Betran replied, "and before that? Ours was not the only battle these lonely peaks have witnessed." He sighed. "My brother will have no shortage of company in the afterlife."

Devon's throat tightened, and he eyed the man, seeking some sign of anger. But there was only sadness on the

Trolan's face. He glanced down at *kanker*, his guilt swelling. "You two were close?"

Betran shrugged and took a seat on the boulder next to Devon. "He was my younger brother. I marched to look out for him, more than anything. Little good it did him." He smiled ruefully. "I didn't even see you coming. One moment we were pressing your line back, the next minute you and that hammer of yours had broken our ranks, and my comrades were streaming back around us. Kieran, fool that he was, tried to stand his ground. He was dead before I could reach him."

"I'm sorry," Devon whispered, but the little Trolan only shook his head.

"I think it must be the folly of the young, to want to test their skills against their fellow man. Maybe that's why our nations have been so cursed with war."

"A depressing thought," Devon mused. "You think that means another war is inevitable?"

There was a long pause before Betran answered, and when he spoke, there was an edge to his voice. "What choice do we have?" he murmured. "I'm thirty-five, with a wife and son, but since the war there's been no work. Of the little I do earn, most goes towards the Tsar's taxes. When you showed up, my family was a week away from starvation."

"And you believe a war with Plorsea will free you?"

"No." To Devon's surprise, there were tears on the Trolan's face now. "We would be crushed. But I can sense the hate in my people, even in my own son. One day soon it will spur them to rise up. And the Tsar will return with his armies, with his demons and his dragons, and destroy us once and for all."

Devon swallowed, struggling to find the words to reassure the young man that they could change things. Before he could speak, another voice came from the shadows. "You're wrong, Betran."

Godrin came wandering across the rocky slope. He looked from Devon to Betran before seating himself alongside the Trolan. His hand gripped Betran's shoulder, though his eyes were fixed on Devon. "Your son is right to hate the Plorseans," he said quietly, "and one day, we *will* make them pay for your brother's life, and all those other lives they stole."

Devon saw the hate in the Trolan's eyes. Godrin had agreed to this mission partly because of Enala, partly because they offered him a chance to strike at the Tsar, and save his nation from a long, slow death. But that had done nothing to change his heart. The hate remained, festering, tainting his mind with thoughts of revenge. Seeing it, Devon wished he had the words to mend the fracture in the man's heart, to restore the unity that had once existed between the Three Nations. But Kellian was the one with the silver tongue, and all Devon could do was sit there in silence.

"And what will that achieve?" Betran spoke up, his voice touched with sadness. "My brother will still be dead, but the hate will have spread. When you're done, some young Plorsean will be left to nurse the hatred in his heart. Then one day he will return to take his revenge on the foul Trolans who killed his loved ones."

"It won't be like that."

"How can it not, when you talk only of hatred and revenge?"

"So when the time comes to free our nation, you will not be with us, Betran? Will you hide in the shadows while your comrades fight for your freedom?"

Betran turned cold eyes on the crime lord. "I will be

there, Godrin. I will stand with my people and fight for our right to live, because I believe the Tsar is evil, and evil must be countered wherever it is found. But know this—the day you march on Plorsea, the day the war turns from liberation, to conquest, I will stand against you. And I will implore our people to do the same. Unlike you, I remember our legends. I will not lead our nation into yet another act of folly."

Godrin snorted. "They are only legends, Betran," he said scornfully. "Told to scare unruly children. Or do you truly believe these mountains once came alive, and consumed entire armies?"

"Maybe not, but I choose to see the message behind the words. War has no victors, only survivors. And I will not be a part of it. Should the day come, I will return to my home, and hold my wife and child in my arms. I will do my best to live with love in my heart, and hope that is enough."

"I believe the legends are true," Devon said, as a quiet settled over the mountain slopes. With the mention of the past, his thoughts had turned to Enala, and the tales that were still told of her. Realising the other men were staring at him, he scratched his beard and went on. "Before all this started, I thought the same, that the stories were just that—stories. But in the last few weeks, I have witnessed trees come to life, have fought with a demon and escaped a dragon's flames. I've met a woman over a hundred years old, who fights like a wraith. And I've seen Trolans unite with Plorseans in the hope of freeing their nation." He paused, eyeing the others, a grim smile on his lips. "After all that, who's to say these mountains couldn't eat an army or two?"

Silence fell over the others at his words, and he turned away, looking back out over the valley. He knew the legend of which they spoke. It dated back to a time long before

Archon's reign, when the Great Wars had been fought between Lonia and Trola. The conflict had consumed the lands now known as Plorsea, turning them into lifeless desert. Legends told that a final battle had been fought here, in Brunei Pass. But as the two great armies came together, the surrounding cliffs had snapped closed, entombing thousands in solid rock.

Devon suppressed a shiver at the thought of the towering cliffs closing in on him. Within the pass, there would be nowhere to run, no hope of survival. Five years ago, he had barely given the legend a second thought, but now the old tale sent a shiver down his neck.

The voices from the campfire had quieted now, and Devon was beginning to feel the weight of the day's travel. Yawning, he stretched his arms and stood, sheathing *kanker* on his back. Bidding the two men goodnight, he started towards the camp. The fire had burned low now, and there was little light. Squinting in the darkness, he was still searching for his bedroll when a distant *thud* carried down the valley.

Turning, he scanned the gloom in search of the source. The ground lay open around them, but the moon's light was shrouded in cloud. He could see no sign of movement below them, but as he looked up the valley, he caught a flicker of movement near the cliffs at the top of the pass.

Abandoning the search for his bedroll, Devon wandered back down to where Betran and Godrin still sat talking. They looked up at his approach, their mouths opening to question him, but he waved them to silence. Straining his ears, he listened for further signs of movement, and caught another *thud*, as of a horseshoe on stone.

Silently, Devon lifted *kanker* from his back. The other two rose to stand alongside him, their eyes focused on the darkness at the top of the valley.

"Someone's coming," Devon whispered.

"I know," Godrin said, before something hard struck Devon in the back of the head.

Stars flashed across his vision and he found himself suddenly on his knees, the strength flowing from him. *Kanker* slid from his hands as he swung to see Godrin standing over him. Betran lay on his stomach nearby and for a moment, Devon thought he was dead. Then a low moan whispered through the night, and Betran shifted, his hands curling into fists, but he did not rise.

Devon tried to summon the strength to stand, but the movement caused his vision to swirl. He swayed on his knees as Godrin loomed above him. There was a pause as their eyes met. The man raised his fist for another blow. Devon tried to defend himself, but his arms only lifted weakly in response. Snarling, the Trolan batted them aside, then hammered his fist into Devon's face.

There was a flash of light, followed by a rush of colour—then darkness.

15

Quinn's mind was far away as he walked the ramparts of the citadel, consumed by thoughts of the night before. The meeting with the Tsar had been frustrating, especially after learning he'd been passed over to lead the pursuit after Devon. His frustration was tempered by what had come next, though he could still hardly believe it.

After years spent watching her grow, after the long lessons in magic and watching her as a young woman take lover after lover, Alana had finally come to him. While he was some seven years her senior, Quinn had always felt a shared attraction between them, a tension that neither had quite dared break.

Last night, that barrier had been shattered, the two of them making love long into the night. Even now he rejoiced in their shared passion, savoured the sight of the young woman standing before him naked. Her momentary confusion had given him pause, but at her touch his hesitation had vanished, and he'd spent the rest of the night in a state of ecstasy, their lips locked together, their bodies entwined…

Feeling himself growing aroused, Quinn clenched his jaw and forced his thoughts to other matters. He had risen with the dawn, leaving the still-sleeping Alana to her rest, and headed to the walls for his morning rounds. Relieved of his duties with the Stalkers, the Tsar had placed him in charge of the citadel's defences, along with reporting progress on preparations for the Northland invasion.

When he looked out over the lake, Quinn could just make out the foothills that hid the gathering men. By now, the army would be nearing twenty thousand men and women—a force unlike any the Three Nations had seen in generations. It would be needed if they were to take the north. The Queen's nation spanned more land than the Three Nations combined, and after centuries of poverty, the generosity of their southern neighbours had finally allowed Northland to grow, becoming a power in its own right.

And how did they repay us? Quinn wondered to himself.

Since the Tsar's decree outlawing magic, the Queen had given refuge to hundreds of Magickers. Her motives were obvious—by aiding them today, she joined their power with hers, making her nation a force to be reckoned with. Little good it would do her; the Tsar planned to neutralise the threat before the Queen could exploit her budding force of Magickers.

Quinn paused on his patrol to inspect the uniforms of two guards standing in the northern gatehouse. They stood to attention at his approach, eyes fixed straight ahead as he scanned their chainmail and spears. Quinn drew their swords from their sheaths one by one, inspecting the blades for nicks or rust, but there was not a spot to be seen.

Nodding, Quinn moved on, his thoughts returning to the Northerners.

The biggest risk from the northern invasion was if Lonia or Trola rose up behind the invading army. Already, Stalkers stationed in Trola were reporting unrest amongst the common folk. If the Tsar marched north with most of his forces, there would be little to stop an uprising. Boosting the garrison stationed in Kalgan might squash thoughts of rebellion, but they could ill afford to waste the soldiers.

No, it would be better if the threat were neutralised before it ever began. He made a note to talk with the new Lieutenant of the Stalkers about rounding up potential ring-leaders. The mob would quickly disperse if their leaders were taken.

Reaching the eastern tower, Quinn considered taking another round of the battlements, but dismissed the idea. The men and women guarding the walls were chosen from the best of the city guard. They needed no instruction from him on how best to defend the citadel. All carried the standard spears and short swords of the Plorsean army, and many were also equipped with crossbows. It would take an army to storm the citadel. Even if Devon and his friend managed to evade Darnell's Stalkers, they would meet a quick death if they tried to reach Alana here.

Thinking of the young princess, Quinn's heart beat quicker, and he headed down the nearest stairway from the ramparts. It was still early, and they had been up late into the night. Perhaps she was still asleep, her naked body draped in the silken sheets…

"Quinn!"

Quinn started as a voice shouted out from the ramparts above him. He was surprised to find Krista there, her eyes aflame with anger as she started down towards him. He watched her come, his arms folded and face expressionless.

"What is it, Krista?" he asked, trying to keep the irritation from his voice. He did not appreciate the delay.

"I hear Alana has…returned," she replied, stopping on the step above him. "Is it true?"

Unable to keep the smile from his face, Quinn nodded. "The Tsar helped restore her memories. The true Alana is back with us."

"How very exciting for you," Krista said, her voice like acid. "but where does that leave me?"

Quinn raised an eyebrow. "What do you mean?"

"The young Magickers. What is the Tsar's plan for them?" Krista asked, then continued before Quinn had a chance to respond. "Because I won't stand by and let her take them from me!"

Despite her best efforts, fear lurked behind Krista's eyes. He could well understand it. Alana's return put her position at risk. As the Tsar's daughter, Alana was used to getting what she wanted—or taking it by force, if necessary.

But Alana had made no mention of the young Magickers or Krista the night before. He doubted she would be interested in such trivial matters while her brother was still missing.

"Alana has other things to occupy her right now," he replied gently. Then his face hardened, and stepping up beside her, he gripped her hard by the wrists. "But you should not be concerning yourself with the mind of the Tsar's daughter, Krista. You should be with your charges."

To his surprise, Krista sneered. "From what I hear, you should take your own advice, Quinn."

Anger flared in Quinn's chest at her words, and tightening his grip on her wrist, he pushed her backwards. They were still halfway up the steps to the ramparts, some twenty feet above the ground. The colour drained from Krista's face as she stumbled, her feet slipping on the edge of the stone stairs. Quinn felt a warm sense of satisfaction as he held her there, suspended over the edge. With a sharp tug, he pulled her back and sent her sprawling against the wall.

"I suggest you return to your charges, Krista," he growled. "Before I am forced to report your negligence to the Tsar."

Krista climbed slowly to her feet, her eyes glittering with rage. The soft crackle of lightning came from her fingers, but he only grinned, and after a long moment the energies died away.

"I won't let her take them from me," she said, her voice hoarse. "The Tsar praises strength. If she tries to interfere, I'll show her just how strong I am."

Quinn smirked. "Do as you will, teacher," he replied. "The Tsar will judge you in the end."

With that he turned and continued his way down the stairwell, leaving Krista to her impotent anger.

16

Devon woke to the rhythmic thump of horse hooves beneath him. His head throbbed with every step, and his mouth tasted of dust and vomit. Groaning, he tried to sit up, and found his hands had been tied to the saddle horn. Cracking open his eyes, he stifled a scream as light sliced through his skull.

"Ah, the cowardly hero awakes at last!"

Devon swayed in the saddle as he looked around for the speaker. A woman rode alongside him, her black cloak and pants marking her as a Stalker. The gold diamond-shaped brooch of a captain shone from her breast as she smiled sweetly at him. She patted the haft of his hammer, which she had lying across her lap.

"Thanks for the trophy. I'll be the envy of every regiment with this hanging from my mantle!" She threw back her head and laughed. "Hell, I can't wait to see the look on Quinn's face when I ride through the gates of Ardath with you in tow."

The stars dancing across Devon's eyes were fading now,

and staring at the woman, he struggled to place her. She was young, probably no older than twenty-three years, but she carried about herself an arrogance he'd come to expect from the Tsar's Stalkers. Her auburn hair was tied back in a long ponytail, and her copper eyes watched him like a hawk, as though she still expected him to resist. Prominent cheekbones and a tanned complexion suggested she came from southern Plorsea, though she spoke with the sharp accent of someone raised in Ardath.

It took a long time for Devon's sluggish mind to realise he didn't recognise her. That was not surprising—while most of the Stalkers had been promoted up from those who'd campaigned in Trola, the army had numbered in the thousands—there was no way Devon could have known them all. Transferring his gaze to the rest of their company, he found Kellian on the horse behind him, still slumped unconscious in his saddle. There was no sign of Betran, but further back Godrin and his men were riding at the rear of the column.

Anger clenched around his stomach as he stared at the crime lord. He scowled at the woman riding beside him. "And to whom do I have the pleasure?"

"Captain Darnell, at your service," the woman replied.

His head still pounding, Devon forced a smile. "Nice to meet you, missy," he murmured, "but I doubt you'll earn much respect for arresting an unconscious man. Why don't you hand me back my hammer, and we'll see how well you really fight?"

Darnell grinned. "And I suppose you expect to be set free should you triumph?"

"Only seems fair," Devon grunted.

"Thanks, but I think I'll pass." She pointed a finger at Devon's chest. Around him the temperature plummeted as though a bucket of ice water had been thrown over him. His teeth began to chatter as she went on. "And if you try anything, I'll turn you into an icicle."

His hands tied to the saddle horn, all Devon could do was grit his teeth and nod. After a long moment, the woman clicked her fingers, and the cold vanished, the warmth of the morning sun returning. Chuckling to herself, Darnell heeled her horse forward. As she moved away, the thump of hooves came from behind Devon. He narrowed his eyes as Godrin rode up beside him.

"So much for bringing war to the Plorseans," he growled.

"It's a complex business, politics," Godrin replied genially. "I considered your plan, Devon, truly I did. But this is the only way Trola survives—by proving our loyalty to the Tsar, and living to fight another day."

Devon studied the man, searching for some hint of remorse, but there was no telling what lay behind his hard eyes. "What drivel," he said at last. "I know your kind. Always looking out for yourself, willing to sink to any level, so long as you get to live. I should have known better than to trust a general who would abandon his people in their time of need."

Godrin's face darkened. "I saw a chance to *save* my people."

"You saw a chance to save your own skin," Devon spat.

"And what of you, Devon?" Godrin growled. "You sit there talking of honour, but you never had any intention of liberating my people. You only wanted to rescue your precious friend. For that you expected me to set aside my enmity, to ignore the crimes you committed against Trola? Make no mistake, *friend*, you are the enemy. When I return to Trola, my people will celebrate your death."

"If that were true, why did you not kill us back in Kalgan? You could have made a display of it, followed in the Tsar's footsteps, and staged a public execution."

"Ay, but then word would have gotten back to Enala and the Queen." He shrugged. "As I said, politics are complicated. Northland and its agents are a growing power. I could not afford to alienate them. And besides, death is too good for you, Devon. I want to see you *humbled*, for you to watch as everything you've ever loved is destroyed."

Tasting blood in his mouth, Devon spat on the roadside. "You are a little man," he said. "With such little ambitions."

Godrin's eyes flashed. "I hope the Tsar brings out this girl of yours and kills her in front of you."

Devon shook his head. "And what has this revenge cost you? What happened to Betran? Did your betrayal require his death, too?"

"Fool though he is, I have no grudge against him," Godrin replied, suddenly unable to meet Devon's eyes. "We left him unconscious by the fire. It was all I could do for him. No doubt he'll find his way home, and be the safer for it."

"Glad to see hatred hasn't entirely blinded you to reason." Kellian's voice came from behind them. Devon's friend was sitting up now, a purple lump the size of an egg swelling on his forehead. Swaying in his saddle, he frowned at Devon, his eyes still slightly unfocused. "You know, I hate to say it…" he began.

"Then don't," Devon growled, his head still pounding.

Kellian scratched his chin, turning to Godrin. "So what's the plan now, Trolan? Hand us over to the Tsar and claim the reward—then what? You think your little deception will keep Enala from learning of this?"

"The woman isn't all-knowing," Godrin shot back.

"Might be she's not." Kellian nodded, then gestured at the men riding around them. There were almost twenty black-cloaked Stalkers, plus Godrin's men. "But with all these eyes, she'll hardly have to be all-knowing to find out your role in this."

Around them several of the Stalkers chuckled. Godrin narrowed his eyes. "You talk too much, little man."

Before Kellian could react, the Trolan's fist swept up and struck him hard in the face. With his hands bound, Kellian had no way to defend himself, and he reeled back. Only his bindings kept him from falling to the rocky ground.

Godrin raised his hand to strike Kellian again, but Devon dug his heels into the side of his mount. The horse was well-trained, and it surged forward, bringing him alongside Godrin. As the two horses came together, Godrin's mount flinched away, jostling Godrin. As the man wavered, Devon drove his shoulder forward, catching the Trolan in the small of his back and flinging him from the saddle.

The sharp *thud* of metal and flesh striking the ground echoed through the pass. Around them the Stalkers drew rein, bringing the party to a stop, as on the ground Godrin coughed and groaned, struggling to his feet. He looked up and caught Devon's eye. Snarling, he reached for his sword.

Devon laughed down at him. "Come on then, sonny! Come cut me down, show me how much of a man you are!"

For a moment he thought the Trolan would do it. Godrin stood trembling on the trail, his knuckles turning white as he clenched his blade's hilt. Then a Stalker pushed his horse between them. "Something the matter, Trolan?" he asked gruffly.

A strained silence followed as Godrin turned his hate-filled eyes on the Stalker, before he finally shook his head.

"No problem, *sir*," he said, spitting the last word. He climbed back into his saddle and kicked the horse hard, sending it cantering to the head of the party.

"You know, I'm liking your plan less and less," Kellian commented.

Devon glanced at his friend. His cheek was already beginning to turn purple. Devon's heart sank, his mind turning over as he sought a way out. With a feeling of dread, he realised they had already reached the top of the pass and were descending into Plorsea. Time was running out. Around them the mountains were quickly giving way, the cliffs widening out into the plateaus of western Plorsea. The river still flowed away to their right, but its waters had now split into several channels separated by gravel banks. Ahead, the land still sloped upwards, but the incline was gentle, barren rock turning to open grassland.

"Least we're still heading in the right direction," Devon grunted.

Kellian chuckled dryly. "Ay. Our enemies are no doubt quaking in their boots." He paused, his eyes flicking back the way from which they'd come. "Do you think they really left Betran alive?"

"I can't see why not," Devon replied noncommittedly.

"Good…I liked the man," Kellian said. "Would have been a shame if our folly had left his son an orphan."

Devon nodded. "Ay, I have enough Trolan lives on my conscience."

"How about you stop worrying about the past, and start thinking of a plan that'll get us out of this, old boy?"

"I thought you didn't like my plans."

"True," Kellian mused. "Well, *I* suggest we wait to make our move until the citadel. Since, well, for now we're going in the right direction." He nodded to the way ahead.

Devon groaned as he saw they'd topped a rise, revealing the land for miles around. The river wound away from them, its channels merging and deepening until a single waterway threaded its way past the buildings of a settlement. The plain grey walls and slate roofs gave it an ugly look, of a place that did not quite belong; but then, Onslow was not known for its beauty. The town sat on the trade route between Trola and Plorsea, at the furthest navigable point of the Brunei river before it entered the mountains.

The docks were almost as large as the settlement itself, though there were only a few ships at berth. Times had been hard for the little town since the fall of Trola, and few traders would bother to risk a shipment to the impoverished nation in the middle of winter. At the end of the docks, a ship sat at anchor sporting the jet-black sails of war.

"At least they were kind enough to send us a welcome party," Kellian said.

☙ 17 ❧

Alana strode across the soft grass, her eyes fixed on the trees ahead. The distant laughter of children called her on, drawing her through the ever-blooming roses, through archways and along mosaic paths. Finally, she glimpsed movement through a low-lying hedge, and angled herself towards it.

As she walked, her mind drifted back to the night before, and the long hours spent in Quinn's embrace. His lovemaking had been clumsy and rushed, his hands trembling as he held her. But she had enjoyed his wild, animalistic grunts, the rush of heat through her stomach, his power as she straddled him.

More than anything, Alana had savoured the screams echoing from deep within her mind, the revulsion rising up from that other part of herself. The crumbling of the girl's hope had been ecstasy.

Yet afterwards, there had only been a hollow emptiness in her stomach, a feeling of dissatisfaction she couldn't quite explain. Even as she lay in Quinn's embrace, Alana had felt strangely alone. When he'd risen early in the morning, she had pretended she was asleep, and he had left without a word. Only with him gone did the strange emotions dissipate. A short while later she had risen, determined to reclaim her old life, to restore her purpose in the world.

Now, walking through the gardens, she paused to watch the scene before her. Children were running freely across the lawns, broad smiles on their faces, their voices raised in joy. Only a few were sitting on the nearby benches, their eyes closed in concentration. She could sense the slight flickering of their magic from where she stood, weak and untamed. None were practicing with sword or bow.

Anger touched her as she watched the woman responsible for the chaos. The teacher Krista sat with two children on the benches, her watchful gaze on the children at play. She wasn't even attempting to direct those dedicated enough to be practising their magic.

Alana shook her head, disgust rising like bile in her throat. How would these students ever grow to serve the Tsar, to master their magic, when their teacher did not even care enough to prepare them?

Clenching her fists, she marched towards them. With her eyes on the children, Krista did not notice her approach until the last second. She was smiling as she turned, but the joy fell from her face as she saw her rival.

"Alana." The woman stood, her stance widening as if to brace herself. "I heard you were well."

"I am," Alana replied. She stepped past Krista and looked out at the children. "You may go now."

A stunned silence followed. Then a hand gripped Alana's shoulder and spun her around.

"What?" Krista snapped.

"I said you may go," Alana said, staring at the woman.

"Are you deaf as well as stupid?"

Krista tensed, her teeth showing as her lips drew back into a snarl. "I'm not going anywhere," she hissed. "I was given this appointment by the Tsar himself, when you…fled. You can't just waltz back in here and–"

"Yes, yes, yes," Alana interrupted. "I'm sure my father thought it was a good idea at the time, appointing you." Her lips twisted in a cold smile. "But I'm back now. Your services are no longer required. In fact, I'd say they never were, looking at the damage you've done here."

A soft crackling drew Alana's gaze to Krista's hands. Blue lightning flickered between her fingers as the woman clenched her fists. "I said, I'm not going anywhere," Krista growled through clenched teeth.

Alana raised an eyebrow. "You would strike down the Tsar's daughter?"

"I will do what is necessary," Krista hissed. "I won't let you terrorise these children any longer."

Throwing back her head, Alana let her laughter roll across the gardens. The children nearby turned to stare, their eyes widening at the sight of the lightning dancing across their teacher's fingers. Alana allowed the smile to fall from her face.

"Your kindness will destroy them," she said. "You have allowed them to become soft. Now where will they be when it comes time for their exams?"

"I don't take orders from you, *girl*," Krista shot back. She lifted a hand and pointed it at Alana's chest. Lighting hissed along her skin without leaving so much as a mark. "Now go, before I make you."

Alana sighed, her shoulders slumping. "Very well."

As she turned away, she glimpsed the surprise in Krista's face. She paused, watching the tension drain from the woman, the lightning beginning to die. Instantly she spun back, her hand snapping out to catch the woman. Krista's eyes widened, the colour fleeing her face. She opened her mouth, a single word slipping out.

"No..."

Then Alana's magic flared, burning its way down her arm and into the other woman. A roaring sounded in Alana's ears as the power poured into Krista, scorching its way through her mind, tearing and rending at her consciousness. The woman began to shake beneath Alana's grip, her body growing taut, as though trying to flee. But there was nowhere left for her to run. Alana's power was within her, and there was no escape.

The thrill of her own power filled Alana as she chased down the woman's mind, harrying her spirit, tearing at the flickering light that was the teacher's consciousness. With every blow, she watched memories spill out into the void, to be consumed by the flames of her magic. Krista's spirit shrank, its flight slowing, allowing Alana's magic to engulf it. Swallowing it whole, she washed away the last of the woman-who-had-been-Krista, until only the stark emptiness of the void remained.

Finally satisfied, Alana released Krista's hand and stepped back. Her knees shook and a sudden weakness came over her. Gasping for breath, Alana staggered, and inwardly cursed her other self for wasting her power. Two days had now passed, and still her magic was as weak as a new-born fawn. Still, she was stronger than she'd been the day she woke, and more than strong enough to deal with one as weak as the teacher.

Smiling, Alana straightened and stepped up to the woman, inspecting her work. Krista stood there dumbly, her vacant eyes fixed on some distant point. Alana placed a hand on her shoulder, and the teacher blinked, the light slowly coming back into her eyes. Her brow creased as she found Alana standing in front of her.

"Who are you?" she asked. Then she staggered, clutching at her chest. "Who am *I?*"

Alana smiled to herself. To the woman, she said: "You are no one." Her voice was cold, and she showed no emotion in the face of the woman's distress. "And you should not be here."

"I'm sorry," Krista whispered, tears appearing in her eyes. "I don't know how I got here. I think…I think I am lost."

"Very lost," Alana agreed.

Taking the woman by the shoulder, she shoved her in the direction of the exit. Krista stumbled a few steps, and then sank to her knees, tears streaming down her face. "Where am I?" she cried.

Her patience wearing thin, Alana grabbed the woman by the wrist and yanked her back up. "Come on," she snapped.

Taking a firmer grip on the former teacher, she dragged her through the gardens, retracing her steps back inside. They wound their way through the citadel, Krista sobbing all the while, until they finally came to the gates leading out into the city.

The guards stood to attention when they saw Alana. "Your highness," one said, his chainmail rattling as he stepped up to greet her. "What brings…the two of you here today?" His eyes flickered nervously at the crying teacher.

Alana flashed the guard a cold smile. "Open the gates," she commanded. "Krista wishes to walk the city."

The man hesitated. The smile fell from Alana's face, and she stepped towards him. His face blanked, and she savoured his sudden look of fear; he was lifting the crossbar to the gates before she could take another step. The squeal of the steel hinges followed as the heavy wood and iron gates swung ponderously open.

Still with Krista in tow, Alana walked through, leaving the guards to stare after them. She led the former teacher several blocks through the cobbled streets before coming to a stop in a dark alley. The scent of urine wafted up from the stones beneath their feet, and not wanting to spend any more time in the filthy streets than necessary, Alana turned to Krista.

"This is where you belong, woman," she said coldly, releasing the former teacher's hand.

There was open fear in Krista's eyes now. The sun was hidden by the tall walls of the alleyway, and the temperature had barely risen above freezing.

"Where will I go?" she whispered.

Alana shrugged and started to leave, her thoughts already turning to the children waiting for her return. She would have to work them doubly hard now, to make up for the damage Krista had done. But the former teacher reached out and grabbed her sleeve.

"Please! Please…can you at least tell me who I am?"

Alana watched the tears streaming down the woman's pretty face. Her eyes were now shot with red, and her thin yellow dress would do nothing to fend off the winter cold. With her power bound deep within her, it was unlikely Krista would ever rediscover her magic. Without it, she wouldn't last a week outside the citadel.

A wave of pity swept over Alana as she looked on the wreck she'd left of the former teacher, and for a second she considered reversing the spell.

"It didn't have to be this way," she murmured.

Krista stared back at her, confused and fearful, already starting to tremble in the cold air.

Alana sighed. Shaking her head, she reached out to touch the woman, to undo what she'd done, when she sensed a wrongness within her. She frowned and turned her mind inwards, and found that other part of herself hovering in the void. Rage flared in her chest as she realised the girl's weakness had been corrupting her. Summoning her magic, she drove the foolish girl back into the darkness, and the pity faded.

Looking back at Krista, she felt only disgust at the woman's weakness. "Get out of my sight," she spat.

With that, Alana turned away. A cry came from behind her, but Krista made no move to follow her. Within minutes Alana was marching back through the gates of the citadel, the woman's sobs already a distant memory. Her mind was already on the task ahead, on the drills and punishments she would need to burn the weakness from her children.

She would begin with the blades, she decided. They would hack and slash at one another until their arms were dead and their bodies beaten black and blue. The first to drop would be sent before the Tsar, as an example to the others.

Alana was just crossing through into the first courtyard beyond the gates when she realised she'd forgotten something. She hailed the guards. "Gentlemen, be so good as to keep the riffraff out in future. I would be very displeased to see that woman back inside the citadel."

The guards saluted without hesitation this time, and smiling, Alana walked away. Whistling a soft tune, she wandered back through the citadel, already savouring the thought of the torments she had in store for her new charges.

18

Braidon paced quickly around the narrow room, the smooth stone walls seeming to draw closer with every lap he took. Flicking another glance at the steel panelled door, he wondered what was taking place behind it. Surely it couldn't take this long to sort out the misunderstanding. After all, the accusation by the Plorsean emissaries was patently ridiculous—he wasn't the son of the Tsar. His father was a…merchant.

He frowned, struggling to recall his past. The memories rose slowly, though they remained blurred and indistinct, as though viewed through a mist. He remembered his father as a giant of a man, a…traveller who he rarely saw. And then…nothing.

Groaning, he resumed his pacing. He'd been waiting more than an hour now, the pain of the blows he'd taken from the guards forgotten in the face of the Queen's revelation. He still couldn't believe she'd set her men on him—and on the word of some two-faced emissary! That she thought him capable of such deceit….

Braidon froze as the soft whisper of oiled hinges opening came from across the room. He spun, and watched in silence as the Queen and Enala entered the room. The Queen's expression was unreadable, and Braidon turned his gaze on Enala, seeking to find some sign of their decision.

His heart sank as he saw the sadness in her eyes.

"It's not true!" Before he could stop himself, his words were echoing through the chamber.

The Queen froze, and for a moment Braidon thought he saw uncertainty flicker across her face. Then the mask fell back into place, and she strode the rest of the way across the room.

"I'm afraid it is," she said coldly. "Though I understand now it was not you who practiced the deception, but your sister."

"What are you talking about? Alana is the Tsar's hostage!" Braidon shouted, his confusion turning to anger.

"That's not true." The Queen spoke over him, her eyes flashing a warning. Braidon bit his tongue, and she went on. "It seems Alana is a Magicker of some power. She used her magic to wipe your memory, to make you believe you were a simple commoner, instead of the Tsar's only son."

Braidon stood staring at them. "Wha…what?"

Her eyes shining, Enala knelt in front of him. "You are the son of the Tsar, Braidon," she said. Then she was reaching out, pulling him into her arms, holding him tight.

His chest constricted, and Braidon found himself lost for breath. He clutched at the old woman's back, struggling to make sense of the words, even as his mind began to spin. He saw again the images of his father, swirling in the mist, falling back into a void in the centre of his soul. And then he *knew*. The memories remained locked away, but he *knew* Enala's words were the truth.

"No," he whispered, clinging to Enala as though his life depended on it. "I…I don't want it, I don't."

"It's okay," Enala breathed, pulling back from him for a moment. There were tears in her eyes, but she wiped them away.

A tremor swept through Braidon as he looked from her to the Queen. "I don't want to go back."

The Queen looked away. "You must."

"Still you persist on this path, Merydith?" Enala stood. "Can't you see the boy is terrified?"

The Queen did not back down. "I must!" she hissed. "If I refuse him, it will mean war. And we do not have the strength to stand against the Tsar's powers!"

"For years you have given refuge to renegade Magickers. Ask them for their help. They will not deny you!"

"No, they would not. But I gave them sanctuary without obligation—not to make them into an army. It would make a mockery of everything we've worked for."

"And this does not?" Enala snapped. "What makes Braidon any different from the others?"

"He does not face death," the Queen answered, her voice sad. "The emissary says the spell was a mistake, that his sister will reverse it. He will become himself again."

"No!" Braidon cried, scrambling back. "I won't!"

"The boy does not wish to go, Merydith," Enala said, stepping between them. "Will you truly take him by force?"

The Queen stared at Enala, fists clenched, eyes shimmering. "You would have me sacrifice a nation to save one life?" she whispered.

"I would have you hold to the morals your parents held so dear," Enala replied.

"We cannot win," the Queen said. "The Tsar commands tens-of-thousands, has Magickers and demons and dragons by the score. And then there is the man himself…"

"Northland is not without power," Enala reminded her.

"No, but we have no standing army, and our population is too dispersed. It would take months to gather a force capable of matching him, longer still to train it."

Enala sighed, her eyes taking on a haunted look. Gently, she gripped the Queen's shoulder. "I cannot make this decision for you, Merydith. It is yours alone. But think on this—war is coming. If not today, then soon. The Tsar will not allow you to continue outside his rule. I know his mind. Sooner or later, he will seek to conquer the last bastion for magic."

Braidon watched as a strained silence fell between the two women. His heart thumped hard in his chest, and he was still struggling to breathe. Even so, his thoughts were becoming clearer now, his mind working hard to follow the conversation.

"Have you heard any news of Devon?" he asked suddenly.

The two women jumped, as though surprised to find him still standing there. After a moment, Enala shook her head.

"I have heard nothing. I'm sorry."

"Then I'll go," Braidon heard himself saying. The women's eyes widened, and he pressed on before his courage abandoned him. "Not with the emissary, but I'll go. If what you're saying is true, and Alana is really…the Tsar's daughter again, then Devon and Kellian are walking into a trap. We need to warn them."

"It doesn't need to be you, Braidon," Enala replied gently.

"No." Braidon paused, gathering his strength before

continuing. "But I won't remain here while my sister is… imprisoned. You say she is there by choice, but I cannot believe that. And if Devon can't save her, it will have to be me."

Silence answered his words. The two women watched him, their eyes shining in the candlelight. Unable to tell their thoughts, Braidon looked away, his stomach tight with worry.

"You are a brave man, Braidon." He jumped as a hand settled on his shoulder. He was surprised to find the Queen standing over him. Gone was the hardness to her eyes, the anger and the fear. With a long sigh, she went on. "For what it's worth, you may remain in Erachill if your mind changes. I will not betray you to the Plorseans."

His throat tight, Braidon nodded his thanks, as Enala moved up alongside them. "She may not be the same woman you remember, Braidon."

"I know," he said, "but I still have to try."

Enala nodded, her eyes tearing.

"I will go alone if I have to," he said, a smile coming to his lips, "but it would be nice to have a dragon…"

The women blinked, then a grin split Enala's face as she started to laugh. "You will have one," she replied. "On one condition."

"Name it," Braidon answered.

"Master your magic, my child," the old woman replied, "and I will take you to Ardath myself."

19

Alana sighed as she sank into the velvet sofa, a glass of Lonian Red in hand. She was just about to take a sip when a *thump* came from the outer door to her quarters, followed by the soft squeal of hinges as it swung open. Quinn appeared in the doorway, his eyes sweeping the room before settling on Alana.

"Quinn," she said, a smile coming to her lips. After the long day she'd spent putting her new students through the wringer, he was just the man she wanted to see. "Come in, help yourself to some wine."

Wearing a smile of his own, he crossed to a cabinet on the wall and took out a glass. He filled it generously from the bottle on the table, then joined her on the sofa. "So, I hear you didn't waste much time…dealing with your replacement."

Alana sipped her wine, savouring the rich earthliness of the vintage, and she slid closer to Quinn until their legs were touching. "The woman annoyed me," she said simply.

Quinn laughed. "I'd best tread carefully then," he said,

resting his hand on her thigh. With the fire keeping the cold of winter at bay, she had already changed into a loose fitting black skirt, its intricately knitted hem riding up above her knees. "I can't say I ever really liked her myself," he finished.

"I'm surprised you didn't deal with her then," Alana replied, enjoying the warmth of his touch as his hand slid higher, "after her show of disrespect on the battlements."

Quinn's hand stilled. "You heard about that?"

"Of course."

He sighed, glancing away for a moment. "Much as I might have liked to…remove her, I am not the Daughter of the Tsar," he answered carefully. "I have other matters with which to concern myself with, without starting a war with the other Magickers in the citadel."

Alana laughed. Leaning against him, she trailed her fingers up his chest, and looked up at him with playful eyes. "Has my father been keeping you busy?" she breathed. "Is that where you keep sneaking off too?"

Enjoying the slightly panicked look in his eyes, she lifted herself up until their faces were level, and pressed her lips to his. With a moan, he sank back into the sofa as she slid into his lap. Heat spread through her stomach as he stirred beneath her, his hands wrapping around her waist. Supressing a moan of her own, she bit his lip hard, the need swelling within her.

He flinched from the pain, but she held him tight, and a trickle of her magic seeped into him. Relaxing again, his eyelids flickered as a distant look came over his eyes. She grinned, enjoying her power over the man, before drawing her magic back into herself. Groaning, he blinked, coming back to himself. He almost looked surprised to find her straddling him.

Then a stiffness came over his face, an almost primal

look, and Alana gasped as he tossed her down on the sofa alongside him. Before she could think, his weight was on her, pinning her down. A shock raced down her spine as he kissed her neck, and she wanted to scream for him to hurry, to tear apart her clothes and take her…

She fumbled desperately at Quinn's belt as he grabbed at her blouse and ripped it open. Buttons went scattering across the fur rug, and she moaned as his mouth slid down her body, his tongue circling her nipples.

Alana felt a rush of triumph as the belt came loose, then her hands were travelling down, gripping him tight, drawing him in…

Afterwards, they found themselves on Alana's bed, chests heaving, cheeks flushed. Still hot from their exertions, Alana lay back, content for the moment. But slowly the gratification of her triumph faded, replaced by a sudden emptiness, and the smile faded from her lips.

Quinn curled up alongside her, his muscled arms enfolding her in an embrace. The show of affection took her off-guard, especially after the way he'd taken her at the end. There had been an animalistic gleam in his eyes as he threw her down on the bed and flipped her onto her stomach…but now, as he kissed her gently on the cheek, she saw only warmth in his expression.

Devon's face drifted across her thoughts, and Alana felt a rush of irritation. Suddenly, she wanted nothing more than to be left alone. Wriggling clear of his arms, she struggled to keep her anger from showing. Within, she sensed no interference from her other self. Unable to pick the source of her disgruntlement, she lay back and stared at the mosaiced ceiling above her poster-bed.

"I saw the children earlier." Quinn didn't seem to have noticed her change in mood.

Alana was glad for the change in topic. "What did you think?" she asked. Recalling her efforts earlier with the young Magickers, she felt a warm sense of satisfaction. Krista had left a troop of weak and unruly children in her wake, but Alana was determined to turn them into the Battle Magickers her father needed. "They have a long way to go, but I think they can be saved."

Quinn grunted. "You don't think you might be pushing them too hard?"

"What?" Alana hissed, sitting up. Her irritation turned to anger as she swung on him. "How *dare* you?"

"Let's not have this discussion again," Quinn replied with a sigh.

"No, let's," Alana growled.

She rolled from the bed. Scooping up a nightdress, she slipped into the soft silk, though it did little to conceal her curves. Quinn stared back at her, a pained look on his face, but it did nothing to quell her rage.

"Alana..." he started, then trailed off. Silently he reached for her, but she pushed him away. "Alana...it's just....beating them, running them until they drop, that's not how I trained you."

"No," she answered coldly, "that is what my father taught me." Quinn said nothing, but seeing the defiance in his gaze, she went on: "You may have taught me how to control my power, but it was the Tsar who forged me into a weapon, who gave me the strength to resist my magic's call."

"You were already strong..."

"Not strong enough," Alana snapped. For an instant, she recalled the first time she'd reached for her power, the icy chills that had engulfed her as the emerald Feline rose in the void. Shivering, she forced the image away. "If it had been up to you, I would have been lost. The magic would have taken me, turned me, made me into a demon."

"So now all your students must suffer the same torment that you did?"

Alana laughed, the sound harsh in the stone confines of her quarters. "I am letting them off easy, compared to what my father subjected me to."

Quinn's eyes were sad now. "And what about your brother? Is that what you wish for him, when he returns?"

The retort died in Alana's throat, and she stood staring at Quinn, mouth open. Ice spread through her stomach as she imagined delivering her brother to the Tsar, the agony he would suffer, the fear and dread, and eventually, the awful hatred.

"What about the boy, Liam?" Quinn went on, taking a step closer. "I saw him in the corner of the dining hall, bruised black and blue, all alone. The others told me he is to take his examination tomorrow. I spoke with him—he's not ready, not even close. If he goes before the Tsar, he *will* fail."

"Then he will die, and my father will have another demon to serve him!" Alana screamed, her rage washing away all thoughts of her brother.

"You're condemning him to a fate worse than death."

"Get out," Alana roared, pointing at the doorway.

For a moment it looked as though he would refuse. Teeth bared, Alana stepped towards him, hand outstretched, her power bubbling in her chest. His eyes widened in fear, and before she could reach him, he spun and retreated through the outer doors. The *thud* of them closing behind him echoed loudly through her bedchamber.

Lowering her arm, Alana stared at the place where he had stood. The anger drained from her, slipping away until she felt only emptiness. Her shoulders slumped, and retreating to the bed, she dropping onto the satin duvet. Closing her eyes, she tried to bring back the anger, to feel anything but the awful void in her chest. But it would not come, and tossing and turning amidst the cushions, she drifted slowly into sleep.

20

Night was falling as the Stalkers led Devon and Kellian through the gates of the citadel. The day had been a hard one for both of them, sitting helpless on their horses as they drew ever closer to Onslow. The Stalkers had taken no chances with either of them. Kellian had been searched as he lay unconscious, all his knives taken from him. And not even Devon's prodigious strength could break their bindings. Even if they were to slip free, there were still more than twenty warriors and the captain's magic to deal with.

So instead, they had waited with growing frustration as they were loaded into the shallow-bottomed barge like sacks of grain. On the water, they had no hope of escaping, and the day had stretched out, the sun hot on their faces despite the cool winter breeze. Sailing upriver, Devon had watched as the waterway converged and broadened out into the great expanse of Lake Ardath.

Overhead, the black sails had creaked and groaned, a constant reminder of days long since passed, when Devon had first marched to war. The army had set off from Ardath with the rising sun, its scarlet rays staining the waters of the lake red. Standing on the deck of his ship, Devon had felt a thrill in his heart, a rush of joy as the trumpets sounded. Five years later though, there was only sorrow as he looked on the black sails of war.

Now, standing beneath the gates of the citadel, Devon couldn't help but wonder where everything had gone so wrong. He had been in his prime when the war ended, a warrior renown across the Three Nations. Fame and fortune had been his for the taking, if only he'd remained with the army. Instead, he had turned his back on his career as a soldier, and embraced a life of misery and despair.

Yet, as the gates swung shut behind them, he realised he felt no regret, and a smile came to his face.

"What are you grinning about, traitor?" Darnell snapped, coming alongside him. She was carrying *kanker* loosely in one hand.

Still smiling, Devon shook his head. "The folly of the young," he said.

Her face darkened and her fist lashed out to catch him in the solar plexus. His hands tied behind his back, Devon was unable to avoid the punch, and he doubled over, gasping for breath. But it was not the first blow he'd suffered that day, and after a moment he straightened with a laugh.

"You pack quite the punch, missy," he grunted, "but next time try putting your hips into–"

He broke off as she struck him again, a blow to the side of his head sending him reeling. Stars flashed across his vision and he almost fell, only the wall of the corridor keeping him upright.

"One more word, and you'll lose more than just your wits, traitor," Darnell said, her hand resting on the pommel of her sword.

This time, Devon decided to keep his mouth shut. Beside him, Kellian was in even worse shape than himself. His quick tongue had earned him several beatings on the voyage across the lake, but he had fallen silent now, his face a mess of purple and blue.

Marching deeper into the citadel, they followed the Stalkers through dimly lit courtyards and long marble hallways. Outside, the sun had dropped below the citadel walls, and here and there they encountered servants running about with fresh lanterns. As they passed through another courtyard, Devon glanced up and saw the stone lattices shielding the upper floors. Idly he wondered what unseen eyes might be watching their progress through the citadel, before they disappeared into yet another corridor.

Curiously, there weren't many guards in sight, though those they did see were heavily armed, their steel-plated armour shining in the lantern light. Most of their company had departed now: Godrin's men had remained outside while he continued with them, and most of the Stalkers had peeled off during their passage through the citadel. By the time they finally stopped outside a set of double doors, there was only the captain and two of her Stalkers left alongside Godrin. Together, they entered a white-walled chamber lined with steel doors.

One of the Stalkers entered one of the doors, while the other helped Godrin shepherd the two prisoners after him—though neither Devon nor Kellian attempted to resist. With their arms still tied behind their backs, they would be quickly overtaken if they did. No, the time to strike would be when their bindings were finally loosened.

Devon turned as the door clanged closed, watching their captors with a wary eye. The room in which they found themselves was unadorned but for several sets of chains hanging from the stone walls. There were no windows, and the only exit was the door through which they'd entered. His eyes were drawn to a single table set in the corner. Ice slid down his spine as he saw the implements laid out on the wooden surface.

"This isn't the dungeons," he murmured.

"You thought I would share my glory with the dungeon master?" Darnell replied, brushing a lock of hair from her face. Moving to the table, she unbuckled her sword belt and placed it on the table, then set *kanker* down beside it. "No, these are my private...quarters. Jarson, Olie, if you could introduce Devon and his friend to their new accommodations?"

Devon tensed as the two Stalkers moved forward, readying himself. This was their chance. They would have to loosen his and Kellian's bonds before chaining them to the walls; in that instant, there would be a moment when he could act. The Stalker to his right was a woman, almost as large as himself, while the man on his left was slightly smaller. Beyond them, Darnell and Godrin were standing too far back to interfere immediately. If he could down the two Stalkers, steal one of their weapons, he would stand a chance.

As the woman closed on him, he gathered himself, preparing to unleash bloody chaos the moment his bonds were loosened. But the moment the woman touched the ropes around his wrists, Darnell raised her hand. Before Devon could react, a sharp, piercing cold wrapped around his skull. Crying out, his legs crumpled beneath him, but the Stalkers caught him before he could fall. Through the agony, he hardly felt their jostling as they tore the ropes from his arms and shoved him up against the wall.

A sharp *click* sliced through the pain, and the cold

vanished as quickly as it had come. He blinked, light dancing before his eyes, and he realised with dismay his arms had already been cuffed to the wall. Slumping against the cold stone, he watched in growing despair as the same procedure was repeated with his friend.

"And you have the gall to call me a coward," he finally managed to croak as the spell was lifted from Kellian.

Darnell only smiled. "One can only make use of the tools with which they were gifted." She said. "It is not my fault you chose to spurn yours, Devon. I know your story. You were blessed beyond all other warriors, a legend amongst the Tsar's soldiers, but you threw everything away." Stepping back, she shook her head. "Thank the Tsar I had a strong teacher, or I may never have mastered this power."

"Whoever he was, he sure did a fine job of turning out monsters," Kellian groaned, lifting himself to his feet and taking the weight off the chains now fastened around his wrists.

The captain smiled. "*She* is a great woman, and the daughter of the Tsar." She turned to one of her Stalkers. "Go and fetch Quinn, tell him I've brought him Devon. I can't wait to see his face when he learns it was *I* who finally brought the cowardly hero to justice!"

The black-cloaked Stalker nodded and left the room, the heavy wooden door slamming closed behind her. Watching her go, Devon strained against the chains holding him to the wall, testing their strength. The one holding his left arm seemed to move slightly; letting off the pressure, he stared at their three remaining foes.

The captain was no longer paying them any attention. She turned towards the table in the corner, then seemed to notice Godrin standing nearby. "Trolan, what are you still doing here?"

Devon pulled against the left-hand chain again as Godrin coughed. "There is the small matter of my payment, captain."

Darnell narrowed her eyes. "You'll get your gold, Trolan. But not now, it's late. Go back to your men, return in the morning. You'll receive your payment then."

"Do you think me a fool, captain?" Godrin murmured, stepping in close. He gestured at Devon and Kellian. "The second I step through that door, my involvement in this whole affair will be forgotten."

"You overstep yourself, Trolan," the captain growled. Raising her fist, she opened her fingers. Blue light seeped across the room.

The sight gave Godrin pause. He stepped back, his hands raised in deference. "My apologies, captain," he said quickly. His eyes went to the other Stalker, who stood close to the prisoners, then back to Darnell. He lowered his hands. "It will be as you say. I shall return in the morning."

Darnell waited until he turned away before lowering her fist. Smiling, she faced Devon and Kellian. Gritting his teeth, Devon strained against his bindings, feeling the bolt in the wall beginning to give…

"Only one thing, captain," Godrin said suddenly, pausing at the door.

Growling, Darnell swung towards him, her hand coming up. "And what is tha–"

She never got to finish her sentence. As she turned, Godrin's hand whipped out, and a knife flashed across the room to bury itself in her throat. Darnell gasped, her hand reaching for the ivory hilt. Blood bubbled between her fingers as she tried to pull it free, but then the strength fled from her and she toppled silently to the ground. A pool of blood began to spread across the floor, almost black in the dim light.

"What the *hell?*" The one remaining Stalker stood stunned, looking from his captain to Godrin.

He scrambled for his sword as Godrin started towards him. The Trolan had left his sword at the gates, but he already had a fresh knife to hand. Steel scraped on leather as the Stalker drew his blade and roared.

Before the two men could meet, Devon yanked again at the weakening bolt. With a sharp *crack*, it came free. The Stalker had his back to the prisoners, but at the noise he glanced back, and Devon's fist crunched into his face. The blow sent him staggering backwards out of Devon's reach, straight into Godrin's dagger. Twisting the blade, Godrin dragged it back, and the man collapsed in a heap alongside his captain.

Leaning down, Godrin wiped his dagger clean on the man's shirt. Calmly he recovered a short sword and the keys from Darnell. Then, still smiling, he stepped towards Devon and Kellian.

"Time to be going, don't you think?"

21

"What the hell is going on?" Devon asked, gaping in disbelief at the bloody corpses on the floor.

Godrin shrugged. "You said you needed a way into the citadel. I arranged one."

"I didn't mean in bloody chains!"

The Trolan held up the keys. "Easily fixed."

Devon stared at them for a moment, then snapped. "Well what are you damn well waiting for?"

Feeling his anger mounting, Devon strained against the remaining chain holding him to the wall. When it wouldn't budge, he stilled, and a tremor shook him. Despite his earlier bravado, for a moment he had truly thought they were doomed, and the shock of that realisation was just beginning to touch him.

Godrin stepped towards them, then paused, his smile faltering. He glanced at Kellian, then back to Devon. "Sorry about the beatings…had to make it believable, you know?"

Devon bared his teeth. "Delaying isn't helping your cause. Now get these damn chains off of us!"

Godrin showed his hands. "Gladly!" He paused. "Just… we're all friends here okay? No need to rehash the last few hours."

Straining his arms, Devon tested the remaining chain again, but there was no give in it. He let out a long sigh and looked at the Trolan. "Just get us out of here, before the Stalker returns with Quinn," he said, trying to keep his voice calm.

Godrin watched them a moment longer before apparently making up his mind. Moving forward, he unlocked the chain from around Devon's wrist, then moved to do the same for his friend. Kellian groaned, slumping slightly against Godrin before finding his feet. Rubbing his wrists, he pushed the Trolan away from him. Godrin stumbled back, opening his mouth to complain, but broke off when he saw Kellian sweep up a fallen knife.

"Hey, what–"

Kellian's empty fist caught Godrin in the jaw before he could finish the question. The blow sent the Trolan reeling sideways. His foot caught on the Stalker's lifeless body and he went down hard. Gasping, he rolled onto his knees and tried to rise, only to freeze as Kellian's blade touched his neck.

Kellian raised an eyebrow at Devon. "What do you think, should I kill him?"

Still on his knees, Godrin glowered at them. "Typical Plorseans, can't trust a single one of ya."

"That's rich, coming from you," Kellian snapped. His face was swollen, and a cut above his eyebrow was seeping blood.

"I did what I said I would," Godrin said coldly. "I never said it would be easy. You're lucky I got you this far."

"Am I?" Kellian leaned down, the blade pressing harder.

Devon saw the Trolan flinch back, bleeding now from a shallow cut on his neck.

Godrin reached up to touch the wound, his hand coming away wet with blood. As he turned his gaze back on them, Devon saw the familiar hate lurking behind his eyes. It seemed not everything had been an act. Stepping up beside his friend, Devon gently lowered Kellian's hand.

"What a world we live in, when it's the butcher who stays the innkeeper's hand," Godrin spat. Rising slowly to his feet, he glared at Kellian. "Well?"

Kellian didn't answer, leaving Devon to address the Trolan. Devon sucked in a breath, seeking to quell his own anger, even as Kellian circled the room, collecting a sword and several more knives from the fallen Stalkers.

"I'm…sorry for our anger," he said at last. "You were true to your word, I can't fault you that, sonny. Might be you could have found a…gentler subterfuge, but you have my gratitude for getting us this far."

Godrin smiled coldly. "If you don't mind, I require a little more than just gratitude." He walked across to the table and hefted *kanker.*

Devon narrowed his eyes, his heartbeat quickening at the sight of the Trolan holding his ancestor's weapon. "That's mine," he said.

"Yes, well, times change," Godrin replied. When Devon said nothing, he sighed and waved at the door. "You came here to save your friend. I understand that, though I can't bring myself to wish you luck. I only came here to kill the Tsar."

"You're welcome to him," Devon growled. "What does *kanker* have to do with it?"

Godrin grinned. "You didn't think I hadn't heard the rumours, did you, Devon?" he asked. "The whole Empire has been talking of it, how you defeated a demon, and fought off a hoard of Stalkers, even one with magic. It's simply not possible for a mortal to have accomplished such feats—not even for a warrior like you. Not unless..." he trailed off, his eyes drifting to the hammer, "not unless you had a magic hammer."

Devon swallowed, his words abandoning him, and Godrin nodded.

"I thought so."

"You can't have it," Devon hissed.

"Think of it as a loan," Godrin said.

"We don't even know if its powerful enough to defeat his magic," Devon argued.

"Yes, well, that's a risk I'm going to have to take," Godrin murmured. "If it's not...then at least I'll be making up for running away while your army overtook Kalgan." As he spoke, a haunted look came over his face, and Devon caught a glimpse of the pain within.

The fight went from Devon then, as he realised the crime lord shared Devon's own sense of shame over his decisions during the war. Yes, he had saved lives by fleeing the city with his cohort and a ship full of civilians. But in doing so, Godrin had abandoned his comrades, leaving them to their death.

He sighed. "Fine," he said, "just make sure you don't get any scratches on her."

Godrin chuckled. "I'll take good care of her." He paused as Kellian returned to stand alongside Devon. Silently, he handed over a short sword, then turned his gaze on the crime lord. Godrin coughed, only finding his voice after several seconds of strained silence. "As for your friend...I asked some of the Stalkers about her, told them you were looking for her..."

"Yes?" Devon pressed when the Trolan did not continue.

"They laughed," Godrin said, his eyes on the floor. "They said…they said she'd be the death of you, Devon. If you ever found her."

Devon frowned. "What are you talking about?"

"They didn't elaborate. But she's here, in the citadel. I got that much from them."

"In the dungeons?"

"No, the eastern wing. From what I managed to discern," Godrin said.

"Can you take us there?" Devon asked.

"You know I can't," Godrin replied. "I have my own mission. If I wait until you free the girl, the chance will be lost. No, we must part ways here. I can only send you in the right direction."

Swiftly he outlined the passageways they would need to take to reach the eastern wing of the citadel. They were close, fortunately, but once there Godrin's instructions ran dry. They would need to locate Alana's room themselves, and find a way to avoid any guards stationed in the hallways along the way.

"Good luck, to the both of you," Godrin said finally.

Devon swallowed, then stretched out his hand. Godrin took it after a moment's hesitation. "I expect you to live, sonny," Devon grunted. "Don't you go disappointing me. I like that hammer."

"I'll do my best." Godrin grinned.

"I can't say it's been a pleasure," Devon added as they broke apart.

Godrin laughed. "Oh, I don't know about that," he replied. "I got to beat the Butcher of Kalgan, after all. Something to tell the young ones about one day."

"You'll be telling them how you lost your teeth in a minute," Devon growled, but the Trolan was already disappearing through the door.

Alone now with Kellian, he glanced at his friend. "I have to say, he's starting to grow on me."

"He would," Kellian replied wryly. He rolled his shoulders, wincing in pain, before looking at Devon again. "Well, shall we get on with it? The night's already old, and we've got a princess to save."

Gripping the unfamiliar short sword in one hand, Devon nodded, and together the two of them passed through the door, and out into the passageways of the citadel.

22

"Sir, a moment?"

Quinn looked up from the reports he was reading, irritated at the interruption. Unable to sleep after his argument with Alana, he had headed for his office, intent on finalising his reports on the army's preparation. But his irritation faded as he recognised the Stalker standing in the doorway as one of Darnell's squad, the ones who'd been tasked with hunting down Devon. He rose to his feet and waved the woman inside.

"Has something happened?" he asked, his heart beating faster.

If Darnell had made a mistake and let Devon slip through her fingers, the hammerman might even now be close, in the city even, seeking a way into the citadel. A sliver of ice seeped into his stomach as he thought of facing the man again.

Gripping his desk, he lowered himself back into his chair and indicated for the Stalker to do the same. Unconsciously he reached for his magic and felt it surge within him. The fear subsided, replaced with a cold determination. If Devon came, he would be ready. Hammer or no, the man could not face all the forces at the Tsar's command and expect to survive.

"No, sir."

Quinn's head jerked up at the woman's words. The Stalker sat nervously across from him, her eyes flickering from Quinn to the doorway. His irritation returning, Quinn scowled. "No?" he growled. "Then why are you here, soldier?"

"I…Darnell sent me," she said quickly. "She wants you in her chambers."

"In her chambers?" Quinn said, momentarily confused. "She's here?"

"Yes, sir," the Stalker replied, "we arrived just after sunset."

Speechless, Quinn stared at the woman for a long moment, before finally finding his words. "She has given up the pursuit of Devon and Kellian already?"

The Stalker swallowed. "That's…not for me to say, sir," she said. "The captain only said for you to come as quickly as possible. She wishes to brief you herself."

Quinn glared at the Stalker, and watched with satisfaction as she shrank in her seat. "The captain thinks to command *me?*"

"I…no…she only requested…your presence, sir," the woman finished lamely, her eyes blinking rapidly in the fading light of a single candle.

"Tell me why you're here," Quinn growled, "instead of chasing down the renegades, as you were *commanded* by the Tsar."

The woman blanked. "We…we already have them… sir," she managed.

"What?"

"We caught them," the Stalker said. "They were taken unaware by the Trolans. All we had to do was march up and arrest them."

"Devon is *here?*" Quinn said, leaping to his feet.

"Yes, sir."

"Then take me to him," Quinn growled.

The Stalker snapped to attention, and sweeping up his sword, Quinn followed her out the door. In the corridor he strapped his sword belt to his waist as they started on their way. The Stalker constantly flicked glances back at Quinn as they walked, revealing her fear. She had betrayed her captain's command, and while Quinn had given her little choice, no doubt Darnell would make her life a living hell for it.

In that moment, Quinn didn't care. His hand drifted to the hilt of his sabre, gripping it tight. The hammerman was *here*. How had that happened?

He's in custody, Quinn reminded himself.

Yet something didn't seem right about the story. Devon and Kellian were wily men; it was unlikely they would be taken unawares by anyone, let alone some washed-up ex-soldiers from Trola. Jaw clenched, he picked up the pace, yelling at his companion to do the same.

They reached Darnell's quarters a few minutes later. A single door hung open and unguarded. Inside, they found the crumpled bodies of Darnell and one of her Stalkers, their life blood spreading slowly across the tiled floor.

The woman who had led Quinn there stood frozen in the doorway as Quinn strode past.

"I…I…" she stuttered.

Ignoring her, Quinn studied the room. Darnell lay face down, a dagger buried in her throat. The other Stalker had managed to crawl a few inches, before he too expired, succumbing to the terrible wound someone had torn in his belly. Of Kellian and Devon, there was no sign.

"Alert the guards. Devon is in the citadel. Send men to the princess's quarters—he'll be heading there," Devon said, swinging on the Stalker still standing in the doorway. When she didn't move, he roared: "*Now!*"

His command echoed loudly in the room and the Stalker leapt to a salute. She made to turn, then paused. "Sir…" she said, her voice fading as he glared at her.

"What?" he snapped.

"There was someone else here: Godrin, the Trolan who betrayed the two renegades."

"Of course," Quinn growled. "Now go!"

So the Tsar's informant had double-crossed them. Darnell should have expected it—Trolans could only be trusted as far as their next bribe. No doubt the thought of being a thorn in the Tsar's side had been too tempting for the man to pass up.

He frowned. Turning back, he surveyed the room, searching for clues, but the Trolan's motive remained a mystery.

Why would the a Trolan help Devon?

His anxiety was growing. With every passing moment, Devon could be drawing closer to Alana's quarters. He fought the urge to go racing there immediately—now that the princess was herself, she was more than capable of taking care of Devon. A smile came to his lips as he thought of the shock Devon would receive if he found her.

The smile faded as his thoughts returned to the Trolan spy. Here was the real mystery—and danger. He knew of Godrin's reputation. He did not take unnecessary risks, certainly not ones that were sure to end in his death. And however impressive his deception was, he couldn't hope to escape the citadel with the Tsar's daughter. Not alive.

No, he had to be here for some other reason. The man had not come all this way to die for a hopeless cause.

Perhaps he wants to assassinate the Tsar.

Quinn smiled at the thought. By all accounts, Godrin had no magic. He wouldn't stand a chance against the wealth of power at the Tsar's command. The man would be destroyed with a whisper.

Yet still something nagged at Quinn, as though he had the jigsaw puzzle before him, but a single piece was missing. He left the dead captain's quarters and started walking. Without thinking, he headed for the Tsar's private quarters. They made up the entire south wing of the citadel, and it wasn't long before he reached their outer limits.

Here he paused, surprised to find no guards standing on the doors. Cursing, he pushed on the double doors, but they were locked against him. His fear growing, Quinn raised a hand and summoned his magic. Outside, the wind swirled, then with a roar, it came racing into the corridor. It hissed around his arm, catching on his cloak. He sent it rushing at the doors with a gesture, caving them inwards.

Striding through, he stopped for a second to inspect the dead bodies of the guards. The head of one was crushed, while the other had been killed when a blunt instrument had caved in his armour. Quinn swore again. There was little doubt the wounds had been caused by *kanker*. Had Devon decided to come for the Tsar instead of rescuing Alana?

Everything he knew of his former comrade said no, and yet...silently, he cursed the reduction in guards around the citadel. If only someone had heard the commotion, the hammerman would have been surrounded the second he engaged with the guards. Instead, he was now inside the Tsar's quarters, with little more than a few patrols standing between his hammer and the ruler of the Three Nations.

Quinn's breath caught in his throat at the thought.

The hammer!

Now he was running, sabre already in hand, his boots slapping hard against the smooth stone. He took the corners without slowing as he mapped out the path to the Tsar's room in his mind. It was still some minutes away. Gritting his teeth, he picked up the pace.

As he turned the final corner, a shout echoed down the corridor. Breathless, Quinn raced towards the open door to the Tsar's rooms, sword raised, magic gathering in his chest. He burst through the door, a roar on his lips, the wind already swirling around him.

Halfway across the room, a man turned and saw him. He held *kanker* in one hand and blood covered his jerkin. For a moment, shock registered on his face. Then, lifting the ancient hammer above his head, he screamed a battle cry and leapt at the poster bed in the middle of the room.

Quinn threw out his arm, and the wind raced from him. Above the intruder's head, *kanker* began to glow. Quinn cursed as he sensed his winds being sucked into the weapon, but he kept on. A strange whisper spread through the room as the gale vanished into the hammer. Yet not all of the gusts were consumed, and with a muffled *thud*, what remained struck the stranger hard in the back.

There was enough power in the blow to send the man toppling forward. Crying out, he flung out his arms, and *kanker* slipped from his fingers to fly across the room. Triumphant, Quinn sent another blast of wind at the man. He went flying backwards and struck the corner post of the

Tsar's bed with a hard *thud.* As he slumped to the ground, Quinn lowered his arm.

Movement came from the bed as the Tsar, looking more mortal than Quinn had ever seen him, sat up. He frowned as he saw Quinn. His gaze transferred to the intruder, and his frown deepened.

"What is going on here, lieutenant?" he said calmly.

Quinn stepped into the room. "The citadel has been… compromised, your majesty."

A groan came from the intruder. His head shifted, his eyes flickering up to look at Quinn.

"You must be Godrin," Quinn said.

Grimacing, the man looked around, assessing the situation. Quinn smiled. *Kanker* lay on the ground at his feet, and idly he placed a foot on the weapon's haft, pinning it down. "Looking for this?" he asked.

But Godrin wasn't looking at him. His eyes were on the bedpost he had come to rest against. Quinn followed his gaze upwards, and saw with horror a sword looped over the corner of the poster bed, just within reach of the intruder.

"Don't–" he started, but the Tsar's voice cut him off.

"You came to kill me?" he whispered, pulling himself from the bed.

The Tsar looked undignified in his silken pyjamas, but Quinn could sense the power radiating from him. Smiling, he relaxed. Without the hammer, the assassin stood no chance now.

Godrin looked from the Tsar to the sword, obviously trying to judge whether he could reach it before being incinerated by the man's powers. Quinn frowned. Was it his imagination, or was there light seeping from its hilt?

"Go ahead," the Tsar said, gesturing at the weapon. "Perhaps you have what it takes."

The Trolan hesitated. The Tsar stood before him, his hands empty and wearing only his night clothes. Even knowing of his power, Quinn could see the temptation. If ever there was an opportunity to strike down the ruler of the Three Nations, this was it.

With a roar, Godrin surged to his feet and swept the blade from its sheath. Light flashed across the room as it slid clear, but to Quinn's surprise, it did not originate from the Tsar. A white glow shone from the blade, bathing the room, forcing Quinn to shield his eyes as he struggled to glimpse the Trolan.

The light died as quickly as it had appeared, revealing the two men still standing in place, unmoved. Quinn looked at the Tsar, noticing the grim smile on his unshaven face, before turning to the Trolan. The breath caught in his throat.

Godrin no longer breathed. The skin of his face had hardened to crystal, his eyes turned as black as coals. His hair had burnt away, leaving his head smooth, shining with the dim light still emanating from the sword. Quinn retched as a putrid stench hit him, of scorched hair and roasted flesh. Perhaps it was his imagination, but he swore a distant scream whispered to him on the breeze.

Then with a suddenness that made Quinn flinch, the Trolan shattered, his body disintegrating before their very eyes. Shards of crystal crashed to the ground and turned to dust. The sword rang as it struck the stone tiles, then lay still, a faint light still dancing in the blade. Silence fell over the room.

Quinn bit his tongue to keep from screaming. An awful voice was yelling at him to run from that place, to flee whatever magic was capable of dealing such an awful ending. Instead, he remained where he stood. Licking his lips, he looked at the Tsar, wondering if he would soon be following the Trolan for allowing an intruder so far inside the citadel.

The Tsar smiled. "My thanks, lieutenant," he said. "Though perhaps next time, you could stop the assassin before he reaches my quarters."

23

"Alana."

The voice whispered through the darkness, soft, rich with sadness. Alana shivered as she found Devon's amber eyes watching her.

"Alana," he called again, sending ripples racing through her spirit.

She went to him then, arms outstretched, soft sobs tearing from her. "Devon," she cried, "please, help me! She's destroying me—please!"

"It's okay," he said as his muscular arms encircled her, holding her tight. She sighed, his warmth filling her with a feeling of safety.

"Please help me," she whispered. "I don't know how to escape her."

"We will face her together," came his reply.

She nodded, pulling back and smiling up at him. Standing on her tiptoes, she made to kiss him. Before their lips could meet, an awful pain tore into her. She cried out and stumbled, her fingers fumbling for the wound and finding the hilt of a dagger piercing her stomach. The strength went from her legs, sending her crumpling to the ground. Green fire rose to encircle her. She tried to scream, but the burning green went pouring down her throat, choking off her cry.

Desperate, she stretched out a hand for Devon, but he was no longer looking at her. He still stood above her, but his eyes were fixed on the woman in front of him. Smiling, he opened his arms to embrace the other Alana. Their lips locked, their spirits joining as they fell against each other. Anguish filled Alana as Devon began to kiss her neck. Cackling, the other woman glanced back, pure malevolence in her steely eyes.

And the darkness rose to claim her once more.

Back in her room, Alana gasped awake, the dream still clinging to her. Heart racing, she smiled as she recalled her other self's screams, the despair that had filled the girl as she took her precious Devon for herself.

"Alana?"

She jerked as a voice spoke from across the room. Sitting bolt upright, her hand fumbled for the sword she kept beside her bed. Her eyes swept the darkness, searching for the intruder, as her hand wrapped around the sword hilt. Beside her, the bed was empty, but the voice was not Quinn's. He wouldn't dare try to approach her yet, not until the light of day. Yet still, it sounded familiar.

"Who's there?" she hissed, rising naked from the bed, sword in hand.

A lantern was unshuttered, illuminating the faces of Devon and Kellian. Alana's mouth dropped open, words slipping unbidden from her mouth. "Devon, how are you here?"

"Nice to see you too, Alana," Kellian muttered as he moved forward, carrying the lantern. His eyes were drawn to the sword in her hand. "They gave you a weapon?"

Alana looked at the blade, then back at the two of them, lost for words. Slowly she closed her mouth. Despite herself, she felt a sudden sadness, a terrible regret for what would come next. "You should not have come here," she heard herself saying.

"Nonsense, princess," Devon replied. "We came to rescue you."

She shook her head, her sadness welling. "But I don't need rescuing, Devon."

The big man frowned, and Kellian shifted on his feet. "What's going on here, Alana?" the innkeeper asked. "Why do you have a sword?"

Alana placed the blade back on her bedside table. As she did so, the realisation she was naked gave her pause. The men seemed to realise it at the same time, and averted their eyes. Her cheeks flushed and she quickly pulled a sheet around herself. Then her anger flared.

What did she care for modesty? She was Alana, Daughter of the Tsar, Princess of an Empire. She took what she wanted. She didn't care what anyone thought of her!

Yet when she glanced back at Devon, the warmth in her cheeks grew, and she kept the sheets wrapped around her.

"Is Braidon okay?" she whispered, seeking to distract herself from the heat in her stomach.

"He's safe," Devon replied, stepping closer. "We knew you'd never forgive us if we brought him along, so we left him with Enala—Tillie, I should say…there's a lot to catch you up on. Anyway, she will protect him. And teach him to use his magic."

Alana nodded, before the meaning of his words struck her. Her head snapped up, a sudden fear clenching at her chest. "No!" she hissed. She grabbed Devon's hand. "He can't…" she trailed off, unable to express where her terror had come from.

For a moment, a memory flickered to life, rising from the missing gaps in her past. She saw Braidon sitting on the lawns of the garden, his eyes wide with dread, but it faded again before she could grasp its meaning. She cursed beneath her breath.

"No?" Kellian asked, frowning. She noticed his hand had dropped to the short sword he wore on his waist. "What's wrong with you, Alana?"

Heart hammering in her chest, Alana clenched her eyes closed. Emotions whirled inside her mind, pulling her in every direction, threatening to tear her apart. The memories of her time with Devon and Kellian were strong, and though that part of herself remained locked away, she could not forget the kindness these men had shown her. Looking at them, she saw again how they'd protected her, how Kellian had argued on her behalf, how Devon had faced down a demon for her.

And she realised no one in her life had ever shown her such loyalty.

"You shouldn't be here, either of you," she said quietly.

"You shouldn't be here either, princess," Devon said. Tentatively, he reached out and patted her shoulder.

A sad smile touched Alana's lips. "You're wrong, Devon," she murmured. "This is exactly where I'm meant to be."

"What?" he whispered.

She looked up at him, her eyes misting despite herself. "I am the Tsar's daughter," she said. "This is my home, my life."

Devon frowned. He shifted on his feet, towering over her. "No, you're wrong," he said. He reached out again, but she flinched away. "He's placed some spell on you–"

"No, Devon," Alana said sharply, cutting him off. "It was me that placed a spell on *you*."

"What are you talking about?"

She forced herself to laugh, to ignore the light in his

eyes. The harsh sound echoed off the walls as she spoke. "That is my power, Devon. I manipulate the minds of men. *That* is why you helped me, why you have crossed the Three Nations to find me." The lie tasted foul on her lips, but she needed them gone, before someone discovered them here. She knew she should turn them in, and yet…

"Go!" she said quickly, even as part of her screamed for her to stop them. "Leave me!"

Devon stood in silence, his eyes sad, staring down at her, and for a second she thought he would obey. Her heart wrenched with the pain of loss. Then he shook his head.

"No," he said quietly, sitting on the bed. "I'm not leaving without you."

A sudden hope swelled in Alana's chest, but as he touched her, her mind shifted, her anger rising. She opened her mouth to warn them, but her jaw snapped closed before she could voice the words. Rage filled her, at her weakness, at her hesitation.

"Very well, Devon," she said.

Smiling, she faced them, letting the sheet fall away. Devon rose cautiously, his cheeks red as he kept his eyes averted from her nakedness. "Alana, what…"

"Get back, Devon!" Kellian said, stepping between them and forcing the hammerman back.

Before Kellian could retreat, Alana stepped forward and placed her hands on his chest. The magic rose within her, the Feline roaring, but she thrust it aside and drew the power to her, pouring it into the helpless innkeeper.

Kellian stiffened, his eyes widening as he tried to pull away, but it was already too late. Her magic rushed through him, overwhelming his thoughts, replacing them with her own. He sagged, and the light went from his eyes. A cold smile on her face, Alana stepped back.

"Kellian, my dear," she said quietly. "Be so good as to secure Devon for me."

"What–?" Devon began.

Before he could finish, Kellian twisted towards him. Moving with frightening speed, he leapt into the air and drove his boot into the side of Devon's head. The blow sent the hammerman staggering back. Losing his balance, he tripped over the sofa and went crashing to the floor.

Kellian followed after him, but Devon surged to his feet, and a meaty fist caught the innkeeper in the stomach. Kellian doubled over, but recovering quickly, he spun on his heel and lashed out with his other foot. The kick went low, sweeping Devon's legs out from beneath him. As he crashed to the ground, Kellian surged forward, his boot slamming down into Devon's face before he could raise a hand to protect himself.

Groaning weakly, Devon slumped to the ground and lay still. Kellian stood over him, statue-like, his hawkish eyes watching intently for signs of movement.

Alana sighed as she strode across to them and looked down at Devon. "You should have left, Devon," she said, a smile twitching on her lips.

Behind her, the doors to her room burst open and guards rushed inside. Swords rasped from sheaths as they saw Kellian beside her, but he did not react. Blades extended, the guards advanced on him. Alana stepped between them, eyes flashing with rage.

"You're a little late, boys," she snapped.

The men paused, frozen by the sight of the naked princess standing before them. She glanced back at the two men, Devon unconscious on the ground, Kellian still trapped by her magic. Smirking, she waved at the guards.

"Get them out of my sight."

24

"Are you ready, Braidon?" Enala asked, her eyes shining in the moonlight.

Braidon sat across from the old woman, seeing the compassion in the softness of her face, the deepening of the wrinkles around her lips. Idly he wondered what had driven her to take him under her wing. There were other Magickers in the city, Magickers less important to the city than she was, who could have been spared to teach him. Yet Enala had never so much as suggested the idea. Perhaps it was their shared journey, their flight across the Three Nations that had bound them together.

Either way, he wasn't about to question it now.

Rubbing the exhaustion from his eyes, he forced his fear back into its cage. They were sitting out under the stars, the cold kept at bay by the flames burning in Enala's palms.

"Okay."

He nodded, and closing his eyes, Braidon sought out his calm centre. It was not an easy task—not after having his entire life turned upside down. Delving down into the darkness, he found himself questioning every memory, every thought. How did he know this was really the right course of action? Was this what he would have done before, in that other life he could not remember?

For a moment, confusion swamped him and he started to panic. His chest constricted, and he found himself hardly able to breathe. Gasping, he sucked in another lungful of air, his hands gripping hard to the rock beneath him.

"Focus, Braidon. I believe in you."

Her words sliced through the panic, though he still felt lost, alone amongst the chaos of his mind. Who was he? What was true, what was false?

His sister's face sprang into his thoughts, crisp and clear, a smile on her pale lips, her eyes shining.

I love you, little brother.

Braidon's shoulders swelled as the words swept through him. He clung to them like a lifeline, the one immovable fact in his unstable past. Instinctively, he sensed the truth behind the words, that their love for one another had in fact been real. Everything else might be false, but Alana was truly his sister.

Holding the image of her in his mind, he allowed all other thoughts to fall away. Slowly he found himself drifting, and a strange otherworldliness came over him, as though his spirit were no longer weighed down by the trappings of his body. Opening his eyes, he looked on the familiar darkness, his spirit a flickering light alone in the void.

Except he wasn't alone.

Turning his eyes outwards, he saw the distant white glowing in the distance, and felt the old fear return.

I need you, Braidon…

He could no longer tell whether his sister's words were real or imagined, but her voice gave him courage, and he shot towards the distant light. It swelled before him, as though it already sensed his approach, could taste its victory. He watched as it shifted, growing larger, changing, until the awful Feline stood, jaws wide, its roar sending ripples through his very soul.

The need to flee rose within him. He shook as the beast approached, the great claws reaching out. His fear was like a tangible force now, turning his strength to water, his courage evaporating like smoke before the breeze. As it had so many times before, it filled him, demanding he turn and run.

Please, Braidon…

Trembling, fists clenched, Braidon stood his ground as the Feline stalked forward. He could sense its hate, its raw hunger radiating out before it, surrounding him, threatening to tear him down. Yet still, he did not move.

Now it stood directly over him, its breath hot, the light quivering dangerously behind its monstrous eyes. Leaning down, it roared, the sound sending vibrations down to the very core of his being. Closing his eyes, Braidon waited for the end to come.

Nothing happened.

After a long moment, he opened his eyes again. He flinched as he found the creature's giant maw mere inches from his face, and for a second it seemed the Feline would lunge forward and tear into his flesh. He was gathering himself to bolt when he heard his sister's voice again, crisp and clear, rising from the vaults of some memory.

I believe in you, Braidon.

He froze. A snarl of hatred came from the Feline, but still it did not move. Slowly Braidon's fear seeped away, fleeing out into the void. His legs ceased to shake, and as he drew in a breath, his spirit swelled. He felt himself growing in size, fuelled by his courage, even as the substance leached away from the beast.

Reaching out, he touched a hand to the Feline's mane. As his hand met the creature, it burst asunder, collapsing in on itself, becoming a swirling pool of light that stretched out before him. Pure heat washed across him, gentle and reassuring. He thrust his hand deep into the pool, and felt a surge of power, the crackling of his magic's energy as it filled him…

Back on the mountainside, Braidon opened his eyes, and smiled.

"I did it," he whispered.

Enala sat across from him, her aged face stretched with worry. She straightened at his words and leaned forward, staring intently into his eyes.

"Is it truly you?" she asked.

"It's me, Enala," he replied.

Within, he could feel the magic swirling, its power spreading to fill every inch of his body. But he no longer sensed a threat from it. Amidst the darkness of the void, he and it had become one, their purpose joined as the beast finally recognised its master. Its power was his to command now.

Working by instinct, Braidon concentrated on the ground beside him, imagining a replica of himself sitting there. Light flickered, and an image sprang into life. Braidon jerked as he suddenly found himself staring into his own crisp blue eyes. It was like staring into his own reflection.

"Wow," he murmured, glancing down at his own hands. They were aglow, a bright white flickering out to dance alongside the fire in Enala's palms.

The flames died away, and Enala embraced him. "Well done, Braidon," she whispered. "I knew you could do it!"

Braidon smiled, and the image of himself vanished. "I'm glad someone did. I thought the beast had me for a moment!"

"But you faced it down!" Enala replied. "You stood your ground like a man. You should be proud."

"It was Alana that gave me the courage."

Enala reached out and gripped his shoulder. "Never forget the power of love, my child. There are some who believe the world should be governed by fear and pain, but in my life, I have found the bonds of love to last far longer. The Tsar's people may fight for him out of fear, but should his power abandon him, so will they. The Northlanders love their Queen—they will fight for her to the end."

"It may come to that, because of me," Braidon whispered.

"No, my child," Enala replied. "War was coming whatever we decided. But perhaps we can find a way to change that, when we reach your sister."

"So you'll come with me?"

"Ay," Enala whispered, her eyes turning to the dark slopes far below. "I should have returned to Ardath a long time ago, when my brother stood against the Tsar. As it is, I fear I will be too weak to make a difference now. Only time will tell."

"I don't know what I'll do when we get there..." Braidon murmured, his heart sinking. "I don't even know how to find Alana."

To his surprise, the old priest smiled at that. "Don't you worry about that, my child," she replied. "Leave the planning to me."

25

For the second time in as many days, Devon woke to a pounding in his head that made him wish he'd never left Northland. Opening his eyes, he watched as strange squiggles of light danced before his eyes, slowly fading to darkness. Blinking, he waited for his vision to clear, but the black remained. For an instant, he wondered if he was dead. Then a low groan came from his right, the rattle of chains from his left. The cold stones beneath him seeped through his leggings, and the stench of what smelt like an open sewer wafted in his nostrils. Retching, he rolled onto his side, and the world finally began to take shape through the gloom.

Concrete walls surrounded him on three sides, a row of bars on the fourth. Beyond the bars he could see candles flickering down the length of a corridor lined with a dozen more cells. Turning away, he ran his gaze over his own cell, and noted he had two companions in the darkness. The first was an old man, his ghostly white hair long and filthy, his skin hanging in bags from his face. The man was asleep, his soft snores whispering lightly from the stone walls.

The other occupant was Kellian. Devon's heart beat faster as he remembered their confrontation with Alana, how Kellian had turned on him at the woman's command. A knife twisted in his chest at her betrayal. Taken by surprise, Devon had hardly been able to get in a blow before Kellian overwhelmed him. His friend was unconscious now, and Devon prayed to the Gods that whatever spell Alana had worked on him would wear off by the time he woke.

He shivered at the thought. Alana had magic! With a single touch, she had taken control of Kellian. His mind reeled at the implications, returning to her words in the darkness of her room.

I am the Tsar's daughter. This is my home, my life.

No, it couldn't be true. He knew her, knew her heart. It wasn't possible for her to have worked such a deception on them, not through all those long days of travel. And then there was Braidon—sweet, innocent, Braidon. He could not have pretended…

And yet, what else could explain her sudden power? Could the woman they'd met have been an imposter?

The thought gave him hope, yet he knew it wasn't true. Alana had recognised them—he had seen it in her eyes. And she had begged them to flee, to leave her behind, before it was too late. In his stubbornness he had refused to listen, to believe her, but the truth had been laid bare now.

I am the Daughter of the Tsar.

He shook his head. It couldn't be true. And yet…he turned the words over in his mind, reliving the events of the past few weeks through different eyes, seeing again how Quinn had seemed to recognise her back in the temple of Sitton, the lengths he and the Tsar had gone to capture

Alana and her brother. Demons and dragons had been sent against them, yet none had attacked Alana or the boy Magicker directly.

An icy cold slid down his spine. The woman he'd encountered in the bedchamber above had been Alana—he couldn't deny it. Yet it had also *not* been her. There had been a hardness about her, a stony cold to her eyes that allowed no emotion.

"It doesn't make sense," he muttered to himself.

"In my long life, I've found little really does," an ancient voice replied from across the cell.

Looking up, Devon found the eyes of the old man on him. The man lifted himself from the floor and propped himself up against the wall, his emaciated limbs seeming to hardly have the strength to move him. His clothes were little more than dishevelled rags, and his skin was so pale that Devon could see the thin blue veins beneath. Weeping sores covered his arms and legs, while a long white beard reached almost down to his waist.

"How long have you been here?" Devon whispered.

To his surprise, the old man smiled. "Not so long," he murmured, his voice sounding weary. "Thirty years, forty?" His eyes flickered closed as he rested his head back against the wall. "What does it matter?"

Devon suppressed a shudder. "How have you survived?" The old man's laughter echoed through the cell, and Devon frowned. "Why do you laugh?"

"Because in my long life, I have faced death many times. It has stalked me through all these years, a constant companion, waiting for me to make a mistake, to take me. And yet here in this dungeon, far from sword and monsters and Magickers, you ask me how I have survived?"

"I only meant…"

"I know what you meant," his companion sighed. He shook his head, and for a second Devon saw the despair lurking behind his eyes. "In truth I never expected to see fifty. Yet here I sit, creeping slowly towards an unremarkable end. I never imagined this would be my fate."

"You were a warrior?" Devon now noticed the thin white streaks of scars on the old man's arms, threading their way between the filth and sores.

His cellmate nodded. "A warrior. A Magicker. Once upon a time."

"A Magicker?" Hope stirred in Devon's chest, before cold hard reality returned to crush it. If the man could have used his powers to escape, he would have done so long ago… "Can you not use your powers to escape?" he asked anyway.

The old man smiled. Lifting his hands, he shook the bracelets he wore on either wrist, fashioned from silver and studded emeralds. "Not with the Tsar's gift," the man said.

"They block your magic?" Devon asked.

"That, and more." The man turned his eyes on Devon. "You must be a dangerous man, to end up in these dungeons. Once they were used to contain the vilest of creatures, though the old kings refashioned them after the fall of Archon. The Tsar only keeps his most dangerous of enemies here."

Devon shrugged, but before he could answer a groan came from across the cell. His heart skipped a beat as Kellian sat up, and he stared at his friend, searching for some sign of recognition. Kellian blinked in the dim light, his gaze finally settling on Devon. Frowning, he touched a hand to his head, and groaned again.

"You always bring me to the most interesting places, Devon…" he murmured.

Relief swept through Devon, and he swept his friend up into a hug. "You're back!"

"Ugh, Devon, get off! My head feels like you hit it with your damned hammer," Kellian said as he tried to disentangle himself from Devon.

Chuckling, Devon released him, though he gave his friend an extra thump on the back for good measure. Kellian winced and quickly retreated across the cell, only slumping back to the ground when he was well out of range. He winced, pain still etched across his face.

"What the hell happened? Where are we?" Blinking, he seemed to notice the old man for the first time. "Who the hell are you?"

The old man laughed. "I could ask the same of the two of you."

"Devon and Kellian," Devon replied quickly. "Former soldiers, current renegades."

"Names…" the old man sighed. "How little meaning they have now. Down here we are nothing, our lives extinguishable at a whim."

"I don't plan on staying long," Devon growled.

The old man did not reply, but his eyes said it all. In the corner, Kellian was still holding his head. "How did we get here, Devon?" he asked. "The last thing I remember was finding Alana…"

Devon swallowed. The words were slow to come, and when he spoke his voice was taut with pain. "Alana betrayed us."

Kellian looked up at that. "What? How?"

"She said she was the Tsar's daughter."

"I remember…" Kellian said after a moment. "But how is that possible?"

"The Tsar's daughter, you say?" The old man said.

Devon shivered as he found the ancient eyes on him. "Not a pleasant woman, from what I've overhead from the guards."

"It's not true," Devon snapped.

"Perhaps," their cellmate replied carefully, "but I have heard of her power. An Earth Magicker, capable of manipulating human minds."

"I..." Kellian frowned, looking at Devon. "She touched me, and everything went black. What happened, Devon?"

Devon looked away, his hands curling into fists. "You attacked me, old friend."

The colour drained from Kellian's face. "I don't remember," he murmured. A strained silence stretched out before he added. "I guess we finally answered the question of who's stronger though..."

"I wasn't exactly fighting for keeps," Devon growled, but his heart wasn't in it. He turned back to the old man. "You were talking about her power?"

"Yes," he sighed. "She's able to manipulate people's minds—their thoughts, memories, actions."

"That explains how she was able to control me," Kellian said, "but...not why she was so different from the woman we knew. She was like a completely different person."

The old man looked thoughtful. "It is strange, but perhaps...perhaps she used her power on herself."

"Why would she do that?" Devon demanded.

"Who could say?" the old man shrugged. "There's only one person who can answer that—and by the sound of it, she's not interested in talking with you any longer."

"You're saying the Alana we first met...was a completely different person from the woman who attacked us?" Devon pressed.

"As I said, it's possible, but only the girl herself could tell you for sure."

Devon sucked in a breath, struggling to comprehend the old man's theory. "If that's true…how can we know which was the true Alana? The woman we helped…" he trailed off, his mind turning to the night he'd spent with Alana in the moonlit springs south of Fort Fall. The image faded, replaced by one of her sneering down at him. "Or the one who had us imprisoned as traitors?"

"I'm sorry, my friend," their cellmate replied, his eyes soft, "but from what you say, her old personality has reasserted itself. Perhaps some of the woman you knew remains, but her true self? That can only be the one able to manipulate her magic. And from what you've told me…" Devon didn't need him to finish.

Tears burned in his eyes and he looked away, a lump catching in his throat. An awful weight settled on his chest. Alana was gone, her existence snuffed out as though she'd never been. In her place was a stranger, a hard and unforgiving woman who hadn't hesitated to set his friend on him. She may have spared their lives…yet what did that matter when they were imprisoned in the Tsar's dungeons? Sooner or later, the man would send for them, demanding retribution for stealing away his children.

"Devon…" said Kellian from across the cell.

Devon shook his head, raising a hand to fend off his friend's words. "Just…leave me, Kellian," he whispered, his voice breaking. "Just…leave me."

Hanging his head, Devon began to sob.

26

Alana's footsteps echoed loudly on the stone floor as she wandered across the andron, the large adjoining chamber set behind the throne room. Royal guards lined the room, their golden helmets gleaming in the morning sun, while in the centre stood a great table of gilded oak. Whispers carried across as she approached, though the men and women seated at the table had yet to notice her.

The Tsar sat at the head of the table, his hands clasped before him as he listened to his advisors. Alana dragged out an empty chair and sat. Silence fell around the table as the advisors turned to stare at her, but she ignored them. Leaning back in her chair, she lifted her legs and rested them on the table.

"Daughter, how nice of you to join us," the Tsar murmured. "How are you this morning? I heard your night was...disrupted."

Alana snorted. Her eyes flickered around to the gathered advisors, enjoying the sudden fear that had appeared behind their eyes. To the Tsar, she raised an eyebrow.

"Yes, and I trust our unexpected guests have been settled into appropriate accommodation?"

The Tsar scowled. "They have been seen to. I will question them later, when more urgent matters have been dealt with. Perhaps we can then ascertain how they were able to get so far inside the citadel."

"You should look to your guards, father," Alana replied with a smirk. She sat up suddenly, her boots slamming back down on the hard floor. The others at the table flinched as she stood, but she barely spared them a glance. She strode across the andron to where the ring of guards stood. "I fear some of your men have grown fat and lazy."

Striding down the line, she studied the face of each man, finally coming to a stop before one she recognised. She stepped in close, and smiled as he looked nervously from her to her father.

"You, what is your name?"

The guard swallowed. "An…Anthony, princess."

"Anthony…" she said. "Tell me, do you remember me?"

He stared blankly at her. "Remember you from where, princess?"

"The Firestone Pub, I believe it was called," she murmured. "I suppose you don't, considering you were lying unconscious in a pile of garbage by the time I arrived."

The guard blinked, uncomprehending. "What?"

Alana stepped in close, so that their faces were only an inch apart. "I was there, *fool*. The night Devon knocked you unconscious, I saw you. If only you weren't such an incompetent warrior, you might have seen me too, might have recognised me. Alas, you allowed a drunken coward to knock you on your ass."

"I...I…I'm sorry, princess," he stammered.

"Don't be," she hissed.

Quick as lightning, her hand flashed down, dragging the dagger from his belt. The guard cried out, scrambling uselessly for his sword hilt, but she buried the blade in his throat before he could draw it. Gasping, he staggered back, his hands clutching uselessly at his throat. A dull gurgling noise came from his chest as she tore the dagger loose. Blood gushed from his neck as he staggered back two steps, then sagged to the floor.

Alana tossed the bloody dagger on his dying body, her gaze turning to the other guards and councillors. Every man and woman in the room stared back at her, open terror on their faces. She laughed.

"Relax, boys and girls!" she shouted. "You look like you've seen a ghost."

Smiling, she wandered back to the council table and resumed her seat. The Tsar's advisors continued to stare at her as she lifted her feet back to the table. Folding her hands in her lap, she let out a long sigh.

"I feel so much better," she said. Seeing the blood on her hands and let out an exasperated snort. She tugged a handkerchief from the breast-pocket of a stunned looking councillor and used it to clean them. "I needed to calm my nerves," she explained to the terrified man as she returned the ruined cloth.

Beside her, the Tsar chuckled. "You truly are yourself again."

"Did you doubt it?" she asked.

"Quinn mentioned you'd been having…trouble with your former self."

"She's under control," Alana snapped, her irritation with Quinn redoubling. Since taking him to her bed, he always seemed to be around, meddling in her affairs. Their argument the night before had only been the latest in a series of growing nuisances. And now he was informing on her for her father…

The Tsar stared at her for a long moment before nodding. "Good. Devon and Kellian's capture will be a blow against Enala. She will have to surrender your brother now, or her beloved Northland will face annihilation."

At the mention of her brother's return, Alana shivered, the hackles rising on her neck. Something tugged at her memory, a fleeting fear that shouted for her to denounce her father. She clenched her teeth, fighting back against the emotion, knowing it was only that other part of her. After a moment it faded, and she brushed a lock of golden hair from her face.

"You think so?" When the Tsar nodded, she smiled. "It will be good to see him again."

"Yes." Her father's voice was distant. "This…delay to his training is unseemly. He should have been ready for his final examination by now."

Unconsciously, Alana's hands balled into fists. A faint anxiety tugged at her, and she stared into space, waiting for the sensation to fade once more…

"Alana?"

She blinked, and found her father staring at her. There was a pause before she realised he'd asked her a question. "Apologies, father, my mind was elsewhere. What did you say?"

He frowned, and for a moment she thought he would press her. But he only waved a hand and said. "Quinn tells me Braidon's power concerns illusions. What else do you know of it?"

Alana shrugged. "Yes, I…*she* didn't know until the end. It was as much our surprise as Quinn's when we realised at

Fort Fall. I cannot remember his power awakening though —my memory of his sixteenth birthday is still lost."

"That is the night you both vanished."

"Interesting," Alana mused, turning the fact over in her mind. Magic could only arise on the anniversary of one's birth. It was curious, that her magic had scoured their minds on the same day her brother's magic had appeared. Surely that could not be a coincidence?

Straining, she sought again to lift the fog from her lost memories, but still they would not come. Finally she shook her head. "It might be there is more to his power than illusions," she said, "but not from what I saw of his wild magic."

The Tsar nodded. His brow creased as he looked at her. "You look tired, my daughter."

"Yes, well, my strength still has not recovered from my…*her* loss of control. My midnight guests did not help."

"Then you should rest, allow your powers to return. You were lucky you had the strength to stop Devon and his friend. Especially after your little…incident with the woman, Krista."

"She was weak." Alana snorted. "It did not take much of my power to remove her. I am surprised you elected such a poor choice of guardian for the children in my absence."

"There were other matters on my mind," the Tsar rumbled, "but…you are right, I should have dealt with her. Still, your students will not miss you for one morning. I will see that Quinn takes over for the day…unless you would rather he attend to you?"

Alana forced a smile to her lips, even as the dream from the night before rose in her mind. In the dream, she had taken Devon to spite her other self, to crush her hopes, to show her everything she'd ever loved was hers now. Yet as she'd imagined herself with him, she'd felt the girl's emotions rising from the void, entangling with her own…

"No," she said sharply, her mouth dry. "And I do not want him near my students…But, it shall be as you say. I will rest, and see to the children in the afternoon."

Rising, she left her father and his advisors to their boring discussions of governance and war, and found her way back to her quarters. There she threw herself down on the bed, sighing as she burrowed into the soft silk sheets. A memory rose from the depths of her mind, of the mud and dirt and cold she had endured on the streets of Ardath.

Alana shivered. How could she have sunk so low, convinced herself she was nothing but a pauper, a street rat to be crushed by better people?

Yet as she recalled the abject poverty she'd condemned herself to, the image shifted, and she saw her brother alongside her. As the days had grown shorter and the temperature had dropped, the two of them had taken to sleeping beneath one blanket, sharing warmth to fend off the winter's chill.

Watching herself embrace the young boy, tears came to Alana's eyes, and for a second she wished she were back in the abandoned hovel with her brother. At least they'd been together then.

She cursed, flinging the thought away and turning her mind to the future. Her brother would return soon, they would be together again. She would no longer be alone.

Yet imaging him back in the citadel, running through the gardens, she felt only fear. There was something strange about the thought, a wrongness that tickled in the back of her mind. The warmth she'd felt when picturing the hovel was missing.

Quinn's words from the night returned to haunt her.

"And what about your brother? Is that what you wish for him, when he returns?"

Rolling over, she punched the pillow, cursing herself for a fool. It was the girl! It had to be, working her feeble emotions, her weakness into her every thought. She was like a parasite, eating at Alana from within, no matter how many times the magic burned her.

Alana sucked in a breath, forcing herself to recall the joy she'd experienced as the guard's hot blood spouted over her hands. Within, she felt a part of her recoil, and laughed to herself. "This is you," she whispered to the empty room. "This is who you are, girl. Accept it!"

There was no voice inside to reply. Finally at peace, Alana closed her eyes, and allowed her weariness to take her…

In her dreams, Alana awoke, and found herself amongst a great forest. Tree trunks rose around her, so high she could not see their canopies. Craning her neck, she sought out the sky, but in place of blue horizons and light, there was only…nothing.

Mist clung to the ground, creeping across the forest floor, though there was no cold, no wind, no movement. Alana spun, looking around and around, trying to recall how she had come to be there, but the memory was lost.

A cold fear gripped her then. Her father's enemies must have come for her, stealing her from the citadel. But they had made a mistake, left her alive. She would make sure they lived to regret it.

Alana set off through the trees, though without any sense of direction, she had no way of knowing where she was headed. The mist seemed to follow her, billowing across her feet, obscuring the ground below. Though there must have been branches and leaves on the ground, there was no sound as she moved. Crouching down, she tried to sweep the fog away. The movement did nothing to pierce the white, and she changed tact, thrusting her arm deep into the fog. It was stopped abruptly by what she presumed was the ground, though it was cold and smooth as glass.

"What is this place?" she whispered, fear gnawing at her stomach.

"My domain," came a girl's voice from the trees.

Her heart racing, Alana sprang back to her feet and reached for her sword. Only then did she realise she was unarmed. Weakened as it was, she turned instead to her magic, and felt it come to life inside her. To her surprise, a green glow lit the forest, seeming to come from her chest itself.

"You would use my own power against me?"

Movement came from the trees, a young girl appearing between the endless trunks. She walked forward, her soft brown curls bouncing with each footstep. A strange light lit her face, revealing a tiny button nose, a smattering of freckles, and dimpled cheeks. She wandered through the trees, no more than a child, a smile on her youthful face.

Alana lowered her arm, as the girl looked up at her, revealing violet eyes. Looking into them, it seemed as though the universe were staring back at her, infinite and terrifying. The strength went from Alana then, and she stumbled, a cry on her lips.

"Who are you?" she gasped.

"The Goddess of the Earth," the girl replied. "Antonia."

Alana shook her head. "No, that isn't possible!" she said. "The Gods are dead!"

"Only our bodies," the girl replied, her eyes aglow. "Our spirits remain, as they always have, and always will. We are a part of the land, a part of the magic within you."

Alana's hand drifted unconsciously to her breast. "My magic?"

"Yes, child. Your power comes from the Earth—but then, you knew that." Alana shivered as the Goddess's eyes hardened. "You have been a great disappointment to me, child."

Alana's anger flared. "I didn't realise you had expectations. I thought you left."

The Goddess looked up, her eyes catching Alana's and holding them. She found her heart suddenly beating hard against her chest, and she sensed in that moment the vast power in the girl before her. Not just that, but an anger, a yearning to reach out and tear Alana's heart from her chest.

Then Antonia blinked, and the moment passed.

Alana swayed on her feet, then sank to her knees.

"I am sorry," Antonia said gently.

She waved a hand, and the towering trees seemed to retreat. Rocks cracked and a boulder lifted through the mist. Moving to it, Antonia seated herself cross-legged atop it, and gestured for Alana to join her.

Still on her knees, Alana sucked in a breath. Unable to summon the will to speak, she shook her head.

"You are not beyond redemption, Alana," the Goddess said, looking down at her from the boulder.

"Who says I need to be redeemed?" Alana hissed, rage giving her courage.

Anger returned to Antonia's face. "I do," she growled, and Alana reeled back before the force of her words.

For a moment the child seemed a giant, with the power to reach out and crush her beneath one thumb. Alana gasped, her will crumbling, and she threw herself flat against the ground.

"Please, don't hurt me!" she begged, and hated herself for it.

Laughter came from the Goddess. Looking up, Alana saw she had returned to normal, though the dark gleam remained in her eyes. "I thought you were strong, Alana. Is that not what your father taught you, to show strength before mercy? Could it be, your strength comes from the part of yourself you seek to crush?"

"No!" Alana yelled, standing now. "She is the weak one!"

"She is only the girl you wished yourself to be—one free of your father's manipulations."

"You lie," Alana snapped. "I would remember." Comprehension came to her and she stumbled back. "I know why you are here!" she

gasped. "You seek to be reborn, to usurp my father and rule Plorsea in his place."

The Goddess looked sad. "My siblings and I have no wish to return to your mortal world. We never wanted a part of it in the first place. But you are right—it is your father who has drawn us back, forced me to interfere once more in the lives of mortals."

"What are you talking about?"

Antonia sighed. "Matters beyond your understanding, my dear Alana." There was a sadness in her face that made Alana shudder. With an inexplicable feeling of shame, she looked away.

"Tell me, girl. Do you wish to know the truth?" Antonia asked.

"The truth?" Alana asked suddenly.

"The truth about what has happened to you. The truth about how you lost your memory."

The breath caught in Alana's throat. She stared at the youthful Goddess, sensing the trap. If she allowed this creature into her mind, who knew what damage she might do, what would happen to her? Would she feed strength to her other self, allowing the girl to bury her back in the darkness?

"I will not harm you," Antonia said, as though already reading her thoughts.

Alana shivered. Despite her suspicions, she believed the girl's words. Still she hesitated, an unknown fear lodging in her throat. What was so important about the month she'd lost, between her brother's birthday and the moment she'd woken in the stepwell? What had changed?

Yet Alana could not allow the fear to rule her. She had learned that lesson once, long ago when she'd first mastered her power. Her father had trained her well, breaking her spirit, crushing her soul, only to reshape it, allowing the Daughter of the Tsar to be born. It was that woman who had first faced her magic, who'd overcome her terror and conquered the force within.

Her decision made, she looked at the Goddess.

"Show me."

27

"Enala!"

Braidon spun as the Queen's voice echoed down the tunnel, his eyes widening to find her standing on the path behind them, her chest heaving, hand clutched at her breast. Without her guards and crown, she no longer looked like the intimidating woman who'd ordered his capture, but vulnerable and human, her eyes shining with emotion.

"Merydith, what are you doing here?" Enala asked.

"Please, Enala, you can't leave us. Not now, when we need you most," the Queen gasped, the words rushing from her in a torrent.

A lump lodged in Braidon's throat. Around the corner ahead, the light of a new dawn beckoned. There, the dragon Dahniul waited to fly them south, deep into the Tsar's territory. Enala had thought to leave in secret without causing upheaval, but apparently the Queen had heard of their plan.

Yet she had come alone, without guards or advisors, to

beseech the ancient Magicker to stay, when she could have brought an army to stop them.

"Merydith," Enala murmured, stepping forward and placing a hand on the woman's shoulder. "You do not need me. You are a brave, intelligent woman. I believe in you. If anyone can lead Northland through this turmoil, it's you."

The Queen swallowed, a tear streaking her cheek. "Through all our short history, you have stood beside us, Enala." She broke off, swallowing hard. "You served my father, and his mother before him. You are the only thing that stands between Northland and chaos."

"That's not true!" Enala said, both hands on the Queen's shoulders now. "For decades I have watched you grow, Merydith, and barely needed to lift a finger to aid you. Northland has its own spirit, its own soul, and *you* are the heart of that. I am but a remnant, a shadow that holds you back. That is why I left the first time, all those years ago, to return to my homeland." She smiled, reaching up to stroke the woman's cheek. "You have outgrown me, girl."

"What if I make a mistake?"

"You won't," Enala insisted.

The Queen took a great, shuddering breath and nodded. Braidon watched as her shoulders straightened, her face settling back into the familiar mask. For a moment, he'd glimpsed the woman behind the crown, seen her humanity, her vulnerability. But now it was the Queen who stood before them once more, regal, untouchable. She sighed, gesturing to the way ahead.

"You would take our most powerful weapon as well?" she asked.

Enala sighed. "You know Dahniul is not ours to command. She has chosen this path—it is not our place to question her."

"Very well." She looked at Braidon, and he shivered as she approached him. To his surprise, she knelt to meet him at eye-level. "I wish you would stay, young Braidon," she said, her voice soft, "but I respect your decision to search for your sister. I pray it does not prove the end of you."

"It won't," Braidon replied. "I know her."

"We can only hope," the Queen replied, drawing him into an embrace. "Good luck."

Braidon nodded, surprised at the warmth in the Queen's voice. "Thank you," he said. Then, as the Queen drew back and stood, he added: "Good luck to you as well. I hope your decision to refuse the Tsar's emissaries does not prove too costly."

The Queen's face hardened at his words. "I am sorry, Braidon, for how I acted. It was wrong, I see that now. Do not concern yourself with us. If the Tsar comes, at least we will meet him as a free people."

"He will come, Merydith," Enala said, moving alongside them, "with all the forces at his command. You must prepare yourselves."

"We have already begun," the Queen replied, a sudden weariness coming over her. "After a century of peace, Northland rises once more. Did you think you'd live to see it, Enala?"

The old woman chuckled. "It is the way of things. The wheel turns, comes full circle. Only now it is your people who fight for freedom, the Three Nations the conquerors. Oh, how my brother would laugh to see it."

With her words, Braidon sensed an awful sadness in his mentor, and for a moment it seemed the weight of all her years had caught up to Enala. Her shoulders sagged, the folds of her aged face deepening. He swallowed, unable to imagine what it must be like for her—over a century old, all her friends and family gone, the last of a golden age of heroes. Reaching out, he squeezed her arm, and the old woman seemed to shake herself free of her melancholy.

"I'm sorry, Merydith, but we must be on our way. Time is short," Enala said.

"Very well," the Queen replied, "but please, be careful, Enala. You have been like a mother to me all my life. I couldn't bear to lose you."

"Of course you could, child," Enala chided, "and if it comes to it, I will die with pride, knowing you will carry on the fight."

The Queen smiled wryly. "Fine, just, do your best to avoid it, okay? The Tsar knows you're alive. He will be waiting for you this time."

Enala waved a hand. "The man isn't half as smart as he thinks. Braidon and I have his number."

"I hope so," the Queen replied with gusto. "If not, I fear we will not be able to stand against him."

"We will never be able to stand against him," Enala replied sadly. "Not unless the Three Nations rise as one against him. We can only pray that the Gods have a plan."

"The Gods are gone."

"No, Merydith. They never left." Enala tapped her chest. "When she was within me, I saw things, felt things… an eon's worth of knowledge. I remember but a fraction of it now, but they were watching over us long before our priests made them flesh. They will continue to do so long after I'm gone. They may be spirits, but their power flows through all of us now."

The Queen looked unconvinced, but she nodded anyway. "I pray you are right."

Enala smiled. "I usually am."

28

"Your friend is dead, Devon," Quinn announced as he stopped outside the squalid cell.

He smiled as he looked through the bars and saw the three men sitting within. Only a few hours had passed, but already their clothes were stained by the grime within, their skin filthy with it. Lifting the lantern higher, he watched the rats go scuffling into their holes. Devon sat on one side of the cell, Kellian on the other, alongside an old man who looked like he'd been in the dungeon for decades.

Blinking in the harsh light, Devon looked up at him. "Quinn," he said, "I might have guessed you'd come."

Grinning, Quinn hefted the bundle he held in his other hand. Pulling back the cloth, he lifted *kanker* into the light. He watched the pain flicker across the hammerman's face, savouring the sight.

"I thought you might be missing this," he said.

Devon glared back at him. "So you killed the Trolan?"

Quinn shrugged. "Didn't need to."

"Tsar did the dirty work for you, did he?"

Chuckling, Quinn leaned against the bar. "Still playing the hero, I see. You think your little act fools me? Look at where you are, man! Food for the rats, while I stand free, a hero in the eyes of the Tsar...and his grateful daughter."

"Bastard!" Devon surged to his feet and threw himself at the bars. "If you touch her…!"

Quinn stepped back quickly and laughed in the man's face. "Me, touch her?" he said, though he hadn't talked to her since their fight. "I can barely keep her hands off *me!*"

"Liar!" Devon roared, straining uselessly against the steel bars.

Shaking his head, Quinn sneered. "You're pathetic, Devon. To think I once considered you a rival. You were a hero, a warrior, and what did you do with it? You threw it all away! How a man descended from Alan could be so weak, I don't understand. Your ancestor would be ashamed, to know his progeny betrayed the nation he gave his life to defend."

Devon fell back, his shoulders heaving, teeth bared. For a moment, his eyes seemed to glow, and despite himself Quinn shivered as he met the fiery gaze. He swallowed, suddenly glad for the bars between them.

"Alan stood to protect the weak from evil," Devon murmured.

"*You* are the weak one," Quinn hissed. "You could have had it all!"

"Is that why I'm here, then?" Devon asked. "Because I refused to use my strength against those who could not defend themselves?" He let out a long breath. "If that's the case, so be it. I'd rather be in here, standing on the side of good, than out there with you, allied with evil."

His anger flaring, Quinn stepped back up to the bars. "Who are you to accuse me of evil?" he snapped. "Was it not you who led the charge against the Trolans, who cracked open their defences, slaughtered their people?"

"Ay, and I'll hold that guilt in my heart to my dying day. But what of yours, Quinn? Does your guilt burn you?"

"There is no guilt!" he yelled. He pointed a finger at Devon's chest. "And you'd best close that mouth of yours, lest I decide to shatter every bone in your body."

Devon did not move, but a soft laughter came from behind him. Inside the cell, the old man lifted himself from the ground and wandered across to join them. Blue eyes glittered as the prisoner stopped and leaned against the bars.

"Quinn, is it?" he asked, his voice rasping with untold age.

Jaw clenched, Quinn nodded before he could stop himself, and the laughter came again.

"I've heard of you," the old man continued. "The guards talk. Nothing much else to do while on duty down here, I suppose. I hear you're a great man: lieutenant of the Stalkers, renown warrior…a Magicker with powers over the wind."

"What of it, old man?" Quinn growled.

The old eyes flickered to the stone ceiling. "Not much of the Sky element this far underground, I think you'll find, lieutenant…"

Quinn bared his teeth. "Let's find out shall we, old man?"

Within, his magic stirred, its blue light seeping out to fill him. There was a moment of resistance, as it sought to break free, but he was no apprentice and quenched it in an instant. Then he was reaching out, extending his consciousness beyond himself, searching for the wind, and finding…nothing.

The ancient prisoner's laughter came again. Quinn's stomach lurched and he felt his cheeks grow hot.

"Guess you're not so great after all, lieutenant!" the old man taunted him. "Next time why don't you bring some wind with you. I could use the fresh air."

Still cackling to himself, the prisoner retreated back into the cell, leaving Quinn staring impotently after him.

Grinding his teeth, Quinn gripped *kanker* tighter in one hand and reached for the door to the cell, ready to crush the insolence from the feeble man. But as he touched the bars, he froze, sensing Devon's eyes on him. The hammerman was watching him, his hands clenched into fists. Beyond, Kellian was crouched on the ground, poised to spring.

His hands trembling, Quinn slowly let out his breath. He turned to Devon and forced a smile. "Enjoy your stay, old friend. I suspect you'll be here a long time."

With that, Quinn turned on his heel and fled up the corridor, his blood still boiling at his embarrassment by the old man. Silently he raced up the winding stairs, repeating the conversation over and over in his mind, seeking where it had gone so wrong.

The stairs opened out into a small room that served as the entrance to the dungeons. Here, two guards quickly stood to attention and saluted on Quinn's approach. He slowed his stride to speak with them.

"Ensure they have no visitors," he ordered.

He strode past them, then paused, the weight in his hand reminding him he still carried the ancient hammer. His stomach twisted in disgust. He had thought to make it a trophy, a prize that could sit on his mantle as a reminder of his conquest over his rival. But looking at it now, he felt only a deep sense of disgust.

Contemptuously, he tossed the hammer on the table

alongside the wall of the guardroom. "Add it to the other confiscated weapons."

Then he was striding through the open door, down a narrow corridor, and out into the hallways of the citadel. Yet even with the hammer discarded, his thoughts kept returning to Devon. The confrontation had not gone as he'd imagined. He'd wanted to see the hammerman on his knees, broken—and he had been so close. Taunting him with Alana had almost pushed the giant over the edge—until the old man had intervened.

"Dammit!" Quinn cursed.

He shook his head, forcing a smile to his lips. Despite the loss of face, Devon was still the one behind bars. And despite her wilfulness, Alana was truly herself once more—her betrayal of her former friends proved it. They might disagree with how to train the new Magickers brought to the citadel, but that was nothing new.

His humour returning, Quinn straightened his shoulders and took the next corridor on his left. After his confrontation with Devon, he felt a need to see Alana again. It was past time they made up. Striding quickly through the citadel, he made his way towards her bedchambers.

He was just nearing the princess's rooms when a scream echoed down the hallways from ahead of him. His heart lurched painfully in his chest and drawing his sword, he sprinted towards the sound. His mind raced, trying to determine who or what could be attacking Alana now. For a second he wondered if there'd been another traitor working with Devon, if their capture had been some ruse…

Turning the last corner, the door to Alana's bedchamber came into sight. The guards that Devon and Kellian had immobilised last night had not been replaced, but the heavy wooden door remained closed. Sabre in hand, Quinn charged forward, bursting into the room with a shout. His eyes swept the gilded interior, taking in the empty sofa, the open curtains, the shining sun, the bed…

He froze as he found Alana staring back at him, her eyes wide with shock. She was sitting up in the bed, the sheets tangled around her naked body, her breasts uncovered. Quinn lowered his sword, swallowing hard as he felt the beginnings of desire.

"Alana," he said quickly, his heart still hammering. "Are you okay?"

She stared at him a moment, her lips parted, face pale. Then she blinked, a frown creasing her forehead. "I'm fine," she answered shortly. For a moment it seemed that was all she would say, and he was about to jump into an apology for the night before, when she shook her head. "No, nothing is okay, Quinn. Everything is wrong. So wrong."

Quinn sheathed his sword and crossed to her. Seating himself on the bed, he drank in her naked body, savouring the sleek curve of her neck, the hollow of her throat, the pale mounds of her breasts. He smiled and reached out a hand to stroke her hair.

"Everything is fine, Alana," he said. Her eyes fluttered closed at his touch, and he went on. "You're safe. Devon and his friend are locked–"

At the mention of Devon's name, Alana flinched away from him. Her eyes snapped open, rage appearing in their stony depths. She pushed him, catching him in the chest and sending him toppling from the bed.

"I didn't say you could touch me," she snarled, climbing from the bed to stand over him.

"Alana…" Quinn murmured, staring at her.

A shudder went through her, and her eyes softened. "I'm

sorry…Quinn," she whispered. She shook her head and turned to the trunk at the foot of her bed.

She rummaged around inside, dragging out a pair of underwear and trousers. Quinn approached cautiously as she began to dress herself.

"Alana, what is going on?" he asked.

"Nothing," she answered, pulling on a pair of breeches.

But her breath was racing, and Quinn could see her hands trembling as she struggled into the clothes. Pulling on a shirt, she turned and tried to get past him, but he stepped into her path.

"What is going on, Alana?" he asked again, his voice hardening.

She tried to sidestep him, but he blocked her way once more. She raised her hand to strike him, but Quinn retreated, and the blow never fell. Letting out a long breath, the anger seemed to flow from her. She lowered her hand to her side.

"I'm sorry, Quinn," she said suddenly, a smile appearing. "I can't right now. Later, I promise."

Stepping forward, she stroked his arm, pulling him to her. Desire rushed through Quinn as he pressed his lips to hers. He shuddered, pulling her tightly against him, and ran his hands through her hair, tangling his fingers in her blonde locks, drawing her deeper into the kiss…

Then a bright light burst across his vision, and somewhere in his mind a voice cried out. Opening his eyes, he found himself on his knees, the strength gone from his legs. Letting out a groan, he swayed and looked around, finding Alana now standing in the doorway. For a moment their eyes met, and he realised with horror she'd used her power against him.

"Alana…" he managed, his voice barely more than a whisper.

"I'm sorry, Quinn," she said sadly. "Truly I am. But I need to talk to my father."

With that, she was gone, and the darkness rose up to claim him.

29

"So, Alan was your ancestor, ay?"

It was a while before Devon registered the old man's question. They had been sitting in silence for hours now, and the cold of the cell seemed to have seeped into his soul. The brief pleasure he'd gotten from Quinn's humiliation had already faded away, replaced by a growing despair. Inside this cell, his physical strength meant nothing, and Quinn's words went round and around in his head, taunting him. He shivered at the thought of spending his remaining years down here in the darkness, while above Quinn breathed fresh air, free to…

"What was that?" he asked, snapping his thoughts free of the images that were circling his mind.

The old man grinned. With an audible click of bones, he stretched his neck. "The boy said Alan would be ashamed of you—I take it that means you are his descendant."

Devon nodded. "Ay, he was my great-grandfather."

"An interesting family. Alan was a legend—even in his

own time. But it was his father-in-law who always had my respect."

"The Magicker?"

"You've heard of him?" The old man seemed surprised. "It is good to hear he has not entirely been forgotten."

"A priest told me of him, though she did not mention his name. Apparently he placed a spell on *kanker*, Alan's hammer."

"Interesting. Does it protect its wielder from magic?" the old man questioned.

Devon blinked. "How did you know that?"

His cellmate scratched his long white beard. "He had a sword with the same power, though it was destroyed during the final war against Archon. It seems reasonable he would create a similar protection for his son-in-law."

"Do you know his name?" Devon asked.

"Alastair." The old man spoke the name with a sigh, almost like a prayer. "A greater man even than Alan, though few know his name now. It was he who thwarted Archon's first invasion. While he enjoyed an extended life span, Alastair was still ancient by the time the Dark Magicker returned. Even so, he answered the call, and gave his life to train a new generation of Magickers to stand against the darkness."

"Like Enala?"

The old man's head whipped up at the mention of the old woman's name. "Enala still lives?"

Devon nodded. "She was the priest I speak of, though she went by Tillie when I met her."

For the first time since he'd woken in the dank cell, Devon saw the light of hope on the old man's face. He sat up straighter, and it seemed some of the wrinkles had fallen from his cheeks.

"Truly? That..." he shook his head, tears appearing in his eyes. "Perhaps...perhaps there may be hope after all."

"I'm not so sure." Seeing his cellmate's confusion, Devon swallowed and went on. "She has the boy, Braidon with her. If...if Alana is truly the Tsar's daughter, then Braidon must be his son. What if it was all a trap, to trick Enala into trusting the boy, or to lure her out of hiding?"

The old man smiled. "Enala will not be fooled so easily. Perhaps she already knew their identity when you met—it would not surprise me. Either way, she won't easily be taken."

Devon sighed. "The two are in Northland. I doubt they'll be venturing south anytime soon."

"No..." Some of the energy went from the man then, and he slumped back against the wall. "No, I suppose not."

A groan came from the corner of the cell as Kellian sat up. "You two are great company, you know?" he muttered, rubbing his eyes. "If you're not going to let me sleep, you could at least find a more pleasant topic!"

Devon felt a sick sense of responsibility settle around him. "I'm sorry, old friend. This is my fault, I should never have dragged you into this business."

Kellian snorted and moved across to join them. "That's hardly fair, I chose to come, didn't I? Alana was my friend as much as yours."

"Some friend," Devon murmured. "Seems she never needed our help to begin with."

"Perhaps, perhaps not," the old man replied. "But it does not lessen your sacrifice."

"Yes, well, if I'm honest I would have preferred avoiding the sacrifice altogether," Kellian added. "As it is, I'd rather not spend the rest of my life here." He coughed. "Err, how long exactly did you say you'd been here?"

"I'm afraid I lost track after the first decade."

"Great," Kellian muttered. "Guess we'll count you out for escape plans. What about you, Devon, any ideas?"

"No," Devon replied, trying to keep the despair from his voice.

"What about your magic then?" Kellian turned back to the old man. "You said the bracelets keep you from using it. Is there any way to remove them? They look fragile enough."

The old man laughed bitterly. "You think I have not tried?"

Kellian sighed. "True. Suppose it's up to me then!" Seemingly nonplussed, he stood looking out through the bars. "What about the other cells? I...what's wrong with them?" His voice rose several octaves as he finished.

Devon frowned at the fear behind Kellian's words. Rising, he joined him at the bars and looked into the opposite cell, watching as shapes formed in the gloom. There were three people sitting on the floor opposite them—two women, and a man. If their cellmate had seemed in poor health, these three looked like the life itself had been drained from them, leaving only empty husks of their former selves. Little more than skin and bone, their flesh was raw and cracked, their eyes lifeless white globes, their hair hanging in tufts from their skulls.

Then he saw the soft rise and fall of their chests. Staggering back, his stomach swirled, and he struggled to keep from throwing up. With one hand he fumbled for the wall, using its solidity to right himself. Taking a great, shuddering breath, he faced the old man.

"What's wrong with them?" he said, repeating Kellian's question.

The old man lifted an emaciated wrist, and the dim light

of the lantern in the corridor caught on the emerald bracelet. "The Tsar's gifts are like a parasite," he said. "To keep our power locked away, they infect us with their dark magic. It harries the spirit, devouring the soul bit by bit. Eventually, there is nothing left but a tiny spark, and the Magicker becomes a shell, a remnant that lives only to serve the Tsar's purpose."

"Then how have you survived so long?"

"Hate," the old man whispered, his eyes shimmering. "Everything else has been lost to me—hope, love, joy. Only the hate remains, burning like a candle within, holding the darkness at bay."

"What did he do to you?" Devon whispered.

"He took someone dear from me," their cellmate replied, looking away. He gazed out at the corridor, an infinite sorrow etched across his ancient face.

Devon swallowed, unable to find the courage to ask who. Instead, he turned the conversation back to the Tsar. "Why is he keeping all of you alive though?" he asked. "I thought the Magickers who defied him were all executed."

"Would that we were," the old man replied bitterly. "No, he can't kill us. He *needs* us. Every Magicker brought before him is offered a choice—serve him, or spend the rest of their lives rotting in these cells. Most choose a life of service, rather than this stinking pit. All but his most trusted Magickers wear the bracelets."

Devon's skin crawled. "What do the cuffs do then, if those above still wear them? Surely there is no need, if they're wielding their magic in service to the Tsar."

There was a haunted look on the old man's face now. "A long time ago, the Tsar discovered a way of robbing Magickers of their power. But there was a flaw in the spell: it required the Magicker's death. He did not realise it in those early days, but with the original Magicker's lifeforce extinguished, the magic he stole could not be renewed. Once used, it was gone. So he devised a new way of taking our magic, one that would allow him unlimited power."

"The bracelets," Kellian hissed.

"Yes," said the old man. "They siphon off our magic one drop at a time, providing the Tsar with a constant source of power. By now, he must have hundreds of Magickers to feed off of, both down here and in his service across the Three Nations. So long as we all live, the Tsar's power is unassailable."

"But if the bracelets are broken, his power would vanish?" Devon asked.

The old prisoner's laughter whispered through the cell. "Mortal strength will not touch them. Only with death will we be released—and even that is denied to us. The other prisoners would have perished long ago, but the bracelets feed their lifeforce, holding them to this world."

Shivering, Devon shook his head. "There must be a way."

"Even if there were, do not forget the countless Magickers who serve the Tsar willingly. Each also lends their power to the Tsar. I see your Stalker friend no longer wears the bracelets…but he would be one of the few."

"We could weaken him at least," Kellian murmured, still standing at the bars to the cell, "if we freed you and the others."

"That is true." The old man shrugged. "But how do you plan on doing that while sitting in this cell?"

"A good point," Kellian replied with a grin. "I guess we'd better set about getting out then."

At his words, the *bang* of the outer doors echoed down the corridor. Footsteps followed, drawing nearer, though there was no sign of light. Devon frowned–usually the guards carried lanterns when they went about their rounds. As he watched, a shadow appeared in the corridor beyond their cell. The shadow approached Kellian, who smiled and leaned towards it. Soft whispers passed between them. Then it was gone.

Smiling, Kellian turned to face them. A jingling sound carried across the cell as he held up a loop of keys.

"Always have a backup plan, old friend," he said.

30

Wind hissed in Braidon's ears as the dragon drifted lower, catching in his hair and sending shivers down his back through a rip in his clothing. Squinting in the bright sunlight, he gasped as they dropped towards the clouds, his stomach lurching uncomfortably. In front of him, Enala let out a whoop of joy as though she were still a ten-year-old girl, and the dragon roared in response.

Despite the cold, Braidon found himself grinning at the old priest's youthful exuberance. Since he'd met her, he had rarely seen beyond the woman's calm, reserved exterior. Only up here, far above the worries of the world, did she seem free. Her eyes flashed as she glanced back at him, a smile of her own on her lips.

"We're close!" she cried out, the rushing air whipping away her words almost before Braidon could comprehend them.

Are you ready, young Braidon? Dahniul's voice spoke in his mind.

"I think so!" he shouted back, his heart beating faster at the thought of the coming challenges.

They had flown all night and day, racing across oceans and desert, mountains and forests, to reach the distant Plorsean capital. Enala had filled him in on her plan while they flew, but now that the time had come, he found himself suddenly doubting her words.

After all, her entire plan rested on his magic.

"I believe in you, Braidon!" Enala said, as though reading his mind.

She stood suddenly. Balancing precariously on Dahniul's back, she turned and lowered herself back down so she was facing him. She reached out and took his hands in hers, her aged face alight with the sun's warmth.

"Have faith, the Gods are with you," she said.

Braidon shivered. "Easy for you to say, you've seen them," he muttered.

Enala laughed. "I've *been* them, but the point is well taken. Have faith in yourself then. You have conquered your magic once already. When you reach for it now, hold to that memory. You *know* you can do this."

He smiled. "Let us see, shall we?"

And closing his eyes, he reached for his power. White light flickered in the void of his mind, rising up, the Feline taking shape. Only now, to Braidon's surprise, he found himself able to face the creature without fear. Bemused, he watched it roar, the great jaw opening wide. Chuckling to himself, he strode towards it, and the beast's power faded away. His hand stretched out, thrusting deep into its core, and the magic collapsed in on itself.

Braidon gasped as white-hot heat filled him, rushing to every pore of his body. Opening his eyes, he saw a world awash with colour. Enala still sat before him, only now it was not the old woman who watched him, but a figure of brilliant, shining red. Braidon gasped as he saw the amber swirling within the dragon, shining out to fill the sky. Further afield, he sensed other spirits, other powers all around, and felt a sudden yearning to go to them.

A strange motion followed, and then Braidon was soaring through the sky, beyond Enala and the dragon, outside his own body. Colours whirled around him, a stream of blue and white and red dancing across the sky. He watched the dragon and its tiny passengers, mystified by their brilliant light.

Only then did his purpose return to him. Enala believed he could use his power to shield them from the Tsar's view, allow them to infiltrate the citadel and find his sister without being detected. His spirit flickered as he considered the problem. The magic of the priest and dragon shone across the sky, his own power small alongside them. If he wanted to shield them from the Tsar, he would need to do more than just hide them from sight.

Drifting closer to Dahniul, he reached out with his spirit to touch the aura surrounding her, and it rippled away from him, changing. He frowned, concentrating on it, willing it to alter, to become one with the sky. To his surprise, the amber colour faded, becoming the same multicoloured light that he had drifted through earlier. Slowly, the dragon faded from the sight of his spirit eyes.

Braidon smiled then, pleased with his success, and quickly turned his attention to Enala and his own flickering power.

When he finally opened his eyes, Braidon let out a long groan as the weight of his body returned. He swayed on the dragon's back, but a firm hand settled on his shoulder, holding him in place. Blinking, he found Enala smiling at him.

"You did it, Braidon!" she exclaimed.

There was a strangeness to Enala's face as he looked at her, and it was a moment before Braidon realised he could see straight through her. His mouth dropped open. "What the...?"

Enala laughed. "A side-effect of your spell," she said, answering his unfinished question. "I *believe* we should now be invisible to anyone outside the spell, while to those within we merely appear...less substantial."

"Are you sure?" Braidon asked. They were still above the clouds, but once they dropped below them...

"Only one way to find out!" Enala replied with a youthful grin. "Dahniul, take us down!"

Before Braidon could reply, his stomach lurched up into his chest as the dragon folded its wings and dived. Screaming, they plunged into the clouds. For a moment, everything vanished, and all Braidon could see was a thick white mist. Only the solidness of the dragon beneath him convinced Braidon he was not plummeting to his death.

Then the clouds were gone, and Braidon was left looking out over the lands of his home. Shining water stretched out below, the waters raging with the afternoon winds sweeping in off the plateau. A sprinkling of ships were racing across the lake, and Braidon's chest tightened at the sight of their pitch-black sails.

Ahead, he saw the towering cliffs of his island home rising from the lake. Here, even more ships bobbed at the docks, their black sails like a stain on the lake around them. Their colour could only mean one thing—the Tsar was preparing for war.

His heart beating faster, he shouted at Enala. "The

emissaries couldn't have reached the city already," he breathed.

"No," Enala replied, voice grim, "the Tsar never intended to honour his offer of peace. Look over there." She nodded to the far side of the lake. Beyond the rolling hills bordering the waters, an army spread across the land as far as the eye could see.

Braidon clenched his jaw. "We have to stop him."

"Yes," Enala replied. "But first, we must find your sister."

At that, Dahniul swept down, and the tall white walls of Ardath's citadel came racing up to greet them.

31

"Where…?" Devon started, then trailed off, too stunned to finish the question.

Laughing, Kellian moved to the iron door. A solid *thunk* followed as the lock disengaged, then a loud squeal of rusty hinges as the door swung open. Kellian gestured them forward.

"Well, don't just stand there! I don't know how much time we have before the real guards return!"

The old man rose with a chuckle. "You know, I think I like you, innkeeper." He wandered past Devon and out into the corridor. Stretching his arms, he groaned. "Ahh, but it's good to be out of that hole. You coming, youngster?" he said to Devon.

Shaking his head, Devon strode after them. "What about the guards?" he asked gruffly, glaring at Kellian. Just moments before, he'd been on the brink of despair. Now it seemed Kellian had had a way out all along.

"Don't look so glum, old friend," Kellian laughed, thumping him on the back. "The guards are taken care of…

or at least, I hope they are. Hard to know how much of my message Betran managed to deliver."

"Betran?" Devon repeated dumbly.

"I left him with some papers to give my contacts in Kalgan, in case anything happened to us. I don't know about you, but I didn't like the idea of spending my remaining days locked in a dungeon when your brilliant plans inevitably unravelled."

"I wouldn't advise it personally," the old man offered.

"Such faith you have in me," Devon grunted, but Kellian only grinned.

"Lighten up, Devon! We're free, aren't we?" he said. "Or we are for now. I think we'd best be leaving. Who knows how much time my patrons have managed to buy us? Old drinking buddies can only get you so far. What's say we see about those bracelets of yours, my friend?" He rattled the keys at the old man.

Their companion sighed. "I'm afraid there's no key for these, innkeeper. Powerful magic locked them in place, and it will take magic equally as powerful to remove them. We'll have to rely on our wits alone to take us the rest of the way."

"Figures," Kellian grunted, lowering the keys. He shared a glance with Devon, then turned to the neighbouring cells. Now that they were in the corridor, they could see down the length of the dungeons—or at least as far as the light reached. There were at least a hundred cells, all full of people. "What about them?"

"There's little we can do for them now," the old man replied. "Not unless you have it in you to kill them?"

Devon's head jerked up. "*What?*"

The old man's eyes shone. "They are the source of the Tsar's power," he replied. "Them, myself, his Magickers upstairs. So long as we live, so long as we wear the bracelets, his power remains."

"We'll wake them…" Kellian began, but the old man was already shaking his head.

"They're past that now," he shot back. "And we cannot carry them." Moving to the front of a cell, he looked in at the occupants and let out a long breath. "But you are right. I don't have the stomach for it either—though no doubt they would thank us for the mercy."

"Well, if we can't help them, let's at least help ourselves," Kellian said briskly, starting towards the stairwell.

Devon offered the old man his shoulder, but now that they were free, their cellmate seemed to have regained his vigour. He sprang after Kellian, leaving Devon to bring up the rear. Ahead, Kellian lifted the single lantern from its bracket and started up the stairwell. The others came close behind, ears straining for sounds of movement from above. The stone steps wound upwards, spiralling past more levels of dungeons. Silently, Devon wondered how many cells there were, how many Magickers the Tsar had imprisoned over the decades.

Shivering, he recalled the Trolan Magickers who'd been captured during the civil war. There had been hundreds—and the Tsar's power had been insurmountable even then. What new feats might he be capable of now?

Finally, the stairwell came to an end, the stone steps giving way to a wide guard chamber. They paused in the doorway, scanning the room for signs of danger. A desk was pushed up against the far wall, two chairs behind it. Two men were seated there, but both were slumped unconscious across the wooden surface. A crevasse of wine stood on the table between them, along with two empty mugs.

Devon looked at Kellian and raised an eyebrow. His friend only shrugged and entered the room. The guards were armed with knives and swords, and he quickly helped himself to them. The old man found himself a short sword, while Kellian secreted several daggers about his person. Hefting a spare short sword, he offered it to Devon.

Scanning the room, Devon's heart leapt as he glimpsed a black haft poking out from beneath the desk. Crouching down, he reached out and gripped the familiar weapon. A weight lifted from his shoulders as he straightened, *kanker* settling easily into his hands.

"I'm beginning to think we might make it out of this alive after all," he said, grinning.

"*Kanker*," their cellmate whispered. He moved slowly across the room, staring at the hammer. "Gods, I never thought I would see it again."

Devon narrowed his eyes. "I told you he was my ancestor."

Their companion smiled. "Yes, but then, I never thought I'd leave that cell either." He paused, swallowing. "It's magic…I wonder…?"

Devon gripped the weapon tighter. "You think it could free you?"

"I'm not sure Alastair's spell will be strong enough."

"Can't hurt to try."

"Oh, it can," the old man replied, "but it's worth the risk."

He held out his hands. Devon extended *kanker* and tapped it lightly to the bracelets around the man's wrists. As it connected, a hiss like a boiling kettle whistled through the room. The old man's face tightened, his jaw clenching as though to muffle a scream. Still, he did not back away.

An instant later, a brilliant flash lit the room, followed by a sharp *crack*. The light faded away with the soft tinkling of metal striking stone. Looking down, Devon saw the old man's wrists were now unadorned.

"It worked!"

Grimacing, the old man rubbed his hands. "Ah, but that hurt," he said. Then he smiled and clenched his fists. To Devon, it seemed the temperature in the room dropped several degrees.

"What now?" Devon asked.

"My friends have done what they can," Kellian answered. "I say we get out of this citadel and this city as quickly as possible, before anyone discovers we're gone."

"We'd best move quickly," the old man added, "before the next shift arrives..." He trailed off as a distant *thud* carried to them from the doorway leading out of the dungeons.

Devon advanced on the exit. The heavy wooden door was closed, but from beyond he could hear footsteps approaching. The scraping of a key in the lock followed, and the door shifted slightly. Then a voice called out.

"Hey, lads, give us a hand will ya? You know it sticks!"

Kanker gripped in one hand, Devon waited on the other side of the door for his moment. The others closed in behind him, but he waved them back. The doorway was narrow, and there wouldn't be room in the corridor beyond for more than one man to fight.

He eyed the door, and seeing it shift, he surged forwards, his boot lashing out to crash against the wood. The door flew backwards with the power of the blow, and beyond, a voice cried out. Then Devon was charging through, *kanker* in hand, and he was amongst them. There was no time to count his foes, only to attack. Taken by surprise, they fell back before his fury, their swords still sheathed at their sides. Scarlet guard-cloaks became tangled around boots, and the first man was still clutching his head where the door had struck him when *kanker* caught him in the chest, hurling him back.

Leaping the fallen body, Devon swung again, slamming his weapon into the face of the following guard. The man was still scrambling for the hilt of his sword, but as the hammer struck, his body stiffened, and the half-drawn blade clattered to the ground.

Beyond, a third guard cried out and turned to flee. Hefting *kanker*, Devon hurled it at the man. The weapon hissed through the air and caught him in the small of his back. He cried out and crashed face-first into the ground, his legs twitching uselessly as he tried to crawl away.

Striding down the corridor, Devon retrieved *kanker*. Looking down at the injured man, his anger flared. These men had sought to cage him, to lock him in the darkness, while blood suckers like Quinn and the Tsar enjoyed the light as heroes. Teeth bared, he lifted *kanker*, ready to bring it down on the man's skull.

"Devon!" Kellian's voice carried down the corridor, halting his blow.

He looked back. "What?"

Kellian walked towards him. "They're done," his friend said softly. "You beat them. Leave him, there's more where they came from."

Devon sucked in a breath, seeing the concern in his friend's eyes. At his feet, the fallen guard was trembling with terror. Still, the anger clutched at Devon, demanding retribution.

"You remind me of him a lot, you know." said the old man, his voice carrying down the corridor.

Devon frowned. "Who?"

The old man joined Kellian. At his feet, the guard groaned. "Your ancestor."

A sharp pain lanced through Devon's chest at the reference. "Alan?" he growled. "How could you possibly have known him?"

"No, not Alan, though he was even larger than you." The old man smiled. "I was talking of Alastair. In his day, there were few Magickers more powerful than him. No mortal foe could hope to stand against him—yet he rarely used his power on those without magic. You are strong, Devon, powerful like him. But are you merciful?"

Devon sighed, his anger dying like flames before the water. "Fine," he agreed. "Let's get out of here, then."

Without waiting for a reply, he turned and started down the corridor, leaving the others to race after him. Pushing through another set of wooden doors, they found themselves in a broad corridor. Devon searched for some point of reference that would tell him where they were in the citadel as the old man strode to a window in the opposite wall. Light was streaming through the glass, and their companion's eyes flickered closed as it bathed his face. He stood still as a statue, the years seeming to fall from him, while in the courtyard beyond, birds chirped.

"I never thought I would see the sky again." The old man's words shook. "I thought I would never leave that place."

Devon reached out and placed a hand on the man's shoulder. "You're free now," he said softly.

To his surprise, the old man shook his head. Reaching up, he wiped the tears from his cheeks, then looked at Devon. "I can never be free," he said. "I did not lie before, my friend. There is nothing left of the man the Tsar sent into the darkness. Only the hate remains. It binds me to him still. I cannot join you."

"You must," Kellian replied. "Even with your powers restored, you cannot hope to match him alone."

The old man smiled. Clenching his fists, he let out a long breath. Devon's ears popped as the windows shattered inwards, and a swirling wind went rushing into the corridor. A dull *boom* echoed around them, and looking down, he saw lightning dancing along the old man's arms.

"Perhaps not," the man said quietly, "but even so, I will try. At the very least, it will give you a distraction."

"You don't need to do this," Devon argued, but the blue eyes turned to stare at him, and the words left him.

"I have lived long past my time, Devon. But my death can still have meaning. I can still leave this world a better place than when I entered it. Now go. Run. Don't turn back."

He started down the corridor, but Kellian's voice called him back.

"Who *are* you?"

The old man paused, his eyes shining as he smiled. "My name is Eric."

Then he was gone.

32

Alana stood before the throne, fists clenched, her whole body trembling as she faced the man who dared to call himself her father. Several of his councillors stood around him. He still hadn't noticed her presence, but the ring of guards were watching her from the dais, their eyes alert. No doubt they were still weary after her earlier display with their comrade. In that moment, Alana hardly cared.

In her mind, she saw again the memories her father had kept from her, the ones Antonia had unlocked. She remembered it *all* now—the reason she had fled the citadel with her brother, why she had wiped their memories.

For years she had marched children off to their examinations, many never to be seen again. Those who survived became Battle Magickers for her father, while the ones who failed were consumed by their magic, becoming the demons her father sent to destroy his enemies. Either way, Alana had never really cared—so long as the Tsar's power grew. At least, not until her brother's time had come…

Braidon.

The name was like a bell tolling within her, filling her with fear, with terror. The Magickers she'd tutored through the years had been beneath her, commoners who lived only at her father's mercy. But her brother…she couldn't face the thought of losing him, of watching him fail. And he would, she knew. Perhaps it was her own love that had made him weak, her mercy that had blighted him…but it mattered little now.

She had known he would fail, long before his magic surfaced. Even after a year of tutoring, of meditation and training, he had still been too soft to face his magic. It would have overwhelmed him, swept away the boy she loved and replaced him with one of the black-eyed creatures who served the Tsar.

And her father hadn't cared.

Alana reached down and drew her sabre from its sheath. The guards tensed as the rasp of steel on leather whispered through the throne room, but she ignored them and advanced up the stone steps towards her father. One of the guards moved towards her, his spear bristling, steel plate mail rattling loudly. His weapon swept down, the point pressing lightly against her chest.

She glanced at the spear, then into the eyes of the man holding it.

"Get out of my way," she commanded.

Magic surged from her, catching on the tip of the spear and racing up the weapon into the man. He shuddered, a battle taking place behind his eyes, but it was one he could not win. With another rattle of metal, he stepped aside, and Alana marched past. The other guards stayed out of reach, but quickly moved to position themselves on either side of her father.

He was watching her now, his eyes following her as she

topped the stairs and came to a stop before the throne. The other councillors fell silent as he stood to meet her.

"Alana, I thought you were resting–"

"I know everything, father," she interrupted, her voice like stone. "I remember."

For half a second, she thought he would deny it. A flicker passed across his face, but then the mask settled back into place, the emotion fading away. He turned to his councillors. "Leave me."

He swung back to Alana without allowing them a chance to argue. They hesitated a moment, before striding past Alana and down the stairs to the exit. The guards remained, spears still bristling, but at a wave from her father, they lowered the weapons and retreated.

"And what is it you remember, my daughter?" the Tsar said finally.

Alana advanced, her skin still crawling at the thought of what he'd wrought on her memories, the hole he'd left when he'd helped restore her past. She felt a sick sense of betrayal rise in her chest.

"*Everything*," she snapped, lifting her sabre to point it at his chest. "You *dared* to interfere with my memories?"

To her surprise, the Tsar chuckled. "Me, daughter? I only did what you asked. It was *you* who made such a mess of them in the first place!"

"To hide from *you!*" Alana shrieked.

The guards started forward again, but she was faster still. She closed in on the Tsar, her sabre lancing forward. He made no move to stop her, and she felt a moment's thrill as the blade plunged towards him. But as the point touched his chest her sword shrieked and grated to a stop, as though she'd struck solid stone. Her hands jarred at the impact, the vibrations almost tearing the hilt from her grasp. Instead of fading, the shrieking sound grew until it reached a fever pitch, and with a sudden *boom*, her blade shattered.

A wave of energy struck Alana, throwing her on her back. Shards of steel rattled on the marble floors as the remnants of her blade scattered across the dais. On the ground, Alana groaned as she struggled to regain her breath. She lay staring up at her father, hate curdling in her stomach.

The Tsar pursed his lips, face impassive. "It was smart, I'll admit," he said pleasantly, as though she had not just tried to stab him. "Altering your own mind, and your brother's, to conceal yourselves from my powers." He shook his head. "I trained you well."

Alana shivered, seeing again the memories Antonia had unlocked, of her brother coming to her before his birthday, his eyes alive with fear.

I can't do it, Alana, he had told her.

Looking into his eyes, she had wanted to tell him it would be alright, that he would discover the strength he needed to master his magic. Yet the words had died in her throat, and all she could see was the bright child she had helped raise after her mother's death; the one good, pure thing in her otherwise joyless existence.

And Alana had seen the truth then—that one way or another, she would lose him. Either he would become the hard, unyielding man their father wanted him to be, or he would perish, consumed by his own magic.

That life of darkness was all Alana had ever known. Long ago, she had come to terms with her place in the world, sacrificing her freedom and embracing her role as the Tsar's daughter. She had hoped she might spare her brother the same fate, but she had only delayed the inevitable.

The day Braidon had come to her, she'd known what

she needed to do. That very night, she had smuggled them both out of the citadel, to what she hoped was freedom. As the midnight bell chimed, Braidon's fear had taken hold, unleashing his magic, but she'd used her own power to render him unconscious before his power could be detected. She'd managed to carry him deep into the city, but slowed down by his dead-weight, they hadn't reached the gates in time. The city guard were already on alert for their disappearance.

So they had taken refuge in the city, concealing themselves from their father's magic in the mass of humanity that was the slums of Ardath. For weeks, they'd fled from abandoned buildings to crumbling shacks, waiting for the hunt to die down. Through all the long days and nights, she had sensed her father's power, humming in the skies overhead as he searched for them. It was only then that she'd realised they could never escape him. The moment they left the crowds of Ardath, their minds would be exposed, and his magic would find them.

Only when the boy's wild magic had set fire to the stepwell, had Alana seen her opportunity. Using his power to mask her own, she had turned her magic on herself and Braidon. Wrapping their minds in bands of green fire, she'd buried their memories deep, allowing their subconscious to form new lives for themselves. They had become new people—people her father would not have recognised, even had he touched their minds with his magic.

Alana was still surprised by the girl who had emerged to replace her. Perhaps she had only unlocked a part of herself she'd never known existed, one buried deep by her father's teachings, consumed by the harsh reality of life as the Daughter of the Tsar.

Thinking of her other self now, Alana's animosity faded,

replaced by a cautious respect. Whatever her faults, the girl had escaped the Tsar's Stalkers, had succeeded in rescuing her brother, where Alana herself had failed. With the release of her final memories, she felt almost at peace with her other self.

Their hatred for the Tsar had united them.

Glaring at her father, Alana climbed slowly to her feet.

"I won't let you bring him back," she said.

"You cannot stop me, my daughter," the Tsar replied. "He must face his examination."

"He will fail!"

"Such little faith, my daughter," her father replied. "He is of the blood of kings. He will prevail—as you once did."

"Ay, I remember how you prepared me," Alana replied bitterly.

"Did you not impart on your students the same preparations?" The Tsar responded. "Did your teachings not prepare them for the challenge, and a life in my service?"

Shame filled Alana as she recalled her charges, their terror as she faced them. She knew the emotion came from her other self, but with memories of her brother's terror fresh in her mind, she embraced it, finally seeing the mindless cruelty of her actions. Her methods had been pointless—only necessary because the young Magickers were given just a month to prepare for their examinations.

In all the time Alana had served as teacher, she had never regretted her students' suffering. After all, their torments were nothing to what her father had subjected her to. She clenched her fists, recalling the agony of losing a limb, only for the Tsar to touch her with his power, restoring it. A shudder swept through her as she looked up into his eyes.

"You are a monster. You will destroy your own son."

"If that is his fate, then so be it," her father replied sadly. "If he does not have the strength to master his magic, he is no son of mine."

"*No!*" Alana shrieked, throwing herself forward. An invisible barrier brought her up short. She slammed her fists against it. "You will not turn him!"

Against her will, she saw again the demon that had come for her on the ship back in Lon, its youthful face and jet-black eyes. She knew now that had not been the first time she'd seen that face, the first time she'd looked into those eyes—though before they had been sky green. With her memories restored, she knew now who he was.

His name was Anish, and he had been her student.

Before his magic took him.

The thought of her brother facing the same fate set her stomach heaving, and she slid down the invisible barrier to the floor. Looking up at her father, she shook her head, sobbing now, powerless before his magic.

"Please," she whispered.

He shrugged. "His fate is in his own hands, daughter," he replied. "When our emissaries return with him, he will face the examination like any other Magicker. I will release the bonds of his magic. He will face the beast, and either defeat it, or succumb to its power. I have no wish to see my son a demon, but I will not save him should it take him."

"But you could!" Alana shrieked. "You saved me!"

"You were not yourself."

"I...I don't want to be myself!" Alana said, her voice fading as she realised it was true. Her eyes burned as she thought of Devon and Kellian, locked away because of her. Pain wrenched at her heart. "I want to be free."

The Tsar moved towards her. "Free?" he sighed. "What is freedom? I have given you *everything,* child! Life, magic, an empire! I have endured your wilfulness for years, yet still you demand more."

"I don't want anything from you."

Her father sighed, his eyes shining. "Then I will take it all. You *will* serve me, daughter. You think your magic can protect you? I have a dozen Magickers in my thrall with the same power."

Ice spread though Alana's stomach as her heart started to palpitate. Her father's eyes had hardened, all traces of kindness draining from them. Taken by a sudden fear, she rose and backed away on trembling legs. Another invisible barrier brought her up short. Her father started towards her.

Alana spun, slamming her hands against the barrier, desperate to escape. But there was nowhere to run, and she froze as a hand clutched her by the shoulder, forcing her to look back. Her mouth parted as she looked up at her father, her vision shimmering.

"No..." she said.

The Tsar shook his head. "Why do you hate me, daughter?" he asked. "Everything I have ever done was to build a better world for you. Yet still you spurn me."

Hot tears ran down Alana's cheeks. "Go ahead and do it," she said. "You have already taken everything from me. My childhood, my joy, my soul. You made me into your executioner, had me drive scores of children into the darkness. And you have the gall to ask me why I hate you?"

"I am sorry," he murmured, still holding to her shoulder. "This is my fault. I thought I could fix you by holding back your memories. But the weakness is rooted too deep."

"And weakness must be destroyed," Alana whispered.

"I will start afresh," her father agreed. His face tightened. "But you will feel nothing."

Before Alana could react, she felt the burning touch of his magic wash through her. She gasped, her own power rising to defend her, but it was nothing to the forces in the Tsar's command. The burning green of her magic was engulfed, swept away like a sandcastle before the incoming tide. Her body shook as she fought him, but it was no use. She opened her mouth to scream…

And the roar of thunder filled her ears.

❧ 33 ❧

Devon stumbled to a halt as a crash echoed through the corridors of the citadel. Kellian drew up alongside him. Together they looked back. Flashes of light burst through the open windows, and it seemed as though the very air was alive with energy. They shared a glance, then returned their eyes to the lightning flickering in the sky.

Somewhere in the citadel, the old man had engaged with the enemy.

Eric.

The name sent a shiver down Devon's spine. It couldn't be true…and yet, surely it could not be a coincidence? Eric was the last Magicker to have seen the Gods alive, the last to have wielded the Sword of Light, one of the few to stand to the end against the Dark Magicker, Archon.

And he was Enala's brother.

"You think he can win?" Devon heard himself asking.

"No," Kellian replied shortly.

Devon nodded, though he wasn't so sure. Somehow Eric had survived the Tsar's corrupting magic, had lived for decades in the darkness below the citadel, where so many others had succumbed. And when he'd looked into the man's eyes, there had been an indomitable will there, a determination to finally have his revenge.

Yet now Eric stood against the most powerful Magicker in the Empire, a man who could draw on the magic of hundreds, who commanded demons and dragons with a wave of his sword.

In the distance, the rumble of thunder died away, and outside the clouds parted. A ray of sunshine burst over the citadel. Seeing it, the hope withered in Devon's chest as he realised Eric's storm magic had been defeated. He turned back to Kellian.

"Let's go," he said.

They started down the corridor, but they'd only made it a few more feet when they heard the soft patter of running boots ahead of them. Before they could react, a squadron of black-garbed Stalkers raced into view. Quinn stood at their head, his eyes widening as he saw them standing in the middle of the corridor.

"What–?" he started.

Hefting his hammer, Devon charged at Quinn, but the man already had his sword drawn, and the blade leapt to meet his attack. Steel clashed as Kellian joined him. Devon ducked as Quinn's sabre slashed for his face, then he dropped his shoulder and drove it into Quinn's chest. The blow hurled his foe back into his comrades, creating a hole. Devon rushed through it, *kanker* sweeping out, catching a Stalker in the head with a sickening crunch.

Then they were clear, the scattered Stalkers turning to follow. Angry shouts chased them down the corridor as Devon glanced back, his heart pounding hard. Kellian was just behind him, a blade in either hand. They shared a grin as a voice chased after them.

"*Devon!*" Quinn roared.

A shriek came from the windows alongside Devon, and he looked up in time to see the glass shatter. Spinning, he lifted *kanker* in time to meet the gale Quinn had summoned with his power. It came rushing into the corridor, but with a hiss it was absorbed by his hammer, though its force still pushed Devon back several steps.

Alongside him, Kellian was not so lucky. Without the protection of *kanker*, Quinn's winds caught him midstride, and hurled him backwards. He struck the marble wall of the corridor with an awful *thud*, his blades skittering loudly on the stone floor, and he slumped to the ground, unconscious.

Devon cried out and started towards him, but Quinn's voice brought him up short.

"Don't move, hammerman," he hissed, "or I'll crush his skull against the bloody wall."

The lieutenant came striding towards him. The Stalkers followed, though Devon noted several lay on the ground behind them, unmoving. He smirked.

"Can't say it's good to see you, sonny," he said.

Fury etched across his face, Quinn stepped up and touched his sabre to Devon's neck. "Drop the hammer."

Devon hesitated, and the wind whistled louder. The *thunk* as *kanker* hit the ground echoed loudly in the corridor.

A dark smile spread across Quinn's face as he withdrew his sabre, then slammed a fist into Devon's stomach. Unprepared, Devon doubled over, the breath whistling between his teeth. He looked up in time to see Quinn's knee rising to catch him in the face, before stars exploded across his vision as he toppled back.

When his vision cleared, he found Quinn looking down at him. "So, the rats escaped their cell."

Devon struggled to find a reply, but Quinn's boot slammed into his ribs. Something went *crack* as pain tore through Devon's chest. Rolling onto his side, he coughed, the agony redoubling as he found himself suddenly breathless.

"Get them up," Quinn said. "I'd like to continue on our way to the throne room. Something is going on with Alana and the Tsar."

Despite himself, Devon's chest clenched at the mention of Alana's name. He groaned as rough hands gripped him beneath the arms and hauled him up. Head swimming, he saw Quinn already moving away. Two more Stalkers had hefted Kellian between them, though his friend still appeared unconscious.

As Devon was dragged down the corridor, he tried to get the lieutenant's attention. "I hope Eric killed him."

Quinn paused. "The old man?" he raised an eyebrow. "*That* was the legendary Eric?" Laughter echoed in the corridor. "I guess age makes fools of everyone, in the end! Now stop delaying, Devon. Or Kellian will suffer for it."

Devon knew he wasn't bluffing. The last of the fight went from him as he slumped in the arms of the men carrying him. His stomach twisted as he realised one held *kanker.*

Quinn chuckled as the Stalkers dragged Devon alongside him. "I must say I'm impressed, Devon," he said conversationally. "You'll have to tell me how you escaped, one day. It's a shame your weakness betrayed you in the end. I mean, you must know you're both going to die now? You could have saved yourself, but instead you chose… what? A pointless death?"

"A man like you wouldn't understand," Devon whispered.

One of the men carrying him paused long enough to slam his fist into Devon's stomach. He cried out as the broken rib sliced deeper into his chest. His vision swirled, red closing in on all sides, but he fought to stay conscious.

"It's no wonder Alana spurned you," Quinn was saying now.

"Where is she?" he gasped, barely able to breathe.

"She's mine now," Quinn snapped, though Devon sensed there was more behind his words.

"Is that so?" he rasped.

Quinn hesitated. His face was dark, his eyes shining with suppressed rage, but he made no move to attack Devon again. After a moment, he shook his head and swung away.

"She'll never be yours, Devon."

Devon was about to reply when a cry came from the Stalkers carrying Kellian. Somehow, he had slipped from their arms, tripping one of them as he tumbled to the ground. The other was bending over them, trying to get them up, but as Devon watched, the man jerked, stiffening suddenly.

"What's going on?" Quinn growled, running towards the men.

In that instant, Kellian rolled, leaving the second Stalker to topple dead to the floor. He held a bloody dagger clutched in one hand, and with a flick of his wrist, sent it hurtling at Quinn.

Quinn saw it just in time. He lurched back, and the blade hissed past, just a hair's breadth from his throat. With a scream, he threw out an arm. The wind roared, rushing down the corridor to catch Kellian where he still crouched on the ground. He flew through the air, his legs slamming awkwardly into the wall, and an awful *crack* echoed down the corridor. Screaming, Kellian crumpled to the ground clutching his leg.

Devon tried to summon the strength to go to his friend, but the two Stalkers only held him tighter as Quinn advanced on Kellian.

"Bastard innkeeper, I'll see you bleed for that," he shouted, drawing his sabre with his left hand.

Kellian tried to scramble back, but Quinn's boot crashed down on his injured leg, forcing a scream from him. Surging forward, Devon fought to reach the man, but a third Stalker stepped in and slammed a fist into his face. He sagged in the men's grip, the red flaring again, filling his vision. Blood pounded in his ears, but over it he heard another scream. Fear for his friend rose within him, but it was too late now. His strength had already fled, and with a cry, Devon felt himself falling away.

34

When the light finally died away, Alana found herself lying sprawled alongside the throne. Groaning, she forced herself to sit up, but a thousand flashing lights danced across her vision, and she slumped back to the ground. A harsh ringing in her ears drowned out all other noise—then with a sharp *pop*, sound returned.

Screams echoed through the throne room. Her vision cleared, revealing men scattered across the marble floors, their bodies blackened, their plated armour now twisted and misshapen. The sight of their scorched skin and torn bodies made Alana's stomach swirl, and rolling onto her side, she vomited. Silence settled like a blanket around her as the last screams died away.

Looking at herself, Alana was surprised to find her own body free of marks. She guessed her lack of armour or sword had saved her from…whatever it was that had struck them. Even so, she ached with the force of being picked up and hurled across the room. Across from her, black smoke still clung to the dais, but it was beginning to clear now, revealing the twisted remains of the golden throne.

And the Tsar still standing atop the stairs, staring down at the open doors.

Her head pounding, Alana followed her father's gaze and saw an old man striding towards the dais. His blue eyes shone with power, though his face was wrinkled and bleached white hair hung down around his shoulders. In his hands, lightning crackled.

"Eric," the Tsar's voice whispered across the room. "So good to see you again. I'm sorry to see the years have not been kind."

Silently, the old man continued his advance, the lightning growing in his hands. Her father laughed, and with a roar, Eric threw out an arm. A bolt of lightning flashed across the throne room, crackling as it went.

Her father lifted a hand, and the lightning froze mid-air, the sound of its thunder still booming off the walls. With a flick of his finger, the Tsar sent it careening up into the ceiling. White light flashed as it struck, almost blinding Alana.

"So you removed the bracelets," the Tsar said conversationally as he started down the steps of the dais. "Fortunately, you are not the only Sky Magicker in my…service."

Baring his teeth, the newcomer spread his arms. A roar came from the windows high above as they shattered inwards. Alana threw herself face first on the ground as glass crashed down around her.

In the middle of the room, her father laughed as the howling wind encircled him. "Have we not had this fight before, old man?" he shouted.

Alana watched in astonishment as ice grew around her father, stretching up from the marble floors. The harsh *crack* of splitting stone rang out, while amidst the ice, her father continued to smile, even as his breath misted before him. He lifted his hand, and fire appeared in his palm, growing and swelling, then rushing out to consume the ice. With a flick of his fingers, he sent the flames rushing towards his foe.

Moving with an agility that belayed his age, the old man hurled himself aside. Behind him, a column of marble was engulfed by the fire, its heat washing across the room to even where Alana lay. Surging back to his feet, the old man drew a sword and rushed at the Tsar.

Her father laughed again. She watched with a sinking heart as the Tsar allowed the intruder to close in on him. Then with a sudden decisiveness, he pointed a finger. Nothing appeared to happen, but the old man came to an abrupt halt, as though held by some invisible force. Sword raised above his head, he glared at the Tsar.

The Tsar gently lifted his hand, and still frozen in place, the old man rose slowly into the air.

"Ah, Eric, why in the Three Nations did you come here?" he asked of the prone Magicker. "You could not defeat me in your prime, what hope do you have now?"

Electricity crackled in the old man's hands. With a *boom*, it shot towards the Tsar. Cursing, her father thrust out a fist, and the bolt shattered into a thousand sparks. But the distraction had freed the old man from his power, and dropping lightly to the ground, the intruder hurled his blade at the Tsar.

Alana gasped as it flew for her father's face, her soul divided between hope and horror, but at the last second it halted mid-air. The Tsar stared at the blade a moment, his face darkening, then sent it spinning off into the corner with a flick of his finger.

Only a few feet separated the Magickers now, and they

stood facing each other, their twin blue eyes shimmering with unrestrained power. Neither was willing to give ground.

"You know I couldn't walk away," the old man said suddenly. "That I couldn't let you live, not after what you did."

Her father sighed. As he spread his hands, the power in his eyes faded. "What would you have me say, Eric? I cannot change the past. I am sorry your son had to die, but he had something I needed."

There was pain in the old man's eyes as he looked at Alana's father. "He was your *friend*," he said. "How could you do it?"

"My friend?" Her father seemed puzzled. "Yes, I suppose it might have looked that way. But no, Calybe was never my friend, no more than you or your sister were. You were *Gods*, Eric, compared to the rest of us mere mortals.

"You were *family*, Theo," the old man whispered.

"Family?" There was anger in the Tsar's voice now. "Maybe in name, but I was never *family* to you, never a part of your plans. Not like Calybe. No, I was just Theo, the magicless, the mortal, forever despised for my weakness."

"We loved you, Theo, Enala loved you," Eric replied. "How could you have betrayed her, betrayed us?"

"Betrayed you?" Her father shook his head. "All I have ever done is try to live up to your examples. I have sacrificed *everything* for the greater good. And I am so close now."

"If your idea of the greater good is locking away hundreds of innocent Magickers, I pity you," Eric replied.

The Tsar spread his hands. "Are you so blinded by hate, Eric, that you cannot see it? Surely even in your black cell, you have heard. For the first time in a thousand years, the Three Nations are truly at peace. There is no war, no great destruction between nations or Gods. Even the scourge of magic will soon be consigned to the pages of history."

"Except for your own," Eric said.

"No," the Tsar responded, "when I am done, not even my own power will remain. I will draw the magic from the land, so there will never again be Gods or Magickers to bring bloody slaughter to the Three Nations. Surely, you of all people understand the pain magic has brought to this world."

Eric laughed. "You must have truly lost your mind, Theo, if you think the genocide of Magickers will be the end of magic."

"Of course not." The Tsar smiled. "I have found another way, one that requires no more to die." His voice dropped a notch. "I am close, Eric, so close now. Your son's sacrifice will not be in vain—if only you could set aside your hatred, you would see it. With your help, we could finally rid this world of magic's curse."

"I will never help you, Theo. And I am done talking!"

With the words, Eric sent a lightning bolt arcing for her father. But the Tsar was ready, and his hands swept out to freeze the blue fire in place. The crackling of lightning hissed through the throne room as he sent it ricocheting backwards. Thunder crashed as it struck the old man in the chest and hurled him across the room.

"Very well, Eric." The Tsar's words boomed over the thunder as he advanced on the fallen man. "Then death it shall be."

He raised a hand, but before he could summon his magic, the sharp squeal of hinges carried across the room. The Tsar swung around, and Alana watched in shock as Quinn and a troop of Stalkers led Kellian and Devon inside.

Quinn paused in the entranceway as he saw the destruction the two Magickers had wrought on the throne room. The bodies of the guards still lay in scattered piles, and fire and lightning had left blackened scorch marks on the walls. In several places, the carpets and curtains were smouldering. Swallowing visibly, Quinn led his men between the bodies to where the Tsar stood.

"I found them trying to run, your majesty," he said. "Someone must have helped them and the old man escape their cell.

"Obviously," the Tsar answered. Turning, he smiled at the old man. "So after all this time, that was to be your final achievement, Eric? Your life thrown away as a distraction, so two mortals could escape me." He shook his head. "How low you have fallen, that you could not even do that."

35

Devon staggered to a stop in the entrance to the throne room and stared at the chaos within. He had seen battle Magickers in action during the civil war, but never before had he seen so much carnage in one setting. The men lying scattered across the marble floors had never known what hit them, and stomach surging, he forced himself to look away.

His heart sank as he saw the old man on his knees, the towering figure of the Tsar standing over him. He quickly averted his gaze, sensing that even to look into the ruler's eyes was to risk annihilation, and found Alana standing nearby. The breath caught in his throat, and he saw an awful sadness cross her face. Her lips parted, and for a moment it seemed she would speak.

"I had intended to interrogate you later, Devon, Kellian."

Devon swung around as the Tsar spoke from nearby, and froze as he found the man's face just a few inches from his own. Despite standing almost a foot taller, Devon took an involuntary step back. Fear flared in his chest and he longed for the feel of *kanker* in his hand. The hammer had broken the Tsar's enchantment on the bracelets—did that mean Enala was wrong, that the ancient weapon *could* defeat the man himself?

Seeing his fear, the Tsar laughed. "It is good to finally meet you, Devon," he said, advancing on him. Devon tried to retreat, but the Tsar's hand rose, and suddenly it felt as though a vice had closed around his neck. Choking, Devon clawed at his throat, but there was nothing there to dislodge.

"Thrice you have defied me," the Tsar continued, his eyes hardening. "But no longer."

Devon gasped as the invisible force hauled him into the air, the vice tightening. His legs kicked out, finding only empty space. Darkness swirled at the edges of his vision as he watched a cold smile spread across the ruler's face.

"I forgave you the first deviance, when you spurned my service. But the kidnapping of my son and daughter, the attempted escape, the freeing of a dangerous Magicker, these transgressions I cannot ignore."

The Tsar gave a contemptuous flick of his hand. A force like a stampeding horse struck Devon in the chest, driving the last breath from his lungs and sending him sprawling across the ground. He came to rest near the old man.

Beside him, Eric was struggling to his feet. Blue lightning crackled in his fingers, but the Tsar swung on him before it could be released.

"*Enough!*"

With the Tsar's roar, the lightning died in Eric's fingers. Now it was the old man's turn to rise ponderously from the ground. He hung, suspended there, as the Tsar turned his attention back to Devon.

"Before I kill you, hammerman, I would like to know

where my son is. I had thought the Northland Queen an intelligent woman, but now I learn she is sending assassins behind my back. Who knows what she might do with my dear Braidon."

Looking into the man's icy eyes, Devon's courage withered. A shudder swept through him, and he tried to look away, but he was trapped now. He was about to blurt out everything he knew about Enala and the Queen and Braidon, when the young boy's face flickered into his mind. He saw again the innocent smile, the sparkling intelligence behind his blue eyes, so like his father's. Yet that was all the two shared. In that moment, Devon knew he would do everything in his power to keep the boy from the Tsar.

Devon climbed to his feet. "He is safe from you, monster. I will not betray him."

"Devon..." Alana's voice came from behind him.

"You will tell me, hammerman," the Tsar interrupted.

With his words, he opened his hands, and a trickle of flame seeped from his fingers. Before Devon could throw himself back, they wrapped around his legs, burning through his leather leggings, searing his flesh. Pain unlike anything Devon had experienced rippled through his body, and he screamed. He tried to flee, to move, but the invisible force had him again, holding him to the fire.

As suddenly as the flames had begun, they died away. Cold spread down his legs, almost as painful, and Devon watched as his melted flesh knitted itself back together again. Sobbing despite himself, he slumped to his knees, tears streaming down his face. Soft footsteps approached.

"I will give you one last chance," the Tsar whispered. "Next time, I'll leave you a cripple."

His vision blurring, Devon looked up into the frigid eyes. "Go to hell!"

"I don't think that I will," the Tsar replied, smiling, "but you may go in my place."

He drew the sword at his waist. For half an instant, Devon thought he saw light flickering in the steel blade, but when he blinked, it had vanished. In its place, he saw his own haggard face reflected there, his unkempt beard and bloodshot eyes, the bruises and cuts. Still on his knees, he looked like a broken man. Looking up at the most powerful man in the Three Nations, he tried to find the strength to stand.

"I have always preferred the sword, you know," the Tsar said. He twirled the blade in his hand before pointing it down at Devon. "After all, that was all I had, in the beginning. The strength of my sword arm, the speed and quickness of my mind. I was like you, hammerman, a warrior born in a Magicker's world. It pleased me to see the magicless advance ahead of those like Quinn. I am afraid you will not live to see it, but one day soon, men like yourself will rule this world."

"You and I are nothing alike," Devon croaked, "I never wished to rule anyone."

The Tsar chuckled. "Yes, perhaps you are right. Watching you during the war, I thought you were a strong man. But you didn't have what it took. There was a weakness in you."

"How is it weakness to refuse to kill the innocent?"

"Innocent?" The Tsar seemed genuinely puzzled. "Were the Trolans innocent when they sent their soldiers into our lands, breaking the peace I had built so carefully? Were they innocent when they attacked our border towns, slaughtering hundreds?"

"You slaughtered *thousands!*" Devon spat.

"And saved tens of thousands," the Tsar said.

Anger fed strength to Devon's limbs. Despite the pain of his burns, he climbed slowly to his feet. "You're a coward," he snapped. "Men like you will always take the easy path, justify anything if it means you can hold onto power. But you're just like the Magickers you so despise, hiding behind your magic. If you truly wish to be mortal again, put *kanker* in my hands, and I'll show you what death feels like."

To his surprise, the Tsar laughed. "Ah, you do not disappoint, Devon!" he said. "And another time, I might have granted you your wish. But there is much to do now, and I have no time to play your games. Still though, I must thank you for your part in the excitement. It has been a long time since anyone put up such a fight."

Devon watched, unable to move, as the Tsar's sword rose, then arced towards his face.

"*No!*"

Suddenly Alana was between them, sword in hand. Steel rang out as the blades met, echoing loudly in the cavernous room.

36

Alana stared up at her father, the sword she'd taken from a fallen guard still vibrating from the deflected blow. Standing there, she could scarcely believe what she'd just done. She saw the same shock reflected in her father's eyes, but it quickly retreated, giving way to rage. His lips tightened.

"Daughter," he hissed. "Get out of my way."

"Alana, what are you doing?" Quinn's voice carried from across the hall.

Ignoring him, she turned the full force of her glare on the Tsar. She knew all it would take was an instant, a second's hesitation, and he would overwhelm her as he had before.

"I won't let you hurt him," she heard herself saying.

The Tsar shook his head. "It seems I underestimated your newfound weakness, daughter," he murmured. "Could it be you *care* for this fool?"

"It is not *weakness* to care for others," she replied, though her voice was wavering now.

"Is it not?" the Tsar asked. "Is that why these new-found friends of yours lie defeated around me? Why you find yourself standing alone?"

"It is a different kind of strength."

Her father laughed. "I see. Well, it will matter naught. I will burn it all from you, and start anew. Perhaps then I will finally have a daughter worthy of my empire."

Alana shivered, the sabre wavering in her hand. With his words, it felt as though a cold hand had reached into her chest and torn out her heart. Looking into his eyes, she could see the truth there, that he would not hesitate to obliterate her, to remake her in a fresh image.

As she had with the teacher, Krista.

"You have no right," she whispered.

"I have every right!" the Tsar boomed, his eyes shining with power. "I am your father, I am the Tsar. No soul lives within my realm except by my consent."

"I would rather die than live beneath your yoke."

"Alana, no!" Quinn called. She heard his footsteps approaching, but didn't dare look at him.

You should listen to your lover, Alana, the Tsar's voice spoke in her mind. *You think this one will want you, when he learns the truth?"*

"Stay out of my head!" Alana shrieked, staggering back from the words shrieking in her skull. But they only rose in volume.

You are mine, Alana! her father thundered. *You think you have the power to defy me?*

She felt a foreign presence enter her then, a darkness slithering into her body, wrapping around her thoughts, seeking out the most intimate corners of her mind. She stumbled back, dropping the sabre and clawing at her skull. And still the voice persisted.

You will not escape me this time.

"*Get out!*" she screamed again.

Somewhere within, her power responded. Surging up from the void, the green flames rushed to meet the Tsar's darkness. A dull *boom* sounded in the confines of her skull, and for a second her spirit soared, her soul swelling with the sudden retreat of her father's power.

But within an instant it pressed back, the darkness growing to dwarf her tiny flame, until it seemed she stood alone amidst the cosmos, with only a lantern to light the way. Even so, Alana clung on, holding to the green, as waves of black fought to sweep her away.

Then with a sudden popping sensation, the darkness vanished, the pressure relenting. Opening her eyes, Alana realised she had fallen to her knees. Her blade lay discarded alongside her, but she made no move to reach it. Looking up, she found her father towering over her.

"You are stronger than I thought, my daughter," the Tsar sighed. "But it will avail you nothing. I shall deal with you later."

He turned away then, exposing his back. Rage swept through Alana at his show of contempt, and clutching the blade, she launched herself at him. But again the blade struck empty air and ground to a halt. She sobbed in frustration as the invisible force held her back.

The Tsar looked back at her, a frown on his lips.

"Stay, daughter."

At his words, the sword in Alana's hand came alive. Tearing itself from her grip, the metal twisted back on itself and lifted into the air. Before she could react, it shot towards her, wrapping itself around her neck. She gasped as the cold steel enclosed her throat, the sharp edges biting into her flesh. Blood trickled across her skin as she staggered back, screaming her fury.

"And be silent," the Tsar added calmly.

Alana gasped as the sword contracted further, stealing away her voice and leaving her barely able to breath. She clawed at the metal, but it had hardened once more, becoming unmovable. Struggling to inhale, the strength slowly fled her legs, and she slumped to the ground, her vision spinning.

Above her, the Tsar turned to Devon. "Any last words, hero?"

Devon's eyes flashed as he stared at the man, jaw clenched, defiant. With a shrug, the Tsar raised his sword once more. Her vision fading, Alana watched in silent horror as her father prepared to strike down her friend.

Then, with a flash of silver, a blade came whirring through the air to bury itself in the Tsar's forearm.

Screaming, he stumbled back, his sword clattering uselessly to the marble floor. For a second, he stood staring down at the blood pumping from his arm, and the blade embedded in his wrist. Pain flashed across his face as he bared his teeth, his eyes sweeping the room in search of his assailant.

Alana stared in disbelief as a pale-faced Kellian surged to his feet and hurled another dagger. Forgotten by his captors, he had been left unconscious in the middle of the throne room while the Stalkers and Quinn encircled those still standing.

Blood was dripping from his forehead, and as the second blade left his hand, Kellian staggered, almost collapsing back to the ground. But his aim was true, and the blade hissed across the room at the Tsar. Only now the Tsar was expecting it, and with a cry of rage, the dagger froze a hair's breadth from his face. He grimaced, and the blade reversed its flight, rushing back to slam into Kellian's shoulder. The blow knocked the last strength from the innkeeper, and groaning he collapsed back to the ground.

Breath whistled between the Tsar's teeth as he tore the dagger from his wrist. He paused for a moment, staring at the wound. In an instant it had healed over, the flesh knitting itself back together as though it had never been torn.

Bloody dagger still in hand, the Tsar advanced on the innkeeper. "Kellian," he spat, unbridled rage in his eyes now. "Another soldier with such potential, another disappointment. Perhaps it was Devon's influence on you, but it no longer matters—you will join one another in death now."

Beside Alana, Devon had managed to regain his footing, but as he tried to follow the Tsar, he was brought up short by an invisible barrier. Crying out, he slammed his fists into it, but could go no further.

Kellian had managed to haul himself back to his knees. He looked up at the Tsar with open scorn. "Go ahead. You cannot change the truth. You are evil, and so long as good men stand against you, you'll never succeed."

"Then I had best kill all the good men, hadn't I?" the Tsar replied.

He surged forward, his dagger plunging into Kellian's stomach. Kellian reared back, a scream on his lips, but the Tsar caught him by the neck and dragged him forward, driving the dagger deeper.

"Happily, I'll start with you," he whispered, the words carrying to every corner of the throne room.

37

All was chaos as Braidon and Enala crept amidst the drifting smoke. Looking around, Braidon felt a sudden sense of déjà vu as a mirror image seemed to superimpose itself over the room. He saw himself, kneeling before the throne, the dark eyed Tsar towering over him, sword in hand. Then he blinked, and the image vanished, leaving only the awful sight of the Tsar plunging his dagger into Kellian's stomach.

In that moment, time seemed to stand still. Braidon stood frozen in place, still concealed by the magic pulsing around him, yet unable to act, unable to do anything but stare in open-mouthed horror as his friend collapsed to his knees. Rooted to the spot, he did nothing as the Tsar released the innkeeper and reached down to retrieve his sword, could do nothing but stare as the blade flashed down.

"*No!*" Braidon cried out as Kellian's body hit the ground, his scream muffled by the spell.

Tears streaked his cheeks as Braidon sank to his knees. In the corner, he glimpsed his sister on the ground, her fingers clawing weakly at what looked like a steel collar around her neck. Beyond her, Devon stood pounding at empty air, as though unable to take another step towards his friends. His impotent cries echoed around the room.

"We're too late, he whispered.

"No."

Enala strode past him, but she did not move against the Tsar. Her eyes were fixed on an old man who lay near the dais. He was on his side, eyes closed and face a paled grey, his breath coming in ragged gasps. Enala knelt beside him. His eyes flickered open as she gripped his hand.

"Eric..." she breathed, tears streaking her cheeks.

Concentrating, Braidon forced his magic to expand, engulfing the old man in his spell.

"Enala," the man whispered. The lines on his face deepened and his eyes took on a haunted look. "You should not have come here..."

"You were here all along..." Enala croaked, ignoring the old man's words. She shook her head, quickly wiping the tears from her cheeks. "I would have come long ago, if only I'd known..."

"Then you would have met the same end as me," he said.

Enala shook her head. "Why did you face him alone, Eric?" she whispered. "We could have taken him, together."

Eric seemed to have regained some of his strength now. He pushed himself up onto one arm, and reached out to grip her shoulder. "When I discovered the truth, I knew...I knew I couldn't do that to you. I thought I could spare you..."

"He was my responsibility," she said.

"He was all of our responsibility," Eric replied.

Enala swallowed. Her lips trembled for a moment, then

a fresh resolve came over her face. "Ours then," she said, tightening her grip on his shoulder. "It's time we ended this. Together?"

Eric sighed. "I'm afraid I have nothing left to give, sis."

Leaning forward, Enala embraced him. "Oh, Eric, what has he done to you?"

"He granted me a fate worse than death, ensuring I lived on long after my son passed from this world," he croaked. "You have no idea how many times I wished for death…"

"I would have come for you..." Enala repeated.

"I know." Eric forced a smile. "I'm glad you didn't. I'm glad you were free."

"Free and helpless," she sighed. "You have no idea the horrors he has wrought through the decades. I wish I knew where we went so wrong."

"You did nothing wrong, Enala," Eric replied sadly. "Somewhere along the path, he lost his way."

"Ay, but is it not a mother's job to lead her son back to the light?"

A chill spread down Braidon's back at her words. He stared at the two siblings in disbelief, but they only had eyes for each other. Silently, he tried to comprehend Enala's words. Could it possibly be true?

But that would mean…

"I need you, Eric," Enala said softly. "I cannot fight him alone."

"I have nothing left…" Eric began, but Enala silenced him by gripping him by the wrist. His eyes widened and he shook his head. "Don't, it's too dangerous. Not even Alastair–"

Eric's words were cut off as his head snapped back, his body suddenly going taut. Red light flashed between Enala's fingers, flowing into Eric's wrists, setting his veins aglow. An unholy fire seemed to light the air around them, and Braidon had to redouble his concentration on his own magic to keep them concealed from view.

Across the room, the Tsar was advancing on Devon. But a low keening from Eric drew Braidon's attention back to the siblings. For a second, Eric's eyes seemed to turn red—then Enala snatched back her hand, and the light died as quickly as it had begun. She slumped beside him, her breath coming in ragged wheezes. It seemed to Braidon the lines on her face had deepened, but after a moment she sat up and climbed back to her feet.

"Are you ready?" she asked her brother.

Nodding, Eric rose slowly. Braidon stared at the old man, shocked to see the wrinkles had faded from his face, his colour returning. He gave a sad smile as he looked at Enala.

"Thank you," he murmured. "Though you could have killed us both."

Enala chuckled. "I'm not still some green apprentice, Eric. I have spent two lifetimes mastering my power. I know what I'm doing. Now come, we have a job to do."

Together, the two Magickers turned to face the Tsar.

38

"No!"

The cry tore from Devon's lips as his friend collapsed, the Tsar's dagger embedded in his stomach. Jumping to his feet, he leapt towards his friend, but the invisible barrier brought him up short. Desperate, he pounded the empty air with his fists, yet even his immense strength could do nothing to pierce it. His eyes met Kellian's. His friend opened his mouth, as though to say something, but he never got to speak the words.

With a flash of silver, the sword in the Tsar's hand swept down. Devon screamed again, a wordless, toneless cry of grief and loss. Across the room, the *thud* of Kellian's lifeless body striking the ground seemed impossibly loud. Blood streamed from Devon's knuckles as he fought to reach the man who'd saved his life so many times before.

Standing over Kellian with bloody sword in hand, the Tsar smiled. Suddenly the barrier vanished, and almost losing his balance, Devon staggered forward. Fists clenched, he rushed to Kellian and dropped to his knees beside him.

But it was already far, far too late. Not even the Northern Earth Magickers could bring him back now. Choking, Devon clutched at Kellian's shirt, hauling him into his arms, overwhelmed. For half a decade they'd had each other's backs, from the very first battle in Brunei Pass. It would be difficult to find two more unlikely friends, yet the war had bound them together, blood brothers forever.

Except now Kellian was gone, his life expunged by the very man whose name they'd fought beneath all those years ago.

A shudder swept through Devon as he saw the Tsar watching him. "Bastard," he hissed.

The Tsar only shrugged, gesturing at the broken body with his sword. "Did you think this could end any other way, Devon?" he asked. "I am the Tsar. The power of five hundred Magickers courses through my veins. I will not be defeated, not by anyone."

Devon slowly climbed to his feet. "I'll kill you."

"You won't," The Tsar shook his head, as though the fact saddened him. "I cannot allow it. My work is not done yet."

"I'll tear you apart with my bare hands," he growled, stepping towards the ruler.

"Very well," the Tsar replied, and tossed his sword aside.

Before Devon could react, the man stepped in close, and a fist hammered into his forehead. Reeling back, Devon shifted his feet, widening his stance to ride with the blow. Then he straightened, surging forward. Blood pounded in his head, washing away the agony of his injuries, leaving only a single, cold-minded determination.

To destroy the man who had killed his friend.

As he charged, the Tsar side-stepped, moving far too quickly for a man three times Devon's age. A blow slammed into Devon's stomach, then another struck him in the jaw, lifting him from his feet.

Growling, he twisted, his own fist careening into the Tsar's forehead. Pain lashed his knuckles as the blow landed —it was as though he'd struck a stone wall. Even so, he followed with two more, smashing a right hook into the ruler's chest, then jaw.

In the past, such blows had shattered bones and left opponents unconscious on the floor. The Tsar only laughed. Stepping back, he wiped a streak of blood from his lip.

"Not bad," he said, "but I'm done playing now."

The Tsar surged forward. Raising his fists to defend himself, Devon managed to deflect the first blow, but agony flared down his arm as something in his wrist went *snap*. Casually, the Tsar battered aside the last of his defences, and slammed a blow into Devon's chest that hurled him backwards off his feet.

Striking the stone floor, Devon gasped, unable to breathe, his strength lost to him. The Tsar approached, the sword in his hand once more.

"It's been fun, Devon," he said, raising the blade, "but now it's time to die–"

A terrible *boom* interrupted his words, and the ground beneath Devon started to shake. A flash of light lit the throne room, followed by a *whoosh* of air and a sharp *pop*, as though the pressure in the chamber had just dropped several points.

Then blue and red fire rushed across the room to engulf the Tsar, and he vanished into the conflagration.

Eric came striding into sight, his sister Enala at his side. Arms outstretched, faces set, they unleashed their combined power against the Tsar. Lightning boomed and flames roared, causing Devon to scramble back, heat searing at his face.

Within the flickering red and blue, a dark shadow writhed, and it seemed to Devon that a soundless voice cried out. Watching the figure, hope surged through Devon. Surely, *surely*, not even the Tsar could survive such an attack? In the old tales, it had been Enala and Eric together who'd thrown back the might of Archon. What was a mortal such as the Tsar to the ancient Dark Magicker?

And still, the two siblings did not relent. Energy poured from them in an endless river, filling the throne room with the stench of burning. Devon saw Eric glance back, and glimpsed the sorrow in his cellmate's face. A sick sense of certainty struck him as he realised the Tsar was not defeated, only delayed. The look in Eric's eyes was a farewell, a plea for Devon to run and save himself.

Because Eric and Enala would not run. Neither would retreat from the Tsar, not this time.

Tears forming, Devon nodded back at the old man and clambered to his feet. Many of the Stalkers were down, caught in the initial explosion of magic. The rest had fallen back, giving Devon a chance to escape.

But as he turned, he saw there was still one left standing.

Quinn.

Anger rushed through Devon's chest. Silently, he started towards the man.

Quinn was staring at the spot where the Tsar had vanished, and did not see Devon's approach. He held *kanker* loosely at his side, and Devon's eyes settled on the weapon. He needed it back. With it, the foul Stalker would not stand a chance.

Slipping behind him, Devon strode forward, readying himself to tackle the Magicker. At the last second, however, his foot scraped against a fallen blade, sending it clattering across the floor. Quinn spun, but Devon was already hurling himself forward, and a straight left caught the lieutenant in the jaw, sending him reeling.

Devon followed after him, hammering a punch into his stomach, and then dragging him forward into a headbutt. The last blow dropped Quinn to his knees. *Kanker* slipped from his fingers, and Devon swept it up. Strength rushed back to his tired limbs as his hand closed around the black shaft.

Taking a breath, he looked down at Quinn. The man's eyes eyelids flickered and he groaned, but he made no attempt to rise. An awful desire rose in Devon, to slam his hammer into the man's face, to crush his skull and end the man forever. Every fibre of his being wanted it…but to do so would be a betrayal of Kellian's final wish: that Devon hold to the path of good. Murdering a defenceless man...as much as Quinn deserved it, Devon could not do it.

Devon quickly surveyed the ongoing battle. The conflagration had lessened, the last sparks of magic dying away from the hands of Eric and Enala. Both were pale now, their eyes suddenly weary, the lines on their faces deepening. It was clear they had given everything they had.

But it had not been enough. Where the Tsar had stood, a great bubble hung in the air, its surface opaque, swirling with the last remnants of the combined attack. Now it grew clearer, until it seemed a sphere of glass hung in the centre of the throne room. Within, the Tsar stood unmoved, his face tight and jaw clenched hard, but unharmed.

The last of Devon's hope fell away then. Looking at Eric and Enala, he considered joining them. Perhaps with *kanker* in hand, he might prove the difference…

He shook his head. If the power he'd just witnessed

could not kill the man, the spell imbued inside *kanker* would be overwhelmed in an instant. No, he needed to escape, to carry the fight on for another day. He could make no difference here.

Silently, he headed for the exit, but a voice, weak and in pain, brought him up short.

"Devon, help me, please."

Devon saw Alana on the floor then, the steel sword the Tsar had brought to life still wrapped tightly around her neck. She lay helpless amongst the chaos, her fingers gripped around the blade, blood streaming down her neck where the sharp edge had bit her.

His heart pounding hard in his chest, Devon watched her. Their eyes met, and he heard her silent beseechment, her pleas for his help. In a rush, he saw the night they'd spent in the spring south of Fort Fall, felt again the quiet companionship, the beginnings of...something, that had begun in his heart.

He stepped towards her, but another image came rushing forward before he could reach her. He saw again Alana in the bedroom of the citadel, her dark eyes filled with scorn, her laughter as she set Kellian against him with her magic. He heard again her words, her confession that everything he'd felt for her had been from some spell she'd cast over him.

And he saw Kellian falling, the dagger in his stomach, the Tsar's sword descending.

Hate rose to drown the warmth in his chest. An icy cold replaced it as he studied the helpless woman.

"No," he said, his voice trembling. "Help yourself."

39

Alana found herself sobbing as Devon strode from the throne room. She tried to summon the strength to call him back, to beg, to use her magic even, but her will had abandoned her. Gasping, she fumbled at the blade around her neck, seeking to bend it back, to allow herself a complete breath. It felt as though the life was slowly being strangled from her, each inhalation barely enough to keep her from blacking out.

Darkness swirled at the edges of her vision, threatening to engulf her. She fought it, knowing if it won she might never wake again. And that if she did, it would not be as herself. Her father had unlimited power now—even her own magic could be his if he wished. He would have no trouble tearing her fractured consciousness from her skull, and remaking her in his own twisted image.

It was why she had wiped her own memory in the first place, to keep him from seeking her out, from tracking her thoughts across the endless miles of the Empire.

Her mouth went dry at the thought of losing herself

again. Seeing the disgust in Devon's eyes, the full weight of her actions had come crashing down on her. With the Goddess's vision, her two personalities had merged, and while there was still a disjointedness about them, she knew now how wrong she'd been. She should never have used her power against Devon and Kellian, against her friends.

Krista's face swelled in her thoughts, and her guilt redoubled. The woman had been innocent, only wanting to defend her students from the brutal teachings of the Tsar's daughter. And Alana had washed her away for it, banishing her to a life with no memory, left her alone to wander the streets of Ardath in squalor.

Alana's hands fell from the blade. Her fingers were sticky with blood where the edge had cut them. She struggled for another breath, knowing that with one wrong movement, the blade would slice through the arteries in her neck. It would be over in moments. Swallowing, she closed her eyes.

You don't deserve to live.

A sob tore from Alana, but she couldn't bring herself to end it all. Screams came from all around, but there was no telling now who they belonged too. Smoke billowed across the throne room, lit by eerie flashes of lights. She sensed movement from somewhere, and rolling onto her side, she saw a figure emerge through the smoke. Quinn appeared, limping now, with a lump on his forehead already turning purple. His eyes had a slightly distracted look, as though he wasn't quite sure where he was, but they cleared when he saw her. Stumbling forward, he crouched beside her.

"Alana…are you okay?"

Alana saw the concern in his eyes, but also the suspicion. He knew now she had used her power against him. And he had seen her earlier, defying the Tsar, defending his rival.

Yet even so, they had known each other for decades, had been the closest of friends long before she'd taken him as a lover…

"Get me out of this, Quinn," she gasped, thinking quickly of a lie that would convince him she was on the Tsar's side again. "Please, the old Magicker, he helped free the girl, the *other* Alana, but I have her under control. My father needs my help!"

Seeing him dither, she drew on the memories of her crueller self.

"*Now!*" she snapped, with all the force she could muster.

He rocked back on his heels. "I'm not sure how…"

"Figure it out," she snapped. With the last of her strength, Alana pushed herself to a sitting position.

The hesitation left him and he closed his eyes. An electric tingling shot down Alana's spine as she sensed his magic building, though it was like a candle to the inferno of magic already bubbling around them. She shivered as a cold breath passed across her neck. Staring into his face, she saw his eyelids flickering, and prayed to the Goddess he knew what he was doing.

The temperature around her plummeted as a freezing wind whirled around her. Slowly it contracted, focusing in on her neck. Within seconds, her teeth were chattering, the metal burning where it touched her flesh. Her breath misted in the air as she wrapped her arms around herself, trying and failing to keep the heat from being sucked from her.

She began to sway where she sat, her skull aching with the change in temperature. Even the small breaths she took now no longer seemed enough, as though the air itself had been drained of oxygen. Her vision faded and all feeling had left her throat now. Pain flared in her chest, a desperate need to lurch upright, to gasp and cough and tear at the sword until she could breathe; but seeing the concentration etched across Quinn's face, she fought the instinct. She had no idea what he was doing, but she had to trust him, had to believe he knew what he was doing.

And if he failed, well, at least she would not become the monster her father wanted her to be.

Her final thought as the darkness rose to claim her was of her brother, running across the gardens, free.

QUINN COULD FEEL HIS MAGIC FADING QUICKLY, ITS ENERGIES burning low. He should have held back against Kellian and Devon earlier, but the two men had a habit of testing him. A habit he was glad had at least been halfway dealt with. If only he hadn't allowed Devon to take him by surprise, he might have finished the job.

His head still ached where the giant had struck him, and in truth he had been surprised to find himself alive a few minutes later, when the darkness had faded. After everything they'd been through that day, he would have killed the hammerman at the slightest opportunity. And with the loss of his friend, Devon had no reason to be offering mercy.

But then, Quinn supposed, the man was weak.

He forced his attention back to his magic, redoubling his efforts to draw the icy winds down from far above the citadel. The task required immense concentration to reach so far outside himself, almost to the bounds of his ability. Where Eric had found the howling winds that were now filling the throne room, Quinn didn't know, but apparently the ancient Magicker's abilities far exceeded his own. It was galling—though ultimately it would mean nothing.

The Tsar would kill him all the same.

Drawing the cold air miles down through the sky, and concentrating it on the sword around Alana's neck, was proving far harder than he had anticipated. The plan had come to him from nowhere, and without time to think, he had set it into motion. He still had no idea if it would work, and if he succeeded, whether Alana would survive the attempt.

Ice had begun to form on the steel blade. Before him, Alana swayed on her knees and started to fall. He caught her and hugged her to his chest, though the winds still flowed around her. She was cold to the touch, the skin around her face blue, her lips quickly turning grey. Her eyes flickered closed, and he knew she didn't have long.

Despite the confusing torment of the last few days, Quinn's heart clenched at the thought of losing her. His only consolation was that he would not be long in following her if he failed—the Tsar would not be pleased if he killed his daughter.

Remembering her rescue of Devon, Quinn felt a pang of jealousy. What was it about the man that inspired such devotion from those around him? And while the glint in Alana's eyes and anger in her voice earlier had been that of the girl he knew, Quinn still found himself wondering what was going on inside her mind…

But it was too late to turn back now. Alana's breathing had all but ceased, and with the sword still clenched around her throat, she was mere moments from death. She needed to breathe, fully and unconstrained. He gritted his teeth as the last drops of magic left him, the wind dying, leaving the ice-covered blade before him.

Lying Alana down, Quinn drew his dagger and held it up before her. He took a breath, readying himself, then brought its hilt down on the ice-encrusted blade with all his strength.

A sharp, shrieking *crack* followed as the frigid steel shattered. Quinn dropped the knife and pulled the broken shards from Alana's neck, cursing as the freezing metal bit his flesh. Throwing it aside, he placed his fingers to Alana's neck, searching for a pulse.

"Come on, Alana!" he whispered, but there was no movement beneath his fingers. Her skin was like ice.

Cursing, he placed his palm against her chest, the other over the top. Shifting so he was crouched over her, he pushed down with all his weight. Again and again he pounded her chest, settling into the rapid rhythm of a drumbeat. Alana's lifeless body jerked like a ragdoll with each compression, but still there were no signs of life.

"Come on!" he screamed.

Leaving the compressions, Quinn leaned over her, holding her nose and pressing his mouth to hers. He exhaled hard, watching her chest rise as his breath filled her lungs. Withdrawing, he waited half an instant to see if she would respond, then leaned in to start the whole manoeuvre again.

Alana jerked beneath him. Her eyes flickered open and she gasped in a fresh breath. Immediately, she started to cough. Quinn helped her onto her side as she groaned. Her tiny body shook beneath his hands as she sucked in great, life-restoring breaths.

When he was sure she was stable, Quinn sat back, his own heart pounding. Relieved of his task, exhaustion swept through him. For a moment, he felt overwhelmed, the terror and relief crashing together inside him. Without thinking, he rubbed Alana's back, feeling the warmth coming back into her body.

"Thank you."

He opened his eyes as she spoke, hearing the raw, unbridled emotion behind her words.

Nodding, he offered a smile. "It's good to have you back, Alana."

She lowered her eyes. Her lips were still blue, but the colour was rapidly returning to her face. An awful bruise and shallow cuts ringed her neck, but she was alive, and that was all that mattered. He reached out a hand and lifted her chin to look at him. Leaning in, he pressed his lips to hers.

For a moment she did nothing, and a trace of doubt entered him. He started to pull away, when suddenly she was kissing him back, hard and fast, her tongue darting out to meet his. Despite his exhaustion and his worry for her condition, he moaned, drawing her to him, feeling the icy touch of her skin against his. Her fingers were in his hair, but then she was pulling away, shaking her head. She looked up at him, her eyes filled with tears.

"I'm sorry, Quinn," she whispered.

"What–?"

Before Quinn could finish his sentence, her fingers tightened in his hair. He tried to jerk away, but a fiery heat rushed into his mind, a green light filling his inner-eye—then all was darkness.

40

Lightning streamed from Eric's fingers and rushed across the room, joining with his sister's flames to strike at the Tsar, only to shatter uselessly a few feet from their foe. Through the flickering blue and red, Eric watched him laughing, the protective barrier flashing with each impact. The Tsar's familiar blue eyes, so like his own, watched them, waiting for the attack to cease. The man knew they could not outlast him.

Already Eric could feel his strength fading, the energy Enala had poured into him consumed by the relentless assault. He fought on anyway, pushing himself beyond all limits, knowing he would soon be consuming his own life-force. He no longer hoped to defeat the man, only to stall him as long as they could, so that the others might escape and fight on another day. The future of the Three Nations no longer rested in their hands, but in those of Enala's grandchildren.

His heart warmed at the thought of them, and at the sight of his sister fighting alongside him. He'd given up hope long ago of ever seeing her again. It had been so long now, decades since Eric had set out upon learning of his son's murder. He hadn't known the truth then, that it was his nephew, Theo, who'd been behind it. In fact, it had been his nephew, the newly crowned king of Plorsea, who he'd turned to for help. The man had sent Eric on a wild goose chase. It had taken a long time for Eric to realise his mistake —and by then, it had already been too late.

Maybe Enala was right, maybe they could have defeated him together, even then. But knowing the agony it would have caused her, Eric had kept his sister in the dark. He hadn't realized how much magic Theo had consumed, how much he had learned and studied, readying himself for the moment Eric came for him.

His heart filled with rage, Eric had returned to Ardath to confront his son's killer. But in his arrogance, he had underestimated the man. After all, this was no Archon, with dark magic to rival the Gods. This was his magicless nephew Theo, who had grown up alongside his only son, who he and his wife Inken had helped to raise.

But when he'd reached the shores of Ardath, Theo had been waiting. And he was no longer the boy Eric had once known, but a master of a dozen magics. Eric had been humbled, his body broken, his magic shackled.

And the endless days of darkness had begun.

He would have preferred death. At least death would have been a release. While he had long outlived her, he knew Inken and their son waited for him somewhere out in the void. Through the long years, he had yearned to join them. Instead, time had crept by, marked only by the slow dwindling of his soul, the corruption of his magic, the withering of his body.

Now, he was far too weak to challenge the man.

But he would not be shackled again.

He glanced at Enala, seeing the strain on her face as she continued the fight. But her power was finite, and the little she'd given Eric had drained her as well. She would not last much longer.

She couldn't be here when the end came. Eric didn't want her to see what he would become, when he unleashed the darkness.

Slim though it was, there was still one possibility of defeating the Tsar now, one chance of striking through his shield and tearing the magic from the man.

If Eric unleashed the demon within.

"Enala!" he called over the raging magic.

She flicked him a look. The fire in her eyes was fading, the red giving way again to blue, and he saw the desperation there. He smiled, attempting to convey all his love and warmth in that one gesture, a final farewell. Surprise registered on her face, but he was already moving, not giving her a chance to respond.

"I'm sorry, sis," he whispered.

Lightning still streaming from one hand, he raised the other, and sent a blast of wind rushing across the room to catch Enala. It picked her up, almost gently, and carried her backwards to where her grandson waited. Collecting him as well, the wind threw them both from the throne room. The door slammed closed behind them, a breath of wind settling in to hold it shut.

Turning back to the Tsar, Eric saw they were alone but for the fallen. Devon and Alana were gone, the Tsar's soldiers and Stalkers lying in piles around the room. Silently, he sent a prayer up to Antonia that Devon would make it out of the citadel alive. In the chaos, there was a chance he could pass unnoticed out into the city.

Eric let out a long breath and lowered his arm, drawing the winds and lightning back to himself. Clenching his fists, he watched the flickering light dance across his skin, then begin to fade into his flesh itself. It was a trick he'd learned a long time ago, one few Magickers could replicate. When he was done, the winds and lightning had vanished, but he could sense them still, lurking within, in the void alongside his magic.

The Tsar moved forward, his leather boots carrying him lightly across the scorched marble.

"You don't think you've saved them, do you?" he asked.

Eric shrugged. "I can only hope."

The Tsar chuckled. "I would have thought you'd learned your lesson by now."

Smiling sadly, Eric shook his head. "It doesn't matter that I cannot defeat you, Theo," he replied. "I don't matter at all, not here, not now." Eric gestured around him. "A mortal has rebelled against you, and lived. Your own children have turned on you. How long do you think it will be before your people follow? Before they learn you are no true God?"

The Tsar sneered. "Then they will die."

"Ay, many will. But you stand alone. You cannot kill them all."

"Time will tell the truth of that, but you will not be around to see it, Eric," he snapped. "I am tired of your company. Goodbye."

The Tsar lifted a hand. Light, brilliant and blinding, shone through his clenched fingers. Eric could feel the magic building, the sheer scale of his power, collected from hundreds of Magickers around the building. It would burn him to ashes.

Eric summoned his own power in response. Its blue light

reared to life within him, the familiar wolf towering over his mind's eye. Eric stared up at it, recalling the terror he'd felt when it had first appeared. It seemed a thousand years ago now. These days the magic was almost like an old friend, the conflict between wolf and man a long played out game, more ritual than actual battle.

Until today.

As the wolf reared above him, Eric opened his arms, and offered his soul up to the beast.

And cried out as razor-sharp fangs tore into him, sinking deep into the dying light of his soul. In the darkness, Eric screamed as the magic encircled him, wrapping his soul in chains of fire. His terror swelled, granting new strength to the beast. Triumphant, it hurled him screaming into the depths of his consciousness.

Back in the throne room, Eric's eyes slid open. Only it was no longer Eric who looked out, but the magic.

"Freedom," the demon whispered, its voice distorted, metallic.

A dark smile twisted its lips as black eyes swept the room, settling on the man standing across from it. Sensing the unbridled power radiating from the clenched fist, the demon hesitated.

"You fool," the man whispered.

Energy crackled in the demon's fists as it faced the man. The magic within it was weak, exhausted by the foolish human. Yet there were other energies to draw on, it knew. The human's lifeforce was still a burning beacon within, a brilliant white against the void. And its former master no longer had any use for such a power.

Cackling, it drew the blue flames of its magic around the white. An awful scream sounded from somewhere deep inside its mind. The blue flames swelled, then roared back to life, the white igniting like wood on a bonfire.

In the throne room, lightning boomed. Gathering in the demon's hands, it doubled, then redoubled in size, the heat of its power washing across the marble surroundings. Bolts shot off around the room, wind swirling inwards to join it, converging on the demon.

Across the room, the man who stood against it cursed and threw out his hand. The power in his fist responded, forming a glowing beam of white. But as the white energies lanced towards it, the demon leapt into the air, and the power slashed harmlessly past. Lightning, more powerful than any its human master could summon, rippled out to hammer into its foe.

The demon grinned as the man staggered back, but to its surprise, he did not go down. Light swirled again in his hands, and the demon hissed as another flash of power slashed at it. Too slow this time, it cried out as the gathered energies of the Light struck its human body, hurling it through the air.

Hissing, the demon recovered. Around it, a maelstrom of wind and rain and lightning gathered as it swung around, searching for its foe. But the man had vanished.

The very air bursting with the gathered energies of the Sky, the demon scanned its surroundings, cursing the Light Magicker for concealing himself from sight. But it would avail the man little. Standing still, the demon threw out its arms, sending a blast of air rushing outward. Stones and tiles and bodies were lifted from the ground, filling the air with a million projectiles.

A cry came from its left, and spinning, the demon sent a flash of lightning at the man who had just appeared behind it. The bolt lanced towards him, but, impossibly, the earth shifted suddenly, a patch of marble rushing up to deflect the blow.

A rumbling began beneath the demon's feet, seconds before the marble stone split open, tearing the floor asunder. The demon leapt into the air, summoning the wind to carry it clear, but before it could escape, another force struck it like an invisible hammer from above. It dropped back towards the gaping fissure.

Rage surged in the demon's chest as it fought against the inexorable force. The human's power was awesome, but unbridled by human fears and limits, the demon would not be defied. Throwing out its arms, the demon sent lightning rushing outwards, filling the room with crackling blue fire.

This time the demon's attack found its mark. Crying out, the human staggered away, and the ground snapped closed once more. The invisible force surrounding the demon dissipated. Floating free, it drifted towards where the man had fallen. He had vanished again now, but the human could not have gone far.

With a roar, the man reappeared to the demon's left. Face mottled red, blue eyes defiant, he threw his arms together. Around the room, the swirling debris halted mid-air as a new force took possession of it. With a hiss, it reversed its track, and rushed inwards at the demon.

Moving with impossible speed, the demon ducked and twisted between the projectiles, but it could not avoid them all. A chunk of marble struck it in the face, shattering bone and splitting flesh, but there was no pain. The magic ruled now—the body was nothing but armour to host its spirit.

The demon regathered its spent lightning, forming a flaming wall of blue around itself to consume any projectile that came near. Then its consciousness soared skywards, seeking out the frozen air currents far above and drawing them down. The temperature plummeted as the icy winds filled the throne room. It might be immune to mortal frailties, but its foe was not.

But in the centre of the room, the man seemed to have given up all interest in fleeing. Flames lit his hands, sweeping outwards to cast aside the cold. Then, to the demon's shock, the wind was torn from its control. Raising his hands, the man sent the winds rushing through the flames, drawing them high to the ceiling before sending them swirling at the demon.

The demon fell back before the flaming vortex. The flames roared and gave chase, even the marble weeping before their heat. Fear touched the demon then, as it sought to understand the man's mastery of all Three Elements. Such a feat was not possible, not even for the Gods. What manner of man was this?

And while mere injuries did not concern it, if the flames consumed its mortal body, the demon too would perish.

Crying out in frustration, the demon sought to reassert its power over the winds, but its energies were burning low now, the last of its host's lifeforce flickering out. All these years the demon had waited for its chance, seeking the moment when it could seize control, to cast aside its master. So many years imprisoned, its power wasted by the cruel human who ruled it, unable to fly free.

Now, in its moment of triumph, it was about to be destroyed.

Rage flickered in the demon's chest as it drew on the last reserves of its strength. A single ball of lightning coalesced before it. Power crackled as the firestorm approached, its heat washing over the demon. Still, it stood its ground. Screaming, it pointed a finger at its foe. The burning ball of lightning rushed forward, tearing through the flames.

Across the room, a voice cried out, and with a sudden *whoosh,* the flames died, the winds dissipating instantly. The demon stared in shock as the smoke cleared, revealing its foe down on one knee, gasping for breath. A black scorch marked his tunic, and his face had paled, but it was clear the man still lived.

Without any magic left to spend, the demon started towards the human. Its eyes caught the glint of a sword lying nearby, and it quickly diverted towards it. Unlike the other weapons in the room, the sword remained intact, its blade somehow untouched by the energies that had melted marble and warped lesser metals. The demon collected the blade and approached the kneeling man.

The man looked up as the demon approached, his mouth wide. "Foul creature," he gasped. "That Eric would stoop to this." He shook his head and stumbled to his feet. "Well, you won't defeat me."

The demon laughed. "You have nothing left to give, mortal," it whispered. Closing on the man, it raised the sword.

A smile twitched on the man's lips. "Ay, but you picked the wrong sword, demon."

Before the demon could strike, the man flicked his fingers. A sudden light burst from the blade in the demon's hand, more brilliant than any it had seen before. The energies burned at it, scorching its already beaten body, lashing out at the spirit within. Hissing, it tossed the weapon aside.

Quick as lightning, the man darted forward and snatched the weapon from the air. Energy crackled as the man grinned, his eyes ablaze with renewed power.

The demon stood in shock, staring at the terrible blade in the man's hand. With his touch, the sword had swelled with light, filling the room, so that it seemed the very air itself were aflame. Sensing the power radiating from it, an awful fear lit in the demon's chest, as somewhere deep within a voice cried out, a memory of its past rising to the surface.

The Sword of Light.

As the realisation came to it, the man pointed the sword. And with a flash of light, the demon died.

41

"No!"

Enala's screams echoed down the corridor as she threw herself at the door, pounding her fists against the polished wood. But the wind still howled on the other side, barring their passage back, sealing Eric within.

"Enala," Braidon said gently.

Stepping forward, he caught the old woman by the hand. She froze at his touch, but he could still feel the tension in her wiry limb, her desperation to save her brother. "Enala, you have to let him go. It's what he wants."

Trembling, Enala turned to look at him. He flinched from the despair in her eyes, the terrible grief. Tears streamed down her withered cheeks. "I only just got him back," she whispered.

He gave her shoulder a squeeze and pulled her into a hug. "He knows what he's doing," he said. "Let's not make his sacrifice in vain. Come on, Dahniul is this way."

She stared at him a moment longer, then sighed. "You heard what was said in there, about the Tsar?"

Braidon hesitated, then nodded. Enala smiled, pulling him into a hug of her own. "Whatever happens with your father and sister, I am proud of you, Braidon. I know Gabriel, your grandfather, would be as well. You have his spirit, his courage."

Braidon's eyes stung at her words and he blinked back tears. "We don't have much time," he said quickly, starting away so she wouldn't see the tears on his cheeks. "I can feel my power fading. Dahniul won't stay hidden forever."

Enala said nothing, but after a moment he heard her footsteps following. Taking the lead, he led them through the winding corridors, taking each turn by instinct, drawing on memories that still lingered just beyond reach.

He shivered as he realised he was leaving Alana behind again. He had glimpsed her only briefly in the throne room. Amidst the chaos, he hadn't noticed her lying in the corner, not until she had staggered to her feet, blood streaming down her neck. He had wanted to go to her, but the swirling vortex of magic had cut them off. She had fled through a set of double doors on the other side of the room without ever knowing he was there.

Silently, he prayed she had escaped. In the brief moments he'd seen her, it had been impossible to tell whether she was still the sister he remembered, or... someone else. Yet something in his soul told Braidon his sibling still lived. He couldn't for a moment believe that woman had been sponged, lost to him forever.

Shivering, Braidon forced his thoughts back to the present. Somewhere in the citadel, Devon and Alana were both at large, but it would be him the Tsar came for first. And Eric's interference had left them only one path to take—up.

In his mind, he called out to Dahniul, hoping the giant

dragon would hear him, that his magic was still casting a protective net over the beast, concealing it from the eyes of the soldiers. It would only take a single flaw in his spell, one glimpse from the guards to send Magickers and Red Dragons after their only ally left standing. And powerful as Dahniul was, even she could not survive against such odds.

Hurry, Braidon!

The dragon's voice was barely audible in his mind, but he felt a thrill of triumph. He glanced at Enala, but her eyes were distant, her movements automatic as she followed Braidon. She wore her grief like a lead blanket, but there was no more time left to comfort her. Within, the last trickles of his magic were fading. They only had minutes before the dragon was discovered.

Footsteps pounded ahead of them. Grabbing Enala, Braidon pressed them up against the wall of the corridor. He held his breath as a troop of guards rushed past, their weapons drawn, eyes fixed straight ahead. Thankfully, not a single one noticed the blurring of air beside them, the slight flicker of movement.

When the men had passed, Braidon led Enala around the next corner and up a twisting stone staircase. Enala was struggling now, her face ashen, her hair hanging in scorched clumps across her face. The battle with the Tsar had cost her dearly, and Braidon wished there was something he could do for her. She had given some of her energy to Eric before the battle…but Braidon didn't even know where he would begin with such a feat. And besides, he had little left to give as it was.

Braidon slowed as they approached the top of the stairwell. Ahead, daylight beckoned, but as Braidon listened he heard the soft whisper of voices from above. It only took one look at Enala's face to know she wasn't up for a fight.

He considered taking the sword from her and tackling whoever it was, but he would be no match for even one trained soldier.

There was no choice for it. They would have to risk his weakening magic in the daylight atop the walls. Silently, Braidon checked the concealment with his mind, sensing the holes appearing but knowing he no longer had the power to fill them. Then he took Enala by the hand, and led her up the last of the stairs.

Emerging into the sunlight, Braidon swallowed when he saw a troop of soldiers lurking nearby, their eyes watchful, hands clenched around their weapons. They stood atop the stairwell, scanning the ramparts and skies around them. Clearly, the explosions from the citadel had them on high alert.

Braidon shivered as Dahniul reared up behind the guards, giant jaws spread wide. The spell still clung to the creature, but like their own it was fading, causing the air to shimmer where the dragon sat crouched atop the walls.

Shall I kill them? Dahniul's voice echoed in their minds.

Braidon looked at the gathered men, remembering the horror that had unfolded in the throne room below, and quickly shook his head. These men were only serving their country, doing their duty. It was not their fault the Tsar had become a monster. He would not kill them if he could help it.

Moving quickly across the ramparts, Braidon breathed a sigh of relief as the men's eyes slid over them, unseeing. Reaching Dahniul's side, Braidon started to climb on to her back. A low rumble came from her chest as he settled into place, and the head of one of the men jerked up.

Braidon shivered as the man looked directly at them. A

frown creased the man's forehead as he took a hesitant step towards the hidden dragon.

Dahniul shifted beneath him, manoeuvring herself to strike the man.

Not yet!

Braidon sent out a desperate plea, and she stilled. Perching himself on her back, Braidon reached down, offering Enala a hand. Silently she sat behind him, too tired to even take her usual position as rider. Braidon's spirits fell as he sensed her despair.

He glanced back at the guard. His stomach clenched as he saw that the man was still approaching. It was obvious he had noticed something, but with the magic still clinging to Dahniul, he still couldn't figure out what it was. They had to be out of range of bow or magic before that realisation came.

Go! Braidon screamed in his mind.

Dahniul shifted towards the edge, her claws scraping loudly against the stone blocks. The hackles on Braidon's neck rose as someone shouted behind them. He risked a look back, and saw the man drawing his sword, the other guards rushing to join him. Crossbows bristled, pointing in their general direction. Then, Braidon's stomach lifted into his chest as Dahniul dove from the edge of the wall.

Letting out a wild scream, he watched the ground rush towards them, the three-pronged spire of a nearby temple seeming to point directly for his heart. Then with a great flap of Dahniul's wings, their descent halted. Another *thump*, and they went rushing upwards.

Crossbows *twanged* behind them as they rose above the ramparts, and Braidon turned in time to see steel arrows slash the sky. Roaring, Dahniul twisted, almost dislodging Braidon from his seat, but the bolts hissed harmlessly past.

Below the men were already reloading, and Braidon realised his magic had abandoned him.

Rising higher, Dahniul swung towards the lake surrounding the island. The men of the citadel were behind them now, but ahead, the outer walls of the city were approaching rapidly. Maybe they could make it after all...

Then Braidon cursed as he realised they weren't yet high enough to avoid the great longbows being hefted by the guards. As he watched, one drew back his string and sent an arrow arcing towards them.

Dahniul turned again, and it flew harmlessly past, but already others were taking aim. Soon, the air would be thick with arrows. Dahniul couldn't avoid them all, and while she was protected by thick scales, her riders were not.

Braidon glanced back, and was shocked to see Enala slumped against the dragon's back. Her skin was so pale he could see the thin blue lines of her veins on her hands, and she was barely holding on. He swallowed and turned his attention back towards their escape.

Turn back, he said silently to the dragon. They needed to gain more height before passing the outer walls. It would bring them over the citadel again, but with the guards there armed with only crossbows, Braidon prayed the dragon would be beyond their range. So long as there were no Magickers waiting now...

Dahniul's wings swept down as she circled back, each wingbeat carrying them ever higher. He could see men gathering on the walls below, pointing in silent frustration, like ants below them. Braidon smiled; then felt the air shifting around them, heard the dragon's wings creak as a blast of wind struck them. Sensing the magic in the wind, Braidon clung to the dragon's scales as the gale tried to tear them from the dragon's back. Fear for Enala filled him, but in that moment there was nothing he could do for her.

Time to try for the walls, I think, came Dahniul's voice.

Braidon nodded, his eyes watering with the cold. All he could do was cling on as the dragon fought to break through the Magicker's winds. He prayed to the Gods that Enala was doing the same.

Then with a roar, Dahniul shot for the outer walls. The move caught the soldiers below by surprise, and they were on them before the first arrow rose to greet them. It made a sharp *crack* as it struck Dahniul's breast, but bounced harmlessly away. Braidon ducked low, knowing there was little else he could do. The hiss of arrows filled the air, and he heard the dragon snarl as one sliced through the soft skin of her wings, but she flew on.

Then the air was silent once more. Sitting up, Braidon saw they had made it past the city, past the walls. The cliffs of the island were already falling away, the glistening waters of Lake Ardath spreading out all around. Braidon shivered as the island shrank into the distance.

Beneath him, Dahniul powered onwards, her great wings carrying them rapidly across the lake. Soon, the water below turned to open fields, a single river winding its way through their expanse. Ahead, the dark trees of a forest approached. Behind, Ardath became a speck of black amidst the silent blue.

Yet as he watched the distant city, it seemed to Braidon that it shimmered, and a light appeared on the walls atop the citadel. He squinted, trying to make out what it was, what was happening. The light grew stronger, its intensity swelling until it blotted out the city.

No... he realised, icy fear turning his limbs to lead. *No... it's coming closer!*

"Dahniul!" he screamed, but it was already too late.

With a *boom* that seemed to come from all around them, the light came boiling up to meet them. Braidon cried out as it struck, an awful *shriek* filling his ears, a searing heat, a swirl of colours blinding him. He screamed as the dragon lurched beneath him, losing his grip on the golden scales.

Then he was falling, plummeting down, and an ocean of green was rising up to greet him…

EPILOGUE

Quinn's legs trembled as he approached the ruined throne, his mind whirring, struggling to come up with some excuse, some justification that would save him. But in the awful silence that had swallowed the throne room, his thoughts had gone blank, and with a growing sense of despair, he sank to his knees before the dais. Hours had passed since the confrontation with Eric, but there was still no sign of the fugitives.

The Tsar towered over Quinn, his once magnificent doublet and leggings now scorched and torn. His eyes were dark as he looked on the lieutenant, giving away nothing of his inner thoughts. A slight twitch to his lips was the only sign of his displeasure.

"Well?"

The sudden break in the silence made Quinn jump, though the Tsar had barely spoken louder than a whisper. A vice clamped around his chest as he struggled to find the words to reply. With painstaking slowness, he unclenched his jaw and swallowed the lump in his throat.

"She was dying." Once the words were out of his mouth, Quinn realised they were the only argument that might work. "She was choking, bleeding to death. I feared she would die before you finished dealing with the intruders..."

His voice trailed off beneath the withering stare of the Tsar.

"Is that all?"

Quinn gulped. "I...I..." He clenched his eyes shut, and bowed his head. "I'm sorry, sir. I failed you. I let your daughter escape. I am prepared to accept my fate."

Despite his words, Quinn flinched as the soft rasp of steel against leather announced the unsheathing of the Tsar's sword. A cold draught slithered down his spine as footsteps padded down the half-melted steps, finally coming to a halt beside him.

"It is I who failed, Quinn," the Tsar's voice came from overhead, touched now with unmistakable sadness. Quinn looked up in surprise, his heart palpitating as the monarch continued. "I should have dealt with Eric long ago, should have known Enala still lived, that she would come for them when she realised what I'd done."

"What did you do?" Quinn whispered, hardly daring to breathe.

The Tsar lifted his sword into the air, and a brilliant white lit the blade. "I did what every Magicker since the fall of Archon has failed to do. I recreated the spell that brought the Gods into the physical realm."

"*How?*"

A smile crossed the Tsar's lips. "It cost me greatly, but we managed it, Eric's son and I. Fool that he was, Calybe volunteered to be the host. We both came from the right lineage, but I guess he took after his father. Eric always was the type for self-sacrifice. Even at the end…" He shook his head, as though to dismiss the memory of the old man, before going on: "We cast the spell, and let the spirit of Darius enter Calybe. Together, we brought the God of Light back to life."

Quinn looked around quickly, as though the reincarnation of Darius might suddenly appear before them. Then his eyes were drawn inexorably back to the sword in the Tsar's hand. It was the same blade the intruder, Godrin, had tried to wield. Merely touching it had crystallised the man. It couldn't be, and yet…

"But the God of Light…where?"

"Here." The Tsar smirked, gesturing to the sword. "That was Calybe's mistake. He thought we could only find peace by bringing back the Gods. But it was quite the opposite."

"But the Gods–" Quinn began.

"Were parasites," the Tsar interrupted, "using their powers to manipulate us, to rule us. They were no different from any other Magicker who has sought to rule us throughout the centuries. No, there is only one way to buy peace—by wiping every last trace of magic from our world. I *knew* I could do it, if only I could recreate the Sword of Light. So when the God of Light possessed Calybe, I was ready. Darius barely had a chance to breathe fresh air, before I plunged my sword between his shoulders, and used the spells I had perfected through the years to send his foul spirit screaming into the blade."

"Then…that truly is…the Sword of Light?"

"Yes." The Tsar smiled faintly. "But though I have spent decades studying its power, still I have failed to achieve my goal."

His shoulders slumped, and he sank to the bottom step

with a soft *thud.* In that moment, Quinn had never seen the Tsar look so mortal. His knees beginning to ache, he sat up slowly, sensing there was more behind the man's words. When he spoke, he picked his words carefully, still half-afraid of incurring his ruler's wrath.

"But…?"

The Tsar did not respond. Then he started to laugh, softly at first but quickly growing louder, until it seemed the walls themselves were trembling. Quinn shrank back as the Tsar stood.

"My children have abandoned me, betrayed everything I stand for. I can no longer ignore their transgressions. For years I searched for another way. With Eric, perhaps it would have been possible. But now I am left with no choice." He looked at Quinn, his eyes aglow. "Bring me my children, Stalker. They are the key to all this. Willingly or not, they *will* serve me in my final purpose."

For a second, Quinn hesitated, thinking of the girl he'd helped raise, who he'd taught and trained and spent long nights entwined with. Then he remembered how she'd used her magic against him, how she had betrayed him again and again. And he knew that he too could no longer ignore the truth. The Alana he yearned for was lost to him.

He bowed his head. "It shall be as you command, sir."

HERE ENDS BOOK TWO OF
THE LEGEND OF THE GODS

Continue the adventure in…
Dawn of War

NEW YORK TIMES BESTSELLING AUTHOR

AARON HODGES

DAWN OF WAR

LEGEND OF THE GODS BOOK THREE

PROLOGUE

Merydith sighed as she entered her bedchamber and swung the door shut behind her. A *thud* followed as the latch caught in the frame, preventing the door from closing. Cursing, she swung back and lifted it more carefully, allowing it to click into place. The faint whisper of laughter from her guards carried through the thick wood. She resolved to have Damyn put them on double shifts for the next few days, but as she turned her back on the door, her exhaustion returned, and the thought drifted away.

The leather sofa beckoned. Staggering across the room, she toppled onto the cushions. She groaned and closed her eyes, giving in to the call of sleep—until the thought of all she had left to do intruded on her peace. Cursing again, she sat back up.

Her quarters had been cleaned while she'd been busy trudging up and down the long corridors of Erachill. Sparsely furnished, the polished walls were mostly of granite, though in places veins of silver streaked the surface. Her room was deep within the mountain city, and there were no windows, but an adjoining chamber led to her washroom. Other than the sofa, her only furniture was a small dining table she used to break her fast, and the double bed in the corner.

The room would no doubt send a southern queen into a fit, but it was all Merydith needed. Indeed, it was far more than her ancestors had enjoyed in the dark days of the past.

Her gaze lingered on the freshly-made bed, but the stench of her unwashed body hung around her like a cloud, and rising, she crossed to the washroom. A smile tugged at her lips as she saw the tub had recently been filled with hot water. Stripping off her long cotton and fur *del*, she lowered herself into the bath.

She sighed as warmth enveloped her, banishing memories of the cold winter draughts that whispered through the tunnels of Erachill. Winter had finally arrived in Northland, and it showed no sign of relenting. Its icy hands would hamper her efforts to muster a defence for their border, but the snows would also slow the enemy, should the Tsar decide to advance.

But then, her enemy's forces were legion, his magic unmatched, and nothing was certain. The man controlled more power than any mortal had a right to.

She and Enala had spoken of the matter many times, about whether her people might find a way to mimic him, but not even Enala's century of wisdom knew how the Tsar had gained such power. So Merydith and her people would face him alone, and pray to the Gods they could match him.

Lying in the hot waters, Merydith's thoughts turned to the old woman. Silently, she wondered where her mentor was now. Enala had been in Merydith's life since before she could remember. After her mother's death, the old priest had become like a third parent to Merydith. But now she needed the woman more than ever, Enala had left, abandoning Northland in the time of its greatest need.

No, Merydith reminded herself, *she has not abandoned us.*

Despite the heat, Merydith shivered, thinking of Enala and Braidon as she'd last seen them, on the back of the Gold Dragon. They had flown off alone, intent on bringing the fight to the Tsar, on ending his darkness before it could spread beyond the reach of the Three Nations.

No, Enala had not abandoned them. The old woman had placed her trust in Merydith, in the girl she had raised to be Queen, to defend the Northland territories as Enala had since the dark days of Archon.

Merydith was determined not to let her down, and yet…she still longed for the old woman's comforting presence, to know she was there should everything fall apart. Instead, there was only Merydith, only the Queen. If she fell, Northland would fall with her.

She had delivered her message to the Tsar's emissaries the night after Braidon and Enala had left, refusing their request to return the boy. The decision still surprised even her—after all, Braidon was the Tsar's own son, though he retained no memory of his past. Yet Enala had been right: Braidon was innocent, and son of the Tsar or not, she could not turn him over to that madman.

The Tsar's people had told her to expect an answer within the day, though they had not mentioned how they planned to communicate her message so quickly across the hundreds of leagues between Erachill and the southern capital of Ardath.

Now, two full days later, she was still waiting for their response. The five southern emissaries had all but vanished, retreating to their quarters. Merydith allowed the faintest of hopes to enter her heart. Could Enala and Braidon's plan have worked? Could they have found a way past the Tsar's defences, and finally put an end to his tyrannical rule?

Merydith quickly quashed the thought. Others could envisage such daydreams, but the fate of Northland rested on her shoulders. She could not afford to indulge in such fantasies. No, until proof of the Tsar's death was placed before her, she needed to prepare as though the man still lived, as though he were planning to march on Northland within the month.

Because in all likelihood, that was the truth.

Rising from the cooling waters, Merydith took a cotton towel from its hook and wrapped it around her body. She wound her long auburn hair in another towel, then wandered out into her bedchamber. A silver mirror hung on the wall above her bed, but she hardly spared it a glimpsed. She didn't need the mirror to remind her of the grey streaks in her hair, nor the faint lines that had appeared around her eyes. At forty-five, she was fitter than most men in their thirties, but even her iron determination could not turn back the slow advance of time.

She started as a knock came from her door. Scowling, Merydith glanced at the wooden panels, wondering who would disturb her at such a late hour. Sleep was beckoning once more, and loath to deny it. She was about to tell them to go away when the knock came again. Grating her teeth, she considered finding something to wear, then decided otherwise.

"Whoever it is, tell them come back in the morning," she called out.

"It's Damyn, your majesty," one of her guards called back. "He says it's urgent."

Merydith closed her eyes and begged the Gods for patience. Damyn was her most trusted advisor and oldest friend, and while he had a habit of overstepping his bounds, even he would not have come to her so late if the matter wasn't truly pressing.

"Send him in," she called back, lifting the latch to unlock the door and then returning to the sofa.

The door creaked as Damyn entered, followed by the click of the latch as he closed it behind him again. He looked as exhausted as she felt as he crossed the room. His black hair was still unwashed, his forty years of age showing in the silver streaks around his temple and the wrinkles across his brow. Shadows ringed his brown eyes, and he grimaced as he looked at her.

"Damyn, what is it?" she asked, sitting up straighter.

Damyn paused when he saw her state of undress, though they had seen each other naked many times while swimming in the mountain rivers as youth. He raised an eyebrow, and she scowled.

"I was just finishing my bath," Merydith replied to his questioning look. She gestured to the space on the sofa beside her. "Now sit down and tell me what's happened."

He nodded and sat, though she noticed there was a distracted look to the way he averted his eyes. "It's Joel, the Tsar's emissary," he said, dispensing with the niceties. "He…he wishes to see you."

Though she kept her expression unchanged, Merydith cursed inwardly. Joel was the Tsar's head ambassador. If he was ready to talk, it meant they had received a reply from the Tsar. Which meant Enala and Braidon had failed…

"He can wait until morning," she replied, her voice hoarse.

"He wants to see you now."

She cast a glare in his direction. "I am the Queen here," she snapped. "Their demands can wait."

Damyn nodded, though the uncertainty remained in his eyes.

Merydith sighed. "Was there something else, Damyn?"

He cleared his throat, obviously uncomfortable. "It's just…he followed me here, Your Majesty."

Merydith closed her eyes in exasperation. "Of course he did." Sucking in a lungful of air, she looked at her companion and shook her head. "It's okay, Damyn. I guess the Tsar's ambassador is not used to being told no." She smiled. "But you will give him my message anyway. With the point of your sword, if needs be."

Damyn grinned at that. His hand drifted to the hilt of the sabre he wore at his side. "It will be as you say, Your Majesty."

Rising, he crossed to the double doors and tugged them open. Before he could step outside, a shadow flickered in the doorway, and a slender man slipped inside. Wearing a sickly smile on his pale face, he sidestepped the startled Damyn. Merydith rose smoothly to her feet as Joel slid towards her, his movements almost snakelike.

"Your Majesty, so nice of you to see me at this late hour," he said smoothly.

"Get out," she snarled, pointing a finger at the door. "Before I have my guards drag you to the dungeons."

The man smiled in the face of her rage. Coming to a stop a few feet away, he spread his hands. "My apologies, Your Majesty," he said as Damyn moved alongside him, eyes narrowed. "But my message could not wait. The Tsar was most displeased with your news regarding his son."

"What message could you possibly have that could not wait until morning?" she snapped.

The smile faded from Joel's face. "Death."

Before Merydith or Damyn could react, a dagger

appeared in the man's hand. Caught off guard, Merydith gasped as he lunged forward, the steel blade flashing for her throat. Beside the emissary, Damyn shouted, his hand snaking out to catch the southerner's cloak. But the assassin was already too close.

Reacting with the instincts of a thousand childhood drills, Merydith spun on her heel, twisting into a fighting stance—even as her hand whipped down to strike his wrist. She gasped as fire sliced across her thigh, but she had managed to deflect the dagger from a killing blow.

Her other hand caught her assailant by the arm. Twisting into her attack, she slid her shoulder beneath his arm. He cried out as she thrust back with her hips, heaving him over her shoulder and driving him into the ground. His skull gave a satisfying *crack* as it struck the polished granite, but she still did not release his wrist.

Wrenching his arm, she drove her knee into the back of his elbow, shattering the joint. The dagger clattered to the ground as he screamed. Driving her weight into his chest, she swept up the blade and pressed it to his throat.

"*Traitor!*" she hissed. "Why?"

The man groaned, his eyes whirling in his skull. They had glazed over, but as he looked up and saw her crouched over him, they cleared a little.

"For the Tsar," he breathed.

Before Merydith could say anything else, the man started to shake. His eyes rolled up into his skull, and a long, hissing whisper escaped his throat. Red bubbles burst from his mouth in a sudden cough. Then the life seemed to drain from his body, and he breathed no more.

Dropping the dagger, Merydith stood and staggered back. Her towel had been lost in the scuffle, but she was too horrified to care. She stared at Damyn, seeing the fear in his eyes, a mirror of the terror that had already taken lodge in her heart.

"What does this mean?" he whispered.

Merydith shook her head, her gaze traveling back to the dead emissary. "It means Enala failed. It means war is coming to Northland."

✣ I ✣

K*eep going, Alana.*

Agony encircled Alana's throat as she followed the voice through the forest, her strength fading with every step. Her shirt was wet with the blood dripping from the wounds around her neck, and the past few hours had turned to a blur. She wasn't sure when the voice had first made itself known—only that in her desperation she had followed it, though she couldn't say whether it was real or a product of her fractured consciousness.

Hardly.

Was it her, or did the voice seem amused by her plight?

Gasping, she continued on, only dimly aware that the light was fading, beckoning in the night. Inside her head, her last moments in the throne room played out again and again, and she saw her father, the Tsar, standing over her, felt the bite of the sword as it wrapped around her neck.

Only Quinn's foolishness had saved her, his weakness showing as he gave in to her pleading. No doubt he would pay for it when her father discovered his part in her escape.

As would the guards she had coerced into aiding her. She had found them while staggering through the endless corridors of the citadel, before the voice had appeared to guide her. The squadron had not heard of her betrayal, and had leapt to obey their princess. They had led the injured Alana deep into the bowels of the citadel, to a private passageway down through the cliffs to the royal docks.

There she had commandeered a skiff and left the guards behind. Unable to summon the strength to wipe their memories with her magic, she had ordered them to remain at their posts until she returned. She wondered how long it had taken her father to find them.

Was he even now searching for her with his power?

No, his powers are exhausted for the moment, the voice came again.

In a moment of clarity, she recalled it had first come to her on the skiff, as she set sail across the lake. In her exhausted state, she had mistaken it as that other part of herself, the gentler, more innocent personality she had created as a mask the first time she'd escaped her father.

Go west, the voice had said, and Alana had obeyed.

On its urging, she had abandoned the skiff on a bend in the Brunei River, pushing it back out into the current after she'd disembarked. Now she was lost in an unknown forest, pursued by whatever dark creature her father might send next, still following the voice of some unknown entity, which for all she knew might be leading her into even greater danger.

Not very trusting, are you?

"Oh, do shut up," Alana muttered. She flinched at her own words, her footsteps slowing.

Her voice had echoed loudly in the forest, accentuating

the silence blanketing the trees. After a moment she picked up the pace, her thoughts turning to bandits and the dark creatures that might lurk in the night.

Paranoid, too, I see, the voice returned.

"I'm lost in the woods in the middle of the night, I'd hardly call myself paranoid," Alana replied, then swore beneath her breath. "Great, now I'm talking to myself."

Silent laughter whispered in her mind. Gritting her teeth, Alana resolved to ignore any further instructions from her mysterious guide. She was lost enough as it was.

Branches rustled overhead as a breeze blew down the deer trail she was following. Alana shivered as she tasted ice on the wind, and guessed snow was on its way. This deep in winter, the limbs of the surrounding trees were naked, offering little shelter from the elements. If the snow came, the ground would be covered by morning.

Struggling to ignore the growing cries of her injured body, Alana pressed on, though her every breath seemed to reignite the agony encircling her throat. She needed a healer, someone with the magic to heal her wounds. Unfortunately, the only ones left in the Three Nations were held in her father's sway. Teeth chattering, she continued through the trees, the temperature plummeting around her.

Slowly the last of the light faded, until it was all she could do to keep to the trail. Exhaustion tugged at her mind, calling for her to rest, and she staggered to a stop. Grasping at a tree to steady herself, she sucked in a great, agonising mouthful of air.

You must go on…

"I can't!" she screamed, then groaned as the action tore open her wounds. "I can't," she sobbed again to the empty forest.

The cold seeped through her thin clothing, draining away the last of her strength. She clutched at the tree, knowing that if she sat she would never get up again. In desperation she reached for her magic, for the warming heat of its power, but there was nothing there. Despair gripped Alana as she remembered she'd used the last of it to overwhelm Quinn. Her power was gone, at least until she could stop and rest, recover.

So this is how the Daughter of the Tsar meets her end? the voice sneered. *Lost and defeated, with hardly a whimper of defiance.*

Alana's breath hissed between her teeth as she exhaled. Pushing against the tree, she staggered upright and continued along the trail. She was surprised to see snow on the ground. She hadn't noticed it falling before, but now the air was thick with snowflakes, though Alana hardly felt the cold. A dull thudding began in her temples, spreading outwards across her skull and down the back of her neck.

She staggered as an unseen tree root tripped her, then cursed as the sword she'd taken from one of the guards slammed against her knee. In rage she tore at the scabbard, determined to hurl it into the trees, before sense returned and she only rearranged it on her belt. Without her magic, the blade was her only defence against any unsavoury characters lurking in forest.

"How much longer?" she croaked to the darkness.

Almost there.

Alana shook her head, struggling to hold back her despair. All her life, the Tsar had taught her to be strong, had beaten and tortured her until all that remained was unyielding iron. Yet in the aftermath of the throne room, Alana had been left in pieces. Her father's teachings had done nothing to prepare her for Kellian's death, nothing to ready her for the pain of watching her friend die.

Nor had she been ready for Devon's revulsion. Even now, she could see the loathing in his eyes as he looked at her, his disgust, his hatred. He had seen her suffering and turned his back on her. In that moment, Alana's strength had meant nothing, instead becoming a blade that seemed to drag through her very core.

Now she was lost and alone, at the very edge of her endurance, with nothing but dark forest and silence for company.

The thought brought a frown to her face, and slowing, she lifted her head to scan the darkness. It was a moment before she realised what had changed—that the trees were no longer silent. A soft whisper carried through the night. Overhead, snowflakes glittered in the faintest sliver of moonlight.

Alana started forward again, the whisper calling her on. The voice had silenced now, and she cursed beneath her breath, her hand drifting to the hilt of her sword. She gripped the pommel, willing strength to her weary limbs.

Squinting, she noticed some of the trees around her had been damaged. Jagged branches stretched across the trail, and it was a moment before she realised that several tree trunks had been snapped in two, as though a giant had come crashing through the canopy.

Her heart beating painfully against her ribcage, Alana stepped from the trail, following some instinct she couldn't quite describe. Moving amongst the broken trees, she scanned the shadows, wondering if a tornado had torn through this section of the forest. Yet they were rare here on the Plorsean plateau, and the area seemed too small…

Alana froze as the trees suddenly gave way to a clearing. Breath held, eyes straining, she watched as a giant shape took form from the gloom. Great, clawed limbs stretched out across the clearing, where deep grooves had torn the earth. Broad wings of scaled skin draped over the broken trees, and a monstrous head lay not too far from where Alana stood, eyes closed. Horns twisted up from its skull, and beyond the body, a massive tail twisted its way into the darkness.

Dragon.

Terror flooded Alana's veins as she recalled her father's Red Dragons, the devastation they had reaped on his enemies. Breath still held, she was about to back away, when she caught the whispering again. It was coming from somewhere in the clearing. She frowned as something moved beside the dragon. With a start, she recognised the sound.

Someone was crying.

A part of her still screamed to run, but another part, one born out of her time with Devon and Kellian, urged her forward. On trembling legs, Alana crept across the clearing. The source of the sobbing came into sight as she moved around one giant foreleg.

An old woman crouched beside the beast, her long robes in tatters, wrinkled skin scorched and blackened from the flames of battle. Her long white hair hung limply against her skull, and there was an air of despair about her as she sat there, head resting against the leather hide of the dragon.

"Tillie..." Alana whispered, then trailed off as she remembered the name wasn't quite right. She swallowed, agony engulfing her throat, and then tried again. "Enala... what happened?"

For a long moment, the old woman said nothing, though the sobbing had ceased at the first word from Alana's mouth. The silence stretched out, heavy with pain, with grief, with anger. Alana opened her mouth, then closed it again when she realised she had nothing else to say.

"Your father happened, girl," Enala whispered, rising to her feet. "My cursed son happened."

2

Darkness stained the world when Braidon woke, a cry on his lips. Gasping, he looked around, his panicked mind struggling to make sense of his surroundings. Slowly, shapes appeared through the black, shadowy and indistinct. The soft creak of tree branches shifting in the wind seeped into his consciousness, and he shivered as a cold draught touched the back of his neck.

A dull ache began in his lower back as he climbed to his feet. Rubbing his arms, he struggled to recall how he had come to be lying alone in the dark. Images flickered through his mind, disjointed and broken, as though they'd somehow become jumbled as he slept. He remembered a man with sapphire eyes looking down at him, a whisper on his lips.

My son.

The image changed, and he saw the same man in a great gilded room. Flames leapt about him as two aged figures charged, swords extended. Thunder crashed and a great roar filled Braidon's ears as the picture faded to black, leaving one word on his tongue.

Tsar.

Another memory appeared, and he saw himself sitting in a garden, a young woman beside him. Her steely grey eyes watched him as they spoke, her blonde hair blowing across her face. She smiled down at him, her mouth forming words he could not hear, and another name rose from his scattered thoughts.

Alana.

Sister.

More memories followed then, still jumbled, so that it took time for him to piece them together. He saw a giant of a man with warhammer in hand, facing off against a child with pitch-black eyes, then an older man with kind eyes telling him they would keep him safe.

Devon and Kellian.

As the names came, the flow of memories jolted, flickering forward in time, and he saw his father the Tsar poised over Kellian, golden sword in hand. He watched in horror as the blade descended, and Kellian died. Grief swept through him, turning his legs to water. Sinking to his knees, Braidon wept for the man who had given his life to save him.

The past continued to flow through his mind, faster now, a river that threatened to wash him away. He saw again their journey across the Three Nations, their meeting with Enala, the conflicts with Quinn and his Stalkers, the awful battle in the throne room, his flight with Enala on the back of the Gold Dragon, Dahniul.

Amongst the memories were some he did not recognise, and with a chill he realised they must have come from his other life, from the time before Alana had wiped his mind. Unfamiliar faces rushed across his thoughts, and for the first time he felt a sense of sadness, of loss for the life he could not remember.

Finally, he saw the shining beam of light that had cut across the sky, heard Dahniul scream and Enala cry out, felt himself coming loose from the dragon's back, falling through empty air…

Braidon shuddered, tearing himself from the flow of memories. Turning his mind to his mentor and her dragon, he sent out a silent prayer to the Gods that they had survived his father's attack. There was no doubt in his mind the burning light had come from him—only the Tsar could have commanded magic across such a distance.

There was nothing he could do for his friends now though, and gathering his thoughts, he turned his mind to his own situation. When he'd fallen, it had still been early in the afternoon. He had no idea which direction the dragon had turned as they fled the citadel; all he could recall from before he fell was a sea of green beneath them.

If only he knew which forest he was in, he might be able to find his way out. Many of the forests around Plorsea spanned hundreds of miles. It was said a man could wander lost in the trees for a lifetime, without ever seeing another soul. If he set out without knowing which direction safety lay in, he might end up walking deeper into the abyss, never to be seen again.

Well, not never. It was only a matter of time before his father sought him out. With the magic at the Tsar's command, it didn't matter how many leagues Braidon put between himself and the capital. There was no corner of the Three Nations the man's magic could not reach out and touch his consciousness. Amidst a city of thousands, he might have hidden for a while, camouflaged by the host of other minds, but out here in the wilderness, his mind would shine out like a candle in the darkness.

Unless…

Closing his eyes, Braidon sought his own magic. Breathing slowly, he sank into the void where his power lurked, searching for the flickering white. But he found only darkness, only emptiness where before there had been life. His heart sank as he returned from his trance.

He had used his magic to conceal himself and Enala as they flew a dragon back from Northland, but the effort had drained his power. Until it regenerated, he could do nothing to hide himself from the Tsar.

Braidon started as a realisation came to him—that Alana had wiped their memories as a way of deceiving their father. Without them, their minds would have been unrecognisable to their father, so that even if he'd touched them with his magic, they would have remained undetected.

A shiver swept through Braidon as he sucked in a breath, tasting the ice on the air. He rubbed his arms and rose to his feet, trying to get his circulation flowing again. The ground crunched beneath his boots, and looking down he noticed a slight sheen to the ground. Brushing his shoulders, his hands came away wet with snow.

His eyes had adjusted to the gloom now, allowing him to cast around for somewhere that would offer shelter. He let out a long breath as he saw the massive buttress roots of a Ficus tree. Twisting away from the trunk, they stood almost a yard off the ground. It was the best shelter he was likely to find in the dark.

He crossed to the tree, and crouching down, crawled into the space between the roots. He moved quickly, collecting as many dry sticks and fallen branches from the grooves between the roots as he could. Protected from the snow, they were still dry, and stacking them in the corner, he started to build a fire between himself and the forest beyond.

Then he paused, realising with a curse he had no way to light it.

As though summoned, a memory came to him, rising from the murky fog that was his past. Born in the citadel atop the cliffs of Ardath, he and his sister had dwelt in luxury—but their lives had never been idle. Their father had wanted them to be strong, ready for any eventuality the world might throw at them.

And Braidon was more than capable of lighting a fire.

Taking out his knife, he cut a slice of bark from the Ficus and placed it on the ground in front of him. Then he took one of the dry branches he'd collected and sliced thin shavings from the wood, collecting them in a pile beside his strip of bark. Selecting a stick from his pile of kindling, he placed its point on the bark, and pressing down, he began to twist it rapidly between his palms.

It took half an hour, several blisters, and Braidon's full assortment of curses before a thin column of smoke rose from the bark. Letting out a yelp of joy, Braidon removed the stick and added the wood shavings to the bark. Carefully he lifted it to his lips and blew gently onto the embers. After a few attempts, the flames leapt to life amongst the kindling. Braidon quickly placed the bark on the ground and added more fuel, until he had a small blaze.

When he was finally satisfied the fire wouldn't go out, Braidon lay back against the tree trunk and closed his eyes, a sigh on his lips as the warmth of the flames bathed his face. Beyond the flickering orange, the forest faded into the darkness, his night vision banished by its light. In that moment he didn't care, so long as he escaped the icy cold creeping through the world beyond his tree.

As his mind relaxed, his thoughts turned back to Enala, and he wondered again at the old woman's fate. She taken him in and taught him to use his magic, had defended him when everyone else had wanted to hand him over to the Tsar. He had wondered why for a long time, but in the throne room Braidon had learned the truth—Enala was his grandmother.

He bit his lip, recalling the moment Enala and the Tsar had faced off. Their words had been bitter, their hatred for one another undisguisable. It saddened him to think of it, and he could only imagine what pain must have come between them to cause such a rift between mother and son.

His mind drifted as the call of sleep beckoned, but he shook himself back awake and added another branch to the fire. The flames leapt at the fresh offering, tongues of orange dancing up to consume the slender wood. He glanced at his small pile, aware it was not enough to last the night. Beyond the flames, the snow was falling faster, piling up in the entrance to his crevice between the Ficus roots. If he didn't want to freeze to death, he'd have to find more before the flames died out. Exhausted as he was, he wouldn't have the strength to relight it.

Even so, Braidon couldn't bring himself to leave the warmth of his shelter. His eyelids drooped again as he leaned against the tree trunk. A loose rock was digging into his backside, but it hardly seemed to matter…

Gasping, Braidon snapped back awake, aware that time had passed but unsure how long. He scrambled up, his heart beating rapidly. The fire was still crackling amongst the wood, and he let out a long sigh of relief. Clutching at his chest, he was about to rise and find more fuel, when a voice spoke from the shadows beyond the flames.

"Evening, sonny."

Braidon gasped as adrenaline burned through his veins. Leaping to his feet, he scrambled for his dagger, until the gentle rasping of laughter reached his ears. Heart still pounding, he paused, squinting into the darkness. The shadows shifted, and a giant of a man appeared. Firelight lit his wiry beard, glinting in his amber eyes. He wore a leather jerkin and steel gauntlets on his wrists, and carried a massive warhammer one-handed. There was a weary smile on his face as he looked down at Braidon.

"You going to stick me with that, sonny, or you gonna invite me to join your camp?" the giant rumbled.

It took an effort of will for Braidon to release the hilt of his dagger. He shook his head, still staring at the warrior in disbelief. "Devon..." He trailed off, swallowing hard. "How...how are you here?"

Devon only grunted. Stepping closer, he brushed the snow from his woollen cloak. The giant warhammer, *kanker*, made a *thunk* as he dropped it, then Devon lowered himself down beside the fire with a groan. "Oh, but it's been a long day," he said quietly, his eyes on the flames. "Can we leave the questions until the morning?"

Braidon stood for a second longer, before the weight of his own exhaustion drew him back to his seat against the tree trunk. His eyes still did not leave Devon, and after a moment the big man sighed.

"Was there something else?"

Stifling a sob, Braidon darted forward and threw himself at his friend. Until the moment Devon had appeared, he hadn't realised how afraid he'd been, out here in the darkness. He had no idea how the hammerman had found him, but he thanked the Gods for his presence.

Clearly stunned by Braidon's sudden show of affection, Devon tottered backwards beneath his weight. Then giant arms wrapped around Braidon, squeezing him into a bear hug. Unable to hold them back any longer, tears came to his eyes, and he sobbed softly into Devon's chest. The warrior's leather vest was cold from the snowy night, but it was warm in the giant's embrace, comforting. After the gruesome scene Braidon had witnessed in the throne room...

His heart lurched at the memory of Kellian's lifeless body toppling to the marble floor, and he jerked back from Devon. Looking up into the familiar face, he saw the warmth there, but even Devon's grizzled featured couldn't hide the grief that lurked behind his eyes.

"I'm sorry," Braidon blurted out, the words seeming meaningless in the wake of what Devon had lost. "I...we... were too late!"

A sad smile touched Devon's cheeks, and his eyes turned distant, as though he were looking off into some other time, some other place.

"It's not your fault, sonny," Devon whispered. "No one..." His voice cracked, and closing his eyes, he averted his face.

Silence fell, punctuated only by the crackling of the fire beside them. Braidon watched as the giant warrior drew in a long breath. "What brought you back here, sonny? I thought you were safe in Northland."

Braidon swallowed. "Enala and the Queen..." He trailed off, struggling to put together the jumbled memories of the past few weeks. "Enala helped me to master my magic," he started again. "We thought...we thought it might make the difference against the Tsar."

There was a tightness to Devon's face as he forced a smile. "Thank you for trying, sonny. But no one could have saved him. Kellian knew what he was doing when he attacked the Tsar. He knew there would be no going back."

Braidon shivered, remembering the scene. He had witnessed it as he first stepped into the throne room: Kellian surging to his feet as the Tsar towered over Devon, the dagger as it flashed through the air, the Tsar's screams as it struck home. In that one act, Kellian had saved Devon's life. But in doing so, he had paid for it with his own.

"Why did he do it?" Braidon whispered.

"Because…" Devon trailed off. In the light of the fire, his skin seemed pale, his eyes cast in shadow. "Because he was Kellian," he finished with a shrug.

"I don't understand."

Devon nodded. "He was a believer—in the Gods, in humanity, in me. He thought there were things worth more than his own life. Things like freedom, and friendship. He died so that I could live." His shoulders straightened almost imperceptibly, and his brow hardened. "So that I could fight on."

The conversation trailed off with Devon's pronouncement, though the forest no longer seemed so quiet now, no longer so empty. Braidon felt his fear for the morning fading. The threat of his father still loomed over his future, but with Devon at his side, Braidon felt a sudden faith that things might work out. The call of sleep beckoned, and he wriggled in his hollow, struggling to find a more comfortable position. His eyes slid closed, but as he started to drift off, a thought came to him.

"Devon, where are we?" he asked, cracking open one eye.

The big man chuckled. "Onslow Forest, sonny."

"Onslow…Forest?" Braidon swallowed as lost memories flickered into his mind. He sat back up. "I know it. It's a refuge for outlaws and bandits—"

Devon's booming laughter drowned him out. The sound echoed from the hollow, reverberating out into the trees, as though he were inviting the dark fiends to come for them. A true grin split the hammerman's face as he patted the haft of his warhammer.

"Don't you worry, sonny," he said. "Whatever's out there, it's no match for *kanker.* Now, why don't you get some sleep, you look like you could use it. I'll keep watch."

Seeing the man's immovable confidence, Braidon relaxed back against the tree. Seated beside the fire, with *kanker* in hand, Devon seemed like some hero out of legend, a warrior of renown who could crush any enemy with one hand. Indeed, Braidon himself had watched the man defeat a demon in single-handed combat. Even in his exhausted state, a few bandits were no threat to such a legend.

He nodded wearily, his eyes already flickering closed.

And slept.

3

"Is it dead?"

Alana blurted out the words before she could process what the old woman had said. Standing there before the giant beast, with its dagger-filled jaws large enough to swallow either one of them whole, she could think of nothing else. Alana had seen her father's dragons up close, but none of the Red beasts came close to the size of the creature lying in the clearing.

Her question was met with stony silence. Tearing her gaze from the beast, Alana focused on the wrinkled face of Enala. She frowned as the woman's words finally seeped through her consciousness.

"You're his *mother?*" she gasped.

In all the years Alana's father had trained her, he had never mentioned his parents—not even in her younger years, when there was still some softness in him, and he had still been given to kindness towards his only daughter. Those had been the years when her mother had been with them, before Braidon had arrived and the last traces of humanity faded from their father.

Across from her, the old woman stepped away from the beast. Despite the darkness, her eyes seemed to glow, and Alana remembered her father's tales of this woman. He may have never mentioned his mother, but he *had* talked endlessly of Enala—the Magicker who had fought against Archon, who with her brother had opposed the Tsar's rise to power.

Now Alana understood why the woman had survived. She had been spared. There could be no other explanation—no one endured her father's wrath.

"You're my grandmother," Alana whispered.

Her words finally drew a reaction from Enala. A tremor swept across the old woman's face, anger replacing grief. "Never!" she snapped. "I know who you are now, *girl*. Your brother may be innocent, but you most certainly aren't. How many young Magickers have you sent to their deaths? How many did you mind wash to do your father's bidding? No, a monster like you will never be a grandchild of mine."

Alana smirked. "On that we can agree."

The old woman glared back. Fists clenched, she advanced a step. "What are you doing here, *girl?*" she spat. "Come to finish the Tsar's dirty work?"

At the mention of her father, Alana's anger flared. Her hand dropped to her sword hilt. "What right do *you* have to judge *me*?" she growled. "The Tsar is *your* making. Everything he is, everything he's done, it's on *you*. If…if…" she stammered, unable to find the words to express her emotions.

She closed her eyes, recalling the pain, the torment of a life spent in thrall of the Tsar, as the enforcer of his will. Even now, memories of her deeds brought Alana a thrill of joy, though they were tainted now with disgust from her other self, from the innocence she had freed when she chained away her own memories. The conflict bubbled within her, until she felt as though she might burst.

"*It's all your fault!*" she screamed, her self-loathing taking voice.

Weariness forgotten, Alana advanced across the clearing. The old woman watched her come, unmoving. Drawing to a stop, they faced off against one another. Alana flicked a glance at the dragon, wondering whether it might wake, but up close her earlier suspicions were proven true.

The Gold Dragon was dead, its shining scales stained grey. One great eye hung half open, the vacant globe clouded white. Torn scales and blood seeped into the earth around it, and in its stomach a great gash had been scorched deep into its hide. She shuddered, and quickly returned her attention to Enala.

Unnoticed, the old woman had crept forward until their faces were only an inch apart. Confronted by the woman's crystal blue eyes, Alana stumbled back, her heart suddenly racing. A cold smile appeared on Enala's lips.

"If you think to stop me, *girl*, you had best keep your wits about you."

Alana clenched her fists. "I don't answer to my father," she hissed. "Go where you want, old woman."

"You think that's an insult?" She laughed, the sound cold and absent of humour. "Ay, I'm old. I have lived a hundred years and more, seen things you could never comprehend. And I have survived them all. Cross me at your peril, girl."

Her cackling echoed between the trees like the whisper of some long dead spirit, raising the hackles on Alana's neck. Finding herself lost for words, she said nothing, only stood and stared at the woman.

Enala smirked. "A good choice, *girl*," she said, then turned her back. "Now if we're done here, I'm returning to Northland."

Without waiting for a reply, the old woman started around the still body of the fallen dragon. Alana watched her go, a lump lodged in her throat. An image rose from her memories, of her father towering over her with sword in hand. She heard her own pitiful cries for help as she stood alone against him, her sense of powerlessness, and her anger came rushing back.

"That's right!" she shrieked. "Go! Leave the rest of us to clean up your mess. Run, like the coward you are."

Enala froze at the edge of the clearing. Her face was pale as she looked back at Alana, her eyes wide and nostrils flaring. "What did you say?"

"I said you're a coward!" Alana shrieked, advancing. "You ran from your own son, left your nation, your people, your grandchildren alone to suffer under his reign. You could have stopped him, you and your brother, all those years ago, but you did *nothing!*"

"*You* dare to lecture *me*, girl?" Enala hissed. "You, who joyed in enforcing your father's laws, who wielded your power against those who could not defend themselves against it?"

"I'm not the one running away."

"No?" Enala raised an eyebrow. "Then why are you here, in this faraway forest, instead of in Ardath, standing against your father?"

Alana's cheek twitched at the mention of her father, a wave of fear washing through her. She recalled his words back in the citadel, his plans to wipe away everything she was, to expunge her memories and consciousness, and create her anew with his powers. If he had his way, the small shred of good she had discovered within herself would be swept away, leaving only the cold, calculating woman she had become to protect her brother.

Looking at the old woman, Alana saw the satisfied smirk she wore, and bristled. "I can't stop him alone," she snapped, "but I won't let you abandon us, not again."

"Try and stop me," Enala growled.

Steel hissed against leather as Alana's sword leapt into her hand. She lunged forward, the point spearing for the old woman's throat. With a speed belying her age, Enala skipped sideways, and the blade cut only empty air. Carried forward by her momentum, Alana stumbled, her exhaustion returning with the rush of blood to her limbs.

Swaying, she turned to follow the old woman, and barely managed to parry a thrust from Enala's sword. The sharp shriek of steel on steel rang out across the clearing. Alana twisted her blade, slipping the point beneath the old woman's guard and stabbing upward. But again, Enala was too quick, and her blow missed its target.

Alana caught the crunch of twigs beneath boots as the old woman shifted behind her and hurled herself down. A *hiss* came from overhead as Enala's blade cut the space where Alana's head had been. Rolling, Alana came to her feet and spun back toward her grandmother. Face set, Enala strode towards her, blade raised for another blow.

Instinctively, Alana reached for her magic, but there was only the slightest spark of green within. She cried out as she deflected another blow, its impact vibrating down the blade, almost tearing the sword from her grip.

Her breath coming in desperate gasps, Alana switched her attack, seeking to break through the old woman's guard and put an end to the fight. But weakened by blood loss and exhaustion, she was too slow. With each blow, her blade dipped lower, and finally Alana staggered to a stop, allowing the old woman to leap clear.

"Is that all you have, girl?" Enala murmured.

Blood rushed to Alana's head as her face flushed with rage. Roaring, she threw herself forward. She lashed out with the last of her strength, aiming her sword for the old woman's throat. Enala ducked beneath the blow, her shoulder crashing into Alana's chest.

Caught off-guard, Alana was hurled backwards. She staggered on the uneven forest floor, and her feet went out from underneath her. Alana's breath hissed between her teeth as she struck the ground. Gasping, she tried to recover, but her limbs refused to obey her commands. She looked up in time to see a blade flashing towards her face.

☙ 4 ❧

The sun was high in the sky by the time the slanted rooftops of Onslow came into view. Standing on the forward rail of the ship, Quinn's heart quickened at the sight. Behind him, the twenty-odd Stalkers he'd selected for this mission were preparing their mounts alongside the fifty soldiers that were to accompany them. Quinn remained where he stood, watching the village's slow approach, already impatient to be underway. Beyond the docks of Onslow, the mountains of western Plorsea slashed the sky, seeming to tower over the land beyond the village.

West, the Tsar had said, and Quinn had obeyed.

That was where the Gold Dragon had fallen, struck down by the awesome power of the Sword of Light. The Tsar's own powers still had not recovered from the battle the day before, when Devon, Enala and Eric had launched their assault on the throne room. They would return though, just as soon as the Magickers in the Tsar's thrall recovered from the drain on their power.

Fortunately for Quinn and the twenty Stalkers he'd

chosen for their magic, they had long ago earned the Tsar's trust. They had been spared the bracelets worn by most Magickers under the Tsar's thrall, which allowed him to siphon off their magic at will. Quinn could still recall their stinging touch from his childhood—and his relief when he'd earned his lieutenant's badge and been freed of them.

Others though were not so lucky. During the assault, the Tsar had drawn on the collective power of his Magickers like never before, driving many to the point of exhaustion and collapse. Several had perished during the hours the battle raged. In the dungeons beneath the citadel, where renegade Magickers were imprisoned, they had died by the score.

With his Magickers in the city drained, the Tsar had mounted his Red Dragon that morning and flown north to join the army as it marched. There, he would have the powers of his Battle Magickers to draw on, to defend their forces against any underhanded attacks the North might mount.

That left Quinn and his Stalkers the task of tracking down his children. Quinn smiled at the thought of having Alana in his thrall once more. He had drained his own magic to save her life, only to have her betray him, leaving him to suffer her father's wrath. In his mercy, the Tsar had spared him, but Quinn was still determined to make the girl pay. While there had been little word of her since she'd fled the citadel, he was confident wherever Braidon was to be found, his sister would not be far away.

His smile faltered as he thought of the old woman who had escaped alongside the boy. The last time they had met, Enala had carved through his Stalkers like a wolf amongst sheep…

He shook his head, dismissing memories of the slaughter. The twenty men and women he had selected were the finest of the Tsar's Stalkers. Each was capable of significant magic and were renown fighters with sword and dagger. If the old woman still lived, even she could not stand against them.

"Sir, your mount is ready."

Quinn found his aid at his side. Nodding his thanks, he strode across the deck of the barge to where the other Stalkers had gathered. Behind them, his soldiers stood at attention, awaiting their orders.

"The Tsar has commanded us to bring back his children," Quinn boomed. "Their treacherous assault on his person have left his powers fatigued. I do not intend to weary him needlessly with queries on their whereabouts, for are we not Stalkers? Is it not our duty to hunt down renegade Magickers, and bring them before our Tsar?"

He paused, eyeing the men and women gathered before him. They stared back with cold eyes, clearly unimpressed with his speech. His face hardened as he continued more quickly. "I chose each of you based on your reputation. Those reputations were no doubt hard-earned. But do not forget, the Tsar does not accept failure, and his goodwill is easily lost."

There was a stirring amongst the Stalkers now, and he offered them a cold smile. "There has been no word of Alana since she was spotted sailing west across the lake, nor of Braidon since the Gold Dragon he was riding fell from the sky. We know Devon at least took sail on a ship heading for Onslow. Where he goes, I expect the other two will not be far behind. Question the villagers. He will not have gone unnoticed. If they refuse to talk, make them. I expect to be on the road by sunset. Do not fail me, or you will not live to see the Tsar's vengeance."

The Stalkers saluted, their faces carefully blank, their discipline absolute. Many no doubt loathed him for being selected over them to lead this mission. He would have to tread carefully, to ensure they had no cause to offer complaints to the Tsar.

The deck jerked beneath Quinn's feet as their barge banged against the docks. Ignoring the gangplank, he turned and leapt across to the wooden jetty. The *thud* of the gangplank being lowered was followed by the *clip-clop* of hooves as Quinn's aid led his mount across it.

Taking the reins, Quinn vaulted into the saddle and directed the horse down the docks, and out into the town. Several villagers were already gathering. They wore puzzled looks on their faces as they watched the black-garbed Stalkers disembark, before riding into the square to gather around Quinn.

When his entire force was in place, Quinn addressed the villagers from his saddle. "I'm looking for a young woman, a boy, and a renegade soldier by the name of Devon. There's a reward for anyone who comes forward now with information." His hand dropped to the hilt of his sword. "If you refuse..." He trailed off, allowing them to read the threat behind his words.

The dozen or so villagers exchanged glances, their eyes wide with fear, but not a voice spoke. Quinn allowed himself a smile as his horse shifted beneath him.

"Very well then." He pointed to a nearby house and addressed his men. "You can begin there."

5

The hushed voices fell silent as Merydith entered the room. Her chainmail rattled with each step as she crossed to the granite table, the long sabre slapping against her thigh. Iron gauntlets protected her hands, and on her head, she wore the gold-gilded helm of the Northland Queen. Lantern light lit the room, illuminating the faces of the men and women who rose to their feet as she took her place at the head of the council table.

Merydith reached up and unstrapped her helmet before taking her seat. Her council remained standing, until with a gesture, she indicated they could sit. The rustle of clothing followed as they made themselves comfortable once more, though not a voice was heard.

Studying the men and women around her, Merydith was careful to keep any trace of emotion from her face. Silently, she took note of who was present. The aged faces of the twelve men and women gathered around the table were well-known to her. With their greying hair and wrinkled faces, these were the clan leaders who had presided over Northland after her mother's death, before Merydith herself had come of age. There were other leaders from clans further afield, from the prairies and marshlands and forests that spanned far across Northland, but it would take time for her message to reach them. For the moment, these twelve men and women, chiefs of the mountain clans around Erachill, were all she had.

She had summoned them a week ago to discuss treaties and peace, to deliberate over how best to prevent an invasion from the south. They were long past such talk now though. Winter or no, the Tsar was ready to make his move, and they could no longer afford to delay.

Her messengers had taken wing that morning, summoning their nation to war. Given time, Northland could raise an army twice the size of any the Tsar might field against them. But they did not have time. If the Tsar felt bold enough to strike here, in the heart of their nation, then his forces were already on the march. They could not be allowed to cross the Gap unopposed.

"Thank you for coming here today," Merydith said, finally breaking the silence. "I know things are not as we expected when I first summoned you."

"As expected?" an old woman to Merydith's right snapped. Eyes flashing, she rose to her feet. Merydith did not react as the woman jabbed a wrinkled finger at her chest. "A southerner makes an assassination attempt on you, and your response is to declare war against the Three Nations? Who do you think you are, girl? Archon reborn?"

A strained silence fell over the table as Merydith stared the woman down. "Sit, Dyanna of Clan Clennan," she said, her voice so quiet the others in the room had to lean forward in their chairs, "before you find yourself a guest in my dungeons."

The leader of Clan Clennan bared her teeth, and for a moment Merydith thought she was going to have to make good on her threat. Then with a snort, Dyanna slumped back in her chair. Crossing her arms, she averted her eyes from the Queen.

Merydith nodded, her gaze turning to the others at the table. "Would anyone else here care to question my leadership?" she asked, fixing a glare to her face.

Silence met her question, and smiling, she rose to her feet. "Ladies and gentlemen, you all know me, have seen me grow from a child, to the woman I am today. You know I am no warmonger. This was not a decision I came to lightly, but whether we like it or not, war is coming for Northland. The only decision left is where we choose to make our stand."

"What does it matter?" At the other end of the table, an old man climbed to his feet. His long white hair hung down around his shoulders, and there were more winkles on his face than cracks in his aged leather jerkin. "Your family has always led us with honour, Merydith of Clan Kenzie. So tell us truly, what hope do we have against the Tsar, wherever we face him?"

Merydith swallowed as she looked at the speaker. Murdo was one of the oldest clan leaders, though no less fierce for his advanced years. He came from the Crae Clan, who had been bodyguards to her own family for generations. Murdo himself had served her mother. She could still remember the long winter nights as a child, sitting on his lap while her mother was busy in council, listening to his tales of the olden times, before Northland had been freed from Archon's yoke.

"My family have served yours since long before you were born, Merydith," Murdo continued softly. "Do not seek to mislead me. I say again, tell us truly—what chance do we stand?"

Her mouth suddenly dry, Merydith looked into the old man's eyes, and knew she could not lie to him. "No more chance than the Three Nations when Archon led the greatest army that has ever been known against them."

To her surprise, a smile appeared on the old man's cheeks. "Very well," he rasped, sinking back into his seat with a groan. "Then my people and I will march with you. I always wished to see the south."

The others at the table stared at her. Unlike the Crae leader, there was open fear in the eyes of many, as the stark reality of what she was asking struck home. Another stood, his hair jet-black, his face as yet untouched by the ravages of age. He stood there for a moment in silence, scratching his beard as his eyes roamed the others at the table.

"There has to be another way," he said at last, the words tumbling from his mouth in a rush. "We should sue for peace, whatever the cost."

Merydith smiled sadly at the young leader of the Cranook Clan. "I'm afraid that is no longer possible, Mokyre," she replied. "Not since I refused to return the Tsar's son."

Mokyre's face turned a mottled red at her words. "And by what right did you make such a decision?" he spat, slamming his fist down on the table.

Beside him, Dyanna was on her feet again, her face twisted with rage. "You would condemn us all to die, for the sake of one life?"

"I offered mercy to a soul in need," Merydith replied calmly, "as we have done for decades."

"Your mercy has doomed us all!"

Merydith's face hardened as she faced the two. Around

the table the other clan leaders watched on, waiting to see how she reacted. "I did what was *right*," she hissed, her voice as cold as ice. "Perhaps clans Cranook and Clennan are willing to sacrifice a child to protect their own, but I would rather die."

"Then you are a fool," Mokyre spat.

"Perhaps," Merydith replied with a smile. Stepping away from her chair, she walked around the table until she stood before the man. "But I think always of the future. The moment we handed over the boy, Northland would have accepted the Tsar's authority over our nation. And what would he have asked of us next? If we would sacrifice one boy for our freedom, why not two? Or ten? What fresh atrocities would you be willing to commit, to spare your own life, Mokyre? Where would *you* draw the line?"

As Merydith spoke, Dyanna sank back into her chair, though the Cranook leader remained standing. Eyes burning, he glared at her, but offered nothing in response to her condemnation. Merydith smiled, and with a curt nod, turned her back on him.

"No, this is the only way we remain free," she continued as she circled the table, eyeing each leader in turn. "I will not see Northland become some vassal state for the Tsar. We will not be ground into dust, bowing and scraping to some foreign dictator. I will fight to my dying breath before I see our land succumb to the darkness again."

"Hear, hear!" Murdo replied from the other end of the table.

"What about the Magickers who have come to us?" Dyanna asked softly. "Surely they will fight?"

"They might," Merydith answered as she completed her circuit of the table and resumed her seat, "but I will not ask that of them."

"Surely you jest?" Mokyre shouted. Dyanna only frowned, and slumped further into her chair, but others added their voices to the Cranook leader's objection. Emboldened, he stood and continued. "We have given them food and shelter, safety from the Tsar, surely they have an obligation—"

"*No,*" Merydith snapped, her patience pressed to breaking point. She slammed her palm down on the table. Her gaze swept the room, silencing the old men and women. Sucking in a breath, she prayed to the Goddess for strength. "The Magickers came here with their families to escape the Tsar's persecution—not to be used as a weapon against him."

This time, the room remained silent and Merydith continued. "I'm sorry, my friends. There is no easy path here, but there is no longer any point in debating the past. It is done, set in stone—all we can do now is deal with the reality of the present. And the reality is, the Tsar is coming.

"As I said before, we must decide how best to face him. It is my belief he cannot be allowed to cross The Gap. Northland is too large to defend if he gains a foothold on our lands."

"Then what do you propose, Merydith?" Murdo asked, his eyes aglow with a fresh light.

She smiled. "We march."

6

Sitting by the ashes of the fire, Devon watched as the morning's light dawned over the forest, illuminating the snow now lying thick on the forest floor. In their safe haven amongst the Ficus roots, with the tree's broad canopy overhead, he and Braidon had been spared its icy touch. Even so, Devon couldn't help but sigh as he felt the sun's warmth on his face. He'd allowed the fire to die out an hour ago, trusting that the morning would soon warm his aching bones.

He'd dozed lightly through the night, awakening every so often to stoke the fire or search for fresh kindling. Now though, the thought of facing the day filled him with trepidation. Much as he might deny it, the events in the citadel had left him exhausted, both in body and soul. From the moment Alana had betrayed them, it felt as though his entire world had spun out of control. There had been a moment's clarity, when he had recovered *kanker,* the warhammer passed down by his ancestors, but even that had quickly been snatched away by Quinn and his Stalkers.

Then Kellian…

Devon shuddered as his friend's sacrifice played itself out once more in his mind. He had spent much of the night trapped in a loop of self-loathing and despair, as he sought again and again for some way he might have changed things.

If only they had left before Alana had betrayed them.

If only Devon had fought Quinn in the corridors, rather than surrendering.

If only, if only, if only…

Clenching his fists, Devon tore his mind from the scene. He found himself staring down at the still sleeping Braidon. Not for the first time that night, he wondered what force could have brought the two of them together once more.

Devon's memories after his flight from the throne room were little more than a blur now. Distracted by the conflagrations rippling out from the throne room, the remaining guards had paid little heed to Devon as he strode down the long corridors of the citadel. Even at the gates to the city, the men on duty had been too focused on the Gold Dragon flying loops around the citadel to notice a single man slipping out the open doors.

From there it had been an easy matter to escape the city. Order within Ardath had already crumbled into chaos long before he made the outer walls, and the guards had already been swept away by the crowd trying to flee the city.

Along with a dozen other panicked citizens, Devon had boarded the first ship he could find departing the island city. A captain heading for Onslow was only too overjoyed to see so many patrons for the voyage. Aided by the afternoon breeze, the passage across the lake had been swift.

The only disturbance had come when a dazzling beam of light sliced across the sky towards the distant shore.

Several sailors had thrown themselves flat against the deck, while a few of the jumpier townsfolk had leapt overboard. It had cost precious time fetching them back out of the lake, but they had still reached the river mouth to Onslow before night arrived.

It was only on the Onslow River that the uneasy feeling had come over Devon. A sense of wrongness had gripped him, a feeling he was traveling in the wrong direction. Farmland stretched away to either side of the river, offering little cover from the hunters that were bound to follow him.

Then around a bend in the river, the first trees of the mountain forests had come into view. The sight had set his heart pounding. Watching the other passengers, he'd tried to ignore the urge to leap overboard.

Devon…

The voice had begun as little more than sigh in his ear, like the whispers of some long-dead spirit. It had grown stronger as the trees approached, until it seemed someone was screaming from the riverbank, begging him to join them.

Before he'd known quite what he was doing, Devon had found himself leaping from the railings of the ship. He had never been a strong swimmer, and the weight of *kanker* on his back had almost dragged him straight to the bottom. Fortunately, the forgiving currents had carried him closer to the shore, and by the time Devon surfaced, he'd had little left to do but reach out and catch an overhanging branch to drag himself from the icy waters.

Standing freezing and drenched on the riverbank, sense had finally returned to Devon, but by then his ship was already disappearing around the next bend in the river. Cursing beneath his breath, Devon had carried on from there on foot. He'd walked quickly, struggling to keep warm as the cold winds cut through his soaking clothes.

By the time darkness fell and the snow began, Devon's teeth were chattering uncontrollably, and he was beginning to lose hope he would ever find shelter. He'd been busy cursing his rotten luck, when the voice returned.

Without any other options, he'd followed its directions without question. He'd been as shocked as Braidon to find the boy sitting beside the flames, though at the time, Devon had been more interested in the heat radiating from the fire.

Now though, he found himself wondering how Braidon had come to be in the forest in the first place. The boy had claimed Enala brought him, that they had meant to make an attempt on the Tsar's life. Yet as far as Devon knew, Braidon's magic was nothing more than illusions. How could the old woman have thought it might prove the difference against the Tsar?

But then, the ways of Magickers were far beyond Devon's understanding, and he had little desire to change that. He wrapped a hand around the haft of *kanker*, drawing reassurance from its presence. It had been passed down from his ancestor Alan, a hero who had once stood upon the walls of Fort Fall and defied the might of Archon. Until recently, Devon had thought it nothing more than what it appeared—a simple hammer—but in the battles of the past few months, he had discovered it had another ability: it could protect its wielder from magic.

It had saved his life on more than one occasion, and while Enala had told him the protection spell would quickly be overwhelmed by the power commanded by the Tsar, he still felt better with it to hand. At least it might give him a fighting chance.

Beside him, Braidon twitched and gave a soft cry. Devon

thought again of the voice that had called him through the forest, and wondered whether the boy himself might have summoned him with his magic. Or could it have been the old priest, Enala? Or the Tsar himself, in an effort to gather all his prey in one place?

Devon shuddered at the implications. He glanced out at the snow-covered woods. The light had grown, banishing the shadows beneath the trees. A soft *thump* came from nearby as a clump of snow slid from a branch, but otherwise, there was no sign of movement.

Devon sighed, then sat up and stretched his arms. Braidon jerked awake at the movement, his crystal blue eyes blinking in the dawn's light. Groaning, he started when he saw Devon sitting there, almost making it to his feet before he seemed to realise where he was. His cheeks grew red, and rubbing his eyes he sank back to the damp earth.

"You didn't wake me?" he said with a frown.

Devon smiled. Throughout the night, he'd found himself wondering which version of Braidon he sat beside: the young boy he'd come to know on the road from Ardath, or some other boy, one who had been raised by the cruelty of the Tsar.

"I thought you could use the rest," was all he said.

Braidon's face remained uncertain. "So…how *did* you find me?"

"I don't know, sonny," Devon replied. The first calls of the dawn chorus were just beginning, and Devon watched as a blackbird emerged from a nest in the tree above them. "Something about this forest, it called to me," he added finally. "I should have stopped and made camp long before I found you. Yet something, some presence, called me on. I can't really explain it."

To his surprise, Braidon nodded, as though what he'd

said made perfect sense. "Enala said the Gods were still with us, guiding us—"

Devon snorted. "I bet." He chuckled quietly. "Gods, magic, exhaustion-induced hallucinations. Whatever, here we are." He raised an eyebrow in the boy's direction. "So, if you're here…you know the truth about your sister?"

Braidon swallowed visibly. "The news reached us in Erachill, about who she was…who I am," he replied softly.

"So which Braidon am I speaking to then?"

"The only one you've ever known," the boy replied. "If *you* know the truth, then…did you…did you meet my sister?"

Devon's chest tightened. "Best we not talk about that, sonny," he replied bluntly. Before the boy could argue, he rose to his feet, groaning as his joints cracked from the disuse. His stomach rumbled as he looked down at the boy. "How about we walk and talk? I could use a fresh meal, and I don't think we'll find one between the roots of this tree."

Accepting Devon's help, Braidon stood and stamped out the last embers of their fire. Since neither of them knew quite where they were, they set off in a random direction and hoped for the best. Despite Devon's words, they walked in silence, each lost in his own private thoughts.

Thankfully, it wasn't long before Devon caught the distant whisper of running water. The ground sloped down beneath them as they headed towards it, then dropped away sharply into a steep valley. Ivy covered the slope, and moving with care, the two of them picked their way down towards the stream. The dirt beneath their feet turned to loose rocks, and Devon was forced to rely on the thick vines clinging to the slope to keep his balance.

At the bottom, they were rewarded for their efforts by a fast-running stream. Further upstream, the crystal clear waters rushed over a cobble bed, but where they stood, a cluster of boulders had partially damned the flow, creating a small pool around a turn in the valley. Kneeling beside the water, Devon drank gratefully, then sat back and made space for Braidon to do the same.

When he was done, Braidon knelt beside the stream and eyed the water with the intensity of a soldier readying himself for battle. Devon opened his mouth to ask what he was doing, then thought better of it. Moving to a nearby boulder, Devon lay back in a patch of sunlight and watched as the boy lowered his hands into the stream. There he sat, unmoving, as time slowly crept past, until Devon began to wonder whether the boy had lost his mind after all. Coming from far up in the Sandstone Mountains, the waters of the stream must have been freezing.

Still drowsy from the long night, Devon was just beginning to drift off, when a shout snapped him back to wakefulness. Leaping to his feet, he was still scrambling for the haft of his hammer when Braidon's laughter carried to his ears. He frowned. Looking around, he found Braidon standing beside the river, a grin as wide as The Gap on his youthful face. At his feet, a rainbow trout flapped helplessly amongst the gravel, its pink and orange scales shining in the sunlight.

Devon's mouth dropped open. "How?"

Braidon beamed. "It must have been something I knew in my…other life." He gestured up the slope in the direction they'd come from. "It was the same with the fire last night."

Crouching beside the trout, he pulled his dagger from his belt and stabbed it through the eye. Blood gushed onto the stones and the fish ceased flapping. Holding it in the air, he waved it like a trophy at Devon. "Since the citadel, little bits have been coming back to me, snippets of memories. It seems our…father wanted us to be self-sufficient."

Devon could only shake his head. His mind turned back to the night he'd shared with Alana in northern Lonia. The young woman had disappeared for an hour, finally returning with a dead rabbit in tow. She'd claimed to have killed it with a stone. At the time he'd wondered how a girl from the city had learned such a skill.

Now he knew.

His thoughts drifted, turning as they so often did to later that night, when they'd swum together in the moonlit pool. Standing suddenly, Devon forced the painful memory from his mind. "I'll get a fire started," he snapped, then clambered up the slope in search of dry firewood.

He sensed Braidon's gaze on his back, but ignored him. How could he possibly explain his sense of betrayal to the boy, the loss and rage that burned his soul whenever he thought of Alana, and the role she'd played in Kellian's death?

If it hadn't been for her, they would never have been captured.

If it hadn't been for her, they would never have been in that throne room, and Kellian would never have found himself face-to-face with the Tsar.

Sheltered from the worst of the weather, only a thin frosting of snow had fallen in the valley, and Devon was able to gather a stack of firewood in less than an hour. Returning to the stream, he set about lighting a fire between two boulders that lay on a flat piece of ground just up from the water. He wasn't much of a woodsman, but with his flintstone he managed to get a fire burning.

By then, Braidon had successfully tickled two more trout from the stream. Devon wandered over to help the boy with the fish. They had both lost just about everything but the clothes on their back and the contents of their pockets, but

Devon managed to fashion them each a skewer from his stack of kindling. Spearing a fish on the end of each, they braced them over the fire, then sat back and waited, hungry eyes on the roasting flesh.

"Devon…" There was a touch of fear in the boy's voice, and he trailed off without saying anything more.

Devon looked up, knowing what Braidon wished to ask, but not knowing how he should answer him. Their eyes met, and he looked away, a vice closing around his throat.

"What happened to Alana?" Braidon finished in a whisper.

Staring into the flames, Devon saw again those final moments in the throne room, as he'd looked down on the helpless woman. With the twisted sword wrapped around her throat, Alana had begged him to help her, to use his prodigious strength to free her, to carry her clear—anything that might spare her from her father's wrath.

But Devon had walked away.

Guilt wound around his stomach, and clenching his jaw, he struggled to find an answer. "She didn't make it," he said finally, the lie foul on his tongue. "I'm sorry, sonny. The girl we remember is gone."

He looked up as a sob came from across the fire. Tears streaked Braidon's face, and there was desperation in his eyes. In that instant, Devon knew his lie had been the right choice. If he'd told Braidon the truth, nothing in the Three Nations would have stopped the young man from trying to find her, to rescue her.

Just as Devon had done, to his folly.

"I'm sorry," Devon repeated, shuffling around the fire and pulling the young man into a hug. "There was nothing any of us could have done. She was already lost long before we reached that citadel."

"What?" Braidon's question came between sobs, half-muffled by Devon's chest. "But…I saw her in the throne room."

Devon bit his lip, regretting his slip of tongue. He gave Braidon's shoulder a squeeze. "That…that wasn't her, sonny. That was someone else, the woman she used to be, the Daughter of the Tsar. When Kellian and I tried to save her, she betrayed us, had us locked away in the dungeons."

"I'm sorry, I didn't know."

"It wasn't her, sonny," Devon murmured, his eyes burning with remembered pain. "Not the woman we knew, anyway."

The boy fell silent then, his eyes fixed on the running waters of the stream. His face had taken on a faraway look, as though he were recalling some event from long ago. When he spoke, his words were barely more than a whisper.

"But it was," he said. "I have a memory of her, from the old days, sitting with me in some gardens. She…she was kind, loving, vulnerable. She's afraid of our father. It was as though there in that garden, our father's darkness couldn't touch her, and she could let down her guard." He swallowed, his eyes flicking up to look at Devon. "That was why she took our memories. I…I remember now. She was trying to save us, to save *me* from our father."

Silence fell as Braidon trailed off. Devon felt the guilt swell within him as he watched the boy, and saw again the young woman they had travelled with, her sweet smiles and fiercely protective nature. Then he saw her again the night he and Kellian had come for her, how she had tried to tell them to run, to leave her behind.

He looked away as tears came to his own eyes. "I'm sorry," he whispered, struggling to hide his own grief. "I'm sorry I never saw that side of her, sonny."

7

Alana woke to a sharp throbbing in her temples. Stars danced across her vision as she opened her eyes. A muffled shriek tore from her lips as the light drilled into her skull. Rolling onto her side, her stomach heaved, and she choked as the remains of her last meal came rushing up. A convulsion shook her as she vomited on the forest floor.

It was only when she finally lay back and spat out the acrid taste of bile that Alana realised she was alive. Sitting bolt upright, she looked around for the old priest. Red lights swirled at the edges of her vision, threatening to draw her back down into the darkness. Her stomach swirled again, but she had nothing left to throw up, and a moment later it settled.

Soft laughter came from behind her, and turning, Alana was surprised to find the old woman sitting nearby, the remains of a fire still smouldering between them. Light streamed through the branches above. In the dawn's light, Enala looked younger, less world-weary, and Alana supposed she'd had the night to rest, while she, apparently, had spent it in a coma.

Scowling, Alana pulled herself to her knees. "What are you laughing at, woman?"

Enala grinned and gestured at the mess she'd left on the icy ground. "The Daughter of the Tsar, vomiting in the forest." Still smiling, the old woman reached down and produced a makeshift wooden bowl shaped from tree bark. Within, Alana spied a crude stew of tubers and some kind of meat. She raised an eyebrow.

"It's not poisoned," Enala said when Alana didn't move to take it.

Alana bit her lip, hesitating, until a growl from the void where her stomach was usually located pushed her into action. "Thank you," she muttered as she took the bowl.

The old woman did not reply, and using her hands, Alana set about eating her breakfast. The stew was bland and the meat as tough as old leather, but in her exhausted, injured, half-starved and quite possibly half-mad state, she hardly cared. While still warm from the fire, the stew had cooled enough not to burn her fingers, and she wolfed it down in a matter of minutes.

Putting the bowl aside, Alana sat back and contemplated the old woman once more. "Why didn't you kill me?" she asked, her hand drifting to the lump on her forehead. It was the size of a goose egg. Enala must have turned her sword at the last second, striking her with the flat edge of the blade.

The old woman shrugged, her eyes still on the ashes. "Bad luck to kill a grandchild."

Alana snorted. "Glad to know you're so sentimental."

Enala lifted her head. "Care to go again, girl?"

Just the thought of picking up her sword caused the pain

in her head to redouble, and Alana quickly lowered her eyes.

"Thought so." Enala cackled.

Branches cracked as Enala lifted herself to her feet and wandered to where Alana sat. She was carrying another bowl, though this one was filled with some kind of green paste speckled with black flakes. Groaning, the old woman crouched beside her.

"Those cuts around your neck don't look good," she said matter-of-factly. "If they get infected, we'll have to amputate."

"Very funny," Alana growled, though she found herself shrinking away from the old woman's presence.

A withered hand shot out and caught her by the wrist. "Where are you going, girl?" Enala asked with a grin as she tried to pull away.

"What do you *want?*" Alana shouted, her panic rising.

"Oh, calm down," Enala snapped. "I'm trying to help." She hefted the bowl of paste. "I'm afraid I can't heal you. Unlike your father, I only command one power, and that tends to have the opposite effect on people." She chuckled at her own joke before continuing: "Luckily for you, I've learnt a few tricks over the years. This should help with the pain, and the healing."

Alana paused, the throbbing around her throat impossible to ignore. Combined with the pounding in her skull, she'd certainly had better days. Her stomach twisted as she eyed the sickly paste, before finally nodding. "Fine."

"So grateful," Enala muttered as she settled herself down and scooped paste from the bowl.

Alana flinched when the poultice touched her skin, a gasp tearing from her throat. It felt as though a burning brand was being pressed into her flesh. She was about to pull away again, when the sensation faded as quickly as it had begun. An icy cool replaced it, radiating out from where Enala had applied the paste, granting instant relief. She sighed at the absence of pain, her eyes flickering closed.

"Thank the Gods," she whispered,

A snort came from the old woman as she applied her poultice to the rest of Alana's wounds. "The Gods have nothing to do with it," she said. "You can address your thanks to me."

"Yes…thank you…Enala." She said the old woman's name reluctantly.

"You're welcome," Enala replied.

Sitting back on her haunches, the old woman inspected her work. Alana watched her, feeling suddenly uncomfortable with the old woman's kindness. She cleared her throat, thankful to find the pain almost completely numbed.

"They're not his powers, you know," she murmured, remembering Enala's comment about her father. "He tried to hide the truth, but it's difficult to keep secrets from me, even for him. He draws his magic from the Magickers in his command. And in the dungeons."

"I gathered as much, after I saw Eric."

"Your brother," Alana whispered, remembering the old man from the throne room. His attack had kept her father from completing his spell, from wiping away her memories and remaking her in his own vision. "He…saved me."

"Yes, he made a habit of doing that," Enala said, and for a moment Alana thought she caught tears in her eyes. The old woman fell silent for a moment, then gestured at Alana. "I can show you how to make more, which plants to use."

Alana nodded her thanks. Without the pain, her mind

was growing sharper now. She looked back at Enala, her lips growing tight as a thought occurred to her.

"Devon said you were looking after my brother. In Erachill. What are you doing here?"

"You didn't see him in the throne room?"

For a second, Alana thought she'd misheard. She stared at Enala, a sudden pounding in her ears as her heart began to race. In a rush, she surged to her feet.

"You brought him to the capital?"

For the first time in their encounter, the old woman managed to look ashamed. She quickly looked away, and when she spoke, Enala's words were soft, hesitant. "I thought he might shift the balance in our favour."

"He plays with illusions!" Alana shrieked, lashing out at the remains of the fire. A half-burnt log went flying across the clearing. "*Damnit!* What were you thinking, you stupid hag? What could he possibly have done to stop my father?"

Looking all her hundred-and-twenty years of life, Enala climbed to her feet. "I thought he could hide us. I thought if I could get close enough, my son..."

"You *fool*. His magic protects him."

"No, he must summon his power like any other Magicker. He is not untouchable, not if taken unawares. Did you not see Kellian's blade pierce him?"

Enala hesitated, recalling the bloody dagger jutting from her father's arm. It had caused him pain, but once he had pulled it out, the wound had healed in moments. "But even had you been successful, his magic would have held him to life."

"Perhaps," Enala whispered. There was a haunted look in her eyes, and Alana suddenly realised then what it must have cost her, to try and murder her son. "But I had to try."

A wave of pity swept through Alana, but even so, she

shook her head. "So you were willing to put my brother's life at risk, on a hunch? It could never have worked. Even with my brother's power, he would have sensed *you* well before you could strike him."

Enala's eyes returned to the forest floor. "Yes, well, it doesn't matter now, does it?" she muttered to the leaves. "I failed. We'll get no second chances now."

Something in the old woman's tone raised the hackles on Alana's neck. She took a hesitant step towards Enala, ice sliding down her spine. "Enala, where's my brother?"

"He's dead, girl," Enala snapped, swinging to face her. "My son killed him, like he killed everyone else I ever loved. And he'll be coming for us next. If you don't want to end up like your brother, I suggest we get moving."

Alana hardly heard anything after Enala's first two words. Blood pounded in her ears, drowning out all other sound. She stood staring into space, her lips parted, breath caught in her throat. She shook her head, slowly at first, then harder, as though something as simple as denying the old woman's words could change what was.

"Did you hear what I said, girl?" Enala whispered, stepping in closer. "Your father is coming, we can't stay here."

Blinking, Alana managed to focus on the old woman's face. "He can't be dead," she croaked. "He's…he's the one good thing…I gave up *everything* for him."

Enala's face softened. Unspilt tears shimmered in her eyes as she reached out and gripped Alana's shoulder. "I'm sorry, Alana," she whispered. "So, so sorry. You're right, I never should have brought him here. But nor could I stop him. When Braidon found out what had happened to you…he said he would come alone if he had to."

Alana swallowed. "That was Braidon," she whispered.

"Even before my magic..." She swallowed. "He always cared."

A frown creased Enala's forehead. "Why...why did you take both of your memories?"

"He can find you anywhere, once he knows you," Alana replied in a whisper, barely knowing what she was saying. "But I found a way to deceive him."

Enala inhaled sharply. "You did it to hide," she breathed.

Alana nodded. "Without our memories, our minds were unrecognisable to him." Her vision blurred and she swayed on her feet. "How...how did my brother die?" Her voice broke on the last word, and only Enala's grip on her shoulder kept Alana on her feet.

"He...he fell from Dahniul, when your father struck us down."

"I need to see him," Alana whispered, her eyes on the trees.

"Your father—"

"*I need to see him!*"

Alana's eyes flashed, and her magic stirred within, though it was still far too weak to be of use. Enala stared back, and for a long moment Alana thought the old woman would try to stop her. But in the end, Enala closed her eyes, and nodded.

"Very well," she murmured. "Then let us find him."

☙ 8 ❧

Sunlight coloured the horizon red as Merydith climbed the crumbling steps up the side of the mountain. Far below, darkness was already creeping over the Northland steeps, and she hoped she could make it to the peak before it reached her. Above, the fractured cliffs loomed, their crevice-riddled stone a maze leading up to her remote perch. She had hoped to arrive earlier, and spend one last quiet evening contemplating the setting sun, but preparations for the coming march had occupied her well into the afternoon.

She shivered, thinking of what was to come on the morrow. At sunrise, she would lead five thousand men and women south through the crags of the Northland mountains, through caves and tunnels and narrow canyons that would bring them out onto the plains above the southern stronghold of Fort Fall.

So few…

"And yet so many," she whispered, trying to reassure herself.

The words only reminded her of the responsibility she now carried on her shoulders. Her legs trembled, and she paused her climb for a moment to steady herself.

Five thousand.

Mothers and fathers, sons and daughters, even a few grandparents, they were the cream of the Northland clans surrounding Erachill.

The Tsar's army would outnumber them ten to one, yet they were all she had. Word had already reached them of a southern army on the march, making their slow way up through northern Plorsea. If they were allowed to reach The Gap and retake the abandoned fortress, the war would be over before it began.

Looking out over the dizzying expanse of the land below, Merydith found herself wishing for the powers of the Dark Magicker, Archon. With his magic, he had swept across the unending span of their fledging nation, summoning his people to war, marshalling them from every corner of the land. But Merydith had no such sorcery, and while messengers had gone out, it would be weeks before there was any response.

She didn't have weeks. So she would make do with her five thousand, and pray it was enough to hold them. At the least, her force was well-trained, with most coming from the warrior clans that guarded the mountain fortress of Erachill.

Merydith was within the cliffs now, making her slow way up towards the mountain peak. Shadows clung to the narrow passageways, making the going slow, and she breathed a sigh of relief when she finally dragged herself back into the sunlight.

Emerging from the crag at the top, she sat herself down on the edge of the cliff. Despite her worries, a smile came to her face as she looked out over the fading plains. This place, more than any other, reminded her of Enala. Scaling these treacherous paths with the wily old woman had become a ritual for Merydith since the time she first learned to walk. Tears welled in her eyes as she remembered the old priest.

"Where are you, Enala?" she whispered to the howling winds. "I need you."

No, you have outgrown me, girl.

Merydith swallowed as she recalled the old woman's words when she'd seen her last. At the time, the old woman's faith had filled her with pride. Yet that had been the day Enala had left. Ever since, things had gone from bad to worse, and Merydith couldn't shake the growing despair in her heart. Without Enala, they were naked in the fight against the Tsar, exposed to his nightmarish powers. The few native Magickers she had under her command could do little against the Tsar.

Demons and dragons and Magickers would come against them, and Northland had only cold hard steel to answer with.

Lowering herself onto a boulder, Merydith pulled her cloak more tightly around her to fend off the cold. The climb up the mountainside had kept her warm, but now that she'd stopped, she was already beginning to shiver. The winds were harsh on the slopes, strong enough to scrape the stones clean of snow and ice.

In the silence, she contemplated the task she faced in the morning. She would be expected to ride at the head of the army, to show no fear in the face of the challenge they faced. There was no one else—certainly no one she could trust. She had already appointed several clan leaders to oversee Northland in her absence, but most of her best were marching south with her. It was there the war would be won or lost.

Even if we win, how many of us will return?

Merydith shivered at the thought. Like most of her people, she had lived her whole life in the north. Now she would lead five thousand men and women south to die on foreign soils, far from the lands of their birth, from those who loved them. If she failed, they might all be lying in the cold hard ground by the summer.

The thought sent a tremor through her soul.

Rising, she was about to start back down to the entrance into Erachill, when a crunch of stones echoed from the crag below. Her hand dropped to her sword hilt as she scanned the shadows. Ever-vigilant since the assassination attempt, her guards had insisted on scouring the mountain paths before her hike, and then taken up position at the exit to ensure she enjoyed the last few hours of daylight undisturbed.

Her heart beat faster as she wondered if her guards had been slain like the ones outside her room, when the Tsar's assassin had come for her. Her fear only lasted a second, as her advisor Damyn appeared on the path between the cliffs. Letting out a long breath, the tension left her body. Another figure appeared alongside him, and together the two dragged themselves clear of the crevice.

It took her a moment to recognise the rugged features of the woman who stood alongside Damyn, and a few moments more to recall her name.

"Helen." She frowned. "What brings you here?" The woman was one of the Magickers who'd fled the Tsar's rein—one of the first, in fact. She and her family had sought passage on a cargo vessel departing Lon. They'd been discovered in the Northland port of Duskendale and brought overland to Erachill to face her judgement. Merydith hadn't spoken with Helen in years, and she wondered what matter was urgent enough for the woman to seek her out now.

Helen shifted on her feet and glanced sidelong at Damyn. Clearing his throat, Damyn stepped forward. While he still looked exhausted, the man seemed to have regained some of his vigour since she'd seen him last. It was a welcome sight, given she had promoted him to captain. He would command a cohort of five hundred cavalry, and she needed him at his best.

"Merydith," he said swiftly, and she was surprised to hear the excitement in his voice. "Helen brings news!"

"Does she?" she asked, her tone a gentle rebuke at his familiarity in the presence of others.

For once, Damyn didn't seem to notice. He gestured the Magicker forward, and Helen hesitantly moved up alongside him.

"Be at ease, Helen," Merydith said gently, trying to dispel the woman's nerves. "Say what you have come to say. It must be important, to brave these mountain paths at so late an hour."

"Thank you for seeing me, Your Majesty," Helen began after another second's hesitation. "I know you must have much on your plate, with the army to march at first light. But..." She trailed off, swallowing visibly. "But I...or that is to say, *we*, have decided, Your Majesty, to accompany you south."

"Accompany me south?" Merydith asked, not understanding.

Eyes downcast, Helen fiddled absently with the cuffs of her robe. "Yes..." she murmured. "We, I, *we* would like to help you, against the Tsar."

Merydith blinked, surprised at the woman's words. Standing there on the mountainside, far from any danger, Helen was as jumpy as a hare in an open field. Folding her arms, Merydith appraised the woman. She must have been fifty years of age by now, though her mousy brown hair had yet to see the streaks of age. At five-foot-five with rounded cheeks and smile lines streaking her face, she was not an imposing figure, and magic or no, Merydith could hardly imagine the woman capable of harming a fly.

Letting out a long sigh, Merydith shook her head. "Helen, that's not necessary," she said, trying to let the woman down gently. She needed Magickers desperately, but she also could not afford weakness in her army. If there was a single fault, a single soul who broke and fled, her entire force might crumble. "I offered you and the others sanctuary, so that you would be safe, so that you might raise your families free of the darkness of the Tsar. I can't ask you to march back into the fire."

"With respect, Your Majesty," Helen replied sharply, "I wasn't asking." Lifting her head, she met the Queen's eyes for the first time. Merydith was surprised to see the ferocity burning there. "I know what you think of me, that I am old and afraid, that I would run at the first clash of swords. Well you're wrong. I have known this day would come since I first came here, that one day the Tsar would set his sights on Northland. And I will not stand idly by when I might do something to stop him. Nor will the others."

"The others?" Merydith asked, shocked at the woman's defiance.

"Yes," the Magicker growled. "When I first heard the news the Tsar was marching, I went to my fellow Magickers, to the other refugees who fled here to escape his wrath. I brought them together, gathered them to see who else wished to fight for their adoptive nation. And I am here to tell you that myself, and a hundred others, are ready to march on the morrow, Your Majesty. And we're not asking."

Helen trailed off into silence, as though suddenly realising she'd gone too far, overstepped her bounds. Silently she dropped her gaze back to the rocky trail.

Merydith was too shocked by her news to care. She stood staring at the woman, struggling to comprehend what her news meant.

A hundred Magickers.

They could prove all the difference, might even be enough to hold off the dark powers of the Tsar. But what Helen was offering went against everything Merydith believed in, everything she'd sacrificed to save the refugee Magickers.

"Are you sure, Helen?" she tried one last time, though her words sounded half-hearted, even to herself.

Helen smiled. "Northland opened its arms for us, took us in when we had nowhere else to go. This is our home now, and the Tsar threatens it. We will march beside you to defend its freedom, will die if needs be, to ensure our families live on in peace."

Merydith nodded, her eyes shining. "So be it."

9

Alana swallowed as the aroma of roasting fish drifted to where she sat on a rounded boulder. Her mouth salivated as the old woman turned the makeshift spit they'd erected over the flames. A howling wind swept through the valley, adding to the watery chorus of the running stream and causing the fire to flicker dangerously. Shadows danced across Enala's face, and it seemed to Alana that the abyss was calling to the woman, summoning her to her grave.

An icy draft slid down Enala's spine and shivering, she looked away. They had spent the long day combing the forests around where Enala and her dragon had crashed, searching, seeking, hunting for any sign of her brother…

A lump lodged in her throat at the thought of him lying somewhere in the frozen snow, his face pale with death, staring off into nothing. Closing her eyes, Enala summoned an image of her father. Hatred rose within her, sweeping aside the grief. She shuddered and clung desperately to the emotion, determined not to allow herself the weakness of sorrow.

It was no use though. The other part of her cried out within, her anguish slicing through Alana's hatred like a knife to pierce her heart. She choked back a sob as tears spilt down her cheeks.

She had done her best to hold herself together during the search, to conceal her emotions from the old woman who strode alongside her. Even when they'd broken for the night to set up camp, Alana had thrown herself into the old routine with zest, determined to keep herself distracted. Collecting firewood, tickling a trout from the stream, building the fire—she'd kept her emotions in place through all of it.

Now though, in the silence of the night, they returned to haunt her.

Looking at the old woman, Alana recalled the grief on her aged face as she'd knelt beside the dragon. She had thought it strange at the time, but now she wondered whether her sorrow had been for the beast, or for Braidon. Clutching desperately at the distraction, she rose from her boulder and jumped down beside the fire.

Enala glanced up, one eyebrow raised in question.

"How did you come to know the dragon?" Alana asked tactfully.

"I once knew many Gold Dragons, in my youth," the old woman replied with a smile. "My parents raised me in Dragon Country, when the Gold tribe still ruled that land. They were allied to my family, bound by an ancient pact with the old king of Trola." She paused, her eyes flickering in Alana's direction. "To *our* family."

Alana swallowed. "How did the beast end up in Northland then?"

"Her name was Dahniul," Enala admonished, "and she was there because she came with me. After the war against

Archon, Gabriel and I returned to Dragon Country. It was there we raised your father, alongside my brother's family. But the Gold Dragons had suffered terribly against Archon. After losing so many of their numbers, they failed to prosper. Dahniul was the last of her kind, as I suppose, I am the last of my generation."

"So she joined you when you left for Northland?"

Enala nodded and was about to reply, when a *thump* came from the trees lining the slope of the valley. They were both on their feet in an instant, swords leaping into their hands.

Alana squinted into the darkness beyond their fire, suddenly all too aware of Onslow Forest's reputation. This was a land for rough and wild company. Two women alone in the wilderness would likely be seen as an easy target.

Gripping her sword hilt tighter, Alana smiled at the surprise any wood-be robbers would get if they tried to attack.

The shadows at the edge of their firelight shifted, and a giant figure loomed in the darkness. Alana's eyes widened, her heart skipping a beat. Devon's name was on her lips as the man stepped into the light.

The word died in her throat as she stared at the stranger looming over them. A terrible scar ran from one side of the man's face to the other, and his hazel eyes seemed to glow in the darkness. His jet-black hair had been pulled into a bun that would have been comical on a smaller man, but with this giant it only seemed add to his ferocity. White streaked his matted beard, though with a massive double-blade axe in hand, Alana wasn't thinking about his age.

He stood there in the light of their campfire, appraising them in silence. Alana shifted nervously on her feet, eyes on the axe. Though she didn't doubt the two of them could best him, with such a weapon there would be no room for mistakes. One blow from that monster would end her life.

"What do you want?" Enala asked, her voice edged in steel.

The giant chuckled as he looked over at the old woman. "Such a frosty greeting from a priest," he rumbled.

Enala smirked. "Yes, well, the Goddess didn't see it fit to bless me with much patience."

Their visitor laughed again. "Ay, I bet." He scratched his beard, as though contemplating his next move. "Well, to be honest, I came here to see whether you might have anything of value."

Alana tensed, but the giant continued before she could make a move. "But I see now I've stumbled across the campfire of a priest. Seems like it would be bad luck to harm a servant of Antonia, being in her own forest and all. Wouldn't want a vengeful Goddess after me, would I?"

Alana exchanged a glance with the old woman. "Since when does a thief care about the Gods?"

The giant's face darkened at her words. "The name's Joseph," he growled. "And I'm a Baronian, not a thief."

Alana frowned. "Baronian? My father hunt—"

"As far as I recall," Enala interrupted her, "Baronians hunt in packs. Not much of a terror by yourself, are you Joseph?" As she finished, the old woman flicked a glance at Alana, silently reprimanding her for the near-mistake.

"You've got a tongue like acid, priest," Joseph replied good-naturedly. "Glad I don't have to fight you, if you're half as ferocious with that sword." He picked at his sleeve. "And pack or not, I am a Baronian. Why else would I be all in black?"

"You look like a poor knockoff of the Tsar's Stalkers,"

Alana snapped. She glanced at Enala, irritated the woman hadn't ordered the man to leave yet.

Instead, Enala threw back her head and howled with laughter. Alana jumped, and stared at the old woman, open-mouthed.

"The girl is right, you do look like you've seen better days, Baronian. So sit," she said, ignoring Alana's apocalyptic look. "No need for you to go away with an empty stomach as well as empty-handed."

Shocked into silence, all Alana could do was watch as the giant took a seat on a rock near the fire. Sheathing her sword, Enala joined him, and the two started to talking like long-lost friends who had just been reunited. Alana stood there a moment longer, sword still in hand, but the two seemed to have forgotten her very existence.

Finally she sank back to her seat, though she laid her sword alongside her rather than returning it to her sheath. Enala took the fish from the flames and sliced it into three morsels. Handing Alana her portion, she turned back to Joseph. The two continued to talk as they picked at the soft flesh of the trout that Alana had frozen her hands off to catch.

Alana's anger built as she watched them eat, and she barely touched her own fish. She began to wonder whether the loss of her dragon had caused Enala to snap, if the old woman suddenly had a death wish, inviting the self-proclaimed Baronian to share their fire. The Baronians had been stamped out by her father in the early days of his rein, but she recalled tales of their people well. Great tribes of them had once roamed the wild lands of the Three Nations, harrying travellers and settlements at will. The kings of the time had been powerless to stop them, so great were their numbers.

That is, until the Tsar had come.

"You're awfully quiet, girly."

Alana jumped as she realised the giant had addressed her. She looked up from her food and glared at him. "My name's Alana," she snapped, a scowl curling her lips. "And I'm not used to sharing my food with scum."

"Is that so?" Joseph replied with a hairy grin. "Good to know." His eyes narrowed. "You know, word is there's another Alana in these parts, Daughter of the Tsar or some sort. Lot of folks looking for that one, Stalkers and the like. Causing a lot of trouble in my forest."

Ice ran down Alana's spine. She dropped her hand to her sword, preparing to launch herself at the rogue.

But Joseph only shrugged, another chuckle whispering through the smoke-filled air. "It's a good thing you're not *that* Alana, right?" He looked at her with one eyebrow raised.

Watching him, Alana slowly relaxed, and took her hand from the sword. "I guess so."

Nodding, Joseph turned to where he'd discarded his axe and pack. Rummaging inside, he came back with a bottle of what Alana took to be spirits. He offered it to her, but Alana only shook her head. Grinning, Enala took the bottle instead, and their conversation resumed, though Alana caught the old woman flash her a warning glare.

Alana rose and wandered away. Enala could take care of herself, she decided. Determined not to let her hard-earned fish go to waste, she finished her remaining portion and then tossed the bones into the stream for the crayfish to finish.

As the night grew older, she found a place near the fire and settled herself down. Enala and Joseph were still conversing, but she curled up without offering either another word and closed her eyes. At least the giant's appearance had distracted her momentarily from her brother, though thoughts of him returned now to haunt her. It was a long time before the darkness finally rose to claim her.

In the morning, Alana woke with a start. Sitting up, she looked around to find Enala already at the fire, a pot of stew bubbling over the flames. She frowned, then suppressed a groan as pain came from her neck.

"I made you a fresh batch," Enala said, as though reading her mind. The old woman nodded to a makeshift bowl of paste sitting beside Alana.

She took it gratefully. The relief as she applied it was instant, and she closed her eyes, almost willing to sing the old woman's blessings. Almost.

Rising, Alana crossed to the fire. "Where did that come from?" she asked, gesturing to the pot and stew.

"Joseph left it for us," Enala replied, a smile that screamed I-told-you-so on her lips.

"How nice of him," Alana said sarcastically. "You sure it's not poisoned?"

"You need to open your mind, girl," the old woman snapped. She took a breath, her eyes flickering closed, as though she were in pain. "Sorry, I guess I'm not as young as I used to be."

Alana grinned despite herself. "You think?"

"Watch it, girl," Enala shot back, though there was no venom in the words. She sighed, her face turning serious. "Before we start today, I need to know, what are you trying to achieve, looking for Braidon?"

Alana quickly looked away. "I need to see him."

"Is that all of it?"

The words caught in Alana's throat as she looked up to refute the old woman's unspoken accusation. She swallowed them back. "No," she croaked. "I…he could still be alive."

Enala sighed. "I don't think so, Alana. Not with the fall he took."

"Even so…I want to see him, *need* to see him, or I'll never…"

"It won't be long, you know, before the Tsar regains enough magic to sense us. My magic is rebuilding, yours must be too. His own Magickers won't be far behind. Once his power is restored, there will be no place left for us to hide."

"So be it," Alan replied.

"So be it," Enala repeated. She grinned then, gesturing at the bubbling pot. "Well, if I'm to fight alongside someone, I'd appreciate it if she were at least a half-decent swordswoman."

"*What?*" Alana spluttered. "I am—"

"You're competent, I'll give you that, but you're no master, girl," Enala replied.

"I can take you, old woman," Alana growled.

Enala only grinned. Reaching behind her, she lifted two long sticks from behind the boulder she was perched on. She tossed one at Alana's feet.

"Then show me."

10

Quinn wore a grim smile as he listened to the crackling of the flames, their roar as they rushed up the sides of the wooden houses, the *boom* as roofs collapsed in on themselves. Great pillars of smoke spiralled upwards, merging with the grey winter sky. His men moved with swift efficiency between each house, dragging out all occupants before tossing flaming torches through the open windows.

The *whoosh* as the new building took light was music to Quinn's ears. He looked at the gathered villagers, on their knees in the centre of the settlement. They wore a mixture of grief and rage on their faces, though none moved to try and stop Quinn and his men. Nor did any come forward with information, and he grated his teeth at their continued obstruction.

Someone had to have seen them. Four renegades could not have gone unnoticed in this forest. With her blonde hair, Alana might have passed for a local, but not the others. Certainly not a young boy barely of age accompanied by an old priest, nor the giant that was Devon. A traveller, a passerby, a villager, someone, *anyone* had to have glimpsed them, even if they had kept to the backtrails.

Yet there had been no word for six days, not since the village of Onslow. There, at least, he had found a witness to Devon's precipitous disembarking from the trading ship. The man was no fool, and had obviously decided making his way through the forest was a better option than taking the Gods Road to Trola.

Of Alana and Braidon and Enala though, there had been not a whisper.

Quinn was starting to grow desperate. This was the fourth village they had burned, and the other Stalkers were becoming restless. They had taken to questioning his orders, challenging his authority at every turn. He was loathe to call on the Tsar's aid, and lose whatever respect he had left, but if there was no word soon he would have no other choice.

Turning to the villagers, Quinn strode across to where they knelt in the mud. "Any sudden recollections yet?" he growled.

The villagers glared back at him, tears streaking their cheeks. Ash fell heavily around them, staining their faces and clothes, all that remained of their livelihoods.

"You would rather see your village burned than betray a couple of renegades?" he asked, shaking his head.

"What can we tell you when we know nothing?" one of the men spat back.

"Liars!" Quinn shrieked, his sabre hissing as it left his sheath. He pointed the tip at the man's throat, but the villager barely moved.

"We do not lie," he replied. "You are mad, Stalker. The Tsar will hear of what you've done."

Quinn smirked. "The Tsar sent me to rat out these traitors. He does not care if I burn a few others along the way."

"But we are loyal—"

The man's protest was cut short as Quinn drove his blade through the man's throat. Screams went up from the other villagers as the dying man clutched at the wound, trying hopelessly to stem the bleeding. The others tried to scramble up and flee, but Quinn's Stalkers intercepted them and forced them back to their knees. Finally, the man gave a soft groan, and toppled face-first to the ground.

Looking at the next villager in line, Quinn raised his bloody sword. "Well?"

"Please, don't hurt me!" the man screamed. He tried to scramble away, but a Stalker gripped him by the shoulder and shoved him down.

"Where is the renegade known as Devon? The blonde girl, Alana, the black-haired boy, Braidon?"

"I don't know!"

"Then die."

The man cried out, but Quinn's blade took him in the heart before he could put up any fight. He sagged against the impaling sword, then toppled sideways as Quinn dragged back his weapon.

"Who's next?" he growled, swinging his sword in an arc that spanned the remaining villagers.

"The Baronians!" a man at the end of the line shrieked as the blade stopped at an older woman.

Quinn glanced along the line. "What?"

The man paled, and he shook his head as though trying to recall the words. At a gesture from Quinn, one of the Stalkers grabbed him by the scruff of his neck and dragged him across to where the lieutenant stood. Quinn rested the cold point of his blade against the man's chest.

"Well?"

Swallowing visibly, the villager glanced from Quinn to the woman he had threatened. "Please, you have to promise to leave us alone, if I tell you."

Quinn scowled. "First tell me what you know, peasant."

"I…it's not much, only a rumour I heard."

Lowering his sword, Quinn walked around the man to where the older woman knelt. "I take it she is something to you, lad?" he asked, resting his blade against the woman's neck. She flinched away from its touch, though her eyes remained defiant.

"Please don't hurt her!" The man tried to rise, but a shove from the Stalker at his side sent him face-first into the ground.

"Then *speak*," Quinn hissed.

"There's a tribe of Baronians here, they passed by a few days ago, to collect their ransom. I overhead one of them talking about two women he'd met in the forest."

"Yes?" Quinn said, trying to keep the excitement from his voice.

"He said one was a priest, seems she impressed him."

"And the other?"

The villager cleared his throat. "He described her in… some detail," he whispered, "but…he mentioned she had blonde hair."

A fire lit in Quinn's stomach at the villager's words. He had no doubt the so-called Baronian had been speaking of Alana. Who else but she would be cavorting with the thugs inhabiting these woods? He had no idea how she had come to be travelling with the old priest, Enala, but the two of them together presented a serious threat. He would need to find a way to trap them.

If he could find them at all.

"Where?" Quinn grated as he returned to the man's side.

"West of here," the villager replied quickly. "In the forested valleys leading up towards the Sandstone Mountains."

"Very good," Quinn replied. They weren't too far from the western mountains now, though finding the two women in such dense wilderness would be another matter. He was about to move away when another question occurred to him. "You spoke of Baronians? How is that possible, the Tsar hunted them to extinction decades ago. You had best not be lying to me."

"No, I swear!" The man swallowed. "They came here a year ago, took up residence in the forest. Word was sent to the Tsar when they began raiding our villages, but no one ever came. Eventually we agreed to a ransom to keep them away from us."

Quinn stared at the man to the count of ten, but he could see no sign of deceit in his young eyes. Finally he nodded and moved away from the villagers, aware his Stalkers were watching him. This was the first substantial news they'd had since leaving Onslow, and it was still little enough at that. Time was running out and another failure would spell the end for Quinn.

"Mount up!" he shouted, spinning back to his Stalkers.

There was a moment's hesitation amongst the black-garbed men and women of his regiment. Then one stepped forward, a smirk on his face. "Are you sure, Quinn?" the man rasped. "Would it not be better for you to call on your master?"

The anger that had begun with the villager's news of Alana roared. Quinn clenched his fists, struggling to keep control of himself. He would gain nothing by rising to the man's provocation.

"You want me to distract the Tsar from his conquest, Zarent?" he asked quietly. "To call him here when we are still empty-handed? Is that truly what you want, to look him in the eye and tell him *we* have failed?"

Silence answered his question as the man Zarent blanked, and Quinn nodded.

"Very well then. If there are no other questions...? Then *mount up!*"

II

Topping the rise, Braidon stumbled to a stop, his breathing heavy as he looked up and saw Devon already extending the distance between them. Letting out a groan, Braidon started after him again, trying to ignore the burning in his calves. Six days of marching through the wilderness had taken their toll, and while he thought he'd done a good job of keeping up with Devon's massive strides, he had a feeling the hammerman was holding back now.

Ahead, Devon glanced back at a bend in the narrow game trail, and Braidon picked up the pace, determined not to show the giant warrior any weakness.

A grin spread across his companion's face as Braidon marched up. "You've got stones, sonny," he said, slapping Braidon on the back.

Braidon staggered beneath the blow, his trembling legs barely managing to keep him upright. By the time he recovered, Devon was already several feet ahead. Braidon poked his tongue out at the man's retreating back, then shaking his head, continued after him.

They had no particular destination or goal in mind, and many of their six days on the road had been spent wandering the backtrails of Onslow Forest. All Braidon knew was that they were working their way west towards the Sandstone Mountains. The going was slow in the dense forest, with its low-lying scrub and steep valleys, but Devon was sure that the only alternative, the road through Brunei Pass, would be guarded against them.

Braidon came alongside Devon as the path widened once more. Glancing at the hammerman, he wondered how the man maintained such a pace for so long, seemingly without exertion. Especially with the giant warhammer *kanker* strapped to his back.

"Is it heavy?" he asked, suddenly curious if some spell on the weapon made it lighter than it appeared.

Devon cast him a sidelong look and grinned. "Try it for yourself." Unsheathing *kanker*, he tossed it into the air as though it weighed no more than a sack of feathers, caught it by the head, and offered it to Braidon.

For a full five seconds, all Braidon could do was stare at the ancient weapon, but finally he found his nerve, and reached out to grip the black haft. Still grinning, Devon released the hammer. Braidon cried out as the hammer's weight almost dragged the weapon from his hands. His other arm snapped up to grip the haft in a two-handed grip.

"Gods, how much does this *weigh?*" he groaned.

Chuckling, Devon retrieved the weapon and sheathed it.

"Not so much for a giant like me, sonny," he said. He eyed the dagger on Braidon's belt. "But maybe we can find you something a little more suitable for a growing lad."

Braidon glanced up sharply. "Really?" Alana had never let him have a sword—at least, not that he could remember.

"Why not?" Devon replied, resuming his march down the winding dirt track.

"I don't know how to use one," he mused as he caught up. "Or at least, I can't remember how… It does seem like something my father would have taught me."

"What's it like?" Devon asked, tapping his head. "Having these other memories you can't quite…remember?"

Braidon frowned, his attention distracted by a blackbird as it raced squawking across their path. "It's not easy," he said finally. "What I *can* remember of my other life, they don't seem like my memories at all. It's like they belong to some other Braidon, if that makes sense?"

"I'm not quite sure it does," Devon admitted, scratching his wiry beard.

Closing his eyes, Braidon tried to find some way to explain. "There's only a few, enough for me to know I truly was the Son of the Tsar. I can *see* them as clear as day, I can see myself in them. But I can't remember what I was thinking or feeling when I was doing those things."

"Ah, I think I get it!" the warrior grinned. "So it's kind of like watching bards performing a play, with you as the main character?"

"That seems like a very specific example," Braidon said, eyeing Devon thoughtfully.

"Yes, well," Devon grunted. "There might have been a play or two featuring yours truly after the civil war. All ancient history now, of course. You were probably too young to remember them. There was one, *The Butcher of Kalgan,* think it was. Pretty popular in the local taverns of Ardath. Well, until word got out that I'd rescinded my commission in the army."

"Yes!" Braidon exclaimed. "I *do* remember!" A grin

spread across his cheeks as he looked at the hammerman. "They changed the title though: *The Cowardly Hero*, I think they called it."

Devon's own smile vanished as he glared at Braidon. "I prefer—"

Before the warrior could finish his rebuke, a high-pitched scream echoed through the trees. Braidon and Devon shared a glance. The cry sounded again; this time it was clear it came from the path ahead. Reaching up, Devon drew *kanker* and started down the track.

"Stay there," he shouted over his shoulder to Braidon as he leaped a half-buried tree root.

Braidon stood frozen to the spot and watched as the giant charged off. Another scream came from ahead. Putting aside his fear, Braidon raced after his companion. He reached down and drew his dagger as he ran, already wishing he had a larger blade to hand.

Around the bend, Braidon looked ahead, expecting to see Stalkers or soldiers with weapons at the ready. He had been waiting for them for days now, thinking at any moment that his father's warriors would come leaping from the trees. His magic restored, Braidon had hidden them both from the Tsar's powers, but with an army under his command, it was only a matter of time before they were flushed from their hiding place.

Yet as the track straightened and the source of the commotion was revealed, Braidon was surprised to find a very different scene playing out before him.

Devon was still charging ahead, but beyond the giant hammerman, a desperate battle was taking place around a small horse-drawn wagon. A man and woman stood on the seat of the wagon, longswords in hand, each struggling to keep a surging crowd of black-garbed men at bay. They might have been mistaken for his father's Stalkers, if not for their threadbare clothing and half-rusted weapons.

His heart beat faster as Devon shouted a war cry. Chasing after him, Braidon's gaze was drawn to the wagon as one of the assailants leapt, his blade catching the woman's weapon near the handle. The impact tore the sword from her grip, but screaming out in rage, she drew a blade from her belt and plunged it into the man's eye. Blood blossomed as she ripped it loose. Her attacker crumpled in a pile, but another one of his comrades was quick to take his place.

Roaring, Devon surged into the fray, his warhammer clutched one-handed. Braidon watched in awe as he carved through the bandits gathered around the wagon. The first of them went down without a sound, taken unawares by Devon's sudden attack. Next to him, another assailant staggered as the body of his comrade fell across his feet. He spun around in time to catch *kanker* squarely between the eyes. Braidon winced as the man crumpled.

There were still a dozen left, and alerted by their friends' deaths, several turned to face Devon. A man carrying a rust-speckled axe charged, the others reforming behind him. Braidon was still several yards behind Devon. He rushed forward, desperate to offer his aid.

Helped by the narrow path, Devon knocked aside a vicious blow from the axe-man, then reversed his hammer and slammed it into the bandit's chest. Striding over the falling body, he ducked a wild slash of a sword, then caught his attacker with a right hook. The man reeled back clutching his nose, until a blow from *kanker* ended the threat.

Leaping the first of the bodies, Braidon rushed forward, but Devon's bulk filled the narrow animal track, and there was no way for him to enter the fray. The big man was laughing now, his mirth bellowing out with each swing of his hammer.

As Braidon watched, another man came at the giant. A sword thrust beneath Devon's guard, but a swing of his gauntleted wrist smashed the blade aside. Before the bandit could react, Devon's hand flicked out, catching the assailant by the shirt and dragging him into a headbutt. There was an audible *crunch* of breaking bone. Tossing the unconscious man aside, Devon continued forward.

On the wagon, the man had downed one of his assailants, while the woman had recovered a sword and was making short work of a bandit trying to gain a foothold beside her.

Suddenly a cry went up, and as Braidon watched, the remaining bandits turned tail and fled. Devon dispatched a bandit and then swung around, searching for his next opponent. He blinked, a frown creasing his forehead as he observed the suddenly empty trail.

Seeing the last of the men vanishing into the woods, he bellowed after them, "Cowards!" His cry echoed loudly on the trail, though none of the thieves stopped to challenge his accusation.

"They're thieves, Devon," Braidon muttered, moving alongside him. "It's not like they're the stuff of legend."

The big man glanced down at him. Blood matted his beard, and there were several cuts on his arms, but otherwise he didn't seem injured. His frown faded, and Braidon watched as the tension slowly drained from the warrior's body.

"True," Devon grunted, finally.

A shriek from the wagon drew Braidon's attention back to the couple. One of the bandits they'd downed was climbing to his knees, but before he could stand, the woman leapt from the wagon. Her sword cleaved his spine and he crashed back to the ground. Hurling aside her sword, the woman kicked him in the side.

"Serves. You. Right." She punctuated each word with another kick. "Trying. To. Rob. Us. Good. For. Nothing. *Bastard!*"

"Enough, Elynor!" Sheathing his sword, the man came up behind the woman and grabbed her arm.

She screamed at his touch and swung a fist to fight him off. The man staggered back from the blow, raising a hand to fend off further attack, but seeing it was him, the woman lowered her hand. "Just making sure he got the point."

Braidon glanced at the bandit. Blood slowly spread out around him, forming a scarlet pool in the hard-packed earth.

"I'd say he gets it," Devon rumbled. Braidon nodded his agreement.

On the path, the two spun to face them. The man raised his sword and the woman quickly recovered hers. Braidon raised his hands, but Devon only chuckled.

"Is that any way to treat your saviours?" the giant warrior asked, gesturing to the bandits he'd felled.

The woman scowled. "We had things handled," she snapped, but her sword lowered a fraction. Beside her, the man did the same.

Grinning, Devon wandered towards them, surveying the fallen men as he went. "What were there, a dozen?" He glanced back at Braidon. "How many would you say made it into the woods, sonny?"

"Six?" Braidon replied uncertainly.

"A few more than a dozen then," Devon replied.

Beyond, the couple shared a glance. They were well-dressed in warm woollen coats and thick leather boots.

Though the snow from earlier in the week had thawed, Braidon found himself wishing he was similarly attired. However, the clothing worn by the slain bandits was even shabbier than his own fraying jerkin and boots. His eyes settled on a sword pitted with dents and rust. Thinking it might be better than his tiny dagger, he scooped it up.

"Yes, well, whatever our chances were," the man was saying, "I thank you for your help, hammerman." Striding forward, he offered his hand. "My names Carcia, and this is my wife, Elynor. The two of us are in your debt."

Devon shook the man's hand, though Braidon noticed his eyes were on the wagon. The bandits had managed to tear off the blanket covering the back, and Braidon could see a handful of household items lying in a cluttered pile. It looked as though the two had packed in a hurry. They might have been well-dressed, but Braidon guessed they had fallen on hard times to find themselves so far from the Gods Road without so much as a sellsword to help guard their belongings.

"What brings you so far into the forest with a rocking chain and spindle?" Devon asked, sheathing his hammer on his back. Braidon removed a sword belt from one of the bandits and put away his new sword. With their weapons secured, the couple seemed to relax.

"Elynor and I are running away," the man explained. "We've had enough of the wars, so we're getting out." He paused, his eyes flickering to the hammer on Devon's back. "Just like you, if my suspicions about that hammer are correct."

Devon shrugged. "True enough." He gestured at the wagon. "How about the two of you mount up and we continue this conversation on the road. Who knows if there's more of them scum out there."

Casting nervous glances at the woods, the couple nodded and returned to their wagon. Carcia took a moment to inspect the horse as Elynor climbed into the seat and picked up the reins. A few moments later Carcia joined her, apparently assured the gelding was okay. Braidon guessed the bandits had been intent on taking the beast as their own —after all, it was the most valuable thing he could see in the couple's possession.

With a flick of the reins, the horse started off. Devon strode along beside it, his eyes on the trees, and Braidon hurried to catch up. Now that the adrenaline was fading from his body, his exhaustion returned, and he looked at the back of the wagon with longing.

"Don't suppose you've got room up there for the boy?" Devon asked as Braidon reached them.

Braidon opened his mouth to argue, but the woman was already nodding, and before he could react Devon was scooping him up and tossing him down amongst the wooden chairs and furnishings.

"There's probably room for you as well," Carcia offered, though his face betrayed his doubt.

Devon shook his head. "I'm just as happy walking, sonny," he replied. "Good for the heart."

Brushing dust from his clothes, Braidon climbed forward until he could seat himself behind the couple. "Thanks for the ride," he said sheepishly. "The name's Braidon, by the way. I guess you already know Devon's."

"Least we could do after you helped us out," Carcia replied, though beside him his wife snorted. He flicked her a scowl before continuing. "What brings you so far from the capital, young Braidon?" he asked. "That's an Ardath accent, if I'm not mistaken?"

Braidon shared a glance with Devon. "Same as you, I

suppose," he said hesitantly, belatedly attempting to add a more rustic tone to his voice. "Devon was a friend of my parents, before…they passed. He's looked after me ever since. I'm fifteen last year, and Devon thought it best we leave before I was conscripted into the war."

Alongside the wagon, Devon's eyebrows rose at the lie, before he quickly nodded in response to the couple's inquisitive stares. "We're heading into the Sandstone Mountains," the warrior said. "See if we can make a life for ourselves out here, least until the war dies down.

"I hear the Queen is marching on us with the Northland army," Carcia said in a hushed tone, as though the woman were close by, and not a thousand leagues to the north."

"That'd be the day," Devon grunted. "More likely, the damned Tsar is looking for an excuse to conquer another kingdom."

Braidon's heart skipped a beat at Devon's treasonous words. A strained silence followed. Braidon looked at the couple out of the corner of his eye, trying to judge their reactions by the expressions on their faces. Beside the wagon, Devon's face blanked and his hands tightened into fists.

"I suppose that could be true," Carcia said, then laughed. "By the Three Gods, it's nice to hear some plain speaking for once!"

The woman was still eyeing Devon closely, but after another moment she seemed to shrug his comment off. "Perhaps, but whatever his faults, I'd still rather have the Tsar ruling us, than those barbarians in the north. Might not be such a bad thing to put them in their place, either. The Gods know they can't be trusted."

Anger flared in Braidon's chest. Remembering the kindness the Northland people had shown when they'd taken him under their protection, the woman's words grated on him. Clenching his teeth, he swallowed back an insult.

"Can't say I've ever had a problem with 'em," Devon said diplomatically. "Their traders have certainly proven more trustworthy than some of the Lonians I've dealt with."

Elynor snorted. "They might pretend they've changed, but a Feline doesn't change its stripes. They've tried to invade—twice. Now that they've got this new Queen, Merydith or whatever her name is, what's to stop them trying it again?"

"Respect, trade, peace?" Braidon asked.

"Those might mean something to a rational leader, little boy, but who's to say we're dealing with someone rational?"

"And what would you prefer?" Devon rumbled. "We invade them unprovoked?"

"If needs be."

"How would that make us any better than those who marched under Archon?" the hammerman asked.

"We're the Three Nations," Elynor replied as though the answer were obvious. "We're the good guys."

"Tell that to Trola," Devon grunted.

An awkward silence stretched out between the four of them as they continued on their way. Braidon shared a look with Devon, but with nothing left to say, they let the conversation drop. Lying back in the wagon, Braidon closed his eyes, pleased for the chance to rest. The soft creaking of the wooden wheels played in his ears like a lullaby, the gentle rocking of the wagon beckoning him to sleep.

12

"Woah, boy!" Merydith said, pulling back on the reins.

Her mount came to a stop on the hilltop, and she allowed herself to glance back over her shoulder. Away to the north, the towering mountains of Erachill rose from the foothills she and her army had just traversed. The tall bows of beech trees rose from the hillslopes, their canopies thick with leaves even in the depths of winter, concealing her forces below.

Turning her gaze to the way ahead, Merydith looked on the empty hillside leading down the last ten miles to the coast. There, the land fell away sharply to the raging waters of two oceans—except where the narrow stretch of land known as The Gap spanned the channel. The ramparts of Fort Fall rose from the earth there, its granite walls standing in defiance of the centuries.

Once, it had been the impenetrable fortress of the Three Nations, the bane of her people. From its gates the southerners sallied out to raid the clans of the north, crushing any hint of rebellion—until Archon had united them beneath his dark cause. Only once had the fortress fallen, during Archon's first coming.

Now, thankfully, its gates stood open to them. Merydith breathed a sigh of relief to see the Tsar's people had not yet reached the fortress. Her plans relied on crossing into the Three Nations before Fort Fall could be secured against them. Once they had a foothold in northern Lonia, the Tsar would be forced to bring his army against her, or risk having his supply lines cut when he tried to march farther north.

With luck, Merydith and her five thousand would lead him a merry chase, buying enough time for those back in Erachill to gather the rest of their army.

Supplying her own forces would quickly become difficult though, if her allies in Lonia and Trola fell through. She had sent messengers before their departure from Erachill, but so far there had been no word on whether they had reached their destination. Like so many other parts to her plan, all she could do was pray.

"We made it." Damyn brought his horse alongside her.

Merydith smiled at her childhood friend and new captain. "Did you doubt it?"

Damyn rolled his eyes. "Do you have to ask?"

Chuckling, Merydith shook her head. "I hope you didn't let your cohort see it."

She had placed him in command of the vanguard. His soldiers were gathering around them even now, their horses kept in tight formation. Steam rose from their flanks in the morning chill, and the men wore thick woollen coats over their chainmail. Most wore steel helmets and were armed with sabres and iron bucklers for shields. They looked to her in anticipation, awaiting the command to advance.

A smile touched her lips as she raised her hand. With a

shout, Damyn kicked his horse forward. The thunder of five hundred horses rumbled across the slopes as the vanguard followed him. Watching them ride, she found herself wondering at the change time had wrought. Whereas a century ago, her people had united with dreams of conquest and destruction, today they rode south in defence of their nation. Her heart swelled at the sight, and with a shout she started down the slope after them.

Ahead, her five hundred cavalry slowed as they neared Fort Fall. Damyn knew his orders well. He was to search the fortress and ensure no ambush waited, before continuing south to scout out the enemy's position. She hoped they had time yet before the Tsar arrived, but she had no desire to be taken unawares.

"The true test begins now." Murdo's dry, rasping voice came from behind her.

Merydith smiled at the sight of the old man in the saddle. In the warmth of the southern sun, he looked younger than she'd seen him in years. Her smile faded as she recognised the figure who rode beside him.

"The beginning of the end," Mokyre said bitterly.

"Did you want Clan Cranook to join the vanguard, Mokyre?" she asked coldly. Distasteful as she found his presence, Merydith had disliked the prospect of leaving the Cranook clan leader behind in Erachill even less. She didn't need enemies stirring things up behind her back while she was risking her life in the south.

The man scowled, but wisely kept his silence. Merydith nodded her approval, as Murdo chuckled, a mischievous grin on his face.

"So, my Queen, the invasion begins. Did you ever dream you'd end up leading an army against the Three Nations?"

Merydith smiled despite herself. "I can't say I did," she replied with a wink, "but after everything they've done for us, I figure it's the least I can do."

Murdo laughed, while Mokyre only scowled and looked away.

Silence fell as they approached the walls. Damyn and his vanguard had already disappeared within the fortress. Merydith took the silence as a good sign. With a glance at her guard, she continued towards the walls.

"I always forget how large this place is," Murdo murmured, his old eyes on the granite walls. "A wonder it was ever taken."

"Hardly difficult with the magic at Archon's command," Merydith replied.

"Do you think he has become more powerful than Archon? The Tsar, I mean?" the old man mused.

"I don't know or care," Merydith answered. "I just hope Helen and her Magickers are powerful enough to hold him back."

"They will be," Murdo said with confidence. Alongside him, Mokyre snorted but said nothing.

"They will or they won't. There's nothing I can do to change it," Merydith sighed. "Much as I might wish it otherwise."

Merydith's thoughts returned to Enala and Braidon. She found herself wondering again what had happened to them, what had gone wrong. Because if the Tsar was marching north with an army, it could only mean they had failed. As for Devon and Kellian, she hadn't heard a single whisper of them since they'd made contact with Enala's connection in Trola.

"She will return to us," Murdo said from beside her. "She always has."

Glancing at the old man, Merydith sighed. She'd forgotten her face was like an open book to him. Her eyes burned at his words and she quickly blinked back the unspilt tears. "This time was different. This time, she said goodbye."

"The woman isn't one to go down without a fight," Murdo murmured. "We'll see her again, you'll see."

Merydith nodded, though she couldn't bring herself to believe the old man's words. The morning Enala had said her goodbyes, Merydith had known in her heart it would be the last time she saw her. But she could not let the others see her despair.

"I know," she replied, forcing a smile to her lips. "I'm just afraid the stubborn old woman has bitten off more than she can chew."

"Better not let her hear you call her that." The old man winked.

As they approached the walls of Fort Fall, Merydith directed her horse towards the open gates. The two clan leaders followed, her guard bringing up the rear. While Merydith had passed this way many times as a child, of the others only Murdo had seen the fortress in person, having been her mother's bodyguard during her journeys south.

Despite his opposition to their quest, the Mokyre's awe for the fortress was clear from the way his mouth hung open as they passed through the first of the gate tunnels. There were three walls in total, each thicker and taller than the last, with wide killing grounds spaced between them. The land rose beneath them as they passed through each gate, so that the defenders did not have so high to climb to reach the ramparts. Beyond the third wall, the gates led into the citadel itself, the tunnel giving way to a series of courtyards overlooked by marble mezzanines and passageways lined with murder holes. Finally, they emerged into the courtyard before the southern gate.

Here Merydith paused to rest her horse, taking the time to look around. For the first time, she saw the damage Enala and Dahniul had wrought when they had come to the rescue of Devon and his friends. A smoky stench still hung around the southern gate tunnel, and a mezzanine had collapsed into the courtyard, as though a giant hand—or a dragon's wing—had smashed it.

Shaking her head, Merydith led her companions into the gate tunnel, eager to be rid of the fortress. Together they rode out onto the plains of northern Lonia.

"Congratulations, Your Majesty," Murdo declared in a solemn voice. "You just invaded the Three Nations."

"Ay," she replied, her eyes on the horizon.

There, ten miles beyond the wasteland, a dust cloud rose from the hooves of racing horses. Silence fell across their company as they watched the horsemen approaching. It was a full minute before Merydith recognised the flashing blue colours of Damyn's scouts. Behind them, the horses of her army slowly formed up beneath the walls of the fortress.

When the first scout reached them, Merydith rode forward and dismounted, even as the man leapt to the ground before her. Several more were approaching rapidly. There was no sign of the rest of her vanguard, and she prayed Damyn and his force were already safely concealed within the woods south of the wasteland.

"Your Majesty!" the scout gasped.

"Tell me," Merydith said.

The man looked at her, his eyes alive, shining with fear and excitement. "It's the Tsar," he said in a rush. "He has an advance force, already in the forest. They're on foot, but less than a day's march out."

"Did they spot you?"

"No." The man shook his head. "We pulled back as soon as we sighted them."

"Good," Merydith said. "Then I have orders for your captain."

13

Alana woke, as she had every morning for the last week, to a sharp kick in her ribs. Cursing, she rolled on her side and glared up at the old woman standing over her.

"Enough, I'm awake!" she growled as Enala drew back her foot in preparation for another kick.

Offering a grim smile, Enala tossed a wooden branch down beside Alana and turned away. Alana muttered something choice beneath her breath as she picked it up and climbed to her feet. Around them the forest was still dark with shadow, the first traces of light only just beginning to filter through the canopy.

"Ready?" Enala asked, turning back and raising her makeshift practice sword.

Alana stifled a groan. Wiping the last of the sleep from her eyes, she squared off against the old woman. Over the past few days, the ancient Magicker had shown Alana exactly how little she measured up against a master swordswoman. While the cuts around Alana's neck were now almost healed, her grandmother had ensured she woke to fresh bruises each morning.

Even so, Alana wasn't willing to admit defeat. Spinning her stick in one hand, she nodded. There were no angry words left to offer now, and she approached the old woman with caution, weapon extended, watching for the slightest hint of movement.

"Show me," Enala murmured.

Alana surged forward, her stick lancing for the old woman's throat. Her grandmother spun away, her own stick leaping up, and Alana was forced to divert her attack to block the would-be deadly thrust. The *clack* of their weapons meeting echoed through the trees as Alana shifted on her feet, seeking to use her height and power to force the old woman back.

Despite her age, Enala was no pushover, and before Alana could bring her weapon to bare, the old woman's shoulder crashed into her chest. The attack sent Alana reeling off-balance. Red flashed across her vision as her grandmother's branch struck her temple. Cursing, Alana thrust upwards, and to her surprise felt the blow connect.

Her grandmother gasped, and Alana took advantage to retreat out of range. They stood staring at one another for a moment, before a smile crossed Enala's face.

"Better," she said, "if you hadn't already been dead."

Alana scowled. Baring her teeth, she brought up her makeshift sword and darted forward in a feint. Her grandmother's branch leapt to meet her, but Alana spun on her heel, aiming low at Enala's thigh. Showing surprising agility, the old woman jumped and Alana's attack sliced empty air. Unbalanced, Alana staggered forward and caught a boot to her jaw.

The blow spun her on her feet, and she had to thrust out

a hand at a nearby tree to keep from falling. Gasping, she righted herself. The crunch of dry leaves warned her of Enala's approach, and she dived to the side. The old woman's branch careened from the tree trunk with a *thud*.

Recovering finally, Alana surged forward. Trapped by the tree, Enala spun, her branch coming up to meet Alana's attack. The *clack-clacking* of their makeshift swords sounded sharply in her ears. Fighting desperately, Alana pressed her advantage, trying to force the old woman back against the tree. When her grandmother had nowhere left to retreat, Alana thrust out with her makeshift sword, seeking what would be a killing blow.

Enala's cloak swept up as she sidestepped, entangling Alana's stick in the heavy fabric. Before she could dislodge it, Enala's weapon slammed down on the branch close to where she held it. The force of the strike tore the stick from Alana's fingers, and she cursed as Enala's branch rose to rest gently on her throat.

"Impatience will be your downfall, girl," Enala said, offering Alana her weapon back.

Alana gave a quick nod and snatched the branch from her grandmother's hands. Another thirty minutes of humiliation and defeat followed. Enala was never cruel, nor savage as her father had been, but for Alana, her softly spoken reprimands were almost as bad. All her life, Alana had been taught to conquer, to beat down her enemies with sheer force and unyielding determination, to never give an inch. After all she had suffered at her father's hands, Alana had believed herself skilled with a blade.

Enala had disavowed her of that illusion over the past week. It was galling to find herself squarely outmatched by the old woman, though Alana had to admit she was improving, as her usual battle rage was honed by freshly-taught intuition.

When they finally finished, Alana slumped down beside the dead fire, a fresh set of bruises now covering her arms, torso and fingers. The soft scuffling of boots on broken leaves followed as Enala sat beside her, a weary smile on her lips.

"You were better today," she said. "We may make a swordswoman of you yet."

Alana snorted. "I doubt we have the time," she murmured.

Over the last week, Alana's fear of her father had grown daily, until now it was all she could do to close her eyes at night. She could almost feel him at the periphery of her vision, watching from afar, amused by her feeble attempts to foil him. At least Enala's training proved a distraction, though each day the burnt-out villages they passed through reminded them of his hunters' presence.

So far they had managed to evade the black-clad Stalkers. Signs of them were everywhere in the forest though, and Alana could almost feel the noose closing around her throat. She wasn't sure why they hadn't already found them; the Tsar could have led his Stalkers directly to their campsite with his magic.

Meanwhile, their hunt for her brother had continued through the endless days and nights. At first Alana had despaired at her grandmother's belief that Braidon was dead; now though, Alana found herself clinging to the hope the old woman was wrong. How else could he have just vanished, if he had not survived the fall? The thought of her brother alone out in this forest, defenceless against monsters and Baronian thugs like Joseph, terrified Alana, but it was still better than the alternative.

Alana knew her grandmother still could not bring herself to believe it. Looking at her now, Alana couldn't help but wonder how much life the old woman had left in her. The week in the forest had drained her grandmother of colour, and while she still moved with shocking speed during combat, there was no forgetting the woman was over a century old. During the days, Alana had begun to notice her grandmother struggling to keep up, and their progress had slowed as the week endured.

Sudden warmth bathed Alana's face, and glancing up, she gaped at the gently crackling fire. The surge of magic was already dying away, but Alana looked at her grandmother in horror.

"You used your magic!" she gasped. "My father, he'll—"

"He already knows where we are, child," Enala replied. "If our magic has returned, so has the Tsar's."

"Obviously," Alana snapped. "But…" She trailed off, and her grandmother nodded sadly.

"He's watching us, toying with us. He knows we can't escape him, not with his Stalkers so close. We should have fled long ago. I fear it is too late now. The only way to escape his gaze…"

"No," Alana hissed, shaking her head.

She knew what her grandmother was suggesting, but she couldn't bear the thought of turning her magic on herself again and wiping her memories. The last time had almost destroyed her. She couldn't risk adding a third personality to the two already crowding her mind. It would drive her insane; she was close enough to it already.

Enala nodded. "I thought as much," she sighed. "Then…it's time we left this forest. I'm sorry for what happened to your brother, but we've run out of time."

A lump lodged in Alana's throat. She quickly looked

away, struggling to keep the tears from her eyes. Whether Braidon lived or not, there was wisdom in the old woman's words. Braidon could hide himself from their father's magic; Alana and her grandmother could not.

"I..." Thorns of iron wrapped their way around Alana's heart at the thought of abandoning her brother. "No, not yet." She stood suddenly, eyes flashing. "One more day."

Enala looked back at her, a sad twist on her lips, sapphire eyes shining. They were so like her father's, her brother's, that Alana had to look away. Her own granite-grey eyes she'd gotten from her mother—something she had always been glad of. She hated looking into her father's icy eyes, and though she saw only kindness when she looked at her brother, she couldn't help but doubt at times, couldn't help but wonder what else of their father Braidon had inherited.

Alana had done all she could to protect him, to keep him from the Tsar's darkness, but she still feared the monster her father wanted him to become.

Looking into Enala's eyes now, Alana recognised the same hard glint as her father, the unyielding strength that would break before it bent. Enala's son took after her more than the woman cared to admit. Alana dug in, preparing herself to argue, but her grandmother only nodded.

Drawing herself to her feet, the old woman gathered her cloak and gestured to the woods. "Lead the way, granddaughter," she said, not unkindly.

A tingling sensation slid down Alana's spine. It was the first time Enala had called her "granddaughter," and she did not deny the title. Swallowing, she looked at the trees, and picking a direction, set off through the growing light.

They walked for the first hour in silence, as the sun slowly crept higher into the sky. Its heat rarely reached the shadows beneath the canopy, but the light still improved Alana's mood. At least during the day, she could see her father's Stalkers coming. At night, they were forced to take shifts, to sit staring out into the icy dark and pray nothing came near.

As they entered the second hour of their trek, Alana decided to break the silence. Over the last week, she and Enala had settled into a truce, forming a routine between them. Her grandmother would wake Alana each morning to receive her daily bruising, before they broke their fast and set off for the day's search. If they were lucky, one of them would catch a trout or hare for food, but for the most part they walked in silence. Now though, Alana had seen a touch of her grandmother's gentler side, and she found herself wondering at the old woman.

"Did you know?" she asked abruptly as they stopped beside a creek for water. Enala looked perplexed, and Alana elaborated. "Did you know who we were, when you first found us?"

When Alana and her brother had first met the old woman, she'd called herself Tillie. It seemed beyond the realms of coincidence that she should turn out to actually be their grandmother…and yet, no one else had known Alana and Braidon would be in that forest.

Enala straightened beside the creek. "No," she said, "I was only following orders. It seems Antonia still has a sense of humour, even after all these decades."

"Antonia sent you?" Alana asked. Her heart quickened as she remembered the Goddess from her dream, the small girl's awesome rage. She swallowed. "You're…on speaking terms with her?"

Her grandmother smiled. "In a sense," she replied. "She was a part of me once. It is a curse of our bloodline, it seems, that we alone can be hosts for the Gods. Antonia returned my body, but she still drops by from time to time with messages for me."

Alana shuddered. "I see."

So, Antonia had been meddling in her life since long before Alana's dream back in the citadel. A part of her was horrified: their father had raised her to mistrust the Gods. But the other, gentler side of her warmed, reassured at the thought there was something out there, keeping an eye out for her.

The conversation petered out, and leaving the stream, they continued on their way. Feeling more confident now, Alana walked alongside the old woman, asking questions occasionally about her past, of the lands to the north of the Three Nations and the Queen that ruled them. Alana found herself wondering what her life might have been like had Enala been there during her childhood, if she had taken them before their father's cruelty could touch them…

Alana tore her mind from the thoughts of 'what if'. She pursed her lips. The past was set, and her grandmother had made her choice. It was a long time now since the glory days of the old woman's youth. Once, she might have protected Alana and Braidon from her son's wrath; now though, Enala was a woman out of time, the sole survivor of a generation long since gone.

A lump formed in Alana's throat as she finally realised how lonely it must have been, to watch everyone and everything she'd ever loved wither and die, to see her only child turn from her into darkness, for her grandchildren to grow up without her and suffer because of it.

Swallowing the lump, Alana followed after her grandmother, all questions gone from her mind. The day grew older, as they wandered down goat track after game trail, always searching for sign of the boy who had fallen from the dragon. In the dense forest, they'd encountered no one but the self-proclaimed Baronian over the last week. They had avoided settlements for the most part, except where the buildings had obviously been abandoned or burnt-out.

The last of the light was just beginning to fade when Alana sensed the magic come rushing through the trees towards them. She swung towards the presence, expecting an attack, only realising it was not directed at them when she found empty forest before her. The hairs on the back of her neck stood on end as the metallic taste of magic filled her mouth.

Ahead, Enala had frozen in her tracks and was staring in the same direction as Alana. They shared a glance, though neither could quite put into words the sudden hope that sprang between them.

The magic in the woods was far off, but unmistakable.

It tasted of the Light.

Alana was running through the trees before her mouth could form her brother's name.

"*Braidon!*"

☙ 14 ❧

It was nearing nightfall by the time Devon, Braidon and the couple reached a settlement. As the flickering lights of torches came into view between the trees, Devon couldn't help but let out a groan. Their newfound travel companions had been convinced there was a village ahead, but they hadn't known whether it was close enough to reach before dark. Having already fended off one group of bandits that day, Devon hadn't been looking forward to the prospect of spending another night exposed to any would-be thieves.

Thankfully the approaching lights promised a soft bed and hot meal, and he couldn't help but grin. Reaching into the back of the wagon, he gripped Braidon by the shoulder and shook him awake. The boy snorted and looked at him through sleepy eyes.

"What is it?" he asked, fumbling for his sword.

"Easy sonny," Devon said. "We're here. Time for a hot meal and a bath, I think."

Nodding, Braidon climbed from the wagon as Elynor directed the horse into the small square around which the settlement was built around. Taking care not to trip over the short sword strapped to his belt, he frowned at Devon.

"Do we have any money?" he asked.

Devon shook his head and turned towards the couple, but Elynor and Carcia were practically fleeing towards the inn in their haste to avoid them. Devon looked back at Braidon.

"Guess we're on our own on that one," he chuckled. "I'm sure we can manage a bit of work for a bed and meal for the night."

Braidon's eyebrows lifted into his mop of curly black hair, and still laughing, Devon moved off. The settlement they'd found themselves in only consisted of a few dozen wooden buildings laid out in a circular pattern around the square of hard-packed earth in which they stood. The inn stood out as the only building with a sign, though the faded red paint spelling its name could not be read. With Braidon in tow, Devon headed for the wooden steps leading up to the front door through which their former companions had already disappeared.

As they approached, the door swung open and a woman with auburn hair and russet-brown eyes stepped out onto the inn's porch. Her gaze swept the square, settling on Devon and Braidon.

"Suppose you're looking for a room?" she asked, raising her slender eyebrows.

Devon scratched his wiry beard and offered a sheepish grin. "Ay, we are. Got any space?"

"Got any money?" she countered.

"A few coppers…" he trailed off, then spread his hands. "There was trouble in Ardath. We left in a hurry."

"So I heard." Her eyes narrowed, and Devon wondered what the couple had told her. "You'd best not be bringing any of that trouble into my establishment." She jerked her head at the alleyway leading to the rear of the inn. "You'll find some uncut wood rounds out back. When you're done, there'll be a hot meal and straw bed for each of you. Don't go tramping any of that mud inside."

Before either of them could reply, she disappeared back into the building. Devon grinned at Braidon as the door slammed behind her. "What'd I say, sonny?"

Braidon groaned but said nothing, and together the two of them wandered around back. Devon hesitated as he saw the pile of wood waiting for them. Stacked along the rear wall of the building, it came almost up to his shoulders.

"Don't suppose you've got a shilling tucked away somewhere, sonny?" he asked.

The boy grunted, his knitted brow revealing his displeasure. Two blocks of wood had been left out, an axe head buried in each. Unstrapping his sword belt, Braidon wandered over and gripped the haft of the first axe with both hands. He placed his boot on the block of wood and yanked. The haft slipped from his fingers and he went stumbling back, toppling over the second round of wood.

Devon roared with laughter as the boy scrambled to his feet. "This is ridiculous!"

"Oh relax, sonny." He wandered over to the axe Braidon had attempted to free and yanked it clear. Tossing it into the air, he caught it by the head and offered it to the red-faced Braidon. "Here, I'll show you how it's done. Together we'll make short work of that stack."

Braidon studied the axe suspiciously before accepting it. Devon retrieved the second blade, then took a round from the wood pile and placed it on the chopping block.

The axe whistled as he hefted it above his head and slammed it into the round. The power of his swing drove the blade clean through, splitting the wood in a single strike and embedding the axe in the block beneath. Twisting the haft, he jerked it free and knocked the cut pieces aside.

"Grab me another, would ya sonny?" he asked with a grin.

His eyes wide, Braidon leapt to obey. They continued for twenty minutes, Devon chopping, Braidon fetching the uncut rounds and stacking the cut pieces in a fresh pile for firewood. Each worked in silence, content to go about the business of earning their dinner as the last daylight faded beneath the trees at the edge of the settlement.

The woman from the inn appeared at the back door, a lit lantern in hand. She took a moment to inspect the pile Braidon had been stacking before hanging the lantern in a bracket and retreating into the building.

Wiping sweat from his brow, Devon shared a grin with Braidon. "Think it might be time you took a turn, sonny."

Braidon looked at the round he'd just placed on the block, then cast an apprehensive glance at the axe in Devon's hand. "Are you sure?"

Reversing the axe, Devon offered it handle first. "It'll help put some muscle on you. You'll need it if you're gonna use that sword of yours. Promise I won't laugh."

The boy pursed his lips, but he took the axe and moved to stand in front of the block. Casting a final glance at Devon, he hefted the tool above his head and slammed it down on the waiting wood. His aim was poor, and the blade struck with a dull thud, then rebounded from the round and struck the block beneath.

Devon's laughter boomed out across the courtyard, and Braidon's face turned red in the light of the lantern. "Hey!" He pointed the axe at Devon as though it were a sword. "You promised not to laugh!"

Grinning, Devon shook his head. "Sorry, sonny. Won't happen again." Moving to stand beside Braidon, he used his boot to push the boy's feet further apart. "You need to widen your stance," he explained. "Most of the swing comes from your hips. You're far too rigid, so when you swing the axe, you have no power, no accuracy."

Braidon *hmph*ed, but he obeyed, and standing back, Devon nodded for him to try again.

This time the blade struck true, but only made it a third of the way through the round. Braidon yanked at the handle, trying to free the blade, but the round came with it. Its weight tore the axe from his hands, and Braidon cursed, leaping back as axe and wood toppled to the ground.

Devon retrieved the round and pulled the axe loose as Braidon unleashed a string of words that impressed even Devon.

"Relax, sonny, you'll get it," he said, offering the axe once more.

"I'm not strong enough!" Braidon snapped, eyes flashing. "I'm not a monster like you, I don't have arms the size of a bear."

"Then use what you've got!" Devon replied. "Those legs of yours have kept up with me all this way, *use* them."

Braidon snorted. "Sure. And how exactly can I do that?"

"Like I said, the swing comes from your hips, same as everything else. This time when you go to swing, take a step towards the log. Focus on transferring the momentum from your hips up through your chest, into your arms. Go on, try it," he added, when Braidon still didn't move.

Muttering under his breath, the boy hefted the axe and moved back into position. This time he positioned himself farther back from the log. He paused a moment, the breath whistling in his nostrils, then nodded, as though reassuring himself he could do it. Lifting the axe, he stepped forward and drove it down into the round.

There was a soft *thunk* as the blade sliced clean through the wood and struck the stump beneath. Wandering forward, Devon grinned at the surprised look on Braidon's face.

"Told ya sonny," he rumbled, slapping Braidon on the back. Then he crossed to the stack of uncut rounds, and placed another before the boy. "Now let's see you do it again."

They continued for another half hour with roles reversed. Their pace was slower with Braidon handling the woodcutting, but nonetheless, Devon was proud of the way the boy took to the task. He might have been raised in a palace, but Braidon was no shirker for hard work.

They were toiling by lantern light alone when the woman reappeared at the back door. Surveying their work, she gave a satisfied nod. "I suppose that'll do." She cast an appraising eye over Devon before adding, "There'll be no trouble in my establishment, understood?"

Devon agreed, and she waved for them to join her. They had started up the steps when she suddenly turned back, her nostrils flaring. "On second thought, you'd best take a bath. The smell of the two of you would drive a sow from its pigsty. There's a trough over there. Join me when you smell less like a horse's ass."

She vanished, leaving Devon staring dumbly up at the closed door. Anger rumbled in his chest as he clenched his fists, but beside him, Braidon chuckled.

"She's right you know, you *stink!*"

Devon turned slowly to look at the boy. "Is that so?"

Braidon blanked, but before he could react, Devon

scooped him up over his shoulder. The boy's protests range out across the courtyard, but in three quick strides Devon reached the trough. Normally, he guessed it was used to water horses, but Devon had no doubt it doubled for the stable-hand's bath when the crotchety owner demanded it. With a grin, he hefted Braidon and dropped him into the ice-cold water.

The boy vanished beneath the surface and came up screaming. Water sloshed over the sides as he scrambled to his feet. He spluttered wordlessly as torrents ran from his face and clothes. His teeth chattering, he pointed a trembling finger at Devon.

"You *bastard!*" he shrieked.

Devon started to laugh, but Braidon surged forward, using his feet to send a wave splashing up out of the trough. The water caught Devon in the chest, soaking him to the skin, and cursing, he stumbled back. By then it was too late —his pants and shirt were already soaked.

"Thanks," he said wryly.

Braidon glared at him, looking ready to do much worse. Chuckling, Devon stripped off his shirt and pants before any further damage could be done.

By the time the two of them wandered into the warmth of the inn's dining room, they were both frozen to the core. Devon had done his best to wring the water from their clothes, but without anything else to wear, they'd been forced to put them back on still damp. Teeth chattering, they shuffled across to where a fire burned in the giant hearth.

"There, isn't that better?"

Devon turned to find the innkeeper standing behind them, a wry smile on her face. Despite himself, he found himself grinning back. "Not really."

"Oh well, better for the rest of us at least." She carried a bowl of stew in each hand. Handing them over, she wandered off to serve the rest of her customers.

Steaming bowl in hand, Devon followed the woman's path through the dining room. He saw the couple they had rescued at a table in the corner, but the two were now studiously ignoring him. Sighing, he rolled his eyes. It seemed their gratitude hadn't even outlasted the daylight. His gaze continued around the room, but there were only a few locals present, old men mostly, too engaged in their evening meals and the day's gossip to notice Devon or Braidon. It seemed whatever pursuit the Tsar might be mounting, it hadn't yet reached this part of the Onslow Forest.

Not that they had much forest left. They were nearing the mountains now, and he hoped the crevasses and canyons of the Sandstone peaks would be enough to shield them from the roaming eyes of the Tsar's dragons.

The broth the innkeeper had served them was bland, but its warmth at least helped thaw the ice that had lodged in Devon's chest. When they'd finished, she returned with a tankard of ale and a plate stacked with mashed potatoes, beans and sausages. They accepted both offerings with thanks, their stomachs still aching from the measly rations they'd managed to scavenge on their trip through the forest.

Finally Devon sat back with a groan, his stomach full for the first time in weeks. "Well, sonny, how does it feel to earn your own meal?"

Braidon smiled, but before the boy could reply, a harsh *bang* came from the entrance to the inn. He trailed off, his eyes flickering to the shadow that had appeared in the doorway. Devon followed his gaze, and watched as a man larger than any he'd ever seen stepped into the room. Sharp hazel eyes scanned the occupants from beneath brows as thick as slugs, and a terrible scar ran from one side of his face to another. His hair had been pulled into a bun atop his scalp.

Leather boots thumped loudly on the wooden floors as he strode across the inn. Every inch of fabric he wore had been stained black—even the haft of the giant axe he carried one-handed. Not a man or woman spoke as he came to a stop in the centre of the room.

"You all know who I am," he growled. "I'm here for the bastard that killed my men."

Devon's heart quickened as the hazel eyes found him from across the room. As the newcomer's words trailed off, he rose to his feet.

"That would be me, sonny," he said. "Who's asking?"

☙ 15 ❧

Braidon watched in horror as the newcomer came to a stop beside their table. The man was so large, even Devon barely reached his shoulder. A shiver slid down Braidon's spine, and he scrambled from the bench to stand alongside Devon. No one else in the establishment so much as moved a muscle. Then a flicker of movement came from behind the bar, and the innkeeper appeared, her thin lips pursed.

"What are you doing here, Joseph?" she asked, her voice a low hiss. "We have an arrangement."

The giant glanced in her direction. "Ay, we do, Selina," he rumbled. "Last I checked it didn't include you harbouring those who murder my people."

"Murder?" Braidon squawked.

Alongside him Devon chuckled. "Since when is it murder to kill a few good-for-nothings intent on theft and murder?"

"They were *Baronians*, little man," Joseph growled, "and you'd best show some respect."

He swung an arm at Devon, as though to bat him aside, but the hammerman blocked it with his forearm and shoved the giant hard in the chest. Caught off-guard, Joseph staggered back a step. His hideous face twisted and his bushy eyebrows knitted together into a ferocious scowl.

"We doing this here?" Devon snapped before the man could speak. "Or shall we step outside?"

The giant blinked, momentarily taken aback by Devon's forwardness. He stood glowering down at the hammerman for a full second, then glanced at the innkeeper. With a sigh, he shook his head and started to chuckle.

"You've got balls, little man," he rumbled. Turning on his heel, he started for the doorway. "Outside. Selina's paid her due. No need for her to be cleaning your blood off her walls."

Braidon stared in disbelief as Devon followed the giant through the double doors. Hinges squealed as the doors swung shut behind them, loud in the silence that had swallowed the room. Looking around at the other occupants of the inn, Braidon searched for someone that might help, but not a man or woman would meet his gaze.

A steely resolve settled over Braidon as he realised it was up to him to help his friend. He clutched the table for a moment, struggling to control the trembling in his knees. Then he drew his sword and stumbled towards the exit.

The sight that met him outside froze him in his tracks. Standing on the inn's porch, he looked out at the square. A hundred men and women stared back at him, their pitch-black clothing seeming to merge with the night. The swords and axes in their hands shone in the light of a dozen bonfires that now lit the settlement.

A chill spread through Braidon's stomach, and he

clenched his sword tight, remembering the man's words inside the inn.

Baronians!

It wasn't possible. The last of the Baronian tribes had vanished decades ago, their brutal traditions expunged from the Three Nations in the early years of the Tsar's rule. A few tribes were said to have fled to Northland, beyond his father's reach, but even those were believed to have died out.

Yet the proof before them was undeniable. With their black-garbed leather armour and rusted weapons, the people gathered below him were like an illustration from the history books, drawn from a time when hordes of Baronian tribes had plagued the wildlands of the Three Nations, waylaying travellers and wreaking havoc at will.

Below, the giant axeman the innkeeper had called Joseph was leading Devon through the horde. The crowd parted before him like he was a king, backing away until a ring formed around the two men. Devon walked a few feet behind the Baronian, his face impassive as he surveyed the surging crowd.

Braidon couldn't understand how his friend could be so calm. With Devon surrounded, there was no way for Braidon to reach him, and he stood frozen on the porch, watching as the two came to a stop in the centre of the square. The doors squealed behind Braidon, and then the innkeeper Selina appeared beside him. Arms crossed, she studied the scene outside her establishment.

"Hope your friend can fight," she said impassively.

Braidon nodded, unable to find the words to speak.

Joseph raised his axe, and a hushed silence fell over the crowd. A grin on his lips, he turned to face Devon. "So, hammerman, how do you wish to die?"

"With *kanker* in hand, as my ancestors did before me." Devon smirked. "But my time hasn't come yet, old man."

To Braidon's shock, Joseph threw back his head and howled with laughter. The sound echoed through the square like thunder as the crowd joined in. The rattle of shields followed as they began to chant.

"*Death, death, death!*"

Braidon wilted as the sound washed over him, the roar of the crowd's bloodlust draining away his courage, feeding his fear until it was all he could do to remain standing.

Devon watched on, arms crossed, face impassive as the crowd screamed for his death. *Kanker* still hung sheathed on his back, even as Joseph thrust his axe skyward, encouraging his followers to greater excess.

Finally he turned back to Devon. With a gesture of his axe, silence returned to the square. To Braidon, the sudden change was shocking, the absence of sound almost as bad as the screams. He swallowed hard, willing his mind to piece out some escape. His thoughts turned to his magic, and he wondered whether he could make them both invisible and flee. Yet surveying the crowd, he realised that even invisible, there was nowhere for them to run. Looking at Devon, he prayed the man had the strength to prevail.

"My followers disagree, little man," Joseph roared. "But draw your hammer, and I will grant you your final wish."

Devon sighed. His head dropped, and Braidon's heart lurched as Devon spread his empty hands. "What about your final wish, elder?"

Joseph's face darkened. "I don't need one," he snapped.

"Very well."

Before anyone could react, Devon surged forward, his fist flashing up to catch the giant Baronian square in the chin. Taken unawares, the blow lifted Joseph to his toes. He staggered back, and for a second it seemed he would lose his footing and fall. Devon moved after him, but snarling Joseph lashed out with the axe, forcing the hammerman back.

For a moment the two stood facing each other. Then Devon reached up and drew *kanker* from its sheath, and the battle began in earnest.

Air hissed as the axe sliced for Devon's head. Ducking low, the hammerman sidestepped the giant's charge and swung out with *kanker*. Joseph spun, revealing a speed that belied his size, and wrenched his axe down, the massive muscles in his arms rippling with the effort, and an awful shriek rang out as the two weapons collided.

Sparks flew as the warriors leapt back, and Braidon winced at the power behind the blows. He was shocked Joseph's axe had not shattered with the impact, though as the Baronian hefted his weapon, Braidon saw a dent had been left in the steel blade.

Recovering almost as quickly, Devon straightened, hefting his hammer. The magic-blessed weapon didn't show so much as a scratch, and grinning, the hammerman started forward. Braidon held his breath as the two colossal warriors clashed again, the shrieking of their weapons sending shivers down his spine. This was no duel between master swordsmen; there would be no minor wounds inflicted before the end came. One touch with either weapon meant dismemberment or death.

Braidon wanted desperately to tear his eyes away, to turn and flee back into the sanctuary of the inn, to the half an hour earlier when he had sat enjoying a warm meal with his friend. Instead, he stood and watched as Devon battled on. He would not run while the man fought for their very lives, would not leave the hammerman alone to face the Baronians.

In the first clashes of the battle, the two giants had seemed evenly matched, but as the fight drew on, it seemed to Braidon that Devon was gaining ground. Joseph's blows had lost some of their power, and his movements were growing slower, even as Devon ploughed on with seemingly endless vigour. A slight sheen of sweat on his brow was his only sign of exertion, while lines had crept into Joseph's face, as though the fight had aged him a decade. Even the white in his beard appeared more prominent.

The crowd was silent now, the black-cloaked Baronians watching on in awe of the two warriors. Another clash echoed from the settlement as axe and hammer met, the combatants spinning away, each unharmed. They paused, eyes glittering as they faced one another. Then with a dull *thud*, the steel blade of Joseph's axe cracked in half and fell to the ground. The Baronian stared dumbly at the weapon for a moment, then up at Devon.

Adrenaline surged through Braidon's veins and he lifted his fist in triumph. "Finish him, Devon!" he yelled, his voice strained to a shriek by the stress of the fight.

Below, the hammerman looked up at him, his face still impassive. They shared a glance, and then Devon returned his eyes to the Baronian. He lowered his hammer and gestured at his opponent.

"Time for a water break, don't you think, sonny?" he asked, panting softly.

Joseph stood fixed in place, the broken haft of his axe still in hand. After a moment, he nodded. "Good idea."

Tossing aside his broken weapon, he gestured to a Baronian. The man raced forward with a water skin, and wordlessly the axeman pointed at Devon. After a second's hesitation, the Baronian offered the skin to Devon first.

On the porch, Braidon looked on, mouth wide, heart in

the pit of his stomach. He shook his head, unable to understand what Devon was doing, why he was sparing the thug's life.

Below, Devon nodded his thanks and placed *kanker* on the ground beside him before accepting the water skin. Lifting it to his lips, he took a long swing and then handed it back to the attendant. The man scampered across to Joseph, who drank deeply as well.

Afterwards, the Baronian gestured at his broken axe. "Mind if I find another weapon?"

Devon grinned. "Won't help you much, sonny," he replied, "but by all means."

Joseph laughed, and shaking his head, he wandered around the circle of Baronians, inspecting their weapons until he found one that suited him. One look at the owner was all it took for the man to hand it over. Hefting the new axe, he returned to the centre of the ring and faced Devon.

"Ready?" he asked.

"Ay," Devon replied, and the battle resumed.

Anger burned in Braidon's chest, and he looked away, cursing Devon for his stupidity. With their lives on the line, the hammerman had thrown away an opportunity to save them both. Worse than that, Devon had given the Baronian time to rest, when it was obvious he was on his last legs. Now Joseph was fighting with renewed vigour and Devon had lost his advantage.

"Noble man, your friend," Selina said from beside him.

Braidon jumped. He'd been so engrossed with the battle he'd forgotten she was there. Shaking his head, he looked up at her in disbelief. "Noble? He had the man! Why did he throw away his chance?"

"Because it wouldn't have been honourable," she replied, her thin lips drawn back into a smile.

"He's fighting a thief!" Braidon countered. "There's no honour amongst such people."

Selina raised an eyebrow. "You shouldn't judge so quickly, young man. Whatever he might appear, Joseph has a code of his own, twisted as it might seem to some. He protects his people, whatever the cost. That is why he is here, why he will continue this fight, even if he may have bitten off more than he can chew."

"Baronian scum," Braidon spat. "I'm glad m…the Tsar drove them from our land."

The innkeeper sighed. "So judgmental for one so young," she said softly. She gestured at the crowd. "Yes, they call themselves Baronians. But look at them, youngster, look at them closely. You think they chose this path, wandering these backroads in the middle of winter, with hardly a cloak between them? Most of those you see here are refugees, runaways from Trola or the capital, where the Tsar's taxes drove them to the edge of poverty. Joseph found them, brought them under his wing. Yes, they might be bandits, but they are only what desperation has made them."

"You defend them?"

Selina shrugged. "Five years ago, before Joseph, the people in this settlement could barely go a month without someone coming under attack. These forests were filled with bandits—vicious, warring factions that were merciless to their victims. Then Joseph came. The worst of the bandits were driven off or brought under his rule. This village, and many like it, came to an arrangement with them. We pay them a small fee, and he and his people do us no harm, nor any harm to those travellers who visit with our permission. It is an unusual arrangement, I admit, but twice as many people live here now, than before the Baronians came."

A cry rang out across the square, and Braidon whipped

around, his heart racing once more as he remembered the battle taking place below. Sunlight flickered on steel as the two warriors battled on, but now Devon was being forced back. Joseph's battle cry echoed around the square as his axe rose and fell.

Growling, Devon deflected a wicked blow with his hammer, but using his awesome strength, Joseph wrenched his weapon back and struck again before Devon could counter. The hammerman sidestepped the blow, but lost his footing and stumbled. Joseph rushed forward, his shoulder catching Devon in the chest and hurling him to the ground.

Kanker flew across the dirt. Unarmed, Devon rolled as Joseph's axe bit the earth where he'd fallen. Joseph hefted his axe for another blow, but as Devon scrambled for the hilt of his hammer, he seemed to hesitate for half a second. It was enough, and gripping *kanker* tight, Devon surged back to his feet.

The Baronian snarled and swung his axe, but the blow was wild and clumsily made. Devon deflected it easily and then thrust out with his hammer, catching the black-garbed man in the chest. With its blunted head it did little damage, but in Joseph's tiring state, it was enough to throw him off-balance.

Leaping forward, Devon attacked again. The axe lifted to counter, but Joseph had misjudged his aim, and instead of catching the hammer with the blade, Devon's weapon crunched home into the Baronian's wrist.

A scream of pure agony rang out across the square as Joseph staggered back, the axe toppling from his hand. Then his mouth clamped shut, cutting off his cries as he cradled his right arm against his chest. Head bowed, he sank to his knees in front of Devon.

"Do it quick," he croaked through clenched teeth.

"Ay," Devon replied.

His boot lashed out and caught Joseph in the side of the head. The Baronian toppled silently to the ground, unconscious. Around the square, not a soul moved, as the Baronians stared on in silence.

Devon looked back at them, lips tight, eyes hard. He lifted *kanker* above his head and let out a cry. "Your leader is defeated," his voice boomed. "If any one of you wishes to join him, step forward now, and I will gladly oblige."

Whispers spread around the square as the crowd shifted, the black-garbed watchers sharing glances. Braidon sensed the mood turning dark, the anger of the Baronians building, as hands clenched at sword hilts. Fear gnawed at Braidon's stomach as he watched Devon standing defiantly against the horde. The hammerman could not face them alone, and they knew it. All it would take was one…

Silently Braidon closed his eyes, and allowed his consciousness to plunge inwards. His breath settled into a gentle rhythm, concentrating his mind, carrying his thoughts away to the nothingness within. In an instant, he found himself drifting in the peaceful black at his core, felt the weight of his body falling away. Time seemed to stand still…and then the light of his magic appeared in void.

It formed before him, twisting and morphing into the familiar Feline. Once, the sight of it had filled him with terror, sending him fleeing through the darkness. Now though, need gave him courage, and reaching out, he gripped it with his mind, banishing the beast with the force of his will, making its power his own.

Opening his eyes, Braidon looked out over the square. Only a moment had passed, but he could sense the impasse coming to a close. There were only seconds to spare.

An image flickered into Braidon's mind, of Devon the

night he'd appeared beside his campfire. The man had loomed out of the darkness like a giant from of legend. A smile came to Braidon's lips.

Reaching across with his power, he wrapped loops of shining white around Devon, altering his image, changing the appearance of reality.

In the light of the burning fires, it seemed the hammerman grew larger as he stood there. Darkness cloaked him as his iron gaze scanned the watchers, promising death. To every eye in the square, it was no longer a mortal who stood amongst them, but a demigod, his power unrivalled. A crackling filled the air as overhead, thunder boomed, blue fire lighting up the sky.

It was all only illusion, a manipulation of the Light, but it was all Braidon could offer his friend. Looking down at the circle of Baronians, he prayed it was enough.

16

Exhaustion weighed on Alana as she pushed through the trees, struggling to keep pace with her grandmother. Ahead, Enala threaded through the dense undergrowth as though she were born to it, seemingly untouched by the clinging vines and vicious thorns.

The explosion of Light magic had returned some of the vigour to the old woman, and now it was Alana who was flagging, the endless journey through the dark forest sapping her energies. Several of the cuts on her neck had opened again, and she could feel the steady trickle of blood down her back. Even so, she refused to slow, knowing if her brother had used his magic so blatantly, he had to be in trouble. He needed her, needed them both.

The light of a new day was just beginning around them now, casting light across the forest. A *hiss* came from ahead as Enala tossed aside the burning torch they'd used to light their way, then stamped it out on the damp earth.

Walking up beside her, Alana studied the woods ahead. Shadows still clung beneath the trees, but she could make out the ground clearly now. After spending much of the night being tripped by hidden roots, the sight was a relief. She could still sense the lingering tang of Light magic on the air around them. Its aftertaste was growing weaker by the hour, but they were close to its source now.

"There's still no way of knowing it was him," Enala reminded Alana, though her face said she thought otherwise.

Alana only nodded. Striding past, she took the lead. Whatever lay at the end of their journey, there was no turning back now. All through the night, they had forged their own path through the forest, unable to find a path leading in the direction the magic had come from. It was another hour before they finally came to a wider track of hardened earth.

Enala loosened her sword in its scabbard. "Ready yourself, granddaughter," she said quietly. "It's not far now."

There was a hardness to her grandmother's eyes, and Alana nodded her agreement. Her hand drifted to the hilt of her sword. The old woman's lessons were still fresh in her mind, but she found herself now filled with doubt, with fear she was not the swordswomen she'd once thought herself.

Nonsense, she growled to herself. *You are the Daughter of the Tsar.*

Alana straightened her shoulders. "Let's go."

It wasn't far before the track widened again. Studying the ground, Alana was alarmed to find overlapping bootprints in the hard-packed earth. It looked as though a large force had passed this way not long ago. It was difficult to know their numbers, but she guessed there were at least a hundred. Her stomach clenched as she picked up the pace, her thoughts on her brother.

Around a bend in the track, Alana stumbled to a halt as she found herself facing a small forest settlement. She paused, scanning the nearest buildings, looking for any sign of the owners of the bootprints in the earth beneath her feet. There was no sign of movement or damage, and she shared a glance with her grandmother as the old woman joined her.

"Where is everybody?" she asked.

"There's one," Enala replied, nodding at one of the buildings.

A door had just opened in the only two-storeyed house in the settlement. A middle-aged woman appeared and started down the steps. Her eyes were on her feet, but suddenly they swept up and saw them standing on the other side of the square. She started, then glanced back at the door. It seemed she would retreat back inside, but then reconsidering, she continued her way down.

Enala strode forward, making her way towards the woman. "Excuse me, ma'am," she said, her voice loud enough to carry through the entire settlement. Catching herself, Alana started after her grandmother. "We were wondering if you might help us."

The woman made it to the bottom of the steps, but paused there, looking up at the approaching Enala. "Depends what help you're looking for," she murmured. "Do you need a room for the night?"

Reaching the woman, Enala shook her head. Glancing around at the silent buildings, she raised one eyebrow. "What happened here?"

"We're full-up at the moment," the villager replied, seeming not to hear Enala's question, "if you're looking for a room." Her eyes distant, she turned and started back up the stairs.

"We're looking for a boy!" Alana shouted. "His name is Braidon."

On the steps, the woman froze. Glancing over her shoulder, she pursed her lips. "What did you say?"

Alana's heart quickened. "You've seen him?" she asked desperately. "Please, is he okay?"

The woman bit her lip. "He's alive," she replied.

"Where?" Enala demanded.

The woman looked at them, then at the buildings surrounding the settlement. Alana thought she glimpsed fear in her eyes, but a second later it was gone. With a gesture, she continued up the steps. "Look, we'd best talk inside, okay?" she called down to them.

Enala followed after the woman, but Alana hesitated, her heart palpitating painfully in her chest. Something about the settlement seemed wrong. Where had all the people gone? Why had her brother been here? Why had he used his magic? The woman had already disappeared into the door at the top of the stairs, and Enala was drawing close.

Swallowing her doubt, Alana raced after her grandmother, catching her just before she reached the doorway. She stepped past her and entered the inn, dropping her hand to the hilt of her sword. Though it was daylight outside, the interior was still dark, the lanterns unlit. In the gloom, Alana could just make out the shadow of a bar and several tables and chairs scattered about the room.

"Light a lantern would you?" Alana asked, searching for the woman who had invited them in, but she was nowhere in sight.

A *bang* came from behind them as the door slammed shut, plunging the room into pitch-black. Alana started back towards the door, when a sudden light erupted through the room. Shocked, she stumbled sideways, struggling to shield her eyes.

"Wha—?" she cried out, as shadows flickered through the room.

Blinking, she strained to see through the brilliant white. Movement came from the tables as black-cloaked men rose from their seats. Her hand was still scrambling for the hilt of her sword when a cold voice spoke from behind her.

"Alana, how good it is to see you again."

SITTING IN THE DARKNESS, QUINN ALLOWED HIMSELF A SMILE as Alana and the old woman came blundering into the inn. The innkeeper had done her job well, as he'd known she would. After all, her life depended on it. Alana and the old priest were nothing to her; she'd had little choice but to accept Quinn's proposition.

Not that it would have mattered in the end. Whether the innkeeper lured them inside or not, he had the numbers to ensure success. Taking them by surprise simply meant a cleaner victory.

His only regret was that they'd missed the boy. Braidon had miscalculated, using his magic on those outside the shield that protected him from magical sight. But at least his mistake had allowed Quinn to flush Alana and the old woman out of hiding.

He'd already sent for the Tsar the night before. Now he had only to capture Alana in preparation for her father's arrival.

Rising, he shielded his eyes and gestured for his Stalkers to make their move. A brilliant white lit the air, illuminating the room and blinding the two women.

Silently Quinn moved behind them, cutting off their escape.

"Alana, how good it is to see you again," he whispered when she staggered towards him.

She spun, her hand going for her sword, but Quinn was faster still. His fist flashed out, catching her hard in the base of the skull, and she collapsed without making a sound.

He looked up as warmth bathed his face. Flames crackled in the old woman's hands as she stepped towards him, her face contorted with rage. Quickly Quinn drew his blade and pressed it to the unconscious Alana's throat.

"Enough, woman," he hissed. "One more move, and your granddaughter dies."

"Go ahead!" Enala growled, the fire in her palms leaping higher.

Quinn smiled. "Look around you, woman. You're surrounded. Give up, Enala."

Blinking in the light of his Stalker's magic, Enala hesitated. With fire in both hands, she looked for all the world like an avenging demon, but Quinn knew better. She was weak, the same as her brother. He watched as her gaze swept the room, taking in the dozen Stalkers Quinn had stationed inside the inn. Half stood with crossbows aimed, the other six with magic crackling in their hands. The fight went from the woman's face, but she did not lower her hands.

"I have no wish to kill the Tsar's mother," Quinn said. "I'm sure he has plans of his own for you. But I won't hesitate if you make me. Now, dismiss your magic," Quinn commanded, his voice ringing from the glass windows.

For a moment he thought the old woman would refuse. Crossbows rattled as she stepped towards him, but he raised a hand to halt their release. A low groan came from the girl at his feet, and Enala's gaze dropped to look at her granddaughter. Alana started to move, but froze as Quinn pressed his blade harder against her throat.

"What, oh..." she trailed off as her eyes flickered open and saw Quinn standing over her.

Quinn looked at Enala, and smiled as the fire slowly died from her hands, her eyes returning to crystal blue.

"The sword, too," he ordered.

Unclipping her sword belt, she tossed the weapon to the ground between them. Quinn gestured for one of his Stalkers to retrieve it, then grinned at Enala.

"I knew you would come," he said conversationally, gesturing with his sabre. "I told the Tsar the boy's magic would draw you here."

"You have my brother?" Alana asked from the floor.

Quinn stepped back, allowing Enala to join her granddaughter. Crouching beside Alana, the old woman offered her shoulder, and together the two rose unsteadily to their feet. A scuffling came from across the room as one of his Stalkers dragged the innkeeper forward, one arm twisted up behind her back.

"You said you'd leave us alone!" she snarled as they approached.

"Yes, yes, yes." He and his men had arrived at first light to find the boy already departed, but it had been a small matter of rounding up the villagers to find out where they'd gone. The other occupants of the settlement were currently locked up in the roughshod temple, overseen by a few of his men. "When we're done. Now, would you *please* tell the girl what happened to her brother? She's so eager to hear about his fate."

The innkeeper looked down at Alana. "I'm sorry," she whispered. "The Baronians have him."

"*What?*"

Alana sounded as disbelieving as Quinn had first been. Though he'd heard rumours of a resurgence in the rebel tribes, Quinn hadn't paid them much credence until now.

"So Joseph was telling the truth." Beside Alana, the old woman looked calm. "The Baronians have returned." She smiled at Quinn. "Your Tsar's power fades by the day, Stalker. Or does he no longer care to protect his people?

Rage bubbled up in Quinn's chest and he pointed his blade at the old woman's chest. "Silence, woman," he growled.

Enala crossed her arms and smirked. "Oh, *now* you're going to kill me are you, Stalker?" she asked. "I thought my son had plans for me?"

Quinn clenched his teeth and sucked in a breath. Struggling to quell his anger, he forced a smile. "Ay, and I hope you live to regret those words." He turned to the innkeeper. Striding forward, he stood face-to-face with the woman. "But you have not told them all of it. Finish the story, innkeeper." He lifted the tip of his sword and rested it against her chest to emphasise his point.

She flinched away from the steel, but the Stalker holding her only tightened his grip. Terror showed on her face, but with a deep breath, she stilled. She met Quinn's gaze with hatred in her eyes.

"Don't worry, girl," she said, still looking at Quinn, "your brother is fine. His friend defeated the Baronian leader. He leads them now."

"His friend?" Alana asked.

"Devon."

Before the innkeeper could say more, Quinn stepped forward, driving his blade through her chest. She gasped, stiffening as the cold steel sliced through her heart.

Collapsing back into the arms of the man holding her, a soft whisper came from her lips. With a jerk, Quinn yanked back his blade and watched the woman's lifeblood pump from the wound. Then he gestured, and his Stalker released her, allowing the innkeeper's body to thud to the floor.

"*Why?*" Alana screamed.

Quinn spun, bloody blade raised. "Because she *lied* to me. It took an hour to get the truth from her, and she thought I would still spare her for finally telling it?" He laughed as he looked at Alana, hatred twisting its cold coils around his soul. "Just like you lied to me, Alana."

Stepping forward, he pointed the tip of his sword at her throat, though he was careful not to touch her with it now that she was conscious. When she was desperate, Alana's magic could transfer along metal, and he had no wish to be used by her again. "You betrayed me."

Alana stared at him a moment, then to his surprise, she bowed her head. "I know," she whispered. "I'm sorry."

Quinn blinked, momentarily confused by her repentance—until he recalled the weakness that had infected her, the soft girl she had become when she'd escaped the citadel. His jaw hardened, his anger returning.

"Sorry? *Sorry?* What do your sorries matter to me? You manipulated me with your power, *used* me, and still I saved you. And how did you repay me?"

"I..."

"You left me to face your father's wrath. By rights he should have killed me a thousand times for allowing you to go free. If not for his mercy..."

Alana snorted. "My father, mercy?"

"Do not speak ill of my Tsar," Quinn hissed.

Summoning his magic, Quinn drew the wind to him. The windows shook, then shattered inwards as the winds gathered around him. With a gesture, he sent them against her, hurling her back against the wall, pinning her there. He walked slowly forward.

"Your father spared me, trusted me to find his children, so that he might lead our army to glory. I will not fail him, not this time. He will have you, and your brother. And I will have my heart's desire."

He lifted a hand to touch her face, but stopped himself at the last second. She stared back at him, her grey eyes set like stone.

"And what is your heart's desire, *my love?*" she asked mockingly.

Quinn scowled and raised a fist, and Alana's eyes flashed. With an effort of will, Quinn controlled himself.

She laughed. "What, are you *afraid*, my love? Go on, *do it*, show me how powerful you are."

Baring his teeth, Quinn swung away from her, and found Enala crouching beside the dead woman. He turned his anger on her. "What do you think you're doing, woman?" he snarled.

"You missed," Enala said, her hands bloody as she pressed a rag to the innkeeper's chest.

Quinn cursed as the woman groaned, her eyelids fluttering. But it was an easy mistake to correct, and hefting his sword, he stepped towards the wounded woman. Before he could reach her, a shout came from outside, followed by a roar that seemed to shake the very foundations of the building.

A smile came to Quinn's lips as he faced the window, and glimpsed the flicker of scarlet scales in the square outside. Lowering his sword, he looked at Alana.

"This should be quite the family reunion."

17

Merydith sucked in a long breath as she directed her horse into the centre of the Gods Road. The wind swirled around her, kicking up dust and causing the treetops to sway violently overhead. The rustle of leaves against branches was almost enough to muffle the distant tread of marching feet.

Almost.

A shiver ran down her spine and she pulled her cloak tighter about her, though it was not the cold that had her trembling. Her hand dropped to the sword resting across her pommel, and she cast a final glance at the trees, searching the shadows for any hint of movement. But Murdo and Mokyre had done their jobs well, and there was no sign of the Northland force concealed there.

The rhythmic *thump-thump* of boots picked up a notch, and Merydith's attention snapped back to the path ahead. The Gods Road continued straight from where she sat for another hundred yards, before disappearing round a bend in the road. Ahead the road narrowed, allowing only enough room for ten men to march abreast. With fifty thousand soldiers under the Tsar's command, the forest had slowed his advance to a crawl.

Merydith intended to halt them altogether.

Her hunters had already taken care of the few scouts the southerners had bothered to send ahead. The Tsar's advance guard were now marching blind, and she intended to take full advantage. Her people had left their mounts half a mile from the Gods Road, at a confluence of several animal tracks that led further up into the Sandstone Mountains. Now they waited on either side of the path, ready to spring her trap.

At the end of the road, shadows flickered as the first line of soldiers marched into view. Their attention on anything but the way ahead, they continued on a dozen yards before a whinny from her mount finally alerted them to her presence. The *thump-thump* of their marching boots rattled to a discordant stop as the front ranks exchanged bewildered glances. Shouts erupted from the following ranks as men marched unawares into the backs of their companions.

"What's going on here?" a man bellowed, forcing his way to the front. A silver star on his breast marked him as a lieutenant. He pointed a cane at one of the soldiers and opened his mouth to scream again.

"Who dares trespass on my land?" Merydith shouted, her voice carrying on the wind to the soldiers.

The lieutenant spun at the sound of her voice. Lines marked his brow as he frowned. "Who goes there?" he called, taking a step towards her.

Merydith smiled as she edged her horse forward. "The Queen of this forest," she bellowed. "You're trespassing on my land."

Beyond the front ranks of the army, further shouting

was breaking out as the sudden halt caused havoc amongst their ranks.

"The Queen of…" the man mumbled, then cursed under his breath. "Get out of our way, woman. This is the Tsar's forest, and he does not take kindly to usurpers." Drawing his sword, he gestured to the men on either side of him. "Take care of the madwoman."

Merydith smiled as the front ranks surged towards her. "Turn back, or you will pay for your insolence," she shouted.

"Kill the b—" The lieutenant's scream was cut short as an arrow blossomed in his throat.

On the road in front of her, the charge faltered as the soldiers glanced back to see what had become of their lieutenant. With their ranks broken and shields still lowered, the first wave of arrows sliced through them like fire in a cornfield. Screams rent the air as men went down, steel-tipped arrows finding their mark in exposed legs and necks and armpits. Only the steel-plated armour of the advance guard stopped the attack from becoming a massacre.

A second volley hissed from the trees, and more soldiers dropped, though fewer this time, as those still standing had turned their shields towards the trees.

Lifting her sabre above her head, Merydith shouted a battle cry. The rumble of hooves came from behind her as a cavalry cohort concealed around the bend came racing into sight. Together, they charged at the enemy.

With their shields turned towards the trees, the Tsar's men were taken unawares, and Merydith's charge carried her people deep into their ranks. Soldiers scattered before her mount or were trampled beneath his iron-shod hooves, and her sabre flashed out, killing any who stood against her.

Alongside her, Merydith's people were doing the same, as the Tsar's soldiers tried to flee back down the Gods Road.

As they neared the bend in the road, Merydith's charge slowed, the ranks of soldiers closing in around them. A sword lanced for her chest, and she swung out with her buckler, turning aside the blow. Lashing out with her sabre, she felt a satisfying *crunch* as it struck home, followed by a scream as the assailant staggered back, blood streaming from his severed arm. His shouts were silenced as her guard closed in, and a sabre cleaved his spine.

Merydith nodded her thanks as her guard spread out around her, forcing the southern soldiers back. She swung around in her saddle, taking the opportunity to gauge the battle. Their charge had carried her cohort deep into the enemy ranks, but now that the element of surprise was lost, the Tsar's soldiers were pushing back. Several had managed to join their shields and were advancing up the path towards them.

"Retreat!" she cried, pulling on her reins to swing her stallion back the way they'd come.

Bodies littered the Gods Road behind them, most of them donned in the scarlet robes of Plorsea. Merydith's heart clenched at the sight, though she knew she'd had no choice but to attack, to be the first to strike. They were only five thousand against fifty thousand. To hesitate now was to face certain defeat.

Her mount leapt forward and the northern army followed her, retreating down the Gods Road as quickly as they had appeared. Arrows hissed after them and several of her people fell. Merydith cursed and crouched lower in the saddle until they were safely around the bend in the road. She prayed her archers had already fallen back, but there was no way of knowing until they reached the rendezvous.

Several riders had pulled ahead, forming ranks around her. The leaders dragged their horses towards the trees, where several trails led deeper into the forest. Merydith and the others followed suit, and together they rushed into the darkness of the trees.

The cries of their pursuers died away, muffled by the dense forest. Despite the still pending danger, Merydith allowed herself a deep breath, her heartbeat slowing a notch. A smile tugged at her lips as she estimated the enemy's losses. The Tsar had lost perhaps as many as three hundred soldiers to death or injury, between those killed by her archers and the cavalry charge. She had counted no more than twenty Northerners amongst the dead.

Not bad, for a distraction.

DAMYN CROUCHED AMONGST THE SCRUB AND PEERED DOWN at the wagons rumbling slowly through the narrow valley. The Gods Road was rutted here, the going slow for the steel-shod wheels of the Tsar's baggage train. A ring of soldiers five men thick marched to either side of the wagons, their eyes alert as they scanned the hills. Damyn allowed himself a smile. With the dense bush covering the valley, there was little chance his cohort would be spotted.

Away to their left, the column disappeared around a bend in the road. They had been marching past for an hour now, and the first hundred ranks of the advance guard had only just given way to the baggage train. Damyn followed their progress up the Gods Road in his mind, along the twisting track through the forest, to where his Queen waited.

When his scout had returned with her plan, he'd found

himself smiling at her boldness. While he would have preferred to fight alongside her, there had been no time to question the intricacies of her trap. His cohort was in place within the hour, and with scouts riding back and forth, their preparations had been finalised.

Now Damyn had only to wait for the chance to strike. From what he'd seen so far of the Tsar's preparations, it would come soon enough. The man thought Northland weak. He knew they had only five thousand soldiers, and had barely bothered to send scouts out ahead of his army. Those had been easily dispatched. Damyn intended to make the Tsar pay for his arrogance.

The distant cry of a bugle carried through the forest, and below, the soldiers to either side of the wagons leapt to the alert. The clash of steel on steel and the screams of dying men followed, whispering through the trees like the ghosts of long-dead souls. Those on the road below closed ranks and drew their weapons, their eyes turning to their commanders. The rumble of wagons ceased as the oxen stumbled to a stop. A dust cloud settled around the convoy, hemming them in.

Along the ridgetop, Damyn felt the eyes of his five hundred men on him. He raised a hand, bidding them to wait. Squinting through the dust, he watched the sunlight flickering from the enemy's armour. The screams had set the southerners on edge, drawing their attention to the path ahead and away from the hillside.

Another bugle cried out. Shouts followed from those below as the Tsar's lieutenants started waving their men forward. Half of the force guarding the train surged forward, the others spreading out to fill the gaps they'd left.

Damyn's heart beat faster as he watched the soldiers march out of sight. He did a quick count of those who remained and cursed beneath his breath. They had been more cautious than Merydith had anticipated. She'd warned him not to attack unless the odds of success were overwhelming, but the Tsar had left close to four hundred men below. His own five hundred had them outnumbered, but if things went wrong and they were delayed, Damyn risked the main body of the Tsar's army catching them in the open.

Letting out a long breath, Damyn made a decision. Merydith had ordered him not to take any unnecessary risks, but the destruction of the Tsar's supplies would be a massive blow to the southland army. With the land still in the grips of winter, they would not be able to advance into Northland until they'd been resupplied. It would buy his people much needed time—perhaps even enough to muster an army that could match the southerners in the field.

Retreating behind the lip of the hill, Damyn mounted up. His five hundred men and women followed suit. Eyes wide, they looked to Damyn for the signal. He swallowed, feeling the weight of their lives on his shoulders. While most had seen combat in the occasional scuffles between clans, none had ever imagined taking on such an army as the one marching up the Gods Road. They knew the odds were against them, but as he looked in their eyes, Damyn knew not a one of them would fail him.

Silently he lifted his sword and pointed it at the valley and army beyond the lip of the hill. A deafening cry went up around him. Damyn kicked his horse into a charge, and five hundred men and woman followed after him.

18

Reclining in the comfortable embrace of a cowhide hammock, Devon couldn't help but smile as he reflected on his sudden change in fortune. Ever since he'd rescinded his commission in the army, it had seemed as though the Gods themselves were against him. His savings had seemed to evaporate overnight, former comrades had turned against him, and everyone from bards to innkeepers had taken great joy in besmirching his name. Since then, his every action, every decision, only seemed to lead his situation from bad to worse.

Until now. Somehow, saving a couple of selfish townsfolk from bandits had led to his ascension to leader of the Baronians. He could only shake his head in amusement at the turn of events.

"Devon, there you are." Craning his head, Devon watched as Braidon walked up. Wearing a scowl on his face, the boy came to a stop beside the hammock and crossed his arms. "Enjoying yourself, are you?"

Devon grinned. "Immensely." Groaning, he levered

himself out of the hammock and stood beside the boy. "Where've you been, sonny?"

Braidon's scowl deepened. "Sleeping in the mud," he snapped.

"Oh..." Devon scratched his beard, a sheepish look coming over his face. "Must have lost track of you somewhere there."

After he'd defeated Joseph, there had been a tense moment when Devon had thought the Baronians were about to tear him to pieces. Strangely, in that moment Devon had felt no fear or anger, only a sense of bemusement that his life would end at the hands of this rabble, rather than the rich and powerful who sought his death.

But instead, the Baronians had one by one fallen to their knees and pronounced him their leader. Devon had felt compelled to accept the title, least their supplication return to rage. Afterwards, they had shepherded Devon and Braidon back to their campsite and shown Devon the hammock. In his exhausted state, Devon had fallen asleep without giving the boy a second thought.

"You think?" Braidon growled.

"Ummm..." Devon was still struggling to produce a satisfactory excuse when a Baronian marched up.

"Hammerman," the Baronian rumbled. "We have prepared your tent, if you'd like to break your fast."

Devon raised an eyebrow at Braidon. "Hungry?" he asked, his tone reconciliatory.

The boy snorted, but eventually offered a nod, and Devon gestured for the Baronian to lead the way. Together they wandered through the roughshod camp the Baronians had created amongst the forest. The undergrowth had been cleared to make space for the cowhide tents, but the trees remained, their upper canopy forming a roof to shield against dragon patrols. Smoke from a dozen cookfires hung heavily in the morning air, and they kept close to their guide as they navigated between the sleeping bodies. It seemed Braidon hadn't been the only one to spend the night without shelter. Devon wondered how they had survived the harsh winter storm that had passed through a week before.

Wagons lined the perimeter of the campsite, drawn up so they formed a makeshift barrier against the world outside. Looking closer at the tents they passed, Devon saw they were as scruffy as the clothes worn by the bandits he'd encountered on the road. Compared to the tales of old, these Baronians seemed a poor relic, impoverished by the necessity of their concealment from the Tsar.

The camp looked to have been there a while—months, at least. The Baronians of old had moved freely from place to place, never staying in one location for long, spreading their terror across the Three Nations. It seemed Joseph had been content to lead his people down a more peaceful route.

"This is your tent, hammerman."

Devon looked up as their guide spoke. He had stopped outside a large tent set in the centre of the camp. A trail of smoke seeped from the tip of the tent, and Devon grinned as he ducked beneath the flap and found a small fire burning in a rusted camp stove. A rough bed of straw was pushed into the corner and several wooden chairs lay strewn around the tent.

He glanced back as Braidon and their Baronian guide followed him inside. "Why didn't you bring us here last night?"

The man scratched his beard, looking uncertain. "Joseph's…belongings had to be removed."

Devon blinked. "This was Joseph's tent?"

"Of course," the man replied. "It is the best tent in the tribe. It belongs to the one who leads us."

Shaking his head, Devon lowered himself into one of the chairs and gestured for Braidon to join him. He scowled at the Baronian as Braidon claimed his seat. "And where is your former leader now?"

The Baronian cleared his throat. "He is a prisoner. We have him held in the prison tent, awaiting your judgement, sir."

Devon sighed. "You'd best bring him here then." The man nodded, and was turning away when Devon's stomach rumbled. "Wait!" He shared a sheepish glance with Braidon before gesturing at the camp stove. "On second thought, we'll break our fast first. I'm sure Joseph can wait another hour."

"Of course, hammerman," the Baronian replied with a grin.

After the Baronian had departed, Braidon snorted with laughter. "Glad you've got your priorities straight."

"Damn right," Devon rumbled. Then he sighed and shook his head. "This is already getting complicated, isn't it? What am I meant to do with the big bastard?"

Braidon frowned. "You already spared his life once. Don't make the same mistake twice."

"Mistake?" Devon asked quietly.

In his mind, he saw again the moment the Baronian's axe had shattered, felt again the thrill of victory. Then Braidon's words had carried through the sudden silence that had fallen over the crowd.

Finish him, Devon!

When he'd looked up, Devon had caught the gleam in the boy's sapphire eyes, recognised the familiar bloodlust. His face contorted with hatred, Braidon had looked for all the world like the Son of the Tsar. Kellian's last words had come back to Devon then, about sparing those who could not defend themselves, and lowering *kanker,* he had given the Baronian a second chance.

"What makes you say it was a mistake to spare him?" he said.

"He tried to kill you!" Braidon exclaimed.

"Ay, but he fought with courage, and honour," Devon replied. He searched the boy's eyes as he spoke, seeking… something, but finding only confusion. With a sigh he went on. "He could have ordered his people to slaughter us, but instead he chose to risk single combat. And he lost everything for it. Is that not enough?"

Braidon shook his head, but before more could be said, the tent flap lifted and their guide returned, carrying two steaming plates. Devon studied the contents as they were placed before them, and was slightly disappointed to see they mostly consisted of rice and tubers dug up from the forest. Thin slivers of beef had been sprinkled through the food, with a generous helping of thyme, but there was little else.

His stomach rumbled, and he looked up to ask the Baronian where the rest was, when he saw the anxiety in the man's eyes. Devon's spirits fell as he realised this was the best these people could offer.

"Cheers, sonny," he rumbled, careful to hide his disappointment. "Give us half the hour, then bring the prisoner."

"Of course, hammerman." The man bowed his head and retreated from the tent.

They were just finishing their meal when the Baronian reappeared with Joseph in tow. The former Baronian leader's arms had been tied behind his back, and he glowered down at them as he was ushered into the tent. A bruise darkened his forehead where Devon had knocked him out. With his injured arm tied behind his back, he must have been in considerable pain, but his face remained carefully blank.

With a nod from Devon, their guide retreated from the tent. Standing before them, Joseph smirked. "I trust the new accommodations are to your liking?"

Devon leaned back in his chair and eyed the giant. When he'd first seen the man, he'd thought him in his late thirties. But after a night tied up in the cold winter air, the lines on Joseph's face had deepened, the silver in his beard becoming more prominent, and now Devon wondered if the man was closer to fifty.

If that were true, the fight he'd put up was all the more impressive. Even now, Joseph refused to bend, facing down his impending judgement with fire in his eyes. Watching Joseph standing there in open defiance, Devon realised he had no desire to see the man killed.

"Seems comfortable enough," Devon mused. "Could use a bit of colour though."

Joseph snorted. "Typical townsfolk."

Beside Devon, Braidon bristled, but the hammerman waved him down. "Strange folks, these Baronians of yours," he mused. "One moment they're cheering for your victory, next they're on their knees proclaiming me their king."

"Baronians don't have kings," Joseph rumbled.

"Leader, whatever," Devon replied, waving a hand.

A strained silence followed, before Joseph sighed and shook his head. "Can't say I understand it myself," he grunted. "Any one of em could have taken my place, if they'd had the guts to put an arrow in ya."

"Glad they couldn't find the courage," Devon replied.

Rising to his feet, he gestured at Joseph's bindings. "If I free you, are you going to play nice?"

"I'll make no promises to you, hammerman."

"Then you can rot for all I care," Devon said, starting to sit.

"Fine," Joseph said quickly, betraying his fear for the briefest of moments.

Grinning, Devon fetched a knife from beside the camp stove and cut Joseph's bonds. The man winced as they came free, and lifted his injured arm to the firelight. His wrist had swollen to twice its original size and had turned an awful black colouring. Pulling up a chair, Devon gestured for the giant to sit.

"Where do you keep the ale around here?" he asked as he stepped back.

Joseph chuckled. "Behind the bed, if Jazz didn't pilfer it already."

Devon found the clay jar where Joseph had said, and fetching a couple of mugs from behind the camp stove, he offered ale to Braidon and Joseph. Finally, he filled a mug of his own and settled back in his chair.

"Quite the predicament we've found ourselves in," he said, lifting his ale to Joseph.

The Baronian chuckled. "You seem to have landed on your feet, from where I sit."

"Ay…" Devon trailed off, remembering the information Braidon had shared the night before about the giant warrior and his people. "Who are you, Joseph? Selina says you and your people just showed up here one day, took over the place."

"Selina talks too much," Joseph rumbled. He shook his head and looked away. Then a smile touched his lips. "I might ask the same of you, hammerman. What kind of man leaves his enemies alive? Or sits down and shares a drink with them, for that matter?"

"Who says we're enemies?" Devon replied, taking a swig of his ale. It was strong, the fiery liquid burning its way down his throat, and he grinned in appreciation.

In the other chair, Braidon took his first swig and started to splutter. Joseph threw back his head and howled with laughter, but Braidon was too busy coughing to complain. When the commotion died down, Joseph leaned forward, his eyes dark.

"I'm serious, hammerman," he said quietly. "If you intend to be rid of me, I'd rather not draw this out."

"I don't kill unless I have to, sonny," Devon rumbled. "So the answer to your question is entirely up to you. When we're done here, you'll have your freedom. I'll warn you though, don't cross me. I give no second chances." He eyed the man. "Now, where did you and these Baronians of yours come from?"

Joseph sighed. "They're farmers, mostly. A few of us are descended from the old folks; have the blood of true Baronians flowing in our veins. But our people have always welcomed exiles, and there's no shortage of those nowadays. I fell on hard times myself a while back, decided the Three Nations could use a bit of the old days."

Devon grinned. "As I heard it, the old days were filled with monsters and Dark Magickers intent on world domination."

"Hasn't changed much, has it?" Joseph replied, sculling his ale. "Just the titles we give em that differ."

Devon gestured for Braidon to fetch the jar of ale. Rolling his eyes, the boy rose and wandered across and retrieved it. Lifting it from the nook where it had been stored, he was just turning back towards them when he stumbled, a sudden cry tearing from his lips.

Throwing back his chair, Devon leapt to his feet. Moaning, Braidon straightened, his breath coming in ragged gasps. His eyes met Devon's, his pupils dilated, as though he were staring away into nothing. Devon took a quick step forward as the boy started to shudder, a low keening coming from the back of his throat.

"Braidon, what's wrong?" he hissed.

Braidon's pale face lifted slowly to meet his gaze. "It's them," he whispered. "It's my sister and Enala. They're in trouble!"

19

Alana screamed as her magic rose from the depths of her consciousness and wrapped its thorny tendrils about her mind. Daggers of fire tore into her thoughts, dragging her down, trapping her in bonds of agony. Beside her, she could hear someone else screaming, and over it all, their assailant's laughter, mocking her.

The green light of her magic filled her. Its voice whispered in her ear, as her own personal demon took joy in its sudden freedom. Mustering her courage, she tried to face it, as she had so many times before, but now her courage seemed nothing beside the beast. It was as though the gates of its cage had been thrust open, unleashing it on her defenceless soul.

An image flickered into her mind, of her father standing over her, shining white sword in hand. Where once before he had thrust her magic back down, saving her from the demon within, now he was using the power of the Sword to unlock the chains of her own magic, handing the beast its freedom. It was devouring her from the inside out, and there was nothing she could do to protect herself.

Just as Alana was sure her mind would crumble, her magic vanished, its sickly green energies going rushing back down into the void within. Its absence was so sudden Alana gasped out loud. Her body shook, and the metallic taint of blood filled her mouth. Collapsing to the ground, she sobbed into the wooden floor as a voice spoke from overhead.

"That should bring the boy running," her father was saying. "Go prepare for his arrival, lieutenant."

The hard *thump* of boots on wood came from nearby, followed by the *thud* of the door being closed. Alana cracked open her eyes as another set of footsteps approached, and found her father crouching beside her. There was no sign of Quinn or the other Stalkers in the inn. The Tsar's eyes shone as he reached out and stroked her hair.

"Oh, my daughter, why must you torment me so?"

Alana shuddered, but when she tried to move away, she found the bonds of his magic holding her tight. The Tsar was taking no chances on her escaping this time.

"I am sorry it had to come to this," he continued, sadness in his voice. "I searched for so long for another way, but your betrayal has forced my hand. I must complete my task, before my enemies find a way to stop me."

"I won't serve you, Father," Alana croaked. "I would rather die."

The Tsar straightened. "And death is what you shall have," he said, his voice suddenly cold. "You're right, no matter my power, I could never fix what's broken in you. But you can still serve me, one last time."

"Never!" Alana spat.

Ignoring her, the Tsar turned his attention to the figure

lying alongside Alana. "And you, Mother…" He trailed off as Enala pushed herself to her knees, pain etched across her aged face. His lips pursed into a thin line. "Why must you fight me? I have only ever done what you raised me to do, to fight for the greater good, to protect our nation from the ravages of war and magic."

Enala's eyes shone like sapphires in the light of the Tsar's sword. "And how did murdering the God of Light and trapping him in your sword serve our nation?" she murmured, gesturing to the blade. "Did you think I would not recognise his power? No wonder the Goddess came to me."

The Tsar shrugged. "It was only a matter of time before they sought to rule us again."

"You're wrong, son," Enala croaked. "They left because they no longer wanted any part of our world. It is the only reason you exist."

"Lies!" the Tsar roared, pointing the Sword of Light at Enala. "You were corrupted by her touch, admit it! You are not the Enala you once were, before Antonia consumed your soul."

Enala smiled sadly. "Perhaps I am not," she murmured. "But that is no fault of Antonia's. It was my choice, to give her my body—and hers to return it."

The Tsar bared his teeth. "And it will be *mine* to finally see an end to her."

The old woman's laughter filled the room. "Antonia is not her brother. You will not fool her so easily, my son. That shoddy copy of a *Soul Blade* will not stop her."

"Copy?" the Tsar cackled. "I spent years studying Archon's work, but I surpassed him long ago. This is no copy, it is an improvement. When I'm done, I won't need others to help me wield the power of the Gods. This blade will contain them all."

"You cannot!" Enala hissed, her eyes widening. "The power will destroy you!"

"I command the magic of five hundred Magickers, Mother. The power of the Gods does not frighten me."

"It should," Enala whispered. She shook her head. "But it does not matter, you will never trap the Goddess. Or do you think she will submit meekly to your blade?"

The smile fell from the Tsar's face as his gaze drifted back to Alana. "No," he whispered. "That is why I need my children. Only they have the bloodline to host their power."

Alana's blood turned to ice at his words. Her mouth fell open, but the words failed to form in her throat. Sword in hand, her father stepped towards her. She tried to scramble back, but at a gesture from him, the bands of power tightened their grip. Slowly they lifted her up, dragging her off her feet until she dangled helplessly before him.

"I am sorry, my daughter," the Tsar whispered. "I wish there were another way."

"Please, don't." Still reeling from the bite of her magic, Alana found herself sobbing. In the past weeks, she had suffered more than she could ever have imagined, and now she could hold herself together no longer. She screamed, fighting to tear herself free of the Tsar's power. Tears spilled down her cheeks as she hurled abuse at the man who dared to call himself her father, and her feet kicked helplessly at empty air.

When she finally stilled, her father stood unmoved before her. Reaching out, he wiped a tear from her cheek, his eyes shining with a grief all of his own. "There is no other way," he whispered. "It is my life's duty to sponge the curse of magic from this land. For years I tried to use the power of the Light to wipe it clean, but the deed requires the Three. I must return the Gods of the Earth and Sky to flesh, so that I might use their power to save our people. You and Braidon are the only hosts left."

"No!" Enala's voice rang from the walls. "I won't let you have them." Flames gathered in her palm as she pointed at the Tsar.

The Tsar only shook his head. "You do not have the power to stop me, Mother. Your brother, your dragon, they're gone now. Look around: you're all alone, there is no one left to help you."

Enala did not back down, but Alana could see the defiance in the old woman's eyes falter, then turn slowly to despair. The soft crackling of her magic died away, and her arm dropped to her side. Her eyes flickered to Alana, her pain reflecting in the light of the Tsar's sword. The lines on her face deepened as she looked back at the Tsar.

"Spare the girl," Enala said. "She and her brother are not the only ones. Take me instead."

20

"*No!*" Alana screamed at her grandmother. Desperately, she fought to reach her across the wooden floor of the inn, but the Tsar's bonds refused to bend. "Please, don't do this, Enala!"

Enala's face wrinkled into a smile. "Ah, but I must, Granddaughter."

Alana shook her head, her heart burning with newfound pain, an awful ache she had never before experienced. "But…I'm not worth it," she whispered.

The smile fell from her grandmother's face. "Nonsense, girl," she growled. "You are the future."

"No, you can't..."

"I can, and I will," Enala replied. "My time is done; yours is only just beginning, Alana."

Between them, the Tsar chuckled. "If you ladies are quite done?" He flicked a finger in Enala's direction, and the old woman rose ponderously into the air. Another gesture, and she drifted towards him. "And I thank you,

Mother. Your sacrifice will allow my daughter to begin her life anew, once I am done shaping it."

"Monster," Enala spat, though she made no attempt to free herself.

Straining her arms, Alana fought to break her father's magic, but the invisible bindings refused to give. She sagged in their grip, a sob tearing from her throat, and watched in despair as the Tsar rested a hand on her grandmother's shoulder.

"Why have you always hated me, Mother?" he asked, his voice reflective.

"I *loved* you," Enala murmured, her voice little more than a croak.

"No." The Tsar shook his head. "I remember your disappointment, the day you discovered the gift wasn't in me, the day you realised I took after my *father.*"

"I only ever wanted the best for you."

"*Lies!*" the Tsar snapped, pointing a finger. "I was never enough for you, always lacking, always the magicless son you never wanted. In all your tales and stories, it was always *magic* that brought wonder to your eyes. I could never live up to that. Just like my father."

"I never—"

"You think I couldn't see it?" the Tsar interrupted. "Your scorn for him, your disappointment as he aged, as his mortality began to show?"

The Tsar trailed off, and Enala hung there in silence, her eyes shining. Finally, she swallowed and spoke, her words barely a whisper. "I loved Gabriel until his dying day. Every wrinkle, every new white hair, was a blessing. I love him still. Even now I hope to see him again, to find him waiting for me on the other side. Though I pray he cannot see what his son has become."

"My father would be *proud* of what I have accomplished," the Tsar roared. His fingers bent like claws as he raised a fist. "And you will see him soon, Mother. That I promise you."

Turning away, he reached into his scarlet robes and withdrew a leather pouch. Glass rattled as he slapped it down on the inn's counter and unfurled it, revealing an array of glass vials. A mortar and pestle appeared next. Taking up vial after vial, the Tsar began to add them to the mortar, whispering beneath his breath all the while.

"What are you doing, Father?" Alana asked, her voice laced with venom. "Making us a cocktail?"

The Tsar flicked an irritated glance over his shoulder, and then returned to his work.

"You really think you can face her, son?" Enala cut in.

Slamming the mortar onto the bar, he spun towards them. The Sword of Light leapt into his hand, its blade aglow with power. "I have *this*, don't I?" he snapped. "With power over *all* magic, what chance does the Goddess of the Earth have?"

Enala smiled. "So much knowledge, and yet so little wisdom. Can you truly be so ignorant, my son?"

The Tsar's face turned a mottled red. Baring his teeth, he took a step towards the old woman before catching himself. With an effort of will, he forced himself back to his work. Taking up the pestle, he resumed his muttering as he ground the ingredients into a paste. When he was done, he lifted it to the light, inspecting it closely before nodding to himself.

"It's done," he announced, facing Enala.

"Are you afraid, Father?" Alana asked as he stepped towards her grandmother. A frown crossed his brow as he seemed to hesitate, and emboldened, she went on. "Don't worry, she's only an old woman. Or is it the Goddess who has your knees trembling? I've seen her, you know. She's about ten years old. I'm sure you can take her, though. Go on, get on with it."

The words burned in her mouth, but she felt a moment's satisfaction as her father's face darkened. Baring his teeth, he appraised her with cold eyes.

"Keep it up, my daughter. It will only quicken your fate."

Returning to Enala, he grabbed the old woman's face and forced open her mouth. As she cried out, he poured half the potion down her throat and then held her jaw closed until she swallowed. Finally he released her and swallowed the rest of the potion himself.

"Bah, but that tastes almost as bad as Jonathan's muck," Enala spat.

The Tsar snorted. "That lunatic knew nothing of magic," he said, leaning casually against the bar. "His experiment would never have worked, not with you dead. Natural magic requires a *soul.* With yours in the void, the power he stole would have withered and died. That is why I am so careful to preserve the lives of my Magickers."

"By condemning them to a life without a past," Alana snapped.

Her father raised an eyebrow. "A task you savoured until quite recently, as I recall."

Alana shuddered as she remembered the part she'd played in her father's reign. Placed in charge of the young Magickers, she had the task of preparing them for their initiation. When the time came, she would take them before her father, and he would unlock their power, forcing them to face the beast within.

Those who survived, she took with her own magic,

wiping the memories from them, reshaping them forever as her father's servants. And those who failed…

Her heart twisted as she saw again her charges changing, their eyes darkening to black as they succumbed to the demons within. Even then they could not escape her father's will. Using his power, he had bound their powers to his, to be his creatures, his assassins in the night.

Shame welled in Alana, not just for the horror of her deeds, but for the delight she had taken in them, that she still took in them, in the depths of her soul. She had joyed in her power over the young Magickers—their helplessness in the face of her magic. And when they had dared defy her…

"I was only what you made me," she whispered.

Her father laughed and turned away. She cursed at his back, but with a wave from her father the air changed, and she was hurled backwards against the wall. The breath hissed from her chest as she struck, leaving her gasping desperately for breath.

"Now, now, my daughter," her father's voice carried across the room. "Don't break my concentration. If this goes wrong, you may end up host to the Goddess after all."

"I hope she tears you in two," Alana gasped.

Her father had his back to her now, though, and didn't seem to hear. His voice boomed out in some strange language, and lifting his arms, he advanced on Enala. As he neared the old woman, his eyes became unfocused, and Alana recognised the look of someone reaching for his magic. A second later she sensed it arrive. Its power bubbled through the rundown inn, seeming to set the very air aflame.

Reaching Enala, the Tsar reached out and placed a hand on her shoulder. The old woman flinched at his touch, but wrapped up in his magic, there was nowhere for her to go. Eyes shining, Enala turned to look at Alana. To Alana's surprise, it wasn't fear or anger that shone from her grandmother's eyes, but a look of peace. Her lips moved silently, forming the words she dared not speak.

I love you, granddaughter.

Tears burned in Alana's eyes as the Tsar tightened his grip on her grandmother. A sudden convulsion shook the old woman, her mouth opening wide.

"*No!*" Alana screamed, but the two of them had entered the trance now, and neither heard.

"I summon you, Goddess of the Earth!" Her father's words rang out like thunder. A moan came from the floor near Alana, and she was surprised to see the innkeeper clawing her way towards the door. Another shout from the Tsar returned her attention to the centre of the room. "I summon you, Antonia, return to this mortal realm. I bid you, take host in this vessel, in the body of the woman marked by the name Enala."

His voice dropped to a low hiss then, his words becoming rapid and indistinct, and while Alana strained to hear the rest, she could not make them out. Her eyes were drawn back to her grandmother.

Alana's heart froze in her chest as she saw the old woman's face. Gone was the familiar sapphire of her grandmother's eyes; in its place shone the violet gaze of the Goddess Antonia. An icy fear spread through Alana's veins as she glimpsed the rage in those ancient eyes. When she had met Antonia in her dreams, the Goddess's anger had seemed fleeting, passing in an instant. But here, now, there was a timelessness to her rage, an anger that promised to never die.

The air wavered as the Goddess turned on the Tsar. With a flick of her hand, the forces holding Enala's body in the air shattered, and Antonia dropped lightly to her feet. Folding her arms, she studied the Tsar, her lips twisting into a scowl. Her foot tapped impatiently on the wooden floor as she waited for him to respond.

But Alana's father was still chanting under his breath, his eyes distant, unaware of the change that had come over the old woman. Arms raised, he seemed to be building to a finish. Alana was baffled—why was her father still trying to summon the Goddess, when Antonia was already standing before him? She shuddered as the violet gaze flickered in her direction. To her surprise, the slightest smile touched the Goddess's lips.

"By the *Gods!*" Antonia burst out suddenly. "Are you going to stand there all day mumbling to yourself?" She stamped her foot as though to emphasise her point.

The Tsar jerked as though he'd been stung. His eyes widened when he saw the old woman standing free of his bindings. He cried out as he recognised the violet eyes shining from her face.

"That's…that's not possible!" he gasped. Stumbling back, he lifted the Sword of Light, placing it between himself and the Goddess.

"What would you know, *mortal?*" Antonia growled. She advanced on him, the earth trembling with each step.

Alana gasped as the powers pinning her to the wall snapped as though they'd been severed by an axe. She staggered slightly as she landed, her muscles burning with the disuse. As she recovered, a wave of warmth swept through the room, radiating out from the glowing figure. The magic wrapped around Alana, every pain, every ache vanishing at its touch. Looking at her arms, Alana gaped as her bruises faded away, her cuts and scrapes healing in an instant. The pounding in her head from the blow Quinn had struck vanished.

A groan came from nearby as the innkeeper sat up. Her hands clutched at her chest where Quinn's sword had pierced her, but now the skin was whole. The only trace of the wound that remained was the blood staining her clothes. She looked at Antonia in wonder, tears brimming in her eyes.

"Thank you, Goddess," she whispered.

"*Stop this!*" the Tsar boomed.

He raised the Sword of Light. A brilliant radiance lit the inn, and Alana moaned as the warmth was sucked from the room. It had done its work though, and her strength restored, she crouched down and crept to where the innkeeper sat. Silently she offered her a hand, then turned to watch her father face off against the Goddess of the Earth.

"Your power is *mine*, Goddess," he hissed through clenched teeth. "You cannot harm me."

Antonia only smiled. "I have no wish to harm you, Theo. I never wanted to return to this realm. It was I who first gave up this body, all those years ago, so that you might be born. It pleased me to watch Enala grow, to become the woman I knew she could be. I am only sorry she lived long enough to see her child become a monster." The Goddess's eyes flickered to Alana. "But perhaps it is not too late for her grandchildren."

"Enough!" the Tsar shrieked. "You do not fool me, Goddess. Your tyranny ends today. No longer shall you and your siblings wield your power over this realm."

He lifted the shining sword, but as Antonia stepped towards him, he faltered. Swirling green light appeared in her hands, and the Tsar's eyes widened with fear. A smile touched Antonia's face. With a flick of her finger, power went crackling through the inn. Alana gasped as her ears popped, the pressure building until she thought for sure her skull would crack.

Go, Alana, a voice whispered in her mind. *Save yourself, as your grandmother wished.*

Alana gasped as she recognised the voice as the one who had led her to her grandmother. A sob tore from her as she looked at the Goddess, and saw her head dip in acknowledgement. Eyes burning, Alana swung away, grabbing the innkeeper as she did so. Somewhere behind them was the door to the outside, though how they could avoid Quinn and his Stalkers, Alana didn't know. All she knew was they had to get out, had to escape that room before the end came.

"You cannot defeat the Light!" Alana heard her father bellow. Together with the innkeeper, she staggered toward the door.

"No," came Antonia's reply. The rumbling energies burning through the room went out as though quenched by a bucket of water. Alana glanced back to see the Goddess standing alone, bathed in the eerie white of her father's sword. "But I do not need to."

For a moment her words gave the Tsar pause. He towered over the Goddess, confusion on his ageless face. Then a sneer twisted his lips, and with a bellow of laughter, he lifted the Sword of Light and drove it through the Goddess's chest.

21

"You sure about this, sonny?" Devon rumbled.

Braidon flicked Devon a nervous grin as they paused on the edge of the settlement. Still in the treeline, he had not yet summoned his magic, and raising a hand, he gestured for the others to halt. The twenty Baronians they had selected to join them came to a stop, their blackened leather armour fading into the shadows beneath the dense canopy.

"As sure as I'll ever be," Braidon muttered.

Movement came from nearby as Joseph crouched beside Devon. Irritation cut through Braidon's fear, but he fought to keep it from his face. The man's injured arm was strapped to his chest, but even wounded, he was a threat. Braidon couldn't believe Devon had let the former leader join them, not when so much was at stake. But his friend had been firm, insisting they needed the man's knowledge of the territory, and of his people.

Shaking his head, Braidon returned his gaze to the settlement. It was too late now to reconsider the Baronian's presence, though looking at what faced them, he wondered if Joseph was already regretting his decision to join them. A dozen Stalkers could be seen wandering the narrow alleyways between the buildings, and in the centre of the square…

"You'd better be, boy," Joseph hissed, his dark eyes transfixed on what faced them.

"Don't worry about the beast," Devon whispered. "It won't lift a claw unless the Tsar wills it."

"How reassuring," Joseph muttered. "But if it's all the same to you, I'd rather not risk my people against a *dragon*."

"Good thing they're not your people anymore, isn't it?" Braidon snapped.

Between them, Devon raised his hands in a consolatory gesture. "Easy," he said. "Don't want to be giving ourselves away just yet." His amber eyes turned on the Baronian. "As for your people, what about the ones in that settlement? Did you not make a deal with the people here to protect them?"

"Against other rogues, not the Tsar himself," Joseph argued, but his head dropped imperceptibly, and after a moment he went on. "The dragon won't attack, you say?"

"Not your people," Devon replied. "Not when Braidon and I have the Tsar's mother and daughter. If everything goes to plan, it'll be coming after *us*. We only need you to free the villagers and distract the Stalkers long enough for them to get away."

"Fine. Just make sure you shake the beast before the rendezvous."

"Don't worry, your safety is our *top* priority," Braidon said spitefully. "Now, if you're done?" Joseph glared at him, but said nothing, and Braidon nodded curtly. "Then we'd better get going, Devon. I can sense something happening in there."

Even as he spoke, the power he sensed in the inn redoubled. Magic rippled through the air, shifting and building, until it seemed his very bones were vibrating with the strength of it. Swallowing his doubt, he reached down and stoked the flames of his own power.

A roar answered his call as it lifted from the depths of his soul. Ignoring the beast that took shape before him, Braidon gripped it with his mind, forcing it to his will. He reached out with the power in hand and wrapped ghostly threads of white around himself and Devon. As they touched the brilliant blue of Devon's lifeforce, they changed, seeming to merge with the green of the forest. He did the same for himself, and beside them Joseph slowly faded until he was just a silhouette against the world around him.

Blinking, the Baronian looked around as though he could no longer see them. "That's incredible," he murmured. "Are you still there?"

"Remember, ten minutes," Devon hissed.

Then they were up and racing across the open ground between the treeline and the settlement. Braidon held his breath as a Stalker appeared ahead of them, his long strides carrying him around the edge of the square. His eyes swept the forest, fixating for a second on Braidon and Devon, and then passing on. Air whistled between Braidon's teeth as he released his breath.

Moving quickly, they crossed the square and made the inn, taking care to avoid the wings and tail of the Red Dragon. It had taken up residence in the centre of the square, its massive body curled around the couple's wagon. The carcass of their pony lay alongside the beast, its bloody bones all but unrecognisable.

Shuddering, Braidon fixed his eyes on their destination. Checking his spell was still in place, he continued on, Devon keeping fast to his side. Despite the big man's words, Devon had one eye on the beast, and Braidon could sense the fear radiating from his friend.

The magic spreading through the square grew stronger as they approached the stairs to the inn. He no longer sensed Alana or Enala's power, but the confusing mixture of Light, Earth and Sky magic could only have come from his father. Something else stained the air though, a cold tang of Earth and Light far more potent than even his father's magic.

"You sure they're in there?" Devon whispered.

Braidon nodded and they started up the stairs. The wooden boards creaked beneath Devon's weight, and Braidon glanced back quickly to see if the watchers had noticed. The black silhouettes of the Stalkers continued their slow march around the square. None of the ones hiding in the shadows moved, but the Red Dragon lifted its head, a low rumble coming from its chest. A vile stench carried across to them as it snorted, then took up a piece of bone and began to chew.

"Disgusting creatures," Devon muttered. "I hope Enala still has Dahniul lurking somewhere nearby."

Braidon's throat clenched as he recalled the beam of light that had caught the Gold Dragon, hurling him from its back. Yet both he and Enala had survived; why not the dragon?

He spun back around as an awful shriek came from inside the inn. Braidon's heart leapt into his throat as he felt the magic in the air changing. Gripping Devon by the arm, he raced for the door. As he reached for the handle, a howl came from the forest behind them, announcing the arrival of the Baronians.

Braidon didn't have time to see whether the Stalkers

were successfully distracted. If everything went to plan, the Baronians would kill a few and then disappear back into the forest. Hauling open the door, Braidon raced inside.

Green and white light raced out to greet him, and for half a second Braidon felt his power swell, as though fed by some other force. A moment later Devon appeared beside him, *kanker* in hand. Braidon sensed his spell tearing, drained by the spell cast over the hammer—then they were standing in the doorway to the inn for all the world to see.

Before he could restore his illusion, a scream drew Braidon's attention to the centre of the room. His father stood there, glowing white sword in hand, Enala bowed before him. Before anyone could move, the blade flashed down, tearing through his grandmother's chest.

Braidon's heart lurched and he screamed, reaching out a hand as though by will alone he could undo what his father had done. Another scream came from his right, and Devon rushed past, his face a mask of determination. Braidon was still staring in horror when Devon returned an instant later, Alana now swung over his shoulder.

"Go, Braidon!" he bellowed. Another voice echoed his cry, and Braidon was shocked to see the innkeeper, Selina, racing before the hammerman. "*Go!*" Devon screamed again.

But Braidon was unable to look away from the terrible scene. His grandmother still stood, her eyes burning violet, her body bent around the awful sword. Magic bubbled from the wound up into the Tsar's blade, green and white mixing and merging, seeming to flow into the steel itself.

The Tsar showed no sign he had noticed Alana's rescue, nor his son's presence. Slowly the magic began to fade, then as though she were a fire dashed by water, the light in Enala's eyes died. She slumped against the sword, and wrenching back his blade, the Tsar allowed her body to tumble to the ground. Power swirled as he lifted the sword aloft, awesome, terrifying.

A sudden fear fill Braidon then, and tearing himself free of his shock, he turned away. Tears streamed from his eyes as he chased after Devon. He could feel his grief within, his rage and hatred rising, becoming entangled in the threads of his magic. Unbidden it rose again, igniting a flickering light in his palms. Stumbling outside, Braidon focused on his grandmother's lessons, concentrating on his breathing, seeking the calm within the storm of his emotions.

As his magic came back under his control, he gripped it tightly, seeking to wrap a fresh layer of concealment around the four of them. But as the magic touched Devon, there was a strange sucking sensation, and he realised with a curse that his friend still held *kanker* in one hand.

"Devon!" he called, his voice echoing through the square. "Sheathe your hammer!"

Devon was already at the bottom of the steps. To Braidon's relief, most of the Stalkers had vanished, presumably chasing after the Baronians that had attacked the settlement. Below, Devon looked back, confusion in his eyes, but seeing Braidon's desperation, he did as he was bid. As he reached up to sheathe *kanker*, Alana shrieked, seeming to come alive in his grip. An elbow struck him in the face, and he staggered back as she dropped lightly to her feet. Eyes dark, she started towards the steps.

"You can't help her, girl." Selina blocked the way back to her inn. "And you can't stop him."

Braidon rushed down the steps as Alana raised a hand towards the woman. He sensed her power building and opened his mouth to scream a warning, but at the last moment his sister hesitated. Some of the rage left her face as she closed her eyes, a shudder sweeping through her. She slumped forward, and Selina stepped quickly forwards to catch her.

Reaching them, Braidon wasted only a second to check that Alana was okay, before diving back into his magic. Sensing their peril, it rose in an instant. Acting by a will of its own, the white light wrapped around them, and they faded from view.

"Fine, then I'll make them all pay."

Braidon looked around as his sister straightened once more. Her eyes glowed as she stalked past him. Concealed now by her power, she strode towards the dragon, which had awoke amongst the chaos and was now staring at the space where they had vanished. Just as Devon had predicted, it had made no move against them without being bidden by his father. Casting a quick glance back at the inn, Braidon wondered how long it would be before the command came. Whatever had happened between the Tsar and Enala was obviously still keeping him preoccupied, and he prayed to the Goddess it continued for a while yet.

Alana was approaching the Red Dragon now, and as its tail twitched, she darted forward and gripped it in both hands. Braidon's ears popped as he sensed the power surge from her into the beast. An awful roar rent the air as it threw back its head. Alana leapt away as the tail whipped about, narrowly missing her.

Then the dragon drew suddenly still, the great globes of its eyes fixating on the distant trees. Alana stepped forward again, resting her hands on its foreclaws.

"Go," her voice rang through the square. "Destroy them all, the ones who caged you, the ones who sought to rule you."

The beast roared again, but now the sound was filled

with an awful glee. Wings spread, it crouched flat against the dirt, and then bounded into the air. A sharp *crack* sounded in the square as the dragon lifted skywards, its great neck circling to stare down at the settlement. Fire built in the cavern of its jaws as it turned towards them.

"*Run!*" Braidon screamed.

22

Blood thumped in Alana's ears as she raced through the trees, drowning out the dragon's roar and the screams of dying men. Smoke hung heavy in the air, its stench choking, blinding. Around them the forest was aflame, the world in chaos. Alana cared nothing for any of it.

Enala was dead.

Her grandmother, the woman she had hated until just a few days ago, had been murdered, and there was nothing Alana could do to change it.

"Come on!"

Someone was screaming from ahead of her, but whether it was Devon or Braidon or the strange woman from the inn, she couldn't tell. Head down, she continued through the forest, her footsteps growing shorter as despair ate her resolve. The magic it had taken to break her father's spell over the Red Dragon had cost her greatly, and now the beast was as likely to kill them all as it was her father's Stalkers.

Tears stung her eyes as she finally staggered to a stop,

overwhelmed. The fire was somewhere behind her now, but smoke still blanketed the forest. It rose to claim her as she slumped to the ground, stealing away her breath.

How long she crouched there, she couldn't say, but suddenly she sensed her brother alongside her. Her heart beat faster as she looked at him, still hardly believing he was there, that he was alive. After all those days thinking he was gone…

"Braidon," she murmured. "You're alive."

"Of course I am, sis," he said as he knelt in the dirt. "What are you doing here?"

Her vision blurred as the pain of their grandmother's loss cut through her joy. "We have to go back," she croaked. "We have to save her."

The pain in her brother's eyes reflected her own, but he shook his head. Reaching out, he drew her into his arms. Alana sobbed as she breathed in the scent of him, felt his heart beating in concert with her own.

He's alive, he's really alive.

"We can't, sis," Braidon whispered into her ear. "We can't, she's already gone."

"But she's our grandmother," Alana sobbed, trying to pull herself together, to summon the unyielding resolve her father had built within her. Yet the moment Enala had been struck down, all that strength, all that resolve, had been shattered. "She sacrificed herself for me," she burst out, and buried her face in Braidon's shoulder.

Braidon said nothing, only held her tighter. For a while they knelt together in silence, eyes closed, listening as the sounds of the world faded away, until it seemed only the two of them remained. A sweet peace settled around Alana, calming her heart, drying her tears. Finally, she pulled back from her brother and opened her eyes. The forest had vanished, replaced by the softest blanket of white.

"You're doing this?" she whispered.

"It's only an illusion," he murmured. "We have to return, before the fires reach us."

The thought of returning to a world without the crotchety old woman filled Alana with dread. She sucked in a breath, savouring the nothingness around them, the peace of it all, and then nodded at Braidon. With a flick of his fingers, the white vanished, returning them to the chaos of the forest.

Slowly he drew Alana to her feet. "Are you ready?" he asked. "My magic won't hide us forever, not while we're so close."

"I know," Alana whispered.

They started off again. Alana had no idea which direction Braidon was leading her in, but as they continued on, the smoke grew thinner, and the bellows of the dragon faded, until the silence of the forest resumed. It wasn't long before they caught up with Devon and the woman from the inn. Seeing them, Devon turned and started off through the forest without saying a word.

The sight twisted a dagger in Alana's heart, but she said nothing, knowing she deserved every bit of his hatred. Her gaze turned to Braidon, who strode along behind Devon like he knew exactly where they were going. She frowned, thinking back to the last time she had seen him, the young, apprehensive boy she'd left before the gates of Fort Fall.

He had seemed so small then, so frail; she would have done anything to protect him. Now though, it was Braidon who had saved her, who had mustered a rescue from right beneath their father's nose. In the brief time they had been separated, the boy that had been her brother had mastered his magic, had come into his own. He was a man now, though Alana wondered whether she could ever think of him as anything but her little brother.

The roar of the dragon sounded through the quiet of the trees, but it was still some distance away, and after a moment's pause the company started off once more. Between Devon's obvious rage and Alana's shock, little was said amongst the four of them. No doubt there would be time for swapping stories later, though Alana doubted Devon would want to a hear a word of what she had to say. For now though, they needed to get away. With Braidon's power concealing them, the Tsar would struggle to detect their minds or magic. But that would not stop his Stalkers from encircling them.

That is, if the Red Dragon didn't burn them first.

They continued on, the trees growing denser around them. After an hour, when they still hadn't heard more from the dragon, Alana sensed her brother release his concealing spell. They shared a glance and she nodded her approval. His magic still protected them from their father's invisible gaze, but the physical concealment required far more energy. Braidon could not have kept up such a magic forever, not without drawing on his own lifeforce.

The trees thinned out again, the light amongst the undergrowth brightening as the canopy grew fainter. Brambles appeared, their vines as thick as fingers. Devon took the lead, his leather jacket and pants giving him some protection from their bites. Following behind him, the others struggled through the broken bushes he left behind, cursing as stray thorns cut their flesh.

Dusk approached, and the soft whine of insects arrived. Alana cursed as the creatures slipped through the cracks in her clothing to fasten themselves on her flesh. She slapped her arm, and her hand came away streaked with blood. A few seconds later, another insect took the mosquito's place.

Finally the last of the forest gave way, but as Alana looked around, it wasn't open ground that greeted her, but a towering cliff of blood-red sandstone. Her heart sank as she scanned the mountain range, her eyes alighting on a slightly darker patch of shadow. In the fading light, it wasn't until they grew closer that she realised it was a thin passage leading through the cliffs.

As they neared the crevice, the buzz of voices carried to their ears. Alana slowed, her hand dropping to her empty sword sheath. She cursed, realising she'd left the blade behind on the floor of the inn, but Devon was still striding forward, seemingly uncaring of the voices. Sharing a glance with her brother, she watched as he disappeared into the shadows of the Sandstone Mountains.

Quinn winced as the door clicked shut behind him. In the silence within the inn, the noise seemed unbelievably loud, echoing through the dark interior of the building like a gong. He froze, taking a moment to prepare himself before facing the Tsar.

"They escaped?"

The words were softly spoken, yet they sliced through the silence, filling the room with their power. Quinn's head whipped around, searching the shadows for his master. He found the silhouette of a man near the bar, head bowed, sword still in hand. As Quinn's eyes adjusted, his gaze was drawn to the pile of rags at the Tsar's feet. The slight sheen of blood pooling there was the only hint that the rags were more than they appeared. Swallowing, he looked back at his master.

"Yes, sir—"

The words had barely left his mouth when he sensed an invisible force invade his body. He gasped, the shining blue of his magic rising to defend him. Yet even as it rose, the other force sliced through his resistance as though he were no more potent than a child and wrapped his mind in chains of fire.

A scream tore from Quinn's lips as agony engulfed him. Then, as quickly as it had come, the force departed, and he found himself gasping on the floor of the inn. Shivering, he dragged himself to his knees and looked at the Tsar.

"Speak," came the Tsar's command.

"Yes…sir," he managed. "The Baronians…they attacked. We…chased them into the forest…others were behind us…they freed the villagers…" He trailed off, his eyes drawn to the dark silhouette of his master.

"And?"

"The Red Dragon, it broke free," Quinn whispered, his voice more steady now. "It burned the forest, half our number, probably the Baronians, too. We…we had to kill it."

Quinn didn't mention the delight he had taken in tearing the beast from the sky. Ever since its mockery of him during his first hunt for Alana, he had despised the creature. He'd been all too happy to combine his magic with the other Stalkers and destroy the Red Dragon, Feshibe.

"And my daughter?"

"One of my men caught a glimpse of her, sir," he replied, "as they left the inn. She was with Devon, and your son."

"So all our enemies, they were here, in this settlement? And you failed to capture them, lieutenant?"

Quinn swallowed. "Yes, sir."

"You disappoint me."

The tone in the Tsar's voice froze the blood in Quinn's veins. He looked up in time to see the soft flicker of lightning as it gathered in the Tsar's hand. Crying out, Quinn stumbled back, but there was no escaping the violence dancing in his master's eyes. With a roar of thunder, it flashed across the room. Catching him around the legs, the blue fire burnt through clothes and flesh alike.

Quinn's back arched, but as he tried to scream he found his jaw clamped tightly shut. The strength went from him as agony engulfed his entire body. Desperately he clawed at his legs, and screamed again as he saw his flesh melting, the shining white of bone peeking through. Another bolt of lightning struck him, and Quinn twisted, his mind falling away…

And then there was nothing.

Blinking, Quinn cried out at the sudden absence of pain. Still clutching his legs, he opened his eyes, and gaped to find the Tsar still standing over him, the Sword of Light pointed at his chest. Except the glow of its power was no longer white, but a brilliant, shining emerald. It streamed from the blade to bathe his legs, cooling wherever it touched. Quinn watched in astonishment as his flesh regrew from nothing, making him whole once more.

"The Goddess is mine," the Tsar whispered. "So I will forgive you this one last time, Quinn." He waved a hand, and light filled the inn, illuminating the broken body of the old woman.

Rising unsteadily to his feet, Quinn bowed. "They won't get far, I promise you."

"I trust not," the Tsar replied. "Take the remaining Stalkers, and the soldiers. There are still more than enough to deal with the hammerman and his newfound allies."

"Yes, sir."

The Tsar regarded him coldly. "Do not betray me, Quinn," he said finally. He gestured to the dead woman. "Or what happened to her will seem a dream compared with your fate."

"Yes, sir," Quinn repeated, dropping to his knees. "I will not fail you."

To his surprise, the man snorted. "You probably will," he cackled. "But for the moment, there is no one else in this forest I can trust." Turning, the Tsar started for the doorway.

"Sir?" Quinn called him back, rising to his feet. "What of the dragon? How will you return to the army?"

"Feshibe's children are already on their way," he replied. His face darkened. "The Northland army has launched an ambush on our forces in Lonia."

"They dare to attack us?"

"Ay, it seems they could not wait for death to come to them. No matter, it will find them soon enough."

23

Damyn had just moments to glimpse the horror on the faces of his enemies before his force slammed into their flank, driving them back up against the wagons. Hampered by the overburdened vehicles and their own oxen, the soldiers struggled to bring their weapons to bear against the northern cavalry. Scores went down before any sort of resistance could be mounted.

By then, Damyn's forces outnumbered the defenders two to one, yet the enemy refused to break. Soldiers streamed through the gaps between the wagons as those caught on the other side of the baggage train reinforced their comrades. Linking shields, they sought to push back the horses.

Glancing along the road, Damyn cursed as he saw men streaming back through the trees towards them. The forces who'd marched to reinforce the vanguard hadn't gone far, and now Damyn only had minutes before they were surrounded. He looked at the wagons, so close and yet still so tantalisingly far away.

A scream came from one of the oxen in the baggage train, and suddenly it was charging forward. Wagon still attached, it slammed into the men standing between Damyn and his goal, shattering their line. Panicked, another oxen followed suit, the traces holding its load in place shattering as it twisted and leapt away.

The scattered soldiers made easy targets, and screaming an order, Damyn pressed his horse forward. His sabre sliced left and right, cutting a path to the broken wagons. Finally, the southerners broke, first one, then dozens turning and fleeing up the Gods Road towards their reinforcements.

Well-trained, Damyn's men dragged back on their reins when the soldiers were clear of the baggage train, turning their attention to the wagons themselves. Swords flashed, freeing the last of the oxen of their burdens, before torches appeared. Damyn lit his own and hurled it into the back of the nearest wagon. His men did the same, and within the minute thick columns of smoke stained the sky, rising high in the thin winter air.

Turning his horse, Damyn surveyed their work. A grin split his bearded cheeks as he waved to his men.

"Back to the hi—"

An ear-splitting roar drowned out his cry as a shadow passed across the sun. Beneath him, Damyn's horse gave a scream of pure terror and reared. He tugged desperately at the reins as it hit the ground running, seeking to turn it, to bring it back under his control. Around him he sensed others doing the same, even as the *thump, thump, thump* of scarlet wings drove a spike of despair deep into his heart.

Finally, Damyn's horse staggered to a halt, its coat drenched in sweat, its powerful body trembling from head to tail. Hardly daring to breathe, Damyn turned the gelding back towards the hillside. With a shout, he kicked his horse into a run, setting his sights on the distant hilltop.

"Pull back!" he bellowed, though his men were scattered around the Gods Road now, and few could hear him.

The shadow passed across the sun again before Damyn could reach the treeline. The Red Dragon came barrelling down, mouth wide, fire blossoming in the void of its throat. Warmth bathed his face as it gushed forth, engulfing the forest.

A dozen or more of his men had already reached the trees. Their screams were terrible to behold as the inferno swallowed them up. Manes aflame, several horses came racing from the forest, but their riders had already succumbed to the awesome heat.

Damyn's horse stumbled to a stop. Its breath coming in ragged snorts, it stood trembling beneath him, too terrified even to run. Around him, what remained of Damyn's cohort did the same. Each knew there was no longer any point in running; death had come for them, and there would be no escape.

The earth shook as the dragon slammed into the hillside, its wings scattering fire in all directions. Giant jaws stretched wide, revealing endless rows of glistening teeth. Talons tore the earth as it crept towards them, the yellow slits of its eyes speaking of an endless hunger. But it was not the sight of the dragon that filled Damyn with despair; it was the scarlet-cloaked figure perched on its back.

Light flashed from the sword in the man's hand, rippling from white to green. The dragon bent low, offering one awful paw for the man to dismount. Leaping clear, the cloaked figure gestured again with his sword, and the beast leapt back into the sky.

Damyn hardly saw it go. His eyes were trapped in the

sapphire gaze of the man before them, in the unyielding gaze of the Tsar. With casual slowness, the man advanced down the hill to where Damyn and his cohort waited. He was one against hundreds, and yet not a single northerner dared raise their sword against him.

The blackened earth crunched beneath the Tsar's boots as he came to a stop before Damyn. Hands clasped before him, he appraised the captain in silence, face impassive. Sitting on his horse, Damyn tried to think of some way of fighting back, but his whole body seemed frozen, as though the man's very presence was enough to rob him of his will.

A crease marked the Tsar's brow as he looked beyond the horsemen at the burning wagons. Raising a hand, he gestured at the flames. A *whoosh* came from behind Damyn as the fires they'd started flickered out.

"I take it the Queen sent you," the Tsar said, his voice deceptively quiet.

Damyn swallowed, his words failing him. The Tsar's rasping laughter whispered through the burning forest as he took a step closer.

"Get down, Captain," he hissed.

"No—" Damyn broke off as he felt something cold pierce his chest.

He gasped and looked down, expecting to see an arrow or blade impaling him, but there was nothing. Yet the sensation was already spreading, seeping out from his chest to fill him with icy fire. Opening his mouth, he tried to scream, even as the cold reached his throat. His shriek came out as a whimper and he slumped in the saddle, his every nerve alive with agony, yet unable to so much as squeak.

"Down," the Tsar repeated.

To Damyn's horror, his body responded without question. His horse whinnied nervously as he dismounted and moved to stand in front of the Tsar. The icy fire still setting his mind aflame, he sank to his knee before the leader of the Three Nations.

Smiling, the Tsar reached down and laid his hand on Damyn's head. Whatever pain he'd felt before redoubled as a terrible force slid through his consciousness. His back arched and he longed to draw his sword and lash out at his assailant, but there was no fighting this man, no resistance against the power gripping his body.

Finally, the Tsar withdrew, his magic going with him. Crying out, Damyn slumped to the ground. A thousand pinpricks needled his every muscle as he tried to move, to run or even crawl away from the man's awful power. But all he could manage was the pitiful moans of a dying man.

"So the Queen is close," the Tsar mused. "She must have powerful Magickers to have shielded herself from me."

"Bastard," Damyn spat. Finally regaining some of his movement, he managed to drag himself to his knees. "You will never conquer us."

"Conquer?" the Tsar said sadly. He gestured to the burnt-out wagons, a smile appearing on his face. "It was not I who invaded a foreign nation, who ambushed and slaughtered innocent soldiers."

"You left us no choice."

"That is not how history will remember it," the Tsar laughed. "If it remembers you at all."

"You will never win," Damyn choked.

"I have heard that before," the Tsar murmured. Leaning down, he touched Damyn's cheek. His skin was soft, the gesture almost tender, and Damyn jerked away. Chuckling, the Tsar straightened and turned to the other Northerners. "And yet I always do."

"Just kill us," Damyn growled, anger giving his words strength. "You'll get nothing from us."

"Oh, but you have already given me *everything*, young Damyn. Your Queen flees for the Sandstone Mountains, seeking to draw us away from her own people."

"No," Damyn whispered.

An awful rage took him then, fed by hatred and the realisation he had failed his Queen. A scream ripped from his throat as he scrambled to his feet. Sabre in hand, he hurled himself at the Tsar...

He made it two steps before a force like a raging bull struck him in the chest. Something went *crack* as he was hurled from his feet. Agony lanced through his chest as though he'd been stabbed. The breath went from him in a rush as he struck the ground.

Footsteps crunched as the Tsar appeared overhead. "Your loyalty is to be admired," he murmured. "A shame your Queen was unworthy of it."

"She will destroy you."

"She will die, like all the rest." The Tsar lifted his sword. "As will all of your people."

"Get on with it then," Damyn spat.

Lowering his sword, the Tsar smiled. The sight filled Damyn with a sudden dread, even before the man spoke. "Get on with it?" He shook his head, gesturing to the ruined wagons. "But you have brought me such pain, Captain. I cannot simply send you all to the void, without repaying the favour."

Fear spread through Damyn like a poison as he looked into the darkness in the man's eyes and saw his fate. In that instant, he saw what he had to do, and screaming, he surged to his feet. His sword lay just a foot away. He hurled himself at the hilt, sweeping it up and lifting it high.

Then he reversed the blade and drove it into his stomach.

Pain tore through him as the point struck home. The metallic taste of blood filled his mouth as he slumped back to his knees. He looked up at the Tsar, his vision swirling, slowly fading away, and smiled.

"She *will* stop you," he gasped, blood bubbling from his lips.

Darkness closed in as the Tsar leaned down and tore the blade from his stomach. By then Damyn could feel nothing. But as the Tsar knelt beside him, warmth washed over him. He groaned as the darkness receded, the world returning, and with it the pain.

A smile touched the Tsar's face as he stroked Damyn's brow. "Don't go leaving just yet, Captain," he murmured. "I'm not done with you."

24

Devon waited until darkness before he allowed the Baronians to light their fires, knowing that even in the mountains, the smoke would be seen for miles around. He would have preferred a cold camp, but with the mountains in the grips of winter, half their number would freeze to death before morning without heat. As it was, the threadbare clothing of the Baronians was hopelessly inadequate.

But there was no turning back now. Braidon had been able to cloak their small group of leaders from the Tsar's roaming eyes, but there was no hiding their tracks. Quinn and his Stalkers would not be far behind. It was unlikely the Baronians and their wagons could outrun the hunters, but they could at least make it harder for them.

At least the dragon was dead. Joseph himself had seen it fall from the sky, struck down by magic and a dozen crossbow bolts. They had Alana to thank for that, though Devon would never admit as much to the young woman. He still could not bring himself to speak with her.

Without the beast prowling the skies, Devon only had to

concern himself with the Stalkers on their trail. From what he'd seen in the settlement, the Baronians had Quinn and his men badly outnumbered. Even poorly fed and armed, the weight of their numbers might have been enough to overwhelm their pursuers.

If not for the magic of the Stalkers.

Devon had considered setting an ambush further up in the mountains, but quickly dismissed the idea. Even with *kanker* and Braidon and Alana, they were badly outmatched by the powers Quinn and his followers could command. Forcing a pitched battle would be to risk everything on the hope the Stalkers didn't react quickly enough to bring their magic to bear. Sadly, Devon knew Quinn well enough to realise that was unlikely.

No, their only chance for the moment was to retreat into the mountains, and pray to the Gods they could lose the Stalkers in the maze of caves and gullies.

Fat chance of that, Devon thought as he surveyed the camp.

The Baronians had taken the loss of their permanent camp in stride, though they'd been forced to leave many of their tents and wagons behind. A few had refused to come, and had remained behind with their measly possessions, but some five hundred had followed Devon into the mountains.

He had been surprised by their loyalty, though the weight of responsibility hung heavy on his shoulders now. In the brief moments they'd had to plan Alana's rescue, he hadn't thought this far ahead, about what it would mean to lead so many people into the mountain passes. Now though, Devon wondered whether he was escorting them to their doom, if his recklessness had finally caught up with him.

Devon looked up as the flaps of his tent parted and Joseph stepped inside. The former Baronian leader offered a nod, and then wandered over and took a seat on the other side of Devon's camp stove. Holding his hands out to the hot iron, he grinned. "Glad to see this made it into the wagons."

In no mood for company, Devon only grunted and waited for the man's reason for being there. Seeing Alana again had left him feeling confused and dejected. When he'd first stepped into the inn and seen her standing there alive, Devon had experienced a surge of elation, quickly followed by despair as he remembered the Alana standing before him was no longer the woman he loved.

Unlike Braidon, he hadn't been able to move past what had happened, what the woman who looked like Alana had done. When the boy had walked into camp with Alana in tow, there had been smiles all around, though the Baronians did not know what they were celebrating. But Devon had taken no joy from the occasion, and had quickly excused himself. Alone, Devon had found himself longing for the quiet comradery he'd enjoyed with the boy this past week, the tranquil peace as they wandered the forest paths, the silence of the night as they cooked their evening meals.

Instead, Devon now found himself alone but for a man who had tried to kill him just days ago.

"What do you want, Joseph?" he snapped after a minute, when the man still had not spoken.

"Grouchy, aren't you?" The giant chuckled. "And I thought *I* was the old man. Thought you'd be overjoyed to have the woman back."

"I'm happy she's alive," Devon growled.

"Truly?" Joseph asked. "Because you looked ready to scream murder when the boy led her into the camp."

"It's complicated," Devon said. Picking up the iron poker, he stabbed at the coals inside the camp stove.

"Ah, complicated, I see," Joseph replied, as though Devon had just spilled his heart. "Never fun, complicated."

"She killed my friend!" Devon burst out. Jabbing a little too hard with the poker, a coal spilled out and struck the cold earth with a *hiss*. Devon cursed and stamped it out with his boot. "Or close enough to it," he added in a whisper.

Joseph shook his head. "You don't strike me as a man who leaves a friend unavenged." He sat back in his chair, his eyes boring into Devon. "So if she's responsible, why did you rescue her?"

Devon looked away. "Because she reminds me of someone I used to know," he murmured, remembering the fiery woman that had fought her way across the Three Nations to protect her brother. "Because I love her."

"Complicated thing, love."

Unable to find the words to reply, Devon only shook his head, and they fell back into silence. After a few minutes, Joseph groaned and rose to his feet.

"Anyway, she's waiting for you outside," he said. "I'll leave you to it."

"Wait—" Devon started to his feet, but the Baronian had already vanished through the tent flaps.

Alana took his place, a hesitant smile on her face. "Devon," she said formally.

"Alana," he replied, his voice tight.

Her eyes slid to the floor as she let the tent flap fall behind her. Silently she wandered around the tent, her hands trailing over the canvas walls. Circling the room, Alana came to a stop beside the camp stretcher. There she crouched for a moment, then stood again with something in hand. As she turned, Devon saw she now held *kanker*. She pressed it into his hands.

Devon took the weapon with a frown. "What?"

"Use it," she said, the words tumbling from her in a rush. "I can't stand this anymore: the guilt, the pain, the loss. I never loved anything or anyone before, no one except my brother. Now I do, and all it's given me is pain. I saw how much you hate me, back in the throne room. You were right to leave me to die, right to hate me. Kellian died because of me. So do it, please."

Devon's hand tightened on *kanker's* haft. He stared silently into her stone-grey eyes, seeing the tears shining there. Gone was the hardness, the anger of the woman he'd seen in the citadel. Looking at her now, he could almost, *almost* bring himself to believe this was the Alana he knew, the Alana he loved.

"Who *are* you?" he whispered.

She shook her head. "I don't know." Her voice cracked. Sinking to her knees, she wrapped her arms around herself. "Why did she sacrifice herself for me?" she asked, looking up at him. "She *hated* me, and she saved me. *Why?*"

Before Devon could think about what he was doing, he was on his knees beside her. *Kanker* lying discarded beside them, he pulled Alana into his arms, hugging her to his chest. "Because that's who she was," he mumbled. "That was Enala. She dedicated her entire life to others."

"I don't deserve it," Alana sobbed.

"Maybe none of us do," he replied, drawing back from her.

Hiccupping, Alana nodded. She seemed to regain some control over herself then, and wiping the tears from her eyes, she stood. Devon rose with her.

"Devon, I'm so, so sorry." The words came in a rush. "For Kellian, for betraying you, for everything."

Devon nodded, the hope withering in his chest. "So… you are still *that* Alana?"

"No..." She trailed off, her gaze distant. "Yes. I'm her, but also...the other girl as well. Both at once, and neither."

"Not like your brother then," Devon sighed. Wandering past her, he recovered the poker from where he'd discarded it earlier. He added another log to the fire and stirred the coals. "He loves you, you know. Thinks you're a good person, whichever version of yourself you are."

"I—"

Devon slammed the door to the camp stove shut, cutting her off, and then strode across the tent to where she stood. Alana did not shrink away as he towered over her, though her eyes betrayed her doubt.

"He's a good man, your brother," he murmured. "I trust him."

"Then..."

Taking a deep breath, Devon offered his hand. "Why don't we start over?" he said. "The name's Devon. It's nice to meet you...Alana."

There was a moment's pause as Alana stared at his outstretched hand. Then, with a hesitant smile, she reached out and took it.

25

"Form rank, shields to the front! Archers, nock arrows!"

Merydith's cry carried down the line as her lieutenants passed along her orders. The rattle of metal echoed from the cliffs as her men shifted into position. The horses had already been taken further up the pass with the bulk of the army, but Merydith had remained with the rearguard. After the loss of Damyn and his cohort, she couldn't bring herself to entrust the task to anyone else.

Not for the first time in the past few days, the weight of grief pressed down on Merydith's shoulders. She swallowed it back, unwilling to give in, to admit to her own weakness. The loss of her childhood friend had hit her hard, but worse still was the effect on morale. For a few brief, golden hours, the Northland army had celebrated their triumph on the Gods Road, but their elation had turned to ash when word reached them of the disaster that had befallen Damyn's cohort.

Astride his monstrous Red Dragon, the Tsar had come, and slaughtered them all. Without the northern Magickers to protect them, Damyn's forces had never stood a chance. Her scouts reported his cohort had been slaughtered to a man—though not before the Tsar had had his fun.

A fresh wave of grief swept through Merydith. Clenching her sword hilt, she drew the blade and lifted it above her head.

"For Northland!" Her cry carried down the line, echoing loudly from the cliffs that rose towering above them.

Striding to the front of the line, Merydith looked down on the forces arrayed before them. In their plated armour and cloaks of scarlet and emerald, the army below looked for all the world like their ancestors before them—champions of freedom, defenders of the weak, defiant in the face of evil. She couldn't begin to understand how the once noble lands of the south had become so corrupted.

Yet even as her own nation grew from infancy to adulthood, the Tsar had led the Three Nations into darkness. Now he led them against Northland, and it rested on her to champion the cause of freedom.

"We hold them here!" she shouted.

Even as she spoke, Merydith tasted the bitter tang of despair. The men and women around her knew this wasn't the plan. After their attack on the advanced guard, they were meant to lead the Tsar and his forces on a merry chase through northern Lonia. Damyn was to have rejoined them, and if his attack on the wagons had been successful, they were to retreat to Northland. Without his supplies, the Tsar could not have followed, not while winter still gripped the lands of the north.

But the Tsar had saved his wagons, and sent a cohort of his own north to cut them off from their homeland. With the bulk of his forces to the east and south of them, Merydith had been left with no other options but to forge a path into the Sandstone Mountains.

Now, far from home and with only a week's supplies remaining, their sole hope was to find a pass through to Trola and their allies there. Yet the Sandstone Mountains were a maze, made up of a thousand gullies and hillsides so steep that not even the mountain goats could scale some of them. Without a map, it would take days for her scouts to find a path through.

Until then, all Merydith could do was pray they did not encounter a dead end. Her rear guard could not hold back the Tsar's forces long, only slow his advance. And while Helen and her Magickers had joined their powers to keep the Tsar from attacking them directly, they had nothing left to use against the thousands who marched against them.

Movement came from the men at the bottom of the canyon as their lines shifted, parting to make way for a single man. Merydith watched in astonishment as the distant figure staggered forward, half-tripping on the uneven ground. He wore little more than a loincloth, and his limbs were so emaciated she wondered how he could stand. Bruises marked his chest, where his ribcage stood out starkly against his pale skin.

Only as he neared did Merydith finally recognise him. A cry tore from her throat as Damyn dropped to a knee, his face stretched with exhaustion. His moans carried up the valley to the watching army, and stumbling back to his feet, he continued towards them, eyes wide, mouth gasping.

Merydith stood frozen in place, unable to believe the change that had been wrought on her friend in just a matter of days. There was little left of the man she'd sent to raid the Trolan supplies. Only a shadow remained of him.

As he neared the Northland army, his cry came again.

Tearing herself from her shock, Merydith ran to him. He started to fall, but she caught him and lifted him into her arms. Shocked by how little he weighed, she turned and strode back towards her soldiers. Men and women parted wordlessly as she staggered past, then closed together in silence behind her.

Reaching the final ranks of the rear guard, Merydith caught herself. Taking a breath, she looked back. Her people needed her; she could not abandon them to tend to Damyn, not now, with the enemy so close.

Stones crunched as Mokyre appeared alongside her. She closed her eyes, unable to summon the strength to face the man just then. His position amongst the clans had demanded she name him captain, but she'd had little patience for him since the meeting with the other clan leaders.

"Take him," he murmured. Merydith looked at him sharply as Mokyre went on. "He needs you. Don't worry, I'll handle the bastards down there."

Merydith stared at the man, seeing the rage in his eyes as he looked at Damyn. Whatever their differences might be, Mokyre was a Northlander. What the Tsar had done to their people, what he had done to Damyn, was an affront to everything they believed in. Mokyre might not have wanted to go to war against the Tsar, but now that he had joined the battle, he would fight to the end for his nation.

Letting out a long breath, Merydith nodded. "Make them pay."

With that, she turned and started up the valley. From behind her she heard the rhythmic *thump* of marching boots as the Tsar's army advanced. Mokrye's voice rang out in answer, ordering the archers to draw. The *twang* of bowstrings was followed by the whistling of arrows, then the screams of dying men rose from the valley below.

The first clashes of steel sounded as Merydith reached her tent and carried Damyn inside. Her stretcher was unmade but she laid him down over the twisted sheets, ignoring the stains his wounds left on her bedding.

"Your Majesty, is everything okay?" a voice called from the entrance to the tent.

Merydith turned, recognising the speaker. "Helen, what are you doing here? Shouldn't you be with the others, holding off the Tsar?"

The Magicker nodded. "I wanted to check on things when I heard the battle begin. Then I saw you with... Damyn..." She trailed off as her eyes were drawn to the broken body of her friend. "Gods, what did they do to him?"

"I don't know," Merydith whispered. Away from the eyes of her people, she felt the beginnings of tears. She sucked in a deep breath. "Can you help me?" she asked in a rush.

Helen closed her eyes for the count of ten, and then nodded. "They can cope without my strength, for the moment." She moved to stand beside the bed. "But he may be beyond even my powers to help."

"Just do what you can," Merydith replied. It had been so long since Enala had departed, she had already given the woman up for dead. But she couldn't cope with losing Damyn as well, not now, not like this.

Crouching beside the camp-stretcher, Helen held her hands out towards the captain. Green light spread from her fingers. Where it touched Damyn's emaciated body, he groaned, his face scrunching tight, though he did not wake.

Merydith sat alongside the woman and stroked her friend's forehead, whispering quiet reassurances.

Behold the fate of your people, Queen.

Merydith flinched as the words whispered in her ear, the voice as clear as if it had been spoken out loud. She spun, her sword slashing the air behind her, but there was nothing there. Laughter taunted her, seeming to come from all around her. Fear wrapped around Merydith's gut as the voice continued.

Every man, every woman, every child who stands against me will suffer thus. Your Magickers will not keep me from them. Even now they falter. I will crush them and burn your army from my land. I will take you and any who survive and make you my prisoners, to suffer like the good captain has suffered. And I will march into your lands and put an end to your rebellion. Northland will be returned to wasteland, as it was always destined to be.

"What do you want?" Merydith groaned.

Bow, Queen, the voice whispered. *Bow to your Tsar. Hand over your renegade Magickers, and you and your people may live.*

Merydith's eyes were drawn to the hunched form of Helen. Light still seeped from her hands, and she did not seem to have heard the voice whispering through the tent. A knife twisted in Merydith's gut at the thought of betraying the kindly woman, and yet…

Images entered her mind, of her people entombed in the tunnels of Erachill, of the northern steeps burning, and the screams of a million voices ringing out across her land. The clash of steel came again from beyond the walls of her tent, the cries of the dying. Her head bowed beneath the weight of her responsibility.

Then Enala's face flickered into her mind, and she remembered how the old woman had stood against the darkness of Archon, even when all hope seemed lost. No matter how dark things became, she and her brother and the man, Gabriel, had never backed down.

Opening her eyes, Merydith saw a dark fog coalescing before her. Slowly the shape of a man took form, vague and indistinct, and yet unmistakable. The Tsar watched her with ghostly eyes for a long time before he spoke again. This time, his voice rang loudly though the tent, instead of within her own mind.

"What is your decision, Queen?"

Merydith drew herself up and faced the phantom. "I will defy you to my dying breath," she spat.

"So be it." The phantom raised his hands.

Merydith flinched, but beside her Helen staggered to her feet. Terror showed on her face, but her eyes glowed with power. Raising her arms, she cried out.

"Brothers, sisters, on me!"

Light flashed across the tent, and a spiralling vortex of multicoloured magic descended on the woman. It gathered around Helen for half a second, and then rushed from her at the spectre. The air crackled as it sliced through the tent and a cry rang out, followed by a dull *boom*. Darkness swallowed the room as all the lanterns flickered out, followed by absolute silence.

Staggering sideways, Merydith squinted through the gloom. The dark canvas blacked out the daylight, but as her eyes adjusted she saw the Tsar had vanished, and Helen on her knees. Heart in her throat, she stepped toward the Magicker. Groaning, the Magicker rose slowly back to her feet. A frown touched the woman's face as she looked away, but a smile replaced it as her eyes alighted on Merydith.

"You're okay. Thank the Gods."

Merydith nodded. Suddenly weary, she sat on the

stretcher beside Damyn. "I thought you said the others could cope without you."

Helen smiled sheepishly. "I guess not."

A voice called to them from beyond the walls of the tent, and then light spilled inside as someone lifted the flap. "Your Majesty!" One of her guards stood there, his face the picture of concern. "Is everything okay? We heard shouting."

Merydith nodded. "Fetch some fresh lanterns, Marcus." The guard nodded and darkness returned to the tent as he departed. Turning her attention to her friend, Merydith reached out and touched his throat. His pulse was erratic but strong. "Is he okay?" she asked the Magicker.

The smile fell from Helen's face. "I've done what I can. Whether he lives is up to him now."

"Thank you, Helen. For everything." She hesitated. "What was that before, when the light appeared?"

"Something very dangerous," the Magicker replied. "While none of us are powerful enough to threaten the Tsar alone, we have been able to combine our magics in a spell, one that keeps the Tsar from entering our camp. Mostly. But just then, when we forced him out, our power needed to be directed. For just a moment, I was its vessel."

"And that's dangerous?"

"If I'd held it a second longer, the force would have torn me to pieces."

Merydith sighed. "So you're saying you couldn't send it against that army down there?"

"I might, though not in the form you just saw. But even if we could manage it, such a feat would cripple us all. It would leave every man and woman here exposed to the Tsar's power." She gestured at Damyn. "And we have seen what he is capable of."

Ice slid down Merydith spine as she nodded. "Very well," she murmured. "Thank you again, Helen, for everything you've done. You should return to the others now, before he tries anything else."

"What about you?" the Magicker whispered, rising to her feet.

Merydith looked down at Damyn. "I will stay with him."

Helen nodded. "May the Gods be with you, my Queen."

Then she was gone, leaving Merydith alone with the man who had stood at her side since she was just a child. Looking at his withered body, she finally allowed her grief to show. Tears burned her eyes as she stroked his cheek.

"Come back to me, Damyn," she said. "I forbid you to die."

Outside, the sounds of battle finally faded away, and silence descended on the tent.

26

Braidon sat in the darkness staring out over the valley, listening as soft voices carried up from the Baronians gathered below. Their campfires glistened in the moonlight, the flicker of movement betraying the chaos of the camp. Where he was sitting though, the world was at peace. He could almost forget the world was at war, that his father was even now leading an invasion of Northland, or that an elite group of soldiers were hunting him.

In his mind, Braidon pictured the warrior Queen Merydith, and wondered where she was now. The woman wasn't one to sit idly by while her people were attacked, and he hoped she would be ready when his father came for her. She had put her trust in Enala and himself to finish the Tsar, but now that they had failed, Northlands fate was in her hands. Though how she could hope to succeed, he couldn't begin to imagine. The Three Nations were too powerful, the Tsar unstoppable.

And now Enala was gone.

He scrunched his eyes closed and shivered as he saw again Enala fall, cut down by his father's sword.

"Her own son," Braidon whispered, still struggling to come to terms with it all.

While he had learned the truth in Ardath, he'd never had the chance to ask his grandmother about their past, about anything. He wondered now who his grandfather had been, and why Enala had kept herself away from them all this time.

His heart ached for the old woman, but while she had shown him kindness, had protected him and taught him to use his magic, he still could not picture her as his grandmother. There was a gap, a great canyon between the images in his mind, one he could not span. Not now that she was gone.

Sadness touched him as he thought of Merydith. It was the Northland Queen who had truly known the old woman. Enala had helped to raise her, had truly been a grandmother to the woman. Braidon swallowed at the thought of having to tell her the truth, that the old woman was gone. He feared it might break her, after their last conversation in Erachill.

You have outgrown me, girl.

He smiled as he recalled Enala's last words to the Queen. However much the news hurt, Enala had had faith in the woman. Merydith would not break, not when the fate of her nation was at stake.

The crunch of footsteps distracted Braidon from his memories. Alana was approaching, her eyes downcast. He smiled, though it still felt strange, knowing she wasn't entirely the sister he remembered.

"How did it go?" he asked, nodding in the direction of camp.

Alana shrugged and took a seat on the boulder beside him. "As well as could be expected," she said, pulling her knees up to her chest. "I'm alive. It's enough."

Braidon's heart twisted at her words. "Is it, though?"

She looked at him sharply, eyebrows raised. "You've grown bold, little brother," she said. "Has your magic so changed you?"

Braidon frowned at her words, wondering whether they were true. He'd come a long way in the months since their escape. Though he remembered little of his old life, he sensed the boy he'd been was not much different than the sheltered child he'd become after their escape. But it was not his magic that had changed him; it was his time with Enala. Her training, her quiet faith; they had given him the courage he'd needed, in a way Alana's protection never had.

"Not my magic, no," he replied, biting his lip. "It's… without you, I had to fend for myself. To grow, to master my fears."

"I'm sorry I wasn't there…"

"No." Braidon grinned. "I'm glad you weren't."

He knew his sister's protectiveness came from love, but her lack of faith had drained his own. Looking back now, he wondered whether he ever would have come to terms with his power, had she remained looking over his shoulder.

Alana's face twisted with hurt. "Well, I guess I'll be on my way then."

"No, I didn't mean it that way," Braidon replied quickly. "It's just…Enala showed me I was strong enough by myself." He clenched his fists, allowing a trickle of magic to seep out. Shielded by the power he was already expending to conceal them from their father, it would not be detected by any nearby Magickers. "I even helped Devon, when the Baronians were preparing to attack him. I made him seem a giant, a hero that could not be defeated. And now…here we are."

"I'm proud of you, little brother," Alana said, though there was sadness behind her words.

He looked at her then, seeing her pain, and wondered what she had been through in the time they had been separated. Somewhere along the way, Alana had lost the fire in her eyes. He had glimpsed it for a moment, back in the settlement when she'd set the dragon on their father's Stalkers, but it had not lasted. Bruised and beaten, her neck ringed by scars, Alana no longer seemed the unstoppable warrior he remembered.

"What happened to you, Alana?" he whispered.

She closed her eyes. "I remembered."

"You remember who you were before?"

"No, I *am* who I was before," Alana croaked. "And who I was with you and Devon and Kellian. It's all tangled up, but I know enough now, enough to hate who I was. I deserve everything that's happened to me."

"No, Alana," Braidon whispered. He reached out and gripped her wrist. "I wouldn't be alive if it wasn't for you."

"Braidon…" Alana sighed. "I love you with all my heart. But that doesn't make up for everything else I've done, the people I've killed, the lives I've stolen. You don't remember—"

"Then *help me* remember," Braidon interrupted. His heart pounded in his chest as he took her hand and placed it on his head.

Alana's eyes widened and she shook her head. "No…"

"Please," Braidon murmured. "There's so much missing, I need to see it, to know the truth. Please, Alana."

"What if you don't like what you see?" He could see the doubt lurking behind her stony eyes.

"You'll still be my sister," he insisted. "It'll be okay."

Swallowing, Alana nodded. Her chest swelled as she drew in a breath, and he sensed her power building. He watched it grow in his mind's eye, saw it swell to a bursting point, and then go from her in a rush, pouring down her arm and into him. He gasped at the icy touch of her power, but there was no pain, only a whispered voice, barely audible, as though heard from a great distance.

"Return to me, brother."

All of a sudden, Braidon was a child, standing on the ramparts of the citadel, looking out over the wide expanse of Lake Ardath. Silver threads crisscrossed the plains beyond its waters, weaving through the countryside like some great tapestry of the Gods. To the east, he could just make out the three shadows of Mount Chole and its nameless brothers. Dark clouds swirled around their peaks, sending life-giving rain down onto the plains below. To the west, snow-capped mountains stretched across the horizon as far as the eye could see.

"It will all be yours one day, son," his father was saying. "Your's and your sister's to rule."

A hand rested on his back, powerful, yet reassuring. Braidon looked up at his father with love in his heart, but the Tsar's gaze was fixed on the waters of Lake Ardath.

"It has been my life's goal to make this land safe for you and our people," his father continued, "but I am afraid." His head dipped, his eyes closing for half an instant. "I am afraid I will fail you."

"Father?" Too young to understand his father's pain, Braidon reached out and gripped his meaty hand. "Are you okay?"

The Tsar glanced down at Braidon. Sadness crinkled the skin around his eyes. "No," he muttered, as though talking to himself. "I have not failed, not yet. It will not come to that."

Braidon shook his head. "What are you talking about, Father?"

A smile touched the Tsar's face. He crouched beside Braidon, his grip tightening on the boy's shoulder. "Do you trust me, son?"

"Of course!"

"Good." The Tsar drew him into a hug. "I cannot fail, not with you and your sister beside me. Together, the three of us can do anything. With our magic, we will finally bring peace to this warring land."

"But I don't have magic." At ten years old, Braidon barely knew his place in the world, but he had seen what those around his father were capable of, knew they could do things he could not.

"Not yet, my son," the Tsar replied, "but I can sense it within you. One day, on an anniversary of your birth, it will appear to you. On that day, you must be strong, must be the master, it the servant. Can you do that for me, son?"

Braidon shivered, his father's words filling him with an unknown terror. Yet he knew the answer his father expected, and nodded. "I can," he said, trying to keep the tremor from his voice.

"Good lad," his father replied, coming to his feet. He looked back out over the lake, a smile on his face. "Every step we take towards a new dawn, there will be those who fight against us. But we will not fail, the three of us. We will stand strong against our enemies, and bring a new era of light into this world."

Braidon shuddered as the vision faded, returning him to the moonlit mountains. He looked at his sister, opened his mouth to speak, to ask about this new vision of their father, but before the words could leave his mouth he was swept away on a fresh tide, swallowed up by a new wave of memories.

Now, Braidon found himself standing in a familiar garden. Birds chirped, and the colours of summer were all around, in the scarlet of the roses and the blue of the sky, the emerald green of the grass lawns, and the smiles of the courtiers as they strode past. His thoughts swirled as he looked up and saw the towers of the citadel spiralling overhead.

Home.

A part of him rebelled at the thought, and yet he knew it to be true.

"Braidon, there you are!" He looked around and saw his sister

walking towards him, a troupe of children following in her wake. "I told you not to go wandering off!"

Braidon scowled. "But I wasn't doing anything, *sis."*

Alana glared at him. "You're too young to do *anything, little brother."*

"I'm older than half of them!" he insisted, gesturing at the other children. "At least let me practice with them."

His sister frowned, and he sensed her resolve wavering. Braidon leapt on the opportunity with both hands.

"Please, sis, I'll be careful, I swear!"

Alana rolled her eyes. "Fine," she growled in her sternest voice, "but don't say I didn't warn you." She gestured for him to join the other children.

They made their way back to the training grounds, where the others collected their practice swords and formed two lines. They eyed his sister nervously as she strode past. Braidon lingered on the periphery, wondering whether Alana had truly meant what she'd said.

Wandering over, she flicked her own practice blade into the air, caught it by the blunted blade, and offered it to him. "You sure you're ready, little brother?" she asked, one eyebrow raised.

Braidon nodded eagerly and took the sword before she could change her mind.

"Be careful with it," she said, a patronising smile on her lips. Before Braidon could say anything, she spun towards the other children. All semblance of kindness left her face. "Anish, get your ass over here!"

A young boy further down the line leapt to obey. "Yes, ma'am!" he said as he joined them.

"Take your new partner through drills one and two. Make sure he's up to speed," Alana snapped.

She walked away before either boy could reply, leaving Braidon staring dumbly at his new sparring partner. The boy nodded, though Braidon didn't miss the fear lurking behind his sea green eyes. As Alana turned, Anish took Braidon through several blocks and counter-

attacks with the blunted swords, while the other children began to spar.

Braidon was surprised by how quickly he began to pant, the subtle movement required to change stances and heft the heavy blade surprisingly exhausting. Within minutes, sweat was dripping down his forehead, but none of the other students so much as paused for a rest, so he kept on, determined to finish what he'd started.

As he shifted back into the defensive section of the drill, his foot slipped on a patch of mud, and off-balance, he toppled forward. Anish cried out, but his blade was already flashing forward. His head low, Braidon cried out as the blunted edge caught him in the back of his skull. A brilliant red light blinded him and the strength went from his legs, sending him crashing to the ground.

Darkness swirled and for a moment he lost consciousness. When he came to, his sister was crouching over him, her brow creased with concern. She reached out a hand and helped him to sit up. A groan whispered up from his throat as he saw the other students standing in silence, their faces pale as ghosts. They remained behind as Alana helped him to the healer's wing of the citadel, where a kindly man took away his pain with a touch.

Back on the hillside, Braidon smiled at the memory of his sister's concern, even as other memories streamed through his consciousness. Alana had been there through them all: fierce and overprotective, but also caring and compassionate, always ready to defend him.

Then a frown touched his lips. The memories from that day in the gardens continued to flow, streaming through his mind in an endless torrent. He witnessed again the drills, experienced the training, the trips into the forests, where he learned to hunt and fish, to survive. In all those memories, Alana was harsh and unyielding, showing no student other than Braidon an ounce of kindness.

But it wasn't her coldness that scared him, nor her anger

or cruelty to those who crossed her. It was the absence he saw now, the missing face he had never noticed in his selfish youth. Because in all the memories he recalled, in all the countless days since his first lesson in the royal gardens, he had never seen Anish again.

At least, not until that fateful day in Lon, when the demon had appeared on their ship, and tried to return them both to their father. Despite the years since their fateful training session, Anish had not aged even a day.

Only his eyes had changed, the sea green giving way to the pitch-black of the demon.

Bile filled Braidon's throat as he staggered to his feet. Alana rose with him, her eyes wide with concern, but as she reached for him he threw her back. Scrambling from the boulder, he slipped on the smooth rock and went crashing to the ground.

"Braidon!" Alana stumbled after him, hands outstretched.

"Stay away from me!" he gasped, holding up his hands to fend her off.

His emotions swirling, he tried to stand. Pain speared his wrist and he was forced to use his other hand to push himself back to his feet. He stared at her, eyes wide, horror wrapping his stomach in iron bands.

"What did you do to him?" he asked. "To Anish?"

Her eyes widened, then dropped to the ground. She shook her head. "You know what I did."

"Say it!"

"He hurt you!" Alana shrieked. Her head snapped up, her eyes aglow in the moonlight. "So I sent him to our father, to be tested, to be judged."

"And he failed," Braidon murmured.

"He failed," Alana agreed. Her eyes softened and she staggered.

"He failed," she said again, though her voice was touched now by horror. She closed her eyes. "Like so many others."

"How could you?" Braidon whispered.

"Braidon…" Eyes wide, Alana reached for him.

"*Don't you touch me!*" Braidon screamed.

Tears streaked Alana's cheeks as she watched him back away. Recalling what he'd felt for her just moments before, Braidon wondered how he could have been so blind. He saw now her overprotective nature came not from love, but a twisted sense of possession. Alana had done whatever she could to ensure he did not mature, that he remained innocent, and therefore malleable.

Even if it meant robbing him of his own past.

"Stay away," he said one last time.

Turning on his heel, he fled down the mountainside back towards the camp.

27

For four nights, the Baronians delved deeper into the mountains, their desperation growing with each passing day. With the Stalkers behind them, they could not turn back, yet as the winter closed in, many began to flag. Their supplies dwindled, and they were soon forced to abandon their wagons, the way proving impassable for even the boldest horses. The paths grew narrower as they pushed higher into the snow-capped peaks. In the thin air, men and women struggled, and the weak began to die.

Though she kept to herself, Alana could sense the resentment building amongst the Baronians. They had started this journey on a whim. The attack on the Tsar had been an act of defiance against the man who had driven them from their homes. Only now did they realise they might pay for it with their lives.

By the fifth day, a ritual had developed in the mornings, as those who had passed in the night were counted and laid to rest. Finally, on the sixth day, they reached the peak of the winding gullies, and began back down into Trola.

Through it all, Devon kept on, refusing to show the slightest hint of weakness. He led them through the mountains with his head held high, often with the ancient hammer in hand, as though the weapon could somehow fend off the creeping cold that had stolen so many of his people's lives.

He walked ahead of Alana now, his gaze fixed on the top of the next bend in the gorge. While he showed no outward sign of his pain, Alana was not deceived. She saw glimpses of it in the way he had begun pushing everyone else away, in his sudden bouts of rage when someone questioned him. More than anything, she wanted to go to him, to ease his grief. But while they had developed an uneasy truce, anything more remained beyond them.

As for Braidon, she had hardly seen him since the day on the hillside. Alana had watched him from afar though, seeing how the magic took its toll, and wishing she could help. Their survival rested on his shoulders, on his ability to keep the Tsar and his Stalkers from tracking them with his magic. While their father himself had departed, she didn't doubt he continued to search for them. If Braidon's magic faltered…

She sighed, forcing her mind back to the way ahead. Her brother had made it clear he wanted nothing to do with her. The knowledge ate at her, but she couldn't blame him. She had done terrible, unforgivable things. Each night, memories of the children she had sent to their deaths haunted her. It didn't help that the Tsar had given her no choice, that she had done it to protect Braidon from his darkness.

Because Alana knew in her heart that she had enjoyed it, had savoured the power she held over her charges, the fear she saw in the eyes of the commoners. She had been the Daughter of the Tsar, her power unrivaled, her nobility unquestioned.

Thinking back on the woman she'd been…

"Hello, princess."

Alana's head jerked up as a gruff voice came from alongside her. Her heart quickened, but her excitement gave way to disappointment when she saw it was only Joseph. They hadn't talked since she'd joined the camp, though she hadn't been surprised to learn he was still around. If Devon could set aside his enmity for her, why not a man he'd fought in mortal combat?

"Princess?" Alana asked archly.

Joseph raised an eyebrow as though to ask if she thought him stupid. Her cheeks warmed and she quickly looked away. "Fine, but keep it quiet, Baronian."

"Of course." Joseph chuckled, but his humour didn't last. As the laughter died away, he looked at her again, sadness in his eyes. "I'm sorry about the old woman," he said at last.

Alana swallowed. She tried to speak, but the words lodged in her throat. Shaking her head, she looked to where Devon still strode at the front of the column.

"I wish he'd saved Enala instead," she managed.

"Heard you and the big man were lovers once," Joseph said.

Alana's head whipped around at his words. Her boot caught an unseen rock and she tripped, and would have crashed face-first into the mountainside had Joseph not caught her by the scruff of her tunic and righted her.

"No!" She burst out finally, flashing the giant a glare. "We were *not!*"

Joseph wore a broad grin on his bearded face. "That

so?" he chuckled, before setting off again along the trail. "Coulda fooled me."

"There's nothing between us," Alana insisted, chasing after him. "He hates me!"

"Ay, he travelled halfway across the world only to have you reject him. You can hardly blame the man for that."

Alana fell silent, her mind turning back to the night Devon and Kellian had snuck into the citadel to rescue her. She'd been shocked by their appearance, but beyond that, there had been a warmth at seeing the two men again, and an urge to throw herself into Devon's arms.

Unfortunately, her darker side had been stronger then.

"I betrayed him," she whispered. "Even if he still loves me, I don't deserve him."

"Maybe not," Joseph rumbled, "but life rarely gives us what we deserve. And the man is hurting."

At that, the Baronian picked up his pace and strode ahead to walk alongside Devon. Trailing behind them, Alana found herself watching Devon, wondering if Joseph's words were true, if there really still was something between them. Her heart twisted as Devon looked back. They shared a glance, but he quickly looked away, returning his attention to the road.

The day stretched out, the sky darkening as the sun fell below the mountain peaks. Finally a call went up from ahead, signalling a break for the night. Around her, men and women sighed and dropped their packs, sinking to the ground in relief.

People began to gather in groups, doffing packs and pulling out food. A familiar loneliness settled over Alana as she saw Devon sitting in conversation with Braidon and Joseph. She yearned to join them and ask what they were talking about, but as she watched, her brother glanced in her direction. The smile faded from his face as he turned back to the others.

Alana's stomach knotted as a roar of laughter came from the three men. She found a boulder off near the cliff and seated herself so she could look back up the valley. The slope they'd spent the morning traversing stretched above her, empty now of movement. Shadows still slung around the top, and she wondered how long they had before Quinn and his Stalkers caught them.

Quinn.

A shiver swept through her at the thought of him. He'd been her companion since childhood, first as a friend, then as a teacher. Back then, she had never thought of him as anything more. But as they'd matured, she'd noticed the change in him, the yearning that had appeared in his eyes.

She had finally reciprocated his desires back in Ardath, thinking to satisfy her own cravings. Yet still he had wanted more, seeking to rule her, to make her his own. And that was one thing Alana would never allow.

His words from back in the inn whispered in her mind.

I will have my heart's desire.

Alana's stomach twisted in disgust, a chill raising the hackles on her neck. For a moment, she wished she'd destroyed him back in the throne room.

"Hungry?"

Alana looked up as a woman's voice came from nearby. Her eyes widened as she saw the old innkeeper, Selina wandering towards her, a stale-looking loaf of bread in hand. Alana looked at the bread distastefully, but there was little enough to go around without being fussy, and she nodded.

Drawing a hunting knife from her belt, the old woman cut the bread in two and offered half to Alana. She sat on the next boulder over as Alana tore off a piece of bread and chewed it slowly.

Selina stretched her arms and lay back with a groan. "I tell you, this isn't what I imagined doing in my retirement," she said. "I'm getting a little old for so much adventure."

Alana glanced at the woman, remembering how she'd lain dying on the floor of her own inn. "What are you doing here?" she asked, curious. "You could have gone anywhere. Quinn wouldn't have come searching for you. Why come with us?"

"The Goddess touched me," Selina murmured. Her eyes drifted out to the forested plains far below their mountain perch. "That means something, it has to. I owe her for saving my life." She raised an eyebrow. "And what about you, miss? Why do you sit alone each day, instead of with your friends and brother?"

Alana shook her head. "It's complicated."

"Step on some toes, did you?"

"You might say that." Despite herself, Alana chuckled at the woman's wording.

"A shame. We need to stand together, us renegades. Tell me, what could you have done to turn even your own brother against you?"

Alana shivered as she ran over the endless list of mistakes that was her existence. "Oh, just destroyed his life," she said finally.

The old woman's cackling echoed from the cliffs. "Is that all?"

"I'm serious!" Alana growled, sitting up on her rock. She jabbed a finger at the innkeeper. "Listen, you little—"

The woman's laughter died away, and her eyes flashed as she looked at Alana. "Yes?" she asked, her voice suddenly dangerous.

Alana gulped back what she'd been about to say. She had faced down demons and Magickers and the leader of the Three Nations, but something about the woman's tone brooked no argument. She tore off another piece of bread and chewed it slowly, seeking something else to say.

"I just mean…I earned this," she said lamely. "I deserve this."

"Pff, probably. But then, if my brother and I had stopped talking every time he ruined my life…well, I guess he'd only have destroyed my business once," she chuckled. "But then, where would the fun have been? Besides, he always made up for it in the end. What about you? Is sitting here moping going to change things between you?"

Alana scowled. "Who says I'm moping?"

The old woman raised a spindly eyebrow, and Alana blushed and looked away. "Fine," she muttered, then shook her head. "But you don't understand, I'm not sure there's anything I *can* do to fix things."

"Whatever you did, you're still family, that means something…"

Alana snorted. "Clearly you haven't met my family."

"Girl, I was dying on that floor, not dead," Selina replied. "I know who your father is, who the old woman was to you."

"Then you know family doesn't mean anything to me."

"It meant something to your grandmother," Selina replied.

The words dried up in Alana's throat. Suddenly she found herself struggling to breathe. Shooting to her feet, she gasped in the icy mountain air. "I didn't ask for her to do that!" she shrieked finally, swinging on the innkeeper.

Selina only smiled. "No, but that is what family does, girl. Loves each other. Protects each other."

Pain locked around Alana's chest and she looked away. "Not my father," she whispered.

"Not your father," Selina agreed. "But it doesn't have to be the same for you, or your brother."

"Then what do you suggest I do?"

"Make peace with young Braidon," the innkeeper murmured. "Protect him from your father."

"I always have," Alana whispered. "It's where this all went wrong."

"Then find a way to work with him," Selina replied. "I think you'll find he's a resourceful young man."

Alana swallowed, fear for her brother's life already swirling within her. She had spent so much of her life protecting him from harm, from their father and his magic, that the thought of *using* him, of working with him to face the man…

"Glad to see you two lasses getting along!" Alana swung around as a voice called down to them from above. Joseph moved towards them, his footsteps crunching on the loose gravel. "Just don't piss her off, Alana. Or you might wake up a few marbles short of a brain."

"What do you want, Joseph?" Selina asked, fixing him with one of her scowls.

Joseph held up his hands in surrender. "Peace, woman, I come in peace." He pointed a thumb over his shoulder. "But Devon wants to see the girl," he said. "You'd best get running, missy."

Alana shared a glance with Selina and then rose to her feet. Her eyes dancing, she fixed a scowl of her own on her lips and stepped towards the giant Baronian. He towered over her, but Alana showed no hint of fear as she rested a hand on his chest.

"This *girl* is the Daughter of the Tsar," she murmured, "and I go where I will."

As she spoke, she allowed a trickle of her power to spread down her arm into his chest. Following the green glow of her magic, she swept through his consciousness. His fear rose before her, a knotted tangle of red and orange. With a few quick twists, she unlocked several threads, sending them spiralling out into the void of Joseph's mind.

A scream echoed from the cliffs as Joseph staggered and dropped to his knees, his eyes wide with terror. Grinning, Alana released him and stepped back, allowing her power to fade.

Blinking, Joseph looked around, as though surprised to find himself back on the mountainside. He frowned, realising he was on his knees looking up at the two women. A scarlet blush touched his cheeks, and scrambling back to his feet, he muttered something incomprehensible and fled.

"That was cruel," Selina commented archly.

Alana chuckled. "I could have left him like that for an hour. *That* would have been cruel."

"You're a hard girl," the innkeeper replied. "Guess it's *me* that should be watching where I step."

Remembering the glare Selina had given her earlier, Alana flashed a grin. "Oh no, you're terrifying enough as it is without any magic. Now I'd best go see what Devon wants. I wouldn't want to keep the leader of the Baronians waiting now, would I?"

28

Exhaustion pressed on Merydith as she forced herself to take a step, then another. Desperately she fought her way up the winding slope, while around her the harsh winds swirled, the sleeting rain whipping at her exposed face. Despite her thick woollen clothing and boots, she had long since lost all feeling in her extremities. But there was no more time to stop and warm themselves, to set camp and cast back the icy chill of winter. The Tsar was coming, and there was no more time for anything.

Her scouts had spotted his forces scrambling up the gullies nearby, seeking to overtake them. If any of his people reached the upper passes first, Merydith and her people would be trapped. While the outriders' numbers were few, they only needed to hold the northern army a day for the Tsar and the bulk of his force to catch them.

Watching her people make their slow way up towards the next pass, Merydith found herself longing for the gentle valleys of the lower foothills. At least there they had been able to ride their horses. Now, the way was so steep that her people had been forced to dismount and lead their mounts on foot.

And even riderless, the horses were struggling. While the mountain clans around Erachill were acclimatised to the thin mountain air, their horses came from the lowland steeps. Despite their massive lungs, the beasts were falling by the dozen now. If they did not escape the freezing mountain peaks soon, more would die, and the northern army would lose their only advantage against the foot soldiers of the Tsar.

At least they had bloodied the man's nose over the last few days. With the way unclear, Merydith had sent her scouts ahead to map out the passes, while she continued to fight a delaying tactic against the southerners. They had barricaded every pass, set ambushes wherever they could, ensuring the Tsar's advance slowed to a snail's pace. Every inch of ground the southerners gained was paid for with their blood.

But now their stock of arrows was running short, as was their food and other supplies. If they didn't find the pass through to Trola soon, her people would starve.

If the Tsar did not catch them first.

She shuddered as an image of Damyn flickered into her mind. He still had not woken, though his condition had improved slightly. With the worst of his injuries healed by Helen, the camp doctors had taken over his care; but it was the scars left on his mind that still haunted him.

Merydith had moved him into her tent, and often she would wake to him screaming in the night, though he never regained consciousness. The Tsar's cruelty had torn apart the bold, humorous man she had known half her life, leaving only a husk in his place. In her darkest moments, Merydith found herself wondering whether she should end his suffering, to offer him the final peace of death.

Yet even as he lay sobbing in her lap, his eyes flickering in the grip of some unknown nightmare, she knew she could never do it. Even if seeing him like this reminded her of the fate the Tsar had promised her, of the fate he had promised all of her people, should they continue to defy him.

Shaking her head, Merydith forced the thought from her mind. Damyn would recover. Her people would reach the pass through the Sandstone Mountains, and descend into Trola. She would raise the people there to rebellion, and together they would wipe the darkness of the Tsar from the history books.

Merydith looked up as footsteps came from above. Through the swirling sleet, she glimpsed a figure take shape. As he neared, she recognised Mokyre's sharp features. He had proven himself on the day Damyn had returned, fighting hard in the frontlines to see off the Tsar's attacks. Under his guidance, her people had inflicted heavy losses to the enemy. She had sent him ahead with several others to scout out the way. Now as he staggered to a stop in front of her, she found herself holding her breath, barely able to bring herself to hear his news.

"Your Majesty!" he burst out, a grin splitting his face. "I've found it!"

"The pass?" she yelled over the wind, her heart clenched with sudden hope.

"The pass!" Mokyre nodded. "It's close. I've sent Tremyl ahead to scout the way."

Forgetting all protocol, Merydith threw herself forward and dragged the man into a hug. The rest of her advance guard let out a cheer that carried on down the canyon, the noise growing as the news passed down through the ranks. Releasing Mokyre, Merydith beamed at her followers.

"The way lies open!" she called out. "One last push! For Northland!"

"For Northland!" The words echoed from the canyon walls as her people shouted their agreement. Merydith turned back and clapped Mokyre on the shoulder. "Are you strong enough to show us the way?"

Despite the ice frosting his beard, Mokyre nodded, and they began the long slog up towards the distant pass. Her limbs filled with a newfound strength, Merydith followed close behind him, the pain in her feet forgotten. She no longer noticed the weight of her sword or buckler; her mind was already far ahead, planning her next move.

Once they took the pass, she would continue into Trola with the bulk of her army, while a rearguard held their rear against the Tsar. If they could pin his forces in the mountains, it would give them time to organise. She already had contacts in Trola, readying themselves for the final battle. Hope warmed Merydith's heart at the thought of fighting alongside the western nation. While few in number, they were ferocious fighters. With them on her side, they might just stand a chance.

Merydith was so lost in thought she didn't notice the second man emerge from the swirling fog on the slopes ahead. A shout from her guards alerted her to his presence, but by then he was almost on top of them. Swords in hand, two guards moved to intercept the newcomer.

A second later they stepped back again as the scout Tremyl stopped before them. Face pale, he stood on the uneven rocks gasping for breath, as though he had run all the way from the pass. Looking into his eyes, Merydith knew what he was going to say before he ever opened his mouth.

"What is it?" she whispered, the wild winds whipping away her words.

"They're ahead of us."

Blood thumped in Merydith's ears, drowning out the words of her guards, the shouts of the other scout, everything but the words he had spoken.

They're ahead of us.

It couldn't be true. The Gods would not allow it. If the Tsar had cut off their escape, all hope was lost. The Northland army would be trapped in this barren canyon, unable to advance, while behind them the unstoppable forces of the Tsar drew ever closer. He would reach them by morning. The weight of his numbers would crush them within a day.

A high-pitched whinny rose above the hiss of rain as a nearby horse toppled to the ground. Merydith stared at the fallen animal, watching as the rapid rise and fall of its chest began to slow, listening to the harsh shuddering of its breath as it tried to stand. But its strength was gone. It slumped back to the earth and lay still.

Merydith's throat contracted as she looked around and saw the eyes of her people on her. She clenched her jaw, struggling to hide her own terror. Death called to them all, but they could not simply lie down and wait for it to take them. If her people were to die here in these barren mountains, they would die as lions, their voices raised in defiance.

"Onwards!" she roared. "Let them try and stop us."

Merydith didn't wait for her people to reply. Pushing past her scouts, she started up the slope. In the swirling winds, she could not hear whether her people followed and she did not risk glancing back. They needed her to be strong now, for their Queen to lead them. After a moment, Mokyre pulled alongside her. She exchanged a glance with the man, remembering his rage back in Erachill, when he had called her a fool. Yet whatever had been said then, he marched with her now, undaunted by the challenge ahead, and she nodded her thanks.

As her guards closed around them, she finally risked a look back. Her people followed below, their faces determined as they marched up through the valley. Tears stung her eyes, and Merydith quickly looked back at the trail.

An hour passed before Mokyre edged alongside her. "Not far now," he whispered, "just over that ridge."

"Front ranks, form lines!" she shouted.

The rattle of steel followed as her guards and the rest of the vanguard formed up around her. She waited a moment, allowing the hundred men and women a chance to catch their breath, and then shouted the order to advance.

As one, the line surged forward. A hundred paces still separated them from the lip of the slope, but as they advanced the pass slowly came into view. To either side the cliffs of the canyon drew closer, narrowing until only half a dozen men could walk abreast. Merydith scanned the fog and shadows that clung to the pass, seeking the first sign of the Tsar's forces.

Weighed down by their armour and the endless days of marching, their charge slowed as they neared the top. Merydith waited for the answering screams of the enemy, the twang of bowstrings and hiss of swords being drawn.

Instead, there was only the howling of the wind through the jagged rocks.

"Draw swords!" Merydith shouted as they topped the rise.

The whisper of blades leaving leather came from around her. Merydith narrowed her eyes, the hackles on the back of her neck lifting. Still, there was no sign of the Tsar's force, and she turned her gaze to the clifftops around them, wondering now whether she was leading her people into some fresh trap.

The ground flattened out as the pass neared. Merydith slowed her advance, shouting an order for her people to do the same. Together they crept towards the shadows, swords in hand, eyes wide as the walls of the canyon rose up around them.

Then they were through, and the ground was falling away before them, sloping back down towards the distant plains of Trola. Merydith stumbled to a stop, unable to believe it, to understand how they had taken the pass. Her gaze drifted out over the mountains, and then froze as movement came from the slopes below.

Merydith frowned as she saw a man standing alone, his woollen cloak billowing around him. Beyond him the land fell sharply, the stark mountains giving way to rolling green hills. For a moment she thought he was alone, until she glimpsed movement against the cliffs further down the slope. Straining her eyes, she spied a large group of men and women camped in the shadows. She could not tell their number, but only a handful would have been needed to hold the pass.

Yet inexplicably, they had made their camp in the most indefensible spot on the mountainside.

Biting her lip, she turned her attention back to the man standing alone. Merydith started as she saw him advancing, but a quick glance at her guards reassured her. Raising a hand to warn them to stay put, she sheathed her sword and stepped towards the man.

"That's far enough," she called when he was still a few paces away, before adding, "What do you want?"

The man came slowly to a stop. He contemplated her in silence for a long time. Anger grew in Merydith's chest as she waited for him to respond, still keenly aware of the Tsar's forces advancing from behind them. Finally, her patience worn to a thread, she dropped a hand to her sword hilt.

"I said, what are you doing here?" she growled.

The man smiled. "Heard there was a war coming."

"Ay," Merydith snapped, "and if you and your men don't move, you'll soon find yourselves in the middle of it."

The man laughed. "I see." He stepped aside and held out an arm, as though to indicate the way was open. "Please, be my guest. Trola stands open for you, my Queen."

"You know who I am?" Merydith asked, blinking.

"Who else would you be?" the man asked.

Merydith opened her mouth, and then closed it, unable to come up with a reply.

"They say you've come to grant freedom to the Three Nations." He paused, a roguish grin crossing his face. "You've got a strange way of going about it."

Speechless, Merydith could only stand and stare at the man. Finally, pulling herself together, she shook her head. "Who in the Gods' names *are* you?"

The stranger crossed his arms. "You don't know me?"

"Should I?"

"Devon and Kellian might have mentioned me?"

"Devon…and Kellian?" Merydith repeated dumbly. "How…I haven't seen either of them in months."

"Oh." The stranger seemed to deflate at the news. "I was sure they'd escaped…" He sighed. "I guess I shouldn't be surprised. It'll be up to us then, I guess." He held out a hand and smiled. "Betran, at your service, my Queen. I helped Devon and Kellian break into the citadel. Now I'm here."

"Betran…" the Queen mumbled, still struggling to catch up. Her eyes flickered to the men and women camped below. They had begun lighting campfires, and laughter now whispered up the valley to where they stood. "And they are…?"

Betran grinned. "Why, that would be the Trolan rebellion, my Queen. We thought we'd come see if you could use some help."

29

As Alana approached the entrance to Devon's tent, the leather flaps lifted and her brother stepped out into the night. She froze, her heart lodging in her throat. Opening her mouth, she tried to voice the words Selina had urged her to say, but they would not come out. Braidon staggered to a stop as he noticed her standing there, and an awkward silence stretched out between them.

Finally, Alana could take it no more. "Is Devon in there?" she blurted out, saying the first thought that popped into her head.

Braidon nodded. "Yes…" he responded, and she cursed herself. It was Devon's tent; where else would he be at this hour?

"Umm, I'd better see him then," she replied.

Her brother shrugged. "Suit yourself." He wandered off without so much as a 'good night.'

Alana watched him go, her throat slowly relaxing. A sudden urge came over her to run after him, to pull him into a hug and beg for his forgiveness. But the tent flaps rustled again, and Devon stepped out into the night with a scowl on his face. He looked as though he was about to call out after his departing guest, then he saw her standing there.

"Alana," he said, a little too forcefully. "What are you doing here?"

Her anger flared as she realised the man had forgotten her. She crossed her arms and glared at him, waiting for him to realise his mistake. It took to the count of ten before his eyes widened and he cursed.

"Sorry, I thought you weren't coming," he grunted, as though that explained his memory lapse. "I wanted you to talk some sense into your brother, but there'll be no getting through to him just now. Come inside, enjoy some warmth." Turning, he disappeared inside without waiting for a response.

Left standing in the darkness, Alana had no choice but to follow him. Devon was already lowering himself into a camp chair as she hesitated in the doorway, suddenly uncomfortable. Silently she gave herself an internal shake.

You are Alana! A voice hissed in her mind. *You fear nothing!*

She dragged a camp chair across the room to the iron brazier and parked herself there, with legs stretched out towards the coals. Leaning back into the fabric, she eyed Devon, taking in the rings beneath his eyes, the added wrinkles that seemed to have appeared overnight. His hair was unkempt, his beard even worse, though he'd never kept either particularly neat.

"You're looking well," she commented wryly.

Devon blinked, rubbing his eyes. Seeing her smile, he chuckled. "I've had better days. Better years, for that matter." Reaching behind him, he lifted a bottle of what looked like malt liquor and swigged a mouthful before offering it to her.

Alana accepted it with a grin, enjoying the burning sensation that spread down her throat as she swallowed a mouthful. Despite the fire, her insides were still frozen, but the liquor was quickly changing that.

"Cheers," she said, then coughed as the aftertaste caught her. "Or maybe not," she gasped finally, wrinkling her nose at the bottle.

"Blame Joseph. Apparently he likes the stuff."

"Better than nothing, I suppose," Alana replied, helping herself to another mouthful.

"Hey, leave some for me, would ya!" Devon laughed, snatching it back.

After they'd passed the bottle back and forth a few times, Alana finally began to feel more…herself. She wasn't sure what that meant nowadays, but sitting with Devon in the quiet of his tent, she could almost imagine herself the innocent girl who had travelled with him all those weeks ago. The girl who had swum and hunted and fought with him, who could never have imagined sending an innocent child to his death because he angered her.

Almost, but not quite.

Eyeing Devon across the tent, she wondered at his words outside, and her encounter with Braidon. She had been too occupied with her own self-loathing at the time, but thinking back now, he had seemed flustered, not the cool young man he had come to be in her absence.

"Why did you want me to talk to my brother?" she asked.

Sitting back in his chair, Devon sighed. "I'm worried about him," he said at last. "Whatever you did with his memories, it's changed him. Before, he told me he remembered a few bits and pieces, but they were more like a play than his own life. He could watch them, hear them, smell them, but it was through the eyes of an observer. Now he remembers *living* them, *feeling* them; it's like there's a whole other Braidon."

Alana looked away. "I know," she whispered. "It's the same for me. But he asked me to do it—to give him his memories back. After everything I've done, I couldn't refuse him."

"Why did you take his memories in the first place?"

"To protect him," she whispered. "To hide us. Without them, our father couldn't find us."

"I see," Devon replied, though his tone suggested otherwise.

She frowned at him. "What?"

"You didn't have any other motives? To hide from your past, perhaps?"

"Maybe," Alana murmured. "But the woman I used to be, she wasn't much for caring about anything."

"Except when it came to your brother," Devon rumbled, his eyes shining.

Alana swallowed. "I did terrible things, Devon…"

"We've all done terrible things, Alana," Devon replied.

She looked at him sharply. From the depths of her memories, she heard his words ringing out, his admission to the horrors he'd committed during the Trolan war.

I killed a child once, he'd said.

At the time, revulsion had curled around her gut at his words, but now when she looked at him, Alana saw only a man in pain. She shook her head.

"I didn't understand before, when you told me what you'd done," she whispered. "I do now. I'm sorry for how I reacted. You're a good man, Devon. Every act you've done since the war has shown it."

Devon said nothing, only offered her the bottle. She

accepted it gratefully and finished the dregs, wondering how Devon survived beneath the weight of so much pain. She hated herself for being responsible for so much of it. Whatever his words earlier, he still hadn't forgiven her. It was in his eyes, even now, in the great gulf that separated them.

Alana swallowed as he looked up and caught her watching him.

"Kellian…he would have been proud of you, helping these people."

Devon grunted. "I'm the reason they're in this mess," he mumbled. "I've led them to their doom."

"No more than if they'd stayed in the forest. Quinn knew about them. When he was done with us, my father would have hunted them down, killed every last one of them."

"It still doesn't seem quite possible, the Tsar being your father."

Alana shrugged. "Perhaps not for you. But for me, for Braidon now, that is who he's always been to us. For as long as I can remember, he has cast his shadow over our lives. My whole life, his way was all I ever knew. Until Braidon came, and I realised I didn't want him to be what I had become. I tried to shield him from it, to protect him…" Alana's throat contracted. "I just wish there had been someone to do the same for me."

"It's really the both of you in there now, isn't it?" Devon whispered.

Despite herself, Alana smiled. "It is, big man," she replied. Then she closed her eyes, and felt a tear streak her cheek. "You still haven't forgiven me, have you?"

"I…I have…" Devon started, but she shook her head.

"Please don't lie to me, Devon," Alana whispered. "It's okay, I understand, but please do not lie."

Devon swallowed, but he nodded, his eyes shining. "How…?"

"You're not a hard man to read, Devon," Alana replied, a smile touching her cheeks. "And you haven't called me 'princess' since the night you came to rescue me."

"Alana…" he started, then trailed off.

Alana looked up, and was surprised to find Devon staring at her. Their eyes met and he quickly looked away. Her cheeks flushed and her stomach clenched. Clearing her throat, she looked at anything but him, embarrassed by her own reaction. The tension built, but still neither said anything.

Then Alana's anger rose to burn away her blush. She wasn't some innocent teenager, no fumbling girl who couldn't say what she wanted. She was Alana, the Daughter of the Tsar, and she would not be denied.

Silently she rose to her feet. Devon's head jerked up as she crossed the room and stood in front of him. Hands clenched at her sides, she looked down at him.

"You want me," she said.

Devon opened his mouth, but all he could manage was an incomprehensible mumble. Smiling, Alana slid onto his lap and draped an arm around his neck. She watched with satisfaction as the shock in his eyes turned to…something else. He tensed beneath her, one arm lifting to grip her waist, and for a moment she thought he would throw her off.

She stroked his brow, her own eyes caught in his amber gaze.

"You want me," she repeated.

Still Devon did not move, and a sudden fear reared within Alana, that the desire she'd seen in his gaze all that time ago had died. She'd thought it was still there, but what if she'd been wrong, what if he didn't want her, and was about to cast her aside, to reject her? Within, she felt the soft green light of her magic stirring. Temptation rose with it, and she reached for it, feeling its warmth bathe her mind. All she needed was to touch him with her power, to bend his mind as she had done to Quinn and so many others.

Don't.

The command whispered through Alana's mind, two voices as one. In that instant she realised if she tried it, she would lose him. It would be a betrayal of their friendship, a final act of evil that would destroy her in his eyes forever.

"Devon…" she whispered, leaning down to press her forehead against his. "Say something."

His eyes flickered closed as he inhaled. The arm on her waist tightened, but he made no effort to throw her aside. Instead, he pulled her closer, so that she could feel the warmth of his broad chest against her breast, his breath on her neck. She trailed her fingers down his giant arms, tracing the outline of his veins, feeling the thump of his powerful heart. Lifting her head, she found herself trapped in his amber eyes, found herself leaning in…

Heat exploded in her chest as their lips met. Her hands went to his head, drawing him deeper into the kiss, as his arm clenched around her. She shivered as their tongues met, tasting the earthly richness of him, feeling his power beneath her. A moan built in her chest and went rumbling from her. Trailing a hand down his neck, she nibbled playfully at his lip. Her fingers tugged at the buttons of his tunic.

Lust rose within her as his hand slide beneath her shirt. She shuddered as his fingers danced across her naked back, tearing another moan from her throat. She wanted more, wanted his hands, his mouth on her flesh. Searching for his other arm, she found it hanging beside the chair. He flinched as she gripped him, her fingers trailing down in search of his own…

Alana froze as she found his hand wrapped around a wooden haft. Her heart lurched in her chest, and pulling back, she looked down to where his arm hung beside the chair. *Kanker* lay there, its steel head shining in the dim light, his meaty hand wrapped around its handle. A sob caught in Alana's throat as she looked at him.

"You don't trust me," she whispered, her eyes burning with unspilt tears.

"Alana…" he started, but she was already pushing away, scrambling to her feet.

"I would *never!*" she all but shouted, even as she recalled the desire that had touched her, the temptation she'd felt to use her magic on him. She shook her head and looked at him. "Never," she repeated in a whisper.

Devon stared back. "I'm sorry," he murmured, but Alana was already shaking her head.

"I'm sorry, too," she said sharply. "Sorry I ever thought this would work."

He opened his mouth, struggling to speak, but Alana was already spinning on her heel. His words fell on deaf ears as she stepped from the tent and fled into the darkness.

30

The rising sun found Braidon sitting alone on the outskirts of the Baronian camp. He watched as the scarlet light touched the mountaintops, and then came creeping down the valley towards him. The morning was clear, and so high up in the mountains, Braidon could see far out across the Trolan lands, where the light of the new day had yet to reach.

Shivering, Braidon averted his eyes, his mind returning to the past. Memories flashed through his mind, a lifetime of sights and sounds, of joy and pain. Worst of all was the rift they caused within him, the warring emotions between the renegade and the Son of the Tsar.

Alana had been wrong to mess with his mind, to rob him of his memories. He was sure now she had done it to escape her own guilt, rather than protect them from their father. Either way, it hardly mattered now—the damage was done. His mind had been fractured, and now he feared he would never piece it all back together.

Warmth flickered in his chest as an image of his father

passed through his mind, of the man holding him tight, his hand casting wide to encompass the great expanse of Plorsea around them. Then the image changed, and he saw again the sword plunging at Enala's chest, heard the old woman's cry as it speared her. He shuddered, feeling the gulf within him widen.

Braidon's old self had feared the Tsar, but amidst that fear there had also been love, born of the knowledge that everything their father did, he did for them. Yet the Braidon he had become under the spell of Alana's magic had loathed and feared the Tsar in equal measure, and he wondered now whether that had also been of his sister's making.

In fact, he found himself questioning everything she'd ever told him, his every memory, every emotion he'd ever felt for her. As a child, he had seen her as his hero, the avenging angel that struck down any who dared threaten him. Looking back over those memories though, he found himself recalling the terror on the faces of her students, the nervousness of even their father's guards in her presence. Alana had never been one to use her power sparingly—who was to say she had not been using it to manipulate him all along?

The thought sent a cold draught down Braidon's spine. Pulling himself to his feet, he stepped down from the boulder and turned in the direction of camp. He staggered as he found Alana standing on the path, her eyes wide, as though he'd just caught her in the middle of some crime. She wore her thick woollen cloak pulled tightly around her shoulders and a sword at her waist.

His heart suddenly beating hard in his chest, Braidon took a step back. "What are you doing here?"

"I..." Alana paused, casting a glance back over her shoulder at the camp. "I...was leaving."

"Leaving?" he asked. "Why?"

She shook her head, and Braidon was surprised to see tears shining in her eyes. "Because there's no place for me here, Braidon."

Braidon's heartbeat slowed. Legs still shaking from the shock of finding her there, he lowered himself back down onto the boulder. "What do you mean?"

"Devon doesn't trust me. *You* don't trust me—"

"Can you blame me?" he cut in, his voice sharp. "After what you did, I can't even trust my own memories!"

Alana's eyes dropped to the gravel-strewn path. "I know," she whispered. "I'm so sorry, Braidon. That's why I have to go, before I cause either one of you any more pain."

Braidon opened his mouth to speak more angry words, but they died in his throat when he looked into her eyes and saw she was serious. Alana was leaving, and she hadn't even intended on saying goodbye. He reeled at the realisation, clutching hard to the stone beneath him to keep steady.

"Alana, you don't have to go..."

Staggering to a nearby boulder, Alana sank to the ground and placed her face in her hands. "I do, Braidon," she said. "I won't stay where I'm hated."

"I don't hate you," Braidon burst out, surprised to find the words were true. Her head jerked up, and he saw the surprise written across her face. Braidon sank to the ground alongside her. Tentatively, he rested a hand on her back.

"Why not?" Alana croaked. "I deserve it."

Braidon smiled despite himself. "Because whatever happens, you're still my sister, Alana."

She looked down at that. "I'm still not sure that counts for much in our family."

"It counts," Braidon replied. He trailed off, distracted by her words, by the memories of their father. "Alana…" he murmured, knowing he had to ask, but still wondering if he could believe her answer. "Our father…I have all these memories of him now, of him smiling, happy. And more than that, I remember *loving* him, and remember his own love for us…"

Alana swallowed. Braidon struggled for the words, for the question he needed to ask. "Why…why is he hunting us? What does he want?"

His sister shook her head, her eyes distant. "He wasn't always so hard," she murmured. "After you came and Mum…died, a part of him died with her. And his ambition, it became everything. I guess somewhere along the way I lost myself as well. But you, Braidon, you were the only pure thing in either of our lives. Yes, he loved you in his own way. That won't protect you though, not so long as you stand in the way of his final goal."

"To end all magic," Braidon breathed. "How do I have anything to do with that?"

Alana shook her head. "The same way I did, until Enala took my place." She looked a Braidon, her eyes gleaming. "He wants you to host the spirit of Jurrien, so he can kill the Storm God and take his power."

"*What?*"

"He already took the power of the Light, when he killed Eric's son. After killing Enala, he has Antonia's God magic as well. Jurrien is the last one left. Once he has all three of the Gods under his sway, he believes he'll be able to wipe all magic from the earth."

"But he needs me to do it?" Braidon asked.

Alana nodded. "He tried to find another way," she whispered, "but after we betrayed him…"

"He no longer cares."

"No," Alana said. She stood sharply. "That's why I still have to go. I can't let him take you, and if I stay here, I'm useless. But if I can get close enough to him, if I take him by surprise, I might be able to—"

"He'll kill you," Braidon said, cutting her off. "He has an army around him, dragons and demons and Magickers. You don't stand a chance."

Alana looked away. A cold wind blew down the valley, catching in her hair and sending it tumbling across her face. "Then he'll kill me."

She reached up to brush the hair from her eyes, but Braidon grabbed her hand and pulled her around. "Damnit, Alana," he snapped. "You don't need to sacrifice yourself for me anymore."

"But—"

"*No,*" Braidon all but shouted. He gestured back at the camp, anger mixing with his terror. "Why can't you see it? Why can't you see what Devon and Selina and all the others can see? I don't *need* you to protect me! I need you to respect me."

Alana opened her mouth, then closed it and swallowed hard. She gave a sharp nod and dragged him into a hug. He held her close, feeling the sobs as they shook her, the silent grief. When they finally broke apart her eyes were wet with tears.

"I'm sorry," she whispered. "You're right, you're not a boy anymore. I should have believed in you back then, given you a chance instead of keeping you from the world. I just..." She trailed off.

"Wanted to protect me," Braidon finished for her. He brushed a tear from her face. "It's okay, sis. But I'm a man now. I won't let you throw away your life for me." He smiled. “Besides, do you even know how to find our father? He could be anywhere in the Three Nations by now.”

Red spread across Alana’s cheeks. “Not exactly.”

Braidon laughed despite himself. “Typical, always leaping before you look.”

“And I suppose you have an idea?”

“As a matter of fact, I just might,” Braidon replied.

Alana shook her head, biting her lip. “Fine, but even if we find him, how do we *stop* him?”

Braidon smiled. “Together.”

31

A cheer went up from the Baronians as they stepped from the canyon out onto the rolling hills of Trola. Leading from the front, Devon forced a smile to his lips, though their joy did little to warm his heart. He stared out over the green hills, and wondered whether Alana and her brother too had survived the mountains, if they had come this way before them, or if they were still lost amongst the crags rising up behind the Baronian travellers.

Two nights had passed since he and Alana had spoken, since their passion had exploded into rage. He had woken the next morning determined to mend the tear he'd opened between them, but he hadn't even managed to step from his tent before the news reached him that she and her brother had vanished.

Panicked, he'd sent out scouts to search for them, to bring them back so he might apologise and make things right, but it had been a hopeless effort. With their memories restored, the Tsar's children were more than capable of disappearing into the wilderness. And with Braidon's power, the Baronians might have been looking straight at them and still never seen them.

The scouts had returned within the hour with no better idea of where the two might have fled. With Quinn still close on their heels, they could not afford to waste time chasing two ghosts through the Sandstone Mountains. With a heavy heart, Devon had ordered the Baronians to break camp, and they had continued their way down through the mountains.

Now that he'd led them safely into Trola, all Devon could think was to turn around and march back into the face of the storm in search of his friends. But all around him, the Baronians were looking to him for guidance. He could not abandon them now, not after taking them from everything they'd ever known to these strange lands.

"Where to now, hammerman?" Joseph asked as he came alongside him.

Devon glanced at the man. His hand no longer hung in a cast and seemed to be healing well, helped in no small part by a paste Selina had created from moss and mountain herbs.

"I hadn't really thought that far ahead, to be honest," Devon grunted. "I'm not exactly popular here."

Joseph glanced behind them, where the snow-capped mountains still towered above. "You think they're still after us, with the two of them gone? They only wanted the boy, didn't they?"

Devon shrugged. "Quinn and I have a bit of a history ourselves," he rumbled. "I doubt he'll give up until I'm six feet under."

"Sounds like we might be better off with another leader," Joseph replied with a grin.

"You thinking about leading a mutiny, sonny?" Devon asked, raising an eyebrow.

Joseph chuckled, rubbing his injured arm. "No thanks. One beating is enough. Besides, we're not on a ship. It's not half as fun when you can't throw the loser overboard."

Shaking his head, Devon returned his eyes to the road ahead. "You're lucky I like having you around," he commented. "Most kings would have hung you for your insolence by now."

"Ay, probably why I've never been fond of kings. Good thing you're a Baronian, not a king."

Devon's laughter rang from the hills. "I'm not a Baronian, sonny."

"Oh? I suppose you're still a Plorsean then?"

The man's words gave Devon pause. "I suppose not," he sighed.

"You're an outcast—that makes you a Baronian!" Joseph slapped him on the back. "Cheer up, there's worse fates in this world of ours."

"Being stuck with you strikes me as one of them."

"Ay, shame you scared off that blonde lassie," Joseph replied with a laugh. "Don't know how you messed that one up, she seemed fond of you."

Devon flashed him a glare, and Joseph raised his hands in surrender. "Alright, alright, still a touchy subject I see," he said. "I can see when I'm not wanted." He fell back into the ranks of Baronians behind them.

"So *do* you have a plan, hammerman?" Selina asked, appearing out of nowhere.

Groaning, Devon raised his eyes to the sky. "You as well?"

"Me as well," she replied, her thin lips drawn tight. "It's only all our lives on the line."

"It's not like we have many options to choose from, woman," Devon grunted. "We either keep running, or turn and fight."

"I know which I would prefer," Selina growled. "I wouldn't mind taking a few pieces off that Quinn, after what he did to my people."

"You'd have to get in line," Devon said. "It's past time the man got his due."

Selina fell silent at that, her eyes growing distant. Devon shivered as he remembered what Alana had told him of the woman, about Quinn stabbing her through the chest and leaving her to die. Only the Goddess's arrival had saved Selina, her Earth magic restoring her to life.

"Quinn, and the Tsar," Selina whispered finally. Her face twitched as though from remembered pain. "He killed the Goddess. What does that mean? Without the Gods… what hope do we have?"

"We've survived well enough without them until now," Devon replied. "I don't know what the Tsar is planning, but I know there are people here in Trola who will stand against him. If we can enlist their help, maybe we can send Quinn and his Stalkers running back to Plorsea with their tails between their legs."

"That's a lot of maybes," Selina said, raising an eyebrow. "Anyone ever tell you you're not much of a planner?"

"Ha!" Devon smiled sadly. "I had a friend who used to say the same. He reckoned the Gods must like me, or I'd have been killed a long time ago."

"Well if that's the case, you'd better hope you're Jurrien's favourite," Selina replied wryly. "I take it your friend is no longer with us?"

Devon looked away at that, pain gripping his chest as he remembered Kellian's death. "No."

"I see." Selina said, and they walked on in silence for a while. Finally she gestured behind them, to the retreating mountains. "Braidon and Alana, why did they leave?"

"I don't know," Devon replied sharply, his heart twisting again.

Thinking of his friends, he felt suddenly alone. First he'd lost Kellian; now Braidon and Alana had left as well. During their time in the forest, he'd grown fond of the young man, watching him come into his own. And Alana…

His cheeks flushed as he remembered their last encounter. Not for the first time in the last few days, Devon cursed himself for his distrust. The pain in Alana's eyes when she'd realised the truth haunted him. He wanted more than anything to take it all back, to return to that night and cast *kanker* aside, to tell her how much she meant to him.

Yet in the moment, what he'd done had seemed right. With the hammer in his hand, her magic could not touch him, could not alter his thoughts, his emotions.

It wasn't until the moment she'd realised his betrayal, that Devon had realised he loved her. Not just the Alana he had travelled with, but the ferocious, confused, and loyal young woman she had become.

But before he could say any of that, she had fled.

Now all Devon could think about was what he'd say when he saw her again.

If he saw her again.

"THEY LEFT THE MOUNTAINS THIS MORNING, SIR," THE Stalker, Zarent, announced as he rode up.

Quinn smiled, relieved to hear they were finally on the right track. For the past week they had trailed the Baronian force deep into the mountains, seeking to head them off before they reached Trolan lands. But with the boy shielding them, finding them had proven more difficult than he'd expected. In the forest, the Baronians and their wagons had left clear tracks for them to follow, but the bare stone of the mountains told little of their passage. The myriad of crevices and valleys that made up the Sandstone Mountains made their task all the more difficult.

Now though, they were finally within striking distance. On their horses, Quinn and his force of Stalkers and soldiers would catch Devon and his followers by evening. Despite the Baronians' greater numbers, Quinn had no doubt they would make quick work of their quarry. Devon, Alana and Braidon might offer a small pocket of resistance, but their power was small compared to the ten Stalkers remaining in Quinn's command. Together, they would break any illusion the boy created, and bring him before the Tsar's justice.

Devon and Alana though, they were Quinn's to deal with. He savoured the thought of the hammerman on his knees, begging for his life. There would be no mercy for him though, nor for any of the Baronians who had followed him. Only the boy would survive untouched, and after what Quinn had witnessed back in the forest, that was no blessing.

As for Alana, Quinn was determined to ensure no harm came to her during the battle. The thought of her still made his blood boil with rage. She had mocked him back in the village, openly derided him in front of his Stalkers. No, after all she had done, death was too good for Alana. He would see her chained and brought before her father, so that he might petition the great man to restore the girl to some semblance of obedience.

First though, he needed to catch them.

"At the canter!" he called out to his Stalkers.

The clatter of horse hooves echoed from the cliffs as they continued down the valley. The stone walls widened around them, slowly giving way to rolling foothills. Further down, grass began to grow once more. The rocky ground turned back to soft earth, the churned up dirt revealing the passage of hundreds of travellers.

Quinn lifted his gaze to the hills ahead of them, watching for the first glimpse of their quarry. It was still only midmorning, and it would be hours yet before he had Devon and the others in his grip, but already his heart raced with anticipation.

Soon.

As the thought touched him, a cold breeze blew across Quinn's neck. Despite the cloudless sky, a shadow seemed to pass overhead. Shivering, Quinn looked up as his gelding gave a cry and staggered to a sudden halt. Around him, the other horses were doing the same. Their screams rolled across the hillside as several reared, throwing off their riders and bolting.

As the downed men chased after their mounts, Quinn dragged back on the reins, bringing his own horse under control. Whispering gently to the panicked beast, he looked around, seeking out whatever had so disturbed the animals.

His heart lurched in his chest as he saw the shadow of a man standing on the path ahead. Cloaked all in darkness, nothing could be seen of his face, yet Quinn recognised him instantly. Hardly daring to breathe, he slid from his horse and dropped to one knee before the Tsar. Seeing him, the other Stalkers abandoned their mounts and did the same.

"Your Majesty," Quinn whispered. "Why are you here?"

Soft laughter whispered across the hillside. "You are too slow, Lieutenant."

"No, sire!" Quinn cried. "We almost have them! No Baronian will be left alive come nightfall, and the boy will be yours."

The figure shook its head. Slowly, the Tsar approached. His feet made no sound on the earth, and Quinn realised with a start that the man was projecting himself from a hundred miles away. He shuddered at the power such a feat must have cost.

"You might catch the Baronians," the Tsar murmured, "but my *son* is no longer with them."

"*What?*" Quinn exclaimed, coming to his feet. "How?"

"Their camp is no longer protected," the Tsar murmured. "Their minds are open to me. My daughter and the boy have abandoned them."

"Why—?"

"*Enough!*" the Tsar's voice boomed, sending their horses bolting again. Quinn staggered back and again dropped to his knees as the shadowed figure loomed. "You have failed me for the last time, Lieutenant," he whispered. "Return to my camp at once."

"What about Devon?" Quinn demanded. "We are so close, I can still destroy him."

"No, Lieutenant," the Tsar growled, blue eyes flashing within the shadows of his hood. "*You* will not. My children are coming here, and I would like my Stalkers at hand to detain them, rather than wandering the countryside carrying out your personal vendettas."

"Devon is dangerous!"

"The man is mortal. He cannot hide from me. I will deal with him when the time is right."

"But—"

"*You!*" Cutting Quinn off, the Tsar turned to a nearby Stalker. Zarent's head jerked up as he realised the Tsar was addressing him, his eyes widening. "You are in charge now. Arrest Quinn. Bring him and the rest of my company to my camp."

The man hesitated, his eyes flickering from Quinn to the other Stalkers, then back to the Tsar. He nodded slowly, his mouth opening and closing as he struggled to adjust to his sudden change of fortunes.

"Can you I trust you to do that, Stalker?" the Tsar asked dangerously. "Or should I find someone else?"

"No, sir!" the Stalker shouted, standing to attention. "It shall be done at once."

"Excellent," the Tsar murmured. His shadowed gaze turned back to Quinn. "Then I shall see you soon, Lieutenant."

With his words, the dark figure faded from sight, leaving Quinn and his Stalkers alone on the hillside.

Except they were no longer *his* Stalkers.

His heart still hammering hard against his ribcage, Quinn faced his former followers. Zarent grinned, reaching for his sword. "You going to come easily, Lieutenant?" he asked as the sword slid free. "Or shall we do this the hard way?"

"Oh, please say hard," another Stalker added as he joined Zarent, blade already in hand.

Panicked, Quinn took a step back. He glanced around, searching for his horse, but in the turmoil inspired by the Tsar's appearance the gelding had galloped clear. Power built in the air as he sensed the black-garbed Stalkers nearest him drawing on their magic, readying themselves for a fight. Slowly they closed in on him.

Silently vowing revenge on his treacherous men, Quinn raised his hands. “I surrender.”

“How disappointing,” Zarent said, before stepping forward and slamming the hilt of his sword into Quinn’s skull.

32

Merydith paused as a breeze blew across the hilltop, savouring the warmth in its touch, the promise it carried of winter's end. The northern army had set up camp on a lonely hilltop overlooking a narrow valley. Her people were busy fortifying their camp for the coming battle. Men and women were hard at work digging a trench along the northeast slope of the hill, facing the distant mountains from which they'd escaped just a few days before. Still trapped in the grip of winter, snow glimmered on the stark peaks.

It was from there the first attack would come. A rider had reached them that morning—their rearguard had been overrun, the few hundred soldiers tasked with slowing the Tsar's advance massacred. Now he was coming for them, and there was nowhere left for the northern army to run.

Merydith had thought to reach Kalgan and make her stand there, but Betran said the city now stood empty, abandoned by its citizens in anticipation of the coming war. Those who believed in the cause had marched with Betran to join her, while the rest had dissipated into the countryside, spreading the news of the rebel Queen far and wide.

In the two days since escaping the mountains, more Trolans had joined them, in ones and twos and groups large enough to fill an inn, though none as great as the thousand Betran led. Many were veterans from the civil war, hard men and women with little give in them. She had given Betran the title of captain and set him to work alongside Mokyre to ready their two forces to work in concert. Together with those who had joined them on the road, her force now numbered a little over six thousand.

Still barely a fraction of what the Tsar would field against them.

Merydith continued along the ridgetop, casting an expert eye over the defensive trench and rampart they were erecting. Unfortunately, the rolling farmland of northern Trola offered little in the way of wood for a palisade, and the rocky soils on the hilltop were making the going hard. At least they still had a day before the Tsar could bring the full force of his army down on them.

Terrified farmers and displaced villagers were already streaming down from the north, fleeing the coming army. Many chose to skirt Merydith's force altogether, seeking to disappear into the wildlands of southern Trola. She could hardly blame them; they had already witnessed first-hand the wrath of the Tsar. It would take a brave soul to face him again, after the devastation he had wrought on the nation during their first rebellion.

Satisfied the ramparts and trench would be completed by nightfall, Merydith returned to her tent.

"How's it looking out there, Merydith?"

Blinking, Merydith's eyes took a few moments to adjust to the gloom. A smile touched her lips when she found the aged figure of Murdo seated in the corner beside Damyn's stretcher. His strength normally unquenchable, Damyn's fate had sapped the old man's spirit. Both members of clan Crae, Damyn was as much Murdo's family as he was Merydith's.

Merydith crossed the room and pulled up a stool beside the clan leader.

"We'll be ready," she murmured, her eyes drawn as always to Damyn. His complexion remained pale, but his breathing was easier now that they had left the mountains. Over the last few days, they had managed to feed him a gruel made of roots and tubers, but still he would not wake.

"He's a strong lad, Merydith," Murdo said, as though reading her mind. "He'll be alright. Just make sure you win this war, so he has something to wake up to."

Merydith smiled. "If only it were so easy."

"Ha!" Murdo cackled. "Don't tell me our relentless Queen is having doubts now?"

"I've had doubts all along, my friend," Merydith replied. "I just keep them to myself."

"Ah, well, don't go bringing down this old man's hopes then, would ya?" he rumbled. "You're of the Kenzie Clan, woman. As far as us Craes are concerned, you're unstoppable."

Merydith snorted. "I never said *I* was the problem," she replied. "I'm just hoping the rest of you can keep up with me tomorrow!"

"You won't have to worry about the Trolans!" Merydith swung around as Betran's voice came from the entrance to the tent. The young Trolan wandered inside, followed a second later by Mokyre.

The latter nodded, adding his agreement: "Ay, they're

tough bastards out there. We'll give the Tsar's army something to think about."

"They'll have to do more than that," Merydith replied, waving for them to pull up stools and join her. "Our scouts report the Tsar's force still numbers close to forty thousand."

The mood in the tent turned sombre at the reminder of their odds. Mokyre was the first to break the silence. "You'll find a way, my Queen," he said softly. "And even if we fail, at least we bought the rest of our people some time." He eyed her through the gloom. "Come what may, you were right to lead us here."

Merydith nodded her thanks as Betran voiced a fresh worry. "What about the Tsar's magic?" he murmured. "Last time, our cities only held as long as our Magickers' stamina."

"Helen and the others remain strong, for now," Merydith replied, thinking of her meeting with the woman earlier in the day.

A great tent had been set in the centre of the camp for Helen and her hundred Magickers. Within, the shadows were lit by a single torch. Men and women sat in circles spreading out from the centre, legs crossed and eyes closed. Even magicless, Merydith had felt the power bubbling on the air as she entered.

Helen had set her people to work in shifts through the day and night, with a quarter of their number rotating to sleep every six hours. Even so, the effort it was taking them to keep the Tsar from the camp was obvious. In the time since they'd stepped foot in the Three Nations, the flesh had vanished from Helen's bones, so that she seemed but a shadow of her former self.

Even so, the Magicker had greeted Merydith warmly, and reassured her they would hold the Tsar to their dying breath. But it was not that for which Merydith had visited them. She had gone in search of a way to attack.

In the end, she'd left without an answer, but Merydith prayed to the Gods that Helen and her people could find a way to turn the tables on the Tsar. Because without *something*, she feared no matter how brave, how daring her people, in the end the sheer weight of numbers would overwhelm them.

"How much longer can they hold for?" Mokyre asked, disturbing her train of thought.

"Helen could not say," Merydith said.

"Then it's a good thing we face them on the morrow," Murdo put in.

"Agreed," Merydith replied. "I just wish we'd found a more defensible position."

"We're on a big hill surrounded by valleys and steep sides," Murdo rumbled. "What more could you ask for?"

"Walls, a well or two, some food or supplies might have been nice."

"Ha, well, beggars can't be choosers, can they?" Murdo laughed.

"Another group of farmers just came in," Betran added. "They brought their livestock with them. A few dozen sheep and a couple of cows. We won't go hungry before the fight."

"Your people are a gift that keeps on giving, Betran," Merydith replied with a smile.

"It is our pleasure, my Queen," he said, stroking his beard. He eyed her closely. "All we have desired for this last decade is our freedom."

Merydith took note of his tone. "And you shall have it, my friend," she responded. Her eyes travelled around the room, taking in the ancient eyes of Murdo, the youthful fire of Mokyre, the unyielding stare of Betran. Unlikely friends, in normal times, but common cause had united them under her banner. "First though, we must win it back. For all of us."

The others nodded. With a wave from her, they departed, each returning to the myriad of tasks needing to be completed before the day was out. Before the Tsar and his army arrived.

Finally alone, Merydith turned and looked down on the sleeping face of Damyn. Gently, she stroked his brow, feeling the warmth of his skin, the cloying dampness of his hair. His cheekbones stood out starkly in the candlelight, so that it seemed he were already half-skeleton.

"Where are you, my friend?" she murmured, a shiver touching her.

They had spent so much of their childhood together, she could hardly imagine a world without him. Back then, before she was Queen, they had just been boy and girl. Two troublesome youngsters, they'd often slipped her guards and disappeared into the winding tunnels of Erachill.

Together they had explored the deepest crevices and highest tunnels, venturing even up to the high peak beneath which the city was built. Upon that viewpoint, it had seemed they could see the entire world, from wild steeps to dense forests to rugged coastlines. Even so far to the north, the three jagged peaks of Mount Chole and its volcanic siblings had just been visible.

As a child, it had scared her sometimes, standing on that peak and looking out on their realm, knowing one day it would be hers to govern. When she'd told Damyn of her fears, he had stood there beside her with a roguish grin on his youthful face, and laughed. He'd told her she had nothing to fear, that her parents and Enala and he would all be there beside her, that together they would lead Northland to greatness.

Now her time had come, Merydith found herself deserted. Her parents were long dead, Enala she knew not where. Even Damyn had abandoned her, his mind fled, leaving Merydith alone to face the darkness that was the Tsar.

"You said you would be here," she whispered, her voice cracking. "You promised."

Closing her eyes, Merydith let the tears fall. How had everything gone so wrong? For the thousandth time, she wondered if she'd made the right decision, protecting the boy. If she had simply handed Braidon over to the Tsar, Northland might never have needed to fear the Tsar's wrath. All those who had given their lives to her cause these past few weeks would still live, happy and safe in the mountains of Erachill.

And the boy would be dead, she tried to convince herself.

Yet still she had heard nothing of Braidon and Enala, nothing but rumour and whispers. It was said a Gold Dragon had been spotted in the skies above Ardath, but it had fled across the lake, never to be seen again. Now she wondered if even her one small act of defiance had been in vain, if the Tsar had taken the boy all the same.

"Was I wrong?" she whispered to the shadows in the tent.

"You could never be wrong, Merydith," a rasping voice responded from beside her. Her head flicked around as Damyn groaned and struggled to sit up. "It's just the rest of the world hasn't figured it out yet."

33

Evening was setting on Devon and his followers as they topped a rise and found themselves looking down on the ruins of Westdale. Devon remembered the town well from the civil war. Close to the mountains, it had once been a place for revellers of all race and creed. Its popularity had done nothing to save it though. The inhabitants had surrendered in the early days of the Tsar's conquest, and been spared, but the city itself had still been gutted.

Now though, Devon was surprised to see fires glowing amongst the burnt-out buildings. A quick count in the dying light estimated there were well over a hundred people camped out in the ruins. Though the Baronians outnumbered them five to one, Devon considered skirting them. On closer inspection though, he realised the people below were kitted out much the same as his own. They sported worn woollen cloaks of various colours, and their weapons consisted of rusted swords and farm hatchets. After a brief discussion with the others, he decided to risk approaching.

No watch had been set, and he was halfway to the ruins

by the time anyone within noticed the approaching tribe. A warning cry carried up the slope as chaos descended on the camp. Devon watched as people rushed in all directions; some gathering up fallen weapons and racing in his direction, while others fled for the wilderness.

"Who goes there!" a voice called up to him.

In the growing darkness, Devon could not make out the man's face, but after a quick check that the Baronians weren't far behind, he lifted *kanker* and shouted a reply. "An enemy of the Tsar!"

Below, the figure staggered to a stop. "Oh!" Before Devon could say anything more, he swung around and shouted to those further down the slope. "It's okay! They're on our side."

Now it was Devon's turn to halt midstride. He frowned, staring at the men and women now gathered on the slope below them. A few carried torches, their soft glow illuminating the hillside. By their light, the first man who had spoken continued forward, a roguish grin on his youthful face. "In that case, well met, stranger!" he said as he strode up.

Devon could only shake his head. The Trolans who'd rushed to defend the camp were already heading back to the ruins, leaving only a few to stand in their path. Beyond, those who had run in the other direction had paused where they stood, and now watched on in silence, as though awaiting the outcoming of the meeting on the hillside. As far as Devon was concerned, they were the smart ones.

"Awfully trusting of you," he said, looking back to the young man. "We might have been lying."

The man looked suddenly unsure of himself, but Devon sheathed *kanker* on his back and waved for his people to do the same with their weapons. Their newfound friend relaxed visibly. Devon was just glad the man hadn't recognised *kanker.* The weapon was infamous amongst the Trolans, and he doubted his reputation had improved at all in the last few months.

"There's not many brave enough to declare themselves enemies of the Tsar," the stranger replied.

"Then what drove a young lad like you to do so?" Devon asked.

"The battle, of course!"

"Battle?" Devon asked.

"You haven't heard?" The man frowned. "Where've you been, mate? The whole of Trola has been talking about it. The Northland Queen has come to liberate us. She's just a little way north of us, camped out on Turkey's Knoll. The Tsar is marching to meet her. We're hoping to reach 'em before the battle begins!" His frown deepened as he glanced over Devon's shoulder, his gaze taking in the Baronians gathered above. "You…aren't from Trola, are you?"

A grin split Devon's matted beard. "No, sonny, but if the Queen's here, that's the best news I've heard all year. What was your name?"

"Corrie." He paused, his eyes narrowing. "And what did you say yours was?"

"I didn't," Devon laughed.

Slapping the man on the shoulder, he strode past, gesturing for the Baronians to join him. Beyond the ruins, the Trolans who had fled were returning to the city. Watching them, Devon wondered what would have happened had it been Quinn who'd come across them first. There were children below, and old men and women bowed with age. Most weren't soldiers at all, though many sported the signs of the last civil war.

They would have been swept away had it been the

Tsar's people who came across them first, the earth stained with their blood. And if Trola was in open rebellion again, there would be no mercy this time. His soldiers would slaughter every man, woman, and child they found.

Walking through the broken walls of the city, Devon wondered at the desperation that had brought these people here. Amongst the crumpled buildings and burnt out hovels, there was no escaping the devastation the last war had left. Their population had been decimated by the Tsar and his army. Devon had played no small part in that massacre. Looking around now, he tasted the familiar tang of guilt in his mouth.

"Where have you all come from?" he asked as he watched a one-armed man walk past him, carrying a stack of firewood.

"Kalgan, Palma, Drata, everywhere in between," Corrie said as he joined Devon.

"And you lead them?"

Corrie shrugged. "No one leads us. I was just the first to notice your people."

"You should have a watch set," Devon grunted. "If the Tsar is in Trola, he will have raiding forces scouring the countryside."

Corrie looked doubtful, and Devon shook his head. "Joseph!" he shouted, turning to the small retinue of Baronians that had followed him into the city.

Joseph stepped forward, his bulk making the young Trolan look tiny. "Yes…sir." He said the title hesitantly, and Devon nodded his thanks at the man for not using his name.

"Take a dozen men and set a watch on the approaches to the city," Devon said, and the man moved away.

Selina stepped up to join them, and the two of them

exchanged glances. "Is there room in the city for our people?" she asked the young Trolan.

Corrie shrugged. "There's only a few hundred of us here. The city used to host a thousand. If your people wish to join us for the night, we won't stop them."

Devon chuckled. "It would have been a bit late if you wanted to," he commented, gesturing to where the Baronians were already streaming through the fallen walls. "Anyway, if your people were intending to join the Queen, we'll march with you." He hesitated, casting another glance around them. "Though I think many of your number would be best left here."

"They'll come, or they won't," Corrie replied. "As I said, I don't lead them." He eyed the black-garbed Baronians. "You still haven't told me where you came from, or who you are, for that matter."

"Ay," Devon replied, his stomach tying in knots.

Clenching his fists, he took a breath. He saw a sudden look of panic on Selina's face, but he could hide the truth no longer. If he was to fight alongside these people, they deserved to know who he was.

"Because I am Devon," he said softly. Reaching up, he drew his hammer. "Because this is *kanker*, and its head is stained with the blood of your people."

Corrie's eyes widened and he took a quick step back. He looked from the fabled weapon to its wielder. Devon watched as hatred blossomed in his eyes.

"You dare to stand here and claim yourself an enemy of the Tsar?" he whispered. "An ally of Trola?"

"I do," Devon rumbled. "Every day since the war ended, I have regretted the part I played in your fall."

"And what is your regret to us, butcher?" Corrie snapped. A crowd was starting to gather around them now.

Devon glimpsed men reaching for sword hilts as they realised what Corrie was saying. "Can your regret help to rebuild our cities, or bring back our Magickers? Can it restore our loved ones to life?"

"No," Devon replied. He stepped towards Corrie, so that he stood just an inch from the man, and looked down at him. Beyond the crowd, several Baronians had taken notice of the commotion and were moving towards them. "But you'll find no greater warrior for your cause, sonny."

"We don't need help from the likes of you."

"You do," Devon snapped, his anger flaring. He threw out an arm, gesturing to the men and women that had gathered around them. "Your army is made of old men and cripples. They're brave, I'll give them that, but it is the *Tsar* you face. His army cannot be defeated by bravery alone. You need warriors, fighters with the strength to see an empire fall. You need me."

As he spoke, Devon had watched the doubt enter the young Trolan's eyes. Like many in his nation, Corrie was hotblooded, quick to anger, but now that he found himself facing the Butcher of Trola, Devon could see his hatred turning to fear. He looked around, seeking strength in those around him, but the crowd had taken an unconscious step back at Devon's outburst.

Selina still stood nearby though, and she advanced, her face radiating calm.

"Devon is not the only one here who carries the weight of your people's fate on his shoulders, Trolan," she said quietly. "I too have Trolan blood on my hands."

"You fought against us, lady?" Corrie asked, taking the chance to retreat from Devon.

"I doubt Devon remembers me, but it was not just

legends who fought beneath the Tsar's banner," Selina replied.

Devon stared at her in disbelief. With her greying hair and slim frame, he'd never guessed for a moment that she too might have fought in the ranks of soldiers who had marched against Trola. Her eyes flicked in his direction, and a knowing smile touched her lips.

"Very well." Devon looked around as the words burst from Corrie. "You and your people may remain, *Butcher*. But do not expect our friendship." With that he turned and vanished through the crowd.

Despite his claims he was not their leader, the crowd dispersed after that, leaving Devon standing alone with Selina.

"Was that true?" he asked when the last of the Trolans had faded away.

Selina raised an eyebrow. "Is that so hard to believe, hammerman?"

Chuckling, Devon shook his head. "No, I should have guessed it sooner, the way you ordered us around back at the inn." He gestured to where several Baronians had already finished setting up his tent. They started towards it as he continued. "So you decided to retire and set up an inn after the war?"

"It was more for the quiet of the forest, but yes," Selina answered, and Devon chuckled.

"I think my friend would have liked you," he said as he ducked beneath his tent flaps.

Selina followed him inside, and Devon waved for her to join him in the camp seats already laid out by the brazier.

"I'll give 'em this," he said as he sat, "at least the Baronians are more organised than these poor souls."

Selina said nothing, and Devon found her staring at the

fire. After a moment she blinked and looked around. Catching Devon watching her, she sighed.

"We never learn, do we?" she said softly.

"What?" Devon asked, nonplussed.

"The folly of war."

Devon frowned. "The Tsar hasn't exactly given us a choice."

"There is always a choice." Selina sighed and leaned forward in her chair. "Tell me, Devon. If you win this fight, what will change? After all this blood and death, after all the orphans you create, what will be left?" There was anger in her voice as she looked at him.

"What do you want from me, Selina?" Devon asked, taken aback. He shook his head, his own anger rising. "I'm no king, no ruler. Those aren't my decisions to make. You think I like this any more than you? I *left* all this, threw everything away to escape it."

"Ay, and what did you do then? What good did you create in this world, to atone for the death you dealt with that hammer of yours?"

"I..." Devon trailed off as the innkeeper's eyes drilled into his.

"Truth is, you did nothing," Selina hissed. "And you expect the Trolans to be grateful, because after you slaughtered them like so many pigs, you hung up your weapon and said, 'Well that's enough.'"

"I lost my *friend*," Devon snapped, surging to his feet. "I might have been late, but I *have* fought for their cause. I have bled and bled for it, gone up against Stalkers and demons and dragons for it. Don't you *dare* say I have done nothing!"

Selina was on her feet now as well. "You have killed for the cause, Devon, but what have you *built?* What legacy will you leave this world, other than one of death and destruction?" She gestured to the people outside in the ruins. "Those people out there, the Tsar destroyed their lives, took everything from them. But every one of them has built more than you. They have families and farms, a home to return to. They are here to protect their own, to strive for a better world for their children."

"So am I—"

"No, Devon," Selina said sadly, "you are here because after the war, you were empty." She slumped back into her chair, the fight going from her in a rush. "I know, because it was the same for me," she said quietly. She swallowed, her eyes on the walls of the tent, as though she could see straight through the fabric, out to where the Trolans made camp. "If men and women like them ruled this world, there would be no more wars. But instead, it's men and women like us who are worshiped. And so the evil spreads across mountains and rivers, on down the centuries, unending."

Devon sank back into his chair, all anger draining from him. "What can I say, Selina, except that I think you are wrong? I know what I am: a soldier, a warrior, a fighter. It's all my family has ever known. Perhaps someday that will change, but it will not change the way of the world. The powerful will always seek to conquer. Some will fight for the light, others a different shade of grey. But when the dark ones come, it's up to men like me to stand against them, to give our lives to ensure men and women like *them*—" he gestured to the unseen Trolans, "can live their lives in peace."

Selina's eyes were sad as she watched him. "I know that, Devon," she murmured. "But do you not think the soldiers who fight for the Tsar believe the same? To them, you and the Baronians and the Trolans are traitors, the Queen a foreign invader, coming to take their land and enslave their families."

"I know, believe me, I know," Devon said. "By the Gods, I fought alongside many of them. And who knows, maybe they're right." He sighed, staring into the dead brazier. It was growing cold in the tent, but he would have to find fuel before it could be lit. "I can only go by what my eyes tell me, Selina. Those Trolans out there, they have suffered because of the Tsar, because of us. And I have met the Queen and the northerners. She's a hard woman, but Northland is no longer the devil it once was. They are thriving and have no reason to invade. She did not come here unprovoked. So I will fight alongside the Trolans, and Northland, and the Baronians, against my former comrades. It may not be what you or I want, but it is what it is."

"Who says that is not what I want?" Selina chuckled.

Devon frowned. "Understanding your words is like wrestling piglets in the mud; soon as I think I have a handle on them, another one slithers free."

"I'm sorry, Devon, if I took my own frustration out on you. It's just, after all our Three Nations has suffered, I thought we were finally done with war. To sit here now, watching more young men and women marching off to fight for their freedom…" She shook her head. "It's hard to see how it will end in anything but more grief."

"Ay, the Tsar will show them no mercy this time."

"You were right, what you said out there," Selina put in. Devon only shrugged, but she went on. "But they will need more than your courage if they're to stand a chance."

"What do you mean?"

"They need a leader, Devon, one who believes in them, who will fight for them to his dying breath."

"Me?"

"Who else?" Selina whispered.

"Rubbish," Devon rumbled. "They despise me."

"Ay, they hate you, because of what you've done. But that is not who you *are*, Devon. Who you are is the man who led the Baronians through the mountains. Show them *that* Devon, and they will follow you to the gates of hell."

"If the Tsar is marching, hell doesn't begin to describe what we face."

"They need you, Devon," Selina said, cutting across his deflection. "You'll see that, come the morrow."

34

Merydith sighed as she sank onto the grass behind the hastily erected ramparts. Silence fell over the men and women stationed there as they broke off their conversations to look at her. She offered them what she hoped was her most reassuring smile. The fear in their eyes told Merydith she was only halfway successful.

"They're beautiful from here, aren't they?" she said, gesturing at the mountains.

The rising sun stained their snowy peaks scarlet, a sign amongst many of her people that a bad day was to come. Bad for whom, though, was yet to be decided. Slowly the red gave way to gold as the burning globe topped the mountains, bathing them all in its warmth. She let out a long breath, her eyes fluttering closed for a moment. They might have left the mountains behind, but winter's chill still lingered over Trola.

"Do you really think we can hold them?" a Trolan woman crouched nearby asked her.

Merydith flashed a grin in her direction. "Hold them?

They should be so lucky! Today we'll see the Tsar's empire fall, I promise you that."

The woman swallowed visibly. Betran moved alongside Merydith. "Trust her, Beth," he murmured. "The Queen has a plan."

"It's just...I never knew there would be so *many*."

"Don't worry about the numbers," Merydith answered in her calmest voice, even as she recalled the sight of the Tsar's horde marching towards them in the fading light of the evening. They had just kept coming, hour upon hour, long after the sun had set and torches were needed to light their way. "We have the high ground, and the courage to use it. When the time comes, we'll slice them in two like a knife through butter."

"I hope so," the Trolan murmured.

"Don't hope, *know*," Merydith said, patting the woman's shoulder as she stood.

Nodding to Betran, the man joined her and they bid the woman and her comrades good luck. Together they moved down the line, Betran greeting men and women he recognised and introducing her. They stopped several more times to talk with the troops, letting them see her, to speak with the Queen they would soon be risking their lives for. Most of those stationed along the ramparts were the Trolan rebels that had joined with Betran, or the volunteers they'd picked up along the way.

If her plan failed, it would fall on these men and women to hold the ramparts long enough for the wounded to be evacuated. Merydith prayed it would not come to that, but she knew if the worst were to happen, it was unlikely she would live long enough to witness the aftermath.

Reaching the end of the northern defences, they climbed the earthen mound that was their ramparts. Merydith looked down at the land below, and the dark shadow that spread around their hilltop. Nestled within the valley, the Tsar had not even bothered to take the slopes to either side of his force. He had stalked her across Lonia, far through the mountains, all the way to this lonely hilltop. And like the wolf at the end of a hunt, he knew they were done, that they did not have the strength to flee any longer.

Or at least, she hoped that was what he thought.

If her plan were to succeed, they needed him to be over-bold, to throw caution to the wind and attack up the long, open slope below their hilltop. He would expect her to sit and wait, to defend her makeshift ramparts and trench to the last man and woman. Looking down at the mass of humanity below, Merydith shivered, and wondered if she were mad to think of attacking such a monster.

The emerald and scarlet of the Lonian and Plorsean soldiers wound up the valley and disappeared out of sight, uncountable, though she knew they numbered around forty thousand. Against her tiny force, the odds seemed insurmountable.

Her eyes drifted to the sky, and she wondered whether the Three Gods were looking down on her today, if they had given their blessing to this desperate gamble.

The *thump* of marching feet rumbled up from the valley below as the first wave of soldiers started forward. Row upon row of ironclad men and women stretched across the valley, wide enough to engage the defenders across the entire rampart.

Despite herself, Merydith allowed herself a smile. The Tsar's battle plan was obvious. He would launch a frontal assault upon their hillside, sending wave upon wave of southern soldiers until the defenders were overwhelmed. A less confident commander might have ordered his forces to surround the hilltop, cutting off their escape. But the Tsar knew she had nowhere left to go, that even if the Queen fled, she would only be delaying the inevitable.

No, the fate of their two worlds would be decided here, and neither the Tsar nor the Queen wished to delay its conclusion any longer.

The rumbling grew as the first wave of soldiers approached the base of the hill. The sound carried up the slope to where the Northland army waited, breaking over them like thunder. Merydith glanced along the line, and smiled when she saw the Trolan defenders standing strong.

She was surprised to find her own fear had evaporated. Looking out at her nemesis, she realised she had been waiting for this day for what felt like a lifetime. Now that it had finally come, she felt a strange indifference to the odds they faced, an acceptance of whatever fate would bring that day.

Even were they to be defeated, Merydith knew the northern battle cry would live on. They had hurt the Tsar these past few weeks, damaged his aura of invisibility. Today, every southern soldier her people slew was one less for their kin back home to face. And if Merydith herself were to die, her death would ring out through the Northland clans, becoming the rallying cry of the free.

The thought brought a sudden melancholy to Merydith, and she pushed it aside.

Death could wait.

Today was for living.

As the sun crept higher into the sky, a single figure broke away from the southern army and started his way up the grass-torn slope. He walked slowly, a white flag flapping above his head. Waving Betran back, Merydith rose and strode down to meet him. Two of her guard followed close behind, the memory of her attempted assassination still fresh in their minds.

"That's far enough," she boomed when the man was still ten paces away.

"I come to discuss terms of surrender!" the man bellowed.

"Excellent!" Merydith shouted back. "Then my terms are this: surrender now, and all but the Tsar may live."

The man stared at her for a long moment, his mouth frozen open. Finally he seemed to shake himself free of his shock. "Pardon?"

"Do you need me to repeat them, sir?" she asked with a laugh. "I thought they were quite simple. Surrender, and you and your soldiers may live."

His face coloured, and baring his teeth, he took a step towards her. "I have not come to negotiate *our* surrender, witch," he spat, "but the surrender of you and your army of heathens!"

Merydith twisted her lips into a pout. "Oh, that *is* a shame. You seem like such a *nice* man. Really, there's no need for you to die here. In fact, I'd rather not see anyone die today, it's such a beautiful morning." She paused. "Other than the Tsar, of course."

"The Tsar is immortal," the man snapped, "and I come under the flag of truce. You cannot kill me."

"Is that so?" Gesturing her guards to remain where they were, she stepped towards the man, her long legs eating up the distance between them. She looked at the white flag he carried. "You think your little flag protects you?" Her sword flashed out to rest against his throat.

The envoy jerked back, his legs stumbling on the uneven ground. With a cry he crashed onto his back. Merydith quickly planted her boot on his chest. Gently she touched her blade to his throat again. He had lost his grip on his flag, and Merydith bent down and picked it up.

"You know, another like you came before me under such a flag." Taking it by the haft, she slammed it into the earth beside his head. "I welcomed him into my city, honoured him as my guest. And how do you think your Tsar repaid me?"

"You…you can't!" the negotiator stuttered.

Lifting her sword, Merydith touched it to his lips, silencing him. "That man tried to kill me," she continued conversationally. "He took his sword and murdered my guards. His assassination almost succeeded. Now another comes before me with a white flag; what am I to do?"

There were tears streaming down the envoy's face now. He managed to blurt out several nonsensical words between sobs.

"Honestly, you're not much of a negotiator. I can't understand a word you're saying. Please, pray, speak more clearly."

The man stilled, his terrified eyes fixing on her. "I have only one message to deliver, witch," he said, his voice hoarse. "Surrender to the Tsar's mercy, and he shall spare half of your people."

Anger rose in Merydith's throat. Teeth bared, she pressed down with her blade, until blood ran from the man's cheek. Silently, she fought the urge to skewer him, aware her people were watching. Whatever crimes the Tsar had committed, she must not let herself sink to his level, lest she become the monster she fought to destroy.

With an effort of will, she withdrew her sword and stepped back. "We reject your terms. Northland will stand to the last against evil."

Turning, Merydith started back towards her people, leaving the man lying in the muck.

His words chased after her, echoing up the hill to the watchers beyond. “Then you will all burn!”

She glanced back, and saw him flinch from the rage in her eyes. “Then you will burn with us.”

35

It took a day and a night for the Stalkers to lead Quinn into the Tsar's camp. Quinn had been surprised to learn the army was already in Trola, but the other Stalkers had been able to ascertain the Tsar's location using their connection to him through their silver bracelets. Their horses were puffing hard by the time the sun broke over their company. Zarent signalled a halt as they topped a rise and looked down at the army camped in the valley below.

Sitting on his horse with his hands tied to the pommel, Quinn realised with a conflicted heart that they had arrived just in time to witness the final battle. Already the Tsar's forces were gathering at the head of the valley, above which the Queen had set her fortifications. An earthen rampart impeded Quinn's view of the rest of the camp, but several hundred soldiers could be seen waiting, their eyes on the army below.

"We're just in time," one of his former Stalkers said with a grin. "Maybe you'll get lucky, *Lieutenant.* The Tsar might send you to the front lines, to die with honour."

Quinn smiled darkly. "Maybe he'll send *you.*"

The Stalker's eyes burned into Quinn. "If my Tsar requires it of me, I will ride into battle with laughter on my lips."

"Of course you would," Quinn spat. "I doubt you've ever had an original thought in that tiny brain of yours."

The Stalker bared his teeth, but the boom of drums drew their attention back to the battlefield. On the hillside beneath the Northland army, a single figure could be seen retreating back to the mass of men and women camped in the valley.

"Guess the negotiations fell through," Quinn commented dryly.

"Let's go," Zarent snapped from the front, urging his horse forward.

Another Stalker held Quinn's reins, leaving him with no choice but to follow the others down the hillside. They rode down towards the camp, where a guard stationed on the outskirts moved to intercept them. The man quickly backed down, though, when he recognised the slick black uniforms of the Stalkers, and they continued on through the campsite, following the familiar layout that was used by the Tsar's army during all campaigns in hostile territory.

Anger coiled around Quinn's gut as they approached the massive tent erected in the centre of the camp. He wanted to hate the Tsar for this betrayal, to rage against Zarent and the other Stalkers, but in the end it was his own failure that had spelt his end. Yet again, the Tsar's children had eluded him. Now the time had come for him to face his judgement.

The other Stalkers dismounted outside the tent, but Quinn was forced to wait until Zarent came and cut his bonds. Clenching his fingers to restore their circulation, he glared down at the Stalker, before climbing from his saddle and joining the others on the ground. Two men took a firm grip on his shoulders and pushed him towards the entrance. Grinding his teeth, he shook them off and strode ahead of them.

Cursing, Zarent pushed past him and took the lead. Quinn followed a step behind as they approached the Tsar's tent. Two guards stood outside, but they parted without hesitation upon sighting the black-garbed Stalkers. A third stood within, spear held at the ready. He retreated into the gloom to announce their arrival. A moment later he reappeared, and waved them forward.

Standing on the threshold, Quinn hesitated. For a moment he wondered whether he should flee, if he should summon his power and blast the Stalkers from his path, and use the chaos that ensued to disappear into the hills. Yet even as he considered it, he dismissed the idea. His doom might wait within the darkness of the tent, but it was a doom to which he had dedicated his entire life. Whatever his fate, Quinn could not abandon the Tsar now, not when he was so close to his final goal.

Besides, where would he go? The Queen, with her reckless defence of Magickers, was anathema to him, and Devon and his Baronian thugs were even worse.

Straightening his shoulders, Quinn strode into the gloom of the tent. Zarent marched eagerly at his side, while the others waited without. Inside, the tent was huge, and it took a moment for Quinn's eyes to adjust. Marble tiles, packed in an oaken trunk and carried by the army each day, covered the floor, their smooth white surfaces a stark contrast to the churned-up mud that was the rest of the camp. A massive poster bed stood on the far side of the tent, while two iron braziers burned to either side of them.

In the middle of the Tsar's quarters, the man himself sat at an ornate table fashioned from polished steel. He looked up as they entered, a frown on his face. There was a plate before him, heaped with steak and sliced potato. Finishing his mouthful, he sat back in his chair and steepled his fingers.

"Lieutenant," he said, ignoring Zarent. "I take it you have news for me."

Surprised at the Tsar's casual words, Quinn glanced at Zarent. The other man said nothing though, just stood staring at the Tsar, his face hard. Clearing his throat, Quinn faced the table. "Ahh, no, sir, you ordered us to return?"

The Tsar stilled at his words, his brow knotting into a frown. "Did I?" he asked, his voice dangerously low. "And how, pray, did I do that?"

"You…you appeared to us, sir," Quinn replied, his stomach suddenly a knotted mess. "You ordered Zarent to take command, and bring me here to face your judgement…didn't you?"

"I did not," the Tsar rumbled.

Face dark, he came slowly to his feet. Quinn opened his mouth, searching for a way of explanation. Around him, the temperature in the tent plummeted, as though all substance were being drawn away. He staggered, his breath misting on the air as he struggled to inhale. Strength fled his muscles as the Tsar walked slowly around the table towards him.

"I…I…it was him!" Clutching at the lifeline that was the other Stalker, Quinn stabbed a finger at Zarent.

Zarent stood staring back, his face impassive, his sapphire blue eyes fixed on the Tsar. Quinn frowned, sensing a wrongness to the man…

"I grow weary of your ineptitude, Lieutenant," the Tsar grated as he came to a stop in front of Quinn. "I have been patient, given you chance after chance, but this final disappointment...it cannot be forgiven."

Blue fire appeared in his palm as he raised his hand. Its heat radiated through the tent, the only warmth in the suddenly frigid air. Quinn gasped, his mind racing, struggling to put sense to what the Tsar was saying.

"We...were tricked!" he gasped.

He tried to inhale, to regain his strength, but it was as though all substance had been drained from the air. His legs shook, and then collapsed beneath him, sending him toppling to the ground. Chest heaving, he looked up at the flame dancing in the Tsar's hand.

"Of course you were, Lieutenant," the Tsar murmured. "Now, goodbye."

"Don't!"

The Tsar swung around as a high-pitched voice shouted from across the tent. His eyes straining, Quinn struggled to find the speaker. He frowned, unable to make sense of the light swirling around Zarent. Then suddenly his vision seemed to clear and the lights faded away. Quinn blinked, struggling to comprehend what he was seeing. Zarent had vanished. In his place now stood the boy, Braidon, his arms folded and sapphire eyes burning with spent magic.

"Please, father," he said, taking a step towards the Tsar. "This is not his fault."

"My son," the Tsar said softly. The fire in his hands died as he faced the boy. "So it was *you* who tricked my lieutenant."

"I needed a way to find you."

The Tsar looked around, searching the tent. "And where, pray, is your sister?"

"Safely away from here," he replied.

"Really?" The Tsar's cocked his head. "That seems unlike her." He raised a hand.

"Stop!"

Quinn looked around as another voice spoke from the corner of the tent. For a moment, he saw nothing, and then Alana stepped forward, a swirling mist falling away from her as she moved.

"I'm here, Father," she said, her eyes on the floor.

"A happy reunion," the Tsar murmured, turning back to Braidon. "You impress me, my son. But pray, what sudden change of heart has brought my children before me?"

"We didn't come here to fight," Alana said, stepping towards the Tsar.

Before she could come close, he lifted a hand and pointed it at her chest. The gesture froze her in place, and Quinn recognised the familiar look of panic on her face as the Tsar's power trapped her. Her mouth opened and closed, but nothing more than a squeak came out. Quietly, Quinn rose to his feet and edged backwards into the shadows.

"I spared your life at Enala's request, daughter, but you no longer play a part in this," the Tsar said. He turned back to Braidon, leaving Alana immobilised. "Now, why have you come, my son?"

Reaching into his belt, Braidon drew a short sword. He stared at the blade for a moment as though deep in thought. Then he tossed it aside.

"My sister thought we might take you by surprise," he said solemnly. "I never thought it would work." He took a step towards the Tsar. "I thought I would call on your mercy, instead."

"My mercy?" the Tsar murmured.

Braidon swallowed. "Yes, Father," he replied. "I know

my past now, I've seen the truth. I know you love me, love both of us in your own way."

"And how do you know this, my son?"

"I remember..." Braidon's voice broke, and Quinn glimpsed tears in his eyes. "I remember a day you took me to the top of the citadel, and showed me our world. You told me that everything you did, you did it for us. Was it not true?"

Shadows hid the Tsar's eyes as he shook his head. "Ah, my son, how I have yearned all these years for you to stand at my side." Moving across the room, he knelt beside Braidon and placed a hand on the boy's shoulder. "I remember that day well. It was the day of my greatest despair, when I thought I had failed."

"What do you mean?"

"That was the day I learned the Sword of Light was not enough to accomplish what I desired, that I would need the power of the other Elements to succeed."

"But why did you despair? You had already claimed the power of one God as your own."

"Because I knew I did not have the strength to do what was needed."

Braidon swallowed. "You knew we would have to be sacrificed."

"Ay," the Tsar replied, standing. "On that day I discovered the true weakness of humanity: not magic or hate or war, but love."

"No," the boy murmured. He tried to take a step back, but the Tsar's magic bubbled through the air, freezing him on the spot.

"Yes," the Tsar whispered. "Fickle, relentless, *dangerous*, it was love that stopped me then. But not now, not ever again." Steel hissed on leather as the Tsar reached down and drew the Sword of Light and Earth.

"Father?" Braidon whispered, staring up at the man.

Tears shone in the Tsar's eyes as he towered over the boy. "Oh, my son," he said, his voice taut. "How this pains me, but I will not stop now. The stakes are too great. My enemies surround me, but with your death, their powers will be dust in the wind before us."

Fear showed on Braidon's face as he struggled in his father's bindings. "Please, you don't have to do this, Father!"

"But I do," the Tsar replied. He raised the Sword, studying the flickering green and white light emanating from the blade. "It is the only way. Jurrien will not possess your sister. Only you can host the God of the Sky. I am sorry, my son, but you must die to seal magic's fate."

36

The Tsar's envoy had barely reached the bottom of the hill before the southern army began to move, its ranks advancing to the rhythmic stomping of boots. Merydith watched from her vantage point atop the earthen ramparts for a few moments, and then retreated beyond the line of Trolan defenders.

"Your mount, Your Majesty," Mokyre said, stepping forward and handing her the reins of her horse.

Merydith nodded her thanks and swung into the saddle. After taking a moment to adjust her buckler, she straightened. Around her, four thousand northern soldiers did the same. The soft whinny of horses whispered across the hilltop, coupled with the ring of steel and creaking of leather.

"Are we ready?" Merydith asked as Mokyre appeared alongside her, freshly mounted.

He nodded, and she turned to look for Betran. She found him standing nearby, his lips twisted in a grim frown. Edging her horse towards him, she shouted to draw his attention.

"Don't look so miserable, Betran," she called when he looked up. "The day is finally here that you get to spit in the face of the Tsar!"

"Oh I know it," said Betran, forcing a smile. "I'm just disappointed I don't get the first stab at him."

"Your time will come, my friend," Merydith replied, though she knew the man did not mean the words.

She glanced back to where the Northland clans were still forming up. Beyond the horses, she could just make out the red steeple of the Magickers' tent. The day's efforts would hinge on not just the courage of those on the battlefield, but on Helen and her people. If they failed, Merydith's gamble would fail with it, and they would all be left exposed to the Tsar's power.

From beyond the ramparts, a distant bugle call drifted up to them. One of the soldiers on watch glanced back at them, his eyes wide with fear. "They're coming!" he called.

Merydith nodded and lifted the gold-enamelled helmet from her saddle. She placed it on her head and then drew her sword. But as she opened her mouth to shout the order to advance, a cry came from behind her, followed by the *thump* of hooves approaching. She swung around, her determination giving way to sudden fear as she saw Damyn riding up.

His face was pale and streaks of red still stained his eyes, but he sat straight in the saddle, a sabre resting across his pommel. He wore no helmet, but his chainmail shone in the morning light. A smile touched his lips when their eyes met, and Merydith's heart gave another twang as she realised there would be no talking him out of joining the fight. Murdo came up behind him, his face more alive than she'd seen it in a decade.

"Save me from the folly of men," Merydith muttered under her breath as the two drew up beside her.

"Were you going to leave without me?" Damyn asked, his voice tight. There was still a greyness to his face, and she wondered where he'd found the strength to leave his stretcher.

Merydith edged her horse closer to the two. "Please don't do this, Damyn," she whispered, trying to keep the panic from her voice. She looked at Murdo, seeking an ally, but the old man only shook his head and gestured at Damyn.

"Please don't try and stop me, Merydith," he replied, his voice shaking slightly. "I can't…I can't just lie here and wait to find out what happens. If we…" His voice broke and he shook his head. "I have to do this."

Understanding touched Merydith as she saw the fear behind his eyes, and she nodded quickly. "Stay close, my guards will protect you." Before he could respond, she turned and lifted her sword once more. "For freedom!"

Trumpets rang out from their camp, and as one, the northern cavalry surged forward. Up the earthen rampart they raced, and down the other side where planks had been tossed across a section of the trench. Then they were on the open hillside for all to see, racing down towards their approaching foe.

Below, the Tsar's forces were already halfway up the hill-side, but their charge faltered when they glimpsed the cavalry come pounding into view. The glee on their faces turned to sudden terror as realisation spread through their ranks. In their eagerness to reach the defenders, they had broken ranks and charged in open formation.

A grin touched Merydith's face as she urged her steed onwards, watching as the panic spread through the Tsar's ranks. The southerners had expected Merydith to hide behind her barricades and wait for them to come to her. Now they found themselves facing a charging horde, the frontmost soldiers were hurriedly staggering to a stop. Some even tried to turn back, but the ranks of soldiers coming up behind prevented them from fleeing the field.

As chaos descended on the southern army, Merydith swung towards the right, so that their charge would strike the enemy's flank. Sabre raised in one hand, the reins in the other, she shouted a cry as the last few yards vanished in the blink of an eye.

Then she was amongst them, her sword hacking and cutting, her momentum hardly faltering as her mount smashed aside a man and trampled him beneath iron-shod hooves. A crash like thunder echoed across the hillside as the rest of her cavalry struck, sweeping aside the leading ranks of footmen like leaves before the autumn winds.

Screaming a battle cry, Merydith charged on. Those beyond the first ranks were still struggling to link shields, and they collapsed inwards as she sliced through their midst. A desperate rage built in Merydith's chest as a man leapt at her, grabbing at her leg and trying to drag her from the saddle. Her sabre flashed down, half-severing his arm before dancing clear. Another cried out as she plunged it through his eye.

Suddenly her horse went down, but she leapt free of the saddle and rolled to break her fall. Surging to her feet, she deflected a wild blow from a charging soldier and then drove her blade into his chest.

Tearing it clear, she swung around and saw one of her men topple from his saddle. The horse reared, scattering the enemy, and she leapt for it. From the corner of her eyes she saw a scarlet-caped Plorsean raise his sword and begin to swing, then Damyn charged into view, and the man disappeared in a flash of hooves.

Catching the riderless horse by the reins, Merydith swung herself into the saddle. She nodded her thanks as Damyn pressed closer. Amidst the sudden calm, she looked around, surprised to find them deep in the enemy formation. Behind them was a broken field of corpses, while ahead the endless ranks of the Tsar's army stretched on towards his distant tent.

A shout came from away to their left, and glancing around, Merydith saw the leftmost ranks of the Tsar's force pressing forward to sweep across the hillside. If they succeeded, the northerners would be cut off from their camp, their flanks exposed. With the impetus of their charge broken, the Tsar's forces would be free to surround them, and cut them down at will.

Watching the advancing ranks, Merydith held her breath, and sent up a silent prayer to the Gods—and Helen. For a moment it seemed time stood still, and she sat there in silence, watching the slow advance of the soldiers as they crossed the hillside behind them, like a giant set of jaws stretching out to swallow the northern soldiers.

Then a *boom* echoed across the churned-up hillside. The sound swept through the battle like a ripple on a lake, as every man and woman paused to seek out its source. Confusion appeared on the faces of those around her, and even Damyn looked in the direction of the Tsar's tent with fear.

A terrible scream tore from the earth as the earthquake struck, hurling men and women from their feet. Merydith's horse screamed and bucked beneath her, but she dragged back on its reins, refusing to give it a second's control. Around her, the northerners struggled to do the same.

An ear-rending *boom* echoed across the battlefield like

thunder, drawing the eyes of all to the hilltop. Together as one, they watched as the earth itself split in two, and a crack raced down towards the Tsar's army. Screams came from the men gathered there, but it was amongst them before any could regain their feet and flee. Like an axe parting a melon, it tore through the centre of the Tsar's forces, hurling hundreds into the void and continuing down the valley towards the distant camp.

Slowly the thunder of the earth faded away, to be replaced by the screams of the dying. Drawing back on the reins of her unfamiliar mount, Merydith brought the gelding under control. Her guards were already doing the same, and she glimpsed Damyn and Murdo nearby, their eyes on the damage Helen and her Magickers had wrought.

Steeling herself, Merydith turned to examine the aftermath of their magic. A gaping crevice now split the slope leading down from their camp, dividing the Tsar's forces clean in two. The left flank that had sought to encircle them was now trapped on the other side of the gulf.

Merydith looked back at the ranks ahead of them.

And smiled.

THE NEXT DAY FOUND DEVON AND THE BARONIANS ON THE road north. Corrie and his Trolans trailed behind them in broken clusters, unorganised and unprepared for the march to come. Within an hour, they were lagging well behind, and Devon was forced to call a stop and wait for the intermittent groups to catch up.

Watching them trail up the hill, he was reminded of Selina's words from the night before. He cursed beneath his breath as Corrie marched up with the last group. Overhead the sun was shining, its warmth already banishing the frost that had set in overnight.

"You're in a bad mood this morning," Joseph said as he joined Devon.

Devon mumbled something unintelligible, but the Baronian only laughed and slapped him on the back.

"Saw Selina leaving your tent last night," Quint replied. "That have anything to do with it?"

"The woman's got a way of getting under a man's skin," Devon grunted.

"That she does," the Baronian agreed. "Usually because she's right, of course."

"Well in that case, you might be interested to hear she wants me to lead all of you, and all of *them*." He waved in the general direction of the Trolans. "Against the Tsar's army."

"Wonderful," Joseph replied. "You think I could reconsider that mutiny?"

"You'd be more than welcome."

Joseph shook his head. "We're already on our way, aren't we?"

"Afraid so," Devon nodded.

"You know he has dragons, right?"

"Yes."

"And demons.

"Yup."

"Magickers too. Don't suppose Alana and her brother have shown up in the night?"

"No," Devon murmured.

Joseph drew his axe from his shoulders and gave it a practice swing. His face twitched, but otherwise his injury didn't seem to bother him. He took a moment to inspect the blade before turning back to Devon.

"You really think the Trolans will follow you?"

"We're about to find out," Devon muttered. Drawing *kanker*, he strode across to where Corrie was sitting with several other Trolans.

The man looked up as he approached, his face darkening. "What do you want, Butcher?"

Devon took a moment to inspect the man before allowing his gaze to travel on, taking in the half dozen men that surrounded him. "Listen up!" he bellowed, his voice carrying across the road to where the other Trolans were gathered. Several faces turned to stare at him. "I'm sure you've all heard about me by now."

"Ay, they've heard," Corrie growled, stepping in front of him. "But they don't need to hear *from* you."

"That's too bad," Devon snapped. Corrie opened his mouth to object, but Devon's hand flicked out, catching him by the shirt. He dragged him close and stared into his terrified eyes. "Listen up, sonny," he murmured. "Whatever you think of me, you can keep on thinking it. Tomorrow. But for today, the past, the future, they don't exist. Because if the Tsar wins, you'll all be dead. Trola will burn. Northland will burn. And there will be no one left to remember any of us. Understand?"

His eyes wide, Corrie's head jerked up and down.

Releasing him, Devon straightened and looked out over the gathered Trolans. "I know you hate me," he started. "I don't blame you. But as I just told your young leader here, today we must set aside our differences. Today, I am not the enemy." He lifted a hand to point the way ahead. "Today, our enemy is the Tsar, and he will destroy us all if we cannot stand together."

"What do you want from us, Butcher?" a voice called from the back of the crowd.

Devon sighed. "I am no king, no general," he replied, "but I understand our enemy, and how he works. These people behind me, they're Baronians." A whisper spread through the crowd at his words. Devon drew *kanker* and lifted it above his head. "*Silence!*" He bellowed. He pointed his hammer at the shocked watchers. "These Baronians, they have already fought against the Tsar, against his Stalkers, against his dragon. Together, we struck a blow against the enemy, and then fled through the mountains. They have followed me through hell and back, and they're still here. Do you know why?"

His gaze swept the gathered Trolans, but not a one of them spoke. He smiled.

"They're here because my name is Devon, and I do not lose."

A cheer erupted from the Baronians behind him as he thrust *kanker* skywards. Looking around, he glimpsed Selina standing amongst them, the slightest hint of a smile on her lips. She nodded as their eyes met, and grinning, he turned back to the Trolans. Silence fell as he lowered his weapon.

"Today, I march against the Tsar. Who will follow me?"

37

Quinn shivered as ripples formed around the Tsar, sheer energy pouring from his outstretched hands, seeming to bend the very fabric of reality. His chant whispered through the tent, incomprehensible, and yet it sent a tingling down to Quinn's very core. He could feel the magic building, coalescing around the boy in the centre of it all.

Sadness touched him as he looked at Braidon. Alana had always kept him at an arm's length from the boy, but seeing the terror in his steely eyes, Quinn felt a wave of pity for him. The boy had come here to call on his father's love. How it must pain him to see now it was not enough, that the Tsar would sacrifice everything he loved to bring about the change he sought.

Tearing his gaze from the boy, Quinn found himself looking at Alana. She barely seemed to notice him, so intent was she on her brother. Teeth bared, the veins on her neck bulging, she strained against the forces holding her in place.

Quinn grinned despite himself, and crossed to where she stood.

"You cannot save him," he murmured. He circled her, barely able to contain his glee at her sorrow. "You cannot even save yourself."

"Quinn," she whispered. "Please, he never did anything to you. Help him."

"Never," Quinn hissed. "The boy may be innocent, but you are not. You brought this on for the both of you, Alana. I—"

He broke off as the ground beneath his feet began to shake. Staggering sideways, he thrust out a hand, using Alana to steady himself. Locked in the Tsar's magic, she didn't so much as stumble. Slowly the shaking faded away, and he straightened. Quinn jerked back his hand as he realised he was still touching Alana and could have been influenced by her magic, but she only had eyes for her brother.

"What was that?" In the centre of the tent, the Tsar had broken off his chanting and was looking towards the Queen's army.

"Let me check," Quinn said quickly, springing to the doorway of the tent.

Ducking outside, he glanced at the stunned faces of the Stalkers, then at the battlefield. His jaw dropped as he took in the jagged tear in the hillside. Half the Tsar's force had been stranded on the green fields on one side, while those on the left were battling furiously with the mounted forces of the Northland Queen.

"What do we do?" one of the Stalkers was saying.

Quinn shook himself free of his shock and swung on the man. "Join the battle," he snapped, pointing up at the hill. "The Tsar is already engaged in the final summons. When he's done, the Queen and her people will be wiped from the field. In the meantime, make sure she's occupied."

His group of Stalkers stared at him, before one stepped forward, a sneer on his lips. "You forget yourself, Quinn," he said. "You're not lieu—"

He never got to finish his sentence, as Quinn's blade plunged through his throat. Dragging back the sword, Quinn glared at the others. "Any other objections?"

As one, the remaining Stalkers turned and fled in the direction of the battle. Quinn followed their progress, wondering whether he should take the chance to escape. It was only a matter of time before the Tsar finished with his work and remembered Quinn's folly. Then there would be a reckoning, one which he was unlikely to survive.

Yet if the Tsar succeeded, there would be nowhere in the Three Nations Quinn could run that he would not be found. Closing his eyes, he returned to the darkness of the tent.

"What's happening out there?" the Tsar demanded. He was at the table now, an assortment of potions and herbs sprawled across its surface.

"The Queen's Magickers have struck. I sent my Stalkers to deal with them," Quinn said quickly.

The Tsar waved a hand. "The Queen will wait, this cannot." Returning to his concoctions, he began mixing ingredients into a mortar.

"Quinn, help me."

Quinn looked around as the boy's voice whispered through the darkness. Swallowing, he clenched his fists. Help him? The boy had tricked him, sentenced him to the same fate as his own. Teeth clenched, he watched as the Tsar worked, as outside the distant roar of voices and clashes of steel carried through the camp.

Finally the Tsar lifted the mortar and held the contents up to the light of a lantern. Nodding to himself, he moved across to where Braidon still stood frozen. He came to a stop before the boy, his face twisted in regret.

"I'm sorry it has to be this way, my son," he murmured.

Braidon's eyes flashed with sudden anger. "Just do it!" he snapped.

Nodding, the Tsar reached out and grabbed his son by the jaw. Forcing his head back, he poured half the contents of the mortar down Braidon's throat, then held his mouth and nose until he was forced to swallow. Then he moved away, and swallowed the remaining potion in one gulp.

The chanting resumed as the Tsar wandered the room, the Sword of Light and Earth now gripped firmly in his hand. Light flickered from the blade, at first brilliant and blinding, then dimming to barely more than a spark.

He returned to stand before the boy and gripped Braidon by the shoulder. His voice grew louder, and finally Quinn understood the words he spoke. Magic bubbled through the tent, and Quinn flinched back at its touch, his own magic boiling up in response. It gathered in the air between the Tsar and his son as the Tsar's voice boomed out:

"I summon you, God of the Sky." At his words, a moan rose up from Braidon's chest. He stiffened, his face taking on a look of terror as he sought to tear himself from his father's grip. "I summon you, Jurrien, return to this mortal realm," the Tsar continued. "I bid you, take host in this vessel, in the body of the man marked by the name Theo. Take his mortal body and return your immortal soul to this world."

Quinn's heart lurched forward at the Tsar's words. Standing there, he struggled to understand whether he'd heard them correctly. He took half a step forward, but the magic pressed against him, forcing him back. Stretching out a hand, he tried to call a warning, but it was already too late. With a triumphant shout, the Tsar slammed his hands together.

A blue light burst into life, blinding, crackling with untold energy. Quinn felt a part of himself respond, drinking it in, his magic exhilarating in the touch of its creator. He gasped as the power of the Storm God swept through him—and then went rushing away. Swirling about the room, the blue light coalesced into a single stream, flowing inwards to a point between the Tsar and his son.

Then with a flash, it vanished.

Letting out a long breath, the Tsar stepped back from Braidon and lifted the Sword of Light and Earth. Braidon stared back at him, his grey eyes shining with a new light, with the triumph of victory. A frown touched the Tsar's forehead as he looked around, saw the horror on Quinn's face, and the joy radiating from the eyes of his two children.

"What is it?" he growled.

"You...you said your own name," Quinn whispered.

The Tsar stared at him blankly, uncomprehending. Before he could respond, a harsh laughter rang through the tent, drawing their attention back to where Braidon stood. Except it was no longer Braidon who stood there.

It was Alana.

A smirk twisting her lips, she folded her arms and raised an eyebrow. "Surprised, boys?"

38

Merydith cursed as her sword caught in the chest of an enemy soldier and was torn from her grip. Screaming, the woman fell back, but another leapt forward to take her place, his spear driving through the thigh of Merydith's horse. The beast screamed and fell, hurling Merydith from the saddle. She came up, dagger in hand, and braced herself as the spearman charged—only for one of her guards to run in and drive a sword through his heart.

Her guard scooped up a discarded blade and tossed it her way. She caught it by the hilt and spun to block a blow from another soldier. Her guard moved alongside her, but another spear came flashing from the ranks of soldiers, taking him in the throat. He staggered back, blood bubbling from the wound, and collapsed alongside her.

Sword and dagger in hand, Merydith killed the second spearman, then leapt back as three red-cloaked soldiers charged her. Movement came from her sides and Damyn and Mokyre stepped up. They had lost their horses as well, and a quick glance told Merydith most of her force were fighting on foot now.

Steel clashed as they met the Plorseans. Turning aside a stabbing sword with her buckler, Merydith lashed out with her adopted sword, catching her assailant beneath the arm. She dragged back the blade as the man cried out, staggering sideways into one of his comrades. Damyn took advantage of the confusion to finish them both, as Mokyre drove his blade through the heart of the soldier to Merydith's left.

Together they pressed forward into the ranks of southern soldiers, desperately trying to turn back the tide of scarlet and emerald. Despite being cut off from half their number, the Tsar's force still stood strong, and was now beginning to press them back. Inch by inch, the ragged front Merydith's people had formed was bowing beneath the pressure.

Only around their Queen did the northerners still stand their ground. But with both flanks bending back, the Tsar's soldiers were beginning to spread out around her force. If the line was not reinforced, their greater numbers would envelope her people in a ring of iron.

"Forward!" she called, desperately willing her people to hold.

A few of those nearby heard the call and hurled themselves into the battle with renewed fury, but those on the flanks were too far away. The line continued to bend, and she sensed the will of her army flickering, about to give.

Then a cry echoed down the hillside behind them. Merydith glanced back, her heart lifting as she saw Betran and his Trolans streaming down towards them. They split in two, reinforcing the flanks to either side of Merydith. With a roar, they hurled themselves into the battle, and the line straightened.

Merydith shared a grin with Damyn. "We're not done yet!" she shouted over the clash of blades, clapping him on the shoulder.

His face pale, Damyn nodded. Looking for all the world like a dead man walking, he lifted his sword. "Haven't won yet either."

Nodding, Merydith gave his shoulder a squeeze and released him. Stepping back into line, she hurled herself at the enemy with renewed vigour. Damyn joined her, fighting mechanically now, while to her left Mokyre moved with a deadly efficiency. Each time his sword flashed out, an enemy fell back, more often than not clutching at some mortal wound.

Time stretched out unending, but for every southern soldier they slew, another was ready to step forward, fresh and ready for the fight. Hope withered in Merydith's heart as she realised they weren't going to break. The cavalry charge, the earthquake, the Trolan reinforcements, none of them had succeeded in shattering the enemy spirit. Still outnumbered two to one, the only thing the rebels had left to give was their lives.

Merydith's only consolation was the Tsar had not attacked. In splitting his army in two, Helen and her people had burned through most of their strength. Now every man and women on the hillside lay exposed to the Tsar's power.

And yet he had not sought retribution.

Struggling to catch her breath, she stepped back from the line, nodding as another soldier took her place. She looked out over the heads of the enemy, to where their camp stretched out down the valley. The Tsar's tent was easily seen from her vantage point, but it remained silent, dark. A shiver touched her as she looked at the men and women fighting below. Clearly, the Tsar would rather spend their lives to destroy her, rather than waste his own power on so trivial a matter.

A cry went up from the wall of soldiers ahead, and then Damyn was staggering back, Murdo draped over his shoulder. Her heart lurched as she raced forward and helped lower the old man to the ground.

"Murdo!" she called, looking around for someone to carry him back to the camp.

But his eyelids were already fluttering closed, and with a long, rattling exhalation, he died. A sob tore from Merydith's chest as she scrunched her eyes closed, her hand locked in a death grip around the old man's shirt.

"*Damnit!*" she screamed.

In a rage she lurched to her feet and threw herself at the line of soldiers. Her blade flashed as she tore into the enemy. She felt the satisfying crunch of flesh giving way to steel, and watched as a man crumpled beneath the blow. Dragging back her weapon, Merydith advanced.

Men and women launched themselves at her with renewed fury, but her sword and dagger were like extensions of her own body now, their blades flashing out to steal away the lives of her enemies. Decades of training at the hands of Enala flowed through Merydith, turning her into a living weapon that sent opponents falling back in dismay.

But the battle had been raging for hours now, and even she could not last forever. As she began to slow, a man lurched forward, his sword opening up a cut on her arm. Crying out, she drove her dagger through his neck and staggered back. Mokyre leapt to her defence, his sword slamming into the thigh of the next soldier in line.

Gasping, Merydith straightened, surprised to find herself edged on either side by Trolan soldiers. Her gaze travelled back, taking in the scores of Northlanders lying fallen in their wake, the enemy staked high around them.

As she watched, her people on both flanks were thrust aside, and the Tsar's army rush through the gap.

"No," she whispered.

But it was already too late. With the flanks collapsing around them, her dwindling force was pressed back on itself, and surrounded within moments. Shields raised, the enemy launched themselves at their rear.

"Fighting square!" Merydith cried out, desperate now.

The men and women around her moved quickly, those on the flanks and rear of the force spinning to meet the threat. Many of her people had taken up shields from the enemy, and joining ranks, they presented a united front against the mass of humanity surrounding them. As one, the last of the northern army stood and faced the enemy gathering around them.

Her heart hammering, Merydith spun, seeking a way out. Less than two thousand men and women stood with her now. Trolans and Northlanders together as one, they showed no sign of fear as they faced the Tsar's soldiers, though they knew now there was no way out.

Movement came from the ranks of soldiers ahead of Merydith as their line parted, emitting the Tsar's envoy to the front. The two forces were separated now by several yards, and wearing a slick smile, the envoy took a step towards their line. Coming to a stop beside the body of a Northlander, he stared down at the corpse, then back at her.

"Tell me again, Queen, how we will all burn?" he asked softly.

Hatred for the man burned in Merydith's heart. She took a quick step forward and hurled her dagger. The smile on the envoy's face faltered as her blade embedded itself in his unprotected chest. He staggered sideways, looking down at the dagger in disbelief. Without another word, he slumped to the ground beside the dead Northlander.

"Who's next?" Merydith screamed, gesturing at the ranks of Plorsean and Lonian soldiers with her sword.

Not a soul spoke, but with a rattle of steel shields, the front ranks swept closed. A harsh crash rang out as they started forwards.

It was as though a bucket of cold water had been poured over Merydith's rage. Stepping back into line, she lifted her sword and readied herself. The gap between the two forces narrowed, the southern soldiers silent but for the trod of their boots. There were no battle cries or jeering now. The Northland army and their Trolan allies had paid for their respect in blood.

Smoothly, the lines came together, and the screams of the dying resumed.

39

Standing on the edge of the valley, Devon looked down at the battle raging below. The roar of a thousand voices whispered up to his vantage point, more like the buzz of insects than the sound of men and women dying. The morning on the road had stretched out, their progress slowed by the older members of the Trolan party. Now that they were finally here, Devon feared they may already be too late.

Below, a great fissure divided the battlefield in two. On one side, a great force could be seen on the march, seeking to find a way across to the battle raging on the other side. From what Devon could see, the crevice stretched out down the valley for well over a mile, dividing even the massive camp that had been set back from the battle.

On the side closest to Devon, the Queen's force stood surrounded by a sea of red and green cloaks. His heart pounded in his chest as he watched the Tsar's army surge forward, slamming into the ranks of the defenders and pressing them back upon one another. If something didn't change, the Queen would be overwhelmed within the hour.

"Still planning on helping out?" Joseph asked from beside him.

Stepping back from the edge, Devon turned and looked back at the thousand men and women gathered behind him. Their numbers had swollen as they came across more stragglers heading for the battle. Now, Baronians and Trolans alike watched him with fear in their eyes. They had not yet seen what waited below, but they could hear the distant screams, the bellowing of trumpets.

They had followed him this far, but he was still unsure whether they would take the final step, if they could set aside their grievances and find common cause with himself and the Baronians. Now though, the time had finally come to find out.

"The battle has been joined," Devon called out. "The Tsar's army has been sundered, but a mighty force still remains. They have the Queen and her people surrounded."

A nervous whispering spread through his followers, but he raised a hand, his eyes fixing them with a glare. Silence fell, and he went on.

"She is not finished yet. *We* are not finished yet."

Devon sucked in a lungful of air and drew *kanker* from its sheath. Looking out at the faces of those who had followed him across the mountains and through these rolling hills, he wondered how it had come to this. These men and women were farmers and potters, bakers and butchers—not soldiers. This was not their life, not their calling. And yet they looked at him with trust in their eyes, believing he would guide them through the coming storm.

Standing amongst the crowd, Selina's lips moved, mouthing the words: *Lead them.*

"I know many of you don't want to be here." The words were out of his mouth before he had time to consider what he was saying. "I know you would rather be safe in your homes, back with your families, anywhere but on this barren hillside. This isn't your place, but you're here anyway, ready to lay down your lives for what you believe in."

"And what do *you* believe in…Devon?" Corrie's voice emerged from the crowd of faces.

Devon smiled. "Love, life, a future for us all," he said simply, lifting *kanker* up in the sunlight. "This is *kanker*. You know it well. With it, I carved my name into your legends. But a legend needs an ending. Today, we will carve that ending in the blood of your enemies, and write a new future for the Trolan nation."

An eerie silence fell over the hillside as he lowered his weapon. All eyes seemed to shift to Corrie. The young man stared back at Devon, his eyes shining. Swallowing visibly, he reached down and drew his sword.

"For Trola!" he cried.

"*For Trola!*" the call echoed off the hillside, lifting Devon up, feeding him strength.

He shared a glance with Corrie. Then he turned and strode over the edge of the hill into the valley beyond.

And a thousand warriors followed after him.

40

Exhilaration swept through Alana as her brother's illusion melted away, revealing her to the room. Across from her, she watched her own face flicker, then vanish, revealing Braidon standing in her place. Beside her brother, horror was written across Quinn's face. Her father still stood poised in shock, struggling to comprehend what she'd just wrought.

She flashed him a smile. It had been so simple in the end. All she'd needed was physical contact, and just the slightest nudge with her magic. Anything more, and her father might have sensed her power, even through Braidon's illusion. But changing one word, one name, and her magic had slid by undetected.

And instead of inviting the Storm God into his son's body, the Tsar had summoned Jurrien into his own.

Alana watched with growing amusement as realisation came to her father.

"You…how?" he stammered.

Almost immediately, rage replaced his shock, and

raising the Sword, he started towards her. Before he could complete a step, however, a brilliant light flashed from his eyes, and he staggered sideways, a cry tearing from his lips.

"*No!*" he screamed, clutching at his skull, as though that could possibly save him from the Storm God.

"Not so fun now, is it Father?" she hissed, stepping towards him. "It's not fun, having someone else in your head. How does it feel, when it's *you* being controlled, when it's *your* mind being burnt away?"

Her father had sunk to his knees now. Another scream whipped the canvas as the Sword of Light and Earth slipped from his fingers. He scrambled for its hilt, but she kicked it away, and then drove her boot into his face, flipping him onto his back. Plucking her dagger from where she had tossed it while disguised as Braidon, she crouched beside him.

Groaning, the Tsar looked up and saw her kneeling there. "Please, daughter, help me!" His eyes flickered, the sapphire blue deepening for half an instant.

"Help you?" she hissed, pressing the dagger to his throat. "You were going to *destroy* me, to sacrifice my brother, *your own son*, all for what? So you could have ultimate power? And now, now you dare ask for my help?"

"Please," he choked, and Alana laughed in his face.

"Nothing was ever enough for you, was it Father? No matter how hard I tried, I was never strong enough, never fast enough, never smart enough. All my life, I tried to satisfy you, but now I see it was your own twisted pain that held us apart. You were always second-best to Eric's son, weren't you? To the *true* Magicker in the family. And even when you killed him, you still couldn't achieve what you had planned. Even with all the powers you had accumulated, even with the Sword of Light, still you wanted more." She laughed, the sound harsh and unforgiving.

She stood and stared down at him. "And where is your power now, father? Even after everything you have achieved, you are *nothing* to the Gods."

Her father stilled at her words. His eyes flickered again as he stared up at her, and with an effort of will he pulled himself to his knees. "You're wrong, Alana," he whispered. "I only ever wanted to save us."

"You wanted to save yourself."

"No…" he groaned, his eyes scrunching closed. "I can…feel him, taking control." He looked up at her again, open panic on his face now. "You can't let him live. He must…not, my daughter. His rage…he will destroy all of it, everything I have created."

"You have created nothing, Father," Alana hissed. "Besides, I have met Antonia. She only ever wanted to help us."

"The Storm God is not Antonia…" The Tsar swayed on his knees. "You think he will show you mercy, after what we have done to his siblings?"

"We?" Alana cried. "It was *you* who killed them!"

"Even so…"

The Tsar dragged himself to his feet. Air hissed between his teeth as he stood there. Alana could sense the power building within him now, the raw energies of the Storm God. Her father was fighting Jurrien with everything he had, no doubt draining the energies from all those in his thrall…but even the Tsar could not fight the power of creation.

"Goodbye, Father," she whispered, stepping back from him.

"Goodbye," Braidon echoed.

"Please, Alana—"

Her father's words were cut off as he stiffened, his eyes darkening to the deep blue of the Storm God. Lightning materialised around him, coalescing in his fingertips, staining the tent white. A howling wind came swirling from nowhere, tearing the tent poles from the earth and flinging the canvas skywards. The Tsar's guards cried out as the black fabric slammed into them, hurling them from their feet.

Standing so close, Alana was forced to her knees by the power of the wind. The temperature plummeted as rain hissed into existence and then froze in an instant. Ice lashed at her face as she strained to see through the swirling vortex that had appeared around her father. Amidst the tempest, she could still see the glow of his eyes, sense the rage that burned behind them. Her ears popped as the pressure built.

"*Where are my siblings?*" The words came from the Tsar's mouth, but it was no longer her father's voice. They boomed across the camp, freezing all who heard it in place.

"Jurrien, we are not your enemies!" Alana had to yell to be heard.

"*Where is my sister? Where is my brother?*" the Storm God screamed.

"Here!" a voice cried from behind the God.

Squinting through the vortex, Alana saw Quinn the second before he acted. The warning was on her lips as he lifted the Tsar's Sword from the ground and leapt. White and green rippled from the blade as it slammed into Jurrien's back.

In an instant, the lightning vanished, the roar of thunder dying away. The wind fell to a whisper, and the soft patter of falling sleet whispered in Alana's ears. Light flashed from her father's eyes one last time as his brow wrinkled in surprise.

A final *boom* sounded, then her father's body slumped to the ground, the blade that had ended his life tearing free.

Mouth wide, Alana stared as Quinn lifted the Sword, his face lit by the flickering white, green, and blue of its power.

41

Fully engaged with the Queen and her soldiers, the Tsar's forces didn't notice Devon barrelling down on them until he was just a few yards away. At the last second, a shout went up from a scarlet-cloaked soldier, but there was no time for them to re-form, and bellowing a war cry, Devon brought his hammer down on the man's skull. The rest of his people followed him, the momentum of their charge driving them deep into the disorganised ranks of the enemy's rear.

Reversing his swing, Devon smashed *kanker* into the chest of another soldier, hurling the man from his feet. Striding into the gap he'd created, Devon lashed out around him, each swipe of his weapon downing another soldier. His people poured into the gap after him, forming a wedge with Devon at its tip.

Then Joseph was alongside him, Selina on the other, and together the three of them sliced forward through the Tsar's forces. Already he could see men beginning to panic, their courage strained to breaking point by the new turn of events. On his left, Joseph was like death itself, his twin-bladed axe rising and falling with terrifying proficiency, while Selina seemed to dance through the southern soldiers like grace embodied. They fell to her blade all the same.

In the ranks ahead, frightened soldiers tried to pull back, terrified of finding themselves crushed between the Queen and this new threat. Beyond, Devon glimpsed the Queen herself. Wearing her gold-embossed half-helm, she hefted a sword in each hand and led her people against the mass of soldiers separating them, fury written across her face.

Throwing himself back into the fight, Devon was swallowed up by the fury of combat. His thoughts, his heartbeat, everything fell away before the rhythm of the battle. A screaming man came at him and died, then another and another, each falling to a single blow.

Joseph and Selina struggled to stay with him as he surged forward, forcing the Tsar's soldiers back. Selina staggered as a blade sliced her arm, but Joseph downed the man with a swing of his axe. Towering over Selina, he dragged her back to her feet.

Devon was barely aware of his comrades' plight. As they pressed the enemy back, his eyes alighted on the black tent peaking up from the campsite. His heart beat faster as he recognised the tent of the Tsar from his days in the civil war. It was there that the battle would be won or lost. Why had the man not acted yet…?

A flash of blue light suddenly lit the distant tent, then a clap of thunder seemed to shake the very earth. Around Devon, men and women froze, turning to stare at the distant campsite. As they watched, the Tsar's tent seemed to lift from its support, as some invisible force hurled it skyward and then sent it crashing down again some half-mile away.

There was a moment's silence as the opposing forces

stood staring at the scene in shock. Unsure of what would come next, they stood waiting for the Tsar to show himself, to hurl his wrath down on the Queen and her allies.

But nothing came, and hefting his hammer, Devon shouted a cry.

"Get em!"

It might not have been the most creative speech, but around him the Trolans and Baronians roared and threw themselves at the enemy. Still stunned by their Tsar's absence, the southern soldiers fell back in disarray. An echoing shout went up from the Queen as the Northland army pressed the attack from the other side.

Leaping forward, Devon pushed ahead once more, carving a path through the gathered bodies. For a moment it seemed as though the enemy would hold. Then a man appeared before Devon, his eyes wide with terror. Glimpsing the giant warrior descending on him, he gave a terrified scream and threw down his sword.

"Run!"

His scream carried through the Tsar's ranks like the plague as others picked up the call. Suddenly, what had been a battle turned into a rout, as half the enemy turned tail and fled. Those who remained found themselves alone, surrounded. Devon's people swarmed over them like ants, and they vanished beneath hacking swords and axes.

Across the battlefield, the Queen's soldiers chased the fleeing men, driving them back towards the camp. Men and women stumbled amidst the tents, tripping over canvas lines and scattering ashes from the morning's campfires. Flames leapt up amongst the broken army, and smoke swirled through the valley on broken winds.

Stumbling to a stop, Devon gasped, taking a moment to catch his breath. His people swept on around him, harrying the fleeing enemy, but he remained where he was. Looking back over the ground they had crossed, a chill spread to his stomach at the death he had left in his wake. Bodies covered the churned-up ground, many still moving, their desperate cries sounding on deaf ears. Hundreds of Trolans and Baronians lay amongst the fallen, but the Tsar's losses numbered in the thousands. Bile rose in his throat, and scrunching his eyes closed, Devon sank to his knees.

Baronians rushed past him, screaming their triumph. They leapt on the backs of fleeing soldiers and bore them to the ground. Overcome by their sudden victory, the Trolans ran with them, hacking and slashing at anyone they could find wearing the colours of Lonia or Plorsea. Scores of unarmed enemy were torn apart as they tried to surrender.

Horrified, Devon staggered back to his feet and bellowed an order. "Stop!"

But his cried went unheeded amidst the chaos, and the slaughter continued unabated.

"So the sheep become wolves," Joseph said, stumbling up beside him.

Devon was about to snap at the man, when the Baronian slumped to his knees. The words stuck in Devon's throat as he caught the man by the shoulder and knelt alongside him.

"What happened?" he asked urgently.

"Didn't see the bastard," Joseph coughed. Blood splattered his beard as he slumped into Devon's arms. "Got 'em though. We'll walk the dark path together, he and I."

"No, sonny," Devon growled. "Not today." Desperately he looked around, searching for help, but his slaughtering forces had moved on, chasing after the fleeing Plorseans.

Then movement came from nearby, and he let out a breath of relief as Selina appeared. She still carried her sword and blood coated her jerkin, but none of it appeared to be hers. She moved quickly through the corpse-strewn battleground and crouched alongside Devon. Ignoring him, she lifted Joseph's shirt, revealing the tear in his chainmail, and the gaping wound beneath. Blood pulsed down his side, feeding his life to the grassland.

"You were careless, axeman," she murmured, replacing his shirt.

"Too busy keeping an eye out for the boss," he grunted.

"Can you help him?" Devon snapped, lowering Joseph to his back.

Selina shook her head. Her lips twisted in a frown, she gently brushed the hair from Joseph's face. "No, Devon. He's not long for this world." Her eyes flickered up, looking from Devon to the distant screams. "But you are needed elsewhere."

Devon shivered at her words. Looking out at the slaughter, he shook his head. "You were right."

"No, I was wrong," Selina murmured sadly. Devon looked at her sharply, and she went on. "The farmers were as quick to the slaughter as you or I."

"Rubbish," Joseph coughed, blood dribbling down his cheek. "You…watch. Devon'll…lead 'em…home."

Devon squeezed the man's shoulder. "Thank you, Joseph," he said, "for giving me a place in this world."

Joseph forced a grin. "You're welcome, boy." He groaned, his face scrunching with pain. "Oh…" he murmured, "were I…a gambling man…I'd say your woman…had something to do with that." He extended a finger to indicate the Tsar's ruined tent.

Devon's heart clenched at the man's words. Staring out over the campsite, he held his breath, trying to catch a glimpse of what was going on. For a second, he saw flashing lights amongst the tents, but it quickly died back to nothing.

"He's right, Devon," Selina murmured, touching his shoulder.

"Go save the lass," Joseph breathed.

Devon stood. "If you knew her like I did, you'd know she doesn't need saving." His head whipped around as thunder crashed in the camp. "But perhaps she might need a hand."

42

"Quinn, what are you doing?" Alana whispered, staring at the Sword.

He seemed to take a long time to hear her words. Lowering the blade, he looked at her, a frown touching his forehead.

"Alana..." He said her name like it was foreign to him, as though he had all but forgotten her. Then his eyes hardened, and the Sword came up again, pointing at her from across the tiles that were all that remained of her father's tent. "You betrayed me!"

Instinctively, Alana hurled herself to the side. A bolt of lightning arced towards her and struck the tiles with an awful *boom.* Shards of marble sliced Alana's face as she rolled across the ground and came to her knees. Reaching for her sword, she swung around, readying herself for another attack.

But Quinn was standing staring at the Sword again, as though surprised by what he'd done. "Incredible," he murmured.

"Quinn, I am not your enemy," Alana shouted.

"No?" He glared at her, his eyes shining with the power of the Sword. "Then why are you the source of all my pain?"

Baring his teeth, he pointed the sword again. Alana tried to hurl herself aside once more, but it was not lightning that came for her this time. Vines tore through the tiles, rushing upwards to envelop her. Winding around her limbs, they lifted her from the ground and bound her tight. Suspended in the air, she watched as Quinn approached.

"Everywhere I look, everywhere I go, I find you, haunting me. Even when I thought you dead in an alleyway somewhere, there you were, fleeing with your brother across Plorsea. Even when I saved you from yourself, from your own father, you betrayed me, rejected me. And for what? That…that bumbling *brute?*"

Alana strained against the vines, but they held her like steel shackles. Slumping into their grasp, she looked at him with disgust. "I am not some prize for you to win, Quinn. All these years, I thought you were my friend."

"I *loved* you," Quin growled, his face just inches from hers. "I would have done *anything* for you."

"You're sick," Alana hissed. "Twisted, if you think this is what love is."

Quinn shook his head. "You still do not see." He lifted the Sword, his eyes drinking in its power. "But I do. I see *all* of it now. This thing, it is knowledge purified, the very essence of creation." He grinned at her. "Your father was a brilliant man, you know? I read of these blades, when I was young: Archon's greatest creation. But your father perfected them. Where your ancestors struggled with their powers, this Sword leaps to do my bidding."

A shout came from behind them, as forgotten, her

brother charged at him. Quinn spun, and a burst of flame rushing out towards Braidon. Crying out, he vanished, and the flames caught only empty air. Reappearing beside Quinn, he leapt for the Sword.

"Braidon, *no!*" Alana screamed.

Alerted by her cry, Quinn turned back. His fist caught Braidon in the forehead and hurled him to the ground. A gesture from the sword, and fresh vines sprang from the earth to bind him in place. Quinn stood over him a second, sword poised.

"Don't," Alana whispered. "Please."

Shaking himself, Quinn looked at her, a look of bewilderment in his eyes. "I wouldn't hurt the boy," he murmured.

"Thank you," she said, watching as he approached.

"I'm not evil, Alana," he replied. "You don't see it yet, but you will."

He lifted the Sword and held it in front of Alana's face. She squeezed her eyes closed, but even then its light burned dots in her vision.

"Please, don—"

Alana's words were cut off as the cold steel touched her forehead. A gasp tore from her as the Earth magic of the Sword entered her, burning into her mind. Like a wolf tracking its prey, it twisted through her thoughts, hunting out her memories, her consciousness, trapping them in bands of fire. She screamed as the flames swelled, as she felt her mind being consumed.

Unlike her own power, the God magic sought not to trap her memories and lock them away, but to erase them, to scorch them from her consciousness forever. It was like a holy fire, burning away all that its master considered blasphemy.

Tears streamed down Alana's face as she watched, helpless, as her memories of Devon burnt. His rescue, his bravery, his love, all of it was incinerated by the unyielding fire of the Sword. She screamed as her brother was enveloped, as Enala's weathered face was torn from her. Every piece of hope, of goodness she had kept locked away, was hunted out without mercy, condemned to the flames.

She sobbed as that other part of her, the one who had loved and grieved and felt joy, was murdered before her eyes, cried out until all that was left was the hard, unyielding woman her father had shaped her to be.

"There..." Quinn murmured, stepping back. "Now, we shall see."

Alana slumped to the ground as the vines unravelled from her arms and legs. She landed lightly, looking around to see her father's body, his blood pooling slowly on the marble tiles. She crouched beside him. With the loss of his magic, his face had aged, his hair turning white. Yet there was no mistaking the man who had raised her, who had fashioned her into the woman she was today.

"You always were a fool, Father," she said.

As she straightened, Alana saw the boy lying nearby, unconscious and still wrapped in vines. She felt a pang of recognition, but as she looked at his face, she could not recall ever seeing him before. A sword lay nearby and she collected it before turning to face Quinn. Blood stained the flickering blade he carried.

"So, you killed him?" she asked, gesturing at the Tsar.

The lieutenant shrugged, a weary grin on his lips. "It needed to be done."

Laughter bubbled up from Alana as she looked at the destruction around them. "You don't say?"

She moved to Quinn and wrapped her arms around his

waist. Standing so close to the Sword, she could feel its power bathing them both. The Earth magic at its core called out to her own, and she moaned as her own magic rose in response, filling her with the ecstasy of her power. Standing on her toes, she pulled Quinn down into a kiss.

Electricity leapt between them as their lips met, raising every hair on Alana's body. She gasped as Quinn drew her hard against him. Her hands danced along his back, tempting him to greater passions.

Then she paused, noticing the distant sounds of battle, the cry of voices drawing nearer. She pulled back from Quinn and looked around. The tents closest to them had been flattened by some explosion, giving them a clear view of the battlefield beyond the campsite. There, Plorsean and Lonian soldiers could be seen fleeing the field, as Northland soldiers gave chase.

"What is going on?" she murmured.

Before Quinn could reply, movement came from the nearby tents, and a giant of a man stepped into the open. The breath froze in Alana's throat as his amber eyes caught her gaze. She watched his features twist in surprise, even as her own heart leapt in her chest. In her arms, Quinn tensed, and she glanced at him, surprised to see the sudden hatred in his features.

"You're too late, Devon," he laughed. "She's mine." He pushed Alana aside and lifted the Sword of the Gods.

Across the clearing, the man called Devon hurled himself to the ground as lightning slammed into the earth where he had been standing. Moving faster than she would have believed possible for such a large man, he recovered and charged at Quinn. He carried a warhammer with glowing runes carved into its head. With a bellow of rage, he swung at Quinn.

The Sword leapt to meet him, and sparks flew as the weapons collided. A concussion erupted where they met, leaving the men untouched but hurling Alana from her feet. She rolled across the marble tiles and came to one knee, a snarl on her lips. Gaining her feet, she hefted her sword and started towards the intruder.

A harsh shriek sliced the air as the weapons met again, but this time Alana braced herself and remained standing. Devon leapt back as Quinn attempted to slice his head from his shoulders. As he moved, his eyes turned to her. Alana froze in place at the warmth she saw reflected there. She clutched at her chest as something tore in her heart, and closed her eyes, struggling to draw breath.

The sound of battle resumed, the crackling of flames filling her ears, but Alana did not open her eyes. Standing fixed in place, she swayed on her feet, struggling to comprehend the sudden emptiness swirling at her core. The sight of Devon had set her mind adrift, filling her with an awful pain, a loss she couldn't begin to explain.

Across the marble tiles the two men battled. For a moment it seemed the giant warrior might have the best of Quinn. His hammer slammed into the Sword again and again, its shining head absorbing whatever attacks Quinn hurled his way—magic or otherwise. The power in his blows forced Quinn to retreat, his own blade barely keeping measure of the giant.

Then with a curse, Quinn leapt back out of the giant's range. He lifted the Sword and pointed it at Devon. "Your legend ends today, Devon," he screamed.

A beam of pure energy went screeching from the blade, flashing across the tent to strike at the giant. His hammer lifted in response, catching the assault in a tempest of swirling energy. For a moment the energies seemed to vanish

—then the hammer started to glow, and a sharp shriek filled the air. Cracks spread through the hammer like the threads of a web, and with an awful *pop*, the weapon shattered into a thousand pieces.

The forces unleashed from the weapon lifted Devon from his feet and hurled him backwards. He landed with a *thud* on the marble tiles and lay still, his desperate gasping the only sign he still lived.

The breath caught in Alana's throat as Quinn strode across the tiles to stand over Devon.

"Did you really think some old spell would protect you from the power of the Gods?" he asked.

Groaning, Devon struggled to sit up, but the giant's prodigious strength seemed to have given up, and he slumped back to the ground. Wheezing, he ignored Quinn and looked again at Alana.

"*Run, princess,*" he whispered.

The hackles on the back of Alana's neck stood up at his words. She opened her mouth and closed it, her heart racing, though for the life of her she could not say why. Her man had defeated the brute, and now stood poised to take the world. What did she care for the barbarian lying at Quinn's feet?

Yet, each time his amber eyes met hers, she felt something stir within her. And when he had called her 'princess'…

The light in Devon's eyes faded as he saw her stand there, unmoving. He looked back at Quinn. "What have you done to her, Stalker?" he whispered.

"I restored her true self," Quinn replied. "Returned her to the Alana I knew before *you* spoiled her."

"You'll pay—" Devon tried to sit up, but a vine erupted

from the ground beneath him, catching him by the throat and dragging him back down.

Blood pounded in Alana's ears as she listened to them, her mind a whir. What was Quinn talking about? What had he done to her? Sensing her panic, magic leapt to her fingertips. It bubbled through her veins, drawing her inwards, seeking out the change Quinn claimed to have wrought, searching for her missing memories.

But there was nothing.

Nothing locked away, nothing hidden, nothing shielded.

Yet as she searched, Alana could sense a loss, a void within, as though something she loved more than life itself had been stolen away. She shuddered and looked back at the two men, at the grizzled face of the giant who had called her 'princess.' For half an instant, she caught a glimpse of him on his knees in a throne room, a dead man in his arms.

"Will I?" Quinn was saying. His laughter rang out across the campsite. "Tell me, Devon, how will you make me pay?"

Devon groaned as the vine tightened around his throat. He clutched at it with meaty fingers, trying to tear it free, but more erupted from the earth. Thorns appeared along their lengths, ripping at his flesh as they wrapped around his muscular limbs. A scream tore from his throat, but he was helpless before Quinn's magic.

"Quinn, stop!"

The two men turned to look at her, Quinn's eyes wide with surprise. Unable to believe she'd spoken, Alana's own mouth hung open. She watched as the surprise on Quinn's face turned to anger. Looking back at Devon, he lifted the Sword.

"Still you corrupt her," he hissed, "but no longer. Goodbye, Devon."

With a cry of rage, Quinn drove the Sword down.

43

Wrapped in the steely vines, his body in agony, all Devon could do was watch as Quinn lifted the Sword above his head. In that moment, he was surprised to find there was no fear, only a deep regret that in the end, he couldn't save the one thing that mattered to him. He had promised Alana once that he would protect her, that he would keep her safe from the Tsar and his Stalkers. But he had failed.

Quinn had taken her, had used his newfound magic to wipe away the ferocious woman Devon loved, and replaced her with a monster. Lying there, he wondered whether he would find that other Alana in the afterlife, if she had a soul all of her own, and if they would walk the dark road together. Or was she tangled up in the woman standing beside Quinn, bound forever within, doomed to witness the atrocities her twin would commit in her name?

With all his heart, Devon hoped it was the former. But as the Sword came rushing down, he knew he might never know the answer. Closing his eyes, he waited for the end to come.

And waited.

Devon frowned as he realised silence had fallen over the world.

Then he heard Quinn's agonised whisper. "Alana, *why?*"

His eyes snapped open to find Alana standing over him. She stood facing Quinn, hands clutched in front of her. Devon's eyes slid down her back, and the tip of the Sword impaling her. Light still flickered along its blade, stained red by the blood coating its length.

Releasing the Sword, Quinn staggered back, his mouth wide with horror.

"*Why Alana?*" Quinn screamed, stretching out an arm as though he might mend the wound with his hands alone.

Blood pouring down her back, Alana staggered, and then straightened. Her hands reached up to grip the hilt of the Sword, as though to draw it from her. She lifted her head to look at Quinn. Sorrow laced her voice as she spoke.

"You took something from me," she whispered. "Now I'm going to take something from you."

"No..." he said, stepping towards her, still reaching for her. "I can save you!"

"Never," she snapped.

One hand still clenched about the hilt of the Sword Quinn had driven through her stomach, she threw out her other arm. Lightning arced from her fingertips and flashed across the room to catch Quinn square in the chest. For a moment he seemed frozen in its light. His back arched as his body went rigid, his mouth opening wide. A deafening *boom* crashed over the campsite, and the lightning flickered again, blinding all who watched.

When Devon's vision returned, he found himself alone

beside Alana. Nothing but a scorched patch of tiles remained of where Quinn had stood.

He sat up as the vines receded, his heart lodged in his throat. Desperately he scrambled to reach Alana as she swayed and began to topple backwards. Catching her in his arms, he lowered her onto her side, taking care not to move the Sword any further. A whisper came from her lips as he rested her head in his lap.

"Alana," he sobbed. He reached out to touch her, then paused, his hand trembling with indecision.

"Please," she murmured, her eyes fluttering. "Who… who are you to me?" A gurgling rattle came from her chest as a convulsion shook her.

Devon swallowed at the pain written across her face, the grief. "I love you."

A sigh whispered from her chest. "I can't remember…" she breathed, trailing off. Then her eyes snapped open, sudden clarity in their stony depths. "You called me 'princess.'"

Devon smiled, despite himself. "You have always been a princess to me, Alana."

"Good," Alana murmured. "Don't you…forget it."

A sob tore from Devon. Swallowing his fear, he reached for the hilt of the Sword, but she caught him by the wrist.

"Don't," Alana said. "Its magic is all…that's keeping me alive."

"No…" Devon croaked.

"Thank you, Devon," she said, her voice so low he had to strain to hear her.

"For what?"

"For saving me," she replied, her lips twitching in a smile. "For bringing me back."

"Now *stay*," Devon hissed, gripping her hand tight.

"I can't…" Alana murmured, her eyes lifting to stare past Devon at some unseen point in the sky.

"No…" Devon trailed off, and for a moment he thought the worst. Sobbing, he bent over her, tears streaming from his cheeks onto her hair.

"Run," her voice whispered in his ear, so softly he almost thought it a trick of the wind.

Pulling back, he shook his head. "I'm not leaving you."

"You must."

"Please," Alana replied. "I don't want…."

"Alana."

"Please, Devon. If you love me, *run*."

Groaning, she pushed weakly at his hand and struggled to a sitting position. Her face pale, alive with agony, she looked at him. Devon stared back, seeing her courage, her anger and pain, but most of all her grief. He knew then it was not the Alana he knew looking at him, but the old one, the Daughter of the Tsar.

And she had helped him.

It made no sense, and yet he could not deny the truth.

Slowly he stood, wiping his tears away. "Are you…sure?"

She nodded, tears of her own streaking her cheeks. Her gaze darted to where a hunched figure lay nearby. "Take the boy."

Striding across the marble tiles, Devon's heart lurched as he saw it was Braidon lying there. He swung the boy over his shoulder and then glanced back at Alana. She had both hands clasped around the Sword now, concentration etched across her face. As he paused, she glanced up, and a smile touched her lips.

"Run, Devon!"

44

Alana let out a long sigh as Devon disappeared beyond the tents, the boy slung over one shoulder. Slumping against the Sword, she let the pain wash over her. A shriek tore from her lips, and shuddering, she prepared herself for the end.

Don't.

The voice whispered in her mind. It sounded distant, yet it rang with undeniable power.

A frown touched Alana's brow as she looked around, seeking out the source. But she was alone in the campsite now. Not a soul stirred in the tents around her, all her father's soldiers and Stalkers having long since fled. Closing her eyes, she gathered herself.

This is not the way.

Her eyes snapped open, but still there was no sign of movement. "Where are you?" she whispered.

Within, came the reply.

"How?" Alana asked, shaking her head.

Let me show you.

Alana sensed the voice wanted her to let go. Hesitation touched her, her old instincts screaming a warning. But then, she was doomed either way. The second she tore the Sword from her she would die—no amount of God magic would be fast enough to bring her back. So what did she have to lose?

Letting out a long breath, she relaxed, allowing the other presence to take hold…

And woke in a glistening garden, its endless rows of roses lit by a golden light. Alana looked around, surprised by the abrupt change in scenery—and the sudden absence of pain. She touched her stomach and found the flesh whole.

"There is no pain here," a voice spoke from behind her.

Spinning around, Alana watched as a young girl approached through the flowerbeds, her eyes aglow with violet light. Two men walked behind her, one seemingly old beyond time, the other muscular and middle-aged, his beard streaked with white.

The three came to a stop before Alana and appraised her with silent eyes.

"You remember me?" the girl asked.

Alana shook her head. "I remember nothing like this," she whispered. "Nothing good."

"Come then," the girl replied, gesturing Alana forward.

Alana dropped to her knees before the girl. The violet glow of her eyes flickered as she reached out and touched a finger to Alana's forehead. A cool power flooded through her, seeping through her skull, filling her up. Alana sighed, rising into the girl's hold, her whole body coming alive.

And one by one, she felt the pieces of the puzzle appear, her memory restored. She saw again Devon facing off against the demon, her brother Braidon as he outlined his plan to defeat their father, she saw Kellian fall in the throne room, and Enala die beneath her father's blade. A sob tore from her lips as she heard again Devon's words in the wreckage of the Tsar's tent, his whispered 'I love you.'

Alana knew she would never see him again, but more than anything she wished she could have returned those words. She had done so much wrong in her short life, caused so much pain. It had been Devon, with his own dark past, who had led her into the light, drawing her out from beneath her father's sway. Not even Quinn, with all the power of his Sword, had been able to burn that light from her.

Alana looked down at the girl. The Goddess Antonia smiled and gestured at her companions. "You and Jurrien met, briefly," she said, indicating the younger of the two. "My brother, Darius, has watched you from your father's Sword for years."

"I'm sorry," Alana whispered.

Darius smiled, his aged face more wrinkles than skin. "It seems to forever be my fate," he murmured. "Until now."

"I am sorry for my anger, young Alana," Jurrien added, stepping forward and placing a hand on her shoulder. "I could sense Antonia's pain, coming from the Sword." He glanced at the Goddess and smiled. "I have a soft spot for my little sister."

Antonia snorted and rolled her eyes. "Don't blame me for your excesses, brother," she replied. "You were wrecking their ships long before we took flesh."

Jurrien offered a roguish grin. "Yes, well, you two never were much fun."

"If only things could have stayed thus," Darius murmured. His pale white eyes looked to Alana. "But now they must change, permanently this time."

"I am sorry, Alana," Antonia cut in. "With my spirit trapped within the blade, I cannot heal you."

"I know." Alana shrugged, swallowing her grief. "I'm ready."

Antonia nodded. "As are we."

Alana shook her head. "Ready for what?"

"For death."

Alana blinked, looking from Antonia to the other two. "What do you mean, 'death'?"

"You shall not walk the dark path alone, Alana," Darius replied. "We shall walk with you, if you would free us."

"Why?" she whispered. "You're Gods, why would you want to die?"

"Because it is our power that corrupts you, all of you," Antonia replied sadly. "Our spirit, our magic, it touches all things. But only humanity seeks to claim it. It calls to them, driving your strongest, your cleverest, to seek us out. Twice now our powers have been trapped by your people. The last time, we departed the physical realm, in the belief it would be enough. But your father drew us back, took our power for his own."

"You want me to destroy you?" Alana asked.

"We want you to destroy it all," Jurrien replied.

"All magic comes from us," Darius added, "and it will die with us."

Alana stared into the faces of the three Gods, and realised for the first time there was fear in their eyes. These three beings had lived an eternity beyond anything she could imagine, had watched over humanity for eons before the scrambling priests had first summoned them to flesh.

Now they were asking to join Alana on the final journey, to go with her into the darkness of death, and look upon what waited on the other side.

She swallowed. "Are you sure?"

The Three Gods nodded.

"Then tell me how."

45

By the time Merydith gathered her people near the bottom of the valley, the last of the enemy had either fled or been slain. She had found a fresh horse from the few that had survived the battle, and now sat in the saddle, looking out over the weary faces of her people.

Less than a thousand were left, and of those there were few who had emerged unscathed. Even so, they looked back at her with triumph in their eyes. She knew that every one of them was celebrating their life, that of all those who had perished today, they still breathed the fresh evening air.

Helen and what remained of her Magickers had joined them once the enemy had fallen back. The effort required to split the valley in two had cost them dearly. Helen had informed her with sadness that two dozen of their number had collapsed and died soon after. Their sacrifice had won the day, Merydith knew, and she embraced the woman like an old sister.

Looking over the gathered allies, Merydith searched for their other saviour. The hammerman Devon had appeared at the decisive minute, leading a horde of black-cloaked warriors as he charged the enemy's rear. She could see many of his people scattered amongst her ranks, but of the hammerman himself, there was still no sign.

Damyn and Mokyre stood to either side of her, their watchful eyes on the campsite. Her guards had died defending her amidst the chaos of battle, and the two clansmen seemed to have taken the role upon themselves. Weary as she was, Merydith didn't have the strength to argue with them over it.

Turning her horse to face the survivors, she was about to speak when a voice shouted out from the crowd.

"Devon!"

Merydith let out a long breath as she saw the hammerman stumbling from the last of the tents. Her heart lifted at the sight of Braidon in his arms, and almost without thinking, she looked at the campsite, waiting for Enala to emerge. But as Devon neared, it became obvious the hammerman was alone. Her heart twisted, but she forced herself to dismount and stride out to meet Devon.

"Well met, hammerman," she said, an uncharacteristic grin on her face. "Your timing was impeccable."

He paused, offering a nod, and then continued past her. Merydith's smile faded, replaced with irritation, and she followed the hammerman into a cluster of black-garbed warriors. An older woman stepped out to meet him, and together they lowered Braidon to the ground.

"I think he's okay," Devon murmured as the woman crouched beside the boy.

The woman touched a finger to his neck, waited a moment, and then nodded her agreement. "He's sleeping."

"What happened, Devon?" Merydith cut in, her irritation mounting.

Devon glanced in her direction, and sighed. "Sorry, Queen," he croaked. "I…it's been a long day."

Merydith opened her mouth to snap a retort, and then caught herself. Letting out a long breath, she forced a smile. "It has," she agreed. "And as I said, I am grateful for your aid."

"Thank them," he said gesturing to the black-garbed warriors scattered amongst her people.

"In time," Merydith replied. "First, what has happened to the Tsar, do you know?"

"He's dead," Devon grunted. "And all his powers with him."

Merydith's heart swelled at his words. "Truly?"

"Ay," Devon replied. "Though it cost everything."

His voice was tight with barely controlled emotion, and Merydith read the pain on his face. Not knowing what to say, she reached out and squeezed his arm.

"Thank you, my friend," she said. "You have given us everything."

"Not me," he murmured, looking past her to the gathered allies. "The Tsar's Daughter. Alana."

Merydith nodded, though in truth she did not understand what he was saying. A cry came from the ground, and the boy lurched up, his sapphire eyes wild.

"Alana!" he cried.

"Easy, sonny," Devon said gently, moving to his side.

"No, what, where am I?" Braidon gasped, pushing aside the helping hands of his friends.

"You're safe, Braidon," the woman said gently.

"Selina?" he frowned, finally taking in his surroundings. "Where is Alana?"

Selina lifted her eyes to Devon, who quickly looked

away. "I'm sorry, sonny," he said quietly. "I couldn't save her, not this time. She's—"

Before he could finish speaking, a rumbling noise came from the campsite. All eyes turned back to where the dark tents of the Tsar's army lay empty. A light had blossomed there, stretching up into the sky. Green, blue, red, gold, and a thousand other colours crisscrossed the column, growing more intense, until it seemed the world itself would flicker out before its power.

A sharp *pop* sounded, followed by a terrifying *boom* that shook the very earth. The column of light swept outwards. Her people cried out as the magic rushed towards them. Merydith threw herself on the ground and closed her eyes, but even then the light seared at her eyes. Her ears filled with an awful buzzing, and she smelt burning in her nostrils.

Then as suddenly as it had appeared, the light flickered out, leaving Merydith crouched on the grass, untouched. Sitting up, she saw the bewilderment on the faces of her people as they looked around, in disbelief that they were alive. Merydith could hardly believe it either—for a second, she'd thought Devon had been wrong, that the Tsar still lived and had launched a final attack against them.

A harsh sobbing drew her attention back to the present, and standing, she searched for the source. She found Helen and the other Magickers nearby, each crouched with their faces to the ground. Listening to their cries, Merydith could not understand what had happened to them, but she heard the pain of loss in their voices.

"What is it?" she asked, moving to Helen's side.

The Magicker looked up, her eyes red. "It's gone," she whispered.

"What's gone?"

"The Gods, magic, all of it," Helen cried.

Merydith stared at her, uncomprehending. Before she could respond, another cry drew her attention to the other end of the valley. Men and women there were shouting and running towards her, their eyes filled with panic. Her heart beat faster, though she barely had the strength to stand now. The day had just about consumed her last reserve of strength.

She looked beyond her people, out to where the valley twisted out of sight. The crevice that Helen and her Magickers had opened ended there. Marching towards them up the valley was the other half the Tsar's army.

Merydith could have laughed. As Mokyre and Damyn formed up on either side of her, she walked towards the approaching force. Her people parted for her, their eyes wide. She felt no fear though, only a strange nothingness, a knowledge that she had done all she possibly could to save her people.

The thud of twenty thousand marching boots rumbled up the valley as the army neared. When they were still a hundred yards away, a trumpet sounded, and the silence resumed. Merydith came to a stop at the front of her people. Folding her arms, she waited for the enemy to make their move.

A gap appeared in the front line of soldiers, and three men stepped into the open. Merydith exchanged glances with Mokyre and Damyn, and then the three of them walked out to meet them. They came to a stop midway between the two forces. Merydith folded her arms once more as the three men stopped before her.

"My name is General Saryn," the frontmost of the three spoke, his voice clear and crisp, carrying with it the air of command. "What happened here?"

"The Tsar is dead. His army is defeated. The empire is done," Merydith said.

A smile touched the general's face. "Is it?"

"It is," Merydith replied. She sighed, her gaze looking out over the men and women aligned against her. "Have enough not died already, General?"

The smile faded from his face. "It has been a grim day indeed."

"Then shall we put an end to this?"

He sighed. "The Tsar is truly dead?"

"He is," Merydith murmured. "And magic with him."

"Then you shall have your peace," Saryn replied, sinking to his knees. "My Queen."

EPILOGUE

Devon walked slowly up the sloping streets of Ardath, taking his time in the stifling heat. His leg still ached where a shard of his hammer had embedded itself in his thigh, and he couldn't go at much more than a slow amble anyway. With magic gone from the continent, it would take months for the wound to fully heal.

Not for the first time in the past few weeks, he wondered what had gone through Alana's head in those final moments. Had she known what she was doing, when she'd turned the Sword on its makers, destroying the spirits of the Gods, and magic with them? It had been her father's purpose in making the Sword in the first place, but…

He shook his head. There was no point in fretting over it. What Alana had done could not be reversed. The moment she'd broken the Sword, it was too late. Now all the Three Nations could do was move on, and forge a fresh future for themselves in a world without magic.

Meredith had decided to remain in the Three Nations for a time, to oversee the transition of power as the empire broke up. Her aide, Mokyre, had been sent back to Northland to oversee the nation in her absence, while the Queen herself was rarely seen without Damyn at her side. They had ridden hand in hand for much of the trip to the capital, and at night had made little secret of their passion.

Along with Braidon and Selina, Devon had joined them for the journey back to Ardath. First though, he had returned to the site where he had last seen Alana. He had needed to see the truth for himself, to know she was not hiding out there somewhere, alone and afraid. But in the end, there had been nothing left to see. The marble tiles that had marked the spot where the Tsar's tent had stood were gone; even the earth beneath had been torn apart, leaving a crater the size of a house where Alana had lain.

He'd known then she could not have survived, that at the end she had made the ultimate sacrifice. Why, they would never know, but he liked to think she had her reasons.

The surviving Baronians had remained behind with their Trolan comrades. With the Tsar gone, the threat of persecution had lifted, and most had been excited at the thought of returning to a stationary lifestyle.

With plenty of land and few hands to work it, the Trolans had welcomed them with open arms. In the days following the battle, Devon had been overjoyed to learn it had been Betran who had raised the rebellion in Trola. If not for his efforts, the Queen's army would have lost long before Devon and his followers arrived.

Much to his protest, the Queen had named Betran as the next Trolan King. Devon smiled at the thought of the timid-looking man he'd first met in a bar beneath the streets of Kalgan ruling a nation. The idea appealed to him, and he began to whistle a familiar tune as he continued through the maze of alleyways.

Braidon had been cool towards him on the journey home. Devon could not fault him for it. The boy blamed him for Alana's death, for not saving her as Devon had saved him. Devon had tried to explain, but the hurt was too fresh. The loss of Braidon's magic had been a double blow, and for days there had been no reasoning with him. Devon hoped that might change, given time.

The Queen intended to give Braidon the Plorsean crown once he came of age. After watching him grow and prosper over the last few months, Devon thought the boy would make a fine king, though he had no doubt there would be those who watched him closely for hints of his father's madness.

Merydith herself planned to stay out the year and then return to Northland next summer. With Lonia already holding elections to bring a new council to rule, only Plorsea needed her help putting itself back together. They had suffered the most during the battle, with most of their leaders dead or missing. It would take time to find someone trustworthy enough to rule in Braidon's stead until he came of age. Personally, Devon was more than glad to know Merydith's hands were at the helm for the moment.

Devon came to a stop outside the blackened remains of a building. Placing his hands on his hips, he cast an appraising eye over the ruin of the Firestone Inn. The stone walls still stood strong, but the fire had consumed the clay tiles of the roof, and there was nothing left of the wooden steps out front.

Climbing up into the building, Devon stood looking on the ruin, remembering the long days and nights he had spent there with Kellian. Sometimes he'd been a customer, others a bouncer, paying off some damage or debt he'd managed to cost his friend. Regardless, they had been good times, simpler and filled with joy, long before they had rescued the Tsar's children and embarked on a quest that would see an empire topple.

Devon chuckled to himself as he studied the gutted interior, and wondered what his friend would think of him standing there now.

"It's going to take a lot of work, you know." A voice came from the doorway behind him.

Turning, Devon smiled as Selina wandered into the ruin.

"Ay, it will." Devon replied. Reaching into his belt, he hefted an old clawhammer. Dented and rusting in places, it told no stories, held no ancient spells. But it would do. He smiled at Selina. "But I'm game to try. Care to join me?"

Selina laughed. "I just might, hammerman."

HERE ENDS BOOK THREE OF
THE LEGEND OF THE GODS

Discover more adventures from the Three Nations in…
Daughter of Fate

NOTE FROM THE AUTHOR

Wow, what a journey. It still amazes me that the concept for this story came to me in a first year English class for high school. It took another ten years for those first stumbling words of Eric's journey to be introduced to the big wide world. But anyway, thank you to everyone who has joined me on this journey. I hope you enjoyed the Sword of Light Trilogy! And fear not, I will be returning to the Three Nations in the future. But to keep you going, if you signup to my reading group below you will **receive a free short story featuring two beloved characters from the Sword of Light Trilogy.** Enjoy!

And as always, reader feedback is a huge part of its continued success, and all reviews on Amazon would be very much appreciated for Soul Blade.

FOLLOW AARON HODGES...

And receive TWO FREE novels and a short story!

www.aaronhodges.co.nz/newsletter-signup/

NOTE FROM THE AUTHOR

Phew, what a ride! I've gotta say, my stories in the Three Nations are still my favourite to write, even after six novels and a novella or two! And as you might have guessed from their ending, there's still more tales left to explore in this brave new world. They'll have to wait a while though - first I plan on writing something a little different. I'll let you know when I figure out what that is!

In the meantime, you should definitely check out my prequel series - Sword of Light Trilogy. The three books are set a hundred years before events in this series, so they might explain a few gaps you might have noticed in the Dawn of War! Be sure to read on below for a free excerpt…

FOLLOW AARON HODGES…

And receive TWO FREE novels and a short story!
www.aaronhodges.co.nz/newsletter-signup/

THE KNIGHTS OF ALANA

If you've enjoyed this book, you might want to check out another of my fantasy series!

When Knights attack the town of Skystead, seventeen-year-old Pela is the only one to escape. Her mother and the other villagers are taken, accused of worshiping the False Gods. They will pay the ultimate price – unless Pela can rescue them.

DESCENDANTS OF THE FALL

If you've enjoyed this book, you might want to check out another of my fantasy series!

Centuries ago, the world fell. From the ashes rose a terrible new species—the Tangata. Now they wage war against the kingdoms of man. And humanity is losing.

Recruited straight from his academy, twenty-year-old Lukys hopes the frontier will make a soldier out of him. But Tangata are massing in the south, and the allied armies are desperate. They will do anything to halt the enemy advance—including sending untrained men and women into battle. Determined to survive, Lukys seeks aid from the only man who seems to care: Romaine, the last warrior of an extinct kingdom.

ALSO BY AARON HODGES

Descendants of the Fall

Book 1: Warbringer

Book 2: Wrath of the Forgotten

Book 3: Age of Gods

The Evolution Gene

Book 1: The Genome Project

Book 2: The Pursuit of Truth

Book 3: The Way the World Ends

The Sword of Light

Book 1: Stormwielder

Book 2: Firestorm

Book 3: Soul Blade

The Legend of the Gods

Book 1: Oathbreaker

Book 2: Shield of Winter

Book 3: Dawn of War

The Knights of Alana

Book 1: Daughter of Fate

Book 2: Queen of Vengeance

Book 3: Crown of Chaos